高等学校英语专业系列教材

A New Edition of Selected Readings in English Literature

新编英国文学名著选读

张伯香 朱宾忠 龙江 张文 编著

WUHAN UNIVERSITY PRESS
武汉大学出版社

图书在版编目(CIP)数据

新编英国文学名著选读/张伯香,朱宾忠,龙江,张文编著.—武汉:武汉大学出版社,2013.5(2023.1 重印)
高等学校英语专业系列教材
ISBN 978-7-307-10678-9

Ⅰ.新…　Ⅱ.①张…　②朱…　③龙…　④张…　Ⅲ.英国文学—高等学校—教材　Ⅳ.I561

中国版本图书馆 CIP 数据核字(2013)第 070124 号

责任编辑:叶玲利　　责任校对:王　建　　版式设计:马　佳

出版发行:**武汉大学出版社**　(430072　武昌　珞珈山)
(电子邮箱:cbs22@ whu.edu.cn 网址:www.wdp.com.cn)
印刷:武汉邮科印务有限公司
开本:787×1092　1/16　印张:26.5　字数:624 千字　插页:1
版次:2013 年 5 月第 1 版　2023 年 1 月第 3 次印刷
ISBN 978-7-307-10678-9　定价:59.00 元

前　言

随着我国经济、科技、文化的快速发展，社会对英语人才的培养也提出了新的要求，更加强调人文素质和创新能力的培养。为更好地满足新时代英语专业人才培养的需要，也为了更充分地体现教材在文学教学和学术研究中的意义和价值，我们对原有的文学教材进行了较大幅度的改编，推出了这本《新编英国文学名著选读》。其目的是培养学生阅读、欣赏、理解英语文学原著的能力，掌握文学批评的基本知识和方法，同时通过阅读和分析英国文学作品，促进学生语言基本功和人文素质的提高，增强学生对西方文学及文化的了解。

《新编英国文学名著选读》是在《英国文学教程》的基础上修改而成的；它保留了原教材的优点，删除了文学史和部分文学选读的内容，极大地压缩了篇幅，以便更好地适应英语专业文学课程新的教学时数、内容、手段和方法的需要。

《新编英国文学名著选读》吸收了近几年国内外英国文学研究的最新成果，按照选取适合学生阅读又具代表性的经典作品为原则，并结合编者自己多年的教学和研究体会，以英国文学发展的历史为脉络，精选了英国文学史中古时期、文艺复兴时期、启蒙时期、浪漫主义时期、现实主义时期、现代主义时期和当代文学中各种流派的代表作品。选读中，现、当代文学作品占有较重比例，旨在使学生能够接触和学习更富时代气息、更为实用的语言素材。在体裁上，我们注意了诗歌、小说、戏剧与散文的适当比例。每章的内容包括历史文化背景、作者简介、作品选读、注释、思考题等。

《新编英国文学名著选读》是普通高等院校英语专业教材，也可供非英语专业或具有同等英语水平的文学爱好者、出国深造预备人员阅读欣赏。

《新编英国文学名著选读》的问世与武汉大学出版社领导的关心与支持密不可分，更是游径海、叶玲利等责任编辑们辛勤劳动的结晶。在此，我谨代表所有编者向他们表示诚挚的谢意。

张伯香

2013 年 5 月于珞珈山

Contents

Chapter 1

The Anglo-Saxon Period (449-1066)

1.1 Introduction

Since historical times, Great Britain has been successively occupied or conquered by several distinct peoples. The earliest inhabitants of the island were the primitive Celtic tribes known as Britons. In 43 A. D. the Romans invaded Britain and made it a Roman province. The Celts under its rule had to pay tributes or taxes to the Roman Empire; but they still kept their own language, customs and religion. The Romans had ruled Britain for almost 4 centuries. When the Roman Empire declined and its troops left Britain, the tribes of Angles, Saxons and Jutes invaded Britain from Northern Europe around the fifth century. They drove the native Celts away from England into Wales, Scotland, and even Ireland across the sea. The three tribes gradually settled down and merged into a whole people called English. They cultivated also a specific poetic tradition, the formal character of which remained surprisingly constant until the termination of their rule by the Norman-French invaders six centuries later.

The Anglo-Saxons were heathens; they lived partly from fishing and piratical expeditions against the northern and eastern coasts of Europe and partly from a rude sort of agriculture and animal husbandry. Strength, courage, and loyalty to king and comrades were the chief virtues that they admired. They worshipped originally heaven and earth, which were regarded by them as father and mother of all things. The glorious summer god, who was said to be the son of heaven and earth, fought bravely against the evil winter monster and frost giants to protect the people. The Anglo-Saxons also had their own gods such as Woden and Thor, which were the origins of today's Wednesday and Thursday. In the year 597, St. Augustine was sent by the pope in Rome as a missionary to Kent, a small, southerly kingdom in England. About the same time missionaries from Ireland began to preach Christianity in the north. Within a century or so the whole island had been Christianized.

English literature began as an oral one, with songs and poems celebrating heroes and praising Anglo-Saxon ideals. Those early poems were passed on by bards, who often recomposed them in the process of singing to their audience. Through the songs of the bards, the major battles and the feats of the tribes' heroes were told and remembered. In this way heroes could win enduring fame, something that was valued highly. By immortalizing their heroes, the bards also brought a semblance of permanence to a world ruled by a sense of transience and fatal doom.

Written literature did not exist in Britain until about the year 700. It first came to our attention in the work of the Venerable Bede, author of *Ecclesiastical History of the English People*. One of the famous men Bede wrote about was Caedmon, a shepherd, who became a monk and the first English religious poet. Although Bede was Anglo-Saxon, he wrote his *History* in Latin. The first notable written work in Old English was *The Anglo-Saxon Chronicles* (c. 871-1154), which was compiled under the remarkable Anglo-Saxon King, Alfred the Great. Alfred is often considered the greatest king of the Anglo-Saxons. The social organizations and laws that he introduced are still evident in English culture today.

During the Anglo-Saxon period, the English people have produced a rich body of literature. Its chief features are love of home and country, attachment to nature, and an ever-present consciousness that there are things worse than death. These features have, in the main, continued unchanged from those days to the present time, in spite of periods of decadence, or of great development. The earliest poems in Old English have been concerned with journeying in a distant land and with life over the sea. Those Angles, Saxons and Jutes had inhabited maritime regions before they came to Britain; the terror and the majesty and the loneliness of the sea had already cast their natural spells on "far-traveled seafarers" when English literature, as we know it, opens. The passionate joy of the struggle between men and the forces of nature, between sailors and the storms of the sea, finds its expression in the literary creation of *Beowulf*. Often bold and strong, but also mournful and elegiac in spirit, this poetry emphasizes the sorrow and ultimate futility of life and the helplessness of humans before the power of fate.

Generally speaking, all the Anglo-Saxon poetry that has survived can be grouped into two main divisions, secular and Christian. The secular poems are mainly concerned with subject matters like tribes, kings, warriors, loyalty, vengeance, hostile nature, and wars. Most of the poems are laments, evoking the Anglo-Saxon sense of the harshness of circumstance and the sadness of the human lot. *The Wanderer*, *Deor*, *The Seafarer*, and *The Wife's Complaint* are among the most beautiful in this group. The harsh climate of North Sea strongly affected the tone or mood of the poets. The life is sorrowful, and the speakers are fatalistic, though at the same time courageous and determined. The Christian poems are mainly on Biblical themes or on saints' lives. They suggest that the true function of art should not be simply to release human feelings but also to teach people and enhance their devotion. *Genesis A*, *Genesis B* and *Exodus* are poems based on the Old Testament; whereas *The Dream of the Rood* comes from the

New Testament. In this poem, Christ is portrayed as the young warrior striding to embrace death and victory, while the rood (cross) itself takes on the burden of his sufferings.

The communal and oral nature of the Anglo-Saxon poetry accounts for a number of its characteristic features. Firstly, it is strongly characterized with structural alliteration. Each full line has four stresses with a number of unstressed syllables, three of which begin with the same sound or letter. Secondly, almost all this poetry is composed without rhyme; its lines are usually divided into two halves with a pause in between, and each half line has two strongly stressed syllables which give musical effects to the poem with an indeterminate number of unstressed ones. Thirdly, the use of metaphors is perhaps the most conspicuous one in the style. There are a great number of vividly picturesque metaphorical synonyms (technically called *kennings*). Thus, the sea is referred to as the "swan-road" or "whale-path," the sun as "heaven's candle," the ship as a "wave-floater," the soldier as a "shield-bearer," and the dragon's cave as an "earth-hall." These kennings add much imaginative suggestiveness to the otherwise over-terse style, and often contribute to the grim irony. All these qualities of form and spirit are exemplified in the epic poem *Beowulf*.

1.2 *Beowulf*

1.2.1 Characteristic features

Beowulf—romance, history and epic—is a typical example of Old English poetry. It is full of incidents and good fights, simple in aim and clear in execution; its characters bear comparison with those of the *Odyssey* and its style is dignified and heroic. Beginning and ending with the funeral of a great king, and composed against a background of impending disaster, *Beowulf* describes the exploits of a Scandinavian hero, Beowulf, in fighting against the monster Grendel, his revengeful mother, and a fire-breathing dragon. In these battles Beowulf is shown not only as a glorious hero but also as a protector of the people. Furthermore, the rich and leisurely portrayal of the Scandinavian world provides many instances of customs going back to pre-Christian times: the close relationship between lord and man in the war-band, the institutions of the vow before battles, the blood-feud, and the burning of the bodies of the dead. It is these concerns that justify the extraordinary manner in which the *Beowulf*-poet conducts his narrative: the "rambling, dilatory method—the forward, backward, and sideward movements."

Beowulf is essentially an aristocratic poem concerned with the heroic ideal of kings and kingship in North Europe. The social patterns ascribed in the poem are rigidly feudal, highly violent. Battle is a way of life. Strength and courage are basic virtues for both kings and his warriors. The hero-king strove to do better than any one else the things that are vitally important to the happy life of his people. The king should protect his people and show gentleness and generosity to his warriors; in return, his warriors should show absolute obedience and loyalty to the king. By praising Beowulf's wisdom, strength and courage, and by glorifying his death for his people, the poem presents the heroic ideal of a king and his good relations to his warriors and people. The poem is also an example of the mingling of nature myths and heroic legends. For instance, the battle between Beowulf and the Dragon symbolically represents that phase of winter and summer myth in which the summer god, here embodied by Beowulf, fights his last battle against the winter dragon in order to rescue the treasures of earth, that is, the golden corn and ruddy fruits. Having given them back to men, Beowulf himself dies of the winter dragon's breath.

1.2.2 An excerpt from part Ⅰ of *Beowulf*

(in modern English translated by Burton Raffel)

Out from the marsh, from the foot of misty
Hills and bogs, bearing God's hatred[1],
Grendel[2] came, hoping to kill
Anyone he could trap on this trip to high Heorot[3],
He moved quickly through the cloudy night,
Up from his swampland, sliding silently
Toward that gold-shining hall. He had visited Hrothgar's[4]
Home before, knew the way—
But never, before nor after that night,
Found Heorot defended so firmly, his reception
So harsh. He journeyed, forever joyless,
Straight to the door, then snapped it open,
Tore its iron fasteners with a touch
And rushed angrily over the threshold.
He strode quickly across the inlaid[5]
Floor, snarling and fierce: his eyes
Gleamed in the darkness, burned with a gruesome
Light. Then he stopped, seeing the hall
Crowded with sleeping warriors, stuffed
With rows of young soldiers resting together,
And his heart laughed, he relished[6] the sight,
Intended to tear the life from those bodies
By morning; the monster's mind was hot

With the thought of food and the feasting his belly
Would soon know. But fate, that night, intended
Grendel to gnaw the broken bones
Of his last human supper. [7] Human
Eyes[8] were watching his evil steps,
Waiting to see his swift hard claws,
Grendel snatched at the first Geat
He came to, ripped him apart, cut
His body to bits with powerful jaws,
Drank the blood from his veins and bolted
Him down[9], hands and feet; death
And Grendel's great teeth came together,
Snapping life shut. Then he stepped to another
Still body, clutched at Beowulf with his claws,
Grasped at a strong-hearted wakeful sleeper
—And was instantly seized himself, claws
Bent back as Beowulf leaned up on one arm.

That shepherd of evil, guardian of crime, [10]
Knew at once that nowhere on earth
Had he met a man whose hands were harder;
His mind was flooded with fear—but nothing
Could take his talons[11] and himself from that tight
Hard grip. Grendel's one thought was to run
From Beowulf, flee back to his marsh and hide there:
This was a different Heorot than the hall he had emptied[12].
But Higlac's follower[13] remembered his final
Boast and, standing erect, stopped
The monster's flight, fastened those claws
In his fists till they cracked, clutched[14] Grendel
Closer. The infamous killer[15] fought
For his freedom, wanting no flesh but retreat,
Desiring nothing but escape; his claws
Had been caught, he was trapped. That trip to Heorot
Was a miserable journey for the writhing[16] monster!

The high hall rang, its roof boards swayed[17],
And Danes shook with terror. Down

The aisles the battle swept, angry
And wild. Heorot trembled, wonderfully
Built to withstand the blows, the struggling
Great bodies beating at its beautiful walls;
Shaped and fastened with iron, inside
And out, artfully worked, the building
Stood firm. Its benches rattled, fell
To the floor, gold-covered boards grating
As Grendel and Beowulf battled across them.
Hrothgar's wise men had fashioned[18] Heorot
To stand forever; only fire,
They had planned, could shatter[19] what such skill had put
Together, swallow in hot flames such splendor
Of ivory and iron and wood. Suddenly
The sounds changed, the Danes started
In new terror, cowering[20] in their beds as the terrible
Screams of the Almighty's enemy[21] sang
In the darkness, the horrible shrieks of pain
And defeat, the tears torn out of Grendel's
Taut[22] throat, hell's captive[23] caught in the arms
Of him who of all the men on earth
Was the strongest.

That mighty protector of men[24]
Meant to hold the monster till its life
Leaped out, knowing the fiend was no use
To anyone in Denmark. All of Beowulf's
Band had jumped from their beds, ancestral
Swords raised and ready, determined
To protect their prince if they could. Their courage
Was great but all wasted: they could hack at Grendel
From every side, trying to open
A path for his evil soul, but their points
Could not hurt him, the sharpest and hardest iron
Could not scratch at his skin, for that sin-stained demon
Had bewitched[25] all men's weapons, laid spells
That blunted every mortal man's blade.
And yet his time had come, his days

Were over, his death near; down
To hell he would go, swept groaning and helpless
To the waiting hands of still worse fiends.
Now he discovered—once the afflictor[26]
Of men, tormentor of their days—what it meant
To feud[27] with Almighty God: Grendel
Saw that his strength was deserting him, his claws
Bound fast, Higlac's brave follower tearing at
His hands. The monster's hatred rose higher,
But his power had gone. He twisted in pain,
And the bleeding sinews deep in his shoulder
Snapped, muscle and bone split
And broke. The battle was over, Beowulf
Had been granted new glory: Grendel escaped,
But wounded as he was could flee to his den,
His miserable hole at the bottom of the marsh,
Only to die, to wait for the end
Of all his days. And after that bloody
Combat the Danes laughed with delight.
He who had come to them from across the sea,
Bold and strong-minded, had driven affliction
Off, purged Heorot clean. He was happy,
Now, with that night's fierce work; the Danes
Had been served as he boasted he'd serve them; Beowulf,
A prince of the Geats, had killed Grendel,
Ended the grief, the sorrow, the suffering
Forced on Hrothgar's helpless people
By a bloodthirsty fiend. No Dane doubted
The victory, for the proof, hanging high
From the rafters[28] where Beowulf had hung it, was the monster's
Arm, claw and shoulder and all.

☞ **Notes**

1. **bearing God's hatred:** under the weight of God's anger.
2. **Grendel:** a man-eating monster who terrorizes the Danish people, until he is later killed by the warrior Beowulf.
3. **Heorot:** the battle-hall built by Hrothgar to house his men, and show off his victories and fame.

4. **Hrothgar:** the Danish king who is portrayed as "wise, brave, yet troubled" at the end of his life, mainly because of Grendel.
5. **inlaid:** to have a thin layer of another material set into its surface for decoration.
6. **relish:** to enjoy the thought of something that is going to happen.
7. Notice the sentence here is a comment from the narrator.
8. **Human Eyes:** Here they refer to Beowulf's eyes.
9. **bolt him down:** to eat him up very quickly.
10. **That shepherd of evil, guardian of crime:** Both shepherd and guardian here refer to Grendel.
11. **talons:** sharp, powerful curved nails on the foot of some birds that catch animals for food.
12. **emptied:** Here it means savaged.
13. **Higlac's follower:** Here it refers to Beowulf. Higlac, king of the Geats, is both feudal lord to Beowulf, and his uncle.
14. **clutch:** to hold something or someone tightly.
15. **The infamous killer:** Here it refers to Grendel.
16. **writhe:** to twist one's body from side to side violently, especially because one is suffering pain.
17. **sway:** to move slowly from one side to another.
18. **fashioned:** Here it means designed, made or built.
19. **shatter:** to break suddenly into very small pieces.
20. **cower:** to bend low and move back, especially because one is frightened.
21. **the Almighty's enemy:** God's enemy (here referring to Grendel).
22. **taut:** stretched tight.
23. **hell's captive:** Here it refers to Grendel, who is held captive by the hell.
24. **That mighty protector of men:** Here it refers to Beowulf.
25. **bewitch:** to get control over something by putting a magic spell on it.
26. **the afflictor:** the one who makes other people suffer.
27. **to feud:** to continue quarreling with someone for a long time often in violence.
28. **the rafters:** large sloping pieces of wood that form the structure of a roof.

☞ Study questions

1. Briefly describe the battle Beowulf fought with Grendel. How did Beowulf overcome Grendel?
2. In what way do the symbolic light and darkness figure into the scene?
3. The outsider (the outcast, the other) draws the reader's sympathy and fascination. How does Grendel typify the outsider? Is he a sympathetic character?

4. How does the poet vary the narrative point of view in this section? What is his purpose?

☞ Essay topics

1. What are the qualities that make a hero? Cite the qualities in Beowulf's personality that you think are truly heroic.
2. Read the whole poem and try to find out examples of the Christian elements and the pagan (non-Christian) ones in *Beowulf*. Which influence is stronger in *Beowulf*, the pagan or the Christian?

Chapter 2

The Medieval Period (1066-1485)

2.1 Introduction

The Medieval Period covers about four centuries, extending from 1066 to 1485. In 1066, William, the Duke of Normandy, conquered England with his strong army. This conquest brought England more than a change of rulers. Politically, a feudalist society replaced the primitive tribal one; religiously, the Rome-backed Catholic Church had a much stronger control over the country; and the language used in the country was also changed. After the conquest, three languages co-existed in England: French became the official language used by the king and the Norman lords; Latin became the principal tongue used by clergymen in church and scholars in universities; and English was spoken only by the common people. The conquest also brought a new and invigorating influence of Mediterranean civilization into England, though in the immediate presence of the eleventh century it seemed a crushing disaster for the nation. However, literary culture managed to survive in the long run and began in fact to flourish in spite of some crushing factors of the then English society, such as the catastrophic mortality of the Black Death (1347-1351), the military conflicts in the form of the Hundred Years' War and the Wars of the Roses, the Peasants' Revolt (1381), and the rise of Lollardism centered on the religious teachings of John Wycliffe. By the 14th century, Britain became a country cresting a wave of success. With the French monarchy relatively weak, Britain was losing its status as a dim little off-shore island and attaining the rank of European power. Its seamen were forging links all over Europe and North Africa; and its merchants were prospering, beginning to form a solid middle-class.

In the early part of the period, i. e. from 1066 up to the mid-14th century, there is not much to say about original literary creation in English. But in the second half of the 14th century, English literature starts to flourish with the appearance of writers like Geoffrey Chaucer, William Langland, John Gower and the unknown author of *Sir Gawain and the Green Knight*. In comparison with the literature of the previous period, medieval English literature is uttered by more voices, dealt with a wider range of subjects and presented in a greater diversity of styles, tones and genres. Popular folk literature also occupies an important place in this period. Its presentation of life is not only accurate but also in a lively and colorful way, though the originality of thought is often absent in the works of this period. Besides, the medieval literature strongly reflects the principles of the medieval Christian doctrines, which are primarily concerned with issues of sin redemption and soul delivery. An emphasis has also been placed on the humanity of Christ and the imagery of human passion. Love has largely superseded fear, and explorations into undiscovered regions of the heart offer fresh possibilities for introspection.

Although medieval poetry is still concerned with narrative, it is distinguished from earlier narrative verses by a greater sophistication of technique and a more articulate concern with the thematic point of stories—a moral or theological significance. Its stories are controlled and directed by that kind of clear thinking about moral and religious matters.

The main kinds of literature in this period are romances, religious works, folk ballads, lyrics of love and religion, and songs of political and social life. In all these, French influence is very strong, but there gradually appear some English elements, which are beginning to hold their own.

Romance, which uses narrative verse or prose to sing knightly adventures or other heroic deeds, is a popular literary form in this period. It has developed the characteristic medieval motifs of the quest, with the hero descending into a world of darkness or catastrophe where he encounters the evil giant and meets with the beautiful beloved. The hero is usually the knight, who sets out on a journey to accomplish some goals—to protect the church, to attack infidelity, to rescue a maiden, to meet a challenge, or to obey a knightly command; there is often a liberal use of the improbable, sometimes even supernatural, things in romance such as mysteries and fantasies; romantic love is an important part of the plot; characterization is standardized, so that heroes, heroines and wicked stewards can be easily moved from one romance to another; the structure is loose and episodic; and the language and style are simple and straightforward. The importance of romance itself can be seen as a means of showing medieval aristocratic men and women in relation to their idealized view of the world. If epic reflects an age of heroism, the romance reflects one of chivalry.

Sir Gawain and the Green Knight is the most accomplished example of medieval romance and a poem of rich psychological and moral interest. Its unknown author was Chaucer's contemporary, but his alliterative verse form was old-fashioned even in his own day, and his dialect, that of northwest England, is also very difficult for the modern reader. However, the poem is an account of a typical chivalric adventure, a combination of a number of the best-known motifs of Arthurian romance—a challenge by a mysterious superhuman knight, a bargain which turns out to have unforeseen consequences, a lone quest, and an attempted seduction of a Christian knight by a bewitching temptress. The courtly romances have also married to archetypal folk myths and to religion.

2.2 Geoffrey Chaucer

2.2.1 Life and career

Chaucer (ca. 1343-1400) was born into a wealthy wine merchant's family. From 1357 to 1358, he served as a page to the wife of Lionel, Duke of Clarence. As a young man, he fought as a soldier for King Edward Ⅲ. In the battlefield, he was captured by the enemy side, and was ransomed back by the king later on. In 1366 Chaucer got married to one of the queen's ladies-in-waiting. Then, he started to pursue a public life, holding various jobs as Italian diplomat, Customs official, and a Justice of the Peace. His active career during all these years as courtier, soldier, diplomat, and civil servant provided him not only with knowledge but also experiences, which accounted for the wide range of his writings.

Chaucer's poetic career was generally divided into three periods. His early writings followed French trends. *The Book of the Duchess*, with dream vision and allegories, was a product of such style, which was more to the taste of the medieval than of modern people. His poetry of the second period was inspired by the poet's own journeys to Italy as a royal emissary. Influenced by the vigor of three great Italian writers—Dante, Petrarch and Boccaccio—Chaucer brought to his own verse a new strength. During this period he produced one of his two masterpieces: *Troilus and Criseyde*, a long narrative poem based on Boccaccio's retelling of a classical love story set during the legendary Trojan War. In his final period, Chaucer broke away from French and Italian models and fully realized his own style in his native tongue. The greatest achievement of this period was *The Canterbury Tales*, which is unique for its variety, humor, grace, and realism. Because of this, Chaucer became the first great poet of the English nation and gave strong influences over the development of English literature.

The influence of Renaissance was already felt in Chaucer's literary creation when he was learning from the great Italian writers in the last part of the 14th century. In his works, Chaucer affirmed man's right to pursue earthly happiness and opposed asceticism; he praised man's energy, intellect, quick wit and love of life; he exposed and satirized the social vices, including religious abuses. It thus can be said that though essentially a medieval writer, Chaucer bore marks of humanism and anticipated a new era to come.

As a work of Chaucer's masterpiece, *The Canterbury Tales* represents his final poetic achievement. For the depth of interest, the wealth of human comedy, and the mature wisdom, it is unrivaled among the medieval English literary works. It is more than just a collection of stories; it is a pageant of 14th century English life. Ranging in status from a Knight to a humble Plowman, the pilgrims are a microcosm of English society.

The General Prologue is usually regarded as the greatest portrait gallery in English literature. It is largely composed of a series of sketches differing widely in length and method, and blending the individual and the typical in varying degrees. Its purpose is not only to present a vivid collection of character sketches, but also to set the tone for the story-telling, to make clear the plan for the tales, to motivate the tale-telling and to introduce the pilgrims and the occasion of the pilgrimage.

In *The Canterbury Tales*, there are all together 24 tales with the Knight's tale at the beginning, the Parson's tale at the end, and others stretching in between. Though the stories vary greatly both in subject and style, *The Canterbury Tales* should be read as a whole poem and not simply as a collection of tales strung together by some loose thread. In its total impression, The Canterbury pilgrimage is the procession of the human comedy itself. The diversity of the tales fulfills the promise of that initial diversity of pilgrim "characters" presented in the Prologue, who are both individuals and representatives in the moral and social sense. In the interludes between the tales, these "characters" are set in action, chatting, arguing and quarreling with one another; and the tales themselves are a lively extension of their talk. These tales are the entertainment the pilgrims provide for each other and at the same time they are a full revelation of the pilgrims themselves, their interests, attitudes and antagonisms.

2. 2. 2 Excerpts from the General Prologue of *The Canterbury Tales*

When in April the sweet showers fall
And pierce the drought of March to the root;[1] and all
The veins are bathed in liquor of such power[2]
As brings about the engendering of the flower[3],
When also Zephyrus[4] with his sweet breath
Exhales an air in every grove and heath
Upon the tender shoots, and the young sun
His half-course in the sign of the Ram has run[5],
And the small fowls are making melody
That sleep away the night with open eye
(So nature pricks them and their heart engages)
Then people long to go on pilgrimages

And palmers[6] long to seek the stranger strands
Of far-off saints, hallowed in sundry lands[7],
And specially, from every shire's end
In England, down to Canterbury they wend[8]
To seek the holy blissful martyr[9], quick
To give his help to them when they were sick.
It happened in that season that one day
In Southwark[10], at The Tabard[11], as I lay
Ready to go on pilgrimage and start
For Canterbury, most devout at heart,
At night there came into that hostelry[12]
Some nine and twenty in a company
Of sundry folk happening then to fall
In fellowship, and they were pilgrims all
That towards Canterbury meant to ride.
The rooms and stables of the inn were wide,[13]
They made us easy, all was of the best.
And shortly, when the sun had gone to rest,
By speaking to them all upon the trip
I soon was of them in fellowship
And promised to rise early and take the way
To Canterbury, as you heard me say.
But nonetheless, while I have time and space,
Before my story takes a further pace,[14]
It seems a reasonable thing to say
What their condition[15] was, the full array[16]
Of each of them, as it appeared to me,
According to profession and degree,[17]
And what apparel[18] they were riding in;
And at a Knight I therefore will begin.

* * * *

There also was a Nun, a Prioress[19];
Her way of smiling was simple and coy[20].
Her greatest oath was only "By St. Loy!"[21]
And she was known as Madam Eglantyne,
And well she sang a service[22], with a fine
Intoning through her nose, as was most seemly,
And she spoke daintily in French, extremely,

After the school of Stratford-atte-Bowe[23];
French in the Paris style she did not know.
At meat her manners were well taught withal;
No morsel from her lips did she let fall,
Nor dipped her fingers in the sauce too deep;
But she could carry a morsel up and keep
The smallest drop from falling on her breast.
For courtliness[24] she had a special zest.
And she would wipe her upper lip so clean
That not a trace of grease was to be seen
Upon the cup when she had drunk; to eat,
She reached a hand sedately for the meat.
She certainly was very entertaining,
Pleasant and friendly in her ways, and straining
To counterfeit a courtly kind of grace,
A stately bearing fitting to her place,
And to seem dignified in all her dealings.
As for her sympathies and tender feelings,
She was so charitably solicitous
She used to weep if she but saw a mouse
Caught in a trap, if it were dead or bleeding.
And she had little dogs she would be feeding
With roasted flesh, or milk, or fine white bread.
And bitterly she wept if one were dead
Or someone took a stick and made it smart;
She was all sentiment and tender heart.
Her veil was gathered in a seemly way,
Her nose was elegant, her eyes glass-gray;
Her mouth was very small, but soft and red,
Her forehead, certainly, was fair of spread,
Almost a span[25] across the brows, I own;
She was indeed by no means undergrown.
Her cloak, I noticed, had a graceful charm.
She wore a coral trinket on her arm,
A set of beads, the gaudies[26] tricked[27] in green,
Whence hung a golden brooch of brightest sheen
On which there first was graven a crowned A,
And lower, *Amor vincit omnia.* [28]

* * * *

A worthy *woman* from beside Bath city
Was with us, somewhat deaf, which was a pity.
In making cloth she showed so great a bent[29]
She bettered those of Ypres and of Ghent[30]
In all the parish not a dame dared stir
Towards the altar steps in front of her
And if indeed they did, so wrath was she
As to be quite put out of charity.[31]
Her kerchiefs were of finely woven ground;[32]
I dared have sworn they weighed a good ten pound,
The ones she wore on Sunday, on her head.
Her hose were of the finest scarlet red
And gartered tight; her shoes were soft and new.
Bold was her face, handsome, and red in hue.
A worthy woman all her life, what's more
She'd had five husbands, all at the church door,
Apart from other company in youth;[33]
No need just now to speak of that, forsooth.[34]
And she had thrice been to Jerusalem,
Seen many strange rivers and passed over them;
She'd been to Rome and also to Boulogne,
Saint James of Compostella and Cologne,[35]
And she was skilled in wandering by the way.
She had gap-teeth, set widely, truth to say.
Easily on an ambling horse she sat
Well wimpled up, and on her head a hat
As broad s is a buckler or a shield;
She had a flowing mantle that concealed
Large hips, her heels spurred sharply under that.
In company she liked to laugh and chat
And knew the remedies for love's mischances,
An art in which she knew the oldest dances.[36]

☞ Notes

1. **pierce the drought of March to the root:** The gentle spring rain penetrates the very roots of the plants. Here drought of March refers to the general situation on the European continent, not specifically to Britain, for March in Britain is not very dry.

2. **The veins are bathed in liquor of such power:** Spring rain provides enough water for every rib of the leaves, thus endowing the plants with its power.
3. **the engendering of the flower:** the budding of the flower. Here, engendering means springing up.
4. **Zephyrus:** the west wind (personified).
5. **the young sun /His half-course in the sign of the Ram has run:** The sun is young because it has run only half way through the Ram, which is the first sign of the Zodiac. The sun runs through the sign of the Ram annually from March 21st to April 21st.
6. **palmers:** pilgrims, so called because they carried palms to show that they had been to Jerusalem.
7. **the stranger strands/ Of far-off saints, hallowed in sundry lands:** the foreign shores where there were the distant shrines of the saints, which were considered as holy places in different countries.
8. **wend** (archaic): go.
9. **the holy blissful martyr:** Here it refers to Thomas a Becket who in his lifetime was Chancellor of Britain and Archbishop of Canterbury. He resisted the efforts of King Henry Ⅱ to deprive the church courts of part of their power. As a result of the quarrel, four of Henry's knights rode to Canterbury and murdered Thomas in the cathedral. Thomas was later considered a martyr and worshipped as a saint, and his tomb at Canterbury became one of the most famous shrines in England.
10. **Southwark:** a suburb of London.
11. **The Tabard:** an inn at Southwark.
12. **hostelry:** an inn, a lodging house.
13. **wide:** spacious.
14. **Before my story takes a further pace:** Before I proceed with my story.
15. **condition:** social status, position.
16. **the full array:** the complete outfit (dress and appearance).
17. **degree:** rank.
18. **apparel:** clothing.
19. **Prioress:** a nun corresponding in rank to a prior (i. e. the superior of a convent).
20. **coy:** The word carries two slightly different meanings: (1) "shrinking from contact or familiarity;" (2) "marked by cute, coquettish, or artful playfulness."
21. **"By St. Loy":** a very mild oath. St. Loy was a well-known French goldsmith in the 6th century.
22. **sang a service:** sang hymns in a church service.
23. **Straford-atte-Bowe:** a monastery near London. Chaucer is making fun of the prioress by describing her speaking of French with a strong local accent.
24. **courtliness:** courtly behaviour, refined manners adopted by courtiers and ladies of

the court.

25. **a span:** the maximum distance between the tips of the thumb and the little finger.
26. **gaudies:** A gaud is a large bead placed between every ten beads in a rosary to mark a division in a prayer.
27. **tricked:** decorated.
28. **Amor vincit omnia** (Latin): Love conquers all.
29. **bent:** a natural skill.
30. **Ypres and Ghent:** cities in Belgium known for clothmaking in Chaucer's time.
31. **put out of charity:** to lose temper.
32. **ground:** texture.
33. **Apart from other company in youth:** not including other lovers she had in her youth.
34. **forsooth** (archaic): truly, no doubt.
35. **Boulogne, / St. James of Compostella and Cologne:** Boulogne, a seaside city in France; Compostella, a city in Spain; and Cologne, a city in Germany. In Chaucer's time, the shrines of these places attracted many pilgrims.
36. **An art in which she knew the oldest dances:** She got to know all the old tricks of the art (of love).

☞ Study questions

1. What is the "framing device" that Chaucer used for his collection of stories?
2. Study lines 1-18 of the "General Prologue." What seems to be the motives offered for the pilgrimage? In what way are the season and the nature imagery important factors?
3. Based on Prioress's portrait, can you deduce a possible reason why she is undertaking this pilgrimage?
4. What details indicate the Prioress is a bit "worldly" in her concerns and behavior?
5. Why does the Wife of Bath travel?
6. How does Chaucer reveal his attitude towards the Wife of Bath?

☞ Essay topics

1. Do you think the Prioress is portrayed by Chaucer as a perfect lady or a perfect nun? Why?
2. Do some research into Chaucer's use of irony in *The Canterbury Tales* and discuss how he makes ironic portraiture of the pilgrims, especially the Prioress.

2.3 Folk Ballad

2.3.1 Characteristic features

The folk ballad is a popular literary form. It is said that ballads were originally oral forms of verse to be sung or recited by the unlettered people. As the main form of medieval folk literature, all its stylistic features have derived from the oral tradition. The first feature is its simple language, which is reflected both in the verse form and the colloquial expressions. The main form of ballads is the quatrain, which is known as the ballad stanza, rhyming *abcb*, with the first and third lines carrying 4 accented syllables and the second and fourth carrying 3. By making use of a simple language or dialect of the common people with colloquial expressions in its narration or dialogues, the ballad gives a strong dramatic effect to the reader. The second feature is its wonderful story, which deals only with the culminating incident or climax of a plot. Most of the ballads have a romantic or tragic dimension, with a tragic incident as their subject. Like classical tragedy, ballads have an inevitability, which reflects the folk belief that people are lured into the fatally attractive traps just because all human life is shaped by fate. It is a common pattern of romantic tragic balladry that if one lover dies the other must follow suit. The third feature is its dominant mood or tone, either tragic like "Sir Patrick Spens," which tells a story of treachery, or comic like "Get up and Bar the Door," which presents a funny scene of the domestic life. Furthermore, to strengthen the dramatic effect of the narration, ballads also make full use of hyperbole; actions and events are much exaggerated. This hyperbolic style partly comes from a desire to astonish, for the poor folk would be delighted to hear of the larger-than-life exploits of ballad people. Another impressive feature of the ballad is the using of refrains and other kinds of repetitions. Poetically the refrains are decorative; musically they are absolutely essential. Through refrains and repetitions, the narration is lent a quality of liturgy, or of incantation. Magic or supernatural force, the perpetual presence of impossibility, is a rich narrative source of balladry. In the ballad world, things happen suddenly and without warning; only the help of magic or supernatural force can overcome the fatal powers of destruction. Love, adventure, courageous feats of daring, and sudden disaster are frequent topics of the folk ballad.

2.3.2 "The Three Ravens"[1]

There were three ravens sat on a tree,
  Down a down, hey down, hey down,
They were three ravens sat on a tree,
  With a down.

There were three ravens sat on a tree,
They were as black as black might be,
  With a down, derry, derry, derry down, down.

The one of them said to his mate.
"Where shall we our breakfast take?

"Down in yonder green field
There lies a knight slain under his shield.

His hounds they lie down at his feet,
So well they can their master keep.[2]

"His hawks they fly so eagerly,[3]
There's no fowl[4] dare him come nigh."

Down there comes a fallow doe,[5]
As great with young as she might go.

She lifted up his bloody head,
And kissed his wounds that were so red.

She got him up upon her back,
And carried him to earthen lake.[6]

She buried him before the prime;[7]
She was dead herself ere evensong[8] time.

God send every gentleman
Such hawks, such hounds, and such lemman.[9]

☞ **Notes**

1. Instead of the regular ballad form, this ballad basically consists of 11 two-lined stanzas. The second and the fourth lines in the first stanza and the third line in the second stanza are tunes sung by the ballad singer to attract the attention of the listener.
2. **So well they can their master keep:** So well do they keep guard over their master.
3. **His hawks they fly so eagerly:** The hawks he bred fly so fiercely.
4. **no fowl:** no bird.
5. **fallow doe:** reddish brown female deer. Here the doe is alluding to the knight's mistress.
6. **earthen lake:** pit.

7. **prime:** the first hour of the morning.
8. **evensong:** the service of evening prayer in the church.
9. **lemman:** mistress.

☞ Study questions

1. What happens in this ballad?
2. What is the mood of the ballad?
3. What is its theme?

2. 3. 3 "Sir Patrick Spens"

The king sits in Dunfermling town, [1]
  Drinking the blude-reid[2] wine:
"O whar will I get guid sailor
  To sail this ship of mine?"

Up and spak an eldern knicht, [3]
  Sat at the king's richt[4] knee:
"Sir Patrick Spens is the best sailor
  That sails upon the sea."

The king has written a braid[5] letter,
  And signed it wi' his hand,
And sent it to Sir Patrick Spens,
  Was walking on the sand.

The first line that Sir Patrick read,
  A loud lauch[6] lauched he;
The next line that Sir Patrick read,
  The tear blinded his ee. [7]

"O wha[8] is this has don this deed,
  This ill deed done to me,
To send me out this time o' the year,
  To sail upon the sea?

"Make haste, make haste, my mirry men all,
  Our guid ship sails the morn."
"O say na sae, [9] my master dear,

For I fear a deadly storm.

"Late late yestre'en I saw the new moon
Wi' the auld[10] moon in her arm,
And I fear, I fear, my dear master,
That we will come to harm."

O our Scots nobles were richt laith[11]
To weet[12] their cork-heeled shoon,[13]
But lang owre[14] a' the play were played,
Their hats they swam aboon.[15]

O lang, lang may their ladies sit,
Wi' their fans into their hand,
Or e'er they see Sir Patrick Spens
Come sailing to the land.

O lang, lang may the ladies stand,
Wi' their gold kembs[16] in their hair,
Waiting for their ain[17] dear lords,
For they'll see thame na mair.[18]

Half o'er, half o'er to Aberdour,[19]
It's fifty fadom[20] deep,
And there lies guid Sir Patrick Spens,
Wi' the Scots lords at his feet.

☞ Notes

1. **Dunfermling town:** a town in Scotland.
2. **blude-reid:** blood-red.
3. **eldern knicht:** elderly knight.
4. **richt:** right.
5. **braid:** broad.
6. **lauch:** laugh.
7. **ee:** eye.
8. **wha:** who.
9. **na sae:** not so.
10. **auld:** old.

11. **laith:** loath.
12. **weet:** wet.
13. **shoon:** shoes.
14. **owre:** ere.
15. **aboon:** above.
16. **kembs:** combs.
17. **ain:** own.
18. **mair:** more.
19. **half o'er to Aberdour:** halfway over to Aberdeen (in Scotland).
20. **fadom:** fathoms.

☞ Study questions

1. What is the conflict of this ballad?
2. What image in the first stanza foreshadows a tragedy?
3. Why does Sir Patrick Spence go on the trip even after he knows it is a death-mission?
4. How would you describe Sir Patrick's character?
5. What can you learn from this ballad?

2. 3. 4 "Get Up and Bar the Door"

It fell about the Martinmas[1] time,
  And a gay time it was then,
When our good wife got puddings to make,
  And she's boild them in the pan.

The wind sae cauld[2] blew south and north,
  And blew into the floor;
Quoth our goodman to our goodwife,
  "Gae[3] out and bar the door."

"My hand is in my hussyfskap[4],
  Goodman, as ye may see;
An it shoud nae[5] be barrd this hundred year,
  It's no be barrd for me."

They made a paction[6] tween them twa[7],
  They made it firm and sure,
That the first word whaeer[8] shoud speak,
  Shoud rise and bar the door.

Then by there came two gentlemen,
  At twelve o'clock at night,
And they could neither see house nor hall,
  Nor coal nor candle-light.

"Now whether is this a rich man's house,
  Or whether is it a poor?"
But neer a word wad ane[9] o them speak,
  For barring of the door.

And first they ate the white puddings,
  And then they ate the black;
Tho muckle[10] thought the goodwife to hersel,
  Yet neer a word she spake.

Then said the one unto the other,
  "Here, man, tak ye my knife;
Do ye tak aff the auld man's beard,
  And I'll kiss the goodwife."

"But there's nae water in the house,
  And what shall we do than?"
"What ails thee at the pudding-broo,[11]
  That boils into the pan?"

O up then started our goodman,
  An angry man was he:
"Will ye kiss my wife before my een,
  And scad[12] me wi pudding-bree?"

Then up and started our goodwife,
  Gied[13] three skips on the floor:
"Goodman, you've spoken the foremost word,
  Get up and bar the door."

☞ Notes

1. **Martinmas**: November 11th, the feast of St. Martin.
2. **sae:** so; **cauld:** cold.
3. **gae:** go.
4. **hussyfskap:** housewifery.
5. **shoud nae:** should not.
6. **paction:** compact.
7. **twa**: two.
8. **whaeer:** whoever.
9. **wad:** would. **ane**: one (of the husband and the wife).
10. **muckle:** much.
11. **What ails thee:** "why don't you use ..."; **pudding-broo:** pudding-broth.
12. **scad:** scald.
13. **gied:** gave.

☞ Study questions

1. What is the mood of this ballad?
2. What can you learn from this ballad?
3. How is the story told?

Chapter 3

The Sixteenth Century (1485-1603)

3.1 Introduction

Renaissance is commonly applied to the movement in Europe that marks the transition from the medieval to the modern world. Generally, it refers to the period between the 14th and mid-17th century. It first started in Italy, with the flowering of painting, sculpture and literature. From Italy the movement went to embrace the rest of Europe. Renaissance, which means rebirth, is usually regarded as the result of a new emphasis upon the newly discovered Greek and Roman classics and the combination of a newly interpreted Christian tradition and an admired tradition of pagan culture. The movement was stimulated by a series of historical events, such as the rediscovery of ancient Greek and Roman culture, the new discoveries in geography and astronomy, the religious reformation, and the economic expansion. Therefore, Renaissance, in essence, is a historical period in which the European humanist thinkers made attempts to get rid of those old feudalist ideas in medieval Europe, to introduce new ideas that expressed the interests of the rising bourgeoisie, and to recover the purity of the early Christianity from the corruption of the Roman Catholic Church.

Renaissance was slow in reaching England not only because of England's separation from the Continent but also because of its domestic unrest. The century and a half following the death of Chaucer is the most volcanic period of English history. The war-like nobles seized the power of England and turned it into self-destruction. The Wars of Roses are examples to show how the energy of England was violently destroying itself. The frightful reign of Richard Ⅲ marked a savage escalation of the factional fighting between the war-like nobles. Consequently almost all the powerful lords were extinguished in their power struggles. After defeating Richard Ⅲ in 1485, Henry Ⅶ founded the Tudor dynasty, thus establishing a centralized monarchy of a totally new type. In the reign of Henry Ⅷ, the Oxford reformers introduced classical literature to England. Education, based upon the classics and the *Bible*, was revitalized, and literature, already much read during the 15th century, became even more popular. Thus began the English Renaissance, which was perhaps England's golden age. The English Renaissance had no sharp break with the past. Attitudes and feelings which had been characteristic of the 14th and 15th centuries persisted well down into the era of Elizabethan and Jacobean reign.

Humanism is the essence of the Renaissance. But in the medieval society, people as individuals were largely subordinated to the feudalist rule without any freedom and independence; and in medieval theology, people's relationships to the world about them were largely reduced to a problem of adapting to or avoiding the circumstances of earthly life in an effort to prepare their souls for a heavenly life. However, Renaissance humanists found in the classics a justification to exalt human nature and came to see that human beings were glorious creatures capable of individual development in the direction of perfection, and that the world they inhabited was theirs not to despise but to question, explore, and enjoy. Thus, by emphasizing the dignity of human beings and the importance of the present life, they voiced their beliefs that man did not only have the right to enjoy the beauty of this life, but had the ability to perfect himself and to perform wonders. Humanism began to take hold in England when the Dutch scholar Desiderius Erasmus (1466-1536) came to teach the classical learning, first at Oxford and then at Cambridge. Thomas More, Christopher Marlowe and William Shakespeare are the best representatives of the English humanists.

Another important part of this Renaissance movement was the religious Reformation, which was initiated by Martin Luther (1483-1546), a German Protestant. Luther believed that every true Christian was his own priest and was entitled to interpret the *Bible* for himself. Encouraged by Luther's preaching, reformers from northern Europe vitalized the Protestant movement. The colorful and dramatic rituals of the Catholic Church were simplified. Indulgences, pilgrimages, and other practices were condemned. In the early stage of the continental Reformation, Henry Ⅷ was regarded as a faithful son of the Catholic Church and named "Defender of the Faith" by the Pope. Only his need for a legitimate male heir, and hence a new wife, led him to cut ties with Rome. But the common English people had long been dissatisfied with the corruption of the church and inspired by the reformers' ideas from the Continent. So they welcomed and supported Henry's decision of breaking away from Rome. When Henry Ⅷ declared himself through the approval of the Parliament as the Supreme Head of the Church of England in 1534, the Reformation in England was in its full swing. One of the major results was the fact that the *Bible* in English was placed in every church and services were held in English instead of Latin so that people could understand. In the brief reign of Henry's son Edward Ⅵ the reform of the church's doctrine and teaching was carried out. But after Mary ascended the throne, there was a violent swing to Catholicism. However, by the middle of Elizabeth's reign, Protestantism had been firmly established, with a certain extent of compromise between Catholicism and Protestantism. The religious Reformation was actually a reflection of the class struggle waged by the rising bourgeoisie against the feudal class and its ideology.

Strong national feeling in the time of the Tudors gave a great incentive to the cultural development in England. English schools and universities were established in place of the old monasteries. With classical culture and the Italian humanistic ideas coming into England, the English Renaissance began flourishing. One of the men who made a great contribution in this respect was William Caxton, for he was the first person to introduce printing into England. With the introduction of printing, an age of translation came into being. Lots and lots of continental literary works both ancient and modern were translated and printed in English, thus providing numerous books for the English people to read and making everything ready for the appearance of the great Elizabethan writers.

The early stage of the English Renaissance was one of imitation and assimilation. Academies after the Italian type were founded. Petrarch was regarded as the fountainhead of literature by the English writers. Wyatt and Surrey began engraving the forms and graces of Italian poetry upon the native stock. While the former introduced the Italian sonnet into England, the latter brought in blank verse. Sidney followed with the sestina and *terza rima*. Marlowe gave new vigor to the blank verse with his "mighty lines". Poetry, which was regarded as a concentrated exercise of the mind, of craftsmanship, and of learning, came into a great boom. Spenser's *The Shepherdes Calendar* showed how the pastoral convention could be adapted to a variety of subjects, moral or heroic, and how the rules of decorum, or fitness of style to subject, could be applied through variations in the diction and metrical scheme. In "The Passionate Shepherd to His Love," Marlowe spoke with a voice so innocent that it would be very difficult for us to connect it with the voice in his tragedies.

The Elizabethan drama, in its totality, is the real mainstream of the English Renaissance. English drama could be dated back to the Middle Ages. Interludes and morality plays thriving in the medieval period continued to be popular down to Shakespeare's time. But the development of the drama into a sophisticated art form required another influence—the Greek and Roman classics. Lively, vivid native English materials were put into the regular form of the Latin comedies of Plautus and Terence. Tragedies were in the style of Seneca. The fusion of classical form with English content brought about the possibility of a mature and artistic drama. The most famous dramatists in the Renaissance England are Christopher Marlowe, William Shakespeare, and Ben Jonson, who wrote plays with such universal qualities of greatness. By imitating the romances of Italy and Spain, embracing the mysteries of German legend, and combining the fictions of poetic fancy with the facts of daily life, they made a vivid depiction of the sharp conflicts between feudalism and the rising bourgeoisie in a transitional period. With humors of the moment, abstractions of philosophical speculation, and intense vitality, this extraordinary drama, with Shakespeare as the master, left a monument of the Renaissance unrivaled for pure creative power by any other product of that epoch.

3.2 Edmund Spenser

3.2.1 Life and career

Spenser (1552-1599) was born into a poor family in London. Thanks to the patronage of Robert Nowell, he received a good education first at the Merchant Taylors' School and then at Pembroke College, Cambridge. He studied philosophy, rhetoric and languages to prepare himself as a poet. He left Cambridge in 1576 and served as personal secretary to several prominent men, including the earl of Leicester. Later he met the poet Philip Sidney, and they became close friends. Spenser wrote *The Shepheardes Calendar* (1579) and dedicated it to Sidney. In 1580 through Leicester's influence, Spenser was made secretary to Lord Grey of Wilton, the queen's deputy in Ireland. He spent the rest of his life there holding various posts in the government. He later acquired Kilcolman Castle north of Cork for his use. The beautiful scenery of this district appears again and again in his poetry. Spenser fell in love with an Irish woman named Elizabeth Boyle and wrote his sonnet sequence *Amoretti* in her honor. He married her in 1594 and wrote the beautiful "Epithalamion" to celebrate his wedding. In 1598 a fierce Irish rebellion forced Spenser to abandon Kilcolman Castle. Spenser never recovered from the shock of this frightful experience. Suffered from sickness both in body and spirit, he died shortly after his return to London.

Spenser's most notable and ambitious poetic achievement is *The Faerie Queene*, set in the mythical world of King Arthur and his knights. Spenser had planned to write twelve books for this great poem, but he completed only six. According to his own explanation, his principal intention is "to fashion a gentleman or noble person in virtuous and gentle discipline." Each book has a hero knight who performs noble deeds for a glorious fairy queen whom Spenser intentionally associates with Queen Elizabeth I. The knight in each book represents a different moral virtue: justice, courtesy, and so on. The hero of heroes, who possesses all of these virtues, is Arthur, and he is to play a role in each of the 12 major adventures, which serves as a unifying element for the poem as a whole. Another character contributing to the unity of the work is Gloriana, the Fairy Queen. It is from her court and at her bidding that each of the heroes sets out on his particular adventure. Prince Arthur's great mission is his search for the Fairy Queen, with whom he has fallen in love through a love vision. Obstacles the knights encounter in the poem stand for evils and temptations that must be overcome. The reader will find that all these would happen in an enchanted world of dragons, giants, witches, and other marvels.

Spenser uses biblical allegory to tell his story, intending to bring to light his moral virtues and philosophies. In the broad sense, the entire struggle between the good and evil characters in *The Faerie Queene* is to be taken as figuring forth the warfare both in the individual soul and in the world at large between virtue and sin; and in a narrow sense, between Protestantism and Catholicism, and between England and Spain. Many of the single persons of the story bear double or triple roles. Gloriana, the Fairy Queen, is abstractly Glory, but humanly Queen Elizabeth. So likewise the witch Duessa is both Papal Falsehood and Mary Queen of Scots; Prince Arthur both Magnificence and the Earl of Leicester. Other characters also carry different levels of meanings. For instance, the Redcrosse Knight in Book Ⅰ stands for St. George, the patron saint of England; he also represents Holiness, one of the 12 private virtues, as Sir Guyon in Book Ⅱ represents Temperance. The heroes do not possess the virtues they represent at the beginning of the stories; they acquire them in the course of their adventures.

Book Ⅰ of *The Faerie Queene* is in a way an epitome of the whole poem. The purpose of Redcrosse's quest is to free original mankind—the parents of Una—from the power of the Devil. Una and her knight are first seen together in the opening canto when Redcrosse easily routs the dragon of Error in the Wandering Wood. However, the fallen world of man is full of delusion, and the overconfident knight soon falls into the snares of Archimago. He pays for this mistake with suffering, but in the end, this suffering makes way for his recovery in the House of Holiness, aided by Faith, Hope, and Charity. With newfound strength and the grace of God, he is able to conquer the dragon that represents all the evil in the world.

For *The Faerie Queene* Spenser invented a new stanza form, a nine-line stanza, rhyming *ababbcbcc*. The first eight lines are in iambic pentameter; the last line has six iambic feet instead of five and is called an alexandrine. Known now as the Spenserian stanza, this nine-line format was used by later English poets such as Burns, Byron, Shelley, and Keats.

Recognized by his contemporaries as the foremost poet of his time, Spenser is not only a master of meter and language but a profound moral poet as well. The five main qualities of Spenser's poetry are (1) a perfect melody; (2) a rare sense of beauty; (3) a splendid imagination; (4) a lofty moral purity and seriousness; and (5) a dedicated idealism. In addition to the above, Spenser uses strange forms of speech and obsolete words in order to increase the rustic effect. It is Spenser's idealism, his love of beauty, and his exquisite melody that make him known as "the poets' poet."

3.2.2 "Sonnet 75"[1]

One day I wrote her name upon the strand,[2]
But came the waves and washed it away:
Agayne I wrote it with a second hand,
But came the tyde, and made my paynes his pray.[3]
"Vayne man," sayd she, "that doest in vaine assay,[4]
A mortal thing so to immortalize,
For I my selve shall lyke to this decay,
And eek[5] my name bee wyped out lykewize."
"Not so," quod[6] I, "let baser things devize,[7]
To dy in dust, but you shall live by fame:
My verse your vertues rare shall eternize,[8]
And in the heavens wryte your glorious name.
Where whenas death shall all the world subdew,
Our love shall live, and later life renew."

☞ Notes

1. This poem is written in the form of English (Shakespearian) sonnet. Its rhyme scheme is *abab bcbc cdcd ee.*
2. **strand:** seashore.
3. **pray:** prey.
4. **assay:** try.
5. **eek:** also.
6. **quod:** said.
7. **devize:** contrive.
8. **eternize:** make eternal.

☞ Study questions

1. What is the thematic significance of the waves and the tide?
2. What images does Spenser use in order to strengthen the theme?
3. Why does the speaker believe that he is able to immortalize his love?
4. What poetic techniques are used in this sonnet?

3.2.3 An excerpt from Canto 1, Book I of *The Faerie Queene*[1]

1

A gentle Knight was pricking on the plaine,
Ycladd[2] in mightie armes and silver shielde,

Wherein old dints of deepe wounds did remaine,
The cruell markes of many a bloudy fielde;
Yet armes till that time did he never wield;[3]
His angry steede did chide his foming bitt,
As much disdayning to the curbe to yield:[4]
Full jolly knight he seemed, and faire did sitt,
As one for knightly giusts[5] and fierce encounters fitt.

And on his brest a bloudie Crosse he bore,
The deare rememberance of his dying Lord,
For whose sweete sake that glorious badge he wore,
And dead as living ever him ado'd:[6]
Upon his shield the like was also scor'd,
For soveraine hope, which in his helpe he had:[7]
Right faithfull true he was in deede and word,
But of his cheere did seeme too solemne sad,[8]
Yet nothing did he dread, but ever was ydrad.[9]

Upon a great adventure he was bond,
That greatest Gloriana to him gave,
That greatest glorious Queene of Faerie lond,
to win him worship, and her grace to have,
Which of all earthly things he most did crave;
And ever as he rode, his heart did yearn[10]
To prove his puissance[11] in battle brave
Upon his foe, and his new force to learn;
Upon his foe, a Dragon horrible and stern.[12]

A lovely lady rode him faire beside,
Upon a lowly ass more white then snow,
Yet she much whiter,[13] but the same did hide
Under a vele, that wimpled was full low,[14]
And over all a black stole she did throw,
As one that inly mourned:[15] so was she sad,
And heavie sat upon her palfrey[16] slow:
Seemed in heart some hidden care she had,
And by her in a line a milke white lambe she lad.[17]

So pure and innocent, as that same lambe, [18]
She was in life and every vertuous lore,
And by descent from royall lynage came
Of ancient Kings and Queenes, that had of yore
Their scepters stretcht from east to westerne shore,
And all the world in their subjection held;
Till that infernall feend with foule uprore
Forwasted all their land, [19] and them expeld:
Whom to avenge, she had this knight from far compeld. [20]

Behind her farre away a Dwarfe did lag,
That lasie seemed in being ever last,
Or wearied with bearing of her bag
Of needments[21] at his backe. Thus as they past,
The day with cloudes was suddeine overcast,
And angry Jove[22] an hideous storme of raine
Did poure into his Lemans lap[23] so fast,
That everie wight to shrowd it did constrain, [24]
And this faire couple eke to shroud themselves were fain. [25]

Enforst to seeke some covert nigh at hand,
A shadie grove not farr away they spide, [26]
That promist ayde the tempest to withstand:
Whose loftie trees yclad with sommers pride
Did spred so broad, that heanens light did hide,
Not perceable with power of any starre:
And all within were pathes and alleies wide,
With footing worne, and leading inward farre:
Faire harbour that them seemes; so in they entred arre. [27]

☞ Notes

1. The poem is written in the stanza invented by poet himself, the Spenserian stanza, i. e., a stanza of nine lines, with the first eight lines in iambic pentameter and the last line in iambic hexameter, rhyming *ababbcbcc*.
2. **ycladd:** clad.
3. **Yet armes till that time did he never wield:** i. e., the knight had never fought in the battle field, so the weapon was new to him.
4. **His angry steede did chide his foming bitt, / As much disdayning to the curbe to yield:**

His horse, foaming with anger, ground the mouth-piece of the bridle as if too proud to yield to its master's control.

5. **giust:** same as joust, meaning: the encounter of two knights on horseback at a tournament.
6. **And dead as living ever him ador'd:** And always adored him (Jesus Christ) dead as if alive.
7. **Upon his shield the like was also scor'd, /For soveraine hope, which in his helpe he had:** Upon his shield there was also the mark of a Cross, as a sign of supreme hope which he received with the help of the Lord.
8. **But of his cheere did seeme too solemne sad:** But in countenance and bearing he seemed too solemnly grave. "cheere" = countenance.
9. **ydrad:** dreaded.
10. **his hart did earne:** his heart did yearn.
11. **puissance:** strength, power.
12. **stearne:** stern.
13. **Yet she much whiter:** here signifying the surpassing purity and spotlessness of Virgin Una.
14. **under a vele, that wimpled was full low:** Her veil was plaited in folds, falling to cover her face.
15. **As one that inly mourned:** as one who felt sorrowful at heart.
16. **palfrey:** a saddle-horse, esp. for a lady, here referring to Una's ass.
17. **lad:** old form for "led".
18. **as that same lambe:** referring to the Lamb of God, i. e., Jesus Christ.
19. **Forwasted all their land:** here referring to the dragon devastating the country.
20. **compeld:** old form for "compelled".
21. **needments:** things needed.
22. **Jove:** Jupiter, king of gods in Roman mythology.
23. **his Lemans lap:** his sweetheart's lap; Lemans: old form for sweetheart, here referring to earth.
24. **That everie wight to shrowd it did constrain:** that every person was forced to take shelter. "wight" = person, human being.
25. **fain:** glad.
26. **spide:** spied.
27. **Faire harbour that them seemes; so in they entered arre:** It seems to them to be a fair shelter and so they enter it.

☞ Study questions

1. What images does Spenser use to describe Redcrosse Knight?

2. What images does Spenser use to describe the Lady?
3. What would happen according to your anticipation when they took shelter in the forest?
4. Which of the moral virtues does Redcrosse Knight represent?

3.3 Christopher Marlowe

3.3.1 Life and career

Marlowe (1564-1593) was born in Canterbury, the son of a shoemaker. His early education is not known, but he bettered himself by winning scholarships that took him first to the King's School, and then Cambridge. His play, *Tamburlaine*, written before he left Cambridge, turned out to be a sweeping success on the stage. When he came to London in 1584, he became an actor and a playwright. His mind was surging with the ideals of Renaissance, which later found expression in *Dr. Faustus*. While in London, Marlowe moved among a circle of writers known as the "University Wits," graduates of Oxford and Cambridge. His name is often linked with the so-called "School of Night", which had a reputation for dangerous free-thinking. With unbridled passion and conceit of a young man, Marlowe became not only a celebrated poet and playwright but also a notorious freethinker and a reputed militant atheist. He lived a tempestuous life in the following six years since his first great success. On May 30, 1593, Marlowe was killed in a quarrel over a tavern bill in Deptford.

As the most gifted of the "University Wits," Marlowe wrote six plays within his short lifetime. Among them the most important are: *Tamburlaine*, Parts Ⅰ & Ⅱ (1587-1588), *The Jew of Malta* (1590?) and *The Tragical History of Doctor Faustus* (1592-1593). Each of Marlowe's important plays has as a central character, a passionate man doomed to destruction by an inordinate desire for power. The plays are further characterized by beautiful, sonorous language, which is, however, at times unrestrained to the point of bombast. Marlowe's non-dramatic poetry includes *Hero and Leander*, "The Passionate Shepherd to His Love," and a verse translation of Ovid's *Amores*.

Doctor Faustus is one of Marlowe's best works in which the old German legend is freely reshaped. Faustus is a great scholar who has a strong interest in knowledge. With the aid of black magic, he calls up the Devil's servant with whom he makes a compact by surrendering his soul to the Devil in return for 24 more years of life in which he may have the Devil's services to give him everything he desires. Then in the following scenes, Faustus is granted by the Devil all his wishes and desires. Meanwhile, Faustus also experiences much internal conflict, symbolized in the appearances of both Good Angel and Bad Angel. In the final scene, there remains only the terrifying soliloquy in which the anguish of the hero's mind is poignantly expressed. The play's dominant moral is human rather than religious. It celebrates the human passion for knowledge, power and happiness; it also reveals man's frustration in realizing the high aspirations in a hostile moral order. And the confinement to time is the cruelest fact of man's condition.

Marlowe's greatest achievement lies in that he perfected the blank verse and made it the principal medium of English drama. To achieve this, Marlowe employed hyperbole as his major figure of speech, which, instead of referring to the exaggeration of the language, indicates the poetic energy and intensity conveyed through the verse. His second achievement is the creation of the Renaissance hero for English drama. Such a hero is always individualistic and full of ambition, facing bravely the challenge from both gods and men.

Though Marlowe is masterful in handling blank verse and creating dramatic effects, he is not so strong in dramatic construction, and, compared with Shakespeare, his women characters are rather pale. But his brilliant achievement as a whole raised him to an eminence as the pioneer of English drama.

3.3.2 An excerpt from Act 5 of *Dr. Faustus*

Scene 1

[*Thunder and lightning. Enter devils with covered dishes;*
Mephistophilis leads them into Faustus' study. Then enter Wagner.]

WAG. I think my master means to die shortly;
He hath made his will, and given me his wealth,
His house, his goods, and store of golden plate,
Besides two thousand ducats ready coined.
And yet I wonder, for if death were nigh
He would not banquet, and carouse, and swill
Amongst the students as even now he doth,
Who are at supper with such belly-cheer
As Wagner never beheld in all his life.
See where they come; belike the feast is ended. [*Exit.*]
[*Enter Faustus, Mephistophilis, and two or three Scholars.*]

1 SCH. Master. Doctor Faustus, since our conference about fair ladies, which was the beautifullest in all the world, we have determined with ourselves that Helen of Greece was the admirablest lady that ever lived. Therefore, master Doctor, if you will do us that favor as to let us see that peerless dame of Greece, whom all the world admires for majesty, we should think ourselves much beholding unto you.

FAUST. Gentlemen,

For that I know your friendship is unfained,
And Faustus' custom is not to deny
The just requests of those that wish him well,
You shall behold that peerless dame of Greece,
No otherways for pomp and majesty
Than when Sir Paris crossed the seas with her
And brought the spoils to rich Dardania.[1]
Be silent, then, for danger is in words.
[*Music sounds. Mephistophilis brings in Helen; she passeth over the stage.*]

2 SCH. Too simple is my wit to tell her praise
Whom all the world admires for majesty.

3 SCH. No marvel though the angry Greeks pursued
With ten years' war the rape of such a queen
Whose heavenly beauty passeth all compare.

1 SCH. Since we have seen the pride of Nature's works
And only paragon of excellence,
Let us depart, and for this glorious deed
Happy and blest be Faustus evermore.

FAUST. Gentlemen, Farewell; the same I wish to you. [*Exeunt Scholars.*]
[*Enter an Old Man.*]

OLD MAN. O, gentle Faustus, leave this damned art,
This magic, that will charm thy soul to hell
And quite bereave[2] thee of salvation.
Though thou hast now offended like a man,
Do not persever in it like a devil.
Yet, yet, thou hast an amiable soul
If sin by custom grow not into nature;
Then, Faustus, will repentance come too late;
Then thou art banished from the sight of heaven.
No mortal can express the pains of hell.
It may be this my exhortation
Seems harsh and all unpleasant; let it not,
For, gentle son, I speak it not in wrath,
Or envy of thee, but in tender love
And pity of thy future misery,
And so have hope that this my kind rebuke,
Checking thy body, may amend thy soul.

FAUST. Where art thou, Faustus? Wretch, what hast thou done?
Damned art thou, Faustus, damned! Despair and die.
[*Mephistophilis gives him a dagger.*]
Hell claims his right, and with a roaring voice
Says, "Faustus, come; thine hour is almost come!"
And Faustus now will come to do thee right.

OLD MAN. O stay, good Faustus, stay thy desperate steps!
I see an angel hovers o'er thy head
And with a vial full of precious grace
Offers to pour the same into thy soul:
Then call for mercy, and avoid despair.

FAUST. Ah, my sweet friend, I feel thy words
To comfort my distressed soul.
Leave me awhile to ponder on my sins.

OLD MAN. Faustus, I leave thee, but with grief of heart,
Fearing the ruin of thy hapless soul. [*Exit.*]

FAUST. Accursed Faustus, where is mercy now?
I do repent, and yet I do despair:
Hell strives with grace for conquest in my breast.
What shall I do to shun the snares of death?

MEPH. Thou traitor, Faustus, I arrest thy soul
For disobedience to my sovereign lord.
Revolt, or I'll in piecemeal tear thy flesh.

FAUST. I do repent I e'er offended him.
Sweet Mephistophilis, entreat thy lord
To pardon my unjust presumption,
And with my blood again I will confirm
The former vow I made to Lucifer.

MEPH. Do it then, Faustus, with unfeigned heart
Lest greater dangers do attend thy drift.

FAUST. Torment, sweet friend, that base and aged man
That durst dissuade me from thy Lucifer,
With greatest torments that our hell affords.

MEPH. His faith is great; I cannot touch his soul;
But what I may afflict his body with
I will attempt, which is but little worth.

FAUST. One thing, good servant, let me crave of thee:
To glut the longing of my heart's desire,

That I might have unto my paramour,
That heavenly Helen which I saw of late,
Whose sweet embracings may extinguish clear
These thoughts that do dissuade me from my vow,
And keep mine oath I made to Lucifer.

MEPH. This, or what else my Faustus shall desire
Shall be performed in twinkling of an eye.
[*Enter Helen again, passing over between two Cupids.*]

FAUST. Was this the face that launched a thousand ships
And burnt the topless towers[3] of Ilium?
Sweet Helen, make me immortal with a kiss.
Her lips suck forth my soul—see where it flies!
Come, Helen, come, give me my soul again.
Here will I dwell, for heaven is in these lips
And all is dross that is not Helena.
[*Enter old man and stands watching Faustus.*]
I will be Paris, and for love of thee,
Instead of Troy shall Wittenberg be sacked,
And I will combat with weak Menelaus,
And wear thy colours on my plumed crest.
Yea, I will wound Achilles in the heel,
And then return to Helen for a kiss.
O, thou art fairer than the evening air
Clad in the beauty of a thousand stars!
Brighter art thou than flaming Jupiter
When he appeared to hapless Semele,[4]
More lovely than the Monarch of the sky,
In wanton Arethusa's azure arms,[5]
And none but thou shalt be my paramour!
[*Exeunt all except the Old Man.*]

OLD MAN. Accursed Faustus, miserable man,
That from thy soul exclud'st the grace of heaven
And fliest the throne of his tribunal seat.
[*Enter the Devils to torment him.*]
Satan begins to sift me with his pride.[6]
As in this furnace God shall try my faith,
My faith, vile hell, shall triumph over thee!
Ambitious fiends, see how the heavens smiles

At your repulse, and laughs your state to scorn.
Hence, hell! for hence I fly unto my God. [*Exeunt.*]

Scene 2

[*Thunder. Enter Lucifer, Beelzebub, and Mephistophilis.*]

LUC. Thus from infernal Dis[7] do we ascend
To view the subjects of our monarchy,
Those souls which sin seals the black sons of hell.
'Mong which as chief, Faustus, we come to thee,
Bringing with us lasting damnation
To wait upon thy soul; the time is come
Which makes it forfeit.

MEPH. And this gloomy night
Here in this room will wretched Faustus be.

BEL. And here we'll stay,
To mark him how he doth demean himself.

MEPH. How should he but in desperate lunacy?
Fond worldling, now his heart-blood dries with grief,
His conscience kills it, and his laboring brain
Begets a world of idle fantasies
To overreach the devil, but all in vain.
His store of pleasures must be sauced with pain.
He and his servant Wagner are at hand;
Both come from drawing Faustus' latest will.
See where they come.

[*Enter Faustus and Wagner.*]

FAUST. Say, Wagner, thou hast perused my will;
How dost thou like it?

WAG. Sir, so wondrous well
As in all humble duty I do yield
My life and lasting service for your love.

[*Enter the Scholars.*]

FAUST. Gramercies, Wagner. —Welcome, gentlemen.

1 SCH. Now, worthy Faustus, methinks your looks are changed.

FAUST. Ah, gentlemen!

2 SCH. What ails Faustus?

FAUST. Ah, my sweet chamber-fellow, had I lived with thee, then had I lived still, but now must die eternally. Look, sirs! Comes he not? Comes he not?

1 SCH. O my dear Faustus, what imports this fear?

2 SCH. Is all our pleasure turned to melancholy?

3 SCH. He is not well with being over-solitary.

2 SCH. If it be so, we'll have physicians, and Faustus shall be cured.

3 SCH. 'Tis but a surfeit, [8] sir; fear nothing.

FAUST. A surfeit of deadly sin that hath damned both body and soul.

2 SCH. Yet, Faustus, look up to heaven: remember God's mercies are infinite.

FAUST. But Faustus' offense can ne'er be pardoned; the Serpent that tempted Eve may be saved, but not Faustus. Ah, gentlemen, hear with patience, and tremble not at my speeches. Though my heart pants and quivers to remember that I have been a student here these thirty years, O would I had never seen Wittenberg, never read book! And what wonders I have done all Germany can witness, yea, all the world, for which Faustus hath lost both Germany and the world, yea heaven itself—heaven the seat of God, the, Throne of the blessed, the kingdom of joy, and must remain in hell forever, hell, ah hell, forever! Sweet friends, what shall, become of Faustus, being in hell forever?

3 SCH. Yet, Faustus, call on God.

FAUST. On God, whom Faustus hath abjured? on God, whom Faustus hath blasphemed? Ah, my God, I would weep, but the devil draws in my tears! Gush forth, blood, instead of tears, yea life and soul! O he stays my tongue; I would lift up my hands but, see, they hold 'em, they hold 'em!

All. Who, Faustus?

FAUST. Why, Lucifer and Mephistophilis.
Ah Gentlemen, I gave them my soul for my cunning.

All. God forbid!

FAUST. God forbade it indeed, but Faustus hath done it: for vain pleasure of four and twenty years hath Faustus lost eternal joy and felicity. I writ them a bill with mine one blood; the date is expired, this is the time, and he will fetch me.

1 SCH. Why did not Faustus tell us of this before, that divines might have prayed for thee?

FAUST. Oft have I thought to have done so, but the devil threatened to tear me in pieces if I named God, to fetch both body and soul if I once gave ear to divinity; and now 'ts too late. Gentlemen, away, lest you perish with me!

2 SCH. O what may we do to save Faustus?

FAUST. Talk not of me, but save yourselves and depart.

3 SCH. God will strengthen me: I will stay with Faustus.

1 SCH. Tempt not God, sweet friend, but let us into the next room, and there pray for him.

FAUST. Aye, pray for me, pray for me! And what noise soever ye hear, come not unto me, for nothing can rescue me.

2 SCH. Pray thou, and we will pray that God may have mercy upon thee.

FAUST. Gentlemen, farewell. If I live till morning, I'll visit you; if not, Faustus is gone to hell.

All. Faustus, farewell. [*Exeunt Scholars.*]

MEPH. Aye Faustus, now thou hast no hope of heaven;
Therefore despair, think only upon hell,
For that must be thy mansion, there to dwell.

FAUST. O, thou bewitching fiend, 'Twas thy temptation
Hath robbed me of eternal happiness.

MEPH. I do confess it, Faustus, and rejoice.
'Twas I, that when thou wer't i' the way to heaven
Damned up thy passage; when thou tookest the book
To view the scriptures, then I turned the leaves
And led thine eye.
What, weepst thou? 'tis too late. Despair, farewell!
Fools that will laugh on earth must weep in hell. [*Exit.*]
[*Enter the Good Angel, and the Evil Angel at several doors.*]

G. ANG. Ah Faustus, if thou hadst given ear to me,
Innumerable joys had followed thee,
But thou didst love the world.

B. ANG. Gave ear to me,
And now must taste hell's pains perpetually.

G. ANG. O what will all thy riches, pleasures, pomps,
Avail thee now?

B. ANG. Nothing but vex thee more,
To want in hell, that had on earth such store.
[*Music while the throne descends.*[9]]

G. ANG. O, thou hast lost celestial happiness,
Pleasures unspeakable, bliss without end.
Hadst thou affected sweet divinity
Hell or the devil, had had no power on thee.
Hadst thou kept on that way, Faustus, behold,
In what resplendent glory thou hadst sit

In yonder throne, like those bright shining saints,
And triumphed over hell; that hast thou lost.
And now, poor soul, must thy good angel leave thee;
The jaws of hell are open to receive thee.
[*Exit. Hell is discovered.*]

B. ANG. Now Faustus, let thine eyes with horror stare
Into that vast perpetual torture-house.
There are the furies tossing damned souls
On burning forks; their bodies broil in lead.
There are live quarters[10] broiling on the coals
That ne'er can die. This ever-burning chair
Is for o'ertortured souls to rest them in;
These that are fed with sops of flaming fire
Were gluttons, and loved only delicates
And laughed to see the poor starve at their gates.
But yet all these are nothing; thou shalt see
Ten thousand tortures that more horrid be.

FAUST. O, I have seen enough to torture me.

B. ANG. Nay, thou must feel them, taste the smart of all;
He that loves pleasure must for pleasure fall.
And so I leave thee, Faustus, till anon;
Then wilt thou tumble in confusion.[11]
[*Exit. The clock strikes eleven.*]

FAUST. Ah, Faustus,
Now hast thou but one bare hour to live
And then thou must be damned perpetually!
Stand still, you ever-moving spheres of heaven,
That time may cease, and midnight never come;
Fair Nature's eye, rise, rise again and make
Perpetual day; or let this hour be but
A year, a month, a week, a natural day,
That Faustus may repent, and save his soul!
O lente lente currite noctis equi.[12]
The stars move still, time runs, the clock will strike,
The devil will come, and Faustus must be damned.
O, I'll leap up to my God! Who pulls me down?
See, see where Christ's blood streams in the firmament! —
One drop would save my soul—half a drop! ah, my Christ!

Rend not my heart for naming of my Christ;
Yet will I call on him—O, spare me, Lucifer!
Where is it now?'Tis gone; And see where God
Stretcheth out his arm and bends his ireful brows.
Mountains and hills, come, come, and fall on me
And hide me from the heavy wrath of God,
No, no?
Then will I headlong run into the earth:
Earth, gape! O no, it will not harbor me.
You stars that reigned at my nativity,
Whose influence hath allotted death and hell,
Now draw up Faustus like a foggy mist
Into the entrails of yon laboring cloud
That when you vomit forth into the air,
My limbs may issue from your smoky mouths,
So that my soul may but ascend to heaven. [13]
[*The watch strikes.*]
Ah, half the hour is past; 'twill all be past anon.
O God,
If thou wilt not have mercy on my soul,
Yet for Christ's sake, whose blood hath ransomed me
Impose some end to my incessant pain:
Let Faustus live in hell a thousand years,
A hundred thousand, and at last be saved!
O, no end is limited to damned souls!
Why wert thou not a creature wanting soul?
Or why is this immortal that thou hast?
Ah, Pythagoras' metempsychosis[14]—were that true,
This soul should fly from me, and I be changed
Unto some brutish beast. All beasts are happy,
For when they die
Their souls are soon dissolved in elements,
But mine must live still[15] to be plagued in hell.
Curst be the parents that engendered me!
No, Faustus, curse thyself, curse Lucifer
That hath deprived thee of the joys of heaven.
[*The clock striketh twelve.*]
It strikes, it strikes! Now, body, turn to air

Or Lucifer will bear thee quick[16] to hell!
[*Thunder and lightning.*]
O soul, be changed to little water drops,
And fall into the *ocean*, ne'er be found.
My God, my God, look not so fierce on me!
[*Enter Devils.*]
Adders and serpents, let me breathe a while!
Ugly hell, gape not—come not, Lucifer—
I'll burn my books—ah, Mephistophilis.
[*Exeunt Devils with Faustus.*]

☞ Notes

1. **Dardania:** Troy.
2. **bereave:** deprive.
3. **the topless towers:** The towers are so high as if they seem to have no tops.
4. **Semele:** a Theban girl, loved by Jupiter and destroyed by the fire of his lightning when he appeared to her in his full splendor.
5. **Arethusa:** Arethusa was the nymph of a fountain, as well as the fountain itself; no classical myth, however, records her love affair with Jupiter, the "monarch of the sky."
6. **with his pride:** i. e., to test me with his strength.
7. **Dis:** the underworld.
8. **surfeit:** indigestion, the effects of overindulgence.
9. **the throne descends:** A throne suspended by ropes descended to the stage near the end of many Elizabethan plays and was an expected theatrical display. Here the throne clearly symbolizes heaven, as the next speech shows.
10. **quarters:** bodies.
11. **confusion:** destruction, perdition.
12. ***O lente lente currrite equi:*** "Slowly, slowly run, O horses of the night", adapted from a line in Ovid's *Amores*.
13. **You stars … but ascend to heaven:** The seven lines here tell about how Faustus begs his natal stars to draw him up into the cloud, where his body may be compacted into a thunderstone and fall to earth, so that his soul, thus purified, may ascend to heaven.
14. **Pythagoras' metempsychosis:** Pythagoras' doctrine of the transmigration of souls.
15. **still:** always.
16. **quick:** alive.

☞ Study questions

1. What examples of hyperbole can you find in Faustus' speech to Helen of Troy?
2. Is Faustus a Renaissance or medieval hero? Justify your response.
3. What is Faustus' agony during the final scene of the play?
4. What is the significance of the Good Angel and the Bad Angel?
5. In what ways does Dr. Faustus epitomize Renaissance attitudes about knowledge and learning?

☞ Essay topics

1. How is Dr. Faustus representative of the spirit of the Renaissance?
2. Faustus and Macbeth are two men of ambition. How are they alike? How are they different?

3.3.3 "The Passionate Shepherd to His Love"

Come live with me and be my love,
And we will all the pleasures prove[1]
That valleys, groves, hills, and fields,
Woods, or steepy mountain yields.

And we will sit upon the rocks,
Seeing the shepherds feed their flocks,
By shallow rivers to whose falls
Melodious birds sing madrigals.[2]

And I will make thee beds of roses
And a thousand fragrant posies,
A cap of flowers, and a kirtle[3]
Embroidered all with leaves of myrtle;[4]

A gown made of the finest wool
Which from our pretty lambs we pull;
Fair lined slippers for the cold,
With buckles of the purest gold;

A belt of straw and ivy buds,
With coral clasps and amber studs:
And if these pleasures may thee move,
Come live with me, and be my love.

The shepherds' swains[5] shall dance and sing
For thy delight each May morning:
If these delights thy mind may move,
Then live with me and be my love.

☞ Notes

1. **prove:** experience, test.
2. **madrigal:** a short love lyric that can be set to music.
3. **kirtle:** a long dress worn by women.
4. **myrtle:** shrub with evergreen leaves, white or pink flowers, and dark berries. In Greek mythology, a symbol of love.
5. **swains:** country youths.

☞ Study questions

1. What images are used in this poem? Are the images literal, or figurative?
2. Name three promises that the shepherd has made for his love. Why would he make these promises?
3. What ideas are implied by the total impression of the whole poem?

3.4 William Shakespeare

3.4.1 Life and career

Poet and playwright, William Shakespeare (1564-1616) is said to be one of the world's most remarkable authors. But not much is known about his early life. He was born into a merchant's family in Stratford-on-Avon. Although the exact date of his birth is unknown, there is a record that he was christened William on 26th April, 1564. He spent his childhood in that beautiful market town and probably attended the Stratford Grammar School. His real teachers were nature and its people that surrounded him. Shakespeare married Anne Hathaway in 1582. They had three children. It is believed that Shakespeare left Stratford for London in 1586 or 1587. There he worked both as actor and playwright. Shakespeare established himself so well as a playwright that Robert Greene, one of the "University Wits," resentfully declared him to be "an upstart crow." About 1610 Shakespeare left London and retired permanently to Stratford, though he continued to write, both by himself and in collaboration. He died on April 23, 1616, the probable anniversary of his birth.

As the precise dates of many of Shakespeare's plays are still in doubt, critics hold different views to the division of his dramatic career. But generally the four-period division is accepted. The first period was one of the apprenticeship, in which Shakespeare wrote five history plays and four comedies. In the second period, his style and approach became highly individualized. By constructing a complex pattern between different characters and between appearance and reality, he made subtle comments on a variety of human foibles. In this period he wrote five histories, six comedies, and two tragedies. His third period includes most of his tragedies and two comedies. *Hamlet*, *Othello*, *King Lear*, and *Macbeth* are usually considered to be his greatest tragedies. The two comedies of this period do not fit into clear categories because of their dark mood, and are sometimes called problem plays. The last period of Shakespeare's work includes his principal romantic tragicomedies, with *The Tempest* as the best of this group, and his two final plays, which are presumably the products of collaboration.

Shakespeare did not confine his genius merely to the theater. He also wrote poems. In 1593 and 1594, he published two narrative poems, *Venus and Adonis* and *The Rape of Lucrece*. His sonnets, 154 in number, are the only direct expression of the poet's own feelings; for his plays are the most impersonal in all literature. He wrote his sonnets in the popular English form of three quatrains and a couplet. The couplet usually ties the sonnet to one of the general themes of the series, leaving the quatrains free to develop the poetic intensity which makes the separate sonnets memorable. His sonnets constitute a vast landscape of metaphor, surprising often because it seems to anticipate the atmosphere of some of his later plays.

Shakespeare's history plays are mainly written under the principle that national unity under a mighty and just sovereign is a necessity. The three history plays on the reign of Henry Ⅵ are the beginning of his epic treatment of English history. The first and second parts of *Henry* Ⅳ are undoubtedly the most widely read among his history plays. It reveals a troubled reign in the 15th century. Shakespeare presents the patriotic spirit when mourning over the loss of English territories in France. He also dramatizes the class struggle between the oppressors and the oppressed during Jack Cade's rising of 1450. Furthermore, he condemns the War of the Roses waged by the feudal barons in which innocent people were killed. Here Shakespeare has liberated himself from any imitations of the contemporary example.

Shakespeare's greatest romantic comedies are: *A Midsummer Night's Dream*, *The Merchant of Venice*, *As You Like It*, and *Twelfth Night*. In his comedies, Shakespeare takes an optimistic attitude toward love and youth, and the romantic elements are brought into full play. In *The Merchant of Venice*, Shakespeare has created a self-conscious and self-delighting artifice that is at once intellectually exciting and emotionally engaging. The sophistication derives in part from the play between high, outgoing romance and dark forces of negativity and hate. The traditional theme of the play is to praise the friendship between Antonio and Bassanio, to idealize Portia as a heroine of great beauty, wit and loyalty, and to expose the insatiable greed and brutality of the Jew. But after centuries' abusing of the Jews, especially the holocaust committed by the Nazi Germany during the Second World War, it is very difficult to see Shylock as a conventional evil figure. And many people today tend to regard the play as a satire of the Christians' hypocrisy and their false standards of friendship and love, their cunning ways of pursuing worldliness and their unreasoning prejudice against Jews. Compared with the idealism of other plays, *The Merchant of Venice* takes a step forward in its realistic presentation of human nature and human conflict. Though there is a ridiculous touch on the part of the characters restrained by their limitations, Shakespeare's youthful Renaissance spirit of jollity can be fully seen in contrast to the medieval emphasis on future life in the next world.

The successful romantic tragedy is *Romeo and Juliet*, which eulogizes the faithfulness of love and the spirit of pursuing happiness. The play, though a tragedy, is permeated with optimistic spirit.

Shakespeare's greatest tragedies have some characteristics in common. Each portrays some noble hero, who faces the injustice of human life and is caught in a difficult situation and whose fate is closely connected with that of the whole nation. Each hero has his weakness of nature: Hamlet, the melancholic scholar-prince, faces the dilemma between action and mind; Othello's inner weakness is made use of by the outside evil force; the old king Lear who is unwilling to totally give up his power makes himself suffer from treachery and infidelity; and Macbeth's lust for power stirs up his ambition and leads him to incessant crimes. With the focus upon the tragic figure, Shakespeare dramatizes the whole world around the hero. Along with the portrayal of the weakness or bias of the hero, we see the sharp conflicts between the individual and the evil force in the society, which shows that Shakespeare is a great realist in the true sense.

In the plays of Shakespeare's last period, there is a prevalent Christian teaching of atonement. Shakespeare seems to have entered an imagined pastoral world. Thus, he could achieve what he failed to in the real world, i. e. to right the wrongs and to realize his ideals. *The Tempest*, an elaborate and fantastic story, is known as the best of his final romances. The characters are rather allegorical and the subject full of suggestion. The humanly impossible events can be seen occurring everywhere in the play. The wild storm becomes magic, answering Prospero's every signal. The playwright resorts to the supernatural atmosphere and to the dreams to solve the conflict. To Shakespeare, the whole life is no more than a dream. Thus, *The Tempest* is a typical example of his pessimistic view towards human life and society in his late years.

Shakespeare, as a humanist of the time, is shocked by the feudal tyranny and disunity and internal struggle for power at the court, which led to civil wars. In his plays, he does not hesitate to describe the cruelty and anti-natural character of the civil wars, but he does not go all the way against the feudal rule. In his dramatic creation, especially in his histories or tragedies, he affirms the importance of the feudal system in order to uphold social order. "The King's government must be carried on"— but carried on for the good of the nation, not for the pleasure of the King.

Shakespeare is against religious persecution and racial discrimination, against social inequality and the corrupting influence of gold and money. In *King Lear*, Shakespeare has not only made a profound analysis of the social crisis in which the evils can be seen everywhere, but also criticized the bourgeois egoism. He has shown to us the two-fold effects, exerted by the feudalist corruption and the bourgeois egoism, which have gradually corroded the ordered society. On the other hand, there is also a limit to his sympathy for the downtrodden. He fears anarchy, hates rebellion and despises democracy. Thus, he finds no way to solve the social problems. In the end, the only thing he can do as a humanist is to escape from the reality to seek comfort in his dream.

Shakespeare has accepted the Renaissance views on literature. He holds that literature should be a combination of beauty, goodness and truth, and should reflect nature and reality. Based on this consideration, he has claimed through the mouth of Hamlet that the "end" of dramatic creation is to give faithful reflection of the social realities of the time. Shakespeare also states that literary works, which have truly reflected nature and reality, can reach immortality. From his sonnets, we can find quite a few examples in which he sings the immortality of poetry.

Shakespeare's major characters are neither merely individual ones nor type ones; they are individuals representing certain types. Each character has his or her own personalities; meanwhile, they may share features with others. By applying a psychoanalytical approach, Shakespeare succeeds in exploring the characters' inner mind. The soliloquies in his plays fully reveal the inner conflict of his characters. He also portrays his characters in pairs. Contrasts are frequently used to bring vividness to his characters.

Also well-known is the adroit plot construction of his plays. Shakespeare seldom invents his own plots; instead, he borrows them from some old plays or storybooks, or from ancient Greek and Roman sources. In order to make the play more lively and compact, he would shorten the time and intensify the plot. There are usually several threads running through the play, thus providing the story with suspense and apprehension.

Irony is a good means of dramatic presentation. It makes the characters who are ignorant of the truth do certain ridiculous things. There is so much fun that the audience are immediately amused. Disguise is also an important device to create dramatic irony, usually with woman disguised as man.

Lastly, to understand Shakespeare, it is necessary to study the subtlest of his instruments—the language. Shakespeare can write skillfully in different poetic forms, like the sonnet, the blank verse, and the rhymed couplet. His blank verse is especially beautiful and mighty. He has an amazing wealth of vocabulary and idiom. He is known to have used a very large number of different words. His coinage of new words and distortion of the meaning of the old ones also create striking effects on the reader. Shakespeare's influence on later writers is immeasurable. Almost all English writers after him have been benefited from his writings either in artistic point of view, in literary form or in language.

3. 4. 2 "Sonnet 18"[1]

Shall I compare thee to a summer's day?[2]
Thou art more lovely and more temperate:
Rough winds do shake the darling buds of May,
And summer's lease[3] hath all too short a date: [4]
Sometime too hot the eye of heaven shines
And often is his gold complexion dimmed;
And every fair from fair[5] sometimes declines,
By chance or nature's changing course untrimmed; [6]
But thy eternal summer shall not fade,
Nor lose possession of that fair thou ow'st; [7]
Nor shall death brag thou wander'st in his shade,
When in eternal lines[8] to time thou grow'st:
  So long as men can breathe, or eyes can see,
  So long lives this, and this gives life to thee.

☞ Notes

1. This poem is written in the form of English (Shakespearian) sonnet. Its rhyme scheme is *abab cdcd efef gg.*
2. **a summer's day:** Here it may refer to a period or the season of summer.
3. **lease:** allotted time.
4. **date:** duration.
5. **fair from fair:** beautiful thing from beauty.
6. **untrimmed:** stripped of beauty.
7. **thou ow'st:** you possess.
8. **lines:** lines of poetry.

☞ Study questions

1. What images does Shakespeare use in order to strengthen the theme?
2. Discuss Shakespeare's use of the "summer's day." Why does he choose this image?
3. How does Shakespeare use the final couplet for effect?
4. There's a lot of imagery revolving around light and vision in the poem. How do these images work in the thematic structure of the poem?
5. What is the significance of the poem's theme? Is it topical or universal in its application?

☞ Essay topics

Write an essay to compare and contrast Shakespeare's "Sonnet 18" with Spenser's "Sonnet 75".

3.4.3 "Sonnet 73"

That time of year thou mayst in me behold
When yellow leaves, or none, or few, do hang
Upon those boughs which shake against the cold,
Bare ruined choirs,[1] where late sweet birds sang.
In me thou seest the twilight of such day
As after sunset fadeth in the west;
Which by and by black night doth take away,
Death's second self[2] that seals up all in rest.
In me thou seest the glowing of such fire,
That on the ashes of his youth doth lie,
As the deathbed whereon it must expire,
Consumed with that which it was nourished by.[3]
  This thou perceiv'st, which makes thy love more strong,
  To love that well, which thou must leave ere long.

☞ Notes

1. **choirs:** choir lofts; parts of church interiors occupied by choirs.
2. **Death's second self:** that is, sleep.
3. **Consumed with that which it was nourished by:** choked by the ashes of the wood that previously fueled its flame.

☞ Study questions

1. What ideas do the descriptive details in this poem suggest?

2. What metaphors or symbols does Shakespeare use in order to strengthen the theme?
3. The tone in this sonnet is different from Sonnet 18. Compare his use of language to convey tone and meaning.

3. 4. 4 "Sonnet 116"

Let me not to the marriage of true minds[1]
Admit impediments; [2] love is not love
Which alters when it alteration finds,
Or bends with the remover to remove:
O, no, it is an ever-fixed mark, [3]
That looks on tempests and is never shaken;
It is the star to every wand'ring bark, [4]
Whose worth's unknown, although his heighth[5] be taken.
Love's not Time's fool, [6] though rosy lips and cheeks
Within his bending sickle's compass come: [7]
Love alters not with his brief hours and weeks,
But bears it out even to the edge of doom. [8]
If this be error and upon me proved,
I never writ, nor no man ever loved.

☞ Notes

1. **marriage of true minds:** a metaphor for true love.
2. **impediment:** the word is lifted straight from the official Church of England wedding service "If any of you know cause or just impediment why these persons should not be joined together..." (you might recognize its modern equivalent, the whole "speak now or forever hold your peace" section of weddings).
3. **an ever-fixed mark:** a marker that never moves (cf. landmark).
4. **the star to every wandering bark:** i. e., the star that guides every lost ship (guiding star = Polaris).
5. **heighth:** altitude. The star's value is not known, though the star's altitude may be known and used for practical investigation.
6. **Love's not Time's fool:** i. e., love is not at the mercy of Time. Here fool means slave or victim.
7. **Within his bending sickle's compass come:** i. e., physical beauty falls within the range ("compass") of Time's curved blade. Note the comparison of Time to the Grim Reaper, the scythe-wielding personification of death.
8. **the edge of doom:** the brink of the Last Judgment.

☞ Study questions

1. How realistic, in your opinion, is the view of love expressed in this sonnet?
2. What kinds of "tempests" might the poet be referring to in terms of human relationships?
3. Does the poem's proposed view of love function in the real world, or is it simply a utopian ideal?
4. Do you agree with the poet's view of love as eternal and unchanging? Why?
5. The poet implies that love is the only guiding light that we have in this troublesome world. Do you agree or disagree?

3.4.5 An excerpt from Act Ⅳ of *The Merchant of Venice*

Scene 1. Venice. A Court of Justice.

[*Enter the Duke, the Magnificoes,* [1] *Antonio, Bassanio, Gratiano, Salerio,* [2] *and Others.*]

DUKE What, is Antonio here?

ANTONIO Ready, so please your Grace.

DUKE I am sorry for thee: thou art come to answer
A stony adversary, an inhuman wretch
Uncapable of pity, void and empty
From any dram of mercy. [3]

ANTONIO I have heard
Your grace hath ta'en great pains to qualify[4]
His rigorous course; [5] but since he stands obdurate, [6]
And that[7] no lawful means can carry me
Out of his envy's reach, I do oppose
My patience to his fury; and am armed
To suffer, with a quietness of spirit,
The very tyranny and rage of his.

DUKE Go one, and call the Jew into the court.

SALERIO He is ready at the door. He comes, my lord.

[*Enter Shylock.*]

DUKE Make room, and let him stand before our[8] face.
Shylock, the world thinks, and I think so too,
That thou but lead'st this fashion of thy malice[9]
To the last hour of act; and then 'tis thought
Thou'lt show thy mercy and remorse more strange
Than is thy strange apparent[10] cruelty;
And where thou now exacts[11] the penalty,

Which is a pound of this poor merchant's flesh,
Thou wilt not only loose the forfeiture,[12]
But, touched with human gentleness and love,
Forgive a moiety of the principle;
Glancing an eye of pity on his losses,
That have of late so huddled on his back,
Enow[13] to press a royal merchant down,
And pluck commiseration[14] of his state
From brassy bosoms and rough hearts of flint,
From stubborn Turks and Tartars,[15] never trained
To offices of tender courtesy.
We all expect a gentle answer, Jew.

SHYLOCK I have possessed[16] your Grace of what I purpose;
And by our holy Sabbath[17] have I sworn
To have the due and forfeit of my bond.
If you deny it, let the danger light
Upon your charter and your city's freedom.[18]
You'll ask me why I rather choose to have
A weight of carrion-flesh than to receive
Three thousand ducats. I'll not answer that!
But say it is my humour:[19] is it answered?
What if my house be troubled with a rat,
And I be pleased to give ten thousand ducats
To have it baned?[20] What, are you answered yet?
Some men there are love not a gaping pig;[21]
Some, that are mad if they behold a cat;
And others, when the bagpipe sings i' th' nose,
Cannot contain their urine for affection.
Masters of passion sways it to the mood
Of what it likes or loathes.[22] Now, for your answer:
As there is no firm reason to be rendered,
Why he cannot abide a gaping pig;
Why he, a harmless necessary cat;
Why he, a woollen bagpipe; but of force[23]
Must yield to such inevitable shame
As to offend, himself being offended;
So can I give no reason, nor I will not,
More than a lodgéd hate and certain loathing

I bear Antonio, that I follow thus
A losing suit against him. Are you answered?

BASSANIO This is no answer, thou unfeeling man,
To excuse the current of thy cruelty.

SHYLOCK I am not bound to please thee with my answers.

BASSANIO Do all men kill the things they do not love?

SHYLOCK Hates any man the thing he would not kill?

BASSANIO Every offence is not a hate at first.

SHYLOCK What, wouldst thou have a serpent sting thee twice?

ANTONIO I pray you, think you question with the Jew,
You may as well go stand upon the beach,
And bid the main flood[24] bate his usual height;
You may as well use question with the wolf,
Why he hath made the ewe bleat for the lamb;
You may as well forbid the mountain pines
To wag their high tops, and to make no noise,
When they are fretten[25] with the gusts of heaven;
You may as well do any thing most hard,
As seek to soften that—than which what's harder?—
His Jewish heart. Therefore, I do beseech you,
Make no more offers, use no farther means,
But with all brief and plain conveniency,[26]
Let me have judgment and the Jew his will.

BASSANIO For thy three thousand ducats here is six.

SHYLOCK If every ducat in six thousand ducats
Were in six parts and every part a ducat,
I would not draw them: I would have my bond.

DUKE How shalt thou hope for mercy, rendering none?

SHYLOCK What judgment shall I dread, doing no wrong?
You have among you many a purchased slave,
Which, like your asses and your dogs and mules,
You use in abject and in slavish parts,[27]
Because you bought them. Shall I say to you,
Let them be free, marry them to your heirs?
Why sweat they under burthens? Let their beds
Be made as soft as yours, and let their palates
Be seasoned with such viands?You will answer
'The slaves are ours:' so do I answer you:

The pound of flesh, which I demand of him,
Is dearly bought. 'Tis mine and I will have it.
If you deny me, fie upon your law!
There is no force in the decrees of Venice.
I stand for judgment. Answer: shall I have it?

DUKE Upon my power I may dismiss this court,
Unless Bellario, a learned doctor,
Whom I have sent for to determine this,
Come here today.

SALERIO My lord, here stays without
A messenger with letters from the doctor,
New come from Padua.

DUKE Bring us the letters. Call the messenger.

BASSANIO Good cheer, Antonio! What, man, courage yet!
The Jew shall have my flesh, blood, bones and all,
Ere thou shalt lose for me one drop of blood.

ANTONIO I am a tainted wether[28] of the flock,
Meetest[29] for death. The weakest kind of fruit
Drops earliest to the ground; and so let me.
You cannot better be employed, Bassanio,
Than to live still, and write mine epitaph.
[*Enter Nerissa, dressed like a lawyer's clerk.*]

DUKE Came you from Padua, from Bellario?

NERISSA From both, my lord. Bellario greets your grace.
[*Presents a letter.*]

BASSANIO Why dost thou whet thy knife so earnestly?

SHYLOCK To cut the forfeiture from that bankrupt there.

GRATIANO Not on thy sole, but on thy soul,[30] harsh Jew,
Thou mak'st thy knife keen; but no metal can,
No, not the hangman's axe, bear half the keenness
Of thy sharp envy. Can no prayers pierce thee?

SHYLOCK No, none that thou hast wit enough to make.

GRATIANO O, be thou damned, inexecrable dog!
And for thy life let justice be accused.
Thou almost mak'st me waver in my faith,
To hold opinion with Pythagoras,[31]
That souls of animals infuse themselves

Into the trunks of men: thy currish spirit
Governed a wolf, who hanged for human slaughter,
Even from the gallows did his fell soul fleet,
And, whilst thou layest in thy unhallowed dam,[32]
Infused itself in thee; for thy desires
Are wolfish, bloody, starved, and ravenous.

SHYLOCK Till thou canst rail the seal from off my bond,
Thou but offend'st[33] thy lungs to speak so loud.
Repair thy wit, good youth, or it will fall
To cureless ruin. I stand here for law.

DUKE This letter from Bellario doth commend
A young and learnéd doctor to our court.
Where is he?

NERISSA (Clerk) He attendeth here hard by,
To know your answer, whether you'll admit him.

DUKE With all my heart. Some three or four of you
Go give him courteous conduct to this place.
Meantime the court shall hear Bellario's letter.

CLERK OF THE COURT [*Reads.*] Your Grace shall understand that at the receipt of you letter I am very sick; but in the instant that your messenger came, in loving visitation was with me a young doctor of Rome. His name is Balthasar. I acquainted him with the cause in controversy between the Jew and Antonio the merchant. We turned o'er many books together. He is furnished with my opinion, which, bettered with his own learning, —the greatness whereof I cannot enough commend, —comes with him, at my importunity, to fill up your Grace's request in my stead. I beseech you, let his lack of years be no impediment to let him lack a reverend estimation;[34] for I never knew so young a body with so old a head. I leave him to your gracious acceptance, whose trial shall better publish his commendation.

DUKE You hear the learned Bellario, what he writes.
And here, I take it, is the doctor come.
[*Enter Portia,* (*Dr. Balthasar.*)]
Give me your hand. Come you from old Bellario?

PORTIA (Dr. Balthasar) I did, my lord.

DUKE You are welcome: take your place.
Are you acquainted with the difference[35]

That holds this present question in the court?

PORTIA I am informéd thoroughly of the cause.
Which is the merchant here, and which the Jew?

DUKE Antonio and old Shylock, both stand forth.

PORTIA Is your name Shylock?

SHYLOCK Shylock is my name.

PORTIA Of a strange nature is the suit you follow;
Yet in such rule that the Venetian law
Cannot impugn[36] you as you do proceed.
You stand within his danger, do you not?[37]

ANTONIO Ay, so he says.

PORTIA Do you confess the bond?

ANTONIO I do.

PORTIA Then must the Jew be merciful.

SHYLOCK On what compulsion must I? Tell me that.

PORTIA The quality of mercy is not strained,
It droppeth as the gentle rain from heaven
Upon the place beneath. It is twice blessed;—
It blesseth him that gives, and him that takes.
'Tis mightiest in the mightiest:[38] it becomes
The thronéd monarch better than his crown.
His sceptre shows the force of temporal power,
The attribute to awe and majesty,
Wherein doth sit the dread and fear of kings;
But mercy is above this sceptred sway,
It is enthronéd in the hearts of kings,
It is an attribute to God himself;
And earthly power doth then show likest God's
When mercy seasons justice. Therefore, Jew,
Though justice be thy plea, consider this,
That, in the course of justice, none of us
Should see salvation. We do pray for mercy;
And that same prayer doth teach us all to render
The deeds of mercy. I have spoke thus much
To mitigate[39] the justice of thy plea;
Which if thou follow, this strict court of Venice
Must needs give sentence 'gainst the merchant there.

SHYLOCK My deeds upon my head![40] I crave the law,

The penalty and forfeit of my bond.

PORTIA Is he not able to discharge the money?

BASSANIO Yes, here I tender it for him in the court;
Yea, twice the sum. If that will not suffice,
I will be bound to pay it ten times o'er,
On forfeit of my hands, my head, my heart.
If this will not suffice, it must appear
That malice bears down truth.[41] And I beseech you,
Wrest once the law to your authority:
To do a great right, do a little wrong,
And curb this cruel devil of his will.

PORTIA It must not be. There is no power in Venice
Can alter a decree established.
'Twill be recorded for a precedent,
And many an error by the same example,
Will rush into the state. It cannot be.

SHYLOCK A Daniel[42] come to judgment! Yea, a Daniel!
O wise young judge, how I do honor thee!

PORTIA I pray you let me look upon the bond.

SHYLOCK Here 'tis, most reverend doctor; here it is.

PORTIA Shylock there's thrice thy money offered thee.

SHYLOCK An oath, an oath, I have an oath in heaven.
Shall I lay perjury upon my soul?
No, not for Venice.

PORTIA Why, this bond is forfeit;
And lawfully by this the Jew may claim
A pound of flesh, to be by him cut off
Nearest the merchant's heart. Be merciful:
Take thrice thy money. Bid me tear the bond.

SHYLOCK When it is paid, according to the tenor.[43]
It doth appear you are a worthy judge;
You know the law, your exposition
Hath been most sound. I charge you by the law,
Whereof you are a well-deserving pillar,
Proceed to judgment. By my soul I swear
There is no power in the tongue of man
To alter me. I stay here on my bond.

ANTONIO Most heartily I do beseech the court

To give the judgment.

PORTIA Why then thus it is:
You must prepare your bosom for his knife.

SHYLOCK O noble judge! O excellent young man!

PORTIA For the intent and purpose of the law
Hath full relation[44] to the penalty,
Which here appeareth due upon the bond.

SHYLOCK 'Tis very true! O wise and upright judge!
How much more elder art thou than thy looks.

PORTIA Therefore lay bare your bosom.

SHYLOCK Ay, his breast:
So says the bond: —doth it not, noble judge?—
' Nearest his heart. ' Those are the very words.

PORTIA It is so. Are there balance here to weigh The flesh?

SHYLOCK I have them ready.

PORTIA Have by some surgeon, Shylock, on your charge,
To stop his wounds, lest he do bleed to death.

SHYLOCK Is it so nominated in the bond?

PORTIA It is not so expressed; but what of that?
'Twere good you do so much for charity.

SHYLOCK I cannot find it: 'tis not in the bond.

PORTIA You, merchant, have you any thing to say?

ANTONIO But little: I am armed and well prepared.
Give me your hand, Bassanio: fare you well!
Grieve not that I am fall'n to this for you;
For herein Fortune shows herself more kind
Than is her custom. It is still her use[45]
To let the wretched man outlive his wealth,
To view with hollow eye and wrinkled brow
An age of poverty; from which lingering penance
Of such a misery doth she cut me off.
Commend me to your honourable wife:
Tell her the process of Antonio's end.
Say how I loved you, speak me fair in death;
And, when the tale is told, bid her be judge
Whether Bassanio had not once a love.
Repent but you that you shall lose your friend,
And he repents not that he pays your debt;

For if the Jew do cut but deep enough,
I'll pay it instantly with all my heart.[46]

BASSANIO Antonio, I am married to a wife
Which is as dear to me as life itself;
But life itself, my wife, and all the world,
Are not with me esteemed above thy life.
I would lose all, ay, sacrifice them all
Here to the devil, to deliver you.

PORTIA Your wife would give you little thanks for that,
If she were by, to hear you make the offer.

GRATIANO I have a wife, who I protest, I love.
I would she were in heaven, so she could
Entreat some power to change this currish Jew.

NERISSA [*aside*] 'Tis well you offer it behind her back;
The wish would make else an unquiet house.[47]

SHYLOCK These be the Christian husbands. I have a daughter:
Would any of the stock of Barrabas[48]
Had been her husband rather than a Christian! —
We trifle time: I pray thee pursue sentence.

PORTIA A pound of that same merchant's flesh is thine.
The court awards it, and the law doth give it.

SHYLOCK Most rightful judge!

PORTIA And you must cut this flesh from off his breast.
The law allows it, and the court awards it.

SHYLOCK Most learned judge! A sentence! Come, prepare!

PORTIA Tarry a little: there is something else.
This bond doth give thee here no jot of blood.
The words expressly are ' a pound of flesh. '
Take then thy bond, take thou thy pound of flesh;
But, in the cutting it, if thou dost shed
One drop of Christian blood, thy lands and goods
Are, by the laws of Venice, confiscate
Unto the state of Venice.

GRATIANO O upright judge! Mark Jew! O learned judge!

SHYLOCK Is that the law?

PORTIA Thyself shalt see the act:
For as thou urgest justice, be assured
Thou shalt have justice more than thou desir'st.

GRATIANO O learned judge! Mark, Jew: a learned judge!
SHYLOCK I take this offer, then: pay the bond thrice,
And let the Christian go.
BASSANIO Here is the money.
PORTIA Soft!
The Jew shall have all justice. Soft! no haste.
He shall have nothing but the penalty.
GRATIANO O Jew! an upright judge, a learned judge!
PORTIA Therefore prepare thee to cut off the flesh.
Shed thou no blood; nor cut thou less nor more
But just a pound of flesh. If thou tak'st more
Or less than a just pound, be it but so much
As makes it light or heavy in the substance,
Or the division of the twentieth part
Of one poor scruple,[49] nay, if the scale do turn
But in the estimation of a hair,[50]
Thou diest and all thy goods are confiscate.
GRATIANO A second Daniel, a Daniel, Jew!
Now, infidel, I have you on the hip.
PORTIA Why doth the Jew pause? Take thy forfeiture.
SHYLOCK Give me my principal, and let me go.
BASSANIO I have it ready for thee: here it is.
PORTIA He hath refused it in the open court.
He shall have merely justice and his bond.
GRATIANO A Daniel, still say I, a second Daniel!
I thank thee, Jew, for teaching me that word.
SHYLOCK Shall I not have barely my principal?
PORTIA Thou shalt have nothing but the forfeiture,
To be so taken at thy peril, Jew.
SHYLOCK Why, then the devil give him good of it!
I'll stay no longer question.
PORTIA Tarry, Jew:
The law hath yet another hold on you,
It is enacted in the laws of Venice,
If it be proved against an alien
That by direct, or indirect attempts
He seek the life of any citizen,
The party 'gainst the which he doth contrive

Shall seize one half his goods; the other half
Comes to the privy coffer of the state;[51]
And the offender's life lies in the mercy
Of the Duke only, 'gainst all other voice;
In which predicament, I say, thou stand'st.
For it appears by manifest proceeding,
That indirectly, and directly too,
Thou hast contrived against the very life
Of the defendant; and thou hast incurred
The danger formerly by me rehearsed.[52]
Down, therefore, and beg mercy of the Duke.

GRATIANO Beg that thou mayst have leave to hang thyself.
And yet, thy wealth being forfeit to the state,
Thou hast not left the value of a cord;
Therefore thou must be hanged at the state's charge.

DUKE That thou shalt see the difference of our spirit,
I pardon thee thy life before thou ask it.
For half thy wealth, it is Antonio's;
The other half comes to the general state,
Which humbleness may drive unto a fine.[53]

PORTIA Ay, for the state, not for Antonio.

SHYLOCK Nay, take my life and all! pardon not that!
You take my house, when you do take the prop
That doth sustain my house. You take my life
When you do take the means whereby I live.

PORTIA What mercy can you render him, Antonio?

GRATIANO A halter gratis:[54] nothing else, for God's sake.

ANTONIO So please my lord the Duke and all the court
To quit[55] the fine for one half of his goods,
I am content; so he will let me have
The other half in use,[56] to render it,
Upon his death, unto the gentleman
That lately stole his daughter:
Two things provided more, that, for this favor,
He presently become a Christian;[57]
The other, that he do record a gift,
Here in the court, of all he dies possessed.
Unto his son Lorenzo, and his daughter.

DUKE He shall do this, or else I do recant[58]
The pardon that I late pronounced here.
PORTIA Art thou contented, Jew? What dost thou say?
SHYLOCK I am content.
PORTIA Clerk, draw a deed of gift.[59]
SHYLOCK I pray you, give me leave to go from hence.
I am not well. Send the deed after me,
And I will sign it.
DUKE Get thee gone, but do it.
GRATIANO In christ'ning shalt thou have two godfathers.
Had I been judge, thou shouldst have had ten more,[60]
To bring thee to the gallows, not the font.[61]
[*Exit Shylock.*]
DUKE Sir, I entreat you home with me to dinner.
PORTIA I humbly do desire your grace of pardon.
I must away this night toward Padua,
And it is meet I presently set forth.
DUKE I am sorry that your leisure serves you not.
Antonio, gratify this gentleman,
For, in my mind, you are much bound to him.
[*Exeunt Duke and his train.*]

☞ Notes

1. **Magnificoes:** noblemen of Venice.
2. **Gratiano, Salerino:** Bassanio's friends, Gratiano marries Portia's maid Nerissa.
3. **dram of mercy:** little bit of mercy.
4. **qualify:** modify, soften.
5. **rigorous course:** severe proceedings.
6. **obdurate:** hardened in heart or feelings.
7. **that:** since.
8. **our:** The Duke uses the royal "we" to show his dignity.
9. **thou but lead'st this fashion of thy malice:** You are merely keeping up this enmity in appearance.
10. **apparent:** not real.
11. **exacts:** demands.
12. **loose the forfeiture:** give up the penalty.
13. **enow:** enough.
14. **commiseration:** sympathy.

15. **Turks and Tartars:** The Europeans would regard Turks and Tartars as savages.
16. **possessed:** informed.
17. **by our holy Sabbath:** an oath (Sabbath is a rest day appointed for Jews on the last day of the week, i. e., Saturday).
18. **let the danger light/ Upon your charter and your city's freedom:** The point is that if the Duke denies the bond, Venice can no longer be called a free-trading city, and the charter that protects the rights of foreign traders will no longer hold good, thus affecting the income of foreign trade.
19. **humour:** whim, caprice.
20. **baned:** poisoned.
21. **a gaping pig:** a pig prepared for the table, with its month open.
22. **Masters of passion sways it to the mood/ Of what it likes or loathes:** "Masters of passion" refers to "affection" in the previous line. The first "it" refers to "passion," the second, to "affection." The meaning of the sentence is that one's feelings influence one's strong emotions to suit the person's likes or dislikes.
23. **of force:** of necessity.
24. **the main flood:** the sea.
25. **fretten:** fretted, worried.
26. **with all brief and plain conveniency:** with all speed and straightforwardness that is within easy access.
27. **in abject and in slavish parts:** for low, menial services.
28. **tainted wether:** a diseased castrated ram.
29. **meetest:** most suitable to.
30. **Not on thy sole, but on thy soul:** a pun on the words "sole" and "soul" which have the same sound but different meanings.
31. **Pythaporas:** an ancient Greek philosopher who believed in the transmigration of souls, i. e., that souls of some human beings pass after their death into animals and those of animals into some men.
32. **dam:** mother beast.
33. **offend'st:** do damage.
34. **let his lack of years be no impediment to let him lack a reverend estimation:** Though he is young of age, let there be no hindrance to prevent him from obtaining due esteem and respect.
35. **difference:** focus of the dispute.
36. **impugn:** oppose.
37. **You stand within his danger, do you not:** This sentence is addressed to Antonio; "**within his danger**" means in his power.
38. **'Tis mightiest in the mightiest:** It is the greatest thing in the greatest person.

39. **mitigate:** to make less severe.
40. **My deeds upon my head:** Let me responsible for what I do.
41. **malice bears down truth:** Malice crushes honesty.
42. **a Daniel:** an upright judge recorded in the *Bible*.
43. **tenor:** the general purport of the bond.
44. **full relation:** fully applies to.
45. **use:** habit.
46. **with all my heart:** sincerely. There is a pun on the word "heart," as it may literally refer to Antonio's body organ.
47. **would make else an unquiet house:** would otherwise cause a quarrel between husband and wife.
48. **any of the stock of Barrabas:** any descendant of Barrabas, a well-known Jewish bandit in the time of Christ.
49. **scruple:** a small weight.
50. **in the estimation of a hair:** by the difference of the weight of a hair.
51. **the privy coffer of the state:** the secret treasury of the state.
52. **formerly by me rehearsed:** previously described by me.
53. **which humbleness may drive unto a fine:** your humble beg for mercy may reduce your penalty from confiscating half of your property to a fine.
54. **a halter gratis:** a rope to hang him, free of charge.
55. **quit:** remit.
56. **in use:** in trust.
57. **He presently become a Christian:** Notice, the Christian treatment is not so lenient as supposed. For the Jew, to be forced to give up their religious belief would be worse than to take a way their life.
58. **recant:** cancel, withdraw.
59. **a deed of gift:** a legal document which shows benevolence.
60. **ten more**: Ten and two will make up a jury of twelve.
61. **font:** a vessel used to hold the holy water during Christian baptizing.

☞ Study questions

1. Why does Portia, disguised as the lawyer, initially conclude that Shylock's bond must be adhered to?
2. How do the Christians treat the Jews?
3. Do you think Shylock's hatred for the Christians can be justified? Why or why not?
4. Is Shylock in any way a sympathetic character? Why or why not?
5. Would the Elizabethans think it just and proper for Shylock to be forced to convert to Christianity? Why? Does this kind of religious arrogance still exist today? Explain.

6. What are the main themes of the play?

☞ Essay topics

1. How does Shakespeare handle the racial/religious conflicts in the play?
2. Does Shakespeare try to help us understand Shylock's situation as an outsider, a Jew in a Christian world? Why?

3.4.6 An excerpt from Scene I, ACT III of *Hamlet*

[*Enter HAMLET.*]

HAML. To be, or not to be[1]— that is the question;
Whether 'tis nobler in the mind to suffer
The slings and arrows[2] of outrageous fortune,
Or to take arms against a sea of troubles
And by opposing end them.[3] To die: to sleep—
No more— and by a sleep to say we end
The heartache and the thousand natural shocks
That flesh is heir to.[4] 'Tis a consummation
Devoutly to be wished. To die, to sleep—
To sleep—perchance[5] to dream. Ay, there's the rub.[6]
For in that sleep of death what dreams may come
When we have shuffled off this mortal coil[7]
Must give us pause.[8] There's the respect
That makes calamity of so long life.
For who would bear the whips and scorns of time,[9]
Th' oppressor's wrong, the proud man's contumely,[10]
The pangs of despised love, the law's delay,
The insolence of office,[11] and the spurns
That patient merit of th' unworthy takes,[12]
When he himself might his quietus make[13]
With a bare bodkin?[14] Who would fardels[15] bear,
To grunt[16] and sweat under a weary life,
But that the dread of something after death,
The undiscovered country,[17] from whose bourn[18]
No traveler returns, puzzles the will,
And makes us rather bear those ills we have
Than fly to others that we know not of?
Thus conscience[19] does make cowards of us all;

And thus the native hue of resolution
Is sicklied o'er with the pale cast of thought, [20]
And enterprises of great pitch and moment[21]
With this regard their current turn awry[22]
And lose the name of action. [23]

☞ Notes

1. To be, or not to be: to continue to live or to die; to take action or to do nothing but suffering.
2. slings and arrows: injuries; ("Slings" are instruments for throwing stones).
3. **Or to take arms against a sea of troubles/And by opposing end them:** Or to take up arms and fight against numerous troubles and dies in the fighting and thus ends all the troubles in this life.
4. **the thousand natural shocks/That flesh is heir to:** All kinds of sufferings that naturally occur to a human being.
5. **perchance:** possibly, maybe.
6. **There's the rub:** There is the difficulty. A "rub" is an obstacle which diverts the bowl from its course in the bowling game. Here it refers to the doubt or difficulty.
7. **shuffled off this mortal coil:** relieved from the trouble of this life that have been wound round us like coils.
8. **give us pause:** make us hesitate.
9. **the whips and scorns of time:** all kinds of the miseries we suffer in this world.
10. **contumely:** rudeness, insolence.
11. **the insolence of office:** the contempt held by the people in high rank.
12. **That patient merit of th' unworthy takes:** The people of merit have patiently to endure at the hands of those who do not deserve respect.
13. **his quietus make:** end his life ("quietus" = final settlement of an account).
14. **With a bare bodkin:** with a mere bodkin. Bodkin was a name for a small dagger.
15. **fardels:** burdens.
16. **grunt:** groan.
17. **The undiscovered country:** the unknown place (where we go after death).
18. **bourn:** boundary.
19. **conscience:** reflection, thinking.
20. **the native hue of resolution/ Is sicklied o'er with the pale cast of thought:** Over the natural color of resolution is thrown the pale and sickly color of reflection. The reference is to the ruddy color associated with the sanguine temperament as contrasted with the tinge of melancholy.
21. **enterprises of great pitch and moment:** actions of great importance ("pitch" = the

summit of a falcon's flight).

22. **their currents turn awry:** turn away from their original purpose.
23. **lose the name of action:** fail to be put into action.

☞ Study questions

1. What does life consist of according to Hamlet?
2. According to the passage, what do we dread?
3. What does this soliloquy reveal about Hamlet's attitude toward revenge?
4. What specific misgivings does Hamlet voice about seeking revenge for his father's death?
5. What is the central importance of Hamlet's soliloquy: "To be, or not to be"?

☞ Essay topics

1. What is your interpretation of Hamlet? Get inside into Hamlet's mind and explore every niche and crevice. Then, attempt to explain why he acts as he does.
2. Write an informative essay explaining the attitude of people in Shakespeare's time toward supernatural phenomena and the occult.

Chapter 4

The Seventeenth Century (1603-1700)

4.1 Introduction

The seventeenth century, especially the period of the English Revolution (1640-1660), was a time of political and religious turmoil, which was focused on the question whether king or Commons should be supreme in England. Over this question, the English people were divided into two main parties: the Royalists, who upheld the monarch with his theory of the "divine right" of kings, and the Puritans (people largely from the bourgeois class), who stood for the rights of the individual man and for the liberties of Parliament and people.

As early as in the Elizabethan age, the bourgeois class (i. e. traders, merchants, and small craftsmen) grew in strength. When Charles I came into the throne, this newly risen class became increasingly influential in the economic and political life of the country. Parliament, which mainly represented the interests of the bourgeois class, disliked Charles's control of trade and commerce, and his imposing of heavy taxes on the merchants. Thus, the relations between the monarch and Parliament became worse. However, Parliamentary power versus a self-righteous monarchy was not the only cause of the conflicts in this period. Religion was also an important factor. Many members of the Parliament were Puritans. They detested Charles's insistence on the divine right of kings, his restrictions on Puritan preaching, and his several attempts to do without Parliament altogether. In 1642, the conflicts developed into a civil war between the Royalists and the Puritans. Oliver Cromwell, a Member of Parliament and a military genius, brought victory to the Puritans and temporarily ended the monarchy in 1649. When Cromwell became the head of the government, he enacted severe laws to control the nation's morals and to restrict personal liberties. Theaters were shut down; Catholics and Anglicans were denied freedom of worship; and massacres were conducted against those Irish forces that challenged England's Puritan rule. After Cromwell's death, his son failed to rule the country in an efficient way. Actually, there was no man in England strong enough to take Cromwell's place. With the wish to restore the monarchy to a

Stuart king, the Parliament sent an invitation to recall "Prince Charlie" from exile to the throne as Charles Ⅱ in 1660. However, Charles Ⅱ had learned nothing from his father's fate, and proceeded by all evil ways to direct the various tendencies against the moral severity of the Puritan regime.

The next twenty years, which were called the period of the Restoration, meant, in effect, the restoration of all that was objectionable in monarchy. As a result, a large part of the nation, particularly the Court, plunged into an orgy of self-indulgence in which moral restraints almost ceased to be regarded. In 1685, James Ⅱ succeeded to the throne and attempted to establish despotism in Church and state again. This attempt was a direct challenge to the supremacy of Parliament. Therefore, people of the bourgeois class started to stir up again. In 1688, Parliament made a decision to invite James's Protestant daughter Mary and her Dutch husband to take the throne, thus bringing a revolution without bloodshed. In 1689 a Bill of Rights that limited the monarch's power was enacted. As a result, Parliamentary government was firmly established in Britain during the reign of William and Mary.

Literarily, the seventeenth century as a whole, compared with the Elizabethan age, was a time of relaxing vigor. The Renaissance enthusiasm had spent itself. However, the output of literature did not diminish. It spread itself over wider fields with diverse forms and subjects.

Poetry again dominated the literature of the early seventeenth century, with John Donne and Ben Jonson as the originators of two diverse poetic traditions. John Donne and his followers tried to break away from the conventional fashion of the Elizabethan love poetry. They wrote what would later be called metaphysical poetry—complex, highly intellectual verse filled with intricate and far-fetched metaphors. Ben Jonson and his disciples were responsible for a second main style of poetry. They wrote in a more conservative, restrained fashion and on more limited subjects than the metaphysical poets. Above all, Jonson strove for clarity and precision. Some of his followers were known as Cavaliers because their verses often took the form of witty, elegant, and gentlemanly compliments or trifles.

John Milton, a great poet of the century, had a style of his own. He remained outside both Donne's and Jonson's influence, representing the culture of the Renaissance and combining it with the moral earnestness of the Puritan. He was famous in literature for his early poems, which were Elizabethan in spirit; for his controversial prose works, which reflected the strife of the age; and for his epic of *Paradise Lost*, which made him rank with Homer, Virgil, Dante and Spenser.

John Dryden was the outstanding English poet from the Restoration in 1660 to the end of the century. He lived in the present, regarding the Renaissance and Puritanism as both things of the past. He followed the French critics of the period who advocated writing by rule. His poems represented the superbly civilized language of the classical style at its best, dignified, unaffected, precise and always musical. The heroic couplet he used in many of his poems and plays became the dominant poetic style for a century. His satire exerted a fruitful influence on the most brilliant verse satirists of the next century.

Theatre in England continued to thrive after Shakespeare's death, with a host of successful playwrights, who were working independently or in collaboration. Ben Jonson, Shakespeare's most distinguished rival in drama, wrote satiric comedies with more sophisticated stock situations. The strength of his dramatic genius lay in the power of depicting a great variety of characters, and in comedy alone he succeeded in finding a wide field for the exercise of this power.

If the theatre lost its momentum in the years of the English Revolution, it sprang to life joyfully when Charles Ⅱ restored the easygoing, theatre-loving monarchy. Women actresses, like the famous Nell Gwyn, began to play female roles. The drama that came to life in the second half of the seventeenth century was called, aptly enough, Restoration comedy. To be sure, a few tragicomedies from the past were popular on the newly lighted stages. However, during the later seventeenth century French-influenced playwrights created more sophisticated plays, still based on the manners of upper-class society but sharpened with wit and satire.

The prose works that we are concerned with in seventeenth century are works of nonfiction—essays and histories, works about religion and science, and works reflecting a new interest in what was going on in the country. Toward the end of the century, essays on literary criticism began to appear, and criticism became a kind of literature itself.

John Bunyan, a poor tinker and lay preacher, reflected the tremendous spiritual ferment among the common people. His *Pilgrim's Progress* is a good example of a long prose fiction, which draws upon the medieval morality play for its approach and for the kind of character it invents. It is the story of a hero named Christian, who, carrying Sin on his shoulders and a *Bible* in his hand, with the help of another character called Helpful, overcomes obstacles such as Vanity on his journey to heaven. *The Pilgrim's Progress*, its prose modeled on that of the *King James Bible*, was written to provide uplifting entertainment for the poor. No other literary work in the seventeenth century obtained a greater number of readers.

Prose style in the seventeenth century developed in two distinct directions. Early in the century, we find an ornate though often majestic style. Religious leaders including John Donne wrote sermons and other works that were complex and richly seeded with images. After the Restoration the Royal Society declared that its members should use a plainer, more efficient prose style. John Dryden was the leading prose writer of the last third of the century, and his writing attempted to move closer to the rhythms and spirit of actual speech. The development of more modern-sounding prose reminds us that the seventeenth century was in all ways a period of continuing exploration and experimentation—in politics, in religion, in science, and in language.

4.2 Francis Bacon

4.2.1 Life and career

Bacon(1561-1626) was born in London. His father was the Lord Keeper of the Great Seal under Queen Elizabeth Ⅰ. Thus, Bacon had a fortunate heritage and background. He studied at Cambridge and Gray's Inn, entered Parliament, and gradually established his reputation. At the height of his career, under King James Ⅰ, he became Lord Keeper and then Lord Chancellor of England. But he was later accused of taking bribes in office. He admitted accepting presents but defended the justice of his act. After a token imprisonment, Bacon retired in disgrace to spend the last five years of his life.

Bacon had a wide range of knowledge. At the age of 31, he wrote a letter to his uncle, claiming that he was determined to take all knowledge to be his province. His accomplishments would seem to support this extraordinary claim. His works can be divided into three groups: (1) philosophical, (2) purely literary, and (3) professional. The most important works of his first group include *The Advancement of Learning* (1605), which sets down nothing less than the progress of human knowledge up to his own time, and *Novum Organum* (1620), written in Latin. Among his literary works, the most famous are the *Essays* and *The New Atlantis*, which, written in the manner of More's *Utopia*, describes an adventurous journey onto an imaginary island in the Pacific. The two famous works from the third group are *Maxims of Làw* (1630) and *The Learned Reading upon the Statute of Uses* (1642).

Novum Organum is a successful treatise on methodology. The argument is for the use of inductive method of reasoning in scientific study. Bacon promoted the idea that generalizations should be made only after careful consideration of facts. This inductive method of reasoning was revolutionary during Bacon's lifetime, when scholars still preferred deductive reasoning—moving from generalizations to specifics instead of vice versa. In addition, Bacon introduced the concept of hypotheses to scientists, arguing that scientists needed to make initial assumptions before beginning their experiments.

Of all Bacon's writings the most popular remains his *Essays*, which has been recognized as an important landmark in the development of English prose. The essay, a brief prose composition exploring a single subject, was a development of the Renaissance, and Bacon was the first English writer to make use of this new literary form and shape it to his own taste. Unlike the warm, personal essays of Bacon's

European contemporaries, the Baconian essay is objective, compact, and logical. As his essays were published at various times between 1597 and 1625, there was an obvious stylistic change. The sentences in the first edition were charged and crowded with symmetries. But the style of the final edition was much improved. The sentences were mostly short, clear and simple, enriched with Biblical allusions, metaphors and cadence.

4. 2. 2 "Of Studies" from *Essays*

Studies serve for delight, for ornament, and for ability. Their chief use for delight, is in privateness and retiring; [1] for ornament, is in discourse; and for ability, is in the judgment and disposition of business. For expert men[2] can execute, and perhaps judge of particulars, one by one; but the general counsels, and the plots marshalling of affairs come best from those that are learned. To spend too much time in studies is sloth; [3] to use them too much for ornament is affectation; to make judgment wholly by their rules is the humor[4] of a scholar. They perfect nature, and are perfected by experience: for natural abilities are like natural plants that need pruning[5] by study; and studies themselves do give forth directions too much at large, except they be bounded in by experience. Crafty men contemn[6] studies, simple men admire them, and wise men use them, for they teach not their own use; but that is a wisdom without them, and above them, won by observation. Read not to contradict and confute, nor to believe and take for granted, nor to find talk and discourse, but to weigh and consider. Some books are to be tasted, others to be swallowed, and some few to be chewed and digested; that is, some books are to be read only in parts; others to be read, but not curiously; [7] and some few to be read wholly, and with diligence and attention. Some books also may be read by deputy, and extracts made of them by others, but that would be only in the less important arguments, and the meaner sort of books; else distilled books are like common distilled waters, flashy things. [8] Reading maketh a full man, conference[9] a ready man, and writing a exact man. And therefore, if a man write little, he had need have a great memory; if he confer little, he had need have a present wit; [10] and if he read little, he had need have much cunning, to seem to know that[11] he doth not. Histories make men wise; poets, witty; the mathematics, subtle; natural philosophy, [12] deep; moral, grave; logic and rhetoric, able to contend. *Abeunt studia in mores*. [13] Nay, there is no stond[14] or impediment in the wit but may be wrought out by fit studies, like as diseases of the body may have appropriate exercises. Bowling is good for the stone and reins, [15] shooting[16] for the lungs and breast, gentle walking for the stomach, riding for the head, and the like. So if a man's wit be wandering, let him study the mathematics; for in demonstrations, if his wit be called away never[17] so little, he must begin again. If his wit be not apt to distinguish or find differences, let him study the Schoolmen, [18] for they are *cumini sectores*.[19] If he be not apt to beat over matters[20] and to call up one thing to prove and illustrate another, let him study the lawyers' cases. So every defect of the mind may have a special receipt.[21]

☞ Notes

1. **privateness and retiring:** private life and seclusion.
2. **expert men:** men of experience.
3. **sloth:** laziness; idleness.
4. **humor:** (*archaic*) temperament; here peculiar character.
5. **pruning:** cultivating.
6. **contemn:** condemn.
7. **curiously:** with great care.
8. **distilled waters, flashy things:** infusions of herbs, etc., used as home remedies—without real value.
9. **conference:** conversations, meetings.
10. **present wit:** lively intelligence.
11. **that:** that which.
12. **natural philosophy:** science.
13. ***Abeunt studia in mores***: "Studies culminate in manners" (Ovid, *Heroides*).
14. **stond:** obstacle.
15. **stone and reins:** gall bladder and kidneys.
16. **shooting:** archery.
17. **never:** ever.
18. **Schoolmen:** scholastic philosophers.
19. ***cumini sectores***: Latin, meaning "dividers of cumin seeds," i. e., hairsplitters.
20. **to beat over matters:** to discuss a subject thoroughly.
21. **receipt:** cure, prescription.

☞ Study questions

1. What is Bacon's attitude toward study and learning?
2. What sort of advice does he give toward study and learning?
3. What writing techniques does Bacon employ to convey the essay's themes and ideas?

4.3 John Donne

4.3.1 Life and career

Donne (1572-1631) was born in London, the son of a prosperous merchant. As a little boy, he was educated by a private tutor. Then he studied both at Oxford and

Cambridge, but left without taking a degree because of his Roman Catholic background. In 1591, he began his legal studies at the Inns of Court in London, where he spent much of his time studying law, languages, literature, and theology.

Upon completing his studies, Donne became private secretary to Sir Thomas Egerton, the eminent Lord Keeper of the Great Seal. His chances of the worldly success were ruined by his secret marriage with Ann More, lady Egerton's niece, in 1601. For over ten years then on, he had been working hard, fighting against poverty. Donne's conversion to Anglicanism had no single date; rather it was a gradual process. In 1615, after a final attempt at secular advancement, he entered the Anglican Church. He took his new vocation seriously and performed his holy duties exceptionally well, acquiring a great reputation as an impressive deliverer of insightful sermons. After his wife's death in 1617, Donne wrote little secular poetry; instead, he devoted all his time and efforts to his priestly duties, writing sermons and religious poems. He was appointed the Dean of St. Paul's in 1621 and kept that post until his death.

John Donne is the leading figure of the "metaphysical school." His poems show the typical characteristics of the metaphysical poetry: dazzling wordplay, paradox, subtle argumentation, surprising contrasts, intricate psychological analysis, and striking imagery selected from nontraditional areas such as law, physiology, philosophy, and mathematics. He employed a subtle and often deliberately outrageous logic; he was realistic, ironic, and sometimes cynical in his treatment of the complexity of human motives. The mode of his poetry is dynamic rather than static, with ingenuity of speech, vividness of imagery and vitality of rhythms. Thus, his poetry presents a notable contrast to the Elizabethan lyric poems, which are pure, serene, tuneful, and smooth-running.

The Songs and Sonnets, by which Donne is probably best-known, contains most of his early lyrics. Love is the basic theme. He holds that the nature of love is the union of soul and body. The operations of the soul depend on the body. The perfection of human lovers will not be made with souls alone. This thought is quite contrary to the medieval love idea which merely put stress on spiritual love. Donne's interest lies in dramatizing and illustrating the state of being in love. This is also distinctive from the Petrarchan sonneteers, who paid so much attention to physical charms.

Donne's chief power as a religious poet is shown in his *Divine Poems*, which are concerned with human sin, divine grace, and the urgent need for salvation. Like his early lyrics, they are dramatically created, revealing a feeling of a personal and often agonized relationship between the poet and God. Stylistically, Donne's religious poems are characterized by the same sort of witty paradoxes and learned conceits, if not the same subject matter and tone as the *Songs and Sonnets*. Faith in God is expressed through images of worldly sensations.

Donne's great prose works are his sermons, which are both rich and imaginative, exhibiting the same kind of physical vigor and scholastic complexity as his poetry. As a matter of fact, his weekly sermons are an intellectual exercise supplying food for thought, a purging of conscience, and a study of rhetoric. Some of his sermons are carefully contrived with a dramatic, irregular immediacy to express a concern with personal quest for religious experience rather than settled certainties. Donne's parallels and contrasts find brilliant reinforcements in matching alliterations, assonances, grammatical functions and rhythms. Repetitions, necessary to the economy of the sermon, are used by Donne to their great effects. His metaphorical style, dramatic wit and his wide range of knowledge give his preaches and sermons power of great impact and touch of philosophical thinking.

4.3.2 "A Valediction: Forbidding Mourning"

As virtuous men pass mildly away,
  And whisper to their souls to go,
While some of their sad friends do say,
  "The breath goes now," and some say No;

So let us melt,[1] and make no noise,
  No tear-floods nor sigh-tempests move;
'Twere profanation[2] of our joys
  To tell the laity[3] our love.

Moving of the earth brings harm and fears:
  Men recon what it did and meant;
But trepidation of the spheres,
  Though greater far, is innocent.[4]

Dull sublunary[5] lovers' love
  (Whose soul is sense)[6] cannot admit
Absence, because it doth remove
  Those things which elemented it.[7]

But we, by a love so much refined
  That ourselves know not what it is,
Inter-assurèd[8] of the mind
  Care less eyes, lips, and hands to miss.

Our two souls, therefore, which are one,

Though I must go, endure not yet
A breach, but an expansion,
Like gold to airy thinness beat.[9]

If they be two, they are two so
As stiff twin compasses[10] are two;
Thy soul, the fixed foot, makes no show
To move, but doth if the other do.

And though it in the center sit,
Yet, when the other far doth roam,
It leans and hearkens after it
And grows erect as that comes home.

Such wilt thou be to me, who must
Like the other foot obliquely run;
Thy firmness makes my circle just,[11]
And makes me end where I begun.

☞ **Notes**

1. **melt:** part, change state. This line may also refer to the quietness with which pure gold melts.
2. **profanation:** debasement; violation.
3. **laity:** layman, non-clergy. Here, the speaker is implying he and his beloved are like priest and priestess as opposed to the laity.
4. **Moving ... innocent:** Earthquakes are harmful and dangerous, whereas the much greater movements of the celestial spheres are harmless.
5. **sublunary:** under the moon, or earthly. Everything under the moon's sphere, including the earth, was considered subject to change; all beyond that sphere was permanent and perfect.
6. **Whose soul is sense:** Whose essence is the senses, not the mind.
7. **which elemented it:** which constituted its essential nature.
8. **inter-assurèd:** mutually assured.
9. **Like gold to airy thinness beat:** Gold leaf is made by beating gold into tissue-thin pieces. Baser metals would break up under the beating. "Airy" in this line refers to the buoyancy of gold leaf.
10. **twin compasses:** the two legs of a geometrical compass.
11. **just:** true, accurate.

☞ **Study questions**

1. What is the situation apparently addressed by the poem?
2. How does the poet talk about the love between him and his wife?
3. Why should the parting of the lovers not be a cause for mourning?
4. What, if anything, is startling about the speaker's comparing himself and his beloved to the two feet of a compass? Why?
5. Look at the figurative language of the poem—metaphors, similes, analogies, and personification. How do these images add to the meaning of the poem or intensify the effect of the poem?

4.3.3 "The Sun Rising"

Busy old fool, unruly sun,
Why dost thou thus,
Through windows and through curtains call on us?
Must to thy motions lovers' seasons run?
Saucy pedantic wretch, go chide
Late schoolboys and sour prentices,
Go tell court huntsmen that the King will ride, [1]
Call country ants to harvest offices; [2]
Love, all alike, no season knows nor clime,
Nor hours, days, months, which are the rags of time.

Thy beams, so reverend and strong
Why shouldst thou think?
I could eclipse and cloud them with a wink,
But that I would not lose her sight so long;
If her eyes have not blinded thine,
Look, and tomorrow late, tell me,
Whether both th' Indias of spice and mine[3]
Be where thou lefst them, or lie here with me.
Ask for those kings whom thou saw'st yesterday,
And thou shalt hear, All here in one bed lay.

She is all states, [4] and all princes I,
Nothing else is.
Princes do but play us, compared to this,
All honor's mimic, all wealth alchemy. [5]

Thou, sun, art half as happy as we,
In that the world's contracted thus,
Thine age asks ease, and since thy duties be
To warm the world, that's done in warming us.
Shine here to us, and thou art everywhere,
This bed thy center is, [6] these walls thy sphere.

☞ Notes

1. **the King will ride:** King James was addicted to hunting.
2. **harvest offices:** autumn chores. The "country ants" may imply an allusion to the old fable of the ant and the grasshopper.
3. **Indias of spice and mine:** The India of "spice" is East India; the India of "mine" (gold) is the West India.
4. **all states:** all the motions of the world.
5. **all wealth alchemy:** i. e. fraudulent.
6. **This bed thy center is:** As the earth was the center of the sun's orbit (according to the old Ptolemaic astronomy), so the bed will be the new center of the sun's activities, and the walls of the bedroom will outline its motion.

☞ Study questions

1. How does the opening of this poem illustrate the vivid colloquialism of some of Donne's poetry?
2. What is the speaker's attitude towards the sun?
3. How does the speaker use the device of hyperbole for persuasive purposes?
4. How does this poem illustrate Donne's use of the microcosm-macrocosm motif?
5. What is the theme of the poem?

4. 3. 4 "Death Be Not Proud"[1]

Death, be not proud, though some have called thee
Mighty and dreadful, for thou art not so;
For those whom thou think'st, thou dost overthrow
Die not, poor Death, nor yet canst thou kill me.
From rest and sleep, which but thy pictures[2] be,
Much pleasure; then from thee, much more must flow,
And soonest our best men with thee do go,
Rest of their bones, and soul's delivery. [3]
Thou art slave to fate, chance, kings, and desperate men,
And dost with poison, war, and sickness dwell,

And poppy,[4] or charms can make us sleep as well,
And better than thy stroke; why swell'st[5] thou then?
One short sleep past, we wake eternally,
And death shall be no more; Death, thou shalt die.

☞ Notes

1. This poem is written in the form of Petrarchan sonnet. The rhyme scheme is *abba abba cddcee.*
2. **pictures:** images.
3. **And… delivery:** Our best men die willingly, in order to rest their bones and free their souls.
4. **poppy:** opium.
5. **swell'st:** swell with pride.

☞ Study questions

1. Why does the poet tell Death not to be proud?
2. What is the relationship of sleep and Death in this sonnet?
3. In what way can Death be described as being a slave?
4. What is paradoxical about the last two lines?
5. What does the poet achieve by personifying Death?

☞ Essay topics

1. To what extent does Donne's poetry express Christian humanist values?
2. What are the basic characteristics of metaphysical poetry?

4.4 George Herbert

4.4.1 Life and career

Herbert (1593-1633) was born in Wales to a wealthy family. He received his education first at Westminster School and then at Trinity College, Cambridge. It was during this time that Herbert wrote his first known poems, in which he declared that love of God was a more worthy subject for poetry than love of women. After taking his degrees with distinction, Herbert was elected a major fellow of Trinity College. In 1618 he was appointed Reader in Rhetoric, and two years later he was elected public orator. In 1626 he took holy orders within the Church of England and became a country parson at Bremerton outside of Salisbury for the rest of his life. He served faithfully as a parish priest, diligently visiting his parishioners and bringing them the sacraments when they were ill, and food and clothing when they were in want. His spontaneous generosity and good will won him the affection of his parishioners.

As the dominating figure of the metaphysical group after Donne, Herbert wrote his poems by drawing comparisons from the Bible and the liturgy, so that his conceits were involved in the subtleties of commentary and allegory epigram. His religious lyrics in *The Temple* (1633) were the result of many spiritual conflicts that passed between God and his soul. The architectural and spiritual images underlying *The Temple* thus allowed Herbert to offer a picture of the full Anglican life, its public institutions and private struggles. In his earthly life, the recovery of faith was also the recovery of humanity and the true poet.

A great many of Herbert's poems, especially those of spiritual doubt, were written in the period that led up to his time of crisis between 1628 and 1629. In these poems of spiritual conflict the technical qualities are often merged with a colloquial, dramatic immediacy and the use of a single extended conceit. The influence of Donne on Herbert is both strong and permanent. However, his poetry is, in a sense, more abstract than Donne's. His conceits are unexpected; they give rise to a thread of argument that may run through an entire poem, yet they are most often drawn from everyday life, or from the natural world, observed with wonder yet scientific precision. With an exquisite interaction between logical structure and speech-rhythm, an intensely dramatic effect is thus produced in his poetry. *The Temple*, which contained Herbert's best poems, is hugely influential and widely imitated.

4. 4. 2 "Virtue"

Sweet day, so cool, so calm, so bright,
The bridal of the earth and sky:
The dew shall weep thy fall tonight;
    For thou must die.

Sweet rose, whose hue, angry and brave, [1]
Bids the rash gazer wipe his eye:
Thy root is ever in its grave,
    And thou must die.

Sweet spring, full of sweet days and roses,
A box where sweets[2] compacted lie;
My music shows ye have your closes, [3]
    And all must die.

Only a sweet and virtuous soul,

Like seasoned timber, never gives;
But though the whole world turn to coal,[4]
  Then chiefly lives.

Notes

1. **angry:** having the hue of anger, red; **brave:** splendid.
2. **sweets:** perfumes.
3. **closes:** concluding cadences. The expression shows that Herbert intended his poem to be sung.
4. **turn to coal:** be reduced to a cinder at the Last Judgment.

Study questions

1. What metaphors does Herbert use in this poem?
2. How does the third stanza logically summarize the preceding two stanzas in imagery?
3. What is the structure of the poem?
4. With what thought does he conclude the poem?

4.5 Andrew Marvell

4.5.1 Life and career

Marvell (1621-1678) was born in Yorkshire, the son of a vicar. He received his education first at Hull grammar school, then at Trinity College, Cambridge. During the 1640's Marvell traveled extensively on the Continent, visiting France, Holland, Switzerland, Spain, and Italy. It has been suggested that he was deliberately avoiding having to commit himself to one side in the Civil War, which had begun in 1642. However, he did make a decision of sorts on his return to England. In September, 1657, he was appointed assistant to John Milton, Latin Secretary for the Commonwealth. During his last twenty years of life, Marvell was engaged in political activities, taking part in embassies to Holland and Russia and writing political pamphlets and satires. After the Restoration, Marvell was elected M. P. for his hometown of Hull, and he continued to represent it until his death.

Marvell wrote both scathing political satires and complex lyric verses, but he published very little of the poems in his lifetime. So his early reputation was based mainly on his satires, which were widely praised, and emulated by other writers, for example Jonathan Swift. His reputation as one of the greatest poets of the seventeenth century was revived only after T. S. Eliot's highly influential essay on Marvell in 1921.

As a humanist and a high-minded patriot, Marvell could praise Cromwell without defaming Charles, and was able to help secure the safety of Milton after the Restoration.

He campaigned for religious toleration and became a satirist against the court poetry. But he is not a professional writer. He launches his poems quietly. His poetry is urbane, to an extent detached, with recurrent motifs and words and a marked tone that distinguish it from the work of other metaphysical poets. Marvell brings the sophisticated artifice of his love poetry to his religious lyrics and, in "The Coronet," he investigated the problems posed by the pride of the artist when in conflict with the humility of the believer.

His love-poems were mostly tissues of conceits, but in *The Definition of Love* the wit is daringly metaphysical. In his exquisite love poem, "To his Coy Mistress," Marvell, by juxtaposing passion and logic, brings to its apogee one of the great themes of Renaissance classicism: the seizing of erotic pleasure before the onset of inevitable death. The poet begins with a cool and reasonable proposition; the poem gathers speed from that quiet beginning and rushes to the cruelly real resolution. Image follows image with precise brevity, each extending and enriching the idea.

4. 5. 2 "To His Coy Mistress"

Had we but world enough, and time,
This coyness,[1] lady, were no crime.
We would sit down, and think which way
To walk, and pass our long love's day.
Thou by the Indian Ganges'[2] side
Shouldst rubies[3] find; I by the tide
Of Humber[4] would complain. I would
Love you ten years before the Flood,
And you should, if you please, refuse
Till the conversion of the Jews.[5]
My vegetable love[6] should grow
Vaster than empires, and more slow;
An hundred years should go to praise
Thine eyes, and thy forehead gaze;
Two hundred to adore each breast,
But thirty thousand to the rest;
An age at least to every part,
And the last age should show your heart.
For, lady, you deserve this state,[7]
Nor would I love at lower rate.
But at my back I always hear
Time's winged chariot[8] hurrying near;
And yonder all before us lie

Deserts of vast eternity.
Thy beauty shall no more be found,
Nor, in thy marble vault,[9] shall sound
My echoing song; then worms shall try
That long-preserved virginity,
And your quaint[10] honor turn to dust,
And into ashes all my lust:
The grave's a fine and private place,
But none, I think, do there embrace.
Now therefore, while the youthful hue
Sits on thy skin like morning dew,
And while thy willing soul transpires[11]
At every pore with instant fires,
Now let us sport us while we may,
And now, like amorous birds of prey,
Rather at once our time devour
Than languish in his slow-chapped[12] power.
Let us roll all our strength and all
Our sweetness up into one ball,
And tear our pleasures with rough strife
Thorough the iron gates of life:
Thus, though we cannot make our sun
Stand still, yet we will make him run.

☞ **Notes**

1. **coyness:** evasiveness, hesitancy, modesty, coquetry, reluctance; playing hard to get.
2. **Ganges:** River in Asia originating in the Himalayas and flowing southeast, through India, to the Bay of Bengal.
3. **rubies:** gems that may be rose red or purplish red. In folklore, it is said that rubies protect and maintain virginity.
4. **Humber:** River in northeastern England. It flows through Hull, Andrew Marvell's hometown.
5. **Flood … Jews:** Resorting to hyperbole, the young man says that his love for the young lady is unbounded by time. He would love her ten years before great flood that Noah outlasted in his ark (Gen. 5:28-10:32) and would still love her until all Jews became Christians at the end of the world.
6. **vegetable love:** love cultivated and nurtured like a vegetable so that it flourishes prolifically.

7. **this state:** this lofty position; this dignity.
8. **Time's winged chariot:** In Greek mythology, the sun was personified as the god Apollo, who rode his golden chariot from east to west each day. Thus, Marvell here associates the sun god with the passage of time.
9. **marble vault:** the young lady's tomb.
10. **quaint:** preserved carefully or skillfully.
11. **transpires:** erupts, breaks out, gives off.
12. **slow-chapped:** chewing or eating slowly.

☞ **Study questions**

1. What is the dramatic situation that the speaker presents?
2. How does time influence the speaker's relationship with his lover?
3. What is the logical relationship of the three stanzas? How convincing is the argument? Do the frequent exaggerations undermine the logic, or make it work?
4. What does the speaker offer as the logical conclusion to be drawn from the ideas presented in the first two stanzas?
5. Why does this poem, written in the 17th century, remain popular in the 21st century?

4.6 Ben Jonson

4.6.1 Life and career

Jonson (1572-1637) was probably born in London, about a month after the death of his father. He attended the free parish school when he was very young. Then he received a brief education at Westminster School, where he was introduced to the humanist culture by William Camden. Forced into the uncongenial trade of his stepfather, a master-bricklayer, he soon deserted it to enlist among the English soldiers to fight Spaniards in the Low Countries. By about the age of twenty he was back in London and married Anne Lewis in 1594. Later he found himself employed, like Shakespeare, as actor and reviser of old plays in the theatre.

Jonson was an excellent playwright. From 1598 on, he produced fourteen comedies and two tragedies, not including his masques. His play, *Every Man in His Humor*, was performed in 1598 by Shakespeare's company. This play is a model of what is called the "comedy of humors," in which each character's action is ruled by a whim or affectation. Jonson gained fame when he wrote *Volpone, or the Fox* in 1606. In this play, Volpone, as a man governed by an overwhelming love of money for its own sake, plays upon the avarice of the other men to increase his wealth by pretending to be at the point of death. Sickened by the greed which was becoming a predominant feature of the economic system, Jonson is no longer simply drawing an amusing picture of Elizabethan times; he is flatly assailing the morals of the age. Jonson's plays, written along classical lines, are marked by a pungent and uncompromising satire, by a liveliness of action, and by numerous humor characters, whose single passion or oddity overshadows all their other traits. He was a moralist who sought to improve the ways of men by portraying human foibles and passions through exaggeration and distortion.

Jonson also wrote a large number of poems, almost all of them written in response to particular events in the poet's experience. Most of his poetry was written in short lyric forms, which he handled with great skill. His poetic style tends to be simple and unadorned yet highly polished. With his great learning, his ability and his commanding position as poet laureate, Jonson set himself squarely against the romantic tendencies of the age. He also disciplined English, ridding it of floweriness and overwhelming metaphors. Thus, Jonson could be regarded as the forerunner of English neoclassicism, a revival of the style and attitude of classical literature.

4.6.2 "Song—To Celia"[1]

Drink to me only with thine eyes,
    And I will pledge[2] with mine;
Or leave a kiss but in the cup,
    And I'll not look for wine.
The thirst that from the soul doth rise
    Doth ask a drink divine:
But might I of Jove's[3] nectar[4] sup,
    I would not change for[5] thine.

I sent thee late[6] a rosy wreath,
    Not so much honoring thee,
As giving it a hope that there
    It could not withered be.
But thou thereon did'st only breathe,
    And sent'st back to me;
Since when it grows and smells, I swear,
    Not of itself, but thee.

☞ **Notes**

1. This song is little more than a skilful cento of quotations from the love-letters of Philostratus, an obscure Greek sophist.
2. **pledge:** drink a toast.
3. **Jove's:** Jupiter's; referring to the Roman ruler of the gods.

4. **nectar:** the drink of the gods.
5. **change for:** give in exchange.
6. **late:** recently.

☞ **Study questions**

1. Why is drinking one of its most dominant metaphors?
2. What makes Celia's love a "drink divine"?
3. How genuine are the speaker's feelings towards Celia?
4. What does the poem imply about the sending of the wreath of roses?
5. What thematic and imagistic connections are there between the two stanzas?
6. How does this poem illustrate the strategy of courtship on the part of an unrequited suitor?
7. What methods does the poet employ to realize his theme?

4.7 Robert Herrick

4.7.1 Life and career

Herrick (1591-1674) was born into a middle-class family, the son of a goldsmith. Although he was born in London, he spent most of his childhood in Hampton. In 1607 he became apprenticed to his uncle, jeweler to the king, and remained in London until 1613. Six years later, He obtained a release from his apprenticeship and entered St. John's College, Cambridge as a fellow commoner. After graduation in 1620, he took holy orders and commenced duties in a parish in Devon. The solitude there oppressed him at first; the village was dull and remote, and he felt very bitterly that he was cut off from all literary and social associations; but soon the quiet existence in Devonshire soothed and delighted him. He was pleased with the rural and semi-pagan customs that survived in the village. Indeed, the charm of much of his poetry derives from his sophisticated treatment of simple country pleasures. As a Royalist he was forced to give up the parish in 1647, but the Restoration of Charles Ⅱ brought him back to Devon, where he lived out his last yeas quietly.

Herrick was a disciple of Ben Jonson and his lyrics show considerable classical influence. But his greatness rests on his simplicity, his sensuousness, his care for design and detail, and his management of words and rhythms. He wrote on a number of themes, often on the attributes of young women, but also on rural life, religious themes and, in his later life, on his approaching death. Herrick's directness of speech is accompanied by an equally clear and simple presentment of his thought; we have, perhaps, no poet who writes more consistently and earnestly with his eye upon his subject. His principal work is *Hesperides; or, the Works both Human and Divine of*

Robert Herrick, Esq. (1648). The entire collection contains more than 1, 200 short poems, ranging in form from epistles and eclogues to epigrams and love poems. The over-riding message of Herrick's work is that life is short, the world is beautiful, love is splendid, and we must use the short time we have to make the most of it.

4.7.2 "To the Virgins, to Make Much of Time"[1]

Gather ye rosebuds while ye may,
    Old time is still a-flying;
And this same flower that smiles today,
    Tomorrow will be dying.

The glorious lamp of heaven,[2] the sun,
    The higher he's a-getting,
The sooner will his race be run,
    And nearer he's to setting.

That age is best which is the first,
    When youth and blood are warmer;
But being spent, the worse, and worst[3]
    Times still succeed the former.

Then be not coy, but use[4] your time,
    And while ye may, go marry;
For having lost but once your prime,[5]
    You may forever tarry.[6]

☞ **Notes**

1. This poem is written in quatrains of iambic tetrameter alternating with iambic trimeter. The rhyme scheme is *abab*.
2. **lamp of heaven:** the sun.
3. **best, worse, and worst:** referring to the three stages of one's life: the youth, the middle age, and the old age.
4. **use:** enjoy.
5. **prime:** the best part of one's life.
6. **tarry:** stay in a place, linger.

☞ Study questions

1. What is compared to the flower in the first stanza?
2. What implied meaning does the central image in the second stanza carry?
3. What is the best stage of life? And what is the worst?
4. What conclusion can you draw from the last stanza?

4.8 John Milton

4.8.1 Life and career

Milton (1608-1674) was born into a middle class family in London. He grew up in a home which combined the culture of the Renaissance with the piety of early Puritanism. At the age of twelve he was sent to study at St. Paul's School. At sixteen, in 1625, he entered Cambridge, where he was distinguished by his passion for classical poetry, by independence and reserve of spirit, and a pure and simple life. After graduation in 1632, he spent six years at his father's country home on solitary study, greedily drilling the treasures over the fields of languages, literature, science, theology, and music. To complete his preparation for his literary career, he started his travel on the Continent in 1638. From boyhood two major principles seem to have shaped Milton's entire career: one is the love of beauty, of music, literature, and, indeed, of every form of human culture; the other is a steadfast devotion to duty as the highest object in human life.

Milton once had an ambition to write an epic which England would "not willingly let it die." But when the English Revolution broke out, all his dreams were gone with the wind; he was entirely occupied with the thought of fighting for human freedom. He cut short of his journey and returned to England to take part in the struggle for human liberty, thus putting his pen to the service of the revolutionary cause, and later of the Commonwealth. In 1649 he was appointed Latin Secretary to Cromwell's Council of State. Even when his eyesight was threatened with strains, he held steadily to his purpose of using his pen in the service of his country. Milton became totally blind in 1652. After the restoration of Charles Ⅱ, he was imprisoned for a short time and then retired to private life.

With the Restoration all his labor and sacrifice for humanity were apparently wasted. Without anger or bitterness he went back to his early dream of an immortal poem and began with great pains to dictate his grand epic, *Paradise Lost*, which was finished in 1665 after seven years' labor in darkness. Milton died peacefully in 1674.

Milton's literary achievements can be divided into three groups: the early poetic works, the middle prose pamphlets and the last great poems. In his early works, Milton appears as the inheritor of all that was best in Elizabethan literature. "L'Allegro" and "Il Penseroso" are twin poems, which can be appreciated as gracefully evocative studies in mirth and melancholy, action and contemplation. *Lycidas* (1637) is an elegy dedicated to Edward King, a fellow undergraduate of Milton's at Cambridge, who was drowned in the Irish Sea. The poem moves from a sad apprehension of death, through regret, to passionate questioning, rage, sorrow and acceptance. In *Lycidas* Milton follows the conventions of the pastoral elegy by using symbols and images which echo both classical and Biblical traditions. The pamphlets written in the second period make him a great prose writer of his age. And they can be compared with his achievement in poetry, at least not unfavorably. *Areopagitica* (1644) is probably his most memorable prose work. It is a great plea for freedom of the press. After the Restoration in 1660, when he was blind and suffering, and when he was poor and lonely, Milton wrote his three major poetical works: *Paradise Lost* (1667), *Paradise Regained* (1671), and *Samson Agonistes* (1671). Among the three, the first is the greatest, indeed the only generally acknowledged epic in English literature since *Beowulf;* and the last one is the most perfect example of the verse drama after the Greek style in English.

Paradise Lost is a long epic divided into 12 books. Working through the tradition of a Christian humanism, Milton wrote this poem, intending to expose the ways of Satan and to "justify the ways of God to men." At the center of the conflict between human love and spiritual duty lies Milton's fundamental concern with freedom and choice; the freedom to submit to God's prohibition on eating the apple and the choice of disobedience made for love. Eve, seduced by Satan's rhetoric and her own confused ambition—as well as the mere prompting of hunger—falls into sin through innocent credulity. Adam falls by consciously choosing human love rather than obeying God. This is the error wherein his greatness lies. In the fall of man Adam discovered his full humanity. But man's fall is the sequel to another and more stupendous tragedy, the fall of the angels. By lifting his argument to that plane, Milton raises the problem of evil in a more intractable form. Milton held that God created all things out of Himself, including evil. There was evil in Heaven before Satan rebelled: Pride, Lust, Wrath, and Avarice were there. At the exaltation of the Son these forces erupted and were cast forth. But God suffered them to escape from Hell and infect the Earth. And then the tragedy was re-enacted, but with a difference— "Man shall find grace." However, he must lay hold of it by an act of free-will. The freedom of the will is the keystone of Milton's creed. His poem attempts to convince us that the unquestionable truth of Biblical revelation means that an all-knowing God was just in allowing Adam and Eve to be tempted and, of their free will, to choose sin and its inevitable punishment. Thereby, it opens the way for the voluntary sacrifice of Christ which showed the mercy of God in bringing good out of evil. The poem moves with a solemn dignity that befits the subject; yet its rhythm is wonderfully sweet and regular, and the variety in distributing the pauses prevents monotony. Milton achieves this through a syntax that is full of inversions and parentheses. Sentences are long and complicated in structures; the diction is rich and elevated, combining Latinate phrasing with colloquial immediacy; and the actual sounds of vowels and consonants are chiming in alliteration and assonance.

In his life, Milton shows himself a real revolutionary, a master poet and a great prose writer. He fought for freedom in all aspects as a Christian humanist, while his achievements in literature make him tower over all the other English writers of his time and exert a great influence over later ones.

4.8.2 An excerpt from Book I of *Paradise Lost*

Of Man's first disobedience, and the fruit[1]
Of that forbidden tree, whose mortal taste
Brought death into the world, and all our woe,
With loss of Eden, till one greater Man[2]
Restore us, and regain the blissful seat,
Sing, Heavenly Muse, that, on the secret top
Of Oreb, or of Sinai, didst inspire
That shepherd who first taught the chosen seed[3]
In the beginning how the Heavens and Earth
Rose out of Chaos: or, if Sion hill[4]
Delight thee more, and Siloa's brook[5] that flowed
Fast[6] by the oracle of God, I thence
Invoke thy aid to my adventurous song,
That with no middle flight intends to soar
Above th' Aonian mount,[7] while it pursues
Things unattempted yet in prose or rhyme.
And chiefly thou, O Spirit,[8] that dost prefer
Before all temples th' upright heart and pure,
Instruct me, for thou know'st; thou from the first
Wast present, and, with mighty wings outspread,
Dovelike sat'st brooding[9] on the vast abyss,
And mad'st it pregnant: what in me is dark
Illumine; what is low, raise and support;
That, to the height of this great argument,[10]
I may assert[11] Eternal Providence,
And justify the ways of God to men.

Say first, (for Heaven hides nothing from thy view,
Nor the deep tract of Hell), say first what cause
Moved our grand[12] parents, in that happy state,

Favored of Heaven so highly, to fall off
From their Creator, and transgress his will
For one restraint, lords of the world besides?
Who first seduced them to that foul revolt?
 Th' infernal Serpent; he it was, whose guile,
Stirred up with envy and revenge, deceived
The mother of mankind, what time his pride
Had cast him out from Heaven, with all his host
Of rebel angels, by whose aid aspiring
To set himself in glory above his peers, [13]
He trusted to have equaled the Most High,
If he opposed; and with ambitious aim
Against the throne and monarchy of God
Raised impious war in Heaven and battle proud
With vain attempt. Him the Almighty Power
Hurled headlong flaming from th' ethereal sky
With hideous ruin and combustion down
To bottomless perdition, there to dwell
In adamantine chains and penal fire,
Who durst defy th' Omnipotent to arms.
 Nine times the space that measures day and night
To mortal men, he with his horrid crew
Lay vanquished, rolling in the fiery gulf
Confounded though immortal. But his doom
Reserved him to more wrath; for now the thought
Both of lost happiness and lasting pain
Torments him; round he throws his baleful[14] eyes,
That witnessed huge affliction and dismay
Mixed with obdurate pride and steadfast hate.
At once, as far as angels ken, [15] he views
The dismal situation waste and wild:
A dungeon horrible, on all sides round
As one great furnace flamed; yet from those flames
No light, [16] but rather darkness visible
Served only to discover sights of woe,
Regions of sorrow, doleful shades, where peace
And rest can never dwell, hope never comes
That comes to all, [17] but torture without end

Still urges, [18] and a fiery deluge, fed
With ever-burning sulphur unconsumed:
Such place Eternal Justice had prepared
For those rebellious; here their prison ordained
In utter darkness, and their portion set
As far removed from God and light of Heaven
As from the center[19] thrice to th' utmost pole.
O how unlike the place from whence they fell!
There the companions of his fall, o'erwhelmed
With floods and whirlwinds of tempestuous fire,
He soon discerns; and weltering by his side
One next himself in power, and next in crime,
Long after known in Palestine, and named
Beelzebub. [20] To whom th' arch-enemy,
And thence in Heaven called Satan, with bold words
Breaking the horrid silence thus began:
"If thou beest he—but O how fallen! how changed
From him, who in the happy realms of light
Clothed with transcendent brightness didst outshine
Myriads, though bright! if he whom mutual league,
United thoughts and counsels, equal hope
And hazard in the glorious enterprise,
Joined with me once, now misery hath joined
In equal ruin: into what pit thou seest
From what height fallen, so much the stronger proved
He with his thunder: [21] and till then who knew
The force of those dire arms? Yet not for those,
Nor what the potent Victor in his rage
Can else inflict, do I repent or change,
Though changed in outward luster, that fixed mind
And high disdain, from sense of injured merit,
That with the Mightiest raised me to contend,
And to the fierce contention brought along
Innumerable force of spirits armed,
That durst dislike his reign, and me preferring,
His utmost power with adverse power opposed
In dubious battle on the plains of Heaven,
And shook his throne. What though the field be lost?

All is not lost: the unconquerable will,
And study[22] of revenge, immortal hate,
And courage never to submit or yield:
And what is else not to be overcome?
That glory never shall his wrath or might
Extort from me. To bow and sue for grace
With suppliant knee, and deify his power
Who from the terror of this arm so late
Doubted his empire— that were low indeed,
That were an ignominy and shame beneath
This downfall; since by fate the strength of gods
And this empyreal substance cannot fail; [23]
Since, through experience of this great event,
In arms not worse, in foresight much advanced,
We may with more successful hope resolve
To wage by force or guile eternal war,
Irreconcilable to our grand Foe,
Who now triumphs, and in th' excess of joy
Sole reigning holds the tyranny of Heaven."

…

Whereto with speedy words th' arch-fiend replied:
"Fall'n Cherub, to be weak is miserable,
Doing or suffering: [24] but of this be sure,
To do aught good never will be our task,
But ever to do ill our sole delight,
As being the contrary to his high will
Whom we resist. If then his providence
Out of our evil seek to bring forth good,
Our labor must be to pervert that end,
And out of good still to find means of evil;
Which oft times may succeed, so as perhaps
Shall grieve him, if I fail not, [25] and disturb
His inmost counsels from their destined aim.
But see! the angry Victor hath recalled
His ministers of vengeance and pursuit
Back to the gates of Heaven; the sulphurous hail,
Shot after us in storm, o'erblown hath laid
The fiery surge that from the precipice

Of Heaven received us falling; and the thunder,
Winged with red lightning and impetuous rage,
Perhaps hath spent his shafts, and ceases now
To bellow through the vast and boundless deep.
Let us not slip th' occasion, whether scorn
Or satiate fury yield it from our Foe.
Seest thou yon dreary plain, forlorn and wild,
The seat of desolation, void of light.
Save what the glimmering of these livid flames
Casts pale and dreadful? Thither let us tend
From off the tossing of these fiery waves;
There rest, if any rest can harbor there,
And reassembling our afflicted powers, [26]
Consult how we may henceforth most offend
Our enemy, our own loss how repair,
How overcome this dire calamity,
What reinforcement we may gain from hope,
If not, what resolution from despair."

☞ Notes

1. **fruit:** Both "fruit" and "result," just as "mortal" in the next line can mean both "human" and "fatal."
2. greater Man: Christ.
3. **Heavenly Muse ... chosen seed:** The poet is asking for inspiration from the spirit that inspired Moses ("That shepherd"), who taught the Israelites ("the chosen seed") the laws as God pronounced them on Oreb, or Sinai, a mountain in the Holy Land. Moses is also traditionally regarded as the author of the first five books of the *Bible*, including *Genesis*, on which *Paradise Lost* is based.
4. **Sion hill:** hill in Jerusalem on which stood the Temple ("the oracle of God").
5. **Siloa's brook:** stream near Jerusalem.
6. **fast:** close.
7. **Aonian mount:** Mount Helicon, in Greek mythology, home of the classical Muses. Milton has chosen a more exalted theme than the writers of the classical epics.
8. **Spirit:** Holy Spirit.
9. **with mighty wings outspread, /Dovelike sat'st brooding:** A composite of phrases and ideas from *Genesis* 1. 2 ("And the earth was without form, and void; and darkness was upon the face of the deep. And the Spirit of God moved upon the face of the waters"), and *Luke* 3. 22 ("and the Holy Ghost descended in a bodily shape like a

dove upon him"). Milton's mind as he wrote was impregnated with expressions from the *King James Bible*, only a few of which can be indicated in the notes.

10. **argument:** subject matter; theme.
11. **assert:** defend, champion.
12. **grand:** first in importance, by implication, in time also.
13. **peers:** His equals. The sentence mimics Satan's action, piling clause loosely upon clause, and building ever higher, till "with vain attempt" brings the whole structure crashing down. It is a dramatic entry into "the midst of things," where epics begin. Book 6 will recount more largely the war in Heaven, in the full narrative form which Aeneas used to tell Dido of the last days of Troy (*Aeneid* 2).
14. **baleful:** malignant, as well as suffering.
15. **as far as angels ken:** as far as angels can see.
16. **no light:** omitting the verb conveys abruptly the paradox: fire-without-light.
17. **hope never comes /That comes to all:** The phrase echoes an expression in Dante ("All hope abandon, ye who enter here"), but Milton expresses it as a logical absurdity. Hope comes to "all" but not to Hell-dwellers; they are not included in "all."
18. **urges:** afflicts, presses.
19. **As from the center:** the earth. Milton makes use in *Paradise Lost* of two images of the cosmos: (1) the earth is the center of the created cosmos of ten concentric spheres; but (2) the earth and the whole created cosmos are a mere appendage, hanging from Heaven by a golden chain, in the larger, aboriginal, and less shapely cosmos. In the present passage, the fall from Heaven to Hell (through the aboriginal universe) is described as thrice as far as the distance (in the created universe) from the center (earth) to the outmost sphere.
20. **Beelzebub:** a Phoenician deity, or Baal (the name means "Lord of flies"); traditionally, prince of devils and enemy of Jehovah. The Phoenician Baal, a sun god, had many aspects and so many names; most Baals were nature deities. But in the poem's time scheme all this lies in the future; Beelzebub's angelic name, whatever it was, has been erased from the *Book of Life*, and as he has not yet got another one, he must be called by the name he will have later on.
21. **He with his thunder:** God with his thunderbolts.
22. **study:** pursuit.
23. **by fate the strength of gods /And this empyreal substance cannot fail:** The essence of Satan's fault is this claim to the position of a god, subject to fate but to nothing else. His substance is "empyreal" (heavenly, from the empyrean), and cannot be destroyed; but, as he learns in the poem, it can be confounded by God's greater power and weakened by its own corruption and self-contradictions. **Fail**: cease to exist.

24. **Doing or suffering:** Whether one is active or passive.
25. **if I fail not:** Unless I'm mistaken.
26. **afflicted powers:** stricken armies.

☞ Study questions

1. How does Satan feel about being in Hell?
2. For what sin was Satan cast out of heaven?
3. How does Satan explain his defeat?
4. How is Satan's pride as tragic as it is heroic?
5. What is Satan's attitude to his defeat?
6. To what extent is Milton's Satan a heroic figure?

☞ Essay topics

1. How does Milton portray Satan?
2. Why did Satan want to destroy Adam and Eve?

4. 8. 3 "When I Consider How My Light Is Spent"[1]

When I consider how my light is spent
    Ere[2] half my days in this dark world and wide,
    And that one talent which is death to hide[3]
    Lodg'd with me useless, though my soul more bent
To serve there with my Maker, and present
    My true account, lest he returning chide,
    "Doth God exact[4] day-labour, light denied?"
    I fondly[5] ask. But Patience,[6] to prevent
That murmur, soon replies: "God doth not need
    Either man's work or His own gifts: who best
    Bear His mild yoke, they serve Him best. His state
Is kingly: thousands[7] at His bidding speed,
    And post[8] o'er land and ocean without rest;
    They also serve who only stand and wait."

☞ Notes

1. This poem is written in the form of Petrarchan sonnet. The rhyme scheme is *abba abba cde cde*. **light is spent:** This clause presents a double meaning: (a) how I spend my days, and(b) how it is that my sight is used up.
2. **Ere half my days:** Before half my life is over. Milton was completely blind by 1652, the year he turned 44.

3. **And that one talent which is death to hide:** The parable of the talents (Matthew 25) loomed large in Puritan minds, and particularly in Milton's. The servants who put their master's money (talents of gold and silver) out to earn interest while he was away were called "good and faithful;" while one who simply returned what he had been given was deprived of everything and cast into outer darkness. Usury, which under Catholic theology had been a deadly sin, changed its meaning for the Puritans; it became a metaphor, and sometimes more than a metaphor, for "working out one's salvation."
4. **exact:** demand, require.
5. **fondly:** foolishly.
6. **Patience:** Milton personifies patience, capitalizing it and having it speak.
7. **thousands:** that is, of angels.
8. **post:** travel.

☞ **Study questions**

1. What is the speaker lamenting in lines 1-2?
2. What does Patience say God asks for?
3. What two meanings does *talent* have? What is the speaker's "talent," and what kind of "use" does he think he can make of it?
4. How would you evaluate the argument made by "patience"? Do you agree with the idea that everyone has his or her own "yoke" to bear?
5. In what category does the speaker place himself?
6. Does the speaker find consolation? Explain.

4.9 John Dryden

4.9.1 Life and career

Dryden (1631-1700) was born into a middle class family in Aldwinkle, Northamptonshire. He was brought up in the strict Puritan faith. He received his education first at Westminster School and then at Cambridge. Making excellent use of his opportunities, he studied eagerly and became one of the well-learned men of his age. After graduation, he went to London, where he hoped to get political preferment through his relatives in the Puritan party.

Dryden lived in a time of political and religious turmoil, and his own beliefs seemed to shift with the times. His first important poem, *Heroic Stanzas*, extolled the virtues of Oliver Cromwell, the leader of the movement to rid England of a monarchy. Yet with the restoration of the monarchy in 1660, Dryden became a royalist and celebrated the return of King Charles Ⅱ in two poems, *Astraea Redux* (1660) and *Panegyric on the*

Coronation (1661). His marriage with the daughter of an earl secured his social position and for more than fifteen years thereafter his life was fairly successful.

Dryden wrote verse in several forms: odes, poetic drama, and biting satires. Among his most important legacy to the poets of the next century was his mastery of the heroic couplet, paired lines of rhyming iambic pentameter. His satire exerted a fruitful influence on the most brilliant verse satirists of the next century. His poems represented the superbly civilized language of the Augustan style at its best: dignified, unaffected, precise and always musical. With the theatres reopened after the Restoration, the drama offered the most attractive field to one who made a living by writing. So Dryden turned to the stage in 1662 as a source of income. His first attempt failed, but *The Rival Ladies*, a tragicomedy written in 1664, was a success. During the next 20 years, he became the most prominent dramatist in England, written altogether 27 plays. He is well-remembered for his heroic play *The Conquest of Granada* (1670-1672) and his version of Shakespeare's *Antony and Cleopatra*: *All for Love* (1678). As a prose writer, Dryden had a very marked influence on English literature. He set his own stamp on the new informal, persuasive style, by shortening his sentences, and especially by writing naturally, without depending on literary ornamentation to give effect to what he is saying.

What have outlived the drama are Dryden's critical dedications in which he shows his vital interest in criticism. The best known of his critical works is *An Essay of Dramatic Poesy*, a delightful dialogue, published in 1667-1668. It is in intention a defense of drama as the highest type of poetry, and of rhyming and heroic tragedies as the most legitimate offspring of the drama. It discusses the principles of drama and judiciously compares the qualities of Ben Jonson and Shakespeare, which attempts to lay a foundation for all literary criticism. The numerous prefaces to his plays and poems bring a very modern sense of historical perspective to the evaluation of literary works and enrichment of literary language. Dryden's criticism, however, has at its best a breadth and humanity, a judicious and skeptical mistrust of dogmatic theory, which shows the practical writer and widely appreciative reader searching for methods to evaluate, compare and contrast. His critical writings established cannons of taste and theoretical principles that determined the character of neoclassic literature.

Dryden is the greatest literary figure of the Restoration, and in his work we can see an excellent reflection of both the good and the evil tendencies of the age in which he lived. Dryden is the "lock by which the waters of English poetry were let down from the mountains of Shakespeare and Milton to the plain of Pope." This is a quite vivid expression of Dryden's position in English literature. He stands between two very different ages, and serves as a transition from one to another. His position in English literature is strengthened by his great influence on the succeeding age of the Classicism.

4.9.2 An excerpt from *An Essay of Dramatic Poesy*

To begin, then, with Shakespeare.[1] He was the man who of all modern, and perhaps ancient poets, had the largest and most comprehensive soul. All the images of Nature were still[2] present to him, and he drew them, not laboriously, but luckily;[3] when he describes any thing, you more than see it, you feel it too. Those who accuse him to have wanted[4] learning, give him the greater commendation: he was naturally learned; he needed not the spectacles of books to read Nature;[5] he looked inwards, and found her there. I cannot say he is everywhere alike;[6] were he so, I should do him injury to compare him with the greatest of mankind. He is many times flat, insipid;[7] his comic wit degenerating into clenches,[8] his serious swelling into bombast.[9] But he is always great, when some great occasion is presented to him; no man can say he ever had a fit subject for his wit and did not then raise himself as high above the rest of poets,

Quantum lenta solent inter viburna cupressi.[10]

The consideration of this made Mr. Hales of Eaton[11] say, that there was no subject of which any poet ever writ, but he would produce it much better treated of in Shakespeare; and however others are now generally preferred before him, yet the age wherein he lived, which had contemporaries with him Fletcher[12] and Jonson,[13] never equaled them to him in their esteem: and in the last king's court,[14] when Ben's reputation[15] was at highest, Sir John Suckling,[16] and with him the greater part of the courtiers, set our Shakespeare far above him. ...

"As for Jonson, to whose character I am now arrived, if we look upon him while he was himself[17] (for his last plays were but his dotages),[18] I think him the most learned and judicious writer which any theatre ever had. He was a most severe judge of himself, as well as others. One cannot say he wanted wit, but rather that he was frugal of it. In his works you find little to retrench or alter. Wit, and language, and humor also in some measure, we had before him;[19] but something of art was wanting to the Drama, till he came. He managed his strength to more advantage than any who preceded him. You seldom find him making love in any of his scenes, or endeavoring to move the passions; his genius was too sullen and saturnine[20] to do it gracefully, especially when he knew he came after those who had performed both to such an height. Humor was his proper sphere,[21] and in that he delighted most to represent mechanic people.[22] He was deeply conversant in the ancients,[23] both Greek and Latin, and he borrowed boldly from them: there is scarce a poet or historian among the Roman authors of those times whom he has not translated[24] in *Sejanus* and *Catiline*.[25] But he has done his robberies so openly, that one may see he fears not to be taxed[26] by any law. He invades authors like a monarch; and what would be theft in other poets is only victory in him. With the spoils of these writers he so represents old Rome to us, in its rites, ceremonies, and customs, that if one of their poets had written either of his tragedies, we had seen less of it than in him. If there was any fault in his language, 'twas that he weaved it too closely and laboriously, in his serious plays: perhaps too, he did a little too much Romanize our tongue, [27] leaving the words which he translated almost as much Latin as he found them: wherein, though he learnedly followed the idiom of their language, he did not enough comply with the idiom of ours. If I would compare him with Shakespeare, I must acknowledge him the more correct poet, but Shakespeare the greater wit. Shakespeare was the Homer, [28] or father of our dramatic poets; Jonson was the Virgil, [29] the pattern of elaborate writing; I admire him, but I love Shakespeare. To conclude of him; as he has given us the most correct plays, so in the precepts which he has laid down in his *Discoveries*, [30] we have as many and profitable rules for perfecting the stage, as any wherewith the French can furnish us."

☞ Notes

1. **To begin, then, with Shakespeare:** The whole excerpt given here is part of a speech by Neander, whose views have generally been supposed to represent those of the author.
2. **still**: ever, always.
3. **luckily:** happily.
4. **wanted:** lacked.
5. **Nature:** the external world of reality.
6. **I cannot say he is every where alike:** I cannot say that he achieves a similar degree of excellence in all his works.
7. **insipid:** lifeless, dull.
8. **clenches:** (or clinches) referring to puns that play upon words.
9. **his serious swelling into bombast:** his serious thoughts expanding into extravagant language.
10. **Quantum lenta solent inter viburna cupressi:** Latin as the cypresses are wont to tower above the yielding osiers (a line quoted from the ancient Roman poet Virgil's *Eclogues*, Ⅰ, 26).
11. **Mr. Hales of Eaton:** referring to John Hales (1584-1656), a fellow of Eton.
12. **Fletcher**: John Fletcher (1579-1625), English dramatist.
13. **Jonson:** Ben Jonson (1572-1637), English dramatist and poet.
14. **in the last king's court:** referring to the court of King Charles Ⅰ.
15. **Ben's reputation:** the reputation of Ben Jonson.
16. **Sir John Suckling (1609-1642):** English poet.
17. **while he was himself**: when he attained to his usual level of achievement.
18. **his dotages:** his works written in old age when he was in his decline.

19. **we had before him:** we had before his time.
20. **saturnine:** heavy.
21. **Humor was his proper sphere:** i. e., he was especially adept in portraying "humours" or characteristic temperaments of the characters in his drama.
22. **mechanic people:** artisans.
23. **deeply conversant in the Ancients:** very well acquainted with the writers of ancient Greece and Rome.
24. **translated:** carried over, transferred, here meaning borrowed boldly and directly (from "the Roman authors of those times").
25. ***Sejanus* and *Catiline*:** *Sejanus* is a tragedy by Ben Jonson, based on the story of the rise and fall of Sejanus, the favourite of the emperor Tiberius, in ancient Roman history, which was first produced in 1603; *Catiline* is a tragedy also by Ben Jonson, based on the story of the struggle between Catiline and Cicero in ancient Roman history, which was first acted in 1611.
26. **taxed:** accused.
27. **Romanize our tongue:** introduce linguistic elements of Latin (the language of the ancient Romans) into English.
28. **Homer:** a great Greek epic poet, born between 1050 and 850 B. C.
29. **Virgil:** a great Roman poet (70-19 B. C.).
30. ***Discoveries*:** the full title being *Timber, or Discoveries Made upon Men and Matte* (1640), a book of literary criticism by Ben Jonson.

☞ Study questions

1. Why does Dryden say that Shakespeare "was naturally learned?"
2. What strong and weak points does Shakespeare show in his drama according to John Dryden?
3. What strong and weak points does Jonson show in his drama according to John Dryden?
4. Who does Dryden value more when he says that he "admires" Jonson but "loves" Shakespeare?

4.10 John Bunyan

4.10.1 Life and career

Bunyan (1628-1688) was born into a poor tinker's family in Bedfordshire. He received very little formal education. When he was still a little boy, he took up his father's trade, and had the least promise of becoming a writer. But the boy had a profound imagination. His marriage in 1647 with a Christian woman led him to the Lord.

He joined a Non-conformist church and began to preach, by the roadside or on the village green, telling people of his vision and interpretation of God's doctrine. However, he was thrown into prison in 1660 for preaching without receiving permission from the Established Church. He remained in prison for 12 years because of his refusing to take a vow to give up preaching. He was imprisoned again in 1675 on charge of the same offence. It was during this second term in prison that he wrote *The Pilgrim's Progress*, which was published in 1678 after his release. During his last years Bunyan was universally recognized as the leading Puritan clergyman and author. He went on missionary journeys, preaching to all walks of people. Throughout all these activities he had constantly kept his perfect mental balance, his charity and humor in the strife of many sects. He died in 1688 from a bad fever. His other works include *Grace Abounding to the Chief of Sinners* (1666), *The Life and Death of Mr. Badman* (1680), *The Holy War* (1682) and *The Pilgrim's Progress, Part* Ⅱ (1684).

The Pilgrim's Progress is a work of an ordinary people's dream. The first part recounts Christian's journey from the City of Destruction to the Celestial City. The journey includes 10 stages, which symbolize the difficulties and triumphs of the Christian life. In the end, Christian successfully overcomes all the difficulties and temptations and arrives at his destination, where he enjoys eternal life in the fellowship of the blessed. The second part describes the subsequent conversion of Christian's wife and their children, and their similar journey to the Celestial City.

The Pilgrim's Progress is the most successful religious allegory in English language. Its success probably lies in 3 aspects: vivid characterization, simple language and natural way of story-telling. In the past, allegoric characters are merely personified human virtues and vices since the purpose of an allegory is to teach a moral lesson. As a result, they are shallow and unnatural. Bunyan's characters are not like that. He endows different individual qualities to his characters, so that his characters are actually living men and women. Besides Bunyan captures the speech of ordinary people as accurately as he depicts their behavior and appearance. Its language and style are founded on the noble and simple model of the English *Bible*. His passion and loving joy in religion enables him often to attain the poetic beauty and eloquence of his original. Both by instinct and of set purpose he rendered his own style even more simple and direct, partly by the use of homely vernacular expressions. Furthermore, *The Pilgrim's Progress* is a real story. Its predominant metaphor of the story—life as a journey—is simple and familiar. Here the strange is combined with the familiar and the trivial joined to the divine; the objects that Christian meets are homely and commonplace; and the scenes presented are typical English ones. And Bunyan's natural way of telling the story at once makes it both entertaining and morally instructive.

Like most working men at the time, Bunyan had a deep hatred for the corrupted, hypocritical rich who accumulated their wealth "by hook and by crook." As a stout Puritan, he had made a conscientious study of the *Bible* and firmly believed in salvation through spiritual struggle.

4. 10. 2 An excerpt from Part I of *The Pilgrim's Progress*

Then I saw in my dream, that when they were got out of the wilderness, they presently saw a town before them, and the name of that town is Vanity; and at the town there is a fair kept, called Vanity Fair. It is kept all the year long. It beareth[1] the name of Vanity Fair, because the town where it is kept is lighter than vanity, and also because all that is there sold, or that cometh thither,[2] is vanity; as is the saying of the wise, "All that cometh is vanity."[3]

This fair is no new-erected business but a thing of ancient standing. I will show you the original of it.

Almost five thousand years ago there were pilgrims walking to the Celestial City,[4] as these two honest persons are: and Beelzebub, Apollyon, and Legion,[5] with their companions, perceiving by the path that the pilgrims made, that their way to the city lay through this town of Vanity, they contrived here to set up a fair; a fair wherein should be sold all sorts of vanity, and that it should last all the year long. Therefore, at this fair are all such merchandise sold as houses, lands, trades, places, honors, preferments, titles, countries, kingdoms, lusts, pleasures; and delights of all sorts, as harlots, wives, husbands, children, masters, servants, lives, blood, bodies, souls, silver, gold, pearls, precious stones, and what not.

And moreover, at this fair there is at all times to be seen jugglings, cheats, games, plays, fools, apes,[6] knaves, and rogues, and that of every kind.

Here are to be seen, too, and that for nothing, thefts, murders, adulteries, false-swearers, and that of a blood-red color.

And, as in other fairs of less moment,[7] there are the several rows and streets under their proper names, where such and such wares are vended;[8] so here, likewise, you have the proper places, rows, streets, (namely, countries and kingdoms,) where the wares of this fair are soonest to be found. Here is the Britain Row, the French Row, the Italian Row, the Spanish Row, the German Row, where several sorts of vanities are to be sold. But, as in other fairs, some one commodity is as the chief of all the fair; so the ware of Rome and her merchandise[9] is greatly promoted in this fair; only our English nation, with some others, have taken a dislike thereat.[10]

Now, as I said, the way to the Celestial City lies just through this town, where this lusty[11] fair is kept; and he that will go to the city, and yet not go through this town, "must needs[12] go out of the world." The Prince of princes[13] himself, when here, went through this town to his own country, and that upon a fair-day too;[14] yea, and, as I think, it was Beelzebub, the chief lord of this fair, that invited him to buy of his vanities, yea, would have made him lord of the fair, would he but have done him reverence as he went through the town. Yea, because he was such a person of honor, Beelzebub had[15] him from street to street, and showed him all the kingdoms of the world in a little time, that he might, if possible, allure that Blessed One[16] to cheapen[17] and buy some of his vanities; but he had no mind to the merchandise, and therefore left the town, without laying out so much as one farthing upon these vanities. This fair, therefore, is an ancient thing, of long standing, and a very great fair.

Now, these pilgrims, as I said, must needs go through this fair. Well, so they did; but behold, even as they entered into the fair, all the people in the fair were moved; and the town itself, as it were, in a hubbub[18] about them, and that for several reasons: for,

First, The Pilgrims were clothed with such kind of raiment[19] as was diverse from the raiment of any that traded in that fair. The people, therefore, of the fair made a great gazing upon them: some said they were fools; some, they were bedlams;[20] and some, they were outlandish[21] men.

Secondly, And as they wondered at their apparel, so they did likewise at their speech; for few could understand what they said. They naturally spoke the language of Canaan;[22] but they that kept the fair were the men of this world: so that from one end of the fair to the other, they seemed barbarians each to the other.[23]

Thirdly, But that which did not a little amuse the merchandisers was, that these pilgrims set very light by[24] all their wares. They cared not so much as to look upon them; and if they called upon them to buy, they would put their fingers in their ears, and cry, "Turn away mine eyes from beholding vanity," and look upward, signifying that their trade and traffic[25] was in heaven.

One chanced, mockingly, beholding the carriage of the men, to say unto them, "What will ye buy?" But they, looking gravely upon him, said, "We buy the truth." At that there was an occasion taken[26] to despise the men the more; some mocking, some taunting, some speaking reproachfully, and some calling upon others to smite[27] them. At last, things came to an hubbub and great stir in the fair, insomuch that all order was confounded.[28] Now was word presently brought to the great one of the fair, who quickly came down, and deputed[29] some of his most trusty friends to take those men into examination about whom the fair was almost overturned. So the men were brought to examination; and they that sat upon[30] them asked them whence[31] they came, whither[32] they went, and what they did there in such an unusual garb. The men told them they were pilgrims and strangers in the world, and that they were going to their own country, which was the heavenly Jerusalem, and that they had given no occasion to the men of the town, nor yet to the merchandisers, thus to abuse them,[33] and to let them in their journey, except it was for that, when one asked them what they would buy, they said they would buy the truth. But they that were appointed to examine them did not believe them to be any other than bedlams and mad, or else such as came to put all things into a confusion in the fair. Therefore they took them and beat them, and besmeared[34] them with dirt, and then put them into the cage, that they might be made a spectacle[35] to all the men of the fair. There, therefore, they lay for some time, and were made the objects of any man's sport, or malice, or revenge; the great one of the fair laughing still at all that befell them. But the men being patient, and "not rendering railing for railing, but contrariwise blessing," and giving good words for bad, and kindness for injuries done, some men in the fair, that were more observing and less prejudiced than the rest, began to check and blame the baser sort for their continual abuses done by them to the MEN. They, therefore, in an angry manner let fly at them again, counting them as bad as the men in the cage, and telling them that they seemed confederates,[36] and should be made partakers of their misfortunes. The others replied that, for aught they could see, the men were quiet and sober, and intended nobody any harm; and that there were many that traded in their fair that were more worthy to be put into the cage, yea, and pillory too, than were the men that they had abused. Thus, after divers words had passed on both sides, (the men behaving themselves all the while very wisely and soberly before them,) they fell to some blows among themselves, and did harm one to another. Then were these two poor men brought before their examiners again, and were charged as being guilty of the late hubbub that had been in the fair. So they beat them pitifully, and hanged irons upon them, and led them in chains up and down the fair, for an example and terror to others, lest any should speak in their behalf, or join themselves unto them. But Christian and Faithful behaved themselves yet more wisely, and received the ignominy and shame that was cast upon them with so much meekness and patience, that it won to their side (though but few in comparison of the rest) several of the men in the fair. This put the other party yet into a greater rage, insomuch that[37] they concluded the death of these two MEN. Wherefore they threatened that neither cage nor irons should serve their turn, but that they should die for the abuse they had done, and for deluding the men of the fair.

Then were they remanded to the cage again, until further order should be taken with them. So they put them in, and made their feet fast in the stocks.

☞ Notes

1. **beareth:** bears. "th" is used to indicate third person single in ancient English.
2. **cometh thither:** comes there.
3. From *Bible Eccl.* 11:8; see also 1:2-14; 2:11-17; *Isa.* 40:17.
4. **Celestial City:** the heavenly city the pilgrims are going to.
5. **Beelzebub, Apollyon, and Legion:** *Beelzebub*, a "prince of demons" according to the

Bible, is the fallen angel next to Satan in power and crime as described in Milton's *Paradise Lost*. *Apollyon*, a friend against god, who is described early in the book. *Legion*, referring to all those followers of Satan.

6. **ape:** a person who copies the behavior of others.
7. **of less moment:** of less importance.
8. **vended:** offered for sale.
9. **The ware of Rome and her merchandise:** the usage and temporal power of the Roman Catholic Church.
10. **thereat:** at or for that.
11. **lusty:** merry.
12. **must need:** must necessarily.
13. **The Prince of princes:** Jesus Christ.
14. **and that upon a fair day, too:** This alludes to the temptation of Jesus in the wilderness.
15. **had:** led.
16. **the Blessed One:** Jesus Christ.
17. **to cheapen:** to ask the price of.
18. **hubbub:** a mixture of loud noises.
19. **raiment:** clothing; garments.
20. **Bedlams:** lunatics from Bethlehem Hospital, the insane asylum in London.
21. **outlandish:** strange.
22. **language of Canaan:** Canaan is the Promised Land, which was ultimately conquered by the children of Israel and settled by them, hence the pilgrims speak the language of the *Bible* and of true religion. Dissenters were notorious for their habitual use of biblical language.
23. **Barbarians each to the other:** Barbarians to each other; Barbarians, the Greeks and Romans designated all those who spoke a foreign language as Barbarians.
24. **set very light by:** to treat as of little importance.
25. **trade and traffic:** business.
26. **an occasion taken:** a chance made use of.
27. **smite:** strike hard.
28. **confounded:** confused and deeply troubled.
29. **deputed:** entrusted.
30. **sat upon:** judged, questioned.
31. **whence:** from where.
32. **whither:** to what place.
33. **thus to abuse them:** i. e. , to abuse them thus, to treat them in such a rough manner.
34. **besmeared:** smeared, made dirty.

35. **be made a spectacle:** be made an object of public shame, disrespect and laugh.
36. **confederates:** members of a confederacy; allies.
37. **insomuch that:** with the result that; so.

☞ Study questions

1. Why is the market called "Vanity Fair"?
2. Why did Christian and his friend cause noise in the fair?
3. What did people in the fair do to Christian and his friend?
4. What does this episode symbolize?

☞ Essay topics

1. Explain the various elements of allegory in *The Pilgrim's Progress*.
2. Do you think *The Pilgrim's Progress* is still important to the modern reader? Why or why not?

Chapter 5

The Eighteenth Century (1700-1798)

5.1 Introduction

The eighteenth century saw the fast development of Britain as a nation. Abroad, Britain occupied a vast expansion of colonies in Asia, Africa and North America, which provided Britain with both capital and market for further development. At home, *Acts of Enclosure* were putting more lands into the hands of fewer privileged landowners and forcing thousands of small farmers and tenants off their land to become wage earners in industrial towns. This coming together of free labor from the home and free capital gathered or plundered from the colonies was the essence of the Industrial Revolution. So, towards the middle of the eighteenth century, Britain had become the first powerful capitalist country in the world.

Along with the fast economic development, the British bourgeois class also grew rapidly. As the major force of the revolution, it was mainly composed of city people: traders, merchants, manufacturers, and other adventurers such as slave traders and colonists. As the Industrial Revolution went on, more and more people joined the rank of this class. Marx once pointed out that the bourgeois class of the eighteenth-century Britain was a revolutionary class then and quite different from the feudal aristocratic class. They were people who had known poverty and hardship, and most of them had obtained their present social status through hard work. Self-restraint, self-reliance and industriousness were their mottoes. To work, to economize and to accumulate wealth constituted the whole meaning of their life. This aspect of social life is best found in the realistic novels of the century.

The eighteenth century is also known as the Age of Enlightenment, which was a progressive intellectual movement that flourished first in France and then swept through the Western Europe. Enlightenment is an important ideology of the bourgeois class in their fight against superstition and injustice, privilege and oppression. Central to Enlightenment thought were the use and the celebration of reason, the power by which man understands the universe and improves his own condition. The goals of rational man were considered to be knowledge, freedom, and happiness. The enlighteners believed that when reason served as the yardstick for the measurement of all human activities and relations, every superstition, injustice or oppression was to yield place to "eternal truth," "eternal justice" and "natural equality". This belief provided theory for the American War of Independence in 1776 and the French Revolution of 1789. At the same time, the enlighteners advocated universal education. In their opinion, human beings were limited, dualistic, imperfect, and yet capable of rationality and perfection through education. If the masses were well educated, they thought, there would be great chance for a democratic and equal human society. As a matter of fact, literature at the time, heavily didactic and moralizing, became a very popular means of public education.

In the field of literature, the Enlightenment Movement brought about a revival of interest in the old classical works. This tendency, known as Neoclassicism, was a partial reaction against the intricacy, boldness and extravagance of European literature of the late Renaissance, as seen for instance in the works of the metaphysical poets. Neoclassicists were in favor of simplicity, clarity, restraint, regularity, and good sense. They modeled themselves on classical or ancient Greek and Roman authors in order to achieve perfect form in literature. The general tendency was to look at social and political life critically; to emphasize intellect rather than imagination; to repress much of their personal emotion and enthusiasm; and to use precise and elegant methods of expression. Thus, writers tried their best to seek proportion, unity, harmony and grace in literary works, with an effort to delight, instruct and correct human beings.

The eighteenth century witnessed the flourish of English poetry in the classical style, climaxing with John Dryden, Alexander Pope and Samuel Johnson. Much attention was given to the witty expression, artistic form and satirical style of poetry. Mock epic, romance, satire and epigram were popular forms adopted by poets of the time. Besides the elegant poetic structure and diction, the poetic works of this period were also noted for their seriousness and earnestness in tone and constant didacticism.

The greatest achievements of the eighteenth-century literature were in prose. The age gave us not only Johnson's *Dictionary* and Boswell's biography but Britain's first major literary magazines, *The Tatler* and *The Spectator*. These journals, produced by Joseph Addison and Richard Steele, contain serious essays like those of Francis Bacon and less formal essays known for their satiric humor. Literary letters flourish in the hands of Lord Chesterfield, while in the area of literary criticism the outstanding figures are Pope and Johnson. Notable contributions in history and philosophy include the writings of David Hume, Edward Gibbon's *Decline and Fall of the Roman Empire* (1776-1788), Adam Smith's *Wealth of Nations* (1776), and Edmund Burke's *Reflections on the Revolution in France* (1790).

The mid-century was, however, predominated by a newly rising literary form—the modern English novel, which gives a realistic presentation of life of the common English people. This is a natural product of the Industrial Revolution and a symbol of the growing importance and strength of the English middle class. It is also a product of several differing literary traditions, among them the French romance, the Spanish picaresque tale, and earlier English prose models such as John Lyly's *Euphues* (1579), Philip Sidney's *Arcadia* (1590) and John Bunyan's *Pilgrim's Progress* (1684). Daniel Defoe, Samuel Richardson and Henry Fielding are the pioneers of the eighteenth-century novelists.

And from the middle part to the end of the century, there was also an apparent shift of interest from the classic literary tradition to originality and imagination, from society to individual, and from the didactic to the confessional, inspirational and prophetic. Gothic novels—mostly stories of mystery and horror that take place in some haunted or dilapidated Middle Age castles—were turned out profusely by both male and female writers; works such as *The Castle of Otranto* (1765) by Horace Walpole, *The Mysteries of Udolpho* (1794) by Mrs. Ann Radcliffe, and *The Champion of Virtue, a Gothic Story* (1777) by Clara Reeve became very popular. Eulogizing or lamenting lyrics by nature poets like James Thomson, William Collins, and William Cowper, and by such sentimentalists as the "Graveyard School" were widely read. The romantic poems of Robert Burns and William Blake also joined in, paving the way for the flourish of Romanticism in the early next century.

Most eighteenth-century drama continues the traditions of Restoration playwrights, although tragedies were not as fine as in the preceding century. The drama in this period mainly focused on an analysis of social manners, and much of it was satire. John Gay, Oliver Goldsmith and Richard Brinsley Sheridan were the leading figures among a host of playwrights. *The Beggar's Opera* (1728) was a very successful play, in which John Gay recycled popular songs of the day and wrote new lyrics that were both humorous and satirical. Goldsmith's *She Stoops to Conquer* (1771) made a successful revival of comedies of manners, recapturing some of the zest and earthiness of Restoration comedy in the midst of the rather insipid sentimental drama of the age. And Richard Sheridan's *Rivals* (1775) and *School for Scandal* (1777) proved to be bright, amusing comedies that criticized wayward youth, overprotective parents, dishonest financial dealings, and social expectations.

5.2 Jonathan Swift

5.2.1 Life and career

Swift (1667-1745) was born into an English family in Dublin, Ireland. His father died before his birth. Through the generosity of an uncle, he was educated first at Kilkenny Grammar School and then at Trinity College, Dublin. After graduation, he obtained a position as secretary to a distant kinsman, Sir William Temple, a retired diplomat. During those years, Swift read widely at Temple's vast library and had time to discover his talent as a prose satirist. Through contact with Temple and many other well-known politicians, he received a first-rate education in politics, learning much about the vice, hypocrisy and corruption in the political world. He also met and tutored Esther Johnson, the daughter of Temple's housekeeper. They formed a profound and lasting affectionate friendship. To her, he wrote the famous journal letters, later published as *The Journal to Stella*.

From 1699 to 1701 Swift held different clerical posts in Ireland. In 1704 he published two powerful satires on corruption in religion and learning, *A Tale of a Tub* (1704) and *The Battle of the Books* (1704), which established his name as a satirist. Then, for several years, he was a most notable figure in London as the editor of the official Tory organ, *The Examiner*. As a reward for his service to the government, he was appointed, in 1713, dean of St. Patrick's Cathedral in Dublin, where he became not only a popular clergyman, but also a leader in the Irish resistance to the English oppression. In 1724, he published, under the pseudonym of Drapier, a series of letters that called on the whole country to refuse the newly-minted English copper coins which would further debase the coinage of the already poverty-stricken country.

Gulliver's Travels (1726), his greatest satiric work, is an artistic enterprise conceived on multiple levels, touching practically all fields of human endeavor—politics, religion, education, ethics—and holding up to mankind a satirical mirror. In this work, Swift takes great pains to bring to light the wickedness of the then English society, with its tyranny, its political intrigues and corruption, its aggressive wars and colonialism, its religious disputes and persecution, and its ruthless oppression and exploitation of the common people. The ugliness of the eighteenth-century English society is no elsewhere so thoroughly and forcefully exposed and condemned as in this single book. *Gulliver's Travels* can also be described as one of the first novels of modern alienation, focusing on an individual's repeated failures to integrate into societies to which he does not belong. England itself is not much of a homeland for Gulliver, and, with his surgeon's business unprofitable and his father's estate insufficient to support him, he may be right to feel alienated from it. He never speaks fondly or nostalgically about England, and every time he returns home, he is quick to leave again. Gulliver never complains explicitly about feeling lonely, but the embittered and antisocial misanthrope we see at the end of the novel is clearly a profoundly isolated individual. Thus, if Swift's satire mocks the excesses of communal life, it may also mock the excesses of individualism in its portrait of a miserable and lonely Gulliver talking to his horses at home in England.

Swift was a man of great moral integrity and social charm. A man with a bitter life experience, he had a deep hatred for all the rich oppressors and a deep sympathy for all the poor and oppressed. He had always regarded himself as a defender of human freedom, fighting against all forms of hypocrisy, corruption, trickery, and exploitation. His understanding of human nature is also profound. In his opinion, human nature is seriously and permanently flawed. To better human life, enlightenment is needed, but to redress it is very hard. So, in his writings, although he intends not to condemn but to reform and improve human nature and human institutions, there is often an under- or over- tone of helplessness and indignation.

Swift is a master satirist. His satire is usually masked by an outward gravity and an apparent earnestness that renders his satire all the more powerful. His "A Modest Proposal" is generally taken as a perfect model. By suggesting that poor Irish parents sell their one-year-old babies to the rich English lords and ladies as food, Swift is making the most devastating protest against the inhuman exploitation and oppression of the Irish people by the English ruling class. The apparent eagerness, sincerity and detachment of the author add force to the bitter irony and biting sarcasm.

Swift is generally thought to be the greatest prose writer of the eighteenth century. He is almost unsurpassed in the writing of simple, direct, precise prose. He defined a good style as "proper words in proper places." Clear, simple, concrete diction, uncomplicated sentence structure, economy and conciseness of language mark all his writings—essays, poems and novels.

5.2.2 An excerpt from Chapter 3, Part I of *Gulliver's Travels*

My gentleness and good behavior had gained so far on the Emperor and his court, and indeed upon the army and people in general, that I began to conceive hopes of getting my liberty in a short time. I took all possible methods to cultivate this favorable disposition.[1] The natives came by degrees to be less apprehensive of any danger from me. I would sometimes lie down, and let five or six of them dance on my hand. And at last the boys and girls would venture to come and play at hide-and-seek in my hair. I had now made a good progress in understanding and speaking their language. The Emperor had a mind one day to entertain me with several of the country shows; wherein they exceed all nations I have known, both for dexterity and magnificence. I was diverted with none so much as that of the rope-dancers, performed upon a slender white thread, extended about two foot, and twelve inches from the ground. Upon which I shall desire liberty,[2] with the reader's patience, to enlarge a little.

This diversion is only practiced by those persons, who are candidates for great employments, and high favor, at court. They are trained in this art from their youth, and are not always of noble birth or liberal education. When a great office is vacant either by death or disgrace (which often happens) five or six of those candidates petition the Emperor to entertain his Majesty and the court with a dance on the rope; and whoever jumps the highest without falling, succeeds in the office. Very often the chief ministers themselves are commanded to show their skill, and to convince the Emperor that they have not lost their faculty. Flimnap, the Treasurer, is allowed to cut a caper[3] on the strait rope, at least an inch higher than any other lord in the whole empire. I have seen him do the summerset[4] several times together upon a trencher fixed on the rope, which is no thicker than a common packthread in England. My friend Reldresal, Principal Secretary for Private Affairs, is, in my opinion, if I am not partial, the second after the Treasurer; the rest of the great officers are much upon a par.

These diversions are often attended with fatal accidents, whereof great numbers are on record. I myself have seen two or three candidates break a limb. But the danger is much greater when the ministers themselves are commanded to show their dexterity; for, by contending to excel themselves and their fellows, they strain so far, that there is hardly one of them who hath not received a fall; and some of them two or three. I was assured that a year or two before my arrival, Flimnap would have infallibly broke his neck, if one of the King's cushions, that accidentally lay on the ground, had not weakened the force of his fall.

There is likewise another diversion, which is only shown before the Emperor and Empress, and first minister, upon particular occasions. The Emperor lays on a table three fine silken threads of six inches long. One is blue, the other red, and the third green. These threads are proposed as prizes for those persons whom the Emperor hath a mind to distinguish by a peculiar mark of his favor. The ceremony is performed in his Majesty's great chamber of state; where the candidates are to undergo a trial of dexterity very different from the former, and such as I have not observed the least resemblance of in any other country of the old or the new world. The Emperor holds a stick in his hands, both ends parallel to the horizon, while the candidates, advancing one by one, sometimes leap over the stick, sometimes creep under it backwards and forwards several times, according as the stick is advanced or depressed. Sometimes the Emperor holds one end of the stick, and his first minister the other; sometimes the minister has it entirely to himself. Whoever performs his part with most agility, and holds out the longest in *leaping* and *creeping*, is rewarded with the blue-colored silk; the red is given to the next, and the green to the third, which they all wear girt twice round about the middle;[5] and you see few great persons about this court who are not adorned with one of these girdles.

The horses of the army, and those of the royal stables, having been daily led before me, were no longer shy, but would come up to my very feet, without starting. The riders would leap them over my hand as I held it on the ground; and one of the Emperor's huntsmen, upon a large courser, [6] took, [7] my foot, shoe and all; which was indeed a prodigious leap. I had the good fortune to divert the Emperor one day after a very extraordinary manner. I desired he would order several sticks of two foot high, and the thickness of an ordinary cane, to be brought me; whereupon his Majesty commanded the master of his woods to give directions accordingly; and the next morning six woodmen arrived with as many carriages, drawn by eight horses to each. I took nine of these sticks, and fixing them firmly in the ground in a quadrangular figure, two foot and a half square, I took four other sticks, and tied them parallel at each corner, about two foot from the ground; then I fastened my handkerchief to the nine sticks that stood erect, and extended it on all sides till it was as tight as the top of a drum; and the four parallel sticks, rising about five inches higher than the handkerchief, served as ledges on each side. When I had finished my work, I desired the Emperor to let a troop of his best horse, twenty-four in number, come and exercise upon this plain. His Majesty approved of the proposal, and I took them up one by one in my hands, ready mounted[8] and armed, with the proper officers to exercise them. As soon as they got into order, they divided into two parties, performed mock skirmishes, discharged blunt arrows, drew their swords, fled and pursued, attacked and retired; and in short discovered the best military discipline I ever beheld. The parallel sticks secured them and their horses from falling over the stage; and the Emperor was so much delighted, that he ordered this entertainment to be repeated several days; and once was pleased to be lifted up, and give the word of command; and, with great difficulty, persuaded even the Empress herself to let me hold her in her close chair[9] within two yards of the stage, from whence she was able to take a full view of the whole performance. It was my good fortune that no ill accident happened in these entertainments, only once a fiery horse that belonged to one of the captains pawing with his hoof struck a hole in my handkerchief, and his foot slipping, he overthrew his rider and himself; but I immediately relieved them both; for covering the hole with one hand, I set down the troop with the other, in the same manner as I took them up. The horse that fell was strained in the left shoulder, but the rider got no hurt, and I repaired my handkerchief as well as I could; however, I would not trust to the strength of it any more in such dangerous enterprises.

About two or three days before I was set at liberty, as I was entertaining the court with these kinds of feats, there arrived an express to inform his Majesty that some of his subjects, riding near the place where I was first taken up, had seen a great black substance lying on the ground, very oddly shaped, extending its edges round as wide as his Majesty's bedchamber, and rising up in the middle as high as a man; that it was no living creature, as they at first apprehended, for it lay on the grass without motion, and some of them had walked round it several times; that by mounting upon each other's shoulders, they had got to the top, which was flat and even; and stamping upon it they found it was hollow within; that they humbly conceived it might be something belonging to the Man-Mountain, and if his Majesty pleased, they would undertake to bring it with only five horses. I presently knew what they meant; and was glad at heart to receive this intelligence.[10] It seems upon my first reaching the shore after our shipwreck, I was in such confusion, that before I came to the place where I went to sleep, my hat, which I had fastened with a string to my head while I was rowing, and had stuck on all the time I was swimming, fell off after I came to land; the string, as I conjecture, breaking by some accident which I never observed, but thought my hat had been lost at sea. I entreated his Imperial Majesty to give orders it might be brought to me as soon as possible, describing to him the use and the nature of it: and the next day the wagoners arrived with it, but not in a very good condition; they had bored two holes in the brim, within an inch and half of the edge, and fastened two hooks in the holes; these hooks were tied by a long cord to the harness, and thus my hat was dragged along for above half an English mile: but the ground in that country being extremely smooth and level, it received less damage than I expected.

Two days after this adventure, the Emperor, having ordered that part of his army which quarters in and about his metropolis to be in a readiness, took a fancy of diverting himself in a very singular manner. He desired I would stand like a colossus, with my legs as far asunder as I conveniently could. He then commanded his general (who was an old experienced leader, and a great patron of mine) to draw up the troops in close order, and march them under me; the foot[11] by twenty-four in a breast,[12] and the horse by sixteen, with drums beating, colors[13] flying, and pikes advanced. This body consisted of three thousand foot, and a thousand horse. His Majesty gave orders, upon pain of death,[14] that every soldier in his march should observe the strictest decency with regard to my person; which, however, could not prevent some of the younger officers from turning up their eyes as they passed under me. And, to confess the truth, my breeches were at that time in so ill a condition, that they afforded some opportunities for laughter and admiration.

I had sent so many memorials and petitions for my liberty, that his Majesty at length mentioned the matter first in the cabinet, and then in a full council; where it was opposed by none, except Skyresh Bolgolam,[15] who was pleased, without any provocation, to be my mortal enemy. But it was carried against him by the whole board, and confirmed by the Emperor. That minister was Galbet, or Admiral of the Realm; very much in his master's confidence, and a person well versed in affairs, but of a morose and sour complexion. However he was at length persuaded to comply; but prevailed that the articles and conditions upon which I should be set free, and to which I must swear, should be drawn up by himself. These articles were brought to me by Skyresh Bolgolam in person, attended by two under-secretaries, and several persons of distinction. After they were read, I was demanded to swear to the performance of them; first in the manner of my own country, and afterwards in the method prescribed by their laws; which was to hold my right foot in my left hand, to place the middle finger of my right hand on the crown of my head, and my thumb on the tip of my right ear. But because the reader may perhaps be curious to have some idea of the style and manner of expression peculiar to that people, as well as to know the articles upon which I recovered my liberty, I have made a translation of the whole instrument, word for word, as near as I was able, which I here offer to the public.

GOLBASTO MOMAREN EVLAME GURDILO SHEFIN MULLY ULLY GUE, most mighty Emperor of Lilliput, delight and terror of the universe, whose dominions extend five thousand blustrugs (about twelve miles in circumference) to the extremities of the globe; Monarch of all Monarchs; taller than the sons of men; whose feet press down to the center, and whose head strikes against the sun; at whose nod the princes of the earth shake their knees; pleasant as the spring, comfortable as the summer, fruitful as autumn, dreadful as winter. His most sublime Majesty proposeth to the Man-Mountain,[16] lately arrived at our celestial dominions, the following articles, which by a solemn oath he shall be obliged to perform.

First, The Man-Mountain shall not depart from our dominions, without our license under our great seal.

Secondly, He shall not presume to come into our metropolis, without our express order;[17] at which time the inhabitants shall have two hours warning, to keep within their doors.

Thirdly, The said Man-Mountain shall confine his walks to our principal high roads; and not offer to walk or lie down in a meadow, or field of corn.

Fourthly, As he walks the said roads, he shall take the uttermost care not to trample upon the bodies of any of our loving subjects, their horses, or carriages, nor take any of our said subjects into his hands, without their own consent.

Fifthly, If an express require extraordinary dispatch, the Man-Mountain shall be obliged to carry in his pocket the messenger and horse, a six days' journey once in every moon, and return the said messenger back (if so required) safe to our Imperial Presence.

Sixthly, He shall be our ally against our enemies in the island of Blefuscu, and do his utmost to destroy their fleet, which is now preparing to invade us.

Seventhly, That the said Man-Mountain shall, at his times of leisure, be aiding and assisting to our workmen, in helping to raise certain great stones, towards covering the wall of the principal park, and other our royal buildings.

Eighthly, That the said Man-Mountain shall, in two moons' time, deliver in an exact survey of the circumference of our dominions by a computation of his own paces round the coast.

Lastly, That upon his solemn oath to observe all the above articles, the said Man-Mountain shall have a daily allowance[18] of meat and drink sufficient for the support of 1, 728 of our subjects; with free access to our Royal Person, and other marks of our favor.[19] Given at our palace at Belfaborac the twelfth day of the ninety-first moon of our reign.

I swore and subscribed to these articles with great cheerfulness and content, although some of them were not so honorable as I could have wished; which proceeded wholly from the malice of Skyresh Bolgolam the High Admiral: whereupon my chains were immediately unlocked, and I was at full liberty: the Emperor himself in person did me the honor to be by at the whole ceremony. I made my acknowledgments by prostrating myself at his Majesty's feet: but he commanded me to rise; and after many gracious expressions, which, to avoid the censure of vanity, I shall not repeat, he added, that he hoped that I should prove a useful servant, and well deserve all the favors he had already conferred upon me, or might do for the future.

The reader may please to observe, that in the last article for the recovery of my liberty, the Emperor stipulates to allow me a quantity of meat and drink, sufficient for the support of 1, 728 Lilliputians. Some time after, asking a friend at court how they came to fix on that determinate number, he told me, that his Majesty's mathematicians, having taken the height of my body by the help of a quadrant, and finding it to exceed theirs in the proportion of twelve to one, they concluded from the similarity of their bodies, that mine must contain at least 1, 728 of theirs, and consequently would require as much food as was necessary to support that number of Lilliputians. By which, the reader may conceive an idea of the ingenuity of that people, as well as the prudent and exact economy of so great a prince.

☞ Notes

1. **cultivate this favorable disposition:** encourage and develop a general tendency of character.
2. **desire liberty:** beg leave or permission.
3. **cut a caper:** jump about in a joyful manner.
4. **summerset:** somersault.
5. **wear girt twice round about the middle:** wear girdle which goes twice round the waist.
6. **courser:** a swift horse.

7. **took:** jump over.
8. **ready-mounted:** placed on the horse in advance.
9. **close chair:** an enclosed or sedan chair.
10. **intelligence:** news.
11. **the foot:** the foot soldier, infantry.
12. **in a breast:** in a rank (in which the members stand side by side).
13. **colors:** the official flags of the army.
14. **upon pain of death:** with the punishment of death.
15. **Skyresh Bolgolam:** Here it indicates the earl of Nottingham, an enemy of Swift.
16. **Man-Mountain:** It refers to Gulliver.
17. **express order:** urgent order.
18. **allowance:** something provided regularly, provision.
19. **marks of our favor:** persons of importance.

☞ Study questions

1. What are the major political practices satirized in Chapter 3 of Part Ⅰ?
2. How do you see the Lilliputian Emperor?
3. What does Gulliver learn about humanity from the Lilliputians?
4. What aspects of human nature does Swift seem to be satirizing through Gulliver's huge size in Lilliput? Why is this contrast effective?
5. Do you think Swift's technique of ridicule is more or less effective than simple, direct criticism? Why?

☞ Essay topics

1. What does Gulliver discover about human nature? Draw your own conclusion to this question and support it with examples from personal or current events.
2. On the basis of *Gulliver's Travels*, discuss Swift's notions of a good and just government.

5.3 Alexander Pope

5.3.1 Life and career

Pope (1688-1744) was born into a Roman Catholic family in London. Ill health plagued Pope almost from birth. At the age of twelve, a severe illness (tuberculosis of the spine) ruined his health. He developed a hunchback, which resulted in a disfigured body. So he had little regular schooling and was largely self-taught by reading at home. Because of his constant sickness and the family religious background, he was not able to go to university or hold any public office like many of his contemporaries. This confinement led to cultivation of a fine taste for natural beauty and turned him into a precocious poet.

Pope began writing poetry quite early. His first book of poetry *Pastorals* came out in 1709. At the age of 23, he firmly established his reputation as a poet with the publication of *An Essay on Criticism* (1711). The poem was written in heroic couplets outlining critical tastes and standards based on neoclassical doctrines. The next year, he published *The Rape of the Lock*, which immediately made Pope famous as a great poet. The story is based on an actual episode in which a young man attempted to cut a lock of hair from a young lady, thus breaking up the friendship between the two families. Pope was asked to write something to restore peace but he chose to use the mock epic form to ridicule the trivial incident, to emphasize the pettiness of the quarrel and to satirize the foolish, meaningless life of the lords and ladies in the eighteenth century England.

The Dunciad (1728-1743) took Pope over ten years for final completion. It is a scathing satire on dunces and literary hacks in which Pope viciously attacked his enemies. But the poem is not confined to personal attack. It also exposed and satirized, in general, the dullness that was reflected in the corruptness of government, social morals, education and even religion. In 1734, Pope published his most ambitious work, *An Essay on Man*, which was a poetic summary of current philosophical speculations.

As a successful author, pope embarked, between 1715 and 1720, on his verse translation of Homer's *Iliad* with the purpose of securing his financial future. He also produced an edition of Shakespeare's works in 1725. It is said that Pope was the first Englishman to make a living from his pen, free from the shackles of patronage and flattery.

As a representative of the Enlightenment, Pope was one of the first to introduce rationalism to England. He upheld the existing social system as an ideal one, but he was not entirely blind to the rapid moral, political and cultural deterioration. Commercialization and money-worship were invading all aspects of national life. He, therefore, assumed the role of champion of traditional civilization: of reason, classical learning, sound art, good taste and public virtue. Using satire as a weapon, he fought against social corruption and debasement that threatened to undermine the moral and social values of the society.

Pope was the greatest poet of his time. He strongly advocated neoclassicism, emphasizing that literary works should be judged by classical rules of order, reason, logic, restrained emotion, good taste and decorum. He believed that literature had the power to influence and enrich life, to educate and correct people. He set out in his works to fulfill this duty. As a result, he developed a satiric, concise, smooth, graceful and well-balanced style and finally brought to its last perfection the heroic couplet Dryden had successfully used in his plays.

Pope is a great verse satirist. Almost all his works are satires. The aim of his satire is to burn away the falsity and corruption, to repair the decaying world and to restore the society to its original healthy conditions. Also, he uses satire to fight his personal enemies, which might be a personal misfortune for such a great poet. His works are usually products of masterly craftsmanship. They are marked by careful diction, a remarkable rhythmical variety of patterns, precision of meaning, harmony of language and structure, a firm control of the form, and flexibility of styles. But at the same time, they tend to be too formal and too polished that they seem to the modern readers to lack vitality and imagination.

5. 3. 2 An excerpt from *An Essay on Criticism*

Some to conceit[1] alone their taste confine,
And glittering thoughts struck out at every Line;
Pleased with a work where nothing's just or fit,
One glaring chaos and wild heap of wit.
Poets like painters, thus unskilled to trace
The naked nature and the living grace, [2]
With gold and jewels cover every part,
And hide with ornaments their want of art. [3]
  True wit is Nature to advantage dressed, [4]
What oft was thought, but ne'er so well expressed;
Something, whose truth convinced at sight we find,
That gives us back the image of our mind. [5]
As shades more sweetly recommend the light, [6]
So modest plainness sets off sprightly wit;
For works may have more wit than does them good,
As bodies perish through excess of blood.
  Others for language all their care express, [7]
And value books, as women men, for dress.
Their praise is still—the style is excellent;
The sense they humbly take upon content. [8]
Words are like leaves; and where they most abound,
Much fruit of sense beneath is rarely found. [9]
False eloquence, like the prismatic glass, [10]
Its gaudy colors spreads on every place;
The face of Nature we no more survey,
All glares alike, without distinction gay.
But true expression, like the unchanging sun,
Clears, and improves whate'er it shines upon,

It gilds all objects, but it alters none.
Expression is the dress of thought, and still
Appears more decent as more suitable.[11]
A vile conceit in pompous words expressed
Is like a clown[12] in regal purple[13] dressed:
For different styles with different subjects sort,
As several garbs with country, town, and court.
Some by old words to fame have made pretence,
Ancients in phrase, mere moderns in their sense.[14]
Such labored nothings,[15] in so strange a style,
Amaze the unlearn'd, and make the learned smile.
Unlucky as Fungoso[16] in the play,
These sparks[17] with awkward vanity display
What the fine gentleman wore yesterday;
And but so mimic ancient wits at best,
As apes our grandsires in their doublets dressed.[18]
In words as fashions the same rule will hold,
Alike fantastic if too new or old:[19]
Be not the first by whom the new are tried,
Nor yet the last to lay the old aside.

☞ **Notes**

1. **conceit:** pointed wit, ingenuity and extravagance, or affectation in the use of figures, especially similes and metaphors.
2. **to trace / The naked nature and the living grace:** to portray (in their paintings or writings) nature in its plainness and the beautiful objects from real life.
3. **want of art:** lack of artistic skill or talent.
4. **dressed:** adorned or decorated.
5. **Something, whose truth convinced at sight we find, /That gives us back the image of our mind:** True wit, whose truth is constantly convinced when we see it brings back to our mind what we have only an imperfect image or notion of.
6. **As shades more sweetly recommend the light:** The light looks brighter if seen against the background of shade or darkness.
7. **Others for language all their care express:** Other people show all their interest in the language of the poem.
8. **content:** mere acquiescence.
9. **where they most abound, / Much fruit of sense beneath is rarely found:** Where/ When too many words are used, they seldom express much sense.

10. **prismatic glass:** a very up-to-date scientific reference. Newton's Optics, which treated of the prism and the spectrum, had been published in 1704, though his theories had been known earlier.
11. **Appears more decent as more suitable:** The more suitable the expression is, the more decent it appears.
12. **clown:** fool, a position one held at an old royal court, whose function was to keep the king amused and who was usually dressed in silly-looking patterned clothes.
13. **regal purple:** the color supposedly to be dressed in only by the royal members.
14. **Ancients in phrase, mere moderns in their sense:** (They are) ancients when judged by their language but mere moderns judged by the ideas they express.
15. **labored nothings:** elaborate but meaningless expressions.
16. **Fungoso:** a character in Ben Jonson's *Everyman Out of His Humour*, a man who is depicted as one "that follows the fashion far off like a spy. He buys clothes to imitate a spruce courtier, but fails, for the fashion changes so fast that his money is thrown away."
17. **sparks:** (a contemptuous term) men of fashion.
18. **in their doublets dressed:** dressed in the doublets of our grandfathers. ***Doublet***: a tightly-fit dress for men.
19. **Alike fantastic if too new or old:** They are both absurd whether the words used are too new or too old for the ideas.

☞ Study questions

1. What is a conceit?
2. What is Pope's definition of true wit?
3. What metaphor dominates Pope's discussion of wit?
4. Do you think more wit will make a better literary work? Why or why not?
5. What metaphor dominates Pope's discussion of language?
6. What is the metaphorical relationship between thought and expression?

5.3.3 "Ode on Solitude"[1]

Happy the man, whose wish and care
A few paternal[2] acres bound,
Content to breathe his native air,
In his own ground.

Whose herds with milk, whose fields with bread,
Whose flocks supply him with attire,[3]
Whose trees in summer yield[4] him shade,

In winter fire.

Blest! who can unconcern'dly find
Hours, days, and years slide[5] soft away,
In health of body, peace of mind,
Quiet by day,

Sound sleep by night; study and ease
Together mix'd; sweet recreation,
And innocence, which most does please,
With meditation.

Thus let me live, unseen, unknown;
Thus unlamented[6] let me dye;
Steal from the world, and not a stone
Tell where I lye.

☞ Notes

1. The hint for this poem was taken from Horace's well-known Epode 2, which praises the simplicity and innocence of country life, a favorite literary theme in Pope's time. The poem consists of five numbered quatrains. Each quatrain has the rhyme scheme, *abab*.
2. **paternal:** fatherly.
3. **attire:** clothing.
4. **yield:** give.
5. **slide:** to move somewhere quietly without being noticed.
6. **unlamented:** not being feeling sad.

☞ Study questions

1. What function does repetition play in this poem?
2. What images does the poet use to realize his theme?
3. What does the poet celebrate in this poem?

5.4 Daniel Defoe

5.4.1 Life and career

Defoe (1660-1731) was born in London. His father was a poor, but hard-working butcher. The boy was sent to one of the best dissenting academies at Stoke Newington, where he studied science and humanities, preparing to become a Presbyterian minister. Though he gave up this plan later on, his Protestant values endured throughout his life despite discrimination and persecution. By the time he was a young man in his 20s, he became a successful merchant in London. Visiting Holland, France, and Spain on business, he developed a life-long taste for travel. A very shrewd and effective but restless businessman, Defoe would never be contented with what he had achieved but itch to embark on some more adventurous enterprises. Therefore, his business underwent many ups and downs, but he was never beaten. His quick mind, abundant energy and never-failing enthusiasm always brought him back on his feet after a fall.

A man of wide interest and inexhaustible energy, Defoe also had a passion for politics. He considered it his civic duty to take an active part in the political affairs of the state and to offer his opinions for the benefit of the general public. He wrote quite a number of pamphlets on the current political issues. His political verse "The True-born Englishman" (1701) won him friendship from the king. "The Shortest Way with Dissenters" (1702), which ridiculed the religious intolerance of the High Church, made him go through public exposure in the pillory. He had even run a political and literary paper, *The Review*, single-handedly for about 9 years. When he was around the age of sixty, Defoe began writing novels. He published his first novel, *Robinson Crusoe*, in 1719, attracting a large number of middle-class readers. In the following years, he wrote four other novels: *Captain Singleton* (1720), *Moll Flanders* (1722), *Colonel Jack* (1722) and *Roxana* (1724).

Robinson Crusoe, as a story of adventure in a distant and unknown region, speaks thrillingly to the universal human sense of romance. The book records how a plain Englishman overcame all kinds of difficulties in a deserted island through the plain virtues of courage, patience, perseverance, and mechanical ingenuity. It is rich enough to contain a number of overlapping meanings. If it is an adventure story, it is also a moral tale, a commercial account and a Puritan fable. It celebrates the eighteenth-century Western civilization's material triumph and the strength of human rational will to conquer the natural environment. Robinson is the very prototype of the empire builder, the pioneer colonist. His success in building up a comfortable living environment and later a private colony is shown as due to the sturdy qualities in his character, to his own unaided efforts, to his courage and patience, to his practical skill, and to his intelligent persistence. In another sense, Robinson is Everyman, struggling with patience and fortitude through persistent work to conquer nature. So, Robinson is the embodiment of private enterprise and colonization; this is perhaps the most important reason why the novel makes a strong appeal to its contemporary readers and why it is still of interest to the present-day readers.

Defoe was a typical man of the eighteenth-century English middle class: liberal in mind and advanced in opinion. He valued the Puritan ethics and believed in diligence and self-reliance. Like Robinson, he is a man whose personal pride would never allow him to belie his own background and class. At the same time, he had a heart broad and ready enough to embrace all the people, including social outlaws. He was among the first writers ever to give his praise to the hard-working, sturdy middle class and showed his sympathy for the down-trodden, unfortunate poor.

Defoe was a very good story-teller. He had a gift for organizing minute details in such a vivid way that his stories could be both credible and fascinating. Stylistically, he was a great innovator. He used the simple, direct, fact-based style of the middle classes. There is nothing artificial in his language; everything is easy, colloquial and mostly vernacular. His sentences are sometimes short, crisp and plain, and sometimes long and rambling, which leave on the reader an impression of casual narration. His influence in helping to shape modern journalism and modern everyday English style was not only large, but also revolutionary.

5. 4. 2 An excerpt from Chapter 4 of *Robinson Crusoe*

A little after noon I found the sea very calm, and the tyde[1] ebbed so far out that I could come within a quarter of a mile of the ship; and here I found a fresh renewing of my grief, for I saw evidently, that if we had kept on board, we had been all safe, that is to say, we had all got safe on shore, and I had not been so miserable as to be left entirely destitute of all comfort and company, as I now was; this fore'd tears from my eyes again, but as there was little relief in that, I resolved, if possible, to get to the ship, so I pulled off my clothes, for the weather was hot to extremity, and took the water, but when I came to the ship, my difficulty was still greater to know how to get on board, for as she lay a-ground, and high out of the water, there was nothing within my reach to lay hold of. I swam round her twice, and the second time I spy'd a small piece of a rope, which I wondered I did not see at first, hang down by the fore-chains so low, as that with great difficulty I got hold of it, and by the help of that rope, got up into the forecastle of the ship. Here I found that the ship was bulged, and had a great deal of water in her hold, but that she lay so on the side of a bank of hard sand, or rather earth, that her stern lay lifted up upon the bank, and her head low almost to the water; by this means all her quarter was free, and all that was in that part was dry; for you may be sure my first work was to search and to see what was spoiled and what was free; and first I found that all the ship's provisions were dry and untouched by the water, and being very well disposed to eat, I went to the bread-room and filled my pockets with bisket, and eat it as I went about other things, for I had no time to lose; I also found some rum in the great cabbin, of which I took a large dram, and which I had indeed need enough of to spirit me for what was before me. Now I wanted nothing but a boat to furnish my self with many things which I foresaw would be very necessary to me.

It was in vain to sit still and wish for what was not to be had, and this extremity rouz'd my application.[2] We had several spare yards, and two or three large spars of wood, and a spare top-mast or two in the ship; I resolved to fall to work[3] with these, and I flung as many of them over board as I could manage for their weight, tying every one with a rope that they might not drive away; when this was done I went down the ship's side, and pulling them to me, I ty'd four of them fast together at both ends as well as I could, in the form of a raft, and laying two or three short pieces of plank upon them crossways, I found I could walk upon it very well, but that it was not able to bear any great weight, the pieces being too light; so I went to work, and with the carpenter's saw I cut a spare top-mast into three lengths, and added them to my raft, with a great deal of labor and pains; but hope of furnishing my self with necessaries encouraged me to go beyond what I should have been able to have done upon another occasion.

My raft was now strong enough to bear any reasonable weight; my next care was what to load it with, and how to preserve what I laid upon it from the surf of the sea, but I was not long considering this. I first laid all the planks or boards upon it that I could get, and having considered well what I most wanted, I first got three of the seamen's chests, which I had broken open and empty'd, and lowered them down upon my raft; the first of these I filled with provision, viz. bread, rice, three Dutch cheeses, five pieces of dry'd goat's flesh, which we lived much upon, and a little remainder of European corn which had been laid by for some fowls which we brought to sea with us, but the fowls were killed; there had been some barly and wheat together, but, to my great disappointment, I found afterwards that the rats had eaten or spoiled it all; as for liquors, I found several cases of bottles belonging to our skipper, in which were some cordial waters, and in all about five or six gallons of rack; these I stowed by themselves, there being no need to put them into the chest, nor no room for them. While I was doing this, I found the tyde began to flow, tho' very calm, and I had the mortification to see my coat, shirt, and waistcoat which I had left on shore upon the sand, swim away; as for my breeches, which were only linen and open knee'd, I swam on board in them and my stockings. However, this put me upon rummaging for clothes, of which I found enough, but took no more than I wanted for present use, for I had other things which my eye was more upon,[4] as first tools to work with on shore, and it was after long searching that I found out the carpenter's chest, which was indeed a very useful prize to me, and much more valuable than a ship loading of gold would have been at that time; I got it down to my raft, even whole as it was, without losing time to look into it, for I knew in general what it contained.

My next care was for some ammunition and arms; there were two very good fowling-pieces[5] in the great cabbin, and two pistols; these I secured first, with some powder-horns, and a small bag of shot, and two old rusty swords; I knew there were three barrels of powder in the ship, but knew not where our gunner had stowed them, but with much search I found them, two of them dry and good, the third had taken water; those two I got to my raft, with the arms; and now I thought my self pretty well freighted, and began to think how I should get to shore with them, having neither sail, oar, or rudder, and the least cap full of wind would have overset all my navigation.[6]

I had three encouragements: 1. a smooth calm sea; 2. the tide rising, and setting in to the shore; 3. what little wind there was blew me towards the land; and thus, having found two or three broken oars belonging to the boat, and besides the tools which were in the chest, I found two saws, an axe, and a hammer, and with this cargo I put to sea. For a mile, or thereabouts, my raft went very well, only that I found it drive a little distant from the place where I had landed before, by which I perceived that there was some indraft of the water,[7] and consequently I hoped to find some creek or river there, which I might make use of as a port to get to land with my cargo.

As I imagined, so it was, there appeared before me a little opening of the land, and I found a strong current of the tide set into it, so I guided my raft as well as I could to keep in the middle of the stream. But here I had like to have suffered a second shipwreck,[8] which, if I had, I think verily would have broke my heart, for knowing nothing of the coast, my raft run a-ground at one end of it upon a shoal, and not being a-ground at the other end, it wanted but a little that all my cargo had slip'd off towards that end that was a-float, and so fallen into the water. I did my utmost by setting my back against the chests to keep them in their places, but could not thrust off the raft with all my strength, neither durst I stir from the posture I was in, but holding up the chests with all my might, stood in that manner near half an hour, in which time the rising of the water brought me a little more upon a level, and a little after, the water still rising, my raft floated again, and I thrust her off with the oar I had into the channel, and then driving up higher, I at length found my self in the mouth of a little river, with land on both sides, and a strong current or tide running up. I looked on both sides for a proper place to get to shore, for I was not willing to be driven too high up the river, hoping in time to see some ship at sea, and therefore resolved to place my self as near the coast as I could.

At length I spy'd a little cove on the right shore of the creek, to which with great pain and difficulty I guided my raft, and at last got so near, as that, reaching ground with my oar, I could thrust her directly in; but here I had like to have dipt all my cargo in the sea again; for that shore lying pretty steep, that is to say sloping, there was no place to land, but where one end of my float, if it run on shore, would lie so high, and the other sink lower as before, that it would endanger my cargo again. All that I could do was to wait till the tide was at the highest, keeping the raft with my oar like an anchor to hold the side of it fast to the shore, near a flat piece of ground, which I expected the water would flow over; and so it did. As soon as I found water enough, for my raft drew about a foot of water, I thrust her on upon that flat piece of ground, and there fastened or mored her by sticking my two broken oars into the ground, one on one side near one end, and one on the other side near the other end; and thus I lay 'till the water ebbed away, and left my raft and all my cargo safe on shore.

My next work was to view the country, and seek a proper place for my habitation, and where to stow my goods to secure them from whatever might happen; where I was, I yet knew not, whether on the continent or on an island, whether inhabitedor not inhabited, whether in danger of wild beasts or not. There was a hill not above a mile from me, which rose up very steep and high, and which seemed to over-top some other hills, which lay as in a ridge from it northward; I took out one of the fowling pieces, and one of the pistols, and an horn of powder, and thus armed I traveled for discovery up to the top of that hill, there after I had with great labor and difficulty get to the top, I saw my fate to my great affliction, viz. that I was in an island environed every way with the sea, no land to be seen, except some rocks which lay a great way off, and two small islands less than this, which lay about three leagues to the west.

I found also that the island I was in was barren, and, as I saw good reason to believe, un-inhabited, except by wild beasts, of whom however I saw none, yet I saw abundance of fowls, but knew not their kinds, neither when I killed them could I tell what was fit for food, and what not; at my coming back, I shot at a great bird which I saw sitting upon a tree on the side of a great wood. I believe it was the first gun that had been fired there since the creation of the world; I had no sooner fired, but from all the parts of the wood there arose an innumerable number of fowls of many sorts, making a confused screaming, and crying every one according to his usual note; but not one of them of any kind that I knew. As for the creature I killed, I took it to be a kind of a hawk, its color and beak resembling it, but had no talons or claws more than common; its flesh was carrion, and fit for nothing.

Contented with this discovery, I came back to my raft, and fell to work to bring my cargo on shore, which took me up the rest of that day, and what to do with my self at night I knew not, nor indeed where to rest; for I was afraid to lie down on the ground, not knowing but some wild beast might devour me, tho', as I afterwards found, there was really no need for those fears.

However, as well as I could, I barricaded my self round with the chests and boards that I had brought on shore, and made a kind of a hut for that night's lodging; as for food, I yet saw not which way to supply my self, except that I had seen two or three creatures like hares run out of the wood where I shot the fowl.

☞ **Notes**

1. **tyde:** tide. The spelling of some of the words in this novel is different from nowadays.
2. **this extremity rouz'd my application:** This extreme hardship stirred me up to do something.
3. **fall to work:** to begin to work.
4. **which my eyes was more upon:** upon which I looked with greater attention.
5. **fowling-pieces:** light guns used for shooting fowls.
6. **overset all my navigation:** upset all my attempts to sail the raft.
7. **some indraft of the water:** some inward flow of water.
8. **I had like to have suffer'd a second shipwreck:** I nearly suffered from a second shipwreck ("I had like," archaic = it was likely for me).

☞ **Study questions**

1. What does Robinson Crusoe discover when he comes back to the wrecked ship?
2. Describe Crusoe's behavior immediately after the shipwreck.
3. What makes Crusoe think that he could manage to sail his raft to a safe port?
4. What qualities in Robinson Crusoe's character strike you most?

☞ **Essay topics**

1. What kind of man is Robinson Crusoe? Cite examples from the selected reading to illustrate your idea.
2. Why does Daniel Defoe use such great details in his description?

5.5 Henry Fielding

5.5.1 Life and career

Fielding (1707-1754) was born into a genteel family, which was closely allied to the aristocracy. As a boy he received his education at Eton College (1719-1724). In 1728 he went to the University of Leiden in the Netherlands, where he cultivated a wide and genuine taste for the classics. After returning to England, he devoted himself to writing for the stage. During a span of eight years he turned out 25 plays and became a successful playwright of the time. His plays were mostly comedies and farces filled with political and social satire. However, his career as a playwright ended abruptly in 1737 when the political censorship of the Licensing Act went into effect. He then took up law and was admitted to the Bar at the Middle Temple in 1740. He was made justice of the peace for Westminster in 1748 and for the county of Middlesex in 1749. But his legal profession did not bring him enough income to maintain his family, so he became editor of a paper called *The Champion*.

Fielding's fame is established chiefly upon his success as a novelist. He had four major fictional works. His novel *The History of the Adventures of Joseph Andrews* is first intended as a burlesque of the false sentimentality and conventional virtues of Richardson's *Pamela*. But after a number of chapters, Fielding found himself considering all the forces working on humans, and in the end he created what he called "a comic epic poem in prose". The success of *Joseph Andrews* caused Fielding to write more novels in the same style, such as *The History of Jonathan Wild the Great* (1743), *The History of Tom Jones, a Foundling* (1749) and *The History of Amelia* (1751).

Among Fielding's novels, the best known is *Tom Jones*, which established his reputation as a founder of the English novel. It tells the story of the title character from infancy through his marriage to the beautiful and virtuous Sophia Western, the pursuit of whom takes up much of the story. Tom, the hero, overcomes not only all external obstacles but, most importantly, his own weaknesses of character, to win both love and fortune. In a way, Tom is kind of wayfaring Everyman who, having being expelled from "Paradise Hall", must through hard experience gain that knowledge of himself which will enable him to be united with the girl, Sophia.

As *Tom Jones* is some three times the length of *Joseph Andrews*, it is even more richly filled with incidents, scenes, and characters of the English countryside and its capital, London. Social evil in every form is also presented: malice, cruelty, savagery, meanness, hypocrisy, deceit, corruption, and moral degeneration seen in the country, on the open road and in London. And the story is further complicated by the intricacies of an ingenious plot of coincidences and unexpected meetings, thus providing a superb panoramic view of the eighteenth century English life.

While Samuel Richardson is seen as the psychological realist of the early novel, Fielding is the humorist and the inventor of the authorial narrative voice of scope and breadth. Of all the eighteenth-century novelists he was the first to set out, both in theory and practice, to write specifically a "comic epic in prose". The structures of his novel are always well planned and often imitations of the classics. The characters, each indispensable to the development of the plot, are true to life. His writings are also noted for dramatic dialogues and other devices such as suspense, coincidence and unexpectedness. His language style is easy, unlabored and familiar, but extremely vivid and vigorous.

As a great enlightener, Fielding sets out from the very beginning to attack the social injustice and inequality, hypocrisy and vice, and the corruptness of the government. His sympathy is always with the kind, honest poor people. He never hesitates to stand up in their defense and protection and is often beyond himself when he sees injustice and exploitation. As an educated man, Fielding firmly believed in the educational function of literature. He shared the contemporary view of the English enlighteners that the purpose of the novel was not just to amuse, but to instruct. The object of his novel was to present a faithful picture of life, "the just copies of human manners," with sound teaching woven into their texture, so as to teach men to know themselves, their proper spheres and appropriate manners.

5. 5. 2 An excerpt from Chapter 8, Book Ⅳ of *Tom Jones*

Mr. Western had an estate in this parish; and as his house stood at little greater distance from this church than from his own, he very often came to Divine Service[1] here; and both he and the charming Sophia happened to be present at this time.

Sophia was much pleased with the beauty of the girl,[2] whom she pitied for her simplicity in having dressed herself in that manner, as she saw the envy which it had occasioned[3] among her equals. She no sooner came home than she sent for the gamekeeper,[4] and ordered him to bring his daughter to her; saying she would provide for her in the family, and might possibly place the girl about her own person, when her own maid, who was now going away, had left her.

Poor Seagrim was thunderstruck at this; for he was no stranger to the fault in the shape of his daughter. He answered, in a stammering voice, "That he was afraid Molly would be too awkward to wait on her ladyship, as she had never been at service."—"No matter for that," says Sophia; "she will soon improve. I am pleased with the girl, and am resolved to try her."

Black George now repaired to[5] his wife, on whose prudent counsel he depended to extricate him out of this dilemma; but when he came thither he found his house in some confusion. So great envy had this sack[6] occasioned, that when Mr. Allworthy and the other gentry were gone from church, the rage, which had hitherto been confined, burst into an uproar; and, having vented itself at first in opprobrious words, laughs, hisses, and gestures, betook itself at last to certain missile weapons,[7] which, though from their plastic nature they threatened neither the loss of life or of limb, were, however, sufficiently dreadful to a well-dressed lady. Molly had too much spirit to bear this treatment tamely. Having therefore—but hold, as we are diffident of our own abilities, let us here invite a superior power to our assistance.

Ye Muses, then, whoever ye are, who love to sing battles, and principally thou who whilom didst recount the slaughter in those fields where Hudibras and Trulla fought, if thou wert not starved with thy friend Butler, assist me on this great occasion.[8] All things are not in the power of all.[9]

As a vast herd of cows in a rich farmer's yard, if, while they are milked, they hear their calves at a distance, lamenting the robbery which is then committing, roar and bellow; so roared forth the Somersetshire mob[10] an hallaloo, made up of almost as many squalls, screams, and other different sounds as there were persons, or indeed passions among them: some were inspired by rage, others alarmed by fear, and others had nothing in their heads but the love of fun; but chiefly Envy, the sister of Satan, and his constant companion, rushed among the crowd, and blew up the fury of the women, who no sooner came up to Molly than they pelted her with dirt and rubbish.

Molly, having endeavored in vain to make a handsome retreat, faced about; and laying hold of ragged Bess, who advanced in the front of the enemy, she at one blow felled her to the ground. The whole army of the enemy (though near a hundred in number), seeing the fate of their general, gave back many paces, and retired behind a new-dug grave; for the churchyard was the field of battle, where there was to be a funeral that very evening. Molly pursued her victory, and catching up a skull which lay on the side of the grave, discharged it with such fury, that having hit a taylor on the head, the two skulls sent equally forth a hollow sound at their meeting, and the taylor took presently measure of his length on the ground,[11] where the skulls lay side by side, and it was doubtful which was the more valuable of the two. Molly then took a thigh-bone in her hand, fell in among the flying ranks, and dealing her blows with great liberality on either side, overthrew the carcass of many a mighty hero and heroine.

Recount, O Muse, the names of those who fell on this fatal day. First, Jemmy Tweedle felt on his hinder head[12] the direful bone. Him the pleasant banks of sweetly-winding Stour[13] had nourished, where he first learnt the vocal art, with which, wandering up and down at wakes and fairs, he cheered the rural nymphs and swains, when upon the green they interweaved the sprightly dance; while he himself stood fiddling and jumping to his own music. How little now avails his fiddle! He thumps the verdant floor with his carcass. Next, old Echepole, the sowgelder, received a blow in his forehead from our Amazonian heroine,[14] and immediately fell to the ground. He was a swinging fat fellow, and fell with almost as much noise as a house. His tobacco-box dropped at the same time from his pocket, which Molly took up as lawful spoils. Then Kate of the Mill tumbled unfortunately over a tombstone, which catching hold of her ungartered stocking inverted the order of nature, and gave her heels the superiority to her head. Betty Pippin, with young Roger her lover, fell both to the ground; where, oh perverse fate! she solutes the earth, and he the sky.[15] Tom Freckle, the smith's son, was the next victim to her rage. He was an ingenious workman, and made excellent patterns; nay, the pattern with which he was knocked down was his own workmanship. Had he been at that time singing psalms in the church, he would have avoided a broken head. Miss Crow, the daughter of the farmer; John Giddish, himself a farmer; Nan Slouch, Easter Codling, Will Spray, Tom Bennet; the three Misses Potter, whose father keeps the sign of the Red Lion; Betty Chambermaid, Jack Ostler, and many others of inferior note, lay rolling among the graves.

Not that the strenuous arm of Molly reached all these; for many of them in their flight overthrew each other.

But now Fortune, fearing she had acted out of character, and had inclined too long to the same side, especially as it was the right side, hastily turned about: for now Goody Brown—whom Zekiel Brown caressed in his arms; nor he alone, but half the parish besides; so famous was she in the fields of Venus, [16] nor indeed less in those of Mars. [17] The trophies of both these her husband always bore about on his head and face; for if ever human head did by its horns display the amorous glories of a wife, Zekiel's did; nor did his well-scratched face less denote her talents (or rather talons) of a different kind.

No longer bore this Amazon the shameful flight of her party. She stopped short, and, calling aloud to all who fled, spoke as follows: "Ye Somersetshire men, or rather ye Somersetshire women, are ye not ashamed thus to fly from a single woman? But if not other will oppose her, I myself and Joan Top here will have the honor of the victory." Having thus said, she flew at Molly Seagrim, and easily wrenched the thigh-bone from her hand, at the same time clawing off her cap from her head. Then laying hold of the hair of Molly with her left hand, she attacked her so furiously in the face with the right, that the blood soon began to trickle from her nose. Molly was not idle this while. She soon removed the clout from the head of Goody Brown, and then fastening on her hair with one hand, with the other she caused another bloody stream to issue forth from the nostrils of the enemy.

When each of the combatants had borne off sufficient spoils of hair from the head of her antagonist, the next rage was against the garments. In this attack they exerted so much violence, that in a very few minutes they were both naked to the middle.

It is lucky for the women that the seat of fistycuff war[18] is not the same with them as among men; but though they may seem a little to deviate from their sex, when they go forth to battle, yet I have observed, they never so far forget, as to assail the bosoms of each other, where a few blows would be fatal to most of them. This, I know, some derive from their being of a more bloody inclination than the males. On which account they apply to the nose, as to the part whence blood may most easily be drawn; but this seems a far-fetched as well as ill-natured supposition.

Goody Brown had great advantage of Molly in this particular; for the former had indeed no breasts, her bosom (if it may be so called), as well in color as in many other properties, exactly resembling an ancient piece of parchment, upon which anyone might have drummed a considerable while without doing her any great damage.

Molly, besides her present unhappy condition, was differently formed in those parts, and might, perhaps, have tempted the envy of Brown to give her a fatal blow, had not the lucky arrival of Tom Jones at this instant put an immediate end to the bloody scene.

This accident was luckily owing to Mr. Square; for he, Master Blifil, and Jones, had mounted their horses, after church, to take the air, and had ridden about a quarter of a mile, when Square, changing his mind (not idly, but for a reason which we shall unfold as soon as we have leisure), desired the young gentlemen to ride with him another way than they had at first purposed. This motion being complied with, brought them of necessity back again to the churchyard.

Master Blifil, who rode first, seeing such a mob assembled, and two women in the posture in which we left the combatants, stopped his horse to inquire what was the matter. A country fellow, scratching his head, answered him: "I don't know, master, un't I; an't please your honor, here hath been a vight,[19] I think, between Goody Brown and Moll Seagrim."

"Who, who?" cries Tom; but without waiting for an answer, having discovered the features of his Molly through all the discomposure in which they now were, he hastily alighted, turned his horse loose, and, leaping over the wall, ran to her. She now, first bursting into tears, told him how barbarously she had been treated. Upon which, forgetting the sex of Goody Brown, or perhaps not knowing it in his rage—for, in reality, she had no feminine appearance but a petticoat, which he might not observe—he gave her a lash or two with his horsewhip; and then flying at the mob, who were all accused by Molly, he dealt his blows so profusely on all sides, that unless I would again invoke the muse (which the good-natured reader may think a little too hard upon her, as she hath so lately been violently sweated), it would be impossible for me to recount the horse-whipping of that day.

Having scoured the whole coast of the enemy,[20] as well as any of Homer's[21] heroes ever did, or as Don Quixote[22] or any knight-errant in the world could have done, he returned to Molly, whom he found in a condition which must give both me and my reader pain, was it to be described here. Tom raved like a madman, beat his breast, tore his hair, stamped on the ground, and vowed the utmost vengeance on all who had been concerned. He then pulled off his coat, and buttoned it round her, put his hat upon her head, wiped the blood from her face as well as he could with his handkerchief, and called out to the servant to ride as fast as possible for a side-saddle, or a pillion, that he might carry her safe home.

Master Blifil objected to the sending away the servant, as they had only one with them; but as Square seconded the order of Jones, he was obliged to comply.

The servant returned in a very short time with the pillion, and Molly, having collected her rags as well as she could, was placed behind him. In which manner she was carried home, Square, Blifil, and Jones attending.

Here Jones having received his coat, given her a sly kiss, and whispered her, that he would return in the evening, quitted his Molly, and rode on after his companions.

☞ Notes

1. **Divine Service:** religious service held in the church of Mr. Allworthy's parish.
2. **the girl:** referring to Molly, daughter of George Seagrim, the gamekeeper.
3. **occasioned:** aroused.
4. **gamekeeper:** referring to George Seagrim.
5. **repaired to:** went to.
6. **sack:** the night gown which Sophia had given to Molly.
7. **missile weapons:** things that can be thrown to hit people.
8. **Ye Muses, then ... assist me on this great occasion:** You Muses, whoever you are, whoever love to sing of battles, and especially you who in the past had given an account of the fierce battle between Hudibras and Trulla, if you hadn't used up all your power in assistance to the work of your friend Butler, help me now in my account of the "great" fight between Molly and the villagers. **Muses:** Goddesses of Poetry. **Hudibras and Trulla:** heroes in Samuel Butler's (1612-1680) poem "Hudibras" (1663).
9. **All things are not in the power of all:** Not everybody can do everything.
10. **Somersetshire mob:** the men and women who were gathered against Molly.
11. **took presently measure of his length on the ground:** immediately fell flat on the ground.
12. **hinder head:** back of the head.
13. **Stour:** a river.
14. **Amazonian heroine:** Women in Amazon are said to be valiant fighters. Here it refers to Molly.
15. **She salutes the earth, and he the sky:** He fell down on his back, and she fell down on her belly.
16. **in the fields of Venus:** in conquering men. **Venus:** Goddess of Love in Roman mythology.
17. **in those of Mars:** in fighting. **Mars:** God of War in Roman mythology.
18. **fistycuff war:** a fight in which the participants fight with the fists.
19. **vight:** fight.
20. **scoured the whole coast of the enemy:** completely defeated the enemy.
21. **Homer:** a great ancient Greek poet, author of the famous epics *Iliad* and *Odyssey*.
22. **Don Quixote:** hero in the famous romance by Spanish writer Cervantes (1547-1616).

☞ Study questions

1. How does Fielding describe the fighting of the country women?
2. Why does Fielding use Venus, Mars and other classical allusions to describe the

fighting?

3. What is the tone of this selected reading part?
4. What effect does Fielding make by dramatizing a village quarrel in the grand epic style?
5. What is "comic epic in prose"? Cite examples from the selected reading to illustrate your idea.

☞ **Essay topics**

1. The author has employed a series of contrasts to build his narrative. Write an essay on these contrasts and comparisons, citing examples from the novel to illustrate your idea.
2. How does Fielding characterize Tom and Blifil in this novel?

5.6 Samuel Johnson

5.6.1 Life and career

Johnson(1709-1784) was born in Richfield, son of a book-seller. He received his education first at the Richfield Grammar School and then at Oxford University. He had to quit the university without taking a degree when his father died in 1731, which also plunged him into a distressingly painful struggle for existence. In 1735 he married Elizabeth Porter, a widow 20 years his senior. He remained devoted to her until her death in 1752. In hope of establishing himself in society, Johnson first made a futile attempt to set up a school and then went to London to try his fortune as a literary adventurer. The years between 1737 and 1755 were very difficult for him: he did translations, edited magazines and wrote essays and accounts of parliamentary debates for the book-sellers, but earned no more than enough to maintain a meager living. It was only after the publication of his *Dictionary* that his financial status took a turn for the better. In 1762 the government gave him a special pension which freed him from the burden of writing for a living. So during the last twenty years of his life he wrote as little as he decently could and enjoyed a pleasant and easy life, talking about literature and literary men in his famous Literary Club, where he was surrounded with respect by the elite of the literary circles.

Johnson was an energetic and versatile writer. He had a hand in all the different branches of literary activities. He was a poet, dramatist, prose romancer, biographer, essayist, critic, lexicographer and publicist. His chief works include poems: "London" (1738), and "The Vanity of Human Wishes" (1749); a romance: *The History of Rascals, Prince of Abyssinia* (1759); a tragedy: *Irene* (1749); and literary criticism as found in the preface to his edition of Shakespeare and in his comments on 52 poets in

The Lives of Poets (1779-1781). As a lexicographer, Johnson distinguished himself as the author of *A Dictionary of the English Language* (1755), a gigantic task which Johnson undertook single-handedly and finished in over seven years.

Johnson was the last great neo-classicist enlightener in the second half of the eighteenth century. Beneath the rough appearance, Johnson was a man not only of very vigorous intellect and great learning, but also of sincere piety and unusual kindness. In most of his writings, he showed his concerns about the vanity of human wishes, and tried to awaken men to this folly. In literary creation and criticism, he was rather conservative, openly showing his dislike for much of the newly rising forms of literature and his fondness for those writings which carried a lot of moralizing and philosophizing. He insisted that a writer should adhere to universal truth and experience, should please and instruct. Like Pope, he was particularly fond of didacticism. Therefore, it is understandable that he was rather pleased with Richardson's *Pamela* but was contemptuous of Fielding's *Tom Jones*.

Johnson's style is typically neo-classical, but it is at the opposite extreme from Swift's simplicity or Addison's neatness. His language is characteristically general, often Latinate and frequently polysyllabic. His sentences are long and well structured, interwoven with parallel words and phrases. However, no matter how complex his sentences are, the thought is always clearly expressed; and though he tends to use "learned words", they are always accurately used. Reading his works gives the reader the impression that he is talking with a very learned man.

5. 6. 2 "To the Right Honorable the Earl of Chesterfield"

February 7, 1775

My Lord,

I have been lately informed by the proprietor of *The World*[1] that two papers in which my *Dictionary* is recommended to the public were written by your Lordship. To be so distinguished is an honor which, being very little accustomed to favors from the great, I know not well how to receive, or in what terms[2] to acknowledge.

When upon some slight encouragement I first visited your Lordship, I was overpowered like the rest of mankind by the enchantment of your address,[3] and could not forbear to wish that I might boast myself "*le vainqueur du vainqueur de la terre*";[4] that I might obtain that regard for which I saw the world contending;[5] but I found my attendance so little encouraged that neither pride nor modesty would suffer[6] me to continue it. When I had once addressed your Lordship in public, I had exhausted all the art of pleasing which a retired and uncourtly scholar can possess. I had done all that I could; and no man is well pleased to have his all neglected, be it ever so little.[7]

Seven years, my Lord, have now passed since I waited in your outward rooms or was repulsed[8] from your door, during which time I have been pushing on my work through difficulties of which it is useless to complain, and have brought it at last to the verge of publication without one act of assistance, one word of encouragement, or one smile of favor. Such treatment I did not expect, for I never had a patron before.

The shepherd in Virgil grew at last acquainted with Love, and found him a native of the rocks.[9]

Is not a patron, my Lord, one who looks with unconcern on a man struggling for life in the water and, when he has reached ground, encumbers him with help? The notice which you have been pleased to take of my labors, had it been early, had been kind; but it has been delayed till I am indifferent and cannot enjoy it; till I am solitary and cannot impart it; till I am known and do not want it. I hope it is no very cynical asperity[10] not to confess obligations where no benefit has been received, or to be unwilling that the pubic should consider me as owing that to a patron which Providence has enabled me to do for myself.

Having carried on my work thus far with so little obligation to any favorer of learning, I shall not be disappointed though I should conclude it, if less be possible, with less;[11] for I have been long wakened from that dream of hope in which I once boasted myself with so much exultation, my Lord,

your Lordship's most humble,
most obedient servant,
Sam Johnson

☞ Notes

1. **the proprietor of *The World*:** owner of the newspaper, *The World*, in which Lord Chesterfield had praised Johnson.
2. **terms:** language, a particular way of expression.
3. **address:** conversation.
4. ***Le vainqueur du vainqueur de la terre*:** French for "the conqueror of the conqueror of the earth."
5. **contending:** competing for.
6. **suffer:** allow, permit.
7. **be it ever so little:** even if it should be so little.
8. **repulsed:** rejected.
9. **The shepherd in Virgil grew at last acquainted with Love, and found him a native of the rocks:** in a work by Virgil (70-19 B. C.) a shepherd complains that love was born among jagged rocks.
10. **asperity:** roughness of manner or temper.
11. **if less be possible, with less:** (I would like to carry on my work) with less obligations

(help) if less (help) is possible, i. e., I no longer need anybody's help.

☞ **Study questions**

1. Why did Johnson first visit Lord Chesterfield? How was he received?
2. What is Johnson's definition of a patron, according to Paragraph 5?
3. How does Johnson feel about the notice Lord Chesterfield has taken of his work?
4. What appears to be the real purpose of Johnson's letter?

5.7 Richard Brinsley Sheridan

5.7.1 Life and career

Sheridan (1751-1816) was born in Dublin, Ireland, son of a prominent actor. The family moved to London when Sheridan was still a boy. He was educated at Harrow. Then he became a law student of the Middle Temple, but was never called to the bar. In 1770, the family settled in Bath, where Sheridan fell in love with a young woman called Elizabeth Linley. After a romantic elopement and duel fighting, he finally married her. As a young man, Sheridan started his career as a playwright. His first play, *The Rivals*, staged in 1775, proved to be a tremendous success. Before long, he became part owner and director of the Drury Lane Theatre. The year 1777 saw the appearance of his masterpiece *The School for Scandal*, which brought him quite a fortune. His other works include: *St. Patrick's Day* (1775), a two-act farce; *The Duenna* (1775), a comic opera; and *The Critic* (1779), a burlesque and a satire on sentimental drama. But his playwriting career was cut short in 1780 when he was elected M. P. for Stafford. Then, for thirty-two years he held various government offices: Under-secretary of State for Foreign Affairs, Secretary of the Treasury, Treasurer of the Navy, etc. His political career came to an end in 1812 when he had no money for re-election. Then his creditors closed in on him and his last years were harassed by debt and disappointment. He died in neglect and poverty.

Sheridan was the only important English dramatist of the eighteenth century. His plays, especially *The Rivals* and *The School for Scandal*, are generally regarded as important links between the masterpieces of Shakespeare and those of Bernard Shaw. They are also true classics in English comedy. In his plays, morality is the constant theme. He is much concerned with the current moral issues and lashes harshly at the social vices of the day. In *The Rivals*, a comedy of manners, he is satirizing the traditional practice of the parents to arrange marriages for their children without considering the latter's opinion. In *The School for Scandal*, the satire becomes even sharper as the characters are exposed scene by scene to their defenseless nakedness.

Sheridan's greatness also lies in his theatrical art. He seems to have inherited from his parents a natural ability and inborn knowledge about the theatre. His plays are the product of a dramatic genius as well as of a well-versed theatrical man. Though his dramatic techniques are largely conventional, they are exploited to the best advantage. His plots are well organized, his characters, either major or minor, are all sharply drawn, and his manipulation of such devices as disguise, mistaken identity and dramatic irony is masterly. Witty dialogues and neat and decent language also make a characteristic of his plays.

5. 7. 2 An excerpt from Scene I, Act I of *The School for Scandal*

ACT I

Scene I Lady Sneerwell's *Dressing-room*

Discovered LADY SNEERWELL[1] *at her dressing table;* SNAKE *drinking chocolate.*

LDAY SNEER. The paragraph,[2] you say, Mr. Snake, were all inserted?

SNAKE. They were, madam; and, as I copied them myself in a feigned hand, there can be no suspicion whence they came.

LDAY SNEER. Did you circulate the report of Lady Brittle's intrigue with Captain Boastall?

SNAKE. That's in as fine a train[3] as your ladyship could wish. In the common course of things, I think it must reach Mrs. Clackit's ears within four-and-twenty hours; and then, you know, the business is as good as done.

LDAY SNEER. Why, truly, Mrs. Clackit has a very pretty talent, and a great deal of industry.

SNAKE. True, madam, and has been tolerably successful in her day. To my knowledge she has been the cause of six matches being broken off, and three sons being disinherited; of four forced elopements, and as many close confinements; nine separate maintenances,[4] and two divorces. Nay, I have more than once traced her causing a *tête-à-tête*[5] in the *Town and County Magazine*, when the parties, perhaps, had never seen each other's face before in the course of their lives.

LDAY SNEER. She certainly has talents, but her manner is gross.

SNAKE. 'Tis very true. —She generally designs well, has a free tongue and a bold invention; but her coloring is too dark,[6] and her outlines often extravagant. She wants that delicacy of tint, and mellowness of sneer, which distinguish your ladyship's scandal.

LDAY SNEER. You are partial, Snake.

SNAKE. Not in the least—everybody allows that Lady Sneerwell can do more with a word or look than many can with the most labored detail, even when they happen to have a little truth on their side to support it.

LDAY SNEER. Yes, my dear Snake; and I am no hypocrite to deny the satisfaction I reap from the success of my efforts. Wounded myself, in the early part of my life by the envenomed tongue of slander, I confess I have since known no pleasure equal to the reducing others to the level of my own injured reputation.

SNAKE. Nothing can be more natural. But, Lady Sneerwell, there is one affair in which you have lately employed me, wherein, I confess, I am at a loss to guess your motives.

LDAY SNEER. I conceive you mean with respect to my neighbor, Sir Peter Teazle, and his family?

SNAKE. I do. Here are two young men, to whom Sir Peter has acted as a kind of guardian[7] since their father's death; the eldest possessing the most amiable character, and universally well spoken of—the youngest, the most dissipated and extravagant young fellow in the kingdom, without friends or character: the former an avowed admirer of your ladyship, and apparently your favorite; the latter attached to Maria, Sir Peter's ward, and confessedly beloved by her. Now, on the face of these circumstances, it is utterly unaccountable to me why you, the widow of a City knight,[8] with a good jointure,[9] should not close with the passion of a man of such character and expectations as Mr. Surface; and more so why you should be so uncommonly earnest to destroy the mutual attachment subsisting between his brother Charles and Maria.

LDAY SNEER. Then, at once to unravel this mystery, I must inform you that love has no share whatever in the intercourse between Mr. Surface and me.

SNAKE. No!

LDAY SNEER. His real attachment is to Maria, or her fortune; but finding in his brother a favored rival, he has been obliged to mask his pretensions,[10] and profit by my assistance.

SNAKE. Yet still I am more puzzled why you should interest yourself in his success.

LDAY SNEER. Heavens! How dull you are! Cannot you surmise the weakness which I hitherto, through shame, have concealed even from you? Must I confess that Charles, that libertine, that extravagant, that bankrupt in fortune and reputation, that he it is for whom I'm thus anxious and malicious, and to gain whom I would sacrifice every thing?

SNAKE. Now, indeed, your conduct appears consistent: but how came you and Mr. Surface so confidential?

LDAY SNEER. For our mutual interest. I have found him out a long time since. I know him to be artful, selfish, and malicious—in short, a sentimental knave;[11] while with Sir Peter, and indeed with all his acquaintance, he passes for a youthful miracle of prudence, good sense, and benevolence.

SNAKE. Yes; yet Sir Peter vows he has not his equal in England; and, above all, he praises him as a man of sentiment.

LDAY SNEER. True—and with the assistance of his sentiment and hypocrisy, he has brought Sir Peter entirely into his interest with regard to Maria; while poor Charles has no friend in the house, though, I fear, he has a powerful one in Maria's heart, against whom we must direct our schemes.

Enter SERVANT

SERV. Mr. Surface.

LDAY SNEER. Show him up. [*Exit* SERVANT] He generally calls about this time. I don't wonder at people giving him to me for a lover.

Enter JOSEPH SURFACE

JOSEPH S. My dear Lady Sneerwell, how do you do today? Mr. Snake, your most obedient.

LDAY SNEER. Snake has just been rallying[12] me on our mutual attachment, but I have informed him of our real views. You know how useful he has been to us; and, believe me, the confidence is not ill placed.

JOSEPH S. Madam, it is impossible for me to suspect a man of Mr. Snake's sensibility and discernment.

LDAY SNEER. Well, well, no compliments now; but tell me when you saw your mistress, Maria—or, what is more material to me, your brother.

JOSEPH S. I have not seen either since I left you; but I can inform you that they never meet. Some of your stories have taken a good effect on Maria.

LDAY SNEER. Ah, my dear Snake! the merit of this belongs to you: but do your brother's distresses increase?

JOSEPH S. Every hour. I am told he has had another execution in the house yesterday. In short, his dissipation and extravagance exceed any thing I have ever heard of.

LDAY SNEER. Poor Charles!

JOSEPH S. True, madam; notwithstanding his vices, one cannot help feeling for him. Aye, poor Charles, indeed! I'm sure I wish it were in my power to be of any essential service to him; for the man who does not share in the distresses of a brother, even though merited by his own misconduct, deserves—

LDAY SNEER. O Lud![13] you are going to be moral, and forget that you are among friends.

JOSEPH S. Egad,[14] that's true! —I'll keep that sentiment till I see Sir Peter. However, it is certainly a charity to rescue Maria from such a libertine, who if he is to be reclaimed, can be so only by a person of your ladyship's superior accomplishments and understanding.

SNAKE. I believe, Lady Sneerwell, here's company coming: I'll go and copy the letter I mentioned to you. —Mr. Surface, your most obedient.

JOSEPH S. Sir, your very devoted. [*Exit* SNAKE] —Lady Sneerwell, I am very sorry you have put any farther confidence in that fellow.

LDAY SNEER. Why so?

JOSEPH S. I have lately detected him in frequent conference with old Rowley, who was formerly my father's steward, and has never, you know, been a friend of mine.

LDAY SNEER. And do you think he would betray us?

JOSEPH S. Nothing more likely: —take my word for't, Lady Sneerwell, that fellow hasn't virtue enough to be faithful even to his own villainy. —Ah! Maria!

Enter MARIA

LDAY SNEER. Maria, my dear, how do you do? —What's the matter?

MARIA. Oh! there's that disagreeable lover of mine, Sir Benjamin Backbite, has just called at my guardian's, with his odious uncle, Crabtree; so I slipped out, and ran hither to avoid them.

LDAY SNEER. Is that all?

JOSEPH S. If my brother Charles had been of the party, madam, perhaps you would not have been so much alarmed.

LDAY SNEER. Nay, now you are severe; for I dare swear the truth of the matter is, Maria heard *you* were here. —But, my dear, what has Sir Benjamin done, that you should avoid him so?

MARIA. Oh, he has done nothing—but 'tis for what he has said: his conversation is a perpetual libel on all his acquaintance.

JOSEPH S. Aye, and the worst of it is, there is no advantage in not knowing him— for he'll abuse a stranger just as soon as his best friend; and his uncle's as bad.

LDAY SNEER. Nay, but we should make allowance[15]—Sir Benjamin is a wit and a poet.

MARIA. For my part, I confess, madam, wit loses its respect with me, when I see it in company with malice. —What do you think, Mr. Surface?

JOSEPH S. Certainly, madam; to smile at the jest[16] which plants a thorn in another's breast is to become a principal in the mischief.[17]

LDAY SNEER. Pshaw! —there's no possibility of being witty without a little ill nature: the malice of a good thing is the barb that makes it stick. —What's your opinion, Mr. Surface?

JOSEPH S. To be sure, madam; that conversation, where the spirit of raillery is suppressed, will ever appear tedious and insipid.

MARIA. Well, I'll not debate how far scandal may be allowable; but in a man, I am sure, it is always contemptible. We have pride, envy, rivalship, and a thousand motives to depreciate each other; but the male slanderer must have the cowardice of a woman before he can traduce[18] one.

Enter SERVANT

SERV. Madam, Mrs. Candour is below, and if your ladyship's at leisure, will leave her carriage.

LDAY SNEER. Beg her to walk in. —[*Exit* SERVANT]— Now, Maria, here is a character to your taste; for though Mrs. Candour is a little talkative, everybody allows her to be the best natured and best sort of woman.

MARIA. Yes, —with a very gross affectation[19] of good nature and benevolence, she does more mischief than the direct malice of old Crabtree.

JOSEPH S. I' faith[20] 'tis true, Lady Sneerwell: whenever I hear the current running against the characters of my friends, I never think them in such danger as when Candour undertakes their defense.

LDAY SNEER. Hush! —here she is!

Enter MRS. CANDOUR

MRS. CAN. My dear Lady Sneerwell, how have you been this century?—Mr. Surface, what news do you hear?—though indeed it is no matter, for I think one hears nothing else but scandal.

JOSEPH S. Just so, indeed, ma'am.

MRS. CAN. Oh, Maria! child, —what, is the whole affair off between you and Charles? His extravagance, I presume—the town talks of nothing else.

MARIA. I am very sorry, ma'am, the town is not better employed.

MRS. CAN. True, true, child: but there's no stopping people's tongues. I own I was hurt to hear it, as I indeed was to learn, from the same quarter, that your guardian, Sir Peter, and Lady Teazle have not agreed lately as well as could be wished.

MARIA. 'Tis strangely impertinent for people to busy themselves so.

MRS. CAN. Very true, child: —but what's to be done? People will talk—there's no preventing it. Why, it was but yesterday I was told that Miss Gadabout[21] had eloped with Sir Filigree Flirt. —But, Lord! there's no minding what one hears; though, to be sure, I had this from very good authority.

MARIA. Such reports are highly scandalous.

MRS. CAN. So they are, child—shameful, shameful! But the world is so censorious, no character escapes. —Lord, now who would have suspected your friend, Miss Prim,[22] of an indiscretion? Yet such is the ill-nature of people, that they say her uncle stopped her last week, just as she was stepping into the York Mail with her dancing-master.

MARIA. I'll answer for't there are no grounds for that report.

MRS. CAN. Ah, no foundation in the world, I dare swear; no more, probably, than for the story circulated last month, of Mrs. Festino's[23] affair with Colonel Cassino; —

though, to be sure, that matter was never rightly cleared up.

JOSEPH S. The license of invention[24] some people take is monstrous indeed.

MARIA. 'Tis so, —but, in my opinion, those who report such things are equally culpable.[25]

MRS. CAN. To be sure they are; tale-bearers are as bad as the tale-makers—'tis an old observation, and a very true one: but what's to be done, as I said before? how will you prevent people from talking? To-day, Mrs. Clackit assured me, Mr. and Mrs. Honeymoon were at last become mere man and wife, like the rest of their acquaintance. She likewise hinted that a certain widow, in the next street, had got rid of her dropsy[26] and recovered her shape in a most surprising manner. And at the same time Miss Tattle, who was by, affirmed that Lord Buffalo had discovered his lady at a house of no extraordinary fame;[27] and that Sir Harry Bouquet and Tom Saunter were to measure swords[28] on a similar provocation. —But, Lord, do you think I would report these things! —No, no! tale-bearers, as I said before, are just as bad as the tale-makers.

JOSEPH S. Ah! Mrs. Candour, if everybody had your forbearance and good-nature!

MRS. CAN. I confess, Mr. Surface, I cannot bear to hear people attacked behind their backs; and when ugly circumstances come out against our acquaintance, I own I always love to think the best. —By-the-by, I hope 'tis not true that your brother is absolutely ruined?

JOSEPH S. I am afraid his circumstances are very bad indeed, ma'am.

MRS. CAN. Ah! I heard so—but you must tell him to keep up his spirits; everybody almost is in the same way: Lord Spindle, Sir Thomas Splint, Captain Quinze,[29] and Mr. Nickit—all up, I hear, within this week; so, if Charles is undone, he'll find half his acquaintance ruined too, and that, you know, is a consolation.

JOSEPH S. Doubtless, ma'am—a very great one.

Enter SERVANT

SERV. Mr. Crabtree and Sir Benjamin Backbite. [*Exit* SERVANT]

LDAY SNEER. So, Maria, you see your lover pursues you; positively you shan't escape.

Enter CRABTREE *and* SIR BENJAMIN BACKBITE

CRABT. Lady Sneerwell, I kiss your hand—Mrs. Candour, I don't believe you are acquainted with my nephew, Sir Benjamin Backbite? Egad! ma'am he has a pretty wit, and is a pretty poet too. Isn't he, Lady Sneerwell?

SIR BENJ. B. Oh, fie, uncle!

CRABT. Nay, egad, it's true; I back him at a rebus or a charade[30] against the best rhymer in the kingdom. —Has your ladyship heard the epigram he wrote last week on Lady Frizzle's[31] feather catching fire?—Do, Benjamin, repeat it, or the charade you made last night extempore[32] at Mrs. Drowzie's conversazione.[33] Come now; —your first is the name of a fish, your second a great naval commander, and—

SIR BENJ. B. Uncle, now—pr' thee—

CRABT. I'faith, ma'am 'twould surprise you to hear how ready he is at all these sorts of things.

LDAY SNEER. I wonder, Sir Benjamin, you never publish any thing.

SIR BENJ. B. To say truth, ma'am, 'tis very vulgar to print; and as my little productions are mostly satires and lampoons[34] on particular people, I find they circulate more by giving copies in confidence to the friends of the parties. However, I have some love elegies, which, when favored with this lady's smiles, I mean to give the public. [*Pointing to* MARIA]

CRABT. 'Fore heaven, ma'am, they'll immortalize you! —you will be handed down to posterity, like Petrarch's Laura,[35] or Waller's Sacharissa.[36]

SIR BENJ. B. Yes, madam, I think you will like them, when you shall see them on a beautiful quarto page, where a neat rivulet of text shall murmur through a meadow of margin. 'Fore Gad, they will be the most elegant things of their kind!

CRABT. But, ladies, that's true—have you heard the news?

MRS. CAN. What, sir, do you mean the report of—

CRABT. No, ma'am, that's not it. —Miss Nicely is going to be married to her own footman.

MRS. CAN. Impossible!

CRABT. Ask Sir Benjamin.

SIR BENJ. B. 'Tis very true, ma'am: everything is fixed, and the wedding liveries[37] bespoke.

CRABT. Yes—and they do say there were pressing reasons for it.

LDAY SNEER. Why, I have heard something of this before.

MRS. CAN. It can't be—and I wonder any one should believe such a story of so prudent a lady as Miss Nicely.

SIR BENJ. B. O Lud! ma'am, that's the very reason 'twas believed at once. She has always been so cautious and so reserved, that everybody was sure there was some reason for it at bottom.

MRS. CAN. Why, to be sure, a tale of scandal is as fatal to the credit of a prudent lady of her stamp, as a fever is generally to those of the strongest constitutions. But there is a sort of puny sickly reputation, that is always ailing, yet will outlive the robuster characters of a hundred prudes.[38]

SIR BENJ. B. True, madam, —there are valetudinarians[39] in reputation as well as constitution; who, being conscious of their weak part, avoid the least breath of air, and supply their want of stamina[40] by care and circumspection.

MRS. CAN. Well, but this may be all a mistake. You know, Sir Benjamin, very trifling circumstances often give rise to the most injurious tales.

CRABT. That they do, I'll be sworn, ma'am. Did you ever hear how Miss Piper came to lose her lover and her character last summer at Tunbridge?[41]—Sir Benjamin, you remember it?

SIR BENJ. B. Oh, to be sure! —the most whimsical circumstance.

LDAY SNEER. How was it, pray?

CRABT. Why, one evening, at Mrs. Ponto's assembly, the conversation happened to turn on the difficulty of breeding Nova Scotia[42] sheep in this country. Says a young lady in company, I have known instances of it —for Miss Letitia Piper, a first cousin of mine, had a Nova Scotia sheep that produced her twins. —What! cries the Lady Dowager Dundizzy (who you know is as deaf as a post), has Miss Piper had twins? —This mistake, as you may imagine, threw the whole company into a fit of laughing. However, 'twas the next day everywhere reported, and in a few days believed by the whole town, that Miss Letitia Piper had actually been brought to bed of[43] a fine boy and a girl; and in less than a week there were some people who could name the father, and the farm-house where the babies were put to nurse.

LDAY SNEER. Strange, indeed!

CRABT. Matter of fact, I assure you. —O Lud! Mr. Surface, pray is it true that your uncle, Sir Oliver, is coming home?

JOSEPH S. Not that I know of, indeed, sir.

CRABT. He has been in the East Indies a long time. You can scarcely remember him, I believe? Sad comfort whenever he returns, to hear how your brother has gone on!

JOSEPH S. Charles has been imprudent, sir, to be sure; but I hope no busy people have already prejudiced Sir Oliver against him. He may reform.

SIR BENJ. B. To be sure he may: for my part, I never believed him to be so utterly void of principle as people say; and though he has lost all his friends, I am told nobody is better spoken of by the Jews.

CRABT. That's true, Egad, nephew. If the Old Jewry[44] was a ward, I believe Charles would be an alderman: —no man more popular there, 'fore Gad! I hear he pays as many annuities as the Irish tontine;[45] and that whenever he is sick, they have prayers for the recovery of his health in all the synagogues.

SIR BENJ. B. Yet no man lives in greater splendor. They tell me, when he entertains his friends he will sit down to dinner with a dozen of his own securities; have a score of tradesmen waiting in the antechamber, and an officer behind every guest's chair.

JOSEPH S. This may be entertainment to you, gentlemen, but you pay very little regard to the feelings of a brother.

MARIA. [*Aside*] Their malice is intolerable! —[*Aloud*] Lady Sneer, I must wish you a good morning: I'm not very well. [*Exit* MARIA]

MRS. CAN. O dear! she changes color very much.

LDAY SNEER. Do, Mrs. Candour, follow her: she may want your assistance.

MRS. CAN. That I will, with all my soul, ma'am. Poor dear creature, who knows what her situation may be! [*Exit* MRS. CANDOUR]

LDAY SNEER. 'Twas nothing but that she could not bear to hear Charles reflected on, notwithstanding their difference.

SIR BENJ. B. The young lady's *penchant*[46] is obvious.

CRABT. But, Benjamin, you must not give up the pursuit for that: —follow her, and put her into good humor. Repeat her some of your own verses. Come, I'll assist you.

SIR BENJ. B. Mr. Surface, I did not mean to hurt you; but depend on't your brother is utterly undone.

CRABT. O Lud, ay! undone as ever man was. Can't raise a guinea!

SIR BENJ. B. Everything sold, I'm told, that was movable.

CRABT. I have seen one that was at his house. Not a thing left but some empty bottles that were overlooked, and the family pictures, which I believe are framed in the wainscot[47]—

SIR BENJ. B. And I'm very sorry, also, to hear some bad stories against him. [*Going*]

CRABT. Oh, he has done many mean things, that's certain.

SIR BENJ. But, however, as he's your brother—[*Going*]

CRABT. We'll tell you all another opportunity. [*Exit* CRABTREE *and* SIR BENJAMIN]

LDAY SNEER. Ha! ha! 'tis very hard for them to leave a subject they have not quite run down.

JOSEPH S. And I believe the abuse was no more acceptable to your ladyship than to Maria.

LDAY SNEER. I doubt her affections are farther engaged than we imagine. But the family are to be here this evening, so you may as well dine where you are, and we shall have an opportunity of observing farther; in the meantime, I'll go and plot mischief, and you shall study sentiment. [*Exeunt*]

☞ Notes

1. **Lady Sneerwell:** The names of most characters in the play reveal the qualities of the persons.
2. **the paragraphs:** that is, the paragraphs of scandals.

3. **in as fine a train:** in as good order or arrangement.
4. **separate maintenances:** The husband and wife live separately, the livelihood of the wife being maintained by the husband.
5. ***tête-à-tête:*** a private interview.
6. **her coloring is too dark:** that she exaggerates too much.
7. **Sir Peter has acted as a kind of guardian:** Besides taking Maria as his ward, Sir Peter also acts as the guardian of Joseph and Charles Surface during their uncle's absence.
8. **a City knight:** a merchant in the City of London who was conferred the title of knight.
9. **jointure:** a sole estate limited to the wife, to take effect upon the death of her husband, for her own life at least.
10. **mask his pretensions:** hide his intention.
11. **a sentimental knave:** a dishonest and unprincipled man with affected emotions.
12. **rallying:** teasing, ridiculing.
13. **Lud:** Lord.
14. **Egad:** by God.
15. **make allowance:** to be lenient toward.
16. **jest:** a jeering remark with the intention to harm.
17. **a principal in the mischief:** a person directly responsible for the harm.
18. **traduce:** slander.
19. **gross affectation:** outrageously putting on manners that are not one's own.
20. **I' faith:** In faith.
21. **Gadabout:** go about, meaning one who easily changes one's mind.
22. **Prim:** easily shocked by something rude.
23. **Festino:** Italian for festival.
24. **license of invention:** the literary taken in inventing scandals.
25. **culpable:** guilty.
26. **got rid of her dropsy:** The implied meaning is that the widow must have had an abortion.
27. **a house of no extraordinary fame:** a place of bad reputation.
28. **to measure swords:** to be engaged in a duel.
29. **Quinze:** a card game.
30. **charade:** parlor game in which words to be guessed are acted in pantomine.
31. **Frizzle:** to fry, to scorch.
32. **extempore:** without time for preparation.
33. **conversazione:** a social gathering.
34. **lampoon:** a piece of writing that attacks a person with ridicule.
35. **Petrarch's Laura:** Petrarch (1304-1374), the Italian poet, who wrote many sonnets to his lover Laura.

36. **Waller's Sacharissa:** Edmund Waller (1608-1687), a 17th century poet, who wrote many poems to Lady Dorothy Sidney, whom he celebrated as "Sacharissa."
37. **liveries:** distinctive uniforms worn by male servants in a great household.
38. **prudes:** a person of extreme or exaggerated propriety concerning behavior or speech, one who is easily shocked by sexual matters.
39. **valetudinarians:** sickly persons.
40. **want of stamina:** lacking strength or staying power.
41. **Tunbridge:** a hot spring near London.
42. **Nova Scotia:** New Scotland, in the east of Canada.
43. **brought to bed of:** gave birth to.
44. **Old Jewry:** the living quarters of the Jews in London.
45. **tontine**: a financial scheme by which the subscribers to a loan or common fund receive each an annuity during his life, which increases as the number is diminished by death, till the last survivor enjoys the whole income.
46. ***penchant*:** inclination.
47. **wainscot:** wooden panel on the wall.

☞ Study questions

1. What personal qualities can you guess from the names of the characters such as Lady Sneerwell, Mr. Snake, Mrs. Candour, and Sir Benjamin Backbite?
2. What is Lady Sneerwell's motives, trying to destroy the mutual attachment subsisting between Charles and Maria?
3. Why does Maria become the pursuing object of several men?
4. What is your impression about all those characters appeared in the first scene?
5. What is your understanding of the author's attitude towards his characters?

5.8 Thomas Gray

5.8.1 Life and career

Gray(1716-1771) was born into a lower middle class family in London. At the age of eight, he was sent to Eton College, where he had a good classical training. In 1734 he went to study at Cambridge but left without taking a degree. Then he made a grand tour of France and Italy with his friend Horace Walpole. He also had several tours of the Lake District and Scotland in his life. Gray returned to Cambridge at the end of 1742 and received a Bachelor of Civil Law degree the next year. In 1768 he was made professor of History and Modern Languages at Cambridge. Gray was by nature a quiet man who avoided social activities and publicity as much as possible. He declined the Poet laureateship in 1757, and led the uneventful life of a scholar all his life.

During his career, Gray devoted himself to the study of the classics, of the Celtic and Iceland poetry. He was primarily a scholar and perhaps the most learned man of his time. He was not only familiar with the literature and history of the ancient world but of all the important modern nations of Western Europe. In contrast to those professional writers, Gray's literary output was small. His masterpiece, "Elegy Written in a Country Churchyard" was published in 1751. The poem once and for all established him as the leader of the sentimental poetry, earning him a respected and deserved place in literary history. The poem investigates the dangers of the glamorous world and contrasts that with the humble simplicity of the country villagers. While the poet tries to celebrate the simple lifestyle that these rural people lived, even at the expense of reputation or wealth, he also claims that they have been spared from the excesses of power and corruption. As a product of literature in the transitional period, the poem has the ordered, balanced phrasing and rational sentiments of neoclassical poetry on one hand, and tends toward the emotionalism and individualism of the Romantic poets on the other. Its solemn cadence, its majesty of diction, and its vivid though melancholy pastoral imagery have made it into a brilliant work. His other important poems include "Ode on the Spring" (1742), "Hymn to Adversity" (1742), "Ode on a Distant Prospect of Eton College" (1747), "Ode on the Death of a Favorite Cat" (1748), "The Progress of Poesy" (1754), and "The Bard" (1757).

A conscientious artist of the first rate, Gray wrote with sincerity, honesty, and integrity. He wrote of true thoughts, feelings, inspirations, and experience. Every word he wrote reflected upon his emotion. His works were written about peacefulness, passiveness, thoughts of joy, of nostalgia, and most importantly, of innocence. Through his writings about life, he displayed his unique outlook on life. His style is sophisticated and allusive, knitting structure, rhyme scheme, imagery and message into an organic whole.

5.8.2 "Elegy Written in a Country Churchyard"[1]

The curfew[2] tolls the knell[3] of parting day,
  The lowing[4] herd winds slowly o'er the lea,[5]
The plowman homeward plods his weary way,
  And leaves the world to darkness and to me.

Now fades the glimmering landscape on the sight,[6]
  And all the air a solemn stillness holds,
Save where the beetle wheels his droning[7] flight,
  And drowsy tinklings lull the distant folds;[8]

Save that from yonder ivy-mantled tower
  The moping owl does to the moon complain
Of such, as wandering near her secret bower,[9]
  Molest her ancient solitary reign.

Beneath those rugged elms, that yew-tree's shade,
  Where heaves the turf in many a moldering[10] heap,
Each in his narrow cell for ever laid,
  The rude[11] forefathers of the hamlet sleep.

The breezy call of incense-breathing Morn,[12]
  The swallow twittering[13] from the straw-built shed,
The cock's shrill clarion,[14] or the echoing horn,
  No more shall rouse them from their lowly bed.

For them no more the blazing hearth shall burn,
  Or busy housewife ply her evening care;
No children run to lisp their Sire's return,
  Or climb his knees the envied kiss to share.

Oft did the harvest to their sickle yield,
  Their furrow oft the stubborn glebe[15] has broke;
How jocund did they drive their team afield!
  How bowed the woods beneath their sturdy stoke!

Let not Ambition[16] mock their useful toil,
  Their homely joys and destiny obscure;
Nor Grandeur[17] hear with a disdainful smile
  The short and simple annals of the poor.

The boast of heraldry,[18] the pomp of power,
  And all that beauty, all that wealth e'er gave,
Awaits alike the inevitable hour,
  The paths of glory lead but to the grave.[19]

Nor you, ye proud, impute to these the fault,
  If memory o'er their tomb no trophies[20] raise,
Where, through the long-drawn aisle and fretted[21] vault

The pealing anthem swells the note of praise.

Can storied urn[22] or animated bust[23]
Back to its mansion call the fleeting breath?
Can honor's voice provoke[24] the silent dust,
Or Flattery soothe the dull cold ear of Death?

Perhaps in this neglected spot is laid,
Some heart once pregnant with celestial fire;[25]
Hands that the rod of empire might have swayed,
Or waked to ecstasy the living lyre.

But knowledge to their eyes her ample page
Rich with the spoils of time did ne'er unroll,
Chill penury repressed their noble rage,
And froze the genial current of the soul.

Full many a gem of purest ray serene,
The dark unfathomed caves of ocean bear:
Full many a flower is born to blush unseen,
And waste its sweetness on the desert air.

Some village Hampden,[26] that with dauntless breast
The little tyrant of his fields withstood;
Some mute inglorious Milton here may rest,
Some Cromwell guiltless of his country's blood.

The applause of listening senates to command,
The treats of pain and ruin to despise,
To scatter plenty o'er a smiling land,
And read their history in a nation's eyes,[27]

Their lot forbade: nor circumscribed alone
Their growing virtues, but their crimes confined;
Forbade to wade through slaughter to a throne,
And shut the gates of mercy on mankind.[28]

The struggling pangs of conscious truth to hide,

To quench the blushes of ingenious shame,
Or heap the shrine of Luxury and Pride,
With incense, kindled at the muse's flame. [29]

Far from the madding crowd's ignoble strife,
Their sober wishes never learned to stray;
Along the cool sequestered vale of life
They kept the noiseless tenor of their way.

Yet even these bones from insult to protect
Some frail memories still erected nigh,
With uncouth rhymes and shapeless sculpture decked,
Implores the passing tribute of a sigh. [30]

Their name, their years, spelt by the unlettered Muse, [31]
The place of fame and elegy supply:
And many a holy text around she strews,
That teach the rustic moralists to die.

For who to dumb forgetfulness a prey,
This pleasing anxious being e'er resigned,
Left the warm precincts of the cheerful day,
Nor cast one longing lingering look behind?

On some fond breast the parting soul relies,
Some pious drops the closing eye requires;
Even from the tomb the voice of Nature cries,
Even in our ashes live their wonted fires.

For thee, [32] who mindful of the unhonored dead
Dost in these lines their artless tale relate;
If chance, by lonely contemplation led,
Some kindred spirit shall inquire thy fate, [33]

Haply some hoary-headed swain may say,
"Oft have we seen him at the peep of dawn
Brushing with hasty steps the dews away
To meet the sun upon the upland lawn. [34]

"There at the foot of yonder nodding beech
  That wreathes its old fantastic roots so high,
His listless length[35] at noontide would he stretch,
  And pore upon[36] the brook that babbles by.

"Hard by yon wood, now smiling as in scorn,
  Muttering his wayward fancies he would rove,
Now drooping, woeful wan, like one forlorn,
  Or crazed with care, or crossed in hopeless love.

"One morn I missed him from the customed hill,
  Along the heath and near his favorite tree;
Another came; nor yet beside the rill,
  Nor up the lawn, nor at the wood was he;

"The next with dirges due in sad array
  Slow through the churchway path we saw him borne.
Approach and read (for thou canst read) the lay,
  Graved on the stone beneath yon aged thorn."

The Epitaph[37]

Here rests his head upon the lap of Earth
  A youth to Fortune and to Fame unknown.
Fair Science frowned not on his humble birth,
  And melancholy marked him for her own.

Large was his bounty, and his soul sincere,
  Heaven did a recompense as largely send:
He gave to Misery all he had, a tear,
  He gained from Heaven ('twas all he wished) a friend.

No farther seek his merits to disclose,
  Or draw his frailties from their dread abode,
(There they alike in trembling hope repose),
  The bosom of his Father and his God.

☞ Notes

1. As the title indicates, the poem is an elegy. Typically, an elegy expresses feelings of loss and sorrow while also praising the deceased and commenting on the meaning of the deceased's time on earth. Gray's poem reflects on the lives of humble and unheralded people buried in the cemetery of a church. The poem has the traditional four-line stanza, with a rhyme scheme of *abab*.
2. **curfew:** a ringing bell in the evening that reminded people in English towns of Gray's time to put out fires and go to bed.
3. **knell:** a sad, mournful sound.
4. **lowing:** mooing.
5. **lea:** meadow, field of grass.
6. **sight:** eyesight, vision; the view.
7. **droning:** marked by buzzing or humming.
8. **folds:** small valleys; level land between rolling hills; creatures in the distance.
9. **bower:** an enclosure formed by the ivy.
10. **moldering:** crumbling, decaying.
11. **rude:** untaught; robust, sturdy.
12. **incense-breathing Morn:** fragrant smells of the morning.
13. **twittering:** That is, chirping, making a short, shrill sound.
14. **clarion:** trumpet sound; wakeup call; loud sound.
15. **glebe:** soil, land.
16. **Ambition:** In this personification, Ambition becomes a proud person that would poke fun at humble people whose deeds receive little notice.
17. **Grandeur:** In this personification, Grandeur becomes a proud person that would poke fun at humble people whose deeds receive little notice.
18. **heraldry:** noble birth.
19. **The paths of glory lead but to the grave:** This line repeats the anti-glory motif as expressed by Shakespeare (Glory is like a circle) and later expressed by Shelley in "Ozymandias."
20. **trophies:** an ornamental or symbolic group of figures depicting the achievements of the dead man.
21. **fretted:** decorated with interesting lines in relief.
22. **storied urn:** a funeral urn with an epitaph inscribed on it.
23. **animated bust:** lifelike statue showing only the head, neck and part of the trunk.
24. **provoke:** call forth.
25. **Some heart once pregnant with celestial fire:** One of these persons might have had what it takes to perform great tasks.
26. **village-Hampden:** Allusion to John Hampden (1594-1643), who refused to pay an

unfair tax imposed by the king and later died in battle in the English Civil Wars (1642-1651).

27. **The applause ... eyes:** If these buried people had had a chance, they could have made politicians in a senate listen to them, comforted people threatened by pain and ruin, provided great bounty for their nation, and earned a place in history books.
28. **Their lot ... mankind:** Because they were deprived of power, the buried people were also deprived of the temptation to commit wrongs, such as murdering their way to a throne and deny mercy to worthy people.
29. **The struggling ... flame:** The buried people didn't have to lie or perform deeds that brought shame upon them. Nor did they hire writers to pen great stories about them.
30. **Yet even these bones ... sigh:** These humble people do have tombstones decorated with the words of an amateur writer and the pictures of an amateur sculptor.
31. **unlettered Muse:** Muse is an allusion to nine goddesses in Greek mythology. They inspired people to write, sing and dance. Muse is used here metaphorically to refer to a writer inspired to record his thoughts about the people buried in the cemetery. However, the adjective unlettered indicates that he is an uneducated writer, perhaps a humble member of the community like those buried in the cemetery.
32. **thee:** Gray himself.
33. **Some kindred spirit shall inquire thy fate:** Gray is wondering what people would say about him if he died.
34. **Haply ... lawn:** Here Gray begins to speculate about how people would assess him after he dies.
35. **listless length:** his body.
36. **pore upon:** gaze upon; look upon.
37. **The Epitaph:** Here Gray writes his own epitaph (inscription on a tomb).

☞ Study questions

1. What do we learn about the speaker from the details that he notices?
2. What is the tone of the poem?
3. Who or what is the speaker of the poem lamenting?
4. What is the speaker's relationship to those he writes about?
5. What truths common to all humankind do you think Gray is expressing?
6. How does the poem develop its theme?
7. In what ways are Gray's statements about human nature still valid in today's world?

☞ **Essay topics**

1. Discuss the connection between the setting and the speaker's state of mind. Cite examples from the poem to illustrate your discussion.
2. What effect does the Epitaph at the end have on the poem in terms of theme? Why does Gray include an epitaph at the end of the poem?

5.9 Robert Burns

5.9.1 Life and career

Burns (1759-1796) was born into a poor peasant's family in Alloway, Scotland. Like most farm children the opportunity for formal education was limited because children had to help on the farm, especially at harvest time. However, he was encouraged in his self-education by his father, and his mother acquainted him with Scottish folk songs, legends, and proverbs. By the time that he had reached manhood he had a good knowledge of English and a fairly wide acquaintance with the masterpieces of English literature from the time of Shakespeare to his own day. Family financial worries forced Burns to work as a farm laborer. When he was 16, Burns had already become his father's chief helper on the farm. He went in 1781 to Irvine to learn flax dressing; but when the shop burned down, he returned home penniless. He had, meanwhile, composed his first poems. His father died in 1784, leaving him as head of the family.

Burns published his first work, *Poems Chiefly in the Scottish Dialect* in 1786. The book was an instant success and he was invited to visit Edinburgh where he was welcomed as the "Heaven-taught Plowman" by the leading literary figures. But he knew that his prominence would not last long, for his poetic novelty might soon wear off. So after spending a brilliant winter in Edinburgh, he set off on a tour through his native land. In 1788 he returned to farming and became a devoted father. In 1787, Burns met James Johnson and was involved in Johnson's project of collecting Scottish folk songs for an anthology entitled *The Scots Musical Museum*. He contributed to the successive volumes some 200 songs, both original compositions and adaptations of traditional Scottish ballads and folk songs. Burns also put his own poems to music he composed, or to traditional Scottish airs. In 1788, Burns received a commission as an exciseman (tax inspector). He gave up farming in 1791, and traveled widely. Then his physical conditions began to decline, for long-time hard work and undernourishment in his youth permanently injured his health, leading to the rheumatic heart disease from which he eventually died.

The importance of Burns' poetry should firstly be evaluated in the Scottish cultural context. He was much indebted to the highly developed Scottish literary tradition established by Robert Henryson, William Dunbar, and Gavin Douglas in the golden age of Scottish poetry during the 15th and 16th centuries. As a peasant poet, his personal experience of the harsh country life and his close contact with the simple country folk greatly enriched his understanding of the people, while those joys and sorrows, hopes and dreams that he shared with them deepened his sympathy for the poor. Most of his poems are dealing with Scottish life, religion and manners, suggesting a world often harsh, sordid, but attractive.

The songs are Burns' best works. The range of their subjects and emotions is quite wide—love, comradeship, married affection, reflective sentiment, and vigorous patriotism. He also put into them the traditional elements of folk songs in Scotland—simplicity, pathos and humor. Thus, he has not only transmuted them into great poetry, but also immortalized in them the Scottish countryside and humble farm life. Burns is also a keen and discerning satirist who has reserved his sharpest barbs for sham, hypocrisy, and cruelty. His satirical verse, once little appreciated, has in recent decades been recognized widely as his finest work.

5.9.2 "A Red, Red Rose"[1]

O, My Luve's[2] like a red, red rose,
　That's newly sprung in June;
O, My Luve's like the melodie,[3]
　That's sweetly played in tune.[4]

As fair art thou, my bonie lass,[5]
　So deep in luve am I;
And I will luve thee still, my dear,
　Till a' the seas gang dry.[6]

Till a' the seas gang dry, my dear,
　And the rocks melt wi' the sun:
O I will luve thee still, my dear,
　While the sands o' life shall run.[7]

And fare thee weel,[8] my only luve,
　And fare thee weel a while!
And I will come again, my luve,
　Though it were ten thousand mile.

☞ **Notes**

1. This poem is in the metrical form of the ballad stanza. The rhyme falls on the second

and fourth lines of each stanza. The first and third lines each have four feet while the second and fourth each have three feet.

2. **Luve:** love, here referring to the young man's sweetheart.
3. **melodie:** melody.
4. **in tune:** in harmony.
5. **bonie lass:** pretty girl.
6. **Till a' the seas gang dry:** Till all the seas go dry.
7. **While the sands o' life shall run:** as long as I live. "Sands" refers to the sand in the sand-glass, which was used for measuring the passage of time.
8. **fare thee weel:** farewell to you.

☞ Study questions

1. How dose the speaker express his love?
2. What images does the speaker use to show his strong love for his beloved?
3. What other themes does this poem carry beside the love theme?
4. Why is this poem so touching to the reader?

5. 9. 3 "For A' That and A' That"

Is there, for honest poverty,
That hangs his head, an a' that?
The coward slave, we pass him by,
We dare be poor for a' that!
For a' that, and a' that,
Our toils obscure, and a' that,
The rank is but the guinea's stamp, [1]
The man's the gowd[2] for a' that.

What though on hamely fare we dine,
Wear hodden-gray, [3] and a' that;
Gie fools their silks, and knaves their wine,
A man's a man for a' that:
For a' that, and a' that,
Their tinsel show, an a' that;
The honest man, though e'er sae poor,
Is king o' men for a' that.

Ye see yon birkie[4] ca'd a lord,
Wha struts, and stares, and a' that;

Though hundreds worship at his word,
  He's but a coof[5] for a' that:
    For a' that, and a' that,
      His riband, star, and a' that,
    The man of independent mind,
      He looks an laughs at a' that.

A prince can mak a belted knight,
  A marquis, duke, and a' that;
But an honest man's aboon[6] his might,
  Guid faith he mauna fa'[7] that!
    For a' that, and a' that,
      Their dignities, and a' that,
    The pith o' sense, and pride o' worth,
      Are higher rank than a' that.

Then let us pray that come it may,
  As come it will for a' that,
That sense and worth, o'er a' the earth,
  May bear the gree,[8] and a' that.
    For a' that, and a' that,
      It's coming yet, for a' that,
    That man to man the world o'er
      Shall brothers be for a' that.

☞ Notes

1. **guinea's stamp:** picture stamped superficially on a coin to show its value.
2. **gowd:** gold.
3. **hodden-gray:** the coarse gray cloth of the poor.
4. **birkie:** young man.
5. **coof:** fool.
6. **aboon:** above.
7. **mauna fa':** must not get.
8. **bear the gree:** get the reward.

☞ Study questions

1. Who does Burns say is the king in stanza 2?
2. How does the independent man respond to the lord who struts, according to stanza 3?

3. Name three qualities that place the honest man above the marquis and duke, according to stanza 4?
4. In the last stanza for what does Burns pray? What does he say is yet to come?
5. Which characteristics does Burns suggest belong only to the rich? Which only to the poor?
6. What ideas does Burns express in this poem?

5.10 William Blake

5.10.1 Life and career

Blake(1757-1827) was born into a lower middle class family in London. Showing a precocious talent for painting as a child, Blake was sent to a drawing school. Then he was apprenticed to an engraver. After his 7-year term was over, he studied briefly at the Royal Academy of Arts. In 1779, he began to earn his living as an engraver, receiving commissions from publishers both for book illustrations and for engravings from pictures. At the age of 24, Blake married Catherine Boucher. The marriage proved to be a lifelong happiness though there were difficulties for a time. Through all his life, Blake had been both a poet and an engraver. He also printed a few books of his own. He lived a life of seclusion and poverty. More often than not he was misunderstood by other people, who would regard him as gifted but mad. Blake's last years found him chiefly concerned with painting and engraving. Gradually he gathered around him a small group of devoted young admirers. However, Blake's genius in poetry remained unknown in his lifetime; he was recognized only posthumously.

Blake began writing poetry when he was still a boy. His first work, *Poetical Sketches* was published in 1783. Joy, laughter, love and harmony are the prevailing notes. The *Songs of Innocence* (1809) is a lovely volume of poems, presenting a happy and innocent world, though not without its evils and sufferings. His *Songs of Experience* (1794) paints a different world, a world of misery, poverty, disease, war and repression with a melancholy tone. A number of poems from the *Songs of Innocence* also find a counterpart in the *Songs of Experience*. For instance, the "Infant Joy" is matched with the "Infant Sorrow;" and the pure "Lamb" is paired with the flaming "Tyger." The two books hold the similar subject-matter, but the tone, emphasis and conclusion differ.

Childhood is central to Blake's concern in the *Songs of Innocence* and *Songs of Experience*, and this concern gives the two books a strong social and historical reference. The laboring poor in London have furnished him with a sharp awareness of the economic exploitation of children, particularly the practice of selling young children into apprenticeships. The two "Chimney Sweeper" poems are good examples to reveal the relation between an economic circumstance, i. e. the exploitation of child labor, and an ideological circumstance, i. e. the role played by religion in making people compliant to exploitation. The poem from the *Songs of Innocence* indicates the conditions that make religion a consolation, a prospect of "illusory happiness;" the poem from the *Songs of Experience* reveals the true nature of religion which helps bring misery to the poor children.

Blake's *Marriage of Heaven and Hell* (1790) marks his entry into maturity. The poem, which was composed during the climax of the French Revolution, plays the double role both as a satire and a revolutionary prophecy. In this poem, Blake explores the relationship of the contraries. Attraction and repulsion, reason and energy, love and hate, are necessary to human existence. Life is a continual conflict of good and evil, of innocence and experience, of body and soul. "Without contraries," Blake states, "there is no progression." The "marriage," to Blake, means the reconciliation of the contraries, not the subordination of the one to the other.

As Blake grew older, he became more and more caught up in his mystical faith and his visions of a heavenly world. He shifted his poetic voice from the lyric to the prophetic mode. Centering on the Biblical stories of the Fall, the Redemption, and the reestablishment of Eden, he wrote a series of long prophetic books, including *The Book of Urizen* (1794), *The Song of Los* (1795), *Milton* (1802), *The Four Zoas* (1803) and *Jerusalem* (1804). Linked together by an intricate mythology and symbolism of Blake's own creation, these books propound a revolutionary new social, intellectual, and ethical order.

Blake was a total non-conformist and anti-establishment thinker, who asserted his conviction that the established church and state hinder rather than nurture human freedom and the sense of divine love. Like Thomas Paine, Blake remained unswervingly committed to the principles of equality, liberty and justice. He heartily supported the American Revolution in 1775 and the French Revolution in 1789. Blake writes his poems in plain and direct language. His poems often carry the lyric beauty with immense compression of meaning. He distrusts the abstractness and tends to embody his views with visual images. Symbolism in wide range is also a distinctive feature of his poetry.

Blake was largely misunderstood and ignored for being eccentric in his lifetime. However, writers like W. B. Yeats, James Joyce, and D. H. Lawrence found inspiration in his writings, and his poem *Milton* was put to music and became a kind of Christian anthem of the English in the twentieth century.

5. 10. 2 "The Lamb"[1]

Little Lamb,[2] who made thee?
Dost thou know who made thee?
Gave thee life & bid thee feed,

By the stream & o'er the mead;
Gave thee clothing of delight,
Softest clothing wooly bright;
Gave thee such a tender voice,
Making all the vales[3] rejoice!
  Little Lamb, who made thee?
  Dost thou know who made thee?

  Little Lamb I'll tell thee,
  Little Lamb I'll tell thee!
He is called by thy name,
For he calls himself a Lamb:
He is meek & he is mild,
He became a little child:
I a child & thou a lamb,
We are called by his name.
  Little Lamb God bless thee.
  Little Lamb God bless thee.

☞ Notes

1. The poem bears similarities with Charles Wesley's hymn beginning "Gentle Jesus, meek and mild," from *Hymns for Children*, published in 1763. It is written in rhyming couplets with alternating iambic and anapestic feet.
2. **Lamb:** When capitalized, the word carries a religious meaning, symbolizing Jesus Christ. In Christianity, Jesus is compared both to a lamb going to the sacrifice and to a shepherd who protects his flock of lambs and sheep, that is, common Christians.
3. **vales:** valleys.

☞ Study questions

1. How does the use of personification contribute to innocence of the lamb?
2. What kinds of qualities are associated with innocence in this poem?
3. How do "innocence" and "experience" relate to the religious concepts of "good" and "evil"?
4. What do you think the lamb represents? Cite evidence from the poem to support your answer.
5. Describe the overall tone of the poem. Which details contribute to this tone?

5.10.3 "The Tyger"

Tyger! Tyger! burning bright
In the forests of the night,
What immortal hand or eye
Could frame thy fearful symmetry?[1]

In what distant deeps or skies
Burnt the fire of thine eyes?
On what wings dare he aspire?[2]
What the hand, dare seize the fire?

And what shoulder, & what art,
Could twist the sinews[3] of thy heart?
And when thy heart began to beat,
What dread hand? & what dread feet?

What the hammer? what the chain?
In what furnace was thy brain?
What the anvil?[4] what dread grasp
Dare its deadly terrors clasp?

When the stars threw down their spears,
And watered heaven with their tears,[5]
Did he smile his work to see?
Did he who made the Lamb[6] make thee?

Tyger! Tyger! burning bright
In the forests of the night,
What immortal hand or eye
Dare frame thy fearful symmetry?

☞ **Notes**

1. **symmetry:** referring to the well-proportioned body of the tiger.
2. **aspire:** have ambition for something.
3. **sinews:** muscles.
4. **anvil:** iron block on which a smith shapes heated metal by hammering it.
5. **When … tears:** When the smith is hammering the heated metal, the fire sparkles like

shooting stars which are often called angels' tears by children.

6. **Lamb:** symbol of peace and purity. Blake wrote a lyric "Lamb" in *Songs of Innocence*. Here, he refers to the creator who can both create the peace and the violence.

☞ Study questions

1. What central metaphor does the speaker use to describe the tiger's maker?
2. What might the tiger represent? Explain your answer.
3. Why does Blake mention a lamb in this poem?
4. How do you think the speaker would answer the question, "Did he who made the Lamb make thee?"
5. What do the language and rhythms of the poem suggest about the significance of the tiger and the nature of its creator?
6. What does Blake's tone seem to be?
7. What is the symbolic meaning of the tiger? What does Blake want to express?

5. 10. 4 "London"

I wander through each chartered[1] street,
Near where the chartered Thames does flow,
And mark in every face I meet
Marks of weakness, marks of woe.

In every cry of every Man,
In every infant's cry of fear,
In every voice, in every ban, [2]
The mind-forged manacles[3] I hear.

How the chimney sweeper's cry
Every blackening[4] Church appalls;
And the hapless[5] Soldier's sigh
Runs in blood down palace walls.

But most through midnight streets I hear
How the youthful Harlot's[6] curse
Blasts[7] the new born Infant's tear,
And blights with plagues the Marriage hearse. [8]

☞ Notes

1. **chartered:** the rights of people were restricted by charters and corporations.
2. **ban:** curse.
3. **mind:** forged manacles: restraints forged for the mind.
4. **blackening:** the wall of the church was blackened by the smoke.
5. **hapless:** unlucky.
6. **Harlot:** prostitute.
7. **blast:** destroy.
8. **And blights with plagues the Marriage hearse:** spoil the marriage hearse with decease. "hearse," the vehicle for carrying a coffin in a funeral.

☞ Study questions

1. What is the speaker seeing and hearing in London?
2. What sort of world does Blake describe in this poem?
3. What does Blake's tone seem to be?
4. What metaphors and images does Blake use in order to realize his theme of this poem?

☞ Essay topics

1. In what ways is Blake a social critic? Cite examples from his poems to illustrate your ideas.
2. In what ways are Blake's poems symbolic? Cite examples from his poems to illustrate your ideas.
3. For what purposes does Blake bring together opposing images or ideas in various poems?

Chapter 6

The Romantic Period (1798-1832)

6.1 Introduction

Romanticism is a broad artistic and literary movement that affected the whole of Europe and America. It marked a partial reaction against the 18th-century rationalism and physical materialism in literature, philosophy, art, religion, and politics. Just as it is difficult to lend a date to its beginning, it is vain to ascribe the precise time of its ending. However, English Romanticism, as a historical phase of literature, is generally said to have begun in 1798 with the publication of Wordsworth and Coleridge's *Lyrical Ballads* and to have ended in 1832 with Sir Walter Scott's death and the passage of the first Reform Bill in the Parliament.

The Romantic era can be considered as indicative of an age of crisis, which was provoked by two important revolutions: the French Revolution of 1789-1794 and the English Industrial Revolution, which happened more slowly, but with more astonishing consequences. In 1789 there broke out the epoch-making French Revolution, which aroused great sympathy and enthusiasm among the English liberals and radicals. Patriotic clubs and societies multiplied in England, all claiming liberty, equality and fraternity. The revolution also stimulated two influential books: one is Thomas Paine's *Rights of Man* (1791-1792), which justifies the revolution; the other is William Godwin's *Inquiry Concerning Political Justice* (1793), which was more important for its influence over Wordsworth, Shelley, and other poets.

With the British Industrial Revolution coming into its full swing, England itself had experienced profound economic and social changes. The primarily agricultural society had been replaced by a modern industrialized one. The capitalist class came to dominate not only the means of production, but also trade and world market. Though England had increased its wealth by several times, it was only the rich who owned this wealth; the majority of the people were still poor, or even poorer. This cruel economic exploitation caused large-scale workers' disturbances in England; the desperation of the workers expressed itself in the popular outbreaks of machine-breaking known as the Luddite riots. However, the industrial capitalists made use of the workers' struggle to fight for their own supremacy in political power against the landed aristocrats. In 1832, the Reform Bill was enacted, which brought the industrial capitalists into power. But the sharp conflicts between capital and labor did not come to an end.

The Romantics, who were deeply immersed in the most violent phase of the transition from a decadent feudal to a capitalist economy, saw both the corruption and injustice of the feudal societies and the fundamental inhumanity of the economic, social and political forces of capitalism. They felt that the society denied people their essential human needs. Thus, under the influence of the leading romantic thinkers like Kant, Goethe, Rousseau and others, they demonstrated a strong rejection of the dominant modes of thinking of the 18th-century writers and philosophers.

It is Rousseau who established the cult of the individual and championed the freedom of the human spirit; his famous announcement was "I felt before I thought". Under his influence, the Romantics tend to place the individual at the center of art, making literature most valuable as an expression of his or her unique feelings and particular attitudes. Their chief emphasis was upon freedom of individual's self-expression: sincerity, spontaneity, and originality became the new standards in literature, replacing the decorous imitation of classical models favored by eighteenth-century Neoclassicism.

Imagination is defined by the Romantics as a dynamic, active power that creates all art. According to Coleridge, it is in solitude, in communion with the natural universe, that man can exercise this vital power of imagination. To contrast distinctly with the traditional arguments for the supremacy of reason, the Romantics elevate imagination to a position as the supreme faculty of the mind, which, accompanied by spontaneity, intuition and inspiration, "shapes" artistic works.

Nature is apprehended by the Romantics not only as an exemplar and source of vivid physical beauty but as a manifestation of spirit in the universe as well. Nature becomes the stage on which the human drama is played, the context in which man comes to understand his place in the universe, and the transforming agent that harmonizes the individual soul with what the Transcendentalists called the Over-Soul. Thus, the Romantics tend to show a deepened appreciation of nature, connecting it with a love for the remote, the strange, the mystery, the supernatural, and everything that creates wonder.

Romantics also tend to be nationalistic, defending the great poets and dramatists of their own national heritage against the advocates of classical rules who tended to glorify Rome and rational Italian and French neoclassical art as superior to the native traditions.

The Romantic period is a great age of poetry. Among the most prominent poets are William Blake, William Wordsworth, Samuel Taylor Coleridge, George Gordon Byron,

Percy Bysshe Shelley and John Keats, who started a movement that was later regarded as poetic revolution. Poetry has been traditionally regarded as an art governed by rules; but to the Romantics, poetry should be free from all rules. They tend to turn to the humble people and the common everyday life for subjects. Employing the commonplace, the natural, and the simple as their poetic materials, Romantic writers are trying to seek for the absolute, the ideal through the transcendence of the actual. They have also made bold experiments in poetic language, versification and design, and constructed a variety of forms on original principles of organization and style; examples of such can be found in Blake's visionary prophetic poems, in Coleridge's mystic ballad, *The Ancient Mariner*, in Wordsworth's spiritual autobiography, *The Prelude*, and in Shelley's symbolic drama, *Prometheus Unbound*.

The Romantic period is also an age of prose. With education greatly developed for the middle-class people, there was a rapid growth in the reading public and an increasing demand for reading materials. Thus, newspapers, magazines and periodicals run by private enterprises started to flourish in this period. *Edinburgh Review* (founded in 1802), *The Quarterly Review* (founded in 1809), *Blackwood's Magazine* (founded in 1817), *London Magazine* (founded in 1820), were among the most famous. They made literary comments on writers with high standards, which paved the way for the development of a new and valuable type of critical writings. Coleridge, Hazlitt, Lamb, and De Quincey were the leading figures in this new development. Guided by rich knowledge of literature and a profound human sympathy, they read sympathetically the work of a new author, with the sole idea of finding what he had contributed, or tried to contribute, to the magnificent total of the English literature. They also wrote familiar essays.

The two major novelists of the Romantic period are Jane Austen(1775-1817) and Walter Scott (1771-1832). Austen is of the eighteenth century in her moral outlook and in her prose style, though she is fully aware of the new strains of Romanticism. Her view of life is a totally realistic one. She has no sentimentality, no time for emotional excess. She honors the Augustan virtues of moderation, dignity, disciplined emotion and common sense. Not surprisingly she had in her day a small, select circle of admirers. But in modern times, she has become a popular classic and has been admired for her wit, her common-sense, her insight into characters and social relationships.

Walter Scott is the most popular novelist of his day. *Waverley* (1814), *Old Mortality* (1816), *The Heart of Midlothian* (1818), *Rob Roy* (1818), and *Ivanhoe* (1820) are among the most popular ones of his novels. In his depiction of Scotland, England, and the Continent from medieval times to the 18th century, he has shown a keen sense of political and traditional forces and of their influence on the individual. He is the first major historical novelist, exerting a powerful literary influence both in Britain and on the

Continent throughout the 19th century.

Gothic novel, type of romantic fiction that predominated in the late eighteenth century, is one phase of the Romantic Movement. Its principal elements are violence, horror, and the supernatural, which strongly appeal to the reader's emotion. With its descriptions of the dark, irrational side of human nature, the Gothic form exerts a great influence over the writers of the Romantic period. Works like *The Mysteries of Udolpho* (1794) by Ann Radcliffe and *Frankenstein* (1818) by Mary Shelley are typical Gothic romance. Even poets like Blake, Coleridge, Shelley and Keats tend to use those fantastic, grotesque and mysterious elements of Gothic fiction in their poetic works.

Besides poetry and prose, there are quite a number of writers who have tried their hand at poetic dramas in this period. This is partly because the lectures and criticism on Elizabethan drama given by Coleridge and Hazlitt have renewed interest in Shakespeare and led to the rediscovery of his contemporaries. Shelley's *Prometheus Unbound* and *The Cenci* (1819), Byron's *Manfred* (1817), and Coleridge's *Remorse* (1813) are generally regarded as the best verse plays during this period. However, compared with the brilliant achievement in poetry and prose, drama in the Romantic period is less successful. There might be different reasons to explain this, but the chief one might be that none of these poets really understand the theater or have performing experiences. Their plays are seldom if ever amongst the best of the stage plays and they survive for readers, not for audience.

6.2 William Wordsworth

6.2.1 Life and career

Wordsworth (1770-1850) was born into a middle class family at Cumberland, in the Lake region. He received his earlier education at Hawkshead Grammar School near Windermere. During his school vacations, he frequently visited places noted for their scenic beauty, thus developing a keen love of nature in his early life. From 1787 to 1791, Wordsworth studied at St. John's College, Cambridge. A walking tour of the Swiss Alps made in the Cambridge long vacation of 1790 further heightened his response to the grandeur of nature. Another important influence on his life was the French Revolution, with which his heart was stirred and his imagination fired. It seemed to him a new dawn of freedom was breaking on the world. He crossed the Channel and lived through the storm and stress of the Revolution for over a year. There he also had a love affair with a French girl, Annette Vallon, before his return to England.

The chaos of the Reign of Terror in France, the guilt over his inability to marry Annette and the unhappiness at not finding suitable employment finally drove Wordsworth into a period of deep depression. However, his life changed dramatically when he inherited a large sum of money from a close friend in 1795. At this time he also became a friend of Samuel Taylor Coleridge. The two poets collaborated on a book of poems entitled *Lyrical Ballads* (1798), which was distinguished for its radical innovations in poetic practice. The small volume contained what were to become some of the most memorable poems in English.

Wordsworth's Preface, written for the second edition of *Lyrical Ballads* in 1800, explains the principles underlying his and Coleridge's new approach to poetry. Rejecting the contemporary emphasis on form and an intellectual approach that drained poetic writing of strong emotion, Wordsworth asserts that "all good poetry is the spontaneous overflow of powerful feelings," and that "it takes its origin from emotion recollected in tranquility". In poetic practice, Wordsworth and Coleridge have made it their task to write in the simple language of common people, telling concrete stories of their lives.

In 1802 Wordsworth married Mary Hutchinson, a childhood friend. In 1807 *Poems in Two Volumes* was published. The work contains some of his finest poems, notably the superb "Ode: Intimations of Immortality," the autobiographical narrative "Resolution and Independence," and many of his well-known sonnets. His greatest work, *The Prelude*, was completed in 1805, though it was not published until after his death. Its purpose was to recapture and interpret the whole range of experiences that had contributed to the shaping of his mind. In 1842, he was given a government pension, and the following year he became poet laureate.

Wordsworth is the leading figure of the English romantic poetry, the focal poetic voice of the period. He has done much to establish Romanticism as the era's dominant literary movement, by emphasizing on feeling, simplicity, and the pleasure of beauty over rhetoric, ornament, and formality. His verse celebrates the moral influence exerted by nature. The most important contribution he has made is that he has not only started the modern poetry, the poetry of the growing inner self, but also changed the course of English poetry by using ordinary speech of the language and by advocating a return to nature.

6.2.2 "The World Is Too Much with Us"[1]

The World is too much with us; late and soon[2],
Getting and spending, we lay waste our powers;
Little we see in Nature that is ours;
We have given our hearts away, a sordid boon![3]
This Sea that bares her bosom to the moon,
The winds that will be howling at all hours,
And are up-gathered now like sleeping flowers,
For this, for everything, we are out of tune;

It moves us not. —Great God! I'd rather be
A Pagan suckled in a creed outworn[4];
So might I, standing on this pleasant lea, [5]
Have glimpses that would make me less forlorn;
Have sight of Proteus[6] rising from the sea;
Or hear old Triton[7] blow his wreathèd horn.

☞ **Notes**

1. This is a Petrarchan sonnet with a rhyme scheme of *abba*, *abba*, *cd*, *cd*, *cd*.
2. **late and soon:** Our fixation on materialism has been a problem in the past and will continue to be a problem in the future.
3. **sordid boon:** shameful gain; tarnished blessing. This phrase is an oxymoron, a form of paradox that juxtaposes contradictory words.
4. **suckled … outworn:** Brought up in an outdated religion.
5. **lea:** meadow.
6. **Proteus:** in Greek mythology, a sea god who could change shape at will and who possessed complete knowledge of the past, present, and future. The description of Proteus echoes Milton's *Paradise Lost* Ⅲ. 603-604.
7. **Triton:** in Greek mythology, in classical mythology, a figure who was half man and half fish and blew upon a conch-shell horn. The description of Triton echoes Spenser's Colin Clout's "Come Home Again," lines 244-245. Spenser and Milton are the two English poets to whom Wordsworth specifically allied himself.

☞ **Study questions**

1. Does our obsession with "getting and spending" make you sad?
2. Why does the speaker think that being a pagan would make him less sad?
3. Why do you think the speaker is upset that people aren't moved by nature?
4. How do you feel about technological advances?
5. In the context of the poem, what do Proteus and Triton represent?
6. What is the main theme of this poem?

6.2.3 "Composed upon Westminster Bridge, September 3, 1802"[1]

Earth has not anything to show more fair:
Dull would he be of soul who could pass by
A sight so touching in its majesty;
This City now doth, like a garment, wear
The beauty of the morning; silent, bare,

Ships, towers, domes, theaters, and temples lie
Open unto the fields, and to the sky;
All bright and glittering in the smokeless air.
Never did sun more beautifully steep[2]
In his first splendor, valley, rock, or hill;
Ne'er saw I, never felt, a calm so deep!
The river glideth at his own sweet will: [3]
Dear God! the very houses seem asleep;
And all that mighty heart is lying still! [4]

☞ Notes

1. The date of this experience was not Sept. 3, but July 31, 1802; its occasion was a trip to France. The sonnet describes a vivid picture of a beautiful morning in London. It follows strictly the Italian form, with a clear division between the octave and the sestet; the rhyme scheme is *abbaabba*, *cdcdcd*.
2. **steep:** saturate.
3. **The river glideth at his own sweet will:** Wordsworth adds beauty to nature by treating it as a living thing.
4. **all that mighty heart is lying still:** What "mighty heart" refers to is ambiguous; here it might refer to London.

☞ Study questions

1. At what time of day is London being described in this poem?
2. Which descriptive elements are presented objectively and which subjectively?
3. How is the simile "like a garment" developed?
4. What is the effect of personification used in the poem?
5. How might the speaker's appreciation of the city change if it were crowded with people?

6. 2. 4 "London, 1802"[1]

Milton! thou shouldst be living at this hour:
England hath need of thee: she is a fen
Of stagnant waters: [2] altar, [3] sword, and pen,
Fireside, [4] the heroic wealth of hall and bower,
Have forfeited their ancient English dower[5]
Of inward happiness. We are selfish men;
Oh! raise us up, return to us again;
And give us manners, virtue, freedom, power.

Thy soul was like a Star, and dwelt apart;
Thou hadst a voice whose sound was like the sea:
Pure as the naked heavens, majestic, free,
So didst thou travel on life's common way,
In cheerful godliness; and yet the heart
The lowliest duties on herself did lay.

☞ Notes

1. This is a sonnet with a rhyme scheme of *abba abba cddece*.
2. **a fen / Of stagnant waters:** This grotesque image of sickly standing water shows us that there is something rotten in the state of England (**fen:** swamp, bog).
3. **altar:** Here it represents the English church.
4. **fireside:** It stands in for the security of home.
5. **dower:** a kind of gift rightfully owed to the English people.

☞ Study questions

1. What is conveyed about English society of the time by the image of England as "a fen/ Of stagnant waters"?
2. What do altar, sword, pen, and fireside stand for?
3. Based on the second part of the sonnet (lines 9-14), what do you think Wordsworth most admires about Milton?
4. Why would Wordsworth look to a poet for reform, rather than a politician or a religious figure?

6.2.5 "I Wandered Lonely as a Cloud"[1]

I wandered lonely as a cloud
That floats on high o'er vales and hills,
When all at once I saw a crowd,
A host, of[2] golden daffodils;
Beside the lake, beneath the trees,
Fluttering and dancing in the breeze.

Continuous[3] as the stars that shine
And twinkle on the milky way,
They stretched in never-ending line
Along the margin of a bay:
Ten thousand saw I at a glance,
Tossing their heads in sprightly[4] dance.

The waves beside them danced; but they
Outdid the sparkling waves in glee;
A poet could not but be gay,
In such a jocund company;
I gazed—and gazed—but little thought
What wealth the show to me had brought:

For oft, when on my couch I lie
In vacant or in pensive mood, [5]
They flash upon that inward eye
Which is the bliss of solitude; [6]
And then my heart with pleasure fills,
And dances with the daffodils.

☞ Notes

1. Wordsworth wrote this beautiful poem of nature after he came across a long belt of gold daffodils tossing and reeling and dancing along the waterside.
2. **a crowd, / A host, of:** a large number of.
3. **continuous:** extending without break.
4. **sprightly:** lively, full of energy.
5. **in vacant or in pensive mood:** in a mood in which the mind is devoid of any thought or in a deeply thoughtful mood.
6. **They flash upon that inward eye/Which is the bliss of solitude:** When alone, the poet recalls the beautiful scene, which gives him great happiness.

☞ Study questions

1. Why is it unusual to use a word like "host" in connection with daffodils? What is the word's biblical connotation?
2. How does the sensation of something "natural" lead the speaker to imaginative vision? How does Wordsworth's "poetry of nature" in this poem transform itself into the "poetry of self-consciousness"?
3. In what sense is this poem an epiphany for the speaker? How permanent is the feeling he describes — to what extent can it be sustained or revived? What role does memory play in this poem?
4. How much does the speaker's mood depend on nature, and how much does his perception of nature depend on his mood?
5. What is the effect of all the shining and twinkling that occurs in the poem?

6. What is an image or memory that you can always count on to lift you out of the blues?

6.3 Samuel Taylor Coleridge

6.3.1 Life and career

Coleridge (1772-1834) was born in Devonshire, son of a clergyman. When he was nine years old, his father died. Then a year later, he was sent to a charity boarding school in London. In 1791, he went up to Jesus College, Cambridge but left in 1794 without obtaining a degree. As a young man, Coleridge was quite a radical in politics and became a strong supporter of the French Revolution. Inspired by the radical thinkers with their idealism, he joined Robert Southey in a utopian plan of establishing an ideal democratic community in America, named "Pantisocracy." The plan resulted in nothing but his marriage to Sara Fricker, which turned out to be an unhappy one.

In 1795 Coleridge met Wordsworth for the first time. The meeting proved momentous and the two poets soon began their famous poetic collaboration, *Lyrical Ballads* (1798), which became a landmark in English poetry. Coleridge's principal contribution to the joint work was "The Ancient Mariner," which tells of a sailor who kills an albatross and for that crime against nature endures terrible punishments.

Coleridge developed rheumatism early in life and suffered acute pain. To cure the pain, physicians freely prescribed opium for him. He became dependent on the drug, which gradually destroyed his health, happiness and poetic creativity. In 1816, he moved to London with the surgeon James Gillman in order to preserve his health. Despite a life filled with illness and depression, he did a prodigious amount of work. In addition to the "Ancient Mariner," he wrote "Kubla Khan," "Christabel" and some conversational poems, the best of which is "Frost at Midnight." Between 1808 and 1819 he gave his famous series of lectures on literature and philosophy; his lectures on Shakespeare were partly responsible for a renewed interest in the playwright. His *Biographia Literaria* (1817), a prose work of autobiographical memoirs and literary criticism, is considered one of his important works.

Politically, the young Coleridge was an enthusiastic supporter of the French Revolution. But in his later years, he was a fiery foe of Jacobinism. He insisted that a government should be based upon the will of the propertied classes only, and should impose itself upon the rest of the community from above. Philosophically and critically, he opposed the rationalistic trends of the 18th-century thought. He advocated a more spiritual and religious interpretation of life, based on what he had learnt from Kant and Schelling. He believed that art is the only permanent revelation of the nature of reality. A poet should realize the vague intimations derived from his unconsciousness without sacrificing the vitality of the inspiration.

Coleridge is generally recognized today as a lyrical poet of the first rank. His poetic themes range from the supernatural to the domestic. His metaphysical anxiety, anticipating modern existentialism, has gained him reputation as an authentic visionary. He also gives close critical attention to poetry, maintaining that the true end of poetry is to give pleasure through the medium of beauty. In analyzing literary works, he emphasizes the philosophic aspect, reading more into the subject than the text and going deeper into the inner reality than only caring for the outer form. His treatises, lectures, and compelling conversational powers have made him one of the most influential literary critics of the nineteenth century.

6. 3. 2 "Kubla Khan"[1]

In Xanadu[2] did Kubla Khan
A stately pleasure dome decree: [3]
Where Alph, [4] the sacred river, ran
Through caverns measureless to man[5]
    Down to a sunless sea.
So twice five miles of fertile ground
With walls and towers were girdled round:
And there were gardens bright with sinuous rills, [6]
Where blossomed many an incense-bearing tree;
And here were forests ancient as the hills,
Enfolding sunny spots of greenery.

But oh! that deep romantic[7] chasm which slanted
Down the green hill athwart a cedarn[8] cover!
A savage place! as holy and enchanted
As e'er beneath a waning moon was haunted
By woman wailing for her demon lover!
And from this chasm, with ceaseless turmoil seething,
As if this earth in fast thick pants were breathing,
A mighty fountain momently[9] was forced:
Amid whose swift half-intermitted burst
Huge fragments vaulted like rebounding hail,
Or chaffy grain beneath the thresher's flail:
And 'mid these dancing rocks at once and ever
It flung up momently the sacred river.
Five miles meandering with a mazy motion
Through wood and dale the sacred river ran,

Then reached the caverns measureless to man,
And sank in tumult to a lifeless ocean:
And 'mid this tumult Kubla heard from far
Ancestral voices prophesying war!
　　The shadow of the dome of pleasure
　　Floated midway on the waves;
　　Where was heard the mingled measure
　　From the fountain and the caves.
It was a miracle of rare device, [10]
A sunny pleasure dome with caves of ice!

　　A damsel with a dulcimer[11]
　　In a vision once I saw:
　　It was an Abyssinian[12] maid,
　　And on her dulcimer she played,
　　Singing of Mount Abora. [13]
Could I revive within me
Her symphony and song,
To such a deep delight 'twould win me,
That with music loud and long,
I would build that dome in air,
That sunny dome! those caves of ice!
And all who heard should see them there,
And all should cry, Beware! Beware!
His flashing eyes, his floating hair!
Weave a circle round him thrice, [14]
And close your eyes with holy dread,
For he on honeydew hath fed,
And drunk the milk of Paradise.

☞ **Notes**

1. **Kubla Khan:** Mongol emperor, the founder of Yuan Dynasty.
2. **Xanadu:** Xamdu, the place in inner Mongolia where Kubla Khan ascended the throne.
3. **decree:** order to be built.
4. **Alph:** derived probably from the Greek river Alpheus, which flows into the Ionian Sea. Its waters were fabled to rise again in Sicily as the fountain of Arethusa; see Milton's "Lycidas", lines 85 and 132.
5. **measureless to man:** too deep to be measured by man.

6. **sinuous rills:** small streams with many curves.
7. **romantic:** having imaginative appeal.
8. **athwart:** across; cedarn: poetic form of cedar.
9. **momently:** from moment to moment.
10. **device:** design.
11. **dulcimer:** stringed musical instrument.
12. **Abyssinian:** a place situates in the east Africa, now Ethiopia.
13. **Mount Abora:** probably Mount Amara in Milton's *Paradise Lost* into which Abyssian kings once sent his children to avoid the outside disturbance.
14. **Weave a circle round him thrice:** a magic ritual, to protect the inspired poet from intrusion.

☞ Study questions

1. How about the images of the river and the fountain? Do they make a concrete picture in your mind, or do they give you a more general feeling?
2. What images in the second stanza then emphasize that the world outside the dome is "A savage place" (line 14)?
3. What vision is introduced at line 37? What aspect of the vision does the speaker long to recover? What does he want to build?
4. What or whom do you suppose the damsel of the vision represents to the speaker?
5. How does Coleridge make use of contrasting images to illustrate the theme?

6.4 George Gordon Byron

6.4.1 Life and career

Byron(1788-1824) was born into an ancient aristocratic family. When he was three years old, his father died. He was then taken by his mother to Aberdeen, where he was brought up in poverty. To his Scottish upbringing he owed his love of mountains. At the age of ten, Byron inherited the title of a baron and a large estate. He was educated first at Harrow and then Cambridge. He began writing poetry while studying at Cambridge. In 1807, he published his lyric poems entitled *Hours of Idleness*, which was sharply criticized by the influential *Edinburgh Review*. Byron responded with a biting satire entitled "English Bards and Scotch Reviewers."

After graduating from Cambridge in 1809, Byron traveled in Portugal, Spain, and the Near East for two years. His experiences of this journey inspired him to write the first two cantos of *Childe Harold's Pilgrimage* (1812), which presents a view of Europe colored by the violent sensibilities of its melancholic and passionate narrator, Childe Harold. The poem brought Byron instant success in England. As he said at the time that he awoke one morning and found himself famous. In the following two years, he had written a number of long verse-tales, generally known as the *Oriented Tales*. Byron married Anna Isabella Milbanke in 1815. From the start the marriage was doomed by the gulf between him and his unimaginative and humorless wife. But his breaking up with his wife caused such a scandal that he was forced to leave England in 1816.

Byron first went to Switzerland, where he made acquaintance with Shelley. In Geneva, he wrote the third canto of *Childe Harold* and the narrative poem *The Prisoner of Chillon* (1816). He next established residence in Italy, where he produced the verse drama *Manfred* (1817), the first two cantos of *Don Juan* (1818-1819), and the final canto of *Childe Harold* (1818). While in Italy, Byron was in close touch with the Italian patriots and assisted them in an uprising against the Austrian rule. At the news of the Greek revolt against the Turks, Byron not only gave the insurgent Greeks financial help but plunged himself into the struggle for the national independence of that country. Because of several months' hard work under bad weather, Byron fell ill and died. The whole Greek nation mourned over his death.

Don Juan is Byron's masterpiece, a great comic epic of the early 19th century. Byron puts into the poem his rich knowledge of the world and the wisdom gained from experience. Thus, *Don Juan* presents brilliant pictures of life in its various stages of love, joy, suffering, hatred and fear. Byron also invests in Juan the moral positives like courage, generosity and frankness, which, according to Byron, are virtues neglected by the modern society. In addition, though Don Juan is the central figure and all the threads of the story are woven around him, he and his adventures only provide the framework; the poet's true intention is to present a panoramic view of different types of society.

A chief contribution of Byron is his creation of the "Byronic hero," a proud, mysterious rebel figure of noble origin. With immense superiority in his passions and powers, he would carry on his shoulders the burden of righting all the wrongs in a corrupt society, and would rise single-handedly against any kind of tyrannical rules either in government, in religion, or in moral society with unconquerable wills and inexhaustible energies. The conflict is usually one of rebellious individuals against outworn social systems and conventions.

Byron's poetry, though much criticized by some critics on moral grounds, has been immensely popular both at home and abroad. This popularity is owed to his persistent attacks on the social hypocrisy and injustice, to the novelty of his oriental scenery, to the romantic character of the Byronic hero, and to the easy, fluent, and natural beauty of his verse. Across Europe, patriots, poets, painters, and musicians are all inspired by him and his poetry. Actually, Byron has enriched European literature with an abundance of ideas, images, artistic forms and innovations.

6. 4. 2 "She Walks in Beauty"[1]

1

She walks in beauty, like the night
  Of cloudless climes and starry skies;
And all that's best of dark and bright
  Meet in her aspect[2] and her eyes:
Thus mellowed to that tender light
  Which heaven to gaudy[3] day denies.

2

One shade the more, one ray the less,
  Had half impaired[4] the nameless grace
Which waves in every raven tress,
  Or softly lightens o'er her face;
Where thoughts serenely sweet express
  How pure, how dear their dwelling place.

3

And on that cheek, and o'er that brow,
  So soft, so calm, yet eloquent,
The smiles that win, the tints that glow,
  But tell of days in goodness spent,
A mind at peace with all below,
  A heart whose love is innocent!

☞ Notes

1. One of the lyrics in Hebrew Melodies, written to be set to adaptations of traditional Jewish tunes by the young musician Issac Nathan. Byron wrote the lines the morning after he had met his beautiful young cousin by marriage, Mrs. Robert John Wilmot, who wore a black mourning gown brightened with spangles.
2. **her aspect:** Her "aspect" can mean both her facial expression and her overall appearance.
3. **gaudy:** bright and blinding.
4. **half impaired:** partially damaged.

☞ Study questions

1. What is beauty? To what extent does beauty depend on personality?

2. Why does the poet compare the woman to "night" instead of to "day"?
3. How many different binaries, or sets of opposites, does Byron employ to describe this woman's beauty?
4. Why doesn't the woman speak in the poem? How would the poem change if we were given a chance to hear her say something?
5. How are the woman's mind and heart reflected in her appearance?
6. Do you think the speaker is more in awe of the woman's beauty, or her virtue? Why?

6.4.3 "When We Two Parted"[1]

When we two parted
  In silence and tears,
Half broken-hearted
  To sever[2] for years,
Pale grew thy cheek and cold,
  Colder thy kiss;
Truly that hour foretold
  Sorrow to this.[3]

The dew of the morning
  Sunk chill on my brow—
It felt like the warning
  Of what I feel now.
Thy vows are all broken,
  And light[4] is thy fame;
I hear thy name spoken,
  And share in its shame.

They name thee before me,
  A knell to mine ear;
A shudder comes o'er me—
  Why wert[5] thou so dear?
They know not I knew thee,
  Who knew thee too well—
Long, long shall I rue[6] thee,
  Too deeply to tell.

In secret we met—
  In silence I grieve,

That thy heart could forget,
  Thy spirit deceive.
If I should meet thee
  After long years,
How should I greet thee?—
  With silence and tears.

☞ **Notes**

1. The metrical movement of this poem is basically a combination of iambic and anapestic feet, with a rhyme scheme *ababcdcd*.
2. **sever:** separate.
3. **this:** this moment.
4. **light:** of small account.
5. **wert:** were.
6. **rue:** to be sorry for.

☞ **Study questions**

1. Who is the speaker? What does the poem reveal about the speaker's character?
2. By what particular event is the poem occasioned?
3. Is the speaker addressing a particular person? If so, who is that person, and why is the speaker interested in him or her?
4. What is your response to the poem on first reading?

6.5 Percy Bysshe Shelley

6.5.1 Life and career

Shelley (1792-1822) was born into a wealthy family at Sussex. He was a delicate child, both shy and sensitive, who often wandered through the woods near his home. As a student in Eton, he was known for his radical views on politics and religion, earning the nickname "Mad Shelley." At 18, he attended Oxford University, where he read radical authors like Thomas Paine and William Godwin. A year later, he was expelled from Oxford for publishing a pamphlet called *The Necessity of Atheism*. This event resulted in being disinherited by his headstrong father.

Shelley then went to London where he met Harriet Westbrook, a young girl of sixteen. He eloped with her to Edinburgh and married her in order to rescue her from what he regarded as her father's tyranny. After spending their honeymoon in Ireland, they returned to London. Then Shelley became a disciple of the radical social philosopher, William Godwin, whose theories had already influenced him as a student.

In the following year, Shelley drifted apart from his wife and fell in love with Godwin's daughter Mary Godwin, who is now remembered primarily as the author of *Frankenstein*. In 1814, Shelley briefly toured Europe with Mary. Harriet's drowning in 1816 freed him to legalize his union with Mary but caused a scandal in London. His enemies launched such strong attacks on him that he had to leave England for good in 1818.

In the following years, the Shelleys lived a wandering life in Italy, where they saw much of Lord Byron. In a short period of four years, he produced all his major works: *Julian and Maddalo* (1818), *The Revolt of Islam* (1818), *The Cenci* (1819), *Prometheus Unbound* (1819), *Adonais* (1821), *Hellas* (1822), scores of magnificent lyrics, and the major prose essay, *In Defence of Poetry* (1822). Shelley was drowned in 1822 in a storm near La Spezia, at the age of 30. His body was cremated on the seashore and the ashes were buried in Rome.

Shelley expressed his love for freedom and his hatred toward tyranny in several of his lyrics such as "Ode to Liberty," "Ode to Naples," "Sonnet: England in 1819" and so on. One of Shelley's greatest political lyrics is "Men of England." It is not only a war cry calling upon all working people to rise up against their political oppressors, but an address to them, pointing out the intolerable injustice of economic exploitation. The poem was later to become a rallying song of the British Communist Party.

Shelley dedicated all his life to the war against injustice and oppression. However, under the influence of Christian humanism, he took interest in social reforms. He came to see that the evil was actually in man's mind. Thus he warned that even after a revolution, i. e. after the restoration of human morality and creativity, the evil deep in man's heart might again be loosed. He predicated that only through gradual and suitable reforms of the existing institutions could benevolence be universally established and none of the evils would survive in this genuine society, where people could live together happily, freely and peacefully.

Shelley is one of the leading Romantic poets, an intense and original lyrical poet in the English language. Like Blake, he has a reputation as a difficult poet: erudite, imagistically complex, and full of classical and mythological allusions. His style abounds in personification and metaphor and other figures of speech which describe vividly what we see and feel, or to express what passionately moves us.

6.5.2 "Ozymandias"[1]

I met a traveller from an antique land
Who said: Two vast and trunkless legs of stone
Stand in the desert ... Near them, on the sand,
Half sunk, a shattered visage lies, whose frown,

And wrinkled lip, and sneer of cold command,
Tell that its sculptor well those passions read
Which yet survive, stamped on these lifeless things.
The hand that mocked them[2] and the heart that fed:[3]
And on the pedestal these words appear:
"My name is Ozymandias, king of kings:
Look on my works, ye Mighty, and despair!"
Nothing beside remains. Round the decay
Of that colossal wreck, boundless and bare,
The lone and level sands stretch far away.

☞ Notes

1. **Ozymandias:** the Greek name for Ramses Ⅱ, the pharaoh who ruled Egypt during the 13th century B. C. During his rule Ramses Ⅱ conducted an extensive building program and was responsible for the largest statue in Egypt, which bore the inscription: "I am Ozymandias, king of kings; if anyone wishes to know what I am and where I lie, let him surpass me in some of my exploits." Ramses Ⅱ was also known as the pharaoh who oppressed the Israelites. Shelley—always an ardent challenger of oppression—depicts the ironical outcome of the pharaoh's legacy in this sonnet.
2. **The hand that mocked them:** the sculptor's hand that "mocked" (imitated and ridiculed) the ruler's passions.
3. **the heart that fed:** the king's heart which has "fed" his passions.

☞ Study questions

1. What form of irony is at work in this poem?
2. What idea or experience is the poet articulating in this poem?
3. What effect does Shelley achieve by putting the poem in the words of "a traveler from an antique land"?
4. How does the poem view the permanence of art? Do artistic "works" necessarily "decay" like the statue of Ozymandias?
5. What kind of connection exists between a work of art and the culture that produced it? Can art tell us anything about the culture that produced it?

6. 5. 3 "Ode to the West Wind"

I

O wild West Wind, thou breath of Autumn's being
Thou, from whose unseen presence the leaves dead
Are driven, like ghosts from an enchanter fleeing,

Yellow, and black, and pale, and hectic[1] red,
Pestilence-stricken multitudes: [2] O thou,
Who chariotest to their dark wintry bed

The wingèd seeds, where they lie cold and low,
Each like a corpse within its grave, until
Thine azure sister[3] of the Spring shall blow

Her clarion[4] o'er the dreaming earth, and fill
(Driving sweet buds like flocks to feed in air)
With living hues and odours plain and hill:

Wild Spirit, which art moving everywhere;
Destroyer and Preserver; hear, O hear!

Ⅱ

Thou on whose stream, 'mid the steep sky's commotion, [5]
Loose clouds like earth's decaying leaves are shed,
Shook from the tangled boughs of Heaven and Ocean, [6]

Angels[7] of rain and lightning: there are spread
On the blue surface of thine aery surge,
Like the bright hair uplifted from the head

Of some fierce Mænad, [8] even from the dim verge
Of the horizon to the zenith's height,
The locks of the approaching storm. Thou Dirge

Of the dying year, to which this closing night
Will be the dome of a vast sepulcher,
Vaulted with all thy congregated might

Of vapours, from whose solid atmosphere
Black rain and fire and hail, will burst: O hear!

Ⅲ

Thou who didst waken from his summer dreams

The blue Mediterranean, where he lay,
Lulled by the coil of his crystalline streams, [9]

Beside a pumice[10] isle in Baiæ's bay, [11]
And saw in sleep old palaces and towers
Quivering within the wave's intenser day,

All overgrown with azure moss and flowers
So sweet, the sense faints picturing them! [12] Thou
For whose path the Atlantic's level powers

Cleave themselves into chasms, while far below
The sea-blooms and the oozy woods which wear
The sapless foliage of the ocean, know

Thy voice, and suddenly grow gray with fear,
And tremble and despoil themselves: [13] O hear!

IV

If I were a dead leaf thou mightest bear;
If I were a swift cloud to fly with thee;
A wave to pant beneath thy power, and share

The impulse of thy strength, only less free
Than thou, O Uncontrollable! If even
I were as in my boyhood, and could be

The comrade of thy wanderings over Heaven,
As then, when to outstrip thy skiey speed
Scarce seemed a vision; I would ne'er have striven

As thus with thee in prayer in my sore need.
Oh! lift me as a wave, a leaf, a cloud!
I fall upon the thorns of life! I bleed!

A heavy weight of hours has chained and bowed
One too like thee: tameless, and swift, and proud.

V

Make me thy lyre,[14] even as the forest is:
What if my leaves are falling like its own!
The tumult of thy mighty harmonies

Will take from both a deep, autumnal tone,
Sweet though in sadness. Be thou, Spirit fierce,
My spirit! Be thou me, impetuous one!

Drive my dead thoughts over the universe
Like withered leaves, to quicken a new birth!
And, by the incantation of this verse,

Scatter, as from an unextinguished hearth
Ashes and sparks, my words among mankind!
Be through my lips to unawakened Earth

The trumpet of a prophecy! O Wind,
If Winter comes, can Spring be far behind?

☞ Notes

1. **hectic:** relating to the reddening of the face caused by the kind of fever which occurs in tuberculosis.
2. **Pestilence-stricken multitudes:** The leaves are like human beings hit by epidemic disease.
3. **Thine azure sister:** refers to the west wind that will blow in the spring.
4. **clarion:** sound of a trumpet.
5. **'mid the steep sky's commotion:** in the midst of the great turbulence high up in the sky.
6. **tangled boughs of Heaven and Ocean:** a metaphorical representation of the manners in which small pieces of clouds ("leaves") are torn by the wind from the larger clouds ("boughs") that are formed by air and vapour drawn up by the sun from the ocean.
7. **Angels:** messengers.
8. **Mænad:** a female worshiper of Dionysus (Bacchus), the Greek god of wine and vegetation. As vegetation god, he was fabled to die in autumn and to be reborn in spring.
9. **the coil of his crystalline streams:** The currents that flow in the Mediterranean Sea, sometimes with a visible difference in color.
10. **Pumice Isle:** an isle near Naples, Italy, formed by deposits of lava from a volcano.

11. **Baiæ's bay:** a favorite resort of ancient Romans, near Naples.
12. **the sense faints picturing them:** seeing the images so beautiful one feel faint to describe them.
13. **And tremble and despoil themselves:** (Shelley's note) The vegetation at the bottom of the sea sympathizes with that of the land in the change of seasons.
14. **lyre:** refers to the Aeolian harp, a stringed instrument that produces musical sounds when the wind passes over it.

☞ Study questions

1. What does wind signify in this ode? How is it used symbolically?
2. Why, at the end of stanza 1, is the west wind referred to as "destroyer and preserver"?
3. Why must the speaker turn to the West Wind to help him?
4. What relationship does the speaker want to establish between the wind and himself?
5. How does the speaker in stanza 4 compare himself to the wind in terms of power and freedom?
6. What are the things that the West Wind can represent?

6.6 John Keats

6.6.1 Life and career

Keats(1795-1821) was born in London, son of a livery-stable keeper. When he was eight years old, his father died. Six years later, his mother died of tuberculosis. Keats was educated at a nearby school where his literary interests were encouraged by one of his teachers. After he left school at the age of 16, he was apprenticed to a surgeon for four years. During this time his interest in poetry grew. He read much of Spenser, Milton and Homer. The first verses he wrote were in imitation of the Elizabethan poetry. Keats also met some literary celebrities in London, among whom Leigh Hunt, a radical journalist, exerted a vital influence on him. In 1816 Keats became a licensed apothecary but did not practice much of his profession; instead he turned to devote himself to poetry writing.

Keats's first important poem "On First Looking into Chapman's Homer" was published in 1816 in Hunt's paper, the *Examiner*. In 1817, he published his first volume of poems, including the poem, "Sleep and Poetry," which is an expression of his own poetic aspirations. The year 1818 witnessed his long allegorical poem, *Endymion*, which marked a transitional phase in his poetry. However, the reviewers of *Blackwood's Magazine*, the *Quarterly Review* and the *British Critic* launched savage attacks on Keats, declaring *Endymion* to be sheer nonsense, and recommending that Keats give up poetry and go back to his apothecary.

At the close of 1817, Keats set out, with a friend, on a walking tour to the Lake Region and to Scotland. This was Keats's first sight of real mountains. He gloried in the grand scenery. After his return from the tour, Keats became ill with tuberculosis, from which he had never quite recovered. Other troubles crowded in upon Keats. First his dearly loved brother, Tom, died; then he was in trouble about money; the cruel criticisms of his poetry hurt him at the same time; and to this already overcharged heart something else was added: he fell in love. However, love brought to him no joyful rest, but rather passionate restlessness. For he could not marry the one he loved due to his poverty and poor health. It was this yearning and suffering that quickened his maturity and added a new dimension to his poetry.

In the following year, despite ill health and financial problems, he wrote an astonishing amount of poetry, including "The Eve of St. Agnes," "La Belle Dame sans Merci," "Ode on Melancholy," "Ode on a Grecian Urn," "Ode to a Nightingale," and "Ode to Psyche." At the heart of these poems lies Keats's concern with how the ideal can be joined with the real, the imagined with the actual, and man with woman. At the beginning of 1820 Keats started to show more pronounced signs of the deadly tuberculosis that had killed his mother and brother. In September of 1820 Keats sailed to Rome to seek a warm climate for the winter. He died there on February 23, 1821, and was buried in the Protestant cemetery.

Keats is one of the most important figures of the early nineteenth-century Romanticism. His poetry is distinctive for its sensual description, physical concreteness, colorful imagery, and closely-knit construction. Sight, sound, scent, taste and feeling are all taken in to give an entire understanding of an experience. The mythic world of the ancient Greece and the English poetry of the Renaissance provide Keats with the most important imaginative resources. The beauty of nature, the relation between imagination and creativity, the response of the passions to beauty and suffering, and the transience of human life always lie in the center of his poetic concerns. Thus, he is highly praised for his seriousness and thoughtfulness, for his dealing with difficult human conflicts and artistic issues, and for his impassioned mental pursuit of truth.

6.6.2 "On First Looking into Chapman's Homer"[1]

Much have I travell'd in the realms of gold,[2]
  And many goodly states and kingdoms seen;
  Round many western islands have I been
Which bards in fealty[3] to Apollo hold.
Oft of one wide expanse had I been told
  That deep-brow'd Homer ruled as his demesne;[4]

Yet did I never breathe its pure serene[5]
Till I heard Chapman speak out loud and bold:
Then felt I like some watcher of the skies
When a new planet swims into his ken;[6]
Or like stout Cortez[7] when with eagle eyes
He stared at the Pacific—and all his men
Look'd at each other with a wild surmise—
Silent, upon a peak in Darien.[8]

☞ Notes

1. Keats's former schoolteacher, Cowden Clarke, introduced him to Homer in the robust translation of the Elizabethan poet George Chapman. They read through the night, and Keats walked home at dawn. This sonnet reached Clarke by the ten o'clock mail that same morning. This poem is written in the Italian form, and its rhyme scheme is *abba abba, cdcdcd.*
2. **realms of gold:** the world of imagination.
3. **fealty:** loyalty owed by a feudal tenant to his lord.
4. **demesne:** realm, domain; feudal possession.
5. **pure serene:** clear, calm air.
6. **ken:** Range of sight or knowledge.
7. **Cortez:** Balboa, not Cortez, discovered the Pacific Ocean.
8. **Darien:** The Darien mountain range runs the length of the Isthmus of Darien, now called Panama.

☞ Study questions

1. What has the "one wide expanse," described in lines 5-7, that the speaker had not explored in his reading?
2. What, literally, are "the realms of gold" referred to in the first line of this poem?
3. What do the Pacific, the planet, and Homer's poetry have in common with respect to the effects on their beholders?
4. What is appropriate about Keats's choice of metaphors for this sonnet?
5. What simile and metaphor does the poet employ to express his immense respect and the awe-struck feeling?

6. 6. 3 "Ode to a Nightingale"

1

My heart aches, and a drowsy numbness pains
My sense, as though of hemlock[1] I had drunk,

Or emptied some dull opiate to the drains
  One minute past, and Lethe-wards[2] had sunk:
'Tis not through envy of thy happy lot,
  But being too happy in thine happiness, —
    That thou, light-winged Dryad[3] of the trees,
      In some melodious plot
  Of beechen green, and shadows numberless,
    Singest of summer in full-throated ease.

2

O, for a draught of vintage![4] that hath been
  Cool'd a long age in the deep-delved earth,
Tasting of Flora[5] and the country green,
  Dance, and Provençal[6] song, and sunburnt mirth!
O for a beaker full of the warm South,
  Full of the true, the blushful Hippocrene,[7]
    With beaded bubbles winking at the brim,
      And purple-stained mouth;
  That I might drink, and leave the world unseen,
    And with thee fade away into the forest dim:

3

Fade far away, dissolve, and quite forget
  What thou among the leaves hast never known,
The weariness, the fever, and the fret
  Here, where men sit and hear each other groan;
Where palsy shakes a few, sad, last gray hairs,
  Where youth grows pale, and spectre-thin, and dies;
    Where but to think is to be full of sorrow
      And leaden-eyed despairs,
  Where Beauty cannot keep her lustrous eyes,
    Or new Love pine at them beyond to-morrow.

4

Away! away! for I will fly to thee,
  Not charioted by Bacchus and his pards,[8]
But on the viewless[9] wings of Poesy,
  Though the dull brain perplexes and retards:

Already with thee! tender is the night,
And haply[10] the Queen-Moon is on her throne,
Cluster'd around by all her starry Fays; [11]
But here there is no light,
Save what from heaven is with the breezes blown
Through verdurous[12] glooms and winding mossy ways.

5

I cannot see what flowers are at my feet,
Nor what soft incense hangs upon the boughs,
But, in embalmed[13] darkness, guess each sweet
Wherewith the seasonable month endows
The grass, the thicket, and the fruit-tree wild;
White hawthorn, and the pastoral eglantine; [14]
Fast fading violets cover'd up in leaves;
And mid-May's eldest child,
The coming musk-rose, full of dewy wine,
The murmurous haunt of flies on summer eves.

6

Darkling[15] I listen; and, for many a time
I have been half in love with easeful Death,
Call'd him soft names in many a mused rhyme,
To take into the air my quiet breath;
Now more than ever seems it rich to die,
To cease upon the midnight with no pain,
While thou art pouring forth thy soul abroad
In such an ecstasy!
Still wouldst thou sing, and I have ears in vain—
To thy high requiem[16] become a sod.

7

Thou wast not born for death, immortal Bird!
No hungry generations tread thee down;
The voice I hear this passing night was heard
In ancient days by emperor and clown:
Perhaps the self-same song that found a path
Through the sad heart of Ruth, [17] when, sick for home,
She stood in tears amid the alien corn;

The same that oft-times hath
Charm'd magic casements, opening on the foam
Of perilous seas, in faery lands forlorn.

8

Forlorn! the very word is like a bell
To toll me back from thee to my sole self!
Adieu! the fancy cannot cheat so well
As she is fam'd[18] to do, deceiving elf.
Adieu! adieu! thy plaintive anthem[19] fades
Past the near meadows, over the still stream,
Up the hill-side; and now 'tis buried deep
In the next valley-glades:
Was it a vision, or a waking dream?
Fled is that music: —Do I wake or sleep?

☞ **Notes**

1. **hemlock:** a poison made from a herb or a poisonous drink made from that herb.
2. **Lethe-wards:** toward Lethe—in classical mythology, a river in Hades (the underworld). Souls about to be reincarnated drank from it to forget their past lives.
3. **Dryad:** in classical mythology, a nymph or deity of the woods. Dryads or nymphs were female personifications of natural features, like mountains and rivers; they were young, beautiful, long-lived and liked music and dance.
4. **for a draught of vintage:** longing for a drink of wine.
5. **Flora:** in classical mythology, goddess of flowers and fertility.
6. **Provençal:** of Provence, an area in the south of France associated with song, pleasure, and luxury.
7. **Hippocrene:** in classical mythology, a spring sacred to the Muses, located on Mt. Helicon. Drinking its waters inspired poets. (The nine muses were associated with different arts, such as epic poetry, sacred song, and dancing.)
8. **Bacchus and his pards:** in classical mythology, the god of wine, who was commonly portrayed in a chariot drawn by leopards ("pards").
9. **viewless:** invisible.
10. **haply:** perhaps, by chance.
11. **fays:** fairies.
12. **verdurous:** green.
13. **embalmed:** perfumed.
14. **eglantine:** sweetbrier or honeysuckle.

15. **darkling:** in the dark.
16. **requiem:** song or musical service for the repose of the dead.
17. **Ruth:** in the *Bible*, a young window who left her homeland and went with her mother-in-law to work in the fields of Judah. Boaz saw Ruth, the Moabite, working in the fields, fell in love with her and married her; David is one of her descendents (*Ruth* 2: 1-23). She is frequently alluded to by poets for her devotion to her mother-in-law or as a stranger in a strange land. In a sense she has achieved immortality.
18. **fam'd:** reported.
19. **anthem:** (1) a hymn of joy or praise, patriotism, or devotion; (2) a sacred choral song generally based on words from the Bible. Both meanings carry with them intense feelings and high seriousness.

☞ Study questions

1. What is the role of wine, drugs, and drunkenness in the speaker's imaginative journey?
2. What does the speaker find so satisfying about the experience of being in the forest at night?
3. What does the speaker find to upsetting about life and the "real world"?
4. Why is the speaker so desperate to escape?
5. What are the differences between the speaker's world and the natural world?
6. Why are so many plants and flowers featured in the poem, and what might they symbolize?
7. Does the poet view himself as a part of nature or as outside of nature?
8. Have you ever been unable to tell the difference between life and a dream?

6.6.4 "To Autumn"[1]

1

Season of mists and mellow fruitfulness,
  Close bosom-friend of the maturing sun;
Conspiring with him how to load and bless
  With fruit the vines that round the thatch-eaves run;
To bend with apples the moss'd cottage-trees,
  And fill all fruit with ripeness to the core;
    To swell the gourd, and plump the hazel shells
  With a sweet kernel; to set budding more,
And still more, later flowers for the bees,
Until they think warm days will never cease,
  For Summer has o'er-brimm'd their clammy cells.

2

Who hath not seen thee oft amid thy store?
  Sometimes whoever seeks abroad may find
Thee sitting careless on a granary floor,
  Thy hair soft-lifted by the winnowing[2] wind;
Or on a half-reap'd furrow sound asleep,
  Drows'd with the fume of poppies, while thy hook[3]
    Spares the next swath and all its twined flowers:
And sometimes like a gleaner thou dost keep
  Steady thy laden head across a brook;
  Or by a cider-press, with patient look,
    Thou watchest the last oozings hours by hours.

3

Where are the songs of spring? Ay, where are they?
  Think not of them, thou hast thy music too, —
While barred clouds bloom the soft-dying day,
  And touch the stubble-plains with rosy hue;
Then in a wailful choir the small gnats mourn
  Among the river sallows,[4] borne aloft
    Or sinking as the light wind lives or dies;
And full-grown lambs loud bleat from hilly bourn;[5]
  Hedge-crickets sing; and now with treble soft
  The red-breast whistles from a garden-croft;[6]
    And gathering swallows twitter in the skies.

☞ Notes

1. Two days after the poem was composed, Keats wrote to J. H. Reynolds: "I never liked stubble fields so much as now—Aye, better than the chilly green of the spring. Somehow a stubble plain looks warm—in the same way that some pictures look warm—this struck me so much in my Sunday's walk that I composed upon it."
2. **winnowing:** blowing; also, the fanning process by which the wheat chaff is separated from the grain.
3. **hook:** scythe.
4. **sallows:** willows.
5. **bourn:** region.
6. **croft:** a "croft" is an enclosed plot of farm land.

☞ **Study questions**

1. What are the seasonal details Keats chooses to include and how do they color the emotional tone of the poem?
2. How is autumn personified? What kind of person might autumn be?
3. What doe Keats suggest about autumn's beauty and about the cyclic pattern of nature?
4. What examples of tactile imagery—imagery that appeals to the sense of touch—do you find in this poem?
5. How do the three stanzas work together to show different aspects of autumn?

6.7 Jane Austen

6.7.1 Life and career

Austen (1775-1817) was born into a country clergyman's family in Hampshire. Her father was a fine scholar. Austen had almost no formal education, but she had a wide reading of books available in her father's library. She acquired a thorough knowledge of English eighteenth-century literature. As a young woman, she enjoyed dancing and attended balls in many of the great houses of the neighborhood. She also loved the country, enjoying long country walks. She lived a quiet, retired and uneventful life. She seldom left her home place except for some short visits to such places like Bath and Southampton. Her lifelong companion and confidant was her older and only sister, Cassandra, who, like her, never married for the whole life. She started to write novels for family amusement as a child. Her works were later published anonymously due to the prejudice against women writers then. She died in Winchester in 1817.

In her life-long career, Austen wrote altogether six complete novels, which can be divided into two distinct periods. The first period lasted from 1795 to 1798. During this time she wrote *Sense and Sensibility* (1811), *Pride and Prejudice* (1813), and *Northanger Abbey* (1818). *Sense and Sensibility* tells a story about two sisters and their love affairs; *Pride and Prejudice* deals with the five Bennet sisters and their search for suitable husbands; and *Northanger Abbey* satirizes those popular Gothic romances of the late 18th century. Her second period of writing lasted from 1811 to 1816, when her early works received public recognition and she deepened her mastery of subjects and form. All her last three novels deal with the romantic entanglements of their strongly characterized heroines. *Mansfield Park* (1814) presents the antithesis of worldliness and unworldliness; *Emma* (1815) gives the thought over self-deceptive vanity; and *Persuasion* (1818) contrasts the true love with the prudential calculations.

Generally speaking, Austen was a writer of the 18th-century, though her adult life was mainly spent in the nineteenth century. She holds the ideals of the landlord class in politics, religion and moral principles; and her works show clearly her firm belief in the predominance of reason over passion, the sense of responsibility, good manners and clear-sighted judgment over the Romantic tendencies of emotion and individuality. As a realistic writer, she considers it her duty to express in her works a discriminated and serious criticism of life, and to expose the follies and illusions of mankind. She shows contemptuous feelings towards snobbery, stupidity, worldliness and vulgarity through subtle satire and irony. In style, she is a neo-classicism advocator, upholding those traditional ideas of order, reason, proportion and gracefulness in novel writing.

As a novelist Austen writes within a very narrow sphere. The subject matter, the character range, the social setting, and plots are all restricted to the provincial life of the late 18th-century England. In her novels, there is little reflection on the events that stirred the whole Europe at the time, no thrilling adventures, no abstract ideas, no romantic reveries, and even no death scenes. Everything in her novel results in an observation of a quiet, uneventful and contented life of the English country. Here lie her very weak points as well as strong points. Such narrowness apparently comes from the writer's own limited experience and knowledge; yet, by writing within the small range of her experience and by never stepping beyond the limits of her knowledge, it allows her to have a close study of characters and a detailed description of recurring situations so that she can portray them with absolute accuracy and sureness. It is no exaggeration to say that within her limited sphere, Jane Austen is unequaled.

Austen's works, at once delightful and profound, are among the supreme achievements of English literature. With trenchant observation and in meticulous detail, she presents the quiet, day-to-day country life of the upper-middle-class English. Her characteristic theme is that maturity is achieved through the loss of illusions. Faults of character displayed by the people of her novels are corrected when, through tribulation, lessons are learned. Even the most minor characters are vividly particularized in Austen's lucid style. All these show a mind of the shrewdest intelligence adapting the available traditions and deepening the resources of art with consummate craftsmanship. Because of her sensitivity to universal patterns of human behavior, Jane Austen has brought the English novel, as an art of form, to its maturity, and she has been regarded by many critics as one of the greatest of all novelists.

6.7.2 An excerpt from *Pride and Prejudice*

Chapter 1

It is a truth universally acknowledged, that a single man in possession of a good fortune must be in want of a wife.

However little known the feelings or views of such a man may be on his first entering a neighborhood, this truth is so well fixed in the minds of the surrounding families, that he is considered as the rightful property of some one or other of their daughters.

"My dear Mr. Bennet," said his lady[1] to him one day, "have you heard that Netherfield Park[2] is let at last?"

Mr. Bennet replied that he had not.

"But it is," returned she; "for Mrs. Long[3] has just been here, and she told me all about it."

Mr. Bennet made no answer.

"Do not you want to know who has taken it?" cried his wife impatiently.

"*You* want to tell me, and I have no objection to hearing it."

This was invitation enough.[4]

"Why, my dear, you must know. Mrs. Long says that Netherfield is taken by a young man of large fortune from the north of England; that he came down on Monday in a chaise and four[5] to see the place, and was so much delighted with it that he agreed with Mr. Morris[6] immediately; that he is to take possession before Michaelmas,[7] and some of his servants are to be in the house by the end of next week."

"What is his name?"

"Bingley."

"Is he married or single?"

"Oh! single, my dear, to be sure! A single man of large fortune; four or five thousand a year.[8] What a fine thing for our girls!"

"How so? how can it affect them?"

"My dear Mr. Bennet," replied his wife, "how can you be so tiresome! You must know that I am thinking of his marrying one of them."

"Is that his design in settling here?"

"Design! nonsense, how can you talk so! But it is very likely that he *may* fall in love with one of them, and therefore you must visit him as soon as he comes."

"I see no occasion for that.[9] You and the girls may go, or you may send them by themselves, which perhaps will be still better; for, as you are as handsome as any of them, Mr. Bingley might like you the best of the party."

"My dear, you flatter me.[10] I certainly *have* had my share of beauty, but I do not pretend to be any thing extraordinary now. When a woman has five grown up daughters, she ought to give over thinking of her own beauty."

"In such cases, a woman has not often much beauty to think of."

"But, my dear, you must indeed go and see Mr. Bingley when he comes into the neighborhood."

"It is more than I engage for,[11] I assure you."

"But consider your daughters. Only think what an establishment it would be for one of them. Sir William and Lady Lucas[12] are determined to go, merely on that account, for in general, you know, they visit no new comers. Indeed you must go, for it will be impossible for us to visit him, if you do not."

"You are over-scrupulous, surely. I dare say Mr. Bingley will be very glad to see you; and I will send a few lines by you to assure him of my hearty consent to his marrying which ever he chooses of the girls; though I must throw in a good word for my little Lizzy.[13]"

"I desire you will do no such thing. Lizzy is not a bit better than the others; and I am sure she is not half so handsome as Jane, nor half so good humored as Lydia. But you are always giving *her* the preference."

"They have none of them much to recommend them," replied he; "they are all silly and ignorant like other girls; but Lizzy has something more of quickness than her sisters."

"Mr. Bennet, how can you abuse your own children in such a way? You take delight in vexing me. You have no compassion on my poor nerves."

"You mistake me, my dear. I have a high respect for your nerves. They are my old friends. I have heard you mention them with consideration these twenty years at least."

"Ah! you do not know what I suffer."

"But I hope you will get over it, and live to see many young men of four thousand a year come into the neighborhood."

"It will be no use to us if twenty such should come, since you will not visit them."

"Depend upon it,[14] my dear, that when there are twenty I will visit them all."

Mr. Bennet was so odd a mixture of quick parts,[15] sarcastic humor, reserve, and caprice, that the experience of three and twenty years had been insufficient to make his wife understand his character. *Her* mind was less difficult to develop. She was a woman of mean understanding, little information, and uncertain temper. When she was discontented, she fancied herself nervous. The business of her life was to get her daughters married; its solace was visiting and news.[16]

Chapter 2

Mr. Bennet was among the earliest of those who waited on[17] Mr. Bingley. He had always intended to visit him, though to the last always assuring his wife that he should not go; and till the evening after the visit was paid, she had no knowledge of it. It was then disclosed in the following manner. Observing his second daughter employed in trimming a hat, he suddenly addressed her with,

"I hope Mr. Bingley will like it, Lizzy."

"We are not in a way to know *what* Mr. Bingley likes," said her mother resentfully, "since we are not to visit."

"But you forget, mama," said Elizabeth, "that we shall meet him at the assemblies,[18] and that Mrs. Long has promised to introduce him."

"I do not believe Mrs. Long will do any such thing. She has two nieces of her own. She is a selfish, hypocritical woman, and I have no opinion of her."

"No more have I," said Mr. Bennet; "and I am glad to find that you do not depend on her serving you."

Mrs. Bennet deigned not to make any reply; but unable to contain herself, began scolding one of her daughters.

"Don't keep coughing so, Kitty,[19] for heaven's sake! Have a little compassion on my nerves. You tear them to pieces."

"Kitty has no discretion in her coughs," said her father; "she times them ill."[20]

"I do not cough for my own amusement," replied Kitty fretfully.

"When is your next ball to be, Lizzy?"

"To-morrow fortnight."[21]

"Aye, so it is," cried her mother, "and Mrs. Long does not come back till the day before; so it will be impossible for her to introduce him, for she will not know him herself."

"Then, my dear, you may have the advantage of your friend, and introduce Mr. Bingley to *her*."

"Impossible, Mr. Bennet, impossible, when I am not acquainted with him myself; how can you be so teasing?"

"I honor your circumspection. A fortnight's acquaintance is certainly very little. One cannot know what a man really is by the end of a fortnight. But if *we* do not venture,[22] somebody else will; and after all, Mrs. Long and her nieces must stand their chance; and therefore, as she will think it an act of kindness, if you decline the office, I will take it on myself."

The girls stared at their father. Mrs. Bennet said only, "Nonsense, nonsense!"

"What can be the meaning of that emphatic exclamation?" cried he. "Do you consider the forms of introduction, and the stress that is laid on them, as nonsense? I cannot quite agree with you *there*. What say you, Mary? for you are a young lady of deep reflection I know, and read great books, and make extracts."

Mary wished to say something very sensible, but knew not how.

"While Mary is adjusting her ideas," he continued, "let us return to Mr. Bingley."

"I am sick of Mr. Bingley," cried his wife.

"I am sorry to hear *that*; but why did not you tell me so before? If I had known as much this morning,[23] I certainly would not have called on him. It is very unlucky; but as I have actually paid the visit, we cannot escape the acquaintance now."

The astonishment of the ladies was just what he wished; that of Mrs. Bennet perhaps surpassing the rest; though when the first tumult of joy was over, she began to declare that it was what she had expected all the while.

"How good it was in you, my dear Mr. Bennet! But I knew I should persuade you at last. I was sure you loved our girls too well to neglect such an acquaintance. Well, how pleased I am! and it is such a good joke, too, that you should have gone this morning, and never said a word about it till now."

"Now, Kitty, you may cough as much as you choose," said Mr. Bennet; and, as he spoke, he left the room, fatigued with the raptures of his wife.

"What an excellent father you have, girls," said she, when the door was shut. "I do not know how you will ever make him amends for his kindness; or me either,[24] for that matter. At our time of life, it is not so pleasant I can tell you, to be making new acquaintance every day; but for your sakes, we would do any thing. Lydia, my love, though you *are* the youngest, I dare say Mr. Bingley will dance with you at the next ball."

"Oh!" said Lydia stoutly, "I am not afraid; for though I *am* the youngest, I'm the tallest."

The rest of the evening was spent in conjecturing how soon he would return Mr. Bennet's visit, and determining when they should ask him to dinner.

☞ Notes

1. **his lady:** Here refers to Mrs. Bennet.
2. **Netherfield Park:** the name of a land estate in the neighborhood of the Bennets.
3. **Mrs. Long:** a neighbor of the Bennets.
4. **This was invitation enough:** This was enough to encourage Mrs. Bennet to tell.
5. **a chaise and four:** a light carriage driven by four horses.
6. **Mr. Morris:** the landlord of Netherfield Park.
7. **Michaelmas:** a festival celebrated on September 29th in honor of Michael, one of the seven archangels in Christian legend.
8. **four or five thousand a year:** Here it means an income of four or five thousand pounds a year.
9. **see no occasion for that:** see no reason or need for that.
10. **you flatter me:** a polite reply to a compliment. Here Mrs. Bennet does not see the ironical meaning in the remark of her husband.
11. **It is more than I engage for:** It is more than I promise to do.
12. **Sir William and Lady Lucas:** a neighboring couple.
13. **Lizzy:** (shortened form for Elizabeth) the second daughter of the Bennets.
14. **depend upon it:** There can be no doubt about it; you may be sure of it.
15. **quick parts:** Here "parts" in the plural form is used in the archaic sense of "abilities"

and "intelligence."

16. **its solace was visiting and news:** The comfort of her life is to visit her neighbors and gossip with them about trivial things.
17. **waited on:** called on.
18. **the assemblies:** the balls; the dance parties.
19. **Kitty:** (shortened form for Catherine) the fourth daughter of the Bennets.
20. **She times them ill:** She coughs at the wrong time.
21. **To-morrow fortnight:** the day after two weeks, i. e., fifteen days hence.
22. **But if we do not venture:** But if we do not venture to introduce Mr. Bingley to her.
23. **If I had known as much this morning:** If I had known this morning that you were sick of Mr. Bingley.
24. **or me either:** or make me amends either.

☞ Study questions

1. What does the opening sentence of the novel mean? In what ways is the conversation between Mr. and Mrs. Bennet in chapter one a commentary on this sentence?
2. Why does Mrs. Bennet insist that her husband call on the new arrival immediately?
3. Why does Mr. Bennet pretend to have no interest in doing so?
4. How do Mrs. Bennet and his daughters react when Mr. Bennet reveals that he has made their new neighbor's acquaintance?
5. How would you describe the marriage between Mr. and Mrs. Bennet after reading chapters one and two?
6. What is Mr. Bennet like as a husband and father?
7. What is Mrs. Bennet like as a wife and mother?

☞ Essay topics

1. What examples of humor do you find in *Pride and Prejudice*? What does this humor suggest about the tone of the novel?
2. How does Jane Austen use irony? Find examples in her novels.
3. Discuss the importance of dialogue to character development in the novel.
4. What was the political and social status of women during Jane Austen's time?

Chapter 7

The Victorian Period (1832-1901)

7.1 Introduction

The Victorian period covers the major part of the nineteenth century. Chronologically it roughly corresponds to the reign of Queen Victoria who ruled over Britain from 1837 to 1901. This is an extremely diverse and contradictory age. On one hand, it is a time of broad imperial expansion, great political reform and tremendous scientific progress; on the other hand, it is a time of cruel exploitation, social injustice and desperate poverty. While the wealth of the middle class increased, the lower classes, thrown off their land and into the cities to form the urban working class, lived ever more wretchedly. Just as John Morley said it was an age of "paradise for the well-to-do, a purgatory for the able, and a hell for the poor."

In the early years of the Victorian England, industrial development and urbanization were key factors, along with increasing class consciousness and strife. Great advances in science and technology created enormous economic changes to the country. Large amount of profits was accumulated from expanding its foreign trade markets and exploiting its huge-sized colonies. Yet beneath the great prosperity and richness, there existed widespread poverty and wretchedness among the working class. In the towns where new factories and mines bloomed, population grew at a high rate. Workers and their families crowded in the dirty and insanitary slums. The working conditions were unimaginably brutal, especially in textile factories and coal mines where women and child labor were widely employed. The worsening living and working conditions, the mass unemployment and the new Poor Law of 1834 with its workhouse system finally gave rise to the Chartist Movement (1836-1848). The workers got themselves organized in big cities and brought forth the People's Charter, in which they demanded basic rights and better conditions. Although the movement declined to an end in 1848, it did bring some improvement to the welfare of the working class.

The mid-Victorian period was a time of economic prosperity and relative stability, though it was not free of serious social problems. The nation was well ahead of others, reaching its highest point of development as a world power. It had completed its shift from a way of life based on the ownership of land to a modern urban economy based on trade and manufacturing. Political and social progress, though less astonishing, was substantial. The improvement came, partly by the passage of laws, partly by the growth of trades-unions. Among other changes were the democratization resulting from extension of the franchise; challenges to religious faith, in part based on the advances of scientific knowledge, particularly of evolution; people's high literacy due to popular education; and gradual improvement in the role of women. People as a whole were trying to live up to a national spirit of earnestness, respectability and modesty. Common sense and moral propriety, which were ignored by the Romanticists, again became the predominant preoccupation in literary works.

The later part of the Victorian Period witnessed the decline of British Empire and the decay of Victorian values. Abroad, its leadership in industry and military force was already facing challenge from Germany and America. At home, the Irish question remained unsolved. The conditions of the working class were still bad, though the three reform bills gradually gave the vote to most males over the age of twenty-one. Meanwhile, the inequality between men and women prevailed, stimulating a fight for women's equality and freedom, and for their educational and employment opportunities. Radical economic theory, developed by Karl Marx and his associates, gained great force in the second half of the century. In addition, the unsettling of religious belief by new advances in science, particularly the theory of evolution and the historical study of the Bible, drew people into considerations of problems of faith and truth.

The Victorian Period is often regarded as a high point in British literature, which can be compared to the importance of the Elizabethan Age. Victorian literature, in general, truthfully represents the reality and spirit of the age. The high-spirited vitality, the down-to-earth earnestness, the good-natured humor and unbounded imagination are all unprecedented. Essayists and novelists choose to directly address the pressing social problems of the day. These problems range from atrocious labor conditions and rampant poverty to the issue of women's place in the world. While the age is characterized as practical and materialistic, it is also an idealistic age where the great ideals like truth, justice, love, and brotherhood are emphasized by poets, essayists and novelists.

The Victorian Era was the great age of the English novel—realistic, thickly plotted and crowded with characters. It was the ideal form to describe contemporary life and to entertain the middle class. Among the famous novelists of the time were Charles Dickens, William Makepeace Thackeray, the Brontë sisters, George Eliot, Mrs. Gaskell, Thomas Hardy and Anthony Trollope. Although writing from different points of view and with different techniques, they shared one thing in common, that is, they were all concerned about the fate of the common people. They were angry with the inhuman social institutions, the decaying social morality represented by the money-worship and utilitarianism, and the wide spread misery, poverty and injustice. Their truthful picture of life and bitter criticism of the society had done much in awakening public consciousness to the social problems and in the actual improvement of the society. Besides, some of the novels were published in installments in weekly magazines. This style of presentation often affected the content of the work, as popular novels were stretched out to prolong their success and unpopular ones were altered in attempts to win the public affection.

Apart from the novels, the Victorian Period was also a great age for non-fictional prose. Famous historians, critics, scientists and essayists abounded. Thomas Carlyle, Thomas Babington Macaulay, John Henry Newman, John Stuart Mill, John Ruskin and Matthew Arnold are among the best. They brought English prose to a very high point in both prose art and literary criticism.

The poets of this period were mainly characterized by their experiment with new styles and new ways of expression. Its most representative poet was Alfred Tennyson, an independent thinker and a conservative liberal, who combined harmoniously classic perfection with romantic feeling in his poetic writings. His great poem, *In Memoriam* (1850), is an acute pathological study of individual grief and the central Victorian statement of the problems posed by the decline of Christian faith. Robert Browning, Tennyson's chief poetic contemporary, stands in striking artistic contrast to Tennyson—a contrast which perhaps serves to enhance the reputation of both. Browning is the most vigorous and dramatic of all great poets. He transferred the thematic interest from mere narration of the story to revelation of characters' inner world by adopting the novelistic presentation of characters. Other poets like Elizabeth Browning, Matthew Arnold, Edward Fitzgerald, Dante Gabriel Rossetti, Gerald Manley Hopkin and Algernon Charles Swinburne all made their respective attempts at poetic innovations.

An art movement indicative of this period was the Pre-Raphaelites, which included William Holman Hunt, Dante Gabriel Rossetti, Christina Rossetti, and John Everett Millais. Towards the end of the century, an Aestheticism and Decadence movement grew out of the French movement of the same name. The authors of this movement encouraged experimentation and advocated the theory of "art for art's sake," totally opposing "natural" norms of morality.

The nineteenth century was the age of a truly popular theatre. English playwrights produced a large number of plays, most of which were sentimental, melodramatic, and dominated by a few very powerful actors, stars who often overwhelmed the works written for them. The sparkling, witty comedies of Oscar Wilde and those of W. S. Gilbert and Sir Arthur Sullivan were perhaps the brightest dramatic achievements of this period.

7.2 Charles Dickens

7.2.1 Life and career

Dickens (1812-1870) was born in Portsmouth, son of a petty navy office clerk. Being exceptionally bright and articulate, little Charles was often asked to perform before people. Dickens received only slight and irregular education, but he read much fiction, especially eighteenth-century authors. His happy childhood ended in 1822 when the family moved to London. At the age of 12, young Dickens had to work at a shoe-blacking factory because his father was imprisoned for bad debt. Pasting labels on blacking bottles twelve hours by day and sleeping under the counter at night, the child always felt hungry, lonely, and ignored. The hardship and suffering inflicted so early upon such a sensitive boy as Charles Dickens had left an everlasting bitter remembrance in his later life. From 1824 to 1827, Dickens studied at Wellington House Academy. After that he entered a lawyer's office. Two years later he became a Parliamentary reporter for newspapers. The journalistic experience helped him get acquainted with some inside knowledge of the British legal and political system, gave him a chance to meet people of all kinds, and laid a good foundation for his coming literary career.

From 1833 Dickens began to write occasional sketches of London life, which were later collected and published under the title *Sketches by Boz* (1836). While working for the *Morning Chronicle*, Dickens fell in love with Catherine Hogarth, daughter of the *Chronicle*'s music critic. In 1836 Dickens and Catherine got married. In the same year, his first novel, *Posthumous Papers of Pickwick Club* (1836-1837), appeared in monthly installments, which at once lifted him into a position of fame and fortune. After this success, Dickens embarked on a full-time career as a novelist, producing works of increasing complexity at an incredible rate. Besides the 17 novels he wrote, he was editor of several newspapers and magazines. He also spent much time travelling and campaigning against many of the social evils with his pamphlets and other writings. In his last years, he did a lot of recitation of his own work before the public. In 1870, this man of great heart and vitality died of overwork, leaving his last novel unfinished.

Dickens's novels are characterized by attacks on social evils, injustice, and hypocrisy. In his early works, he criticizes one or more specific social evils in each: for example, the dehumanizing workhouse system and the dark, criminal underworld life in *Oliver Twist* (1837-1838); the Yorkshire School where children are not taught anything but actually enslaved at the master's house in *Nicholas Nickleby* (1838-1839); legal fraud in *The Pickwick Paper;* the debtor's prison in *David Copperfield* (1849-1850); the money-worship that dominates people's life, corrupts the young and brings tragedy to Mr. Dombey's family in *Martin Chuzzlewit* (1843-1845) and *Dombey and Son* (1846-

1848), etc. Here, the techniques are relatively straightforward and the objects of his attack are easily recognizable, and once the abuse has been overcome, the way is open to a happy conclusion. This youthful brightness and optimism is also manifest in the constant jokes and laughter.

His later novels show that Dickens tries to move towards a highly conscious artist of the modern type. The physical settings are sometimes a mixture of the contemporary and the recollected past; the stories, though usually double or multiple plotted, are much better structured; and the institutions are important not only in themselves but as metaphors for a repressive social psychology. All of the works, with the exception of *A Tale of Two Cities* (1859), present a criticism of the more complicated and yet most fundamental social institutions and morals of the Victorian England, such as the legal system and practices that aim at devouring every penny of the clients in *Bleak House* (1852-1853), the governmental branches which run an indefinitely procedure of management of affairs and keep the innocent in prison for life in *Little Dorrit* (1855-1857), the Utilitarian principle that rules over the English education system and destroys young hearts and minds in *Hard Times* (1854), and the overwhelming social environment which brings moral degeneration and destruction to people as in *Great Expectations* (1860-1861) and *Our Mutual Friend* (1864-1865). The attack now becomes more urgent and passionate, and this urgency creates novels of great compactness and concentration.

Dickens is one of the greatest writers of the Victorian Age. Coming from the lower middle class and fairly acquainted with the life of the poor people, he is one of their most moving spokesmen. His novels exhibit an astonishing ability to create living characters; his graphic exposures of social evils and his powers of caricature and humor have won him a vast readership. As a humanitarian, he pours all his love and sympathy for those poor, innocent and injured people and fights, with laughter and tears, on their behalf against the soulless cruelty of impersonal institutions of an inhuman society. He is admired and loved not only for the practical reform his works help to bring about but also for that heart that is ready to love and sympathize. It is no wonder that he is welcomed by both the high and the low, both the intellectual and illiterate.

Dickens is also a master story-teller. With his first sentence, he engages the reader's attention and holds it to the end. The settings of his stories have an extraordinary vividness, a result of years' intimacy and rich imagination. His humor and wit seem inexhaustible. Character-portrayal is the most distinguishing feature of his works. Among a vast range of various characters, marked out by some peculiar physical trait, speech or manner, are both types and individuals. In language, he is often compared with Shakespeare for his deftness with the vernacular and large vocabulary with which he brings out many a wonderful verbal picture of man and scene.

7.2.2 An excerpt from Chapter 8 of *Great Expectations*

For such reasons I was very glad when ten o'clock came and we started for Miss Havisham's;[1] though I was not at all at my ease regarding the manner in which I should acquit myself[2] under that lady's roof. Within a quarter of an hour we came to Miss Havisham's house, which was of old brick, and dismal, and had a great many iron bars to it. Some of the windows had been walled up; of those that remained, all the lower were rustily barred. There was a court-yard in front, and that was barred; so, we had to wait, after ringing the bell, until some one should come to open it. While we waited at the gate, I peeped in (even then Mr. Pumblechook[3] said, "And fourteen?[4]" but I pretended not to hear him), and saw that at the side of the house there was a large brewery. No brewing was going on in it, and none seemed to have gone on for a long long time.

A window was raised, and a clear voice demanded "What name?" To which my conductor replied, "Pumblechook." The voice returned, "Quite right," and the window was shut again, and a young lady came across the court-yard, with keys in her hand.

"This," said Mr. Pumblechook, "is Pip."

"This is Pip, is it?" returned the young lady, who was very pretty and seemed very proud; "come in, Pip."

Mr. Pumblechook was coming in also, when she stopped him with the gate.

"Oh!" she said. "Did you wish to see Miss Havisham?"

"If Miss Havisham wished to see me," returned Mr. Pumblechook, discomfited.[5]

"Ah!" said the girl; "but you see she don't."

She said it so finally, and in such an undiscussible way, that Mr. Pumblechook, though in a condition of ruffled dignity, could not protest. But he eyed me severely—as if *I* had done anything to him! —and departed with the words reproachfully delivered: "Boy! Let your behavior here be a credit unto them[6] which brought you up by hand!" I was not free from apprehension that he would come back to propound through the gate, "And sixteen?[7]" But he didn't.

My young conductress locked the gate, and we went across the court-yard. It was paved and clean, but grass was growing in every crevice. The brewery buildings had a little lane of communication with it, and the wooden gates of that lane stood open, and all the brewery beyond, stood open, away to the high enclosing wall; and all was empty and disused. The cold wind seemed to blow colder there, than outside the gate; and it made a shrill noise in howling in and out at the open sides of the brewery, like the noise of wind in the rigging of a ship at sea.

She saw me looking at it, and she said, "You could drink without hurt all the strong beer that's brewed there now, boy."

"I should think I could, miss," said I, in a shy way.

"Better not try to brew beer there now, or it would turn out sour, boy; don't you think so?"

"It looks like it, miss."

"Not that anybody means to try," she added, "for that's all done with, and the place will stand as idle as it is, till it falls. As to strong beer, there's enough of it in the cellars already, to drown the Manor House.[8]"

"Is that the name of this house, miss?"

"One of its names, boy."

"It has more than one, then, miss?"

"One more. Its other name was Satis; which is Greek, or Latin, or Hebrew, or all three—or all one to me—for enough."

"Enough House," said I; "that's a curious name, miss."

"Yes," she replied; "but it meant more than it said. It meant, when it was given, that whoever had this house, could want nothing else. They must have been easily satisfied in those days, I should think. But don't loiter,[9] boy."

Though she called me "boy" so often, and with a carelessness that was far from complimentary, she was of about my own age. She seemed much older than I,[10] of course, being a girl, and beautiful and self-possessed; and she was as scornful of me as if she had been one-and-twenty, and a queen.

We went into the house by a side door—the great front entrance had two chains across it outside—and the first thing I noticed was, that the passages were all dark, and that she had left a candle burning there. She took it up, and we went through more passages and up a staircase, and still it was all dark, and only the candle lighted us.

At last we came to the door of a room, and she said, "Go in."

I answered, more in shyness than politeness, "After you, miss."

To this, she returned: "Don't be ridiculous, boy; I am not going in." And scornfully walked away, and—what was worse—took the candle with her.

This was very uncomfortable, and I was half afraid. However, the only thing to be done being to knock at the door, I knocked, and was told from within to enter. I entered, therefore, and found myself in a pretty large room, well lighted with wax candles. No glimpse of daylight was to be seen in it. It was a dressing-room, as I supposed from the furniture, though much of it was of forms and uses then quite unknown to me. But prominent in it was a draped table with a gilded looking-glass, and that I made out at first sight to be a fine lady's dressing-table.

Whether I should have made out this object so soon, if there had been no fine lady sitting at it, I cannot say. In an arm-chair, with an elbow resting on the table and her head leaning on that hand, sat the strangest lady I have ever seen, or shall ever see.

She was dressed in rich materials—satins, and lace, and silks—all of white. Her shoes were white. And she had a long white veil dependent from her hair, and she had bridal flowers in her hair, but her hair was white. Some bright jewels sparkled on her neck and on her hands, and some other jewels lay sparkling on the table. Dresses, less splendid than the dress she wore, and half-packed trunks, were scattered about. She had not quite finished dressing, for she had but one shoe on—the other was on the table near her hand—her veil was but half arranged, her watch and chain were not put on, and some lace for her bosom lay with those trinkets, and with her handkerchief, and gloves, and some flowers, and a prayer-book, all confusedly heaped about the looking-glass.

It was not in the first few moments that I saw all these things, though I saw more of them in the first moments than might be supposed. But, I saw that everything within my view which ought to be white, had been white long ago, and had lost its luster,[11] and was faded and yellow. I saw that the bride within the bridal dress had withered like the dress, and like the flowers, and had no brightness left but the brightness of her sunken eyes. I saw that the dress had been put upon the rounded figure of a young woman, and that the figure upon which it now hung loose, had shrunk to skin and bone. Once, I had been taken to see some ghastly waxwork at the Fair, representing I know not what impossible personage lying in state. Once, I had been taken to one of our old marsh churches to see a skeleton in the ashes of a rich dress, that had been dug out of a vault under the church pavement. Now, waxwork and skeleton seemed to have dark eyes that moved and looked at me. I should have cried out, if I could.

"Who is it?" said the lady at the table.

"Pip, ma'am."

"Pip?"

"Mr. Pumblechook's boy, ma'am. Come—to play."

"Come nearer; let me look at you. Come close."

It was when I stood before her, avoiding her eyes, that I took note of the surrounding objects in detail, and saw that her watch had stopped at twenty minutes to nine, and that a clock in the room had stopped at twenty minutes to nine.

"Look at me," said Miss Havisham. "You are not afraid of a woman who has never seen the sun[12] since you were born?"

I regret to state that I was not afraid of telling the enormous lie comprehended in the answer "No."

"Do you know what I touch here?" she said, laying her hands, one upon the other, on her left side.

"Yes, ma'am." (It made me think of the young man.)

"What do I touch?"

"Your heart."

"Broken!"

She uttered the word with an eager look, and with strong emphasis, and with a weird smile that had a kind of boast in it. Afterwards, she kept her hands there for a little while, and slowly took them away as if they were heavy.

"I am tired," said Miss Havisham. "I want diversion, and I have done with[13] men and women. Play."

I think it will be conceded by my most disputatious reader, that she could hardly have directed an unfortunate boy to do anything in the wide world more difficult to be done under the circumstances.

"I sometimes have sick fancies," she went on, "and I have a sick fancy that I want to see some play. There there!" with an impatient movement of the fingers of her right hand; "play, play, play!"

For a moment, with the fear of my sister's working me before my eyes, I had a desperate idea of starting round the room in the assumed character of Mr. Pumblechook's chaise-cart. But, I felt myself so unequal to the performance that I gave it up, and stood looking at Miss Havisham in what I suppose she took for a dogged manner, inasmuch as she said, when we had taken a good look at each other:

"Are you sullen and obstinate?"

"No, ma'am, I am very sorry for you, and very sorry I can't play just now. If you complain of me I shall get into trouble with my sister, so I would do it if I could; but it's so new here, and so strange, and so fine—and melancholy—" I stopped, fearing I might say too much, or had already said it, and we took another look at each other.

Before she spoke again, she turned her eyes from me, and looked at the dress she wore, and at the dressing-table, and finally at herself in the looking-glass.

"So new to him," she muttered, "so old to me; so strange to him, so familiar to me; so melancholy to both of us! Call Estella."

As she was still looking at the reflection of herself, I thought she was still talking to herself, and kept quiet.

"Call Estella," she repeated, flashing a look at me. "You can do that. Call Estella. At the door."

To stand in the dark in a mysterious passage of an unknown house, bawling[14] Estella to a scornful young lady neither visible nor responsive, and feeling it a dreadful liberty so to roar out her name, was almost as bad as playing to order. But, she answered at last, and her light came along the dark passage like a star.

Miss Havisham beckoned her to come close, and took up a jewel from the table, and tried its effect upon her fair young bosom and against her pretty brown hair. "Your own, one day, my dear, and you will use it well. Let me see you play cards with this boy."

"With this boy? Why, he is a common laboring-boy!"

I thought I overheard Miss Havisham answer—only it seemed so unlikely— "Well? You can break his heart."

"What do you play, boy?" asked Estella of myself, with the greatest disdain.

"Nothing but beggar my neighbor,[15] miss."

"Beggar him," said Miss Havisham to Estella. So we sat down to cards.

It was then I began to understand that everything in the room had stopped, like the watch and the clock, a long time ago. I noticed that Miss Havisham put down the jewel exactly on the spot from which she had taken it up. As Estella dealt the cards, I glanced at the dressing-table again, and saw that the shoe upon it, once white, now yellow, had never been worn. I glanced down at the foot from which the shoe was absent, and saw that the silk stocking on it, once white, now yellow, had been trodden ragged. Without this arrest of everything, this standing still of all the pale decayed objects, not even the withered bridal dress on the collapsed form could have looked so like grave-clothes, or the long veil so like a shroud.[16]

So she sat, corpse-like, as we played at cards; the frillings and trimmings on her bridal dress, looking like earthy paper. I knew nothing then, of the discoveries that are occasionally made of bodies buried in ancient times, which fall to powder in the moment of being distinctly seen; but, I have often thought since, that she must have looked as if the admission of the natural light of day would have struck her to dust.

"He calls the knaves, Jacks,[17] this boy!" said Estella with disdain, before our first game was out. "And what coarse hands he has! And what thick boots!"

I had never thought of being ashamed of my hands before; but I began to consider them a very indifferent pair. Her contempt for me was so strong, that it became infectious, and I caught it.[18]

She won the game, and I dealt. I misdealt, as was only natural, when I knew she was lying in wait[19] for me to do wrong; and she denounced me for a stupid, clumsy laboring-boy.

"You say nothing of her," remarked Miss Havisham to me, as she looked on. "She says many hard things of you, but you say nothing of her. What do you think of her?"

"I don't like to say," I stammered.

"Tell me in my ear," said Miss Havisham, bending down.

"I think she is very proud," I replied, in a whisper.

"Anything else?"

"I think she is very pretty."

"Anything else?"

"I think she is very insulting." (She was looking at me then with a look of supreme aversion.)

"Anything else?"

"I think I should like to go home."

"And never see her again, though she is so pretty?"

"I am not sure that I shouldn't like to see her again, but I should like to go home now."

"You shall go soon," said Miss Havisham, aloud. "Play the game out."

Saving for the one weird smile at first, I should have felt almost sure that Miss Havisham's face could not smile. It had dropped into a watchful and brooding expression—most likely when all the things about her had become transfixed[20]—and it looked as if nothing could ever lift it up again. Her chest had dropped, so that she stooped; and her voice had dropped, so that she spoke low, and with a dead lull upon her; altogether, she had the appearance of having dropped, body and soul, within and without, under the weight of a crushing blow.

I played the game to an end with Estella, and she beggared me. She threw the cards down on the table when she had won them all, as if she despised them for having been won of me.

"When shall I have you here again?" said Miss Havisham. "Let me think."

I was beginning to remind her that to-day was Wednesday, when she checked me with her former impatient movement of the fingers of her right hand.

"There, there! I know nothing of days of the week; I know nothing of weeks of the year. Come again after six days. You hear?"

"Yes, ma'am."

"Estella, take him down. Let him have something to eat, and let him roam and look about him while he eats. Go, Pip."

I followed the candle down, as I had followed the candle up, and she stood it in the place where we had found it. Until she opened the side entrance, I had fancied, without thinking about it, that it must necessarily be night-time. The rush of the daylight quite confounded me, and made me feel as if I had been in the candlelight of the strange room many hours.

"You are to wait here, you boy," said Estella; and disappeared and closed the door.

I took the opportunity of being alone in the court-yard, to look at my coarse hands and my common boots. My opinion of those accessories was not favorable. They had never troubled me before, but they troubled me now, as vulgar appendages.[21] I determined to ask Joe why he had ever taught me to call those picture-cards, Jacks, which ought to be called knaves. I wished Joe had been rather more genteelly brought up, and then I should have been so too.

She came back, with some bread and meat and a little mug of beer. She put the mug down on the stones of the yard, and gave me the bread and meat without looking at me, as insolently as if I were a dog in disgrace. I was so humiliated, hurt, spurned, offended, angry, sorry—I cannot hit upon the right name for the smart[22]—God knows what its name was—that tears started to my eyes. The moment they sprang there, the girl looked at me with a quick delight in having been the cause of them. This gave me power to keep them back and to look at her: so, she gave a contemptuous toss—but with a sense, I thought, of having made too sure that I was so wounded—and left me.

But, when she was gone, I looked about me for a place to hide my face in, and got behind one of the gates in the brewery-lane, and leaned my sleeve against the wall there, and leaned my forehead on it and cried. As I cried, I kicked the wall, and took a hard twist at my hair; so bitter were my feelings, and so sharp was the smart without a name, that needed counteraction.

My sister's bringing up had made me sensitive. In the little world in which children have their existence whosoever brings them up, there is nothing so finely perceived and so finely felt, as injustice. It may be only small injustice that the child can be exposed to; but the child is small, and its world is small, and its rocking-horse stands as many hands high, according to scale, as a big-boned Irish hunter. Within myself, I had sustained, from my babyhood, a perpetual conflict with injustice. I had known, from the time when I could speak, that my sister, in her capricious and violent coercion, was unjust to me. I had cherished a profound conviction that her bringing me up by hand, gave her no right to bring me up by jerks. Through all my punishments, disgraces, fasts and vigils, and other penitential performances, I had nursed this assurance; and to my communing so much with it, in a solitary and unprotected way, I in great part refer the fact that I was morally timid and very sensitive.

I got rid of my injured feelings for the time, by kicking them into the brewery wall, and twisting them out of my hair, and then I smoothed my face with my sleeve, and came from behind the gate. The bread and meat were acceptable, and the beer was warming and tingling, and I was soon in spirits to look about me.

To be sure, it was a deserted place, down to the pigeon-house in the brewery-yard, which had been blown crooked on its pole by some high wind, and would have made the pigeons think themselves at sea, if there had been any pigeons there to be rocked by it. But, there were no pigeons in the dove-cot, no horses in the stable, no pigs in the sty, no malt[23] in the store-house, no smells of grains and beer in the copper or the vat. All the uses and scents of the brewery might have evaporated with its last reek of smoke. In a by-yard, there was a wilderness of empty casks, which had a certain sour remembrance of better days lingering about them; but it was too sour to be accepted as a sample of the beer that was gone—and in this respect I remember those recluses as being like most others.

Behind the furthest end of the brewery, was a rank garden with an old wall: not so high but that I could struggle up and hold on long enough to look over it, and see that the rank garden was the garden of the house, and that it was overgrown with tangled weeds, but that there was a track upon the green and yellow paths, as if some one sometimes walked there, and that Estella was walking away from me even then. But she seemed to be everywhere. For, when I yielded to the temptation presented by the casks, and began to walk on them. I saw *her* walking on them at the end of the yard of casks. She had her back towards me, and held her pretty brown hair spread out in her two hands, and never looked round, and passed out of my view directly. So, in the brewery itself—by which I mean the large paved lofty place in which they used to make the beer, and where the brewing utensils still were. When I first went into it, and, rather oppressed by its gloom, stood near the door looking about me, I saw her pass among the extinguished fires, and ascend some light iron stairs, and go out by a gallery high overhead, as if she were going out into the sky.

It was in this place, and at this moment, that a strange thing happened to my fancy. I thought it a strange thing then, and I thought it a stranger thing long afterwards. I turned my eyes—a little dimmed by looking up at the frosty light—towards a great wooden beam in a low nook of the building near me on my right hand, and I saw a figure hanging there by the neck. A figure all in yellow white, with but one shoe to the feet; and it hung so, that I could see that the faded trimmings of the dress were like earthy paper, and that the face was Miss Havisham's, with a movement going over the whole countenance as if she were trying to call to me. In the terror of seeing the figure, and in the terror of being certain that it had not been there a moment before, I at first ran from it, and then ran towards it. And my terror was greatest of all, when I found no figure there.

Nothing less than the frosty light of the cheerful sky, the sight of people passing beyond the bars of the court-yard gate, and the reviving influence of the rest of the bread and meat and beer, would have brought me round. Even with those aids, I might not have come to myself as soon as I did, but that I saw Estella approaching with the keys, to let me out. She would have some fair reason for looking down upon me, I thought, if she saw me frightened; and she would have no fair reason.

She gave me a triumphant glance in passing me, as if she rejoiced that my hands were so coarse and my boots were so thick, and she opened the gate, and stood holding it. I was passing out without looking at her, when she touched me with a taunting hand.

"Why don't you cry?"

"Because I don't want to."

"You do," said she. "You have been crying till you are half blind, and you are near crying again now."

She laughed contemptuously, pushed me out, and locked the gate upon me. I went straight to Mr. Pumblechook's, and was immensely relieved to find him not at home. So, leaving word with the shopman on what day I was wanted at Miss Havisham's again, I set off on the four-mile walk to our forge; [24] pondering, as I went along, on all I had seen, and deeply revolving that I was a common laboring-boy; that my hands were coarse; that my boots were thick; that I had fallen into a despicable habit of calling knaves Jacks; that I was much more ignorant than I had considered myself last night, and generally that I was in a low-lived bad way.

☞ Notes

1. **Havisham:** an eccentric old lady who lives in seclusion with her adopted daughter, Estella. She was deserted on her wedding day, and then made it her goal in life to get revenge on men. She lives in the past, wearing her yellowing wedding dress. All the clocks in her estate are stopped on the minute she found out her fiancee left her.
2. **acquit myself:** to do something well, especially something difficult that you do for the first time in front of other people.
3. **Mr. Pumblechook:** Pip's pompous, arrogant uncle. A merchant obsessed with money, Pumblechook is responsible for arranging Pip's first meeting with Miss Havisham.
4. **"and fourteen":** Mr. Pumblechook was fond of arithmetic and kept asking Pip about arithmetic questions in the early part of this chapter. Here he asked Pip an arithmetic question again. "And fourteen" means "and fourteen times nine".
5. **discomfited:** being made to feel slightly uncomfortable, annoyed, or embarrassed.
6. **them:** here referring to Pip's elder sister and his other relatives, including Mr. Pumblechook.
7. **And sixteen:** And sixteen times nine.
8. **Manor House:** a big old house with a large area of land around it; here referring to Miss Havisham's residence, which is called the Satis House.
9. **loiter:** to move or travel slowly, or to keep stopping when you should keep moving.
10. **She seemed much older than I:** She appeared to be much older than I, because of her superiority in manner and knowledge.
11. **luster:** the quality that makes something interesting or exciting.
12. **who has never seen the sun:** who has never been out of the house.
13. **have done with:** to finish dealing with someone, and never deal with them again.
14. **bawling:** shouting loudly.
15. **beggar my neighbor:** a card game in which the aim is to get all your opponent's cards.

16. **shroud:** a cloth that is wrapped around a dead person's body before it is buried.
17. **He calls the knaves, Jacks:** In card games, both "knave" and "jack" refer to the card with a value between the ten and queen. However, upper-class people would call it "knave" and the lower-class people would call it "jack". The two names are now interchangeable, one hopes, at any level of society.
18. **Her contempt for me was so strong, that it became infectious, and I caught it:** Estella's contempt for Pip was so strong that it infected Pip and made him show contempt for himself.
19. **lying in wait:** remaining in hidden in a place and waiting for someone so that you can attack them.
20. **transfixed:** unable to move.
21. **appendage:** something that is connected to a larger or more important thing.
22. **smart:** a feeling that you have when you are upset and offended by something.
23. **malt:** grain, usually barley, that has been kept in water for some time and then dried, used for making beer.
24. **forge:** a place where metal is heated and shaped into objects; here referring to Pip's brother-in-law, Joe Gargery's forge.

☞ **Study questions**

1. In what detail does Pip describe Miss Havisham and her room?
2. What is Pip's impression about Estella?
3. Why does Pip think that Estella seems much older than he?
4. How does Estella treat Pip?
5. What experiences have made Miss Havisham as she is? Is she a believable character?
6. What is the similarity between the brewery and Miss Havisham?
7. What does Pip think about himself as he departs the Satis House?

☞ **Essay topics**

1. How is the theme of social class central to the novel?
2. What does Dickens gain by having Pip narrate the story in retrospect?
3. Discuss Estella as an example of Dickens' social commentary. This discussion should include references to her parents as well as her upbringing under Miss Havisham.

7.3 Alfred Tennyson

7.3.1 Life and career

Tennyson (1809-1892) was born into a clergyman's family at Somersby, Lincolnshire. His initial education was conducted largely by his learned father. The boy showed an early interest in poetic composition, working original poems in a variety of meters. Some of his boyhood poetry was published in collaboration with his brother Charles in *Poems by Two Brothers* (1827). In this juvenile work the influence of Byron and an attraction to oriental themes were shown. When he entered the Trinity College, Cambridge, Tennyson was drawn to a group of brilliant young men, known as "the Apostles," who debated all the great issues of the day. He soon became an intimate friend of their leader, Arthur Henry Hallam. During his years at Cambridge, Tennyson published his first signed work *Poems, Chiefly Lyrical* (1830). Crude as it might be, the elaborate texture, the splendid coloring and the dreaming melancholy were already predicting the birth of a great poet.

In 1831, following the death of his father, Tennyson broke off his study at Cambridge without taking a degree. The next year he published *Poems*, most of which were both beautiful in melody and rich in imagery. However, it received very harsh and hostile criticism. This, together with the death of his friend, Hallam, threw the young poet into a profound spiritual depression. For nearly ten years after that, Tennyson published almost nothing. During this time he devoted himself to the task of perfecting his art. In 1842, his next issue of *Poems* came out. The book was immediately recognized as a better work and was welcomed by readers. In 1845 Tennyson received a government pension of £ 200 a year, which helped relieve his financial difficulties. For the success of "The Princess" and *In Memoriam*, he was appointed as Poet Laureate in 1850, which finally established him as the most popular poet of the Victorian era.

In Memoriam is an elegy on the death of Hallam. The poem is actually a spiritual journey the poet undertook in mourning his friend: it starts from his initial response to Arthur's death, moves to sustained grief, intermixed with speculations on life and death, and then shifts from deep sorrow into more impersonal and philosophical grounds. As a poetic diary, the poem is an elaborate and powerful expression of the poet's philosophical and religious thoughts—his doubts about the meaning of life, the existence of the soul and the afterlife, and his faith in the power of love and the soul's immortality. Such doubts and beliefs were shared by most people in an age when the old Christian belief was challenged by new scientific discoveries, though to most readers today, the real attraction of the poem lies more in its profound feeling and artistic beauty than in the religious reflections.

Tennyson's poetic career is also marked out by *Idylls of the King* (1842-1885), his most ambitious work which took him over 30 years to complete. It is made up of 12 books, based on the Celtic legends of King Arthur and his Knights of the Round Table. *Idylls of the King* is not a mere reproduction of the old legend. It is a modern interpretation of the classic myth. For one thing, the moral standards and sentiments reflected in the poem belong to the Victorians rather than to the medieval people. For the other, the story of the rise and fall of King Arthur is, in fact, meant to represent a cyclic history of Western civilization, which, in Tennyson's opinion, is going on a spiritual decline and will end in destruction.

Tennyson is a great Victorian poet, conscious of the situation of his own age. Although he attacks the evils of his time, especially money-worship, his attacks are more those of a moralist than of a radical reformer. His poetry is full of didacticism. He has made poetry the description of a beautiful and antique world, as if deliberately he is closing his eyes to the ugly industrialism of his own century. His own past, his country's past, the past of mankind and the past of the world are the theme of his poetry.

Tennyson is a great poet of nature. He sees nature as the setting for performances. Sometimes nature seems to echo human feelings; and, sometimes, it seems indifferent to them and irrelevant. Wordsworth arrives at a permanent relation with nature, which gives him insight into permanent sources of joy and consolation for mankind. Whereas in Tennyson's poetry, natural descriptions provide a series of metaphors on the changing state of the poet's mind. In his poem, *In Memoriam*, nature becomes a mechanic principle, amoral, unfeeling and indifferent to the claims of man.

Tennyson is a real artist. He has a sensitive ear, an excellent choice and taste of words. He also has the natural power of linking visual pictures with musical expressions. His poetry is rich in poetic images and melodious language, and noted for its lyrical beauty and metrical charm. His works are not only the products of the creative imagination of a poetic genius but also products of a long and rich English heritage.

7.3.2 "Break, Break, Break"[1]

Break, break, break,
  On thy cold gray stones, O Sea!
And I would[2] that my tongue could utter
  The thoughts that arise in me.

O, well for[3] the fisherman's boy,
  That he shouts with his sister at play!
O, well for the sailor lad,
  That he sings in his boat on the bay!
And the stately[4] ships go on
  To their haven[5] under the hill;
But O for the touch of a vanished hand,[6]
  And the sound of a voice that is still![7]

Break, break, break,

At the foot of thy crags, O Sea!
But the tender grace of a day[8] that is dead
Will never come back to me.

☞ Notes

1. This short lyric is written in memory of Tennyson's best friend, Arthur Hallam, whose death has a life-long influence on the poet. Here, the poet's own feelings of sadness are contrasted with the carefree, innocent joys of the children and the unfeeling movement of the ship and the sea waves. The beauty of the lyric is to be found in the musical language and in the association of sound and images with feelings and emotions. The poem contains four quatrains, with combined iambic and anapestic feet. Most lines have three feet and some four. The rhyme scheme is *abcb*.
2. **I would:** I wish.
3. **O, well for:** O, it would be well for; in a double sense, that is, it is well for him, but not for me.
4. **stately:** the power of this adjective in its context is that the ships, though stately and dignified, are vulnerable.
5. **haven:** harbor.
6. **a vanished hand:** the hand of his friend who has vanished.
7. **a voice that is still:** The voice of his friend can no longer be heard.
8. **tender grace of a day:** the loving kindness of the day when I was enjoying your company.

☞ Study questions

1. What is the speaker's tone in this poem?
2. Why couldn't the speaker utter his thoughts that arise in him?
3. How does the speaker contrast himself with the fisherman's boy and the sailor lad?
4. Why do the pleasant sights often make the speaker sad?
5. Do you think the speaker's grief will be softened with time? Why or why not?
6. Why does the speaker address the sea, and not his dead friend? Is the sea a useful symbol? Why?
7. What is the function of repetition used in this poem?

7. 3. 3 "Crossing the Bar"[1]

Sunset and evening star, [2]
And one clear call for me!
And may there be no moaning of the bar, [3]
When I put out to sea,

But such a tide as moving seems asleep,
  Too full for sound and foam,
When that[4] which drew from out the boundless deep
  Turns again home.

Twilight and evening bell,
  And after that the dark!
And may there be no sadness of farewell,
  When I embark;

For though from out our bourne[5] of Time and Place
  The flood may bear me far,
I hope to see my Pilot[6] face to face
  When I have crossed the bar.

☞ Notes

1. This poem was written in the later years of Tennyson's life. We can feel his fearlessness towards death, his faith in God and an afterlife. *Bar*, a bank of sand or stones under the water as in a river, parallel to the shore, at the entrance to a harbor. "Crossing the bar" means leaving this world and entering the next world.
2. **sunset, evening star, twilight, evening bell:** all images of the end of life.
3. **moaning of the bar:** mournful sound of the ocean beating on a sand bar at the mouth of a harbor.
4. **that:** the soul.
5. **bourne:** boundary.
6. **Pilot:** Here it refers to God.

☞ Study questions

1. With what hopes does the speaker bid the world farewell?
2. What does Tennyson actually mean by "crossing the bar"?
3. In what way does the poem express a consolation to those the speaker leaves behind?
4. How would you characterize the death that the speaker is wishing for?
5. What is the tone of the poem?

7.3.4 "Ulysses"[1]

  It little profits that an idle king,
By this still hearth,[2] among these barren crags,[3]

Matched with an aged wife, [4] I mete and dole[5]
Unequal laws[6] unto a savage race, [7]
That hoard, and sleep, and feed, and know not me. [8]

I can not rest from travel; I will drink
Life to the lees. [9] All times I have enjoyed
Greatly, have suffered greatly, both with those
That loved me, and alone; on shore, and when
Through scudding drifts[10] the rainy Hyades[11]
Vexed the dim sea. I am become a name; [12]
For always roaming with a hungry heart
Much have I seen and known—cities of men
And manners, climates, councils, governments,
Myself not least, but honored of them all[13]—
And drunk delight of battle with my peers,
Far on the ringing plains[14] of windy Troy.
I am a part of all that I have met;
Yet all experience is an arch wherethrough
Gleams[15] that untraveled world whose margin fades
Forever and forever when I move,
How dull it is to pause, to make an end,
To rust unburnished, not to shine in use!
As though to breathe were life! Life piled on life
Were all too little, [16] and of one to me
Little remains; but every hour is saved
From that eternal silence, something more,
A bringer of new things; and vile it were
For some three suns[17] to store and hoard myself, [18]
And this gray spirit[19] yearning in desire
To follow knowledge like a sinking star,
Beyond the utmost bound of human thought.

This is my son, mine own Telemachus,
To whom I leave the scepter and the isle—
Well-loved of me, [20] discerning to[21] fulfill
This labor, by slow prudence to make mild
A rugged people, and through soft degrees
Subdue them to the useful and the good.

Most blameless[22] is he, centered in the sphere
Of common duties, decent not to fail
In offices of tenderness, and pay
Meet adoration to my household gods,[23]
When I am gone. He works his work, I mine.

There lies the port; the vessel puffs her sail;
There gloom the dark, broad seas. My mariners,
Souls that have toiled, and wrought, and thought with me—
That ever with a frolic welcome took
The thunder and the sunshine, and opposed
Free hearts, free foreheads—you and I are old;
Old age hath yet his honor and his toil.
Death closes all; but something ere the end,
Some work of noble note, may yet be done,
Not unbecoming men that strove with Gods.
The lights begin to twinkle from the rocks;
The long day wanes; the slow moon climbs; the deep
Moans round with many voices. Come, my friends,
'Tis not too late to seek a newer world.
Push off, and sitting well in order smite
The sounding furrows;[24] for my purpose holds
To sail beyond the sunset, and the baths
Of all the western stars, until I die.
It may be that the gulfs will wash us down;
It may be we shall touch the Happy Isles,[25]
And see the great Achilles,[26] whom we knew.
Though much is taken, much abides; and though
We are not now that strength which in old days
Moved earth and heaven, that which we are, we are—
One equal temper of heroic hearts,
Made weak by time and fate, but strong in will
To strive, to seek, to find, and not to yield.

☞ Notes

1. In Greek mythology, Ulysses is the king of the Ithaca island. He is the hero in many literary classics. In Homer's *Odyssey* (the Greek name for Ulysses), Ulysses eventually arrives home after the ten-year Trojan war and another ten years'

adventures at sea. However, according to Dante, Ulysses never returns to his home place, Ithaca, but urges his men to go on exploring westward. Tennyson combines these two versions. In this poem, Ulysses is now three years back in his homeland, reunited with his wife Penelope and his son Telemachus, and resumes his rule over the land. But he will not endure the peaceful commonplace everyday life. Old as he is, he persuades his old followers to go with him and to set sail again to pursue a new world and new knowledge. Written in the form of dramatic monologue, the poem not only expresses, through the mouth of the heroic Ulysses, Tennyson's own determination and courage to brave the struggle of life but also reflects the restlessness and aspiration of the age.

2. **this still hearth:** the quiet family life.
3. **these barren crags:** referring to the unproductive rocky island of Ithaca.
4. **an aged wife:** Penelope, who had remained faithful during his long absence.
5. **mete and dole:** measure out carefully; "dole" suggests small quantities, and the phrase strongly suggests day-to-day dullness.
6. **unequal laws:** laws made for a primitive race, in that their weight varies among different classes of society.
7. **a savage race:** referring to the people of Ithaca. Ulysses looks down upon his people.
8. **That hoard, and sleep, and feed, and know not me:** The people of Ithaca only know how to hide money and live like beasts; they don't know me.
9. **I will drink life to the lees:** Here life is compared to a cup of wine; "**lees**" means the dregs of wine. I will keep traveling and exploring till the end of my life.
10. **scudding drifts:** showers of rain driven quickly by the wind.
11. **Hyades:** a cluster of stars whose rising predicted storms.
12. **I am become a name:** I have become a name because of my long absence in my native country.
13. **Myself not least, but honored of them all:** I am not the least important, but honored by all of them.
14. **ringing plains:** plains ringing with war cries.
15. **gleams:** a word of particular meaning in Tennyson, suggesting a light which is to be followed.
16. **Life piled on life/Were all too little:** Even if I should live more than one life, I would still not be satisfied.
17. **some three suns:** three years or so.
18. **to store and hoard myself:** not to take action.
19. **this gray spirit:** referring to Ulysses who is now old but still yearning in desire.
20. **of me:** by me.
21. **discerning to:** clear-sighted enough to be able to.

22. **blameless:** a high attribute in a heroic age, and indeed in any age in which men know that evil exists.
23. **household gods:** gods of the hearth and home.
24. **in order smite/The sounding furrows:** in order to beat the roaring waves vigorously.
25. **the Happy Isles:** The Islands of the Blest, which were supposed in the far-west ocean, were said to be the paradise for those immortal heroes.
26. **Achilles:** is another hero in Homer's *Iliad*. He died in the Trojan War and became immortal after death.

☞ Study questions

1. Who was Ulysses and what had he done before the time of the poem as evidenced in the poem?
2. What does Ulysses want? What is his attitude toward life in Ithaca?
3. What does Ulysses think about the majority of his subjects?About being their king?
4. Why is being the ruler of a great kingdom not enough for Ulysses?
5. How does Ulysses contrast himself with his son? What is his tone of description? Are we meant to admire one more than the other?
6. How do you react to Ulysses and his views on how life should be lived?
7. What does Ulysses value most in life? What is Tennyson's attitude toward these values?

☞ Essay topics

1. What do you think of Ulysses? Should we try to be more like Ulysses?
2. Why do you think this poem has been highly admired?
3. To what extent is Tennyson's Ulysses like Homer's Odysseus? How does he differ from the Greek hero in Homer's epic?

7.4 Robert Browning

7.4.1 Life and career

Browning (1812-1889) was born into a well-off family at Camberwell, London. He attended a boarding school and spent a short time at the newly established University of London. But he was educated primarily through private tutoring. His father, a bank clerk, gave him the freedom to follow his own interest. In his father's library, Browning read widely as a youth and began to write poetry while still quite young. The richness of his family and his liberal-minded parents made it possible for him to pursue the writing of poetry all his life without having to worry about his sustenance. He became a great admirer of the Romantic poets, especially Shelley. In 1833, young Browning published his first poetic work, *Pauline*. However, it attracted little attention. From 1837 to 1846 Browning attempted to write verse drama for the stage. However, too many subtle analyses and too few actions ruined his plays. All these frustrating experiences forced the poet to develop a literary form that gave full swing to his genius, i. e. the dramatic monologue.

When Browning read the collected poems by Elizabeth Barrett, he was delighted to find a flattering reference to himself. He at once wrote a letter to her and this started a significant romance between them. Elizabeth was a helpless invalid woman, daughter of a domineering merchant. But love swept aside all obstacles, leading to their secret marriage in 1846. The couple eloped to Italy that same year and enjoyed remarkable happiness there. Mrs. Browning produced her best known book of love poetry—*Sonnets from the Portuguese* while Mr. Browning presented to the world some of his best poems. After Elizabeth's death in 1861, Browning brought their son back to England and went on writing. His productivity and originality still remained powerful. The publication of *The Ring and the Book* (1869) finally established his position as one of the greatest English poets.

Browning lived a full poetic life and had immense creative energy. *Dramatic Lyrics* (1842), *Dramatic Romances and Lyrics* (1845), *Bells and Pomegranates* (1846), *Men and Women* (1855), *Dramatic Personae* (1864), *The Ring and the Book* (1869) and *Dramatic Idylls* (1880) are but some of his best known poetic works. *The Ring and the Book* was often considered his masterpiece. The poem is inspired by an old book of legal documents that records a trial in Rome in 1698 of Count Guido Franceschini, who brutally murdered his wife Pompilia. As the story goes, Pompilia is accused of having an affair with a young priest, who only tries to help her in her flight from the sadistic husband. In this long poem, the same story is told by nine persons, all participants and spectators, from their different points of view. Like his other characters in their monologues, these people unconsciously reveal their own characters while telling the story.

A contemporary of Alfred Tennyson, Browning is acknowledged by many as the most original poet of the time. His name is often associated with the term: "dramatic monologue," that is, a lyric poem which reveals "a soul in action" through the conversation of one character in a dramatic situation. Although it is not his invention, it is in his hands that this poetic form reaches its maturity and perfection. In his poems, he would choose a dramatic moment or a crisis, in which his characters are made to talk about their lives, and about their minds and hearts. For example, in "My Last Duchess," the Duke, as he talks about the portrait of his last Duchess, reveals bit by bit his cruelty and possessiveness. It is ironical that the Duke's own defensive words should betray and condemn himself.

Browning is very different from that of any other Victorian poets. He is like a weather-beaten pioneer, bravely and vigorously trying to beat a tract through the jungle. His poetic style belongs to the twentieth century rather than to the Victorian age. The rough, grotesque and disproportionate appearance, the non-poetic jarring diction and the clumsy rhythms fit marvelously a life that is just as imperfect and incongruous. In general, his poems are not meant to entertain the readers with the usual acoustic and visual pleasures: they are supposed to keep them alert, thoughtful and enlightened.

7.4.2 "Home-Thoughts, from Abroad"

1

Oh, to be in England
Now that April 's there,
And whoever wakes in England
Sees, some morning, unaware,
That the lowest boughs and the brushwood sheaf
Round the elm-tree bole[1] are in tiny leaf,
While the chaffinch[2] sings on the orchard bough
In England—now!

2

And after April, when May follows,
And the whitethroat builds, and all the swallows!
Hark, where my blossomed pear tree in the hedge
Leans to the field and scatters on the clover
Blossoms and dewdrops—at the bent spray's edge—
That's the wise thrush;[3] he sings each song twice over,
Lest you should think he never could recapture
The first fine careless rapture!
And though the fields look rough with hoary dew,
All will be gay when noontide wakes anew
The buttercups, the little children's dower[4]
—Far brighter than this gaudy melon-flower![5]

☞ **Notes**

1. **bole:** tree trunk.
2. **chaffinch:** a common small European bird.
3. **thrush:** a brown bird with spots on its front.
4. **dower:** endowment, gift.

5. **melon-flower:** large, trumpet-shaped yellow bloom from a melon plant (such as a cantaloupe or pumpkin). Browning contrasts this flower, which is native to a warm climate, with the smaller buttercups seen in early spring in England.

☞ Study questions

1. How does the poet present his longing for his homeland during the spring season?
2. What are the things that a person can see in an April morning in England?
3. What are the changes that May brings to Nature in England?
4. How does the poem appeal to our senses?
5. What does the buttercup in this poem symbolize?
6. Where is the speaker? What contrast between his homeland and present surroundings does the speaker suggest?

7.4.3 "Meeting at Night"[1]

1

The gray sea and the long black land;
And the yellow half-moon large and low;
And the startled little waves that leap
In fiery ringlets from their sleep,
As I gain the cove[2] with pushing prow,
And quench[3] its speed i' the slushy sand.

2

Then a mile of warm sea-scented beach;
Three fields to cross till a farm appears;
A tap at the pane, the quick sharp scratch[4]
And blue spurt of a lighted match,
And a voice less loud, through its joys and fears,
Than the two hearts beating each to each!

☞ Notes

1. This poem is written in a very loose version of iambic tetrameter. It has a very neat and contained rhyme scheme: *abccba abccba*.
2. **cove:** a kind of recess or sheltered space on the coast of an ocean.
3. **quench:** means to extinguish or stop. So "quench its speed" means to "stop" the boat on the shore.
4. **the quick sharp scratch:** here refers to the sound of lighting a match.

☞ **Study questions**

1. How does the speaker's going to meet his lover at night influence the way he sees his natural surroundings?
2. Why does the speaker give so much attention to the sea? Is it more than just scenery?
3. What kinds of obstacles does the speaker face as he tries to meet his lover?
4. This poem tells a story through a series of images. How do the images work to tell that story?
5. How does the stream-of-consciousness style of writing influence your understanding of the speaker's journey and the meeting?
6. Comment generally on the cinematic and dramatic qualities of the poem and how they complement each other.

7.4.4 "My Last Duchess"[1]

Ferrara

That's my last Duchess painted on the wall,
Looking as if she were alive. I call
That piece a wonder, now: Frà Pandolf's[2] hands
Worked busily a day, and there she stands.
Will' t please you sit and look at her? I said
"Frà Pandolf" by design,[3] for never read
Strangers like you that pictured countenance,[4]
The depth and passion of its earnest glance,
But to myself they turned[5] (since none puts by
The curtain I have drawn for you, but I)
And seemed as they would ask me, if they durst,[6]
How such a glance came there; so, not the first
Are you to turn and ask thus. Sir, 'twas not
Her husband's presence only, called[7] that spot
Of joy into the Duchess' cheek: perhaps
Frà Pandolf chanced to say "Her mantle laps
Over my lady's wrist too much,"[8] or "Paint
Must never hope to reproduce the faint
Half-flush that dies along her throat":[9] such stuff
Was courtesy,[10] she thought, and cause enough
For calling up that spot of joy. She had
A heart—how shall I say?—too soon made glad,
Too easily impressed; she liked whate'er
She looked on, and her looks went everywhere.

Sir, 'twas all one! [11] My favor at her breast, [12]
The dropping of the daylight in the West,
The bough of cherries some officious fool
Broke in the orchard for her, the white mule
She rode with round the terrace—all and each
Would draw from her alike the approving speech,
Or blush, at least. She thanked men—good! but thanked
Somehow—I know not how—as if she ranked
My gift of a nine-hundred-years-old name
With anybody's gift. [13] Who'd stoop to blame
This sort of trifling?[14] Even had you skill
In speech—(which I have not)—to make your will
Quite clear to such an one, [15] and say, "Just this
Or that in you disgusts me; here you miss,
Or there exceed the mark"[16]—and if she let
Herself be lessoned[17] so, nor plainly set
Her wits to yours, [18] forsooth, [19] and made excuse
a—E'en then would be some stooping; and I choose
Never to stoop. Oh sir, she smiled, no doubt,
Whene'er I passed her; but who passed without
Much the same smile? This grew; I gave commands; [20]
Then all smiles stopped together. [21] There she stands
As if alive. Will't please you rise? We'll meet
The company below, then. I repeat,
The Count your master's known munificence[22]
Is ample warrant that no just pretense
Of mine[23] for dowry will be disallowed; [24]
Though his fair daughter's self, as I avowed
At starting, is my object. Nay, we'll go
Together down, sir. Notice Neptune, [25] though,
Taming a sea horse, thought a rarity,
Which Claus of Innsbruck[26] cast in bronze for me!

☞ Notes

1. "My Last Duchess" is Browning's best-known dramatic monologue. The poem takes its sources from the life of Alfonso Ⅱ, Duke of Ferrara of the 16th-century Italy, whose first wife, Lucrezia, a young girl, died suspiciously in 1561 after three years of marriage. Not long after her death, the duke negotiated through an agent to marry a

niece of the Count of Tyrol. This dramatic monologue is the duke's speech addressed to the agent who comes to negotiate the marriage. In his talk about his "last duchess," the duke reveals himself as a self-conceited, cruel and tyrannical man. The poem is written in heroic couplets, but with no regular metrical system. In reading, it sounds like blank verse.

2. **Frà Pandolf:** Brother Pandolf, an imaginary painter who painted the portrait of the Duchess ("frà" is an Italian word for "friar," meaning "brother").
3. **by design:** on purpose.
4. **for never read/Strangers like you that pictured countenance:** for strangers like you never looked at that face in the picture.
5. **But to myself they turned:** Strangers always turned to me.
6. **durst:** dare.
7. **called:** caused.
8. **"Her mantle laps/Over my lady's wrist too much":** Her cloak covers up too much of her wrist.
9. **the faint/Half-flush that dies along her throat:** the light reddish blush that gradually disappears along her throat.
10. **such stuff/Was courtesy:** Such foolish words were regarded as acts of politeness and respect.
11. **'twas all one:** It was all the same.
12. **My favor at her breast:** the gift I gave her which she wore at her breast.
13. **she ranked/My gift of a nine-hundred-years-old name/With anybody's gift:** She regarded my gift, the title of the Duchess of Ferrara with a history of 900 years to be of the same value as the gifts given to her by some insignificant persons.
14. **Who'd stoop to blame/This sort of trifling:** Who would lower himself to find fault with this kind of trivial things? Notice the haughty and hypocritical tone of the Duke.
15. **such an one:** referring to the Duchess.
16. **here you miss,/Or there exceed the mark: miss:** You have not done this quite enough, while you have overdone that.
17. **be lessoned:** be given a lesson.
18. **nor plainly set/Her wits to yours:** She didn't argue with you.
19. **forsooth:** indeed.
20. **This grew; I gave commands:** This kind of things grew worse and worse; I gave orders.
21. **Then all smiles stopped together:** Then she died.
22. **munificence:** bountifulness.
23. **just pretense/Of mine:** my well-grounded claim.
24. **disallowed:** refused (to give).

25. **Neptune:** the Roman god of the sea, whose chariot is often shown pulled by sea-horses. The Duke is showing the statue of Neptune to the envoy as they are going downstairs to meet the others.
26. **Claus of Innsbruck:** Claus is an imaginary sculptor; Innsbruck is an Italian city, renowned for its sculpture, that Browning visited in 1838.

☞ Study questions

1. How does the Duke want the people around him to respond to his power?
2. Why is the Duke jealous of the smiles and thanks that the Duchess shows to other people? Does he actually value her smiles and thanks? Does he want her to give all her admiration to him, or to stifle her admiring behavior entirely?
3. Why does the Duke think that it would be "stooping" to explain to the Duchess why he dislikes her smiling and blushing?
4. What does the Duke communicate about himself unintentionally by retelling the story of his murder of the Duchess? How do these unintended meanings slip through the language of the poem?
5. What is the Duke really hoping to communicate by telling the story of his "last Duchess" to the Count's servant? Who is meant to receive the message?
6. How does the bronze statue of Neptune taming a seahorse relate to the portrait of the Duchess? Why does the Duke make a point of showing this second object to the Count's servant?
7. How would you characterize the Duke? What is generally revealed about him during the course of the poem?

☞ Essay topics

1. What is the Duke's opinion of the Duchess's personality? Do we as readers see her personality any differently?
2. What report do you think the emissary should make to the Count about the proposed marriage of his daughter to the Duke?

7.5 Elizabeth Barrett Browning

7.5.1 Life and career

Elizabeth Barrett (1806-1861) was born into a well-to-do family in Durham, England. Her father was a man with a strong sense of power and will to command. Elizabeth had a happy childhood. She received her education largely at home by a tutor. She was a voracious reader and a keen student, studying languages and classical literature. Her fist publication was *Battle of Marathon* (1820). In 1826 her book, *An Essay on Mind and Other Poems*, was published anonymously. Her translation of *Prometheus Bound*, by the Greek dramatist Aeschylus, appeared in 1833 and was highly regarded. For nearly a decade after 1838, Elizabeth lived a life of infirmity and confinement as a result of a childhood spinal injury and lung ailment. Her ill health did not stop her from writing. *The Seraphim and Other Poems* (1838), the first volume of her mature poetry, appeared under her own name. Her *Poems* (1844) made her one of the most popular writers in the land, and inspired Robert Browning to write her, telling her how much he loved her poems. Gradually a significant romance developed between them. Confined by ill health to her bedroom, Elizabeth did not expect to have a lover. However, love conquered all. A year later they secretly married and eloped to Italy, where they remained during their married life.

In her new-found happiness she produced her most enduring work, the *Sonnets from the Portuguese* (1850). This is a collection of love songs, written in secret before her marriage. Critics generally consider the *Sonnets*, one of the most widely known collections of love lyrics in English, to be her best work. The Sonnets draw on a broad classical education, but the doubts and triumphs of a forbidden passion have the force of genuine feeling and show the victory of love over emotional death. This experience is often conveyed in original and powerful imagery, as in Sonnet 24. Here, free at last from the suffocating inertia of Victorian propriety, Elizabeth Browning suggests that the cruel knife of worldly criticism now lies shut in the enfolding warmth of love's hand. Mutual passion has triumphed over social constraint, and a woman has asserted her personal freedom in love.

Later Elizabeth became interested in social problems. Through her pen, she was passionately outspoken on issues of social injustice like slavery, child labor, and oppression of women. "A Curse for a Nation" and "The Cry of the Children" are typical examples of this kind. Her growing interest in the Italian struggle for independence is evident in *Casa Guidi Windows* (1851) and *Poems before Congress* (1860). In her longest and most ambitious work, *Aurora Leigh* (1856), Elizabeth created a work that defends a woman's right to intellectual freedom and discusses issues of gender, class and the relation of art to politics. Recent criticism has resurrected it as a central document of Victorian feminism, a woman writer's powerful claim to establish her independent identity through her work. The poem, written in blank verse, gives the story of an English girl educated with all the advantages of the nineteenth century and thoroughly imbued with its restless progressive spirit. Virginia Woolf argued that *Aurora Leigh*'s heroine, with her passionate interest in the social questions, her conflict as artist and woman, her longing for knowledge and freedom, is the true daughter of her age.

Elizabeth Browning had an original genius, a fervent heart, and an intellect that was exceedingly active. Her works, skillfully planned and carefully wrought out in this noble spirit, fully establish her as one of the noblest female poets of the world. Her unorthodox rhyme and diction, often scorned, have been cited as daring experiments that prefigured the techniques of modern poets. Her candid treatment of political and social issues, too, was bold for her time. She had a great influence on American poet Emily Dickinson and English author Virginia Woolf.

7. 5. 2 "How Do I Love Thee?"[1]

How do I love thee? Let me count the ways.
I love thee to the depth and breadth and height
My soul can reach, when feeling out of sight
For the ends of Being and ideal Grace. [2]
I love thee to the level of everyday's
Most quiet need, by sun and candlelight. [3]
I love thee freely, [4] as men strive for Right;
I love thee purely, [5] as they turn from Praise.
I love thee with the passion put to use
In my old griefs, and with my childhood's faith.
I love thee with a love I seemed to lose
With my lost saints[6]—I love thee with the breath,
Smiles, tears, of all my life—and, if God choose,
I shall but love thee better after death.

☞ Notes

1. This poem is composed in the form of a Petrarchan Sonnet. The rhyme scheme is *abba abba cdcdcd*.
2. **when … Grace:** when my soul feels its way into the spiritual realm (**For the ends of Being:** death or at least a bodily death; **ideal Grace:** heaven).
3. **by sun and candle-light:** Here refers to both day and night.
4. **freely:** willingly—and just as intensely as men who fight for freedom.
5. **purely:** genuinely, without desire for praise.
6. **with … saints:** with a childlike fervor for saints and holiness that I seemed to lose when I grew older.

☞ Study questions

1. How would the poem be different if the opening line was "Why do I love thee"?
2. How many ways of loving does the speaker identify? Do these ways of loving overlap, conflict, or complement one another?

3. Which kind of love described in the sonnet seems most familiar to you? Which seems strangest? Why?
4. What images does the poet use to strengthen the theme of love in this poem?
5. This sonnet is probably the most-quoted love poem in the English language. What qualities, both in its content and its style, make "How Do I Love Thee?" memorable?

7.6 Charlotte Brontë

7.6.1 Life and career

Charlotte (1816-1855) was born into a clergyman's family at Thornton, Yorkshire. She spent her childhood in the small village of Haworth. When she was very young, her mother died, leaving behind six children. Charlotte and three of her sisters were sent away to a Clergy Daughters' School. The harsh conditions of the school permanently affected Charlotte's health and hastened the deaths of her two elder sisters, Maria and Elizabeth. This experience inspired the later portrayal of Lowood School in the novel *Jane Eyre*. During the following years, the four surviving children were left to look after themselves at Haworth. They had a great deal of freedom to explore the surrounding countryside, to read widely, and to write stories about fantasy worlds. When she grew up, Charlotte worked away from home as school teacher or governess. In 1842 Charlotte and Emily went to Brussels to study languages so that the sisters could start their own school. There Charlotte fell in love with a married teacher, who discouraged her letters to him. This passionate yet hopeless love left its marks in almost all her works. Upon their return home, the sisters embarked upon their project for founding a school, but their attempt failed in 1844.

In 1845 the three sisters published a book of *Poems* at their own expense. It received little attention. Then the three sisters turned to novel writing. Charlotte's first novel *The Professor* was rejected by the publisher. But her second one, *Jane Eyre*, proved to be tremendously popular with the public when it appeared in 1847. In the same year, Emily's single and unique work *Wuthering Heights* and Anne's *Agnes Grey* were also published. Just at the height of the creative years of the sisters, their brother Branwell, the only boy in the family, died in September 1848. Emily caught cold at his funeral and died of consumption in December of the same year. Scarcely was she buried, Anne, her close companion, showed signs of the same mortal disease and died the next year. Left in ever-deepening loneliness, Charlotte continued writing. Her next important novel, *Shirley*, a work about the industrial troubles between the mill-owners and machine-breakers in Yorkshire, came out in 1849. Another novel *Villette* appeared in 1853. It is a story about Charlotte's own experiences in a Brussels boarding school. In 1854 Charlotte was married to Mr. Nicholls, her father's curate, a sincere but narrow-minded man. She was happy in the marriage, but died in childbirth a few months later. Her first-written novel, *The Professor*, was published posthumously in 1857.

As a novelist, Charlotte was greatly influenced by Byron and Scott. The major characters of her novels were all strong, intelligent women, who stood up for themselves in a time when women were supposed to be subservient, ruled by dominating males in a patriarchal society. *Jane Eyre* is such a typical example. Instead of the rich, gentle and virtuous beauties of the conventional heroine, this novel presents a small, plain and poor governess who begins her life all alone, with no body caring for her and nothing attractive. What she has is an intense feeling, a ready sympathy and a strong sense of equality and independence. *Jane Eyre* has little of the old conventional stamp upon it, but is full of youthful vigor, of freshness and originality, of nervous diction and concentrated interest. Its settings and scenery are used in a highly symbolic fashion, with Jane's inner development of life and soul portrayed against the backdrop of the natural world. The novel merges elements of three distinct genres. It has the form of a Bildungsroman, focusing on the emotions and experiences that accompany growth to adulthood; it also contains much social criticism, with a strong sense of morality at its core; and finally it has the moody quality and Byronic character typical of Gothic fiction. The style of *Jane Eyre* is highly charged with emotion, almost feverish in its intensity. Sentences are often stuffed with lush adjectives and sensual images. Sometimes the words almost seem to have spilled out onto the page in a headlong, uncontrolled rush of feeling. This style of the novel fits very well with the headstrong, emotional character of Jane Eyre, the narrator. Thus the novel is often considered to be ahead of its time because its heroine, Jane Eyre, speaks up for oppressed women of every age.

Brought up with strict orthodoxy, Charlotte would usually stick to the Puritanical code. She loves the beauty of nature but despises worldly ambition and success. In her mind, man's life is composed of perpetual battle between sin and virtue, good and evil. Besides, she is a writer of realism combined with romanticism. On one hand, she presents a vivid realistic picture of the English society by exposing the cruelty, hypocrisy and other evils of the upper classes, and by showing the misery and suffering of the poor. On the other hand, her writings are marked by intensity of vision and of passion. Her works are all about the struggle of an individual consciousness towards self-realization, about some lonely and neglected young women with a fierce longing for love, understanding and a full, happy life. So, whatever weakness her work may have, the vividness of her subjective narration, the intensely achieved characterization, and the most truthful presentation of the economical, moral, and social life of the time—all this renders her works a never dying popularity.

7.6.2 An excerpt from *Jane Eyre*

Chapter 5

Five o'clock had hardly struck on the morning of the nineteenth of January, when Bessie[1] brought a candle into my closet and found me already up and nearly dressed. I had risen half an hour before her entrance, and had washed my face, and put on my clothes by the light of a half-moon just setting, whose rays streamed through the narrow window near my crib. I was to leave Gateshead[2] that day by a coach which passed the lodge gates at six a. m. Bessie was the only person yet risen; she had lit a fire in the nursery, where she now proceeded to make my breakfast. Few children can eat when excited with the thoughts of a journey; nor could I. Bessie, having pressed me in vain to take a few spoonfuls of the boiled milk and bread she had prepared for me, wrapped up some biscuits in a paper and put them into my bag; then she helped me on with my pelisse and bonnet, and wrapping herself in a shawl, she and I left the nursery. As we passed Mrs. Reed's bedroom, she said, "Will you go in and bid Missis good-bye?"

"No, Bessie: she came to my crib last night when you were gone down to supper, and said I need not disturb her in the morning, or my cousins either; and she told me to remember that she had always been my best friend, and to speak of her and be grateful to her accordingly."

"What did you say, Miss?"

"Nothing: I covered my face with the bedclothes, and turned from her to the wall."

"That was wrong, Miss Jane."

"It was quite right, Bessie. Your missis has not been my friend: she has been my foe."

"O Miss Jane! don't say so!"

"Good-bye to Gateshead!" cried I, as we passed through the hall and went out at the front door.

The moon was set, and it was very dark; Bessie carried a lantern, whose light glanced on wet steps and gravel road sodden by a recent thaw. Raw and chill was the winter morning: my teeth chattered as I hastened down the drive. There was a light in the porter's lodge: when we reached it, we found the porter's wife just kindling her fire: my trunk, which had been carried down the evening before, stood corded at the door. It wanted but a few minutes of six, and shortly after that hour had struck, the distant roll of wheels announced the coming coach; I went to the door and watched its lamps approach rapidly through the gloom.

"Is she going by herself?" asked the porter's wife.

"Yes."

"And how far is it?"

"Fifty miles."

"What a long way! I wonder Mrs. Reed is not afraid to trust her so far alone."

The coach drew up; there it was at the gates with its four horses and its top laden with passengers: the guard and coachman loudly urged haste; my trunk was hoisted up; I was taken from Bessie's neck, to which I clung with kisses.

"Be sure and take good care of her," cried she to the guard, as he lifted me into the inside.

"Ay, ay!" was the answer: the door was slapped to, a voice exclaimed "All right," and on we drove. Thus was I severed from Bessie and Gateshead; thus whirled away to unknown, and, as I then deemed, remote and mysterious regions.

I remember but little of the journey; I only know that the day seemed to me of a preternatural[3] length, and that we appeared to travel over hundreds of miles of road. We passed through several towns, and in one, a very large one, the coach stopped; the horses were taken out, and the passengers alighted to dine. I was carried into an inn, where the guard wanted me to have some dinner; but, as I had no appetite, he left me in an immense room with a fireplace at each end, a chandelier pendent from the ceiling, and a little red gallery high up against the wall filled with musical instruments. Here I walked about for a long time, feeling very strange, and mortally apprehensive of some one coming in and kidnapping me; for I believed in kidnappers, their exploits having frequently figured in Bessie's fireside chronicles.[4] At last the guard returned; once more I was stowed away in the coach, my protector mounted his own seat, sounded his hollow horn, and away we rattled over the "stony street" of L[5]—

The afternoon came on wet and somewhat misty: as it waned into dusk, I began to feel that we were getting very far indeed from Gateshead: we ceased to pass through towns; the country changed; great gray hills heaved up round the horizon: as twilight deepened, we descended a valley, dark with wood, and long after night had overclouded the prospect, I heard a wild wind rushing amongst trees.

Lulled by the sound, I at last dropped asleep; I had not long slumbered when the sudden cessation of motion awoke me; the coach-door was open, and a person like a servant was standing at it: I saw her face and dress by the light of the lamps.

"Is there a little girl called Jane Eyre here?" she asked. I answered "Yes," and was then lifted out; my trunk was handed down, and the coach instantly drove away.

I was stiff with long sitting, and bewildered with the noise and motion of the coach: gathering my faculties,[6] I looked about me. Rain, wind, and darkness filled the air; nevertheless, I dimly discerned a wall before me and a door open in it; through this door I passed with my new guide: she shut and locked it behind her. There was now visible a house or houses—for the building spread far—with many windows, and lights burning in some; we went up a broad pebbly path, splashing wet, and were admitted at a door;

then the servant led me through a passage into a room with a fire, where she left me alone.

I stood and warmed my numbed fingers over the blaze, then I looked round; there was no candle, but the uncertain light from the hearth showed, by intervals, papered walls, carpet, curtains, shining mahogany furniture: it was a parlor, not so spacious or splendid as the drawing-room at Gateshead, but comfortable enough. I was puzzling to make out the subject of a picture on the wall, when the door opened, and an individual carrying a light entered; another followed close behind.

The first was a tall lady with dark hair, dark eyes, and a pale and large forehead; her figure was partly enveloped in a shawl, her countenance was grave, her bearing erect.

"The child is very young to be sent alone," said she, putting her candle down on the table. She considered me attentively for a minute or two, then further added —

"She had better be put to bed soon; she looks tired: are you tired?" she asked, placing her hand on my shoulder.

"A little, ma'am."

"And hungry too, no doubt: let her have some supper before she goes to bed, Miss Miller. Is this the first time you have left your parents to come to school, my little girl?"

I explained to her that I had no parents. She inquired how long they had been dead: then how old I was, what was my name, whether I could read, write, and sew a little: then she touched my cheek gently with her forefinger, and saying, "She hoped I should be a good child," dismissed me along with Miss Miller.

The lady I had left might be about twenty-nine; the one who went with me appeared some years younger: the first impressed me by her voice, look, and air. Miss Miller was more ordinary; ruddy in complexion, though of a careworn countenance; hurried in gait and action, like one who had always a multiplicity of tasks on hand: she looked, indeed, what I afterwards found she really was, an under-teacher.[7] Led by her, I passed from compartment to compartment, from passage to passage, of a large and irregular building; till, emerging from the total and somewhat dreary silence pervading that portion of the house we had traversed, we came upon the hum of many voices, and presently entered a wide, long room, with great deal tables, two at each end, on each of which burnt a pair of candles, and seated all round on benches, a congregation of girls of every age, from nine or ten to twenty. Seen by the dim light of the dips, their number to me appeared countless, though not in reality exceeding eighty; they were uniformly dressed in brown stuff frocks of quaint fashion, and long holland pinafores. It was the hour of study; they were engaged in conning over their to-morrow's task, and the hum I had heard was the combined result of their whispered repetitions.

Miss Miller signed to me to sit on a bench near the door, then walking up to the top of the long room she cried out—

"Monitors, collect the lesson-books and put them away!"

Four tall girls arose from different tables, and going round, gathered the books and removed them. Miss Miller again gave the word of command—

"Monitors, fetch the supper-trays!"

The tall girls went out and returned presently, each bearing a tray, with portions of something, I knew not what, arranged thereon, and a pitcher of water and mug in the middle of each tray. The portions were handed round; those who liked took a draught of the water, the mug being common to all.[8] When it came to my turn, I drank, for I was thirsty, but did not touch the food, excitement and fatigue rendering me incapable of eating: I now saw, however, that it was a thin oaten cake shared into fragments.

The meal over, prayers were read by Miss Miller, and the classes filed off, two and two, upstairs. Overpowered by this time with weariness, I scarcely noticed what sort of a place the bedroom was, except that, like the schoolroom, I saw it was very long. To-night I was to be Miss Miller's bed-fellow; she helped me to undress: when laid down I glanced at the long rows of beds, each of which was quickly filled with two occupants; in ten minutes the single light was extinguished, and amidst silence and complete darkness I fell asleep.

The night passed rapidly. I was too tired even to dream; I only once awoke to hear the wind rave in furious gusts, and the rain fall in torrents, and to be sensible that Miss Miller had taken her place by my side. When I again unclosed my eyes, a loud bell was ringing; the girls were up and dressing; day had not yet begun to dawn, and a rushlight or two burned in the room. I too rose reluctantly; it was bitter cold, and I dressed as well as I could for shivering, and washed when there was a basin at liberty, which did not occur soon, as there was but one basin to six girls, on the stands down the middle of the room. Again the bell rang: all formed in file, two and two, and in that order descended the stairs and entered the cold and dimly lit schoolroom: here prayers were read by Miss Miller; afterwards she called out—

"Form classes!"

A great tumult succeeded for some minutes, during which Miss Miller repeatedly exclaimed, "Silence!" and "Order!" When it subsided, I saw them all drawn up in four semicircles, before four chairs, placed at the four tables; all held books in their hands, and a great book, like a Bible, lay on each table, before the vacant seat. A pause of some seconds succeeded, filled up by the low, vague hum of numbers; Miss Miller walked from class to class, hushing this indefinite sound.

A distant bell tinkled: immediately three ladies entered the room, each walked to a table and took her seat. Miss Miller assumed the fourth vacant chair, which was that nearest the door, and around which the smallest of the children were assembled: to this inferior class I was called, and placed at the bottom of it.

Business now began, the day's Collect[9] was repeated, then certain texts of Scripture were said, and to these succeeded a protracted reading of chapters in the Bible, which lasted an hour. By the time that exercise was terminated, day had fully dawned. The indefatigable bell now sounded for the fourth time: the classes were marshalled and marched into another room to breakfast: how glad I was to behold a prospect of getting something to eat! I was now nearly sick from inanition, having taken so little the day before.

The refectory was a great, low-ceiled, gloomy room; on two long tables smoked basins of something hot, which, however, to my dismay, sent forth an odor far from inviting. I saw a universal manifestation of discontent when the fumes of the repast met the nostrils of those destined to swallow it; from the van of the procession, the tall girls of the first class, rose the whispered words—

"Disgusting! The porridge is burnt again!"

"Silence!" ejaculated a voice; not that of Miss Miller, but one of the upper teachers,[10] a little and dark personage, smartly dressed, but of somewhat morose aspect,[11] who installed herself at the top of one table, while a more buxom lady presided at the other. I looked in vain for her I had first seen the night before; she was not visible: Miss Miller occupied the foot of the table where I sat, and a strange, foreign-looking, elderly lady, the French teacher, as I afterwards found, took the corresponding seat at the other board. A long grace was said and a hymn sung; then a servant brought in some tea for the teachers, and the meal began.

Ravenous, and now very faint, I devoured a spoonful or two of my portion without thinking of its taste; but the first edge of hunger blunted,[12] I perceived I had got in hand a nauseous mess; burnt porridge is almost as bad as rotten potatoes; famine itself soon sickens over it.[13] The spoons were moved slowly: I saw each girl taste her food and try to swallow it; but in most cases the effort was soon relinquished. Breakfast was over, and none had breakfasted. Thanks being returned for what we had not got, and a second hymn chanted, the refectory was evacuated for the schoolroom. I was one of the last to go out, and in passing the tables, I saw one teacher take a basin of the porridge and taste it; she looked at the others; all their countenances expressed displeasure, and one of them, the stout one, whispered—

"Abominable stuff! How shameful!"

A quarter of an hour passed before lessons again began, during which the schoolroom was in a glorious tumult; for that space of time it seemed to be permitted to talk loud and more freely, and they used their privilege. The whole conversation ran on the breakfast, which one and all abused roundly. Poor things! it was the sole consolation they had. Miss Miller was now the only teacher in the room: a group of great girls standing about her spoke with serious and sullen gestures. I heard the name of Mr. Brocklehurst pronounced by some lips; at which Miss Miller shook her head disapprovingly; but she made no great effort to check the general wrath; doubtless she shared in it.

A clock in the schoolroom struck nine; Miss Miller left her circle, and standing in the middle of the room, cried—

"Silence! To your seats!"

Discipline prevailed: in five minutes the confused throng was resolved into order, and comparative silence quelled the Babel clamor of tongues. [14] The upper teachers now punctually resumed their posts: but still, all seemed to wait. Ranged on benches down the sides of the room, the eighty girls sat motionless and erect; a quaint assemblage they appeared, all with plain locks combed from their faces, not a curl visible; in brown dresses, made high and surrounded by a narrow tucker about the throat, with little pockets of holland (shaped something like a Highlander's[15] purse) tied in front of their frocks, and destined to serve the purpose of a work-bag: all, too, wearing woollen stockings and country-made shoes, fastened with brass buckles. Above twenty of those clad in this costume were full-grown girls, or rather young women; it suited them ill, and gave an air of oddity even to the prettiest.

I was still looking at them, and also at intervals examining the teachers—none of whom precisely pleased me; for the stout one was a little coarse, the dark one not a little fierce, the foreigner harsh and grotesque, and Miss Miller, poor thing! looked purple, weather-beaten, and over-worked—when, as my eye wandered from face to face, the whole school rose simultaneously, as if moved by a common spring.

What was the matter? I had heard no order given: I was puzzled. Ere I had gathered my wits, the classes were again seated: but as all eyes were now turned to one point, mine followed the general direction, and encountered the personage who had received me last night. She stood at the bottom of the long room, on the hearth; for there was a fire at each end; she surveyed the two rows of girls silently and gravely. Miss Miller approaching, seemed to ask her a question, and having received her answer, went back to her place, and said aloud—

"Monitor of the first class, fetch the globes!"

While the direction was being executed, the lady consulted moved slowly up the room. I suppose I have a considerable organ of veneration, [16] for I retain yet the sense of admiring awe with which my eyes traced her steps. Seen now, in broad daylight, she looked tall, fair, and shapely; brown eyes with a benignant light in their iris, and a fine pencilling of long lashes round, relieved the whiteness of her large front; on each of her temples her hair, of a very dark brown, was clustered in round curls, according to the fashion of those times, when neither smooth bands nor long ringlets were in vogue; her dress, also in the mode of the day, was of purple cloth, relieved by a sort of Spanish trimming of black velvet; a gold watch (watches were not so common then as now) shone at her girdle. Let the reader add, to complete the picture, refined features; a complexion, if pale, clear; and a stately air and carriage, and he will have, at least, as clearly as words can give it, a correct idea of the exterior of Miss Temple—Maria Temple, as I afterwards saw the name written in a prayer-book entrusted to me to carry to church.

The superintendent of Lowood (for such was this lady) having taken her seat before a pair of globes placed on one of the tables, summoned the first class round her, and commenced giving a lesson on geography; the lower classes were called by the teachers: repetitions in history, grammar, &c., went on for an hour; writing and arithmetic succeeded, and music lessons were given by Miss Temple to some of the elder girls. The duration of each lesson was measured by the clock, which at last struck twelve. The superintendent rose—

"I have a word to address to the pupils," said she.

The tumult of cessation from lessons was already breaking forth, but it sank at her voice. She went on—

"You had this morning a breakfast which you could not eat; you must be hungry. I have ordered that a lunch of bread and cheese shall be served to all."

The teachers looked at her with a sort of surprise.

"It is to be done on my responsibility," she added, in an explanatory tone to them, and immediately afterwards left the room.

The bread and cheese was presently brought in and distributed, to the high delight and refreshment of the whole school. The order was now given "To the garden!" Each put on a coarse straw bonnet, with strings of colored calico, and a cloak of gray frieze. I was similarly equipped, and, following the stream, I made my way into the open air.

The garden was a wide enclosure, surrounded with walls so high as to exclude every glimpse of prospect; a covered verandah ran down one side, and broad walks bordered a middle space divided into scores of little beds: these beds were assigned as gardens for the pupils to cultivate, and each bed had an owner. When full of flowers they would doubtless look pretty; but now, at the latter end of January, all was wintry blight and brown decay. I shuddered as I stood and looked round me: it was an inclement day for outdoor exercise; not positively rainy, but darkened by a drizzling yellow fog; all under foot was still soaking wet with the floods of yesterday. The stronger among the girls ran about and engaged in active games, but sundry pale and thin ones herded together for shelter and warmth in the verandah; and amongst these, as the dense mist penetrated to their shivering frames, I heard frequently the sound of a hollow cough.

As yet I had spoken to no one, nor did anybody seem to take notice of me; I stood lonely enough: but to that feeling of isolation I was accustomed; it did not oppress me much. I leant against a pillar of the verandah, drew my gray mantle close about me, and, trying to forget the cold which nipped me without, and the unsatisfied hunger which gnawed me within, delivered myself up to the employment of watching and thinking.[17] My reflections were too undefined and fragmentary to merit record: I hardly yet knew where I was; Gateshead and my past life seemed floated away to an immeasurable distance; the present was vague and strange, and of the future I could form no conjecture.[18] I looked round the convent-like garden, and then up at the house—a large building, half of which seemed gray and old, the other half quite new. The new part, containing the schoolroom and dormitory, was lit by mullioned and latticed windows, which gave it a church-like aspect; a stone tablet over the door bore this inscription:

"Lowood Institution. —This portion was rebuilt A. D. —by Naomi Brocklehurst, of Brocklehurst Hall, in this county." "Let your light so shine before men that they may see your good works, and glorify your Father which is in Heaven."—St. Matt. v. 16.

I read these words over and over again: I felt that an explanation belonged to them,[19] and was unable fully to penetrate their import. I was still pondering the signification of "Institution," and endeavoring to make out a connection between the first words and the verse of Scripture, when the sound of a cough close behind me made me turn my head. I saw a girl sitting on a stone bench near; she was bent over a book, on the perusal of which she seemed intent: from where I stood I could see the title—it was *Rasselas*;[20] a name that struck me as strange, and consequently attractive. In turning a leaf she happened to look up, and I said to her directly—

"Is your book interesting?" I had already formed the intention of asking her to lend it to me some day.

"I like it," she answered, after a pause of a second or two, during which she examined me.

"What is it about?" I continued. I hardly know where I found the hardihood[21] thus to open a conversation with a stranger; the step was contrary to my nature and habits: but I think her occupation touched a chord of sympathy somewhere;[22] for I too liked reading, though of a frivolous and childish kind; I could not digest or comprehend the serious or substantial.

"You may look at it," replied the girl, offering me the book.

I did so; a brief examination convinced me that the contents were less taking than the title: *Rasselas* looked dull to my trifling taste; I saw nothing about fairies, nothing about genii; no bright variety seemed spread over the closely-printed pages. I returned it to her; she received it quietly, and without saying anything she was about to relapse into her former studious mood: again I ventured to disturb her—

"Can you tell me what the writing on that stone over the door means? What is Lowood Institution?"

"This house where you are come to live."

"And why do they call it Institution? Is it in any way different from other schools?"

"It is partly a charity-school: you and I, and all the rest of us, are charity-children. I suppose you are an orphan: are not either your father or your mother dead?"

"Both died before I can remember."

"Well, all the girls here have lost either one or both parents, and this is called an Institution for educating orphans."

"Do we pay no money? Do they keep us for nothing?"

"We pay, or our friends pay, fifteen pounds a year for each."

"Then why do they call us charity-children?"

"Because fifteen pounds is not enough for board and teaching, and the deficiency is supplied by subscription."

"Who subscribes?"

"Different benevolent-minded ladies and gentlemen in this neighborhood and in London."

"Who was Naomi Brocklehurst?"

"The lady who built the new part of this house as that tablet records, and whose son overlooks and directs everything here."

"Why?"

"Because he is treasurer and manager of the establishment."

"Then this house does not belong to that tall lady who wears a watch, and who said we were to have some bread and cheese?"

"To Miss Temple? Oh, no! I wish it did. She has to answer to Mr. Brocklehurst for all she does. Mr. Brocklehurst buys all our food and all our clothes."

"Does he live here?"

"No—two miles off, at a large hall."

"Is he a good man?"

"He is a clergyman, and is said to do a great deal of good."

"Did you say that tall lady was called Miss Temple?"

"Yes."

"And what are the other teachers called?"

"The one with red cheeks is called Miss Smith; she attends to the work, and cuts out—for we make our own clothes, our frocks, and pelisses, and everything; the little one with black hair is Miss Scatcherd; she teaches history and grammar, and hears the second class repetitions; and the one who wears a shawl, and has a pocket-handkerchief tied to her side[23] with a yellow riband, is Madame Pierrot: she comes from Lisle, in France, and teaches French."

"Do you like the teachers?"

"Well enough."

"Do you like the little black one, and the Madame—? —I cannot pronounce her name as you do."

"Miss Scatcherd is hasty—you must take care not to offend her; Madame Pierrot is not a bad sort of person."

"But Miss Temple is the best—isn't she?"

"Miss Temple is very good and very clever; she is above the rest, because she knows far more than they do."

"Have you been long here?"

"Two years."

"Are you an orphan?"

"My mother is dead."

"Are you happy here?"

"You ask rather too many questions. I have given you answers enough for the present: now I want to read."

But at that moment the summons sounded for dinner; all re-entered the house. The odor which now filled the refectory was scarcely more appetizing than that which had regaled our nostrils at breakfast: the dinner was served in two huge tin-plated vessels, whence rose a strong steam redolent of rancid fat.[24] I found the mess to consist of indifferent potatoes and strange shreds of rusty meat, mixed and cooked together. Of this preparation a tolerably abundant plateful was apportioned to each pupil. I ate what I could, and wondered within myself whether every day's fare would be like this.

After dinner, we immediately adjourned to the schoolroom: lessons recommenced, and were continued till five o'clock.

The only marked event of the afternoon was, that I saw the girl with whom I had conversed in the verandah dismissed in disgrace by Miss Scatcherd from a history class, and sent to stand in the middle of the large schoolroom. The punishment seemed to me in a high degree ignominious, especially for so great a girl—she looked thirteen or upwards. I expected she would show signs of great distress and shame; but to my surprise she neither wept nor blushed: composed, though grave, she stood, the central mark of all eyes. "How can she bear it so quietly—so firmly?" I asked of myself. "Were I in her place, it seems to me I should wish the earth to open and swallow me up. She looks as if she were thinking of something beyond her punishment—beyond her situation: of something not round her nor before her. I have heard of day-dreams—is she in a day-dream now? Her eyes are fixed on the floor, but I am sure they do not see it—her sight seems turned in, gone down into her heart: she is looking at what she can remember, I believe; not at what is really present. I wonder what sort of a girl she is—whether good or naughty."

Soon after five p. m. we had another meal, consisting of a small mug of coffee, and half-a-slice of brown bread. I devoured my bread and drank my coffee with relish; but I should have been glad of as much more—I was still hungry. Half an hour's recreation succeeded, then study; then the glass of water and the piece of oat-cake, prayers, and bed. Such was my first day at Lowood.

☞ Notes

1. **Bessie:** a woman servant in the service of Mrs. Reed.
2. **Gateshead:** the place where Jane's aunt Mrs. Reed lives.
3. **preternatural:** beyond normal.
4. **fireside chronicles:** stories from various chronicles which are told to children at the fireside.
5. **L:** Lowood, a place where a charity school was built.
6. **gathering my faculties:** gathering my physical powers.
7. **under-teacher:** a teacher who is subordinate.
8. **the mug being common to all:** the mug that is used by all.
9. **Collect:** the opening prayer.
10. **the upper teachers:** teachers who have comparatively superior positions in the charity school.
11. **of somewhat morose aspect:** with sullen facial expression.
12. **the first edge of hunger blunted:** the sharp hunger was somewhat eased after having eaten some porridge.
13. **famine itself soon sickens over it:** a hungry person will not feel hungry any more smelling such food.
14. **the Babel clamor of tongues:** the confusing sound of many voices talking together, which is like the situation when the Babel Tower fell down.
15. **Highlander:** one who comes from the Highlands in Scotland.
16. **I have a considerable organ of veneration:** I can easily fall into respect of somebody.
17. **delivered myself up to the employment of watching and thinking:** let myself be occupied with watching and thinking.
18. **could form no conjecture:** could not tell.
19. **an explanation belonged to them:** an explanation is required to understand them.
20. **"Rasselas":** *The History of Rasselas, Prince of Abissinia*, a novel written by Samuel Johnson.
21. **hardihood:** boldness, united with firmness of mind.

22. **her occupation touched a chord of sympathy somewhere:** that she was fully occupied with reading aroused a similar feeling in Jane's mind.
23. **her side:** her waist.
24. **redolent of rancid fat:** suggestive of unpleasant odor of fat.

☞ Study questions

1. Is Jane glad to leave Gatesheas? Why?
2. What is the weather like when Jane first arrives at Lowood Hall?
3. How is Lowood different from what Jane had anticipated?
4. What is Jane's first impression of Miss Temple, the superintendent of Lowood School?
5. What does Jane learn from Helen Burns about Lowood School? Who oversees every aspect of its operation?
6. Why does Brontë give so much detail about the porridge the students at Lowood must eat? What do these details reveal about the school?
7. What is ironic about the strict religious observances at the school and the conditions there?
8. How does this irony help contribute to the development of character and theme?

☞ Essay topics

1. What is the significance of Jane's experiences in the charity school to her later life?
2. Examine the relationship between character and atmosphere in *Jane Eyre*.
3. Show how *Jane Eyre* is a novel that demonstrates the importance of a woman standing up for herself.

7.7 Emily Brontë

7.7.1 Life and career

Emily(1818-1848) was born into a clergymen's family at Thornton, Yorkshire. When she was two years old, her father was appointed curate of Haworth, an isolated village on the moors. In 1821, shortly after Emily's third birthday, her mother died of cancer. In 1824, Emily and her three elder sisters were sent to a school for daughters of impoverished clergymen. The conditions of the school were harsh and an epidemic soon broke out, taking the lives of her two eldest sisters. During the following years, Emily's education was largely provided at home by her father. And her father's bookshelf offered her a variety of reading: the *Bible*, Homer, Shakespeare, Milton, Byron, Scott and many others. She also had a great deal of freedom to explore the surrounding countryside. The lonely purple moors became one of the most important shaping forces in her life. She was a reserved, courageous woman with a commanding will and manner. In 1835, Emily attempted formal schooling for the second time at Roe Head, where Charlotte was then teaching. She managed to stay only three months before she became very sick and had to go home. In 1838 she found a teaching job at Law Hill School, where she managed to work for six months under stress, but she suffered a breakdown and had to return home again. Then in 1842, Emily accompanied her sister Charlotte to Brussels, Belgium, for a year to study languages. During this time she impressed the professor as having a finer, more powerful mind than her sister.

Emily began writing poems at an early age and wrote a substantial body of poetry, which ranges from the lyric to the dramatic. She worked progressively, incorporating new experiences and feelings into her poems. Her nature poems were based on direct experience, reflecting beauty and a sense of enchantment. The last years of her life were critical to her poetry, in which the theme of death came to dominate. She perceived that presence transcended everything, freeing the imprisoned soul and mingling life and death within a single nature. Emily is preeminently a poet of self-conscious expression, of an interior life focused on observation, imagination and introspection. However, she had only twenty one poems published in her life time, together with poems by Anne and Charlotte, in a slim volume titled *Poems* (1846). Her novel, *Wuthering Heights* written between the autumns of 1845 and 1846, was published in December 1847. It did not gain immediate success as Charlotte's *Jane Eyre*, but it has acclaimed later fame as one of the most intense novels written in the English language. In September 1848, Emily had caught cold at her brother's funeral and died of tuberculosis at the age of thirty.

Wuthering Heights is a riddle which has meant so many things to so many people. One way of reading is to treat it as a romantic story. Every character in the novel is in one way or another connected with the triangular love between Heathcliff and Catherine and Edgar. While Edgar seems to have the approval of all the people as the best partner for Catherine, Heathcliff has all the hindrances to overcome before getting his union with her. And yet, the stormy love between Heathcliff and Catherine, with their strong desire of mutual possession and torment, with their mutual belonging in life and in death, makes it a most terrible yet wonderful tale of love. From the social point of view, the story is a tragedy of social inequality. Heathcliff, a waif of the lowest order in society, is eager for love and friendship but is forever looked down upon and rejected by the two families. What is more, he loves Catherine dearly but he can't have her just because of the disparity between their social statuses. Hope and love denied turn into humiliation and result in the brutal revenge and the horrible tragedy.

Wuthering Heights is descriptive-narrative oriented. There is no digressive talk or the omniscient comment and analysis from the author as was the fashion at the time. However, the way of narration is rather complicated and extraordinary. It starts from towards the end when Heathcliff is master of both Wuthering Heights and Thrushcross

Grange and little Cathy and Hareton are still in his clutch, and then goes back to the very beginning and moves back and forth as the occasion requires. Most of the story is told by Nelly, Catherine's old nurse, to Mr. Lockwood, a temporary tenant at Thrushcross Grange. Part of it is told by Mr. Lockwood himself, and part through Catherine's diary and Isabella's letters to Nelly.

Wuthering Heights is Emily's only novel and is generally considered one of the most original works. In many aspects, it is unique and has no counterparts in mode as well as in manner of writing. In the aspect of vitalized, animated nature, Emily proves an even better artist than her elder sister in landscape painting. The typical Yorkshire characters, settings, dialect and the primitive, uncultivated, dark aspects of life there can easily be found in this unique novel. And the novel is also remarkable for its simple, naked statement of violent emotions such as Catherine's dying farewell to Heathcliff. Unlike the works of her two sisters, Emily's *Wuthering Heights* shows no remarkable conventional influence in either idea or form. Readers are especially struck by the apparent absence of social morality in her novel. The reading of the novel makes us contemplate, without evasion, some of the most powerful primal human motives, engaged—against a wild, free, stormy background—in ferocious conflict. It will not be easy for us to find an answer, but the challenge is tempting.

7.7.2 An excerpt from *Wuthering Heights*

Chapter 15

Another week over—and I[1] am so many days nearer health, and spring! I have now heard all my neighbor's[2] history, at different sittings,[3] as the housekeeper[4] could spare time from more important occupations. I'll continue it in her own words, only a little condensed. She is, on the whole, a very fair narrator, and I don't think I could improve her style.

In the evening, she said, the evening of my visit to the Heights, I knew, as well as if I saw him, that Mr. Heathcliff was about the place; and I shunned going out, because I still carried his letter[5] in my pocket, and didn't want to be threatened or teased any more. I had made up my mind not to give it till my master went somewhere, as I could not guess how its receipt would affect Catherine. The consequence was, that it did not reach her before the lapse of three days. The fourth was Sunday, and I brought it into her room after the family were gone to church. There was a manservant left to keep the house with me, and we generally made a practice of locking the doors during the hours of service; but on that occasion the weather was so warm and pleasant that I set them wide open, and, to fulfill my engagement,[6] as I knew who would be coming, I told my companion that the mistress wished very much for some oranges, and he must run over to the village and get a few, to be paid for on the morrow. He departed, and I went upstairs.

Mrs. Linton sat in a loose white dress, with a light shawl over her shoulders, in the recess of the open window, as usual. Her thick, long hair had been partly removed at the beginning of her illness, and now she wore it simply combed in its natural tresses over her temples and neck. Her appearance was altered, as I had told Heathcliff; but when she was calm, there seemed unearthly beauty in the change. The flash of her eyes had been succeeded by a dreamy and melancholy softness; they no longer gave the impression of looking at the objects around her: they appeared always to gaze beyond, and far beyond—you would have said out of this world. Then, the paleness of her face—its haggard aspect having vanished as she recovered flesh—and the peculiar expression arising from her mental state, though painfully suggestive of their causes, added to the touching interest which she awakened; and—invariably to me, I know, and to any person who saw her, I should think—refuted more tangible proofs of convalescence, and stamped her as one doomed to decay.

A book lay spread on the sill before her, and the scarcely perceptible wind fluttered its leaves at intervals. I believe Linton had laid it there: for she never endeavored to divert herself with reading, or occupation of any kind, and he would spend many an hour in trying to entice her attention to some subject which had formerly been her amusement. She was conscious of his aim, and in her better moods endured his efforts placidly, only showing their uselessness by now and then suppressing a wearied sigh, and checking him at last with the saddest of smiles and kisses. At other times, she would turn petulantly away, and hide her face in her hands, or even push him off angrily; and then he took care to let her alone, for he was certain of doing no good.

Gimmerton chapel[7] bells were still ringing; and the full, mellow flow of the beck in the valley came soothingly on the ear. It was a sweet substitute for the yet absent murmur of the summer foliage, which drowned that music about the Grange when the trees were in leaf. At Wuthering Heights it always sounded on quiet days following a great thaw or a season of steady rain. And of Wuthering Heights Catherine was thinking as she listened: that is, if she thought or listened at all; but she had the vague, distant look I mentioned before, which expressed no recognition of material things either by ear or eye.

"There's a letter for you, Mrs. Linton," I said, gently inserting it in one hand that rested on her knee. "You must read it immediately, because it wants an answer. Shall I break the seal?" "Yes," she answered, without altering the direction of her eyes. I opened it—it was very short. "Now," I continued, "read it." She drew away her hand, and let it fall. I replaced it in her lap, and stood waiting till it should please her to glance down; but that movement was so long delayed that at last I resumed—"Must I read it, ma'am? It is from Mr. Heathcliff."

There was a start and a troubled gleam of recollection, and a struggle to arrange her ideas. She lifted the letter, and seemed to peruse it; and when she came to the signature she sighed: yet still I found she had not gathered its import, for, upon my desiring to hear her reply, she merely pointed to the name, and gazed at me with mournful and questioning eagerness.

"Well, he wishes to see you," said I, guessing her need of an interpreter. "He's in the garden by this time, and impatient to know what answer I shall bring."

As I spoke, I observed a large dog lying on the sunny grass beneath raise its ears as if about to bark, and then smoothing them back, announce, by a wag of the tail, that some one approached whom it did not consider a stranger. Mrs. Linton bent forward, and listened breathlessly. The minute after a step traversed the hall; the open house was too tempting for Heathcliff to resist walking in: most likely he supposed that I was inclined to shirk my promise, and so resolved to trust to his own audacity. With straining eagerness Catherine gazed towards the entrance of her chamber. He did not hit the right room[8] directly; she motioned me to admit him; but he found it out, ere[9] I could reach the door, and in a stride or two was at her side, and had her grasped in his arms.

He neither spoke, nor loosed his hold some five minutes, during which period he bestowed more kisses than ever he gave in his life before, I dare say; but then my mistress had kissed him first, and I plainly saw that he could hardly bear, for downright agony, to look into her face! The same conviction had stricken him as me, from the instant he beheld her, that there was no prospect of ultimate recovery there—she was fated, sure to die.

"O, Cathy! Oh, my life! How can I bear it?" was the first sentence he uttered, in a tone that did not seek to disguise his despair.

And now he stared at her so earnestly that I thought the very intensity of his gaze would bring tears into his eyes; but they burned with anguish, they did not melt.[10]

"What now?" said Catherine, leaning back, and returning his look with a suddenly clouded brow[11]—her humor was a mere vane for constantly varying caprices. "You and Edgar have broken my heart, Heathcliff! And you both come to bewail the deed to me, as if you were the people to be pitied! I shall not pity you, not I. You have killed me—thriven on it, I think. How strong you are! How many years do you mean to live after I am gone?"

Heathcliff had knelt on one knee to embrace her; he attempted to rise, but she seized his hair, and kept him down.

"I wish I could hold you," she continued, bitterly, "till we were both dead! I shouldn't care what you suffered. I care nothing for your sufferings. Why shouldn't you suffer? I do! Will you forget me—will you be happy when I am in the earth? Will you say twenty years hence, 'That's the grave of Catherine Earnshaw. I loved her long ago, and was wretched to lose her; but it is past. I've loved many others since—my children are dearer to me than she was, and, at death, I shall not rejoice that I am going to her, I shall be sorry that I must leave them!' Will you say so, Heathcliff?"

"Don't torture me till I'm as mad as yourself," cried he, wrenching his head free, and grinding his teeth.

The two, to a cool spectator, made a strange and fearful picture. Well might Catherine deem that heaven would be a land of exile to her, unless, with her mortal body, she cast away her mortal character also. Her present countenance had a wild vindictiveness in its white cheek, and a bloodless lip, and scintillating eye; and she retained, in her closed fingers, a portion of the locks she had been grasping. As to her companion, while raising himself with one hand, he had taken her arm with the other; and so inadequate was his stock of gentleness to the requirements of her condition, that on his letting go, I saw four distinct impressions left blue in the colorless skin.

"Are you possessed with a devil," he pursued, savagely, "to talk in that manner to me, when you are dying? Do you reflect that all those words will be branded in my memory, and eating deeper eternally, after you have left me? You know you lie to say I have killed you; and, Catherine, you know that I could as soon as forget you, as my existence! [12] Is it not sufficient for your infernal selfishness, that while you are at peace I shall writhe in the torments of hell?"

"I shall not be at peace," moaned Catherine, recalled to a sense of physical weakness by the violent, unequal throbbing of her heart, which beat visibly, and audibly, under this excess of agitation.

She said nothing further till the paroxysm was over; then she continued, more kindly—

"I'm not wishing you greater torment than I have, Heathcliff. I only wish us never to be parted—and should a word of mine distress you hereafter, think I feel the same distress underground, and for my own sake, forgive me! Come here and kneel down again! You never harmed me in your life. Nay, if you nurse anger, [13] that will be worse to remember than my harsh words! Won't you come here again? Do!"

Heathcliff went to the back of her chair, and leant over, but not so far as to let her see his face, which was livid with emotion. She bent round to look at him; he would not permit it; turning abruptly, he walked to the fireplace, where he stood, silent, with his back towards us.

Mrs. Linton's glance followed him suspiciously: every movement woke a new sentiment in her. After a pause, and a prolonged gaze, she resumed, addressing me in accents of indignant disappointment.

"Oh, you see, Nelly! He would not relent a moment to keep me out of the grave! *That* is how I'm loved! Well, never mind! That is not *my* Heathcliff. I shall love mine yet; and take him with me—he's in my soul. And," added she, musingly, "the thing that irks me most is this shattered prison, after all. I'm tired, tired of being closed here. I'm wearying to escape into that glorious world, and to be always there; not seeing it dimly through tears, and yearning for it through the walls of an aching heart; but really with it, and in it. Nelly, you think you are better and more fortunate than I; in full health and strength—you are sorry for me—very soon that will be altered. I shall be sorry for *you*. I shall be incomparably beyond and above you all. I *wonder* he won't be near me!" She went on to herself. "I thought he wished it. Heathcliff, dear! You should not be sullen now. Do come to me, Heathcliff."

In her eagerness she rose, and supported herself on the arm of the chair. At that earnest appeal, he turned to her, looking absolutely desperate. His eyes wide, and wet, at last, flashed fiercely on her; his breast heaved convulsively. An instant they held asunder;[14] and then how they met I hardly saw, but Catherine made a spring, and he caught her, and they were locked in an embrace from which I thought my mistress would never be released alive. In fact, to my eyes, she seemed directly insensible. He flung himself into the nearest seat, and on my approaching hurriedly to ascertain if she had fainted, he gnashed at me, and foamed like a mad dog, and gathered her to him with greedy jealousy. I did not feel as if I were in the company of a creature of my own species; it appeared that he would not understand, though I spoke to him; so, I stood off, and held my tongue, in great perplexity.

A movement of Catherine's relieved me a little presently: she put up her hand to clasp his neck, and bring her cheek to his, as he held her: while he, in return, covering her with frantic caresses, said wildly—

"You teach me now how cruel you've been—cruel and false. *Why* did you despise me? *Why* did you betray your own heart, Cathy? I have not one word of comfort—you deserve this. You have killed yourself.[15] Yes, you may kiss me, and cry; and wring out my kisses and tears. They'll blight you—they'll damn you. You loved me—then what *right* have you to leave me? What right—answer me—for the poor fancy you felt for Linton? Because misery, and degradation, and death, and nothing that god or Satan could inflict would have parted us, *you*, of your own will, did it. I have not broken your heart—*you* have broken it—and in breaking it, you have broken mine. So much the worse for me, that I am strong. Do I want to live? What kind of living will it be when you—oh, God! would *you* like to live with your soul[16] in the grave?"

"Let me alone. Let me alone," sobbed Catherine. "If I've done wrong, I'm dying for it. It is enough! You left me too; but I won't upbraid you! I forgive you. Forgive me!"

"It is hard to forgive, and to look at those eyes, and feel those wasted hands," he answered. "Kiss me again; and don't let me see your eyes! I forgive what you have done to me. I love *my* murderer—but *yours*! How can I?"

They were silent—their faces against each other, and washed by each other's tears. At least, I suppose the weeping was on both sides; as it seemed Heathcliff *could* weep on a great occasion like this.

I grew very uncomfortable, meanwhile; for the afternoon wore fast away, the man whom I had sent off returned from his errand, and I could distinguish, by the shine of the westering[17] sun up the valley, a concourse thickening outside Gimmerton chapel porch.

"Service is over," I announced. "My master will be here in half an hour."

Heathcliff groaned a curse, and strained Catherine closer—she never moved.

Ere long I perceived a group of the servants passing up the road towards the kitchen wing. Mr. Linton was not far behind; he opened the gate himself, and sauntered slowly up, probably enjoying the lovely afternoon that breathed as soft as summer.

"Now he is here," I exclaimed. "For Heaven's sake, hurry down! You'll not meet any one on the front stairs. Do be quick; and stay among the trees till he is fairly in."

"I must go, Cathy," said Heathcliff, seeking to extricate himself from his companion's arms. "But, if I live, I'll see you again before you are asleep. I won't stay five yards from your window."

"You must not go!" she answered, holding him as firmly as her strength allowed. "You shall not, I tell you."

"For one hour," he pleaded earnestly.

"Not for one minute," she replied.

"I must—Linton will be up immediately," persisted the alarmed intruder.

He would have risen, and unfixed her fingers by the act—she clung fast, gasping; there was mad resolution in her face.

"No!" she shrieked. "Oh, don't, don't go. It is the last time! Edgar will not hurt us. Heathcliff, I shall die! I shall die!"

"Damn the fool! There he is," cried Heathcliff, sinking back into his seat. "Hush, my darling! Hush, hush, Catherine! I'll stay. If he shot me so, I'd expire[18] with a blessing on my lips."

And there they were fast again. I heard my master mounting the stairs—the cold sweat ran from my forehead; I was horrified.

"Are you going to listen to her ravings?" I said, passionately. "She does not know what she says. Will you ruin her, because she has not wit to help herself? Get up! You could be free instantly. That is the most diabolical deed that ever you did. We are all done for—master, mistress, and servant."

I wrung my hands, and cried out; and Mr. Linton hastened his step at the noise. In the midst of my agitation, I was sincerely glad to observe that Catherine's arms had fallen relaxed, and her head hung down.

"She's fainted, or dead," I thought: "so much the better. Far better that she should be dead, than lingering a burden and a misery-maker to all about her."

Edgar sprang to his unbidden guest, blanched with astonishment and rage. What he meant to do I cannot tell; however, the other stopped all demonstrations, at once, by placing the lifeless-looking form in his arms.

"Look there!" he said. "Unless you be a fiend, help her first—then you shall speak to me!"

He walked into the parlor, and sat down. Mr. Linton summoned me, and with great difficulty, and after resorting to many means, we managed to restore her to sensation; but she was all bewildered; she sighed, and moaned, and knew nobody. Edgar, in his anxiety for her, forgot her hated friend. I did not. I went, at the earliest opportunity, and besought him to depart; affirming that Catherine was better, and he should hear from me in the morning how she passed the night.

"I shall not refuse to go out of doors," he answered, "but I shall stay in the garden: and, Nelly, mind you keep your word tomorrow. I shall be under those larch-trees. Mind! or I pay another visit, whether Linton be in or not."

He sent a rapid glance through the half-open door of the chamber, and, ascertaining that what I stated was apparently true, delivered the house of his luckless presence.

☞ Notes

1. **I:** here referring to Mr. Lockwood, the new tenant of Thrushcross Grange (Heathcliff is his landlord).
2. **neighbor:** here referring to Mr. Heathcliff.
3. **at different sittings:** on different talks.
4. **the housekeeper:** here referring to Nelly Dean, a servant with the Earnshaws and the Lintons for all her life. She is also one of the main narrators of the novel, and she tells the following part of the story to Mr. Lockwood.
5. **his letter:** a letter by Heathcliff who asked Nelly Dean to pass it to Catherine.
6. **to fulfill my engagement:** That is, to pass the letter and to arrange the meeting between Heathcliff and Catherine.
7. **Gimmerton chapel:** a small church near the Thrushcross Grange.
8. **hit the right room:** to find the room where Catherine was reclining.
9. **ere:** before.
10. **they did not melt:** implies that his eyes did not shed any tears.
11. **clouded brow**: gloomy and sorrowful expression.
12. **I could as soon as forget you, as my existence:** I could not forget you just like that I could not forget my own existence.
13. **nurse anger:** be angry all the time.

14. **held asunder:** stood wide apart from each other.
15. **You have killed yourself:** referring to Catherine's marriage to Linton, which destroyed her life.
16. **soul:** here referring to Catherine.
17. **westering:** going west.
18. **expire:** die.

☞ Study questions

1. Who is telling the story in this chapter?
2. Why does Nelly let Heathcliff in the house to see Catherine as she is dying?
3. What do you think about Heathcliff, and his relationship with Catherine?
4. As Heathcliff and Catherine are talking, they both make many accusations against each other. What do they accuse each other of doing?
5. What does Heathcliff mean when he says, "I love my murderer, but yours! How can I?"
6. What are the key elements in the interaction between Catherine and Heathcliff?
7. How does this chapter explore the notion of romantic love?
8. How is Nelly behaving in this chapter? Do you think this is typical of her?

☞ Essay topics

1. Discuss the novel's narrative structure. Are the novel's narrators trustworthy? Why or why not? With particular reference to Nelly's story, consider what might be gained from reading between the lines of the narration. What roles do the personalities of the narrators play in the way that the story is told?
2. What role does social class and class ambiguity play in *Wuthering Heights*? To what extent is Heathcliff's social position responsible for the misery and conflict so persistent in the book?

7.8 George Eliot

7.8.1 Life and career

George Eliot, pseudonym of Mary Ann Evans (1819-1880), was born at Arbury Farm in Warwickshire. Her father was a carpenter who rose to be a land agent. As a little girl, she was very shy and spent most of her time reading. She received her education in several schools and developed a strong evangelical piety. When her mother died in 1836, she stopped her schooling and became her father's housekeeper. However, she pursued her education rigorously and devoted herself to music and language learning. In 1841 she moved with her father to Coventry, where she became acquainted with religious free-thinkers and began to question the orthodoxy of the Anglican Church. This shift in belief eventually brought her into collision with her family and some of her old friends.

After her father's death in 1849, Evans travelled on the Continent for the first time. On her return to England she became assistant editor to the liberal periodical, *Westminster Review*, in 1851. This connection brought her into contact with many of the famous men of the time: Charles Dickens, William Thackeray, Wilkie Collins, Thomas Carlyle, John Stuart Mill and Herbert Spencer. In London she also met George Henry Lewes, a writer and a critic, who deeply sympathized with her personal, intellectual, and artistic struggles. The two intellectuals went from colleagues to friends and finally to lovers, though Lewes was married with children. Their unconventional union (cohabitation) resulted in their 25 years of alienation from the respectable society.

At the suggestion of Lewes, Evans began fiction writing. At this time she took the pen name George Eliot. Her first work, *Scenes from Clerical Life* (1858), was a collection of stories about the people of Warwickshire. It was followed by her first novel, *Adam Bede* (1859), a tragic love story in which the model for the title character was Eliot's father. The book was a brilliant success, establishing her as a leading novelist. 1860 saw the successful publication of *The Mill on the Floss*, a story of destructive family relations. In the following year, *Silas Marner* (1861), a highly unified novella about learning to love unconditionally and act responsibly, came out. She wrote *Romola* in 1863, *Felix Holt the Radical* in 1866 and *The Spanish Gypsy* in 1868. These novels stress the intimate connection between values at the personal and social levels. In 1867 Eliot began her greatest work, *Middlemarch*, a novel of English provincial life in the early nineteenth century. The work fuses several stories and characters, creating a network of parallels and contrasts. *Daniel Derornda* (1876) was her last important novel published.

In 1878, Lewes died, leaving George Eliot "the perpetual mourner." She wrote no more, devoting herself to preparing his unfinished work for publication. Even though her marriage with John Cross, a man some years her junior and her admirer for many years, finally brought about a kind of reconciliation with her family and the society, she was never able to cast off the sense of depression and dreariness left by Lewes' death. She never took up her pen again. She died, probably of a heart attack, on December 22, 1880.

As a novelist, George Eliot is concerned with the depiction of people and life of her time; her mind is always active, instinctively analyzing and generalizing to discover the fundamental truth about human life. By placing the responsibility for a man's life firmly on the moral choices of the individual, she changes the nature of English novel: character becomes plot. In her works, she seeks to present the inner struggle of a soul and to reveal the motives, impulses and hereditary influences which govern human actions. Her characters are not cast in actions but in thoughts. They are mostly presented to the reader with a brief introduction of the central principles of their behavior and the predominant features of their personality. Whatever they do must be the logical development of their principal character, be it the slow growth or decline. The naturalness and soundness of her presentation, diagnosis and analysis of characters' motives and development make her stand out among the host of writers of her time as the only serious intellectual one. By initiating a new type of realism, she sets in motion a variety of development in novel writing, leading in the direction of both the naturalistic and psychological novel.

In *Middlemarch*, George Eliot has set herself, from the very beginning, to illustrate her own profound conviction that the noblest aims, however faithfully and simply pursued, are apt to be wrecked, at least to outward seeming, in this modern age of distracted life. This novel comprises three separate stories. The main narrative is a classic love story that tells of how Dorothea Brooke and her soul mate Will Ladislaw overcome all the obstacles that threaten to keep them apart. The second story is the tragic tale of how Tertius Lydgate's ambitions to advance medical science are brought to nothing by an injudicious marriage and poor community relations. The third story shows Fred Vincy maturing from an idle rake into a decent hardworking citizen in order to marry his childhood sweetheart, Mary Garth. In this novel, George Eliot is investigating human aspirations, in particular, the aspiration of those extraordinary people to serve and be good to others and society. It includes two aspects. One is the part played in their fight for fulfillment by the individual human being, with his frailties, imperfect self-knowledge and weak will-power; and the other is the limitation set by the society. The issue is between man in his capacity as an individual and mankind as a whole in the society. The study is centered on the fatalities of Dorothea and Lydgate. Confined in Middlemarch, a provincial society with its stereotyped habits of thinking, its limited accessibility to higher ideas, and its rigidities, jealousies and pettiness, both Dorothea and Lydgate, starting with more than ordinary promise, have to rest content with very ordinary achievement; both, seeking something beyond the provincial life, have finally to subject themselves to the limitations of their life.

George Eliot holds that individuals are shaped by a number of determining forces, such as the force of environment or nature, the force of heredity, and the force of human conventions. These forces of human and natural, moral and animal, civilized and primitive are all interwoven and interconnected in determining the fate of an individual. Her determinism, generally speaking, is based on a tragic sense. She sees tragedy as part of human life, to be found not merely in high-life romance or in extreme situations but also in the ordinary course of everyday human life. Her tragic view of human life is particularly manifest in her description of women's destiny. Most of her novels are dealing with women problems. Her favorite heroines are usually women of remarkable intelligence and great potential. They are not content with the common lot of the "weaker sex"; they cherish some manly, great ambitions and make a brave struggle against the stifling society. The brave struggles of her heroines, though ending in failure, have nonetheless paved the way for the 20th-century women to achieve their rights of freedom, equality and independence.

7.8.2 An excerpt from *Middlemarch*

Chapter 28

1st Gent. *All times are good to seek your wedded home Bringing a mutual delight.*
2nd Gent. *Why, true.*
The calendar hath not an evil day
For souls made one by love, and even death
Were sweetness, if it came like rolling waves
While they two clasped each other, and foresaw
No life apart. [1]

Mr. and Mrs. Casaubon, returning from their wedding journey, arrived at Lowick Manor[2] in the middle of January. A light snow was falling as they descended at the door, and in the morning, when Dorothea passed from her dressing-room into the blue-green boudoir[3] that we know of, she saw the long avenue of limes lifting their trunks from a white earth, and spreading white branches against the dun and motionless sky. The distant flat shrank in uniform whiteness and low-hanging uniformity of cloud. The very furniture in the room seemed to have shrunk since she saw it before: the stag in the tapestry looked more like a ghost in his ghostly blue-green world; the volumes of polite literature[4] in the bookcase looked more like immovable imitations of books.[5] The bright fire of dry oak-boughs burning on the dogs seemed an incongruous renewal of life and glow—like the figure of Dorothea herself as she entered carrying the red-leather cases containing the cameos for Celia.

She was glowing from her morning toilette as only healthful youth can glow: there was gem-like brightness on her coiled hair and in her hazel eyes; there was warm red life in her lips; her throat had a breathing whiteness above the differing white of the fur which itself seemed to wind about her neck and cling down her blue-gray pelisse with a tenderness gathered from her own, a sentient commingled innocence which kept its loveliness against the crystalline purity of the outdoor snow. As she laid the cameo-cases[6] on the table in the bow-window, she unconsciously kept her hands on them, immediately absorbed in looking out on the still, white enclosure which made her visible world.

Mr. Casaubon, who had risen early complaining of palpitation, was in the library giving audience to his curate Mr. Tucker. By-and-by Celia[7] would come in her quality of bridesmaid as well as sister, and through the next weeks there would be wedding visits received and given; all in continuance of that transitional life understood to correspond with the excitement of bridal felicity,[8] and keeping up the sense of busy ineffectiveness, as of a dream which the dreamer begins to suspect. The duties of her married life, contemplated as so great beforehand, seemed to be shrinking with the furniture and the white vapor-walled landscape.[9] The clear heights where she expected to walk in full communion[10] had become difficult to see even in her imagination; the delicious repose of the soul on a complete superior[11] had been shaken into uneasy effort and alarmed with dim presentiment. When would the days begin of that active wifely devotion which was to strengthen her husband's life and exalt her own? Never perhaps, as she had preconceived them; but somehow—still somehow. In this solemnly pledged union of her life, duty would present itself in some new form of inspiration and give a new meaning to wifely love.

Meanwhile there was the snow and the low arch of dun vapor[12]—there was the stifling oppression of the gentlewoman's world, where everything was done for her and none asked for her aid—where the sense of connection with a manifold pregnant existence had to be kept up painfully as an inward vision, instead of coming from without in claims that would have shaped her energies.[13]—"What shall I do?" "Whatever you please, my dear": that had been her brief history since she had left off learning morning lessons and practicing silly rhythms on the hated piano. Marriage, which was to bring guidance into worthy and imperative occupation, had not yet freed her from the gentlewoman's oppressive liberty: it had not even filled her leisure with the ruminant joy of unchecked tenderness. Her blooming full-pulsed youth stood there in a moral imprisonment which made itself one with the chill, colorless, narrowed landscape, with the shrunken furniture, the never-read books, and the ghostly stag in a pale fantastic world that seemed to be vanishing from the daylight.

In the first minutes when Dorothea looked out she felt nothing but the dreary oppression; then came a keen remembrance, and turning away from the window she walked round the room. The ideas and hopes which were living in her mind when she first saw this room nearly three months before were present now only as memories: she judged them as we judge transient and departed things. All existence seemed to beat with a lower pulse than her own, and her religious faith was a solitary cry, the struggle out of a nightmare in which every object was withering and shrinking away from her. Each remembered thing in the room was disenchanted, was deadened as an unlit transparency, till her wandering gaze came to the group of miniatures,[14] and there at last she saw something which had gathered new breath and meaning: it was the miniature of

Mr. Casaubon's aunt Julia, who had made the unfortunate marriage—of Will Ladislaw's grandmother. Dorothea could fancy that it was alive now—the delicate woman's face which yet had a head-strong look, a peculiarity difficult to interpret. Was it only her friends who thought her marriage unfortunate? or did she herself find it out to be a mistake, and taste the salt bitterness of her tears in the merciful silence of the night? What breadths of experience Dorothea seemed to have passed over since she first looked at this miniature! She felt a new companionship with it, as if it had an ear for her and could see how she was looking at it. Here was a woman who had known some difficulty about marriage. Nay, the colors deepened, the lips and chin seemed to get larger, the hair and eyes seemed to be sending out light, the face was masculine and beamed on her with that full gaze which tells her on whom it falls that she is too interesting for the slightest movement of her eyelid to pass unnoticed and un-interpreted. The vivid presentation came like a pleasant glow to Dorothea: she felt herself smiling, and turning from the miniature sat down and looked up as if she were again talking to a figure in front of her. But the smile disappeared as she went on meditating, and at last she said aloud—

"Oh, it was cruel to speak so! How sad—how dreadful!"

She rose quickly and went out of the room, hurrying along the corridor, with the irresistible impulse to go and see her husband and inquire if she could do anything for him. Perhaps Mr. Tucker was gone and Mr. Casaubon was alone in the library. She felt as if all her morning's gloom would vanish if she could see her husband glad because of her presence.

But when she reached the head of the dark oak there was Celia coming up, and below there was Mr. Brooke,[15] exchanging welcomes and congratulations with Mr. Casaubon.

"Dodo!"[16] said Celia, in her quiet staccato; then kissed her sister, whose arms encircled her, and said no more. I think they both cried a little in a furtive manner, while Dorothea ran down-stairs to greet her uncle.

"I need not ask how you are, my dear," said Mr. Brooke, after kissing her forehead. "Rome has agreed with you, I see—happiness, frescos,[17] the antique—that sort of thing. Well, it's very pleasant to have you back again, and you understand all about art now, eh? But Casaubon is a little pale, I tell him—a little pale, you know. Studying hard in his holidays is carrying it rather too far. I overdid it at one time"—Mr. Brooke still held Dorothea's hand, but had turned his face to Mr. Casaubon—"about topography, ruins, temples—I thought I had a clew, but I saw it would carry me too far, and nothing might come of it. You may go any length in that sort of thing, and nothing may come of it, you know."

Dorothea's eyes also were turned up to her husband's face with some anxiety at the idea that those who saw him afresh after absence might be aware of signs which she had not noticed.

"Nothing to alarm you, my dear," said Mr. Brooke, observing her expression. "A little English beef and mutton will soon make a difference. It was all very well to look pale, sitting for the portrait of Aquinas,[18] you know—we got your letter just in time. But Aquinas, now—he was a little too subtle, wasn't he? Does anybody read Aquinas?"

"He is not indeed an author adapted to superficial minds," said Mr. Casaubon, meeting these timely questions with dignified patience.

"You would like coffee in your own room, uncle?" said Dorothea, coming to the rescue.

"Yes; and you must go to Celia: she has great news to tell you, you know. I leave it all to her."

The blue-green boudoir looked much more cheerful when Celia was seated there in a pelisse exactly like her sister's, surveying the cameos with a placid satisfaction, while the conversation passed on to other topics.

"Do you think it nice to go to Rome on a wedding journey?" said Celia, with her ready delicate blush which Dorothea was used to on the smallest occasions.

"It would not suit all—not you, dear, for example," said Dorothea, quietly. No one would ever know what she thought of a wedding journey to Rome.

"Mrs. Cadwallader[19] says it is nonsense, people going a long journey when they are married. She says they get tired to death of each other, and can't quarrel comfortably, as they would at home. And Lady Chettam says she went to Bath." Celia's color changed again and again—seemed to come and go with tidings from the heart, as it a running messenger had been.

It must mean more than Celia's blushing usually did.

"Celia! has something happened?" said Dorothea, in a tone full of sisterly feeling. "Have you really any great news to tell me?"

"It was because you went away, Dodo. Then there was nobody but me for Sir James[20] to talk to," said Celia, with a certain roguishness in her eyes.

"I understand. It is as I used to hope and believe," said Dorothea, taking her sister's face between her hands, and looking at her half anxiously. Celia's marriage seemed more serious than it used to do.

"It was only three days ago," said Celia. "And Lady Chettam is very kind."

"And you are very happy?"

"Yes. We are not going to be married yet. Because everything is to be got ready. And I don't want to be married so very soon, because I think it is nice to be engaged. And we shall be married all our lives after."

"I do believe you could not marry better, Kitty. Sir James is a good, honorable man," said Dorothea, warmly.

"He has gone on with the cottages, Dodo. He will tell you about them when he comes. Shall you be glad to see him?"

"Of course I shall. How can you ask me?"

"Only I was afraid you would be getting so learned," said Celia, regarding Mr. Casaubon's learning as a kind of damp which might in due time saturate a neighboring body.

☞ Notes

1. The epigram is supposed to be written by George Eliot herself.
2. **Lowick Manor:** the house of Mr. Casaubon.
3. **the blue-green boudoir:** the bow-windowed room with portraits of old Casaubon members on the wall. In Chapter 9 Dorothea has chosen it as her bedroom.
4. **polite literature:** classic works of ancient Greece and Rome.
5. **immovable imitations of books:** not real books or only having the appearance of books.
6. **cameo-cases:** jewelry containers.
7. **Celia:** Dorothea's younger sister.
8. **bridal felicity:** the happiness of marriage.
9. **the vapor-walled landscape:** the landscape covered with white snow.
10. **in full communion:** share completely or communicate perfectly.
11. **the delicious repose of the soul on a complete superior:** referring to Dorothea's dream of fulfilling something great by marrying somebody superior, somebody who can guide her.
12. **the low arch of dun vapor:** the gray sky which seems low because of the dull weather.
13. **where the sense of connection … her energies:** the desire to live a colorful and meaningful life was only a dream and there was hardly anything she could spend her energies on.
14. **miniatures:** very small paintings, usually of persons.
15. **Mr. Brooke:** Dorothea's uncle.
16. **Dodo:** Dorothea's nickname.
17. **frescos:** paintings made on walls by using watercolor paint on a surface of wet plaster.
18. **Aquinas:** St. Thomas Aquinas (ca. 1225-1274), Italian philosopher, priest and Doctor of the Church.
19. **Mrs. Cadwallader:** Wife of Mr. Cadwallader, also rather kind-hearted, though with a tendency to be a bit of a busy-body. She knows all about neighborhood affairs,

showing perhaps a little too much interest in other people's business.

20. **Sir James:** That is Sir James Chettam, who begins pursuing Dorothea at the beginning of the novel but gives her up for her sister Celia when Dorothea becomes engaged to Casaubon. Chettam is an affable, kind man, who listens ardently to Dorothea's plans for improving the life of rural folk, and then takes great measures to make her plans a reality.

☞ Study questions

1. From what journey did Mr. and Mrs. Casaubon return?
2. In what season does Dorothea start her married life?
3. How does Dorothea feel when she faces the chill, colorless, narrowed landscape, the shrunken furniture, the never-read books, and the ghostly stag in a pale fantastic world?
4. Why is Dorothea not happy when everything is done for her?
5. Why does Dorothea show so much sympathy for her husband's aunt Julia when she observed her portrait on the wall?
6. Do you think Dorothea has found her marriage to be a mistake in this chapter? How?
7. Who have paid a visit to her on the second day of her return from the journey?

☞ Essay topics

1. What conflicts does Dorothea experience between her ideals and her realities? How do these conflicts relate to marriage?
2. Why does Dorothea's marriage fail? Why did she get married to Casaubon? Consider the contradictions between what she needs and what she thinks she wants in a spouse.

7.9 Matthew Arnold

7.9.1 Life and career

Arnold (1822-1888) was born in Middlesex, the son of Dr. Thomas Arnold who later became the famous headmaster of Rugby School. Matthew Arnold was one of the most thoroughly educated young men in the formal institutions of the Victorian middle classes, since he went to both Winchester and Rugby. In 1841, he entered Balliol College, Oxford, where he took the prize for original poetry. After graduation Arnold taught classics for a short time at Rugby and then became private secretary to Lord Lansdoune who was minister of public instruction. In 1851, Arnold began to serve as an inspector of schools in which he labored very hard and faithfully, partly at the expense of his creative work. In 1857, he was elected to the professorship of poetry at Oxford, which he held for ten years. Arnold visited the Continent repeatedly in the interests of education and journeyed twice to the United States as a lecturer, in 1883 and 1886. His life was marked by few striking outward events. His marriage and home were happy.

Arnold started his literary career as a poet. His first volume of verse *The Strayed Reveller and Other Poems* appeared in 1849. His poetical influence increased with the publication in 1853 of a collection of poems under his own name. An elevated, meditative, and elegiac tone is characteristic of his poetry. In form and spirit his poetry is one of the very best reflections of that of Greece, dominated by thought, dignified, and polished with the utmost care. Most of his poetic production is beautiful, often formally impressive, yet he found it difficult to forge an industrial voice, perhaps because he found it difficult to come to terms with the Victorian world. In the "Memorial Verses" written after Wordsworth's death in 1850, "the freshness of the early world" is found to be staled by the adult's "time-ridden consciousness." In his greatest poem, *Dover Beach*, dealing with the slow ebb of religious faith, there is no sense of anguished personal involvement. The poem is not about how he lost his faith, but about what it is like to live in an age in which faith is decaying. Arnold defined poetry as a criticism of life; in his own verse, he realized his definition. His poetry is the expression of his long and tragic spiritual struggle; it is also the expression of a temporary mood of questioning protest. As a poet Arnold is generally admitted to rank among the Victorians next after Tennyson and Browning.

Arnold wrote almost no poetry after the age of forty, turning to the great prose works such as *Culture and Anarchy* (1869) which make him one of the great commentators on Victorian commercial civilization. With characteristic self-confidence and obeying his inherited tendency to didacticism, he appointed himself, in effect, a critic of English national life, beliefs, and taste, and set out to instruct the public in matters of literature, social relations, politics and religion. During his later years he wrote many critical essays, which fall into four classes, literary, social, religious, and political. Some of his essays, like those on "The Function of Criticism at the Present Time," "Wordsworth," and "Byron," are among the best in English, while his "Essays on Translating Homer" present the most famous existing interpretation of the spirit and style of the great Greek epics. As a critic, Arnold defended culture against scientific materialism. He believed that literature shaped culture. His essays and lectures brought a broad and humane critical intelligence to bear on the discussion of literature, social questions and issues of religious belief. His style is one of the most charming features of his prose work. Clear, direct, and elegant, it reflects most attractively his own high breeding; but it is also eminently forceful, and marked by very skilful emphasis and reiteration.

Arnold lived in a transitional time, when the old faith was dead, and the new one as yet "powerless to be born." The restless stirrings of his age appeared to him pitifully unintelligent and devoid of results. He found all modern life a chaos of physical misery and of the selfish, unenlightened, violent expression of untrained wills. For the cure of these evils Arnold's proposed remedy was Culture, which would train, broaden, and refine the whole spirit, including the emotions as well as the intellect, into sympathy with all the highest ideals, and therefore into inward peace and satisfaction.

7.9.2 "Dover Beach"[1]

The sea is calm tonight.
The tide is full, the moon lies fair
Upon the straits[2]—on the French coast the light
Gleams and is gone; the cliffs of England stand,
Glimmering and vast, out in the tranquil bay.
Come to the window, sweet is the night air!
Only, from the long line of spray
Where the sea meets the moon-blanched[3] land,
Listen! you hear the grating roar[4]
Of pebbles which the waves draw back, and fling,
At their return, up the high strand,[5]
Begin, and cease, and then again begin,
With tremulous cadence slow, and bring
The eternal note of sadness in.

Sophocles[6] long ago
Heard it on the Aegean,[7] and it brought
Into his mind the turbid[8] ebb and flow
Of human misery; we
Find also in the sound a thought,
Hearing it by this distant northern sea.

The Sea of Faith
Was once, too, at the full, and round earth's shore
Lay like the folds of a bright girdle furled.[9]
But now I only hear
Its melancholy, long, withdrawing roar,
Retreating, to the breath
Of the night wind, down the vast edges drear
And naked shingles[10] of the world.

Ah, love, let us be true
To one another! for the world, which seems
To lie before us like a land of dreams,
So various, so beautiful, so new,
Hath really neither joy, nor love, nor light,
Nor certitude, nor peace, nor help for pain;
And we are here as on a darkling[11] plain
Swept with confused alarms of struggle and flight,
Where ignorant armies[12] clash by night.

☞ Notes

1. The poem is written in irregular metrical form and rhyme scheme.
2. **the straits:** referring to the Strait of Dover, between England and France.
3. **moon-blanched:** become white in the moon light.
4. **the grating roar:** the rubbing pebbles give forth a rumbling sound. Cf. Wordsworth's "It Is a Beauteous Evening": "listen! the mighty Being is awake, /And doth with his eternal motion make/A sound like thunder—everlastingly."
5. **the high strand:** upper part of a coastline, perhaps what lies just above the tide-marks.
6. **Sophocles:** (ca. 496-405 B. C.) a Greek tragic dramatist, author of *Oedipus* and *Antigone*.
7. **Aegean:** the Aegean Sea, the name used by the Greeks and Romans for that part of the Mediterranean Sea between Asia Minor and Greece.
8. **turbid:** confused.
9. **like the folds of a bright girdle furled:** At high tide the water encircles the shore like the folds of bright clothing which have been compressed.
10. **shingles**: beach gravel composed of water-worn stones or pebbles.
11. **darkling**: lying in darkness.
12. **ignorant armies**: Some scholars think that it might refer to the revolution of 1848 or a reference to the siege of Rome by the French in 1849.

☞ Study questions

1. Who is the speaker of the poem?
2. What is the situation or setting?
3. At what point does Arnold's mimetic description of nature turn into an investigation of emotional and spiritual matters?
4. Describe the mood of the opening lines of the poem. Where and why does the mood

shift?

5. What "social prophecy" does Arnold make about the consequences of Europe's loss of Christian faith?
6. How would you characterize the central concern of the poem?
7. How are the themes of the poem reflected in the arrangement of stanzas?
8. What is the speaker's assessment of the world? How do the sounds of the last stanza reinforce its meaning?

☞ **Essay topics**

1. In what way has the world not changed since the time of Sophocles, according to Arnold?
2. What does Arnold mean by the "Sea of Faith"? Why does he say it was once full but is now withdrawing?
3. Do you think the view of human life presented in "Dover Beach" is applicable to today's world? Why or why not?

7.10 Gerard Manley Hopkins

7.10.1 Life and career

Hopkins (1844-1889) was born into a middle-class family of Welsh ancestry. His father was an insurance agent. He received his education first at Highgate School, then at Oxford. While studying classics at Oxford, he involved himself in the Oxford Movement. In 1866, following the example of Newman, he converted to Roman Catholicism, and in 1868 he decided to enter the priesthood. Yet, Oxford gave him the chance to have Walter Pater as his tutor, thus converting himself to the cult of art. It was also at Oxford that he forged the friendship with Robert Bridges which would be of importance in his development as a poet. In 1882 Hopkins became a teacher at Mount St. Mary's College, Sheffield, and Stoneyhurst College, Lancashire, from where he progressed to professor of Greek at University College Dublin, though remaining a priest. During his lifetime he wrote a fairly small body of poetry and some prose works; but he published none of his poems. It was only through the efforts of his friend, Bridges, that his collected verse was published in 1918.

Hopkins wrote poems between 1875 and 1889. The themes of his poetry concern the relationship of man to God and the problem of man's suffering in a world created by God. His deeply moving poems are the last "dark" sonnets; for here the ruptured syntax, the inversions and the sound patterning answer a violence of spiritual conflict between faith and doubt as intense as any in English poetry. These poems are powerful statements of love and loss, of suffering and un-fulfillment, reflecting the contradictory feelings between his desire for an outlet for his art and his painful awareness of his priestly vocation.

Hopkins was also a great nature poet. The striking quality of his poetry lay in its energy which resulted from his close observation of and his excitement about the natural world. Hopkins could feel nature's beauty upon his pulses, and there was a reciprocal relationship between him and nature. Poems like "Spring," "The Starlight Night," "The Sea and the Skylark," "The Windhover" and "Pied Beauty" are very remarkable nature poems, which communicate the excitement and individuality most immediately.

Hopkins was an important technical innovator in poetry writing. His experiment in meter resulted in "Sprung Rhythm" which allowed for the use in a line of verse of "either monosyllabic stressed feet or of stressed feet with any number of weak or slack syllables." In Hopkins' opinion, this "Sprung Rhythm" could achieve a flexibility rarely found in conventional meter. Hopkins also made full use of resources of language and imagery in his poetry writing. He forced the syntax to fit his thought by omitting the articles, pronouns, by breaking up combinations of words or by creating puns. His visional imagination was also powerful; consequently images play an important part in his poetry.

Hopkins' unconventional rhythm and syntax made his poetry seem very modern, but his concern with the imagination's shaping of the natural and religious world put him in the Victorian tradition.

7.10.2 "The Windhover"[1]

To Christ Our Lord

I caught this morning morning's minion,[2] king-
  dom of daylight's dauphin,[3] dapple-dawn-drawn Falcon, in his riding
  Of the rolling level underneath him steady air, and striding
High there, how he rung upon the rein of a wimpling wing[4]
In his ecstasy! then off, off forth on swing,
  As a skate's heel sweeps smooth on a bow-bend: the hurl and gliding
  Rebuffed the big wind. My heart in hiding
Stirred for a bird,—the achieve of, the mastery of the thing!

Brute beauty and valor and act, oh, air, pride, plume, here
  Buckle![5] AND[6] the fire that breaks from thee then, a billion
Times told lovelier, more dangerous, O my chevalier!

  No wonder of it: sheer plod makes plough down sillion[7]
Shine, and blue-bleak embers, ah my dear,

Fall, gall[8] themselves, and gash gold-vermillion.

☞ Notes

1. This poem is a sonnet. The octet (1st 8 lines) focuses on the bird in flight; the sestet (last 6 lines) moralizes. "Windhover" is a falcon or kestrel, which can hover in the wind by vibrating its wings, glide sideways, and dart for prey.
2. **minion:** darling.
3. **dauphin:** heir (literarily, the title of the eldest son of the King of France); the word carries overtones of chivalry and splendor.
4. **how he rung upon the rein of a wimpling wing:** There is an implied comparison to a horse circling around its trainer at the end of a long rein. **"Wimpling":** rippling.
5. **Buckle:** The verb can be read as imperative or indicative. All three meanings of "buckle" are relevant: to prepare for action, to fasten together, to collapse.
6. **AND:** Hopkins emphasizes the "AND" to draw attention from the admiration of the bird and to the sense of Christ behind it which that admiration brings. A movement from appreciation of the life of nature to a religious sense of the God reflected in nature is found in very many of Hopkins' poems.
7. **sillion:** The ridge between two furrows of a plowed field. Hopkins uses this archaic word perhaps to suggest an overtone from "silica" (the mineral which in the form of gleaming particles of quartz often makes dull rocks shine).
8. **gall:** break the surface of.

☞ Study questions

1. How does the speaker describe the falcon?
2. Why does the bird strike him as the crown prince ("dauphin") of the kingdom?
3. What does the speaker feel when he sees the bird riding like a horse in the sky?
4. What images does Hopkins use in this poem? Are they appropriate to the themes of the poem?
5. What does Hopkins believe about the presence of God in the natural world?
6. What does the octet (the first 8 lines) of this poem focus on?
7. How does the sestet (the final 6 lines) complete the poem's meaning?

7.11 Thomas Hardy

7.11.1 Life and career

Hardy (1840-1928) was born near Dorchester, the son of a stonemason. Delicate and precocious, he was educated at a private school in Dorchester, a few miles from his home. When he reached 16, his father apprenticed him to a local architect who specialized in restoring old churches. Six years later he moved to London, where he studied Gothic architecture under Sir Arthur Blomfield. During his spare time, he continued his general education, by attending classes and reading widely: language, literature, philosophy and art. It was also at this time that Hardy began to write poetry. He submitted his early poems to several magazines, but they were all rejected. In 1870 Hardy met Emma Gifford in Cornwall. They fell in love and married four years later.

Hardy never took architecture as his desired profession. What he was interested was poetry. But he could not make a living by writing poetry. So he turned to write novels. His first novel *Desperate Remedies* was published in 1871. However, the real success came with *Under the Greenwood Tree* (1872). The publication of *Far from the Madding Crowd* in 1874 finally enabled him to give up architecture for writing. In the following twenty-three years he produced over ten local-colored novels. In 1896 when he was tired of those hostile criticisms against his last two novels: *Tess of the d'Urbervilles* (1891) and *Jude the Obscure* (1896), Hardy returned to his first love—poetry writing. From then on, he devoted himself to poetic creation. Of the eight volumes by Hardy—918 poems in all—the most famous is *The Dynasts*, a long epic-drama about the Napoleonic Wars. On January 11, 1928, this last important Victorian novelist died. He was buried with impressive ceremonies in the Poet's Corner in Westminster Abbey.

Hardy's novels are all Victorian in date. Most of them are set in Wessex, the fictional primitive and crude rural region which is really the home place he both loves and hates. His early novels such as *Desperate Remedies*, *Under the Greenwood Tree*, *A Pair of Blue Eyes* (1873) and *Far from the Madding Crowd* are mostly cheerful and idyllic. They are about rural life where young women seek their husbands. However, in his later novels, such as *The Return of the Native* (1878), *The Mayor of Casterbridge* (1886), *Tess of d'Urbervilles* (1891) and *Jude the Obscure* (1896), the tragic sense becomes the keynote. The conflict between the traditional and the modern is brought to the center of the stage. In *Tess of the d'Urbervilles*, Tess, the heroine, is depicted as a victim of the society. Being a beautiful, innocent, and hard-working country girl, she is easily taken in and abused by the hypocritical bourgeoisie, constantly suppressed by the social conventions and moral values of the day, and eventually executed by the unfair legal system of the society. Her absolute obedience to Angel as her husband and her willing suffering and sacrifice to him is not only her weakness in character but also an inevitability in a girl of her upbringing. And most important of all, it is the poverty of the family that forces her to improper relations once and again with Alec, and finally, to his murder and her execution. In this sense, she is cornered and driven into dead-end by the destructive social forces incarnated in the characters of Alec and Angel, with one depriving her of her virginity and purity and the other forcing her back into an immoral relationship and then, catching her at it, reducing her to desperation and self-destruction.

Living at the turn of the century, Hardy is often regarded as a transitional writer. In his novels, there is an apparent nostalgic touch in his description of the simple and beautiful though primitive rural life, which was gradually declining and disappearing as England marched into an industrial country. And with those traditional characters he is always sympathetic. On the other hand, the immense impact of scientific discoveries and modern philosophic thoughts upon the man is quite obvious, too. He also believed that man's fate is pre-determinedly tragic, driven by a combined force of nature and culture.

In his youth, Hardy was very interested in Darwin, Huxley, Spencer, and other scientists and philosophers of the new school. He read Darwin's *Origin of Species* and accepted his theory of "survival of the fittest." His reading of Spencer's *First Principle* inspired his pessimistic determinism and led him to the belief that man's fate was pre-determinedly tragic. Their influence led him to accept a reluctant agnosticism and to see the world as the expression of a mysterious, unconscious "will" uncaring for the individual. The blind thrusts of this indifferent universe, the impulses of the "will" and the operation of chance seemed to him to belong to the realm of evil.

In his works, man is shown driven by a combined force of "nature," both inside and outside, and inevitably bound by his own inherent nature and hereditary traits which prompt him to go and search for some specific happiness or success and set him in conflict with the environment. The outside nature is shown as some mysterious supernatural force, very powerful but half-blind, impulsive and uncaring to the individual's will, passion and suffering. Man proves impotent before Fate. No matter how hard he tries, he seldom escapes his ordained destiny. This pessimistic view of life predominates most of his works and earns him a reputation as a naturalistic writer.

Though naturalism plays an important part in some of his works, Hardy is never far away from the real life and the existing society. Most of his works are devoted to a realistic presentation of life, and there is often bitter and sharp criticism and even open defiance of the wicked, hypocritical and corrupted Victorian institution, convention and morality which strangle the individual will and destroy natural human emotions and relationships. The conflicts between the traditional and the modern, between the old rural value of respectability and honesty and the new utilitarian commercialism, between the old, false social moral and the natural human passion, etc. are all closely set in a realistic background true to the very time and the very place.

Hardy is a great painter of nature. In his hand, nature assumes the form of life and becomes a most powerful, forbidding force with its own life and will. His heroes and heroines, those unfortunate young men and women in their desperate struggle for personal fulfillment and happiness, are all vividly and realistically depicted. They all seem to possess a kind of exquisitely sensuous beauty. They are not only individual cases but also of universal truth. Their plight is not just their own; it applies to any one, any age. And finally, all the works of Hardy are noted for the rustic dialect and a poetic flavor which fits well into their perfectly designed architectural structures. They are the product of a conscientious artist.

7. 11. 2 "The Darkling[1] Thrush"

I leant upon a coppice gate[2]
  When Frost was specter-gray,
And Winter's dregs made desolate
  The weakening eye of day.
The tangled bine-stems[3] scored the sky
  Like strings of broken lyres,
And all mankind that haunted nigh
  Had sought their household fires.

The land's sharp features seemed to be
  The Century's corpse[4] outleant, [5]
His crypt the cloudy canopy,
  The wind his death-lament.
The ancient pulse of germ[6] and birth
  Was shrunken hard and dry,
And every spirit upon earth
  Seemed fervorless as I.

At once a voice arose among
  The bleak twigs overhead
In a full-hearted evensong
  Of joy illimited;
An aged thrush, frail, gaunt, and small,
  In blast-beruffled plume,
Had chosen thus to fling his soul
  Upon the growing gloom.

So little cause for carollings
  Of such ecstatic sound
Was written on terrestrial things
  Afar or nigh around,

That I could think there trembled through
  His happy good-night air
Some blessed Hope, whereof he knew
  And I was unaware.

☞ Notes

1. **darkling:** in the dark.
2. **coppice gate:** a gate leading to a coppice, which is a thicket or small wood.
3. **bine-stems:** twining stems of shrubs.
4. **The Century's corpse:** This poem was written on December 31, 1900, the last day of the 19th century.
5. **outleant:** outstretched.
6. **germ:** seed or bud.

☞ Study questions

1. How does the speaker feel about the approaching Twentieth Century?
2. How would you describe nature as it is presented in the first and second stanzas?
3. Why is it more effective for the thrush to be old and frail than young and strong?
4. In what way is the condition of nature a mirror of the speaker's own frame of mind?
5. In what ways are the poet and the thrush both singers? What other similarities do they have?
6. How does the song of the thrush differ from the speaker's "song" in the first two stanzas?
7. What does this poem suggest about our human position in nature?

7.11.3 An excerpt from *Tess of the d'Urbervilles*

Chapter 35

Her narrative ended; [1] even its re-assertions and secondary explanations were done. Tess's voice throughout had hardly risen higher than its opening tone; there had been no exculpatory phrase of any kind, and she had not wept.

But the complexion even of external things seemed to suffer transmutation[2] as her announcement progressed. The fire in the grate looked impish—demoniacally funny, as if it did not care in the least about her strait. The fender grinned idly, as if it too did not care. The light from the water-bottle was merely engaged in a chromatic problem. [3] All material objects around announced their irresponsibility with terrible iteration. And yet nothing had changed since the moments when he had been kissing her; or rather, nothing in the substance of things. But the essence of things had changed. [4]

When she ceased the auricular impressions from their previous endearments seemed to hustle away into the corner of their brains, repeating themselves as echoes from a time of supremely purblind foolishness.[5]

Clare performed the irrelevant act of stirring the fire; the intelligence had not even yet got to the bottom of him.[6] After stirring the embers he rose to his feet; all the force of her disclosure had imparted itself now. His face had withered. In the strenuousness of his concentration he treadled fitfully on the floor. He could not, by any contrivance, think closely enough; that was the meaning of his vague movement. When he spoke it was in the most inadequate, commonplace voice of the many varied tones she had heard from him.

"Tess!"

"Yes, dearest."

"Am I to believe this? From your manner I am to take it as true. O you cannot be out of your mind! You ought to be! Yet you are not. ... My wife, my Tess—nothing in you warrants such a supposition as that?"

"I am not out of my mind," she said.

"And yet—" He looked vacantly at her, to resume with dazed senses: "Why didn't you tell me before? Ah, yes, you would have told me, in a way—but I hindered you, I remember!"

These and other of his words were nothing but the perfunctory babble of the surface while the depths remained paralyzed. He turned away, and bent over a chair. Tess followed him to the middle of the room where he was, and stood there staring at him with eyes that did not weep. Presently she slid down upon her knees beside his foot, and from this position she crouched in a heap.

"In the name of our love, forgive me!" she whispered with a dry mouth. "I have forgiven you for the same!"

And, as he did not answer, she said again—

"Forgive me as you are forgiven! *I forgive you*, Angel."

"You—yes, you do."

"But you do not forgive me?"

"O Tess, forgiveness does not apply to the case! You were one person; now you are another. My God—how can forgiveness meet such a grotesque—prestidigitation[7] as that!"

He paused, contemplating this definition; then suddenly broke into horrible laughter—as unnatural and ghastly as a laugh in hell.

"Don't—don't! It kills me quite, that!" she shrieked. "O have mercy upon me—have mercy!"

He did not answer; and, sickly white, she jumped up.

"Angel, Angel! what do you mean by that laugh?" she cried out. "Do you know what this is to me?"

He shook his head.

"I have been hoping, longing, praying, to make you happy! I have thought what joy it will be to do it, what an unworthy wife I shall be if I do not! That's what I have felt, Angel!"

"I know that."

"I thought, Angel, that you loved me—me, my very self! If it is I you do love, O how can it be that you look and speak so? It frightens me! Having begun to love you, I love you for ever—in all changes, in all disgraces, because you are yourself. I ask no more. Then how can you, O my own husband, stop loving me?"

"I repeat, the woman I have been loving is not you."

"But who?"

"Another woman in your shape."

She perceived in his words the realization of her own apprehensive foreboding in former times. He looked upon her as a species of imposter; a guilty woman in the guise of an innocent one. Terror was upon her white face as she saw it; her cheek was flaccid,[8] and her mouth had almost the aspect of a round little hole. The horrible sense of his view of her so deadened her that she staggered; and he stepped forward, thinking she was going to fall.

"Sit down, sit down," he said gently. "You are ill; and it is natural that you should be."

She did sit down, without knowing where she was, that strained look still upon her face, and her eyes such as to make his flesh creep.

"I don't belong to you any more, then; do I, Angel?" she asked helplessly. "It is not me, but another woman like me that he loved, he says."

The image raised caused her to take pity upon herself as one who was ill-used. Her eyes filled as she regarded her position further; she turned round and burst into a flood of self-sympathetic tears.

Clare was relieved at this change, for the effect on her of what had happened was beginning to be a trouble to him only less than the woe of the disclosure itself. He waited patiently, apathetically, till the violence of her grief had worn itself out, and her rush of weeping had lessened to a catching gasp at intervals.

"Angel," she said suddenly, in her natural tones, the insane, dry voice of terror having left her now. "Angel, am I too wicked for you and me to live together?"

"I have not been able to think what we can do."

"I shan't ask you to let me live with you, Angel, because I have no right to! I shall not write to mother and sisters to say we be married, as I said I would do; and I shan't finish the good-hussif[9] I cut out and meant to make while we were in lodgings."

"Shan't you?"

"No, I shan't do anything, unless you order me to; and if you go away from me I shall not follow 'ee; and if you never speak to me any more I shall not ask why, unless you tell me I may."

"And if I order you to do anything?"

"I will obey you like your wretched slave, even if it is to lie down and die."

"You are very good. But it strikes me that there is a want of harmony between your present mood of self-sacrifice and your past mood of self-preservation."

These were the first words of antagonism. To fling elaborate sarcasms at Tess, however, was much like flinging them at a dog or cat. The charms of their subtlety passed by her unappreciated, and she only received them as inimical sounds which meant that anger ruled. She remained mute, not knowing that he was smothering his affection for her. She hardly observed that a tear descended slowly upon his cheek, a tear so large that it magnified the pores of the skin over which it rolled, like the object lens of a microscope. Meanwhile re-illumination as to the terrible and total change that her confession had wrought in his life, in his universe, returned to him, and he tried desperately to advance among the new conditions in which he stood. Some consequent action was necessary; yet what?

"Tess," he said, as gently as he could speak, "I cannot stay—in this room—just now. I will walk out a little way."

He quietly left the room, and the two glasses of wine that he had poured out for their supper—one for her, one for him—remained on the table untasted. This was what their Agape[10] had come to. At tea, two or three hours earlier, they had, in the freakishness of affection, drunk from one cup.

The closing of the door behind him, gently as it had been pulled to, roused Tess from her stupor. He was gone; she could not stay. Hastily flinging her cloak around her she opened the door and followed, putting out the candles as if she were never coming back. The rain was over and the night was now clear.

She was soon close at his heels, for Clare walked slowly and without purpose. His form beside her light gray figure looked black, sinister, and forbidding, and she felt as sarcasm the touch of the jewels of which she had been momentarily so proud. Clare turned at hearing her footsteps, but his recognition of her presence seemed to make no difference to him, and he went on over the five yawning arches of the great bridge in front of the house.

The cow and horse tracks in the road were full of water, and rain having been enough to charge them, but not enough to wash them away. Across these minute pools the reflected stars flitted in a quick transit as she passed; she would not have known they were shining overhead if she had not seen them there—the vastest things of the universe imaged in objects so mean. [11]

The place to which they had traveled today was in the same valley as Talbothays, but some miles lower down the river; and the surroundings being open she kept easily in sight of him. Away from the house the road wound through the meads, and along these she followed Clare without any attempt to come up with him or to attract him, but with dumb and vacant fidelity.

At last, however, her listless walk brought her up alongside him, and still he said nothing. The cruelty of fooled honesty is often great after enlightenment, and it was mighty in Clare now. The outdoor air had apparently taken away from him all tendency to act on impulse; she knew that he saw her without irradiation—in all her bareness; that Time was chanting his satiric psalm at her then—

Behold, when thy face is made bare, he that loved thee shall hate;
Thy face shall be no more fair at the fall of thy fate
For thy life shall fall as a leaf and be shed as the rain;
And the veil of thine head shall be grief, and the crown shall be pain. [12]

He was still intently thinking, and her companionship had now insufficient power to break or divert the strain of thought. What a weak thing her presence must have become to him! She could not help addressing Clare.

"What have I done—what have I done! I have not told of anything that interferes with or belies my love for you. You don't think I planned it, do you? It is in your own mind what you are angry at, Angel; it is not in me. O, it is not in me, and I am not that deceitful woman you think me!"

"H'm—well. Not deceitful, my wife; but not the same. No, not the same. But do not make me reproach you. I have sworn that I will not; and I will do everything to avoid it."

But she went on pleading in her distraction; and perhaps said things that would have been better left to silence.

"Angel! —Angel! I was a child—a child when it happened! I knew nothing of men."

"You were more sinned against than sinning, [13] that I admit."

"Then will you not forgive me?"

"I do forgive you, but forgiveness is not all."

"And love me?"

To this question he did not answer.

"O Angel—my mother says that it sometimes happens so! —she knows several cases where they were worse than I, and the husband has not minded it much—has got over it at least. And yet the woman had not loved him as I do you!"

"Don't, Tess; don't argue. Different societies, different manners. You almost make me say you are an unapprehending peasant woman, who have never been initiated into the proportions of social things.[14] You don't know what you say."

"I am only a peasant by position, not by nature!"

She spoke with an impulse to anger, but it went as it came.

"So much the worse for you. I think that parson[15] who unearthed your pedigree would have done better if he had held his tongue. I cannot help associating your decline as a family with this other fact—of your want of firmness. Decrepit families imply decrepit wills, decrepit conduct. Heaven, why did you give me a handle for despising you more by informing me of your descent! Here was I thinking you a new-sprung child of nature; there were you, the belated seedling of an effete aristocracy!"[16]

"Lots of families are as bad as mine in that! Retty's family were once large landowners, and so were Dairyman Billett's. And the Debbyhouses, who now are carters, were once the De Bayeux family. You find such as I everywhere; 'tis a feature of our county,[17] and I can't help it."

"So much the worse for the county."

She took these reproaches in their bulk simply, not in their particulars; he did not love her as he had loved her hitherto, and to all else she was indifferent.

They wandered on again in silence. It was said afterwards that a cottager of Wellbridge, who went out late that night for a doctor, met two lovers in the pastures, walking very slowly, without converse, one behind the other, as in a funeral procession, and the glimpse that he obtained of their faces seemed to denote that they were anxious and sad. Returning later, he passed them again in the same field, progressing just as slowly, and as regardless of the hour and of the cheerless night as before. It was only on account of his preoccupation with his own affairs, and the illness in his house, that he did not bear in mind the curious incident, which, however, he recalled a long while after.

During the interval of the cottager's going and coming, she had said to her husband—

"I don't see how I can help being the cause of much misery to you all your life. The river is down there. I can put an end to myself in it. I am not afraid."

"I don't wish to add murder to my other follies,[18]" he said.

"I will leave something to show that I did it myself—on account of my shame. They will not blame you then."

"Don't speak so absurdly—I wish not to hear it. It is nonsense to have such thoughts in this kind of case, which is rather one for satirical laughter than for tragedy. You don't in the least understand the quality of the mishap. It would be viewed in the light of a joke by nine-tenths of the world if it were known. Please oblige me by returning to the house, and going to bed."

"I will," said she dutifully.

They had rambled round by a road which led to the well-known ruins of the Cistercian abbey[19] behind the mill, the latter having, in centuries past, been attached to the monastic establishment. The mill still worked on, food being a perennial necessity; the abbey had perished, creeds being transient. One continually sees the ministration of the temporary outlasting the ministration of the eternal.[20] Their walk having been circuitous they were still not far from the house, and in obeying his direction she only had to reach the large stone bridge across the main river, and follow the road for a few yards. When she got back everything remained as she had left it, the fire being still burning. She did not stay downstairs for more than a minute, but proceeded to her chamber, whither the luggage had been taken. Here she sat down on the edge of the bed, looking blankly around, and presently began to undress. In removing the light towards the bedstead its rays fell upon the tester of white dimity;[21] something was hanging beneath it, and she lifted the candle to see what it was. A bough of mistletoe.[22] Angel had put it there; she knew that in an instant. This was the explanation of that mysterious parcel which it had been so difficult to pack and bring; whose contents he would not explain to her, saying that time would soon show her the purpose thereof. In his zest and his gaiety he had hung it there. How foolish and inopportune that mistletoe looked now.

Having nothing more to fear, having scarce anything to hope, for that he would relent there seemed no promise whatever, she lay down dully. When sorrow ceases to be speculative sleep sees her opportunity. Among so many happier moods which forbid repose this was a mood which welcomed it, and in a few minutes the lonely Tess forgot existence, surrounded by the aromatic stillness of the chamber that had once, possibly, been the bride-chamber of her own ancestry.

☞ Notes

1. **Her narrative ended:** Tess confessed her affair with Aleck to Angel.
2. **transmutation:** the change of one situation into another.
3. **chromatic problem:** that is, a problem about color.
4. **And yet nothing had changed …the essence of things had changed:** the sentences imply that things around Tess are still the same objects but they have made quite a different impression on her now.
5. **a time of supremely purblind foolishness:** a time of extremely blind foolishness, which refers to their early passionate love.
6. **the intelligence had not even yet got to the bottom of him:** Tess's confession stuns him so much that he is unable to recover from his normal wit.
7. **prestidigitation:** sleight of hand or any artful trick. The word used here to display Clare's feeling that Tess's confession has completely changed herself as if the case of

a prestidigitation.

8. **flaccid:** yielding to pressure readily or without resistance, or lacking firmness.
9. **good-hussif:** (Dial.) bag holding needle and thread.
10. **Agape:** (Greek) love-feast, as held by the early Christians.
11. **objects so mean:** referring to those pools of water in the road.
12. **Behold, when thy face ... pain:** quoted from a chorus in Swinburne's *Atalanta in Calydon*.
13. **You were more sinned against than sinning:** Cf. a man more sinned than sinning (*King Lear*, Ⅲ, 2).
14. **have never been initiated into the proportions of social things:** have never been taught the knowledge of social relationship between different ranks.
15. **parson:** Parson Tringham, who discovers Tess's kindred with the noble D'Urbervilles.
16. **an effete aristocracy:** an aristocracy who decays so much that he is unable in fertility.
17. **'tis a feature of our county:** It is a feature of our Dorsetshire, where there had been a great number of French descendents.
18. **other follies:** referring to Angel's love for and marriage to Tess.
19. **Cistercian abbey:** referring to an abbey in Dorsetshire, which was built by members of a monastic order founded by St. Robert of Molesme in 1098 at Citeaux, France, under an austere Benedictine rule.
20. **the ministration of the temporary outlasting the ministration of the eternal:** material things outlasting the spiritual things, such as religion.
21. **tester of white dimity:** canopy with white stripes (Dimity: stout cotton cloth, with raised pattern, often used for bed-hangings).
22. **mistletoe:** a green shrub with small white berries, which was traditionally believed to bring good luck and fertility. Angel's hanging some over the bed was a light-hearted gesture of paganism.

☞ Study questions

1. What effect does Tess's confession have on Angel?
2. Why is Angel unable to forgive Tess when she just bestowed the gift of forgiveness on him?
3. Why does Tess submit to Angel's anger and take no action to win him back?
4. Why does Angel blame Tess for her family background which he previously thought would make her acceptable to respectable middle class society?
5. What moral differences between men and women in the Victorian period does this chapter reflect?

☞ **Essay topics**

1. Discuss the character of Tess. To what extent is she a helpless victim?
2. How does Angel change in the novel?

7.12 Oscar Wilde

7.12.1 Life and career

Wilde(1854-1900) was born in Dublin, the son of a famous Irish surgeon. As a little boy, Wilde was educated at home. He then went to boarding school in 1864, attending Portora Royal School at Enniskillen. In 1871, Wilde began his study at Trinity College, Dublin. He left Ireland on graduating from Trinity with a First Class Degree in 1874. He moved to Oxford and continued his studies in Latin, Greek and Ancient History. In Oxford Wilde excelled in classics, wrote poetry, and incorporated the Bohemian life-style of his youth into a unique way of life. Also in Oxford, he came into direct contact with the art and philosophy of various strands of Aestheticism including the works of Pre-Raphaelite poets and painters, and the poetry of Swinburne. He was deeply impressed by John Ruskin and Walter Pater who taught him about the central importance of art in life. Wilde became particularly well known for his role in the aesthetic and decadent movements. In 1878 Wilde crowned his undergraduate career by winning the prestigious Newdigate Prize for Poetry.

After his graduation from Oxford, Wilde moved to London into fashionable cultural and social circles. As a leading member of the "art for art's sake" movement, he tried his hand at various literary activities: he published a book of poems, lectured in the United States of America on the new "English Renaissance in Art", and worked prolifically as a journalist in London. He was celebrated for his biting wit, flamboyant dress and glittering conversation. Wilde had become one of the most well-known personalities of his day. In 1884, Wilde married Constance Lloyd, a rich barrister's daughter, and they had two sons.

Afterwards he became the editor of *Woman's World*. During this time he published his most famous fairy tale *The Happy Prince and Other Tales* (1888); he also wrote essays championing the Aesthetic movement. His only novel, *The Picture of Dorian Gray*, a Faustian tale about beauty and youth, was published in 1891. Critics often claimed that there existed parallels between Wilde's and the protagonist's life. His real success with the larger public was as a dramatist with *Lady Windermere's Fan* at the St James's Theatre in 1892. It was followed by *A Woman of No Importance* (1893), *An Ideal Husband* (1895) and *The Importance of Being Earnest* (1895). Wilde, with little dramatic training, proved he had a natural talent for stagecraft and theatrical effects. That brilliant career of Wilde's was cut short in 1895 when he was involved into a homosexual scandal, which resulted in his two years of hard labor in prison. He emerged financially bankrupt and spiritually downcast. *The Ballad of Reading Gaol* (1898), the most powerful of all his poems, was written while he was in prison. The starkness of prison life and the desperation of people interned were revealed in beautifully cadenced language. Prison had ruined Wilde's health and when he was released he went into exile in France where he lived under the name Sebastian Melmoth. He died in 1900.

Throughout the course of his literary career, Wilde produced a variety of literary writings in poetry, fiction, drama, and critical essays. His works often reflect a close connection between his art and his own life. *The Importance of Being Earnest* is considered to be his greatest play, which is about two fashionable young gentlemen and their eventually successful courtship. In this play, Wilde chooses to satirize the life of the English aristocracy, a world with which he was personally familiar. His characters are typical Victorian snobs; they are often arrogant, overly proper, formal, and concerned with money. Lady Bracknell in particular embodies the stereotype of the Victorian English aristocrat. In basing his work on the problems and trials of marriage, Wilde deliberately pokes fun at the institution of marriage, which the aristocracy does not see as an organ of love but rather as a tool for achieving or sustaining social stature. This is the major theme of the play. *The Importance of Being Earnest* is often seen as providing a deep insight into London society at both its finest and its most absurd before the dawn of the twentieth century.

Wilde believed that art should not imitate life but art in an ugly age. He wrote, "To project one's soul into some gracious form" is "perhaps the most satisfying joy left to us in an age so limited and vulgar as our own, an age grossly carnal in its pleasures, and grossly common in its aims." He dared to challenge the English social ideals. In his deeply humane and subversive essay, *The Soul of Man Under Socialism*, Wilde, in fact, heaped scorn on piecemeal approaches to the social ills produced by capitalism. Of the reformers he said, "their remedies do not cure the disease: they merely prolong it. The proper aim is to try and reconstruct society on such a basis that poverty will be impossible." Following Walter Pater, he believed that art had nothing to do with morality, but should exist for its own sake. Artists should be left to pursue their art, without the involvement of the state. Private property should be abolished, since ownership hindered the development and spirit of art. He argued that human beings should cultivate their aesthetic sensibilities, their appreciation of beautiful artistry. His arguments were designed to shock. To assert that "all art is quite useless" and that "all art is immoral" was his provocative way of slaughtering the sacred cows of Victorian thinking on the subject. Life, he was saying, should consist of more than adherence to dull and restrictive notions of what was useful or moral. It should aspire to the freedom of art and the variety of experience it contains.

Wilde is one of the most accomplished writers of his generation. His importance resides both in his art and in his personality. His literary reputation is now as high as it was at the pinnacle of his achievement in the 1890s, and his biography has a unique cultural significance, particularly in the history of gay politics. His views on literature, art, and criticism and their relation to conduct are implicit or explicit in almost everything he wrote. As the most celebrated dramatist in the last decade of the 19th century, Wilde demonstrated a breaking away from the conventional well-made plays of the 1870s and 1880s. He expressed a satirical and bitter attitude towards the upper-class people by revealing their corruption, their snobbery, and their hypocrisy in his plays. In brilliance of verbal wit, Wilde is close akin to George Bernard Shaw.

7.12.2 An excerpt from Act I of *The Importance of Being Earnest*

LADY BRACKNELL. Good afternoon, dear Algernon, I hope you are behaving very well.

ALGERNON. I'm feeling very well, Aunt Augusta.

LADY BRACKNELL. That's not quite the same thing. In fact the two things rarely go together. [*sees* JACK *and bows to him with icy coldness.*]

ALGERNON. [*to* GWENDOLEN.] Dear me, you are smart! [1]

GWENDOLEN. I am always smart! Aren't I, Mr. Worthing?

JACK. You're quite perfect, Miss Fairfax.

GWENDOLEN. Oh! I hope I am not that. It would leave no room for developments, and I intend to develop in many directions. [GWENDOLEN *and* JACK *sit down together in the corner.*]

LADY BRACKNELL. I'm sorry if we are a little late, Algernon, but I was obliged to call on dear Lady Harbury. I hadn't been there since her poor husband's death. I never saw a woman so altered; she looks quite twenty years younger. And now I'll have a cup of tea, and one of those nice cucumber sandwiches you promised me.

ALGERNON. Certainly, Aunt Augusta. [*goes over to teatable.*]

LADY BRACKNELL. Won't you come and sit here, Gwendolen?

GWENDOLEN. Thanks, mamma,[2] I'm quite comfortable where I am.

ALGERNON. [*picking up empty plate in horror.*] Good heavens! Lane! Why are there no cucumber sandwiches? I ordered them specially.

LANE. [*gravely.*] There were no cucumbers in the market this morning, sir. I went down twice.

ALGERNON. No cucumbers!

LANE. No, sir. Not even for ready money.

ALGERNON. That will do, Lane, thank you.

LANE. Thank you, sir.

ALGERNON. I am greatly distressed, Aunt Augusta, about there being no cucumbers, not even for ready money.

LADY BRACKNELL. It really makes no matter, Algernon. I had some crumpets[3] with Lady Harbury, who seems to me to be living entirely for pleasure now.

ALGERNON. I hear her hair has turned quite gold from grief.

LADY BRACKNELL. It certainly has changed its color. From what cause I, of course, cannot say. [ALGERNON *crosses and hands tea.*] Thank you. I've quite a treat for you to-night, Algernon. I am going to send you down with Mary Farquhar. She is such a nice woman, and so attentive to her husband. It's delightful to watch them.

ALGERNON. I am afraid, Aunt Augusta, I shall have to give up the pleasure of dining with you tonight after all.

LADY BRACKNELL. [*frowning.*] I hope not, Algernon. It would put my table completely out. Your uncle would have to dine upstairs. Fortunately he is accustomed to that.

ALGERNON. It is a great bore, and, I need hardly say, a terrible disappointment to me, but the fact is I have just had a telegram to say that my poor friend Bunbury is very ill again. [*exchanges glances with* JACK.] They seem to think I should be with him.

LADY BRACKNELL. It is very strange. This Mr. Bunbury seems to suffer from curiously bad health.

ALGERNON. Yes; poor Bunbury is a dreadful invalid.

LADY BRACKNELL. Well, I must say, Algernon, that I think it is high time that Mr. Bunbury made up his mind whether he was going to live or to die. This shilly-shallying with the question is absurd. Nor do I in any way approve of the modern sympathy with invalids. I consider it morbid. Illness of any kind is hardly a thing to be encouraged in others. Health is the primary duty of life. I am always telling that to your poor uncle, but he never seems to take much notice ... as far as any improvement in his ailment goes. I should be much obliged if you would ask Mr. Bunbury, from me, to be kind enough not to have a relapse on Saturday, for I rely on you to arrange my music for me. It is my last reception, and one wants something that will encourage conversation, particularly at the end of the season[4] when every one has practically said whatever they had to say, which, in most cases, was probably not much.

ALGERNON. I'll speak to Bunbury, Aunt Augusta, if he is still conscious, and I think I can promise you he'll be all right by Saturday. Of course the music is a great difficulty. You see, if one plays good music, people don't listen, and if one plays bad music people don't talk. But I'll run over the program I've drawn out, if you will kindly come into the next room for a moment.

LADY BRACKNELL. Thank you, Algernon. It is very thoughtful of you. [*rising, and following* ALGERNON.] I'm sure the program will be delightful, after a few expurgations. French songs I cannot possibly allow. People always seem to think that they are improper, and either look shocked, which is vulgar, or laugh, which is worse. But German sounds a thoroughly respectable language, and indeed, I believe is so. Gwendolen, you will accompany me.

GWENDOLEN. Certainly, mamma.

[LADY BRACKNELL *and* ALGERNON *go into the music room,* GWENDOLEN *remains behind.*]

JACK. Charming day it has been, Miss Fairfax.

GWENDOLEN. Pray don't talk to me about the weather, Mr. Worthing. Whenever people talk to me about the weather, I always feel quite certain that they mean something else. And that makes me so nervous.

JACK. I do mean something else.

GWENDOLEN. I thought so. In fact, I am never wrong.

JACK. And I would like to be allowed to take advantage of Lady Bracknell's temporary absence …

GWENDOLEN. I would certainly advise you to do so. Mamma has a way of coming back suddenly into a room that I have often had to speak to her about.

JACK. [*nervously.*] Miss Fairfax, ever since I met you I have admired you more than any girl … I have ever met since … I met you.

GWENDOLEN. Yes, I am quite well aware of the fact. And I often wish that in public, at any rate, you had been more demonstrative. For me you have always had an irresistible fascination. Even before I met you I was far from indifferent to you. [JACK looks at her in amazement.] We live, as I hope you know, Mr. Worthing, in an age of ideals. The fact is constantly mentioned in the more expensive monthly magazines, and has reached the provincial pulpits, I am told; and my ideal has always been to love some one of the name of Ernest. There is something in that name that inspires absolute confidence. The moment Algernon first mentioned to me that he had a friend called Ernest, I knew I was destined to love you.

JACK. You really love me, Gwendolen?

GWENDOLEN. Passionately!

JACK. Darling! You don't know how happy you've made me.

GWENDOLEN. My own Ernest!

JACK. But you don't really mean to say that you couldn't love me if my name wasn't Ernest?

GWENDOLEN. But your name is Ernest.

JACK. Yes, I know it is. But supposing it was something else? Do you mean to say you couldn't love me then?

GWENDOLEN. [*glibly.*] Ah! that is clearly a metaphysical speculation, and like most metaphysical speculations has very little reference at all to the actual facts of real life, as we know them.

JACK. Personally, darling, to speak quite candidly, I don't much care about the name of Ernest ... I don't think the name suits me at all.

GWENDOLEN. It suits you perfectly. It is a divine name. It has a music of its own. It produces vibrations.

JACK. Well, really, Gwendolen, I must say that I think there are lots of other much nicer names. I think Jack, for instance, a charming name.

GWENDOLEN. Jack? ... No, there is very little music in the name Jack, if any at all, indeed. It does not thrill. It produces absolutely no vibrations ... I have known several Jacks, and they all, without exception, were more than usually plain. Besides, Jack is a notorious domesticity for John! And I pity any woman who is married to a man called John. She would probably never be allowed to know the entrancing pleasure of a single moment's solitude. The only really safe name is Ernest.

JACK. Gwendolen, I must get christened at once—I mean we must get married at once. There is no time to be lost.

GWENDOLEN. Married, Mr. Worthing?

JACK. [*astounded.*] Well ... surely. You know that I love you, and you led me to believe, Miss Fairfax, that you were not absolutely indifferent to me.

GWENDOLEN. I adore you. But you haven't proposed to me yet. Nothing has been said at all about marriage. The subject has not even been touched on.

JACK. Well ... may I propose to you now?

GWENDOLEN. I think it would be an admirable opportunity. And to spare you any possible disappointment, Mr. Worthing, I think it only fair to tell you quite frankly before-hand that I am fully determined to accept you.

JACK. Gwendolen!

GWENDOLEN. Yes, Mr. Worthing, what have you got to say to me?

JACK. You know what I have got to say to you.

GWENDOLEN. Yes, but you don't say it.

JACK. Gwendolen, will you marry me? [*goes on his knees.*]

GWENDOLEN. Of course I will, darling. How long you have been about it! I am afraid you have had very little experience in how to propose.

JACK. My own one, I have never loved any one in the world but you.

GWENDOLEN. Yes, but men often propose for practice. I know my brother Gerald does. All my girlfriends tell me so. What wonderfully blue eyes you have, Ernest! They are quite, quite, blue. I hope you will always look at me just like that, especially when there are other people present. [*enters* LADY BRACKNELL.]

LADY BRACKNELL. Mr. Worthing! Rise, sir, from this semi-recumbent posture. It is most indecorous.

GWENDOLEN. Mamma! [*He tries to rise; she restrains him.*] I must beg you to retire. This is no place for you. Besides, Mr. Worthing has not quite finished yet.

LADY BRACKNELL. Finished what, may I ask?

GWENDOLEN. I am engaged to Mr. Worthing, mamma. [*They rise together.*]

LADY BRACKNELL. Pardon me, you are not engaged to any one. When you do become engaged to some one, I, or your father, should his health permit him, will inform you of the fact. An engagement should come on a young girl as a surprise, pleasant or unpleasant, as the case may be. It is hardly a matter that she could be allowed to arrange for herself ... And now I have a few questions to put to you, Mr. Worthing. While I am making these inquiries, you, Gwendolen, will wait for me below in the carriage.

GWENDOLEN. [*reproachfully.*] Mamma!

LADY BRACKNELL. In the carriage, Gwendolen! [GWENDOLEN *goes to the door. She and* JACK *blow kisses to each other behind* LADY BRACKNELL*'s back.* LADY BRACKNELL *looks vaguely about as if she could not understand what the noise was. Finally turns round.*] Gwendolen, the carriage!

GWENDOLEN. Yes, mamma. [*goes out, looking back at* JACK.]

LADY BRACKNELL. [*sitting down.*] You can take a seat, Mr. Worthing. [*looks in her pocket for notebook and pencil.*]

JACK. Thank you, Lady Bracknell, I prefer standing.

LADY BRACKNELL. [*pencil and notebook in hand.*] I feel bound to tell you that you are not down on my list of eligible young men, although I have the same list as the dear Duchess of Bolton has. We work together, in fact. However, I am quite ready to enter your name, should your answers be what a really affectionate mother requires. Do you smoke?

JACK. Well, yes, I must admit I smoke.

LADY BRACKNELL. I am glad to hear it. A man should always have an occupation of some kind. There are far too many idle men in London as it is. How old are you?

JACK. Twenty-nine.

LADY BRACKNELL. A very good age to be married at. I have always been of opinion that a man who desire to get married should know either everything or nothing. Which do you know?

JACK. [*after some hesitation.*] I know nothing, Lady Bracknell.

LADY BRACKNELL. I am pleased to hear it. I do not approve of anything that tampers with natural ignorance. Ignorance is like a delicate exotic fruit; touch it and the bloom is gone. The whole theory of modern education is radically unsound. Fortunately in England, at any rate, education produces no effect whatsoever. If it did, it would prove a serious danger to the upper classes, and probably lead to acts of violence in Grosvenor Square. [5] What is your income?

JACK. Between seven and eight thousand a year.

LADY BRACKNELL. [*makes a note in her book.*] In land, or in investments?

JACK. In investments, chiefly.

LADY BRACKNELL. That is satisfactory. What between the duties expected of one during one's lifetime, and the duties exacted from one after one's death, [6] land has ceased to be either a profit or a pleasure. It gives one position, and prevents one from keeping it up. That's all that can be said about land.

JACK. I have a country house with some land, of course, attached to it, about fifteen hundred acres, I believe; but I don't depend on that for my real income. In fact, as far as I can make out, the poachers are the only people who make anything out of it.

LADY BRACKNELL. A country house! How many bedrooms? Well, that point can be cleared up afterwards. You have a town house, I hope? A girl with a simple, unspoiled nature, like Gwendolen, could hardly be expected to reside in the country.

JACK. Well, I own a house in Belgrave Square, [7] but it is let by the year to Lady Bloxham. Of course, I can get it back whenever I like, at six months' notice.

LADY BRACKNELL. Lady Bloxham? I don't know her.

JACK. Oh, she goes about very little. She is a lady considerably advanced in years.

LADY BRACKNELL. Ah, nowadays that is no guarantee of respectability of character. What number in Belgrave Square?

JACK. 149.

LADY BRACKNELL. [*shaking her head.*] The unfashionable side. I thought there was something. However, that could easily be altered.

JACK. Do you mean the fashion, or the side?

LADY BRACKNELL. [sternly.] Both, if necessary, I presume. What are your politics?

JACK. Well, I am afraid I really have none. I am a Liberal Unionist. [8]

LADY BRACKNELL. Oh, they count as Tories. They dine with us. Or come in the evening, at any rate. Now to minor matters. Are your parents living?

JACK. I have lost both my parents.

LADY BRACKNELL. Both? ... That seems like carelessness. Who was your father? He was evidently a man of some wealth. Was he born in what the Radical papers call the purple of commerce, or did he rise from the ranks of the aristocracy?

JACK. I am afraid I really don't know. The fact is, Lady Bracknell, I said I had lost my parents. It would be nearer the truth to say that my parents seem to have lost me ... I don't actually know who I am by birth. I was ... well, I was found.

LADY BRACKNELL. Found!

JACK. The late Mr. Thomas Cardew, an old gentleman of a very charitable and kindly disposition, found me, and gave me the name of Worthing, because he happened to have a first-class ticket for Worthing in his pocket at the time. Worthing is a place in Sussex. It is a seaside resort.

LADY BRACKNELL. Where did the charitable gentleman who had a first-class ticket for this seaside resort find you?

JACK. [*gravely.*] In a handbag.

LADY BRACKNELL. A handbag?

JACK. [*very seriously.*] Yes, Lady Bracknell. I was in a handbag—a somewhat large, black leather handbag, with handles to it—an ordinary handbag in fact.

LADY BRACKNELL. In what locality did this Mr. James, or Thomas, Cardew come across this ordinary handbag?

JACK. In the cloak room at Victoria Station. It was given to him in mistake for his own.[9]

LADY BRACKNELL. The cloak room at Victoria Station?

JACK. Yes. The Brighton line.

LADY BRACKNELL. The line is immaterial. Mr. Worthing, I confess I feel somewhat bewildered by what you have just told me. To be born, or at any rate bred, in a handbag, whether it had handles or not, seems to me to display a contempt for the ordinary decencies of family life that reminds one of the worst excesses of the French Revolution. And I presume you know what that unfortunate movement led to? As for the particular locality in which the handbag was found, a cloak room at a railway station might serve to conceal a social indiscretion—has probably, indeed, been used for that purpose before now—but it could hardly be regarded as an assured basis for a recognized position in good society.

JACK. May I ask you then what you would advise me to do? I need hardly say I would do anything in the world to ensure Gwendolen's happiness.

LADY BRACKNELL. I would strongly advise you, Mr. Worthing, to try and acquire some relations as soon as possible, and to make a definite effort to produce at any rate one parent, of either sex, before the season is quite over.[10]

JACK. Well, I don't see how I could possibly manage to do that. I can produce the handbag at any moment. It is in my dressing room at home. I really think that should satisfy you, Lady Bracknell.

LADY BRACKNELL. Me, sir! What has it to do with me? You can hardly imagine that I and Lord Bracknell would dream of allowing our only daughter—a girl brought up with the utmost care—to marry into a cloak room, and form an alliance with a parcel? Good morning, Mr. Worthing!

[LADY BRACKNELL *sweeps out in majestic indignation.*]

JACK. Good morning! [ALGERNON, *from the other room, strikes up the Wedding March.* Jack *looks perfectly furious, and goes to the door.*] For goodness' sake don't play that ghastly tune, Algy. How idiotic you are!

☞ Notes

1. **smart:** elegantly fashionable.
2. **mamma:** Here the word should be pronounced with accent on second syllable.
3. **crumpets:** a kind of toasted muffin.
4. **the season:** the social season, extending from May through July, when people of fashion came into London from their country estates for entertainments and parties.
5. **Grosvenor Square:** fashionable residential area in the west end of London.
6. **death:** the word play here is on "death duties," i. e., inheritance taxes.
7. **Belgrave Square:** another fashionable residential area in the west end known as Belgravia.
8. **Liberal Unionist:** a splinter group of members of the Liberal Party who, in 1886, led by Joseph Chamberlain, joined forces with the Conservative party (the "Tories") in opposing Home Rule for Ireland.
9. **mistake for his own:** In the four-act version of the play Jack explains further what happened to Mr. Cardew: "He did not discover the error till he arrived at his own house. All subsequent efforts to ascertain who I was were unavailing."
10. **make a definite effort to produce at any rate one parent, of either sex, before the season is quite over:** In the four-act version of the play Jack later comments to Algernon about Lady Bracknell's demands about locating parents: "After all what does it matter whether a man has ever had a father and mother or not? Mothers, of course, are all right. They pay a chap's bills and don't bother him. But fathers bother a chap and never pay his bills. I don't know a single chap at the club who speaks to his father." And Algernon remarks: "Yes. Fathers are certainly not popular just at present. ... They are like these chaps, the minor poets. They are never quoted."

☞ Study questions

1. Why does Gwendolen want to marry an "Ernest"?
2. Examine the proposal scene between Jack and Gwendolen. What are its dynamics?

Are they what the audience would expect? Why or why not?

3. Play around with the account Jack gives of his birth. What is significant about his having been discovered in an ordinary handbag lost in the cloakroom of a railroad car?
4. What are Lady Bracknell's requirements for her daughter's suitor?
5. How does the play make the serious seem trivial or the trivial seem serious?
6. How does the play mock convention? What conventions does it mock?
7. How does the play undermine the power structure in the actual society that it assumes?

Chapter 8

The Twentieth Century

8.1 Introduction

In the second half of the 19th century and the early decades of the 20th century, both natural and social sciences in Europe had enormously advanced. Their rapid development led to great gains in material wealth. But when capitalism came into its monopoly stage, the sharpened contradictions between socialized production and the private ownership caused frequent economic depressions and mass unemployment. The gap between the rich and the poor were further deepened. To crown it all, the catastrophic First World War tremendously weakened the British Empire and brought about great sufferings to its people as well. The postwar economic dislocation and spiritual disillusion produced a profound impact upon the British people, who came to see the prevalent wretchedness in capitalism. The Second World War marked the last stage of the disintegration of the British Empire. Britain suffered heavy losses in the war: thousands of people were killed; the economy was ruined; and almost all its former colonies were lost. The once sun-never-set Empire finally collapsed.

All these radical changes gave rise to all kinds of philosophical ideas in Western Europe. In the mid-19th century, Karl Marx and Friedrich Engels put forward the theory of scientific socialism, which not only provided a guiding principle for the working people, but also inspired them to make dauntless fights for their own emancipation. Darwin's theory of evolution exerted a strong influence upon the people, causing many to lose their religious faith. The social Darwinism, under the cover of "survival of the fittest," vehemently advocated colonialism or jingoism. Einstein's theory of relativity provided entirely new ideas for the concepts of time and space. Freud's analytical psychology drastically altered our conception of human nature. Arthur Schopenhauer, a pessimistic philosopher, started a rebellion against rationalism, stressing the importance of will and intuition. Having inherited the basic principles from Schopenhauer, Friedrich Nietzsche went further against rationalism by advocating the doctrines of power and superman and by completely rejecting the Christian morality. Based on the major ideas of his predecessors, Henry Bergson established his irrational philosophy, which put the emphasis on creation, intuition, irrationality and unconsciousness. The irrational philosophers exerted immense influence upon the major modernist writers in Britain.

Modernism rose out of skepticism and disillusion of capitalism. The appalling shock of the First World War severely destroyed people's faith in the Victorian values; and the rise of the irrational philosophy and new science greatly incited writers to make new explorations on human natures and human relationships.

The French symbolism, appearing in the late 19th century, heralded modernism. After the First World War, all kinds of literary trends of modernism appeared: expressionism, surrealism, futurism, Dadaism, imagism and streams of consciousness. Towards the 1920s, these trends converged into a mighty torrent of modernist movement, which swept across the whole Europe and America. The major figures that were associated with this movement were Kafka, Picasso, Pound, Webern, Eliot, Joyce and Virginia Woolf. Modernism was somewhat curbed in the 1930s. But after the Second World War, a variety of modernism, or post-modernism, like existentialist literature, theater of the absurd, new novels and black humor, rose with the spur of the existentialist idea that "the world was absurd, and the human life was an agony."

Modernism takes the irrational philosophy and the theory of psycho-analysis as its theoretical base. The major themes of the modernist literature are the distorted, alienated and ill relationships between man and nature, man and society, man and man, and man and himself. The modernist writers concentrate more on the private than on the public, more on the subjective than on the objective. They are mainly concerned with the inner being of an individual. Therefore, they pay more attention to the psychic time than the chronological one. In their writings, the past, the present and the future are mingled together and exist at the same time in the consciousness of an individual.

Modernism is, in many aspects, a partial reaction against realism. It rejects rationalism, which is the theoretical base of realism; it excludes from its major concern the external, objective, material world, which is the only creative source of realism; by advocating a free experimentation on new forms and new techniques in literary creation, it casts away almost all the traditional elements in literature such as story, plot, character, chronological narration, etc., which are essential to realism. As a result, the works created by the modernist writers are often labeled as anti-novel, anti-poetry or anti-drama.

The 20th century witnessed a great achievement in English poetry. In the early years of the century, Thomas Hardy and the war poets of the younger generation were important realistic poets. Hardy expressed his strong sympathies for the suffering poor and his bitter disgusts at the social evils in his poetry as in his novels. The soldiers-poets of World War Ⅰ revealed the appalling brutality of the war in a most realistic way. The early poems of Pound and Eliot and Yeats's matured poetry marked the rise of "modern poetry," which was, in some sense, a revolution against the conventional ideas and forms of the Victorian poetry. The modernist poets fought against the romantic fuzziness and self-indulged emotionalism, advocating new ideas in poetry-writing such as to use the language of common speech, to create new rhythms as the expression of a new mood, to allow absolute freedom in choosing subjects, and to use hard, clear and precise images in poems.

The 1930s witnessed great economic depressions, mass unemployment, and the rise of the Nazis. Facing such a severe situation, most of the young intellects started to turn to the left. And therefore the period was known as "the red thirties." A group of young poets during this period expressed in their poetry a radical political enthusiasm and a strong protest against fascism.

With the coming of the 1950s, there was a return of realistic poetry again. By advocating reason, moral discipline, and traditional forms, a new generation of poets started "The Movement," which explicitly rejected the modernist influence. There was no significant poetic movement in the 1960s. A multiplicity of choices opened to both the poet and the reader. Poets gradually moved into more individual styles.

The realistic novels in the early 20th century were the continuation of the Victorian tradition, yet its exposing and criticizing power against capitalist evils had been somewhat weakened both in width and depth. The outstanding realistic novelists of this period were John Galsworthy, H. G. Wells, and Arnold Bennett. The three trilogies of Galsworthy's Forsyte novels are masterpieces of realism in the early 20th century, which revealed the corrupted capitalist world. In his novels of social satire, H. G. Wells made realistic studies of the aspirations and frustrations of the "Little Man;" whereas Bennett presented a vivid picture of the English life in the industrial Midlands in his best novels.

Realism was, to a certain extent, eclipsed by the rapid rise of modernism in the 1920s. But with the strong swing of leftism in the 1930s, novelists began to turn their attention to the urgent social problems. They also enriched the traditional ways of creation by adopting some of the modernist techniques. However, the realistic novels of this period were more or less touched by a pessimistic mood, pre-occupied with the theme of man's loneliness, and shaped in different forms: social satires by Aldous Huxley (*Brave New World*, 1932) and George Orwell (*Nineteen Eighty-Four*, 1949); comic satires on the English upper class by Evelyn Waugh (*A Handful of Dust*, 1934); and Catholic novels by Graham Greene (*The Power and the Glory*, 1940). Another important aspect of realistic novels in this period was the fact that there rose a few working-class writers, who gave a direct portrayal of the working-people's poverty and sufferings, by singing highly of the heroic struggles against capitalism waged by the working class. Among this group, the Scottish writer Lewis Grassic Gibbon was the most outstanding. His trilogy: *Sunset Song* (1932), *Cloud Howe* (1933), and *Grey Granite* (1934) present the social changes and the working-people's life on farms, in towns and cities through the personal experience of Chris Guthrie.

In the mid-1950s and early 1960s, there appeared a group of young novelists and playwrights with lower-middle-class or working-class background, who were known as "the Angry Young Men." They demonstrated a particular disillusion over the depressing situation in Britain and launched a bitter protest against the outmoded social and political values in their society. Kingsley Amis, John Wain, John Braine and Alan Sillitoe were the major novelists in this group. Amis was the first to start the attack on middle-class privileges and power in his novel *Lucky Jim* (1954). Both Braine and Sillitoe came from working-class families. They portrayed unadorned working-class life in their novels with great freshness and vigor of the working-class language.

Having been merged and interpenetrated with modernism in the past several decades, the realistic novel of the 1960s and 1970s appeared in a new face with a richer, more vigorous and more diversified style.

The first three decades of this century were golden years of the modernist novel. In stimulating the technical innovations of novel creation, the theory of the Freudian and Jungian psycho-analysis played a particularly important role. With the notion that multiple levels of consciousness existed simultaneously in the human mind, that one's present was the sum of his past, present and future, and that the whole truth about human beings existed in the unique, isolated, and private world of each individual, writers like Dorothy Richardson, James Joyce and Virginia Woolf concentrated all their efforts on digging into the human consciousness. They had created unprecedented stream-of-consciousness novels such as *Pilgrimage* (1915-1938) by Richardson, *Ulysses* (1922) by Joyce, and *Mrs. Dalloway* (1925) by Woolf. One of the remarkable features of their writings was their continuous experimentation on new and sophisticated techniques in novel writing, which made tremendous impacts on the creation of both realistic and modernist novels in this century. James Joyce is the most outstanding stream-of-consciousness novelist; in *Ulysses*, his encyclopedia-like masterpiece, Joyce presents a fantastic picture of the disjointed, illogical, illusory, and mental-emotional life of Leopold Bloom, who becomes the symbol of everyman in the post-World-War-Ⅰ Europe.

In the works of E. M. Forster and D. H. Lawrence, old traditions are still there, but their subject matter about human relationships and their symbolic or psychological presentations of the novel are entirely modern. Forster's masterpiece, *A Passage to India* (1924), is a novel of decidedly symbolist aspirations, in which the author set up, within a realistic story, a fable of moral significance that implies a highly mystical, symbolic view of life, death, human relationship, and the relationship of man with the infinite universe. D. H. Lawrence is regarded as revolutionary as Joyce in novel writing; but unlike Joyce, he was not concerned with technical innovations; his interest lay in the tracing of the psychological development of his characters and in his energetic criticism of the dehumanizing effect of the capitalist industrialization on human nature. He believed that life impulse was the primacy of man's instinct, and that any conscious repression of such an impulse would cause distortion or perversion of the individual's personality. In his best novels like *The Rainbow* (1915) and *Women in Love* (1920), Lawrence made a bold psychological exploration of various human relationships, especially those between men and women, with a great frankness. Lawrence claimed that the alienation of the human relationships and the perversion of human nature in the modern society were caused by the desires for power and money, by the shams and frauds of middle-class life, and, above all, by the whole capitalist mechanical civilization, which turned men into inhuman machines.

Modernist novels came to a decline in the 1930s, though Joyce and Woolf continued their experiments. After the Second World War, modernism had another upsurge with the rise of existentialism; but it was reflected mainly in drama.

The most celebrated dramatists in the last decade of the 19th century were Oscar Wilde and George Bernard Shaw, who, in a sense, pioneered the modern drama, though they did not make so many innovations in techniques and forms as modernist poets or novelists. Wilde expressed a satirical and bitter attitude towards the upper-class people by revealing their corruption, their snobbery, and their hypocrisy in his plays, especially in his masterpiece, *The Importance of Being Earnest* (1895). Shaw is a more important figure in drama than Wilde. He is considered to be the best-known English dramatist since Shakespeare. His works are examples of the plays inspired by social criticism. John Galsworthy carried on this tradition of social criticism in his plays. By dramatizing social and ethical problems, Galsworthy made considerable achievements in his plays. The *Silver Box* (1906) and *Strife* (1910) are such examples, in which Galsworthy presents not only realistic pictures of social injustice, but also the workers' heroic struggles against their employers.

With their joint efforts, the Irish playwrights like W. B. Yeats, Lady Gregory, and J. M. Synge brought about the Irish National Theater Movement in the early 20th century, thus starting an Irish dramatic revival. Yeats, a prominent poet of the 20th century, was the leader of this movement. He was a verse playwright who desired to restore lyrical drama to popularity. With the heroic portrayal of spiritual truth as his main concern, Yeats wrote a number of verse plays, introducing Irish myths and folk legends; but the plot in his plays was seldom very dramatic. As a result, none of his plays was among the best of his poetical achievement. J. M. Synge was the most gifted dramatist of the Movement. By adopting the vivid figurative language of the Irish peasantry, Synge brought vigor, ironic humor, and dramatic pathos to the Irish stage. His most popular play is the comedy, *The Playboy of the Western World* (1907). Another original and distinguished artist that the Abbey Theater produced was Sean O'Casey, who dealt in his work with political and social themes of the Irish Nationalist Movement, and with the suffering of the Irish townspeople. By combining "richness" with "reality," O'Casey presented an urban drama of Dublin slum life to the Irish audience in plays like *Juno and the Paycock* (1925), and *The Plough and the Stars* (1926).

The 1930s witnessed a revival of poetic drama in England. One of the early experimenters was T. S. Eliot who regarded drama as the best medium of poetry. Eliot wrote several verse plays and made a considerable success. *Murder in the Cathedral* (1935), with its purely dramatic power, remains the most popular of his verse plays, in spite of its primarily religious purpose. After Eliot, Christopher Fry gained considerable successes in poetic drama. His exuberant though poetically commonplace verse drama, *The Lady's Not for Burning* (1948), attracted delighted audience.

The English dramatic revolution came in the 1950s under various European and American influences. This revolution developed in two directions: the working-class drama and the Theater of Absurd.

The working-class drama was started by a group of young writers from the lower-middle class, or working class, who presented a new type of plays which expressed a mood of restlessness, anger and frustration, a spirit of rebelliousness, and a strong emotional protest against the existing social institutions. John Osborne was the man who started the first change in drama by presenting his play, *Look Back in Anger*, in 1956. In a fresh, unadorned working-class language, the play angrily, violently and unrelentingly condemned the contemporary social evils. With an entirely new sense of reality, Osborne brought vitality to the English theater and became known as the first "Angry Young Man."

The most original playwright of the Theater of Absurd is Samuel Beckett, who wrote about human beings living a meaningless life in an alien, decaying world. His first play, *Waiting for Godot* (1955), is regarded as the most famous and influential play of the Theater of Absurd.

8.2 George Bernard Shaw

8.2.1 Life and career

Shaw (1856-1950) was born in Dublin to Irish Protestant parents. He was the son of a financially impractical father and a remarkable mother whose musical talent provided him with an excellent musical background. Bernard attended several schools in his youth, but his family never had the money for him to get university training. So his education stopped at the age of fifteen, when he went to work as a clerk in an estate agent's office. His job was to collect rents in the local district. Through his work he came to know the poor people's miserable life. This experience surely enriched his understanding of the society and the sufferings of the people. In 1876 he went to London, joining his sister and mother.

In London he devoted much of his time to self-education by widely reading in the libraries. Between 1879 and 1883, he wrote 5 novels, but none of them brought him profit or fame. Later Shaw came under the influence of Henry George and William Morris and took an interest in socialist theories. He started to attend all kinds of public meetings and to read Karl Marx in the British Museum. In 1884 Shaw joined the Fabian Society, a socialist organization which advocated the establishment of democratic socialism by gradual legal reforms. He was active in socialistic propaganda, both as a street orator and as a pamphleteer.

In a period of ten years from 1885, Shaw served as a critic of music and drama for a number of magazines and newspapers. As he inherited from his gifted mother a love of music and learned to admire Mozart and Wagner's operas, he introduced a new standard in judging both performers and composers in his music criticism. Being a drama critic, Shaw directed his attacks on the Neo-Romantic tradition and the fashionable drawing-room drama. His criticism was witty, biting, and often brilliant. Those articles were later published in a collection entitled *Our Theaters in the Nineties* (1931). Meanwhile, Shaw highly praised Henrik Ibsen in *The Quintessence of Ibsenism* (1891), regarding him as a realistic and reforming playwright.

As a fervent advocate of the new theatre of Ibsen, he decided to write plays in order to illustrate his criticism of the English stage. His career as a dramatist began in 1892, when his first play *Widowers' Houses* (1892) was put on by the Independent Theater Society. But it was not until 1904 with his play *John Bulls Other Island* that he obtained wide acclaim as a dramatist. In 1898, Shaw met and married the wealthy Charlotte Townshend, who was also a Fabian. It was a childless marriage of companionship and mutual respect rather than of romantic love. After the marriage, Shaw was less involved in public meetings or political lectures. But in 1914 when the First World War broke out, Shaw strongly denounced those imperialist war-launchers in his book, *Common Sense about the War*. Shaw declined the Order of Merit but was persuaded to accept the Nobel Prize in 1925.

In his long dramatic career, Shaw wrote more than 50 plays, touching upon a variety of subjects. His early plays were mainly concerned with social problems and directed towards the criticism of the contemporary social, economic, moral and religious evils. *Widowers' Houses* and *Mrs. Warren's Profession* (1893) can be regarded as the typical representatives of Shaw's early plays. Shaw wrote quite a few history plays, in which he kept an eye on contemporary society. The important plays of this group are *Caesar and Cleopatra* (1898) and *St. Joan* (1923). Shaw also produced several plays, exploring his idea of "Life Force," the power that would create superior beings to be equal to God and to solve all the social, moral, and metaphysical problems of human society. The typical examples of this group are *Man and Superman* (1903) and *Back to Methuselah* (1921).

Shaw's comedic masterpiece is *Pygmalion* (performed 1913). It was a didactic play about phonetics, and its antiheroic hero, Henry Higgins, is a phonetician, but the play is a humane comedy about love and the English class system. The play deals with a phonetician named Henry Higgins who, for a bet, plucks from the streets Eliza Doolittle, a poverty-stricken flower girl, and, through a rigorous program of phonetic, grammatical and social tutoring, enables her to transform herself into a lady of social respectability. The play looks at middle class morality and upper-class superficiality, and reflects the social ills of nineteenth century England, and attests that all people are worthy of respect and dignity. The play also probes important questions about social class, human behavior, and relations between the sexes.

Politically, Shaw was a bourgeois liberal humanitarian and a reformist. He regarded the establishment of socialism by the emancipation of land and industrial capital from individual and class ownership as the final goal; but how to achieve it, he differed greatly from the Marxists. He was against the means of violent revolution or armed struggle in achieving the goal of socialism; he also looked down upon the uneducated working class in fighting against capitalists. He held that only those superior intellectuals could have the ability to shoulder this task. And it was his ideal to bring about evolutionary socialism by legal and democratic means, by revealing the evil capitalists, by spreading socialist ideas and by educating the common people. This reformist view of his caused him a painful, often conscious inner conflict between his sincere desire for the new world and his inability to break out of the snobbish intellectual isolation throughout his life and work.

Artistically, Shaw was strongly against the credo of "Art for Art's Sake" held by those decadent aesthetic artists. He held that art should serve social purposes by reflecting human life, revealing social contradictions and educating the common people. In his opinion, theatre should take itself seriously "as a factory of thought, a prompter of conscience, an elucidation of social conduct, an armory against despair and dullness, a temple of the ascent Man." To further explain his purpose of writing, he said, "I regard much current morality as to economic and sexual relations as disastrously wrong; and I regard certain doctrines of the Christian religion as understood in England today with abhorrence. I write plays with the deliberate object of converting the nation to my opinions in these matters."

Structurally and thematically, Shaw followed the great traditions of realism. As a realistic dramatist, he took the modern social issues as his subjects with the aim of directing social reforms. Most of his plays are concerned with political, economic, moral, or religious problems, and, thus, can be termed as problem plays. One feature of his characterization is that he makes the trick of showing up one character vividly at the expense of another. Usually he would take an unconventional character, a person with the gift of insight and freedom, and impinge it upon a group of conventional social animals, so as to reveal at every turn stock notions, prejudices and dishonesties. Another feature is that his characters are the representatives of ideas that shift and alter during the play, for Shaw is primarily interested in doctrines. His plays have plots, but they do not work by plots. The plot is usually the disregarded backbone to one long, unbroken conversation. It is the vitality of the talk that takes primacy over mere story. Action is reduced to a minimum, while the dialogue and the interplay of the minds of the characters maintain the interest of the audience. The forward motion consists not in the unrolling of plot but in the operation of the spirit of discourse.

8. 2. 2 An excerpt from *Pygmalion*

ACT IV

The Wimpole Street laboratory, Midnight. Nobody in the room. The clock on the mantelpiece strikes twelve. The fire is not alight: it is a summer night.
Presently Higgins[1] *and Pickering*[2] *are heard on the stars.*

HIGGINS. [*calling down to* PICKERING] I say, Pick: lock up, will you? I shant[3] be going out again.

PICKERING. Right. Can Mrs. Pearce go to bed? We dont[4] want anything more, do we?

HIGGINS. Lord, no!

ELIZA. *opens the door and is seen on the lighted landing in all the finery in which she has just won* HIGGINS'S *bet for him. She comes to the hearth, and switches on the electric lights there. She is tired: her pallor*[5] *contrasts strongly with her dark eyes and hair; and her expression is almost tragic. She takes off her cloak; puts her fan and gloves on the piano; and sits down on the bench, brooding and silent.* HIGGINS, *in evening dress, with overcoat and hat, comes in, carrying a smoking jacket which he has picked up downstairs. He takes off the hat and overcoat; throws them carelessly on the newspaper stand; disposes of his coat in the same way; puts on the smoking jacket; and throws himself wearily into the easy-chair at the hearth.* PICKERING, *similarly attired, comes in. He also takes off his hat and overcoat, and is about to throw them on* HIGGINS'S *when he hesitates.*

PICKERING. I say: Mrs. Pearce[6] will row if we leave these things lying about in the drawing room.

HIGGINS. Oh, chuck them over the bannisters into the hall. She'll find them there in the morning and put them away all right. She'll think we were drunk.

PICKERING. We are, slightly. Are there any letters?

HIGGINS. I didnt look. [PICKERING *takes the overcoats and hats and goes down stairs.* HIGGINS *begins half singing half yawning an air from* La Fanciulla del Golden West.[7] *Suddenly he stops and exclaims.*] I wonder where the devil my slippers are!

ELIZA *looks at him darkly; then rises suddenly and leaves the room.*

HIGGINS *yawns again, and resumes his song.*

PICKERING *returns, with the contents of the letter-box in his hand.*

PICKERING. Only circulars,[8] and this coroneted billet-doux[9] for you. [*He throws the circulars into the fender, and posts himself on the hearthrug, with his back to the grate.*]

HIGGINS. [*glancing at the billet-doux*] Money-lender. [*He throws the letter after the circulars.*]

ELIZA *returns with a pair of large down-at-heel slippers. She places them on the carpet before* HIGGINS, *and sits as before without a word.*

HIGGINS. [*yawning again*] Oh Lord! What an evening! What a crew! What a silly tomfoolery![10] [*He raises his shoe to unlace it, and catches sight of the slippers. He stops unlacing and looks at them as if they had appeared there of their own accord*]. Oh! theyre there, are they?

PICKERING. [*stretching himself*] Well, I feel a bit tired. It's been a long day. The garden party, a dinner party, and the reception! Rather too much of a good thing. But youve won your bet, Higgins. Eliza did the trick, and something to spare, eh?

HIGGINS. [*fervently*] Thank God it's over!

ELIZA *flinches violently; but they take no notice of her; and she recovers herself and sits stonily as before.*

PICKERING. Were you nervous at the garden party? *I* was. Eliza didnt seem a bit nervous.

HIGGINS. Oh, she wasnt nervous. I knew she'd be all right. No: it's the strain of putting the job through all these months that has told on me. It was interesting enough at first, while we were at the phonetics; but after that I got deadly sick of it. If I hadnt backed myself to do it I should have chucked the whole thing up two months ago. It was a silly notion: the whole thing has been a bore.

PICKERING. Oh come! the garden party was frightfully exciting. My heart began beating like anything.

HIGGINS. Yes, for the first three minutes. But when I saw we were going to win hands down, I felt like a bear in a cage, hanging about doing nothing. The dinner was worse: sitting gorging there for over an hour, with nobody but a damned fool of a fashionable woman to talk to! I tell you, Pickering, never again for me. No more artificial duchesses. The whole thing has been simple purgatory.[11]

PICKERING. Youve never been broken in properly to the social routine. [*strolling over to the piano*] I rather enjoy dipping into it occasionally myself: it makes me feel young again. Anyhow, it was a great success: an immense success. I was quite frightened once or twice because Eliza was doing it so well. You see, lots of the real people cant do it at all: theyre such fools that they think style comes by nature to people in their position; and so they never learn. Theres always something professional about doing a thing superlatively well.

HIGGINS. Yes, thats what drives me mad: the silly people dont know their own silly business. [*rising*] However, it's over and done with; and now I can go to bed at last without dreading tomorrow.

ELIZA'*S beauty becomes murderous.*

PICKERING. I think I shall turn in too. Still, it's been a great occasion: a triumph for you. Goodnight. [*He goes.*]

HIGGINS. [*following him*] Good-night. [*over his shoulder, at the door*] Put out the lights, Eliza; and tell Mrs. Pearce not to make coffee for me in the morning: I'll take tea. [*He goes out.*]

ELIZA *tries to control herself and feel indifferent as she rises and walks across to the hearth to switch off the lights. By the time she gets there she is on the point of screaming. She sits down in* HIGGINS'*S chair and holds on hard to the arms. Finally she gives way and flings herself furiously on the floor raging.*

HIGGINS. [*in despairing wrath outside*] What the devil have I done with my slippers? [*He appears at the door.*]

LIZA. [*snatching up the slippers, and hurling them at him one after the other with all her force*] There are your slippers. And there. Take your slippers; and may you never have a day's luck with them!

HIGGINS. [*astounded*] What on earth—! [*He comes to her.*] Whats the matter? Get up. [*He pulls her up.*] Anything wrong?

LIZA. [*breathless*] Nothing wrong—with you. Ive won your bet for you, havnt I? Thats enough for you. I dont matter, I suppose.

HIGGINS. You won my bet! You! Presumptuous[12] insect! *I* won it. What did you throw those slippers at me for?

LIZA. Because I wanted to smash your face. I'd like to kill you, you selfish brute. Why didnt you leave me where you picked me out of—in the gutter? You thank God it's all over, and that now you can throw me back again there, do you? [*She crisps her* *fingers*[13] *frantically.*]

HIGGINS. [*looking at her in cool wonder*] The creature is nervous, after all.

LIZA. [*gives a suffocated scream of fury, and instinctively darts her nails at his face!!*]

HIGGINS. [*catching her wrists*] Ah! would you? Claws in, you cat. How dare you shew your temper to me? Sit down and be quiet. [*He throws her roughly into the easy-chair.*]

LIZA. [*crushed by superior strength and weight*] Whats to become of me? Whats to become of me?

HIGGINS. How the devil do I know whats to become of you? What does it matter what becomes of you?

LIZA. You dont care. I know you dont care. You wouldnt care if I was dead. I'm nothing to you—not so much as them slippers.

HIGGINS. [*thundering*] Those slippers.

LIZA. [*with bitter submission*] Those slippers. I didnt think it made any difference now.

A pause. ELIZA *hopeless and crushed.* HIGGINS *a little uneasy.*

HIGGINS. [*in his loftiest manner*] Why have you begun going on like this? May I ask whether you complain of your treatment here?

LIZA. No.

HIGGINS. Has anybody behaved badly to you? Colonel Pickering? Mrs Pearce? Any of the servants?

LIZA. No.

HIGGINS. I presume you dont pretend that *I* have treated you badly.

LIZA. No.

HIGGINS. I am glad to hear it. [*He moderates his tone.*] Perhaps youre tired after the strain of the day. Will you have a glass of champagne? [*He moves towards the door.*]

LIZA. No. [*recollecting her manners*] Thank you.

HIGGINS. [*good-humored again*] This has been coming on you for some days. I suppose it was natural for you to be anxious about the garden party. But thats all over now. [*He pats her kindly on the shoulder. She writhes.*] Theres nothing more to worry about.

LIZA. No. Nothing more for you to worry about. [*She suddenly rises and gets away from him by going to the piano bench, where she sits and hides her face.*] Oh God! I wish I was dead.

HIGGINS. [*staring after her in sincere surprise*] Why? in heaven's name, why? [*reasonably, going to her*] Listen to me, Eliza. All this irritation is purely subjective.

LIZA. I dont understand. I'm too ignorant.

HIGGINS. It's only imagination. Low spirits and nothing else. Nobody's hurting you. Nothing's wrong. You go to bed like a good girl and sleep it off. [14] Have a little cry and say your prayers: that will make you comfortable.

LIZA. I heard your prayers. "Thank God it's all over!"

HIGGINS. [*impatiently*] Well, dont you thank God it's all over? Now you are free and can do what you like.

LIZA. [*pulling herself together in desperation*] What am I fit for? What have you left me fit for? Where am I to go? What am I to do? Whats to become of me?

HIGGINS. [*enlightened, but not at all impressed*] Oh, thats whats worrying you, is it? [*He thrusts his hands into his pockets, and walks about in his usual manner, rattling the contents of his pockets, as if condescending to a trivial subject out of pure kindness.*] I shouldnt bother about it if I were you. I should imagine you wont have much difficulty in settling yourself somewhere or other, though I hadnt quite realized that you were going away. [*She looks quickly at him: he does not look at her, but examines the dessert stand on the piano and decides that he will eat an apple.*] You might marry, you know. [*He bites a large piece out of the apple, and munches*[15] *it noisily.*] You see, Eliza, all men are not confirmed old bachelors like me and the Colonel. Most men are the marrying sort (poor devils!); and youre not bad-looking; it's quite a pleasure to look at you sometimes—not now, of course, because youre crying and looking as ugly as the very devil; but when youre all right and quite yourself, youre what I should call attractive. That is, to the people in the marrying line, you understand. You go to bed and have a good nice rest; and then get up and look at yourself in the glass; and you wont feel so cheap.

ELIZA *again looks at him, speechless, and does not stir.*

The look is quite lost on him: he eats his apple with a dreamy expression of happiness, as it is quite a good one.

HIGGINS. [*a genial afterthought occurring to him*] I daresay my mother could find some chap or other who would do very well.

LIZA. We were above that at the corner of Tottenham Court Road.

HIGGINS. [*waking up*] What do you mean?

LIZA. I sold flowers. I didnt sell myself. Now youve made a lady of me I'm not fit to sell anything else. I wish youd left me where you found me.

HIGGINS. [*slinging the core of the apple decisively into the grate*] Tosh, Eliza. Dont you insult human relations by dragging all this cant[16] about buying and selling into it. You neednt marry the fellow if you dont like him.

LIZA. What else am I to do?

HIGGINS. Oh, lots of things. What about your old idea of a florist's shop? Pickering could set you up in one: he has lots of money. [*chuckling*] He'll have to pay for all those togs you have been wearing today; and that, with the hire of the jewellery, will make a big hole in two hundred pounds. Why, six months ago you would have thought it the millennium to have a flower shop of your own. Come! youll be all right. I must clear off to bed: I'm devilish sleepy. By the way, I came down for something: I forget what it was.

LIZA. Your slippers.

HIGGINS. Oh yes, of course. You shied them at me. [*He picks them up, and is going out when she rises and speaks to him.*]

LIZA. Before you go, sir—

HIGGINS. [*dropping the slippers in his surprise at her calling him Sir*] Eh?

LIZA. Do my clothes belong to me or to Colonel Pickering?

HIGGINS. [*coming back into the room as if her question were the very climax of unreason*] What the devil use would they be to Pickering?

LIZA. He might want them for the next girl you pick up to experiment on.

HIGGINS. [*shocked and hurt*] Is that the way you feel towards us?

LIZA. I dont want to hear anything more about that. All I want to know is whether anything belongs to me. My own clothes were burnt.

HIGGINS. But what does it matter? Why need you start bothering about that in the middle of the night?

LIZA. I want to know what I may take away with me. I dont want to be accused of stealing.

HIGGINS. [*now deeply wounded*] Stealing! You shouldnt have said that, Eliza. That shows a want of feeling.

LIZA. I'm sorry. I'm only a common ignorant girl; and in my station I have to be careful. There cant be any feelings between the like of you and the like of me. Please will you tell me what belongs to me and what doesn't?

HIGGINS. [*very sulky*] You may take the whole damned houseful if you like. Except the jewels. Theyre hired. Will that satisfy you? [*He turns on his heel and is about to go in extreme dudgeon*[17].]

LIZA. [*drinking in his emotion like nectar,* [18] *and nagging him to provoke a further supply*] Stop, please. [*She takes off her jewels.*] Will you take these to your room and keep them safe? I dont want to run the risk of their being missing.

HIGGINS. [*furious*] Hand them over. [*She puts them into his hands.*] If these belonged to me instead of to the jeweler, I'd ram them down your ungrateful throat. [*He perfunctorily thrusts them into his pockets, unconsciously decorating himself with the protruding ends of the chains.*]

LIZA. [*taking a ring off*] This ring isnt the jeweler's: it's the one you bought me in Brighton. I dont want it now. [HIGGINS *dashes the ring violently into the fireplace, and turns on her so threateningly that she crouches over the piano with her hands over her face, and exclaims.*] Dont you hit me.

HIGGINS. Hit you! You infamous creature, how dare you accuse me of such a thing? It is you who have hit me. You have wounded me to the heart.

LIZA. [*thrilling with hidden joy*] I'm glad. Ive got a little of my own back, anyhow.

HIGGINS. [*with dignity, in his finest professional style*] You have caused me to lose my temper: a thing that has hardly ever happened to me before. I prefer to say nothing more tonight. I am going to bed.

LIZA. [*pertly*] Youd better leave a note for Mrs. Pearce about the coffee; for she wont be told by me.

HIGGINS. [*formally*] Damn Mrs. Pearce; and damn the coffee; and damn you; and [*wildly*] damn my own folly in having lavished my hard-earned knowledge and the treasure of my regard and intimacy on a heartless guttersnipe. [*He goes out with impressive decorum, and spoils it by slamming the door savagely.*]

ELIZA *goes down on her knees on the hearthrug to look for the ring. When she finds it she considers for a moment what to do with it. Finally she flings it down on the desert stand and goes upstairs in a tearing rage.*

☞ **Notes**

1. **Higgins:** Henry Higgins who is a professor of phonetics.
2. **Pickering:** Colonel Pickering, the author of Spoken Sanskrit, who is a match for Higgins in his passion for phonetics.
3. **shant:** shan't.
4. **dont:** don't.
5. **pallor:** unhealthy paleness of the skin or face.
6. **Mrs. Pearce:** Higgins's housekeeper and representative mother figure in his bachelor establishment at the Wimpole Street laboratory.
7. **La Fanciulla del Golden West:** *The Girl of the Golden West,* opera by Italian composer Giacomo Puccini (1858-1924).
8. **circulars:** printed letter, notice or advertisement sent to a large number of people.
9. **coroneted billet-doux:** love letter decorated with a small crown.
10. **tomfoolery:** foolish behavior or act.
11. **purgatory:** any place or condition of suffering.
12. **presumptuous:** too bold or self-confident; acting without the necessary authority.
13. **crisps her fingers:** clenches them into fists.
14. **sleep it off:** to recover from something by sleeping.

15. **munch:** to eat with a strong movement of the jaw, especially making a noise.
16. **cant:** hollow words and borrowed phrases, repeated without thought.
17. **dudgeon:** in a state of bad temper or anger caused by hurt feelings.
18. **nectar:** (in ancient Greek and Roman literature) the drink of the gods; any sweet and good-tasting drink.

☞ **Study questions**

1. Higgins says to Eliza, "Now you are free and can do what you like." Is that true? In what ways is Eliza NOT free?
2. What does Eliza say to "shock and hurt" Higgins? Is there a symbolic meaning to Eliza returning to Higgins the ring he gave her? What do you think the ring meant to Higgins when he gave it to her? What did it mean to Eliza?
3. What are the personality changes resulting from the treatments given in the main character Eliza Doolittle?
4. Why does Eliza start speaking in her old manner when she gets emotional?
5. Eliza tells Higgins that she wants to be independent. Does she achieve that independence by the end of the play? Why or why not?

☞ **Essay topics**

1. Discuss the characterization of and the relationship between Eliza Doolittle and Professor Henry Higgins. In your opinion, is Shaw a feminist? If so, can you think of any reasons why?
2. Discuss the symbolic meaning of the title (the legend of Pygmalion and Galatea). In what way is this meaning linked to the theme of the play?

8.3 Joseph Conrad

8.3.1 Life and career

Conrad (1857-1924) was born in Poland (then under Russian rule). His father was an ardent patriot. In 1861 his family was exiled to Northern Russia as a result of his father's participation in the Polish independence movement. Conrad was first educated by his father. From the time spent with his father, Conrad became a lover of literature. By 1869 both his parents had died, and Conrad came under the guardianship of his maternal uncle. He attended schools in Kraków. But during his school years, Conrad was thoroughly bored with life as a student. He fed his imagination on tales of sea life. The ambition to be a sailor took root in his young mind. At his repeated insistence of going to sea, his uncle finally yielded, and Conrad realized his long-cherished dream at the age of 17. He spent the next few years in France, mastering his second language and the fundamentals of seamanship. He also involved himself in gun-running, a passionate love affair, and a duel.

Conrad yet again underwent a drastic change in his life when he joined the British merchant marines in 1878. He began working seriously on his career of seamanship and on learning his English. Within ten years, Conrad rose to the rank of captain and mastered the English language. In 1886, he became a naturalized British subject. During those years, Conrad worked on a variety of British ships to the Mediterranean, the Far East, the South Pacific, South America, and other places. It was this experience that provided him with material on the exotic locations of many of his novels. He began writing his first novel, *Almayer's Folly*, in 1889. In the following year, Conrad took a steamboat up the Congo River into the heart of Africa. This nightmarish adventure, which later found its way into *Heart of Darkness*, not only damaged his health severely, but also made him see the horrible inhuman crimes committed by the European colonialists against the African people.

In 1896 Conrad got married to Jessie George, an Englishwoman. He then settled down in London, devoting himself to novel writing. In his 20 years of literary creation, Conrad wrote 31 novels (including novelettes), several collections of short stories, and quite a number of essays. In his early period of literary career, he mainly wrote sea novels or stories, such as *The Nigger of the Narcissus* (1897), *Youth and Two Other Stories* (1902), *Lord Jim* (1900), *Typhoon and Other Stories* (1903), and *The Shadow Line* (1917). The settings of these works are usually exotic, full of jungle scenes, ocean storms, and romantic atmosphere, which give the reader an impression of special richness and splendor. His stories are more than dangerous adventures of romance over the sea or remote settlements; for Conrad's primary concern is about human beings. The true value of the sea is to provide a background and a symbolical atmosphere; a ship or a small outpost serves as a miniature of the larger world so that the author can explore the moral problems he is concerned with or examine the psychological state of his characters. Thus, his sea novels have stronger social and political significance than those pure adventures. In his second period of creation, Conrad wrote novels, which dealt with social and political subjects. The major ones are *Nostromo* (1904), *The Secret Agent* (1907), and *Under Western Eyes* (1911). These novels have widened the scope of Conrad's presentation of human dilemmas with grim pictures of a world given over to the worship of materialistic values. They offer plenty of evidence that Conrad, coming late to settle life on shore, viewed cynically the "industrial society" (meaning the capitalist society) and the sources of its wealth. With an ironic mask and artistic vision, Conrad presented a panorama of the corrupt capitalist world and its perverted inhabitants. The concern with love and sacrifice became the major themes of the novels written in his later period, which included *Chance* (1913), *Victory* (1915), *The Arrow of Gold* (1919), and others. The relative simple subjects and manner are accompanied by a softening in Conrad's attitude to life. The works of this period also show signs of his artistic decline.

Heart of Darkness is Conrad's most famous novel, which tells the story of Marlow and his journey up the Congo River to relieve Kurtz, the most successful trader in ivory working for the Belgian government. Not only does the title make a reference to the dark and gloomy way of life in the heart of Africa, it also signifies the corruption of Kurtz and touches upon many other examples of moral and physical darkness. Kurtz is a symbol for the faithlessness and inner emptiness of the modern world, the climactic example of all the monstrous colonizers, though he himself was a victim of colonialism. The crimes he committed in Africa have clearly demonstrated the degeneration of the European civilization during the heyday of colonialism.

Conrad was living in an age of imperialist expansion and colonization. What he could see was only an avaricious, predatory and almost psycho-pathetic world. Disillusioned, he fell into a mood of pessimism. He held that there was no way to relate existence and life, no way to evade the tragic contradictions of human situation. This pessimistic view of man's future thrust him into a despairing loneliness.

However as a serious novelist, Conrad was primarily concerned with moral ideas in his writing. Fidelity, solidarity, duty, courage, hard work and self-discipline were the high virtues of his moral code, which served as a kind of self-control in man against corruption and evil. The absence or breaking up of such virtues would cause man to suffer isolation and defeat. The conflicts of his novels are always moral ones between true and false, right and wrong, good and evil. To explore the inner causes of his characters' success or failure, Conrad would choose the moment of crucial moral choice in an individual's life as a test. The simple courageous seamen could always pass the test by clinging to fidelity and duty. But those more sophisticated, more idealistic people would usually fail the test because of the loss or abandon of self-control. The world seen by Conrad was a place of unending contention between the evil forces of dissolution and the ideal of brotherhood. And he held that only moral values of human life could be counted upon to last in such a world.

In his preface to *The Nigger of the Narcissus*, Conrad claims that the artist, like the thinker or the scientist, seeks the truth and makes his appeal. He holds that fiction, as a mode of truth-telling, must appeal to temperament, must create the moral and emotional atmosphere of the place and time, if it at all aspires to be art, like painting or music. He further claims that all art appeals primarily to the senses, and that the artistic aim of literature must also make its appeal through the senses, the sense of pity, the sense of pain, and the sense of beauty, if its high desire is to reach the secret spring of responsive emotions. Influenced by impressionism, Conrad sees his subject as something shifting and somewhat illusory, for forms and colors of objects are not constant but changing from hour to hour and even from moment to moment, with the character of the light in which they are seen. Rejecting the conventional way of direct analysis in novel writing, Conrad presents his materials as they appear in detached momentary impressions. In his novel, Conrad explored the meaning of human situation by recording the fleeting moments of life, by capturing the illusive moods of characters.

Conrad has become a great prose master of his adopted language—English. He writes in a figurative language, using carefully selected similes and metaphors to convey the inner truth of human life. His style is a lush and dense one with piles of sharp images to evoke the emotions of the character or to create an atmosphere of the situation. There is also a poetic quality in his works. The vivid scenes with their heavy rhythms and cunning repetitions can break down easily into effective free verse. Conrad is one of the modernist pioneers. His modernity lies largely in his tragic awareness of man's disillusionment, isolation, and suffering in an alienated and corrupted world of civilization. The most evident examples are the subjects explored in *Heart of Darkness*, *Lord Jim* and *Nostromo*. His narrative techniques are also distinctively modern, though he seems to have had no interest in experiment for its own sake. However, some of his technical innovations have exerted strong influences over writers of later generations.

8. 3. 2 An excerpt from the first part of *Heart of Darkness*

The Nellie, [1] a cruising yawl, swung to her anchor without a flutter of the sails, and was at rest. The flood had made, the wind was nearly calm, and being bound down the river, the only thing for it was to come to and wait for the turn of the tide.

The sea-reach of the Thames stretched before us like the beginning of an interminable waterway. In the offing the sea and the sky were welded together without a joint, and in the luminous space the tanned sails of the barges drifting up with the tide seemed to stand still in red clusters of canvas sharply peaked, with gleams of varnished spirits. A haze rested on the low shores that ran out to sea in vanishing flatness. The air was dark above Gravesend, [2] and farther back still seemed condensed into a mournful gloom, brooding motionless over the biggest, and the greatest, town on earth.

The Director of Companies was our captain and our host. We four affectionately watched his back as he stood in the bows looking to seaward. On the whole river there was nothing that looked half so nautical. He resembled a pilot, which to a seaman is trustworthiness personified. It was difficult to realize his work was not out there in the luminous estuary, but behind him, within the brooding gloom.

Between us there was, as I have already said somewhere, the bond of the sea. Besides holding our hearts together through long periods of separation, it had the effect of making us tolerant of each other's yarns—and even convictions. The Lawyer—the best of old fellows—had, because of his many years and many virtues, the only cushion on deck, and was lying on the only rug. The Accountant had brought out already a box of dominoes,[3] and was toying architecturally with the bones. Marlow sat cross-legged right aft, leaning against the mizzenmast.[4] He had sunken cheeks, a yellow complexion, a straight back, an ascetic aspect, and, with his arms dropped, the palms of hands outwards, resembled an idol.[5] The Director, satisfied the anchor had good hold, made his way aft and sat down amongst us. We exchanged a few words lazily. Afterwards there was silence on board the yacht. For some reason or other we did not begin that game of dominoes. We felt meditative, and fit for nothing but placid staring. The day was ending in a serenity of still and exquisite brilliance. The water shone pacifically; the sky, without a speck, was a benign immensity of unstained light; the very mist on the Essex marsh was like a gauzy and radiant fabric, hung from the wooded rises inland, and draping the low shores in diaphanous folds. Only the gloom to the west, brooding over the upper reaches, became more somber every minute, as if angered by the approach of the sun.

And at last, in its curved and imperceptible fall, the sun sank low, and from glowing white changed to a dull red without rays and without heat, as if about to go out suddenly, stricken to death by the touch of that gloom brooding over a crowd of men.

Forthwith a change came over the waters, and the serenity became less brilliant but more profound. The old river in its broad reach rested unruffled at the decline of day, after ages of good service done to the race that peopled its banks, spread out in the tranquil dignity of a waterway leading to the uttermost ends of the earth. We looked at the venerable stream not in the vivid flush of a short day that comes and departs for ever, but in the august light of abiding memories. And indeed nothing is easier for a man who has, as the phrase goes, "followed the sea" with reverence and affection, than to evoke the great spirit of the past upon the lower reaches of the Thames. The tidal current runs to and fro in its unceasing service, crowded with memories of men and ships it had borne to the rest of home or to the battles of the sea. It had known and served all the men of whom the nation is proud, from Sir Francis Drake to Sir John Franklin,[6] knights all, titled and untitled—the great knights—errant of the sea. It had borne all the ships whose names are like jewels flashing in the night of time, from the *Golden Hind* returning with her round flanks full of treasure, to be visited by the Queen's Highness and thus pass out of the gigantic tale, to the *Erebus and Terror*, bound on other conquests—and that never returned. It had known the ships and the men. They had sailed from Deptford, from Greenwich, from Erith[7]—the adventurers and the settlers; kings' ships and the ships of men on "Change"; captains, admirals, the dark "interlopers"[8] of the Eastern trade, and the commissioned "generals" of East India fleets. Hunters for gold or pursuers of fame, they all had gone out on that stream, bearing the sword, and often the torch, messengers of the might within the land, bearers of a spark from the sacred fire. What greatness had not floated on the ebb of that river into the mystery of an unknown earth! ... The dreams of men, the seed of commonwealths, the germs of empires.

The sun set; the dusk fell on the stream, and lights began to appear along the shore. The Chapman lighthouse, a three-legged thing erect on a mud-flat, shone strongly. Lights of ships moved in the fairway[9]—a great stir of lights going up and going down. And farther west on the upper reaches the place of the monstrous town was still marked ominously on the sky, a brooding gloom in sunshine, a lurid glare under the stars.

"And this also," said Marlow suddenly, "has been one of the dark places of the earth."

He was the only man of us who still "followed the sea." The worst that could be said of him was that he did not represent his class. He was a seaman, but he was a wanderer, too, while most seamen lead, if one may so express it, a sedentary life. Their minds are of the stay-at-home order, and their home is always with them—the ship; and so is their country—the sea. One ship is very much like another, and the sea is always the same. In the immutability of their surroundings the foreign shores, the foreign faces, the changing immensity of life, glide past, veiled not by a sense of mystery but by a slightly disdainful ignorance; for there is nothing mysterious to a seaman unless it be the sea itself, which is the mistress of his existence and as inscrutable as Destiny. For the rest, after his hours of work, a casual stroll or a casual spree on shore suffices to unfold for him the secret of a whole continent, and generally he finds the secret not worth knowing. The yarns of seamen have a direct simplicity, the whole meaning of which lies within the shell of a cracked nut. But Marlow was not typical (if his propensity to spin yarns be excepted), and to him the meaning of an episode was not inside like a kernel but outside, enveloping the tale which brought it out only as a glow brings out a haze, in the likeness of one of these misty halos[10] that sometimes are made visible by the spectral illumination of moonshine.

His remark did not seem at all surprising. It was just like Marlow. It was accepted in silence. No one took the trouble to grunt even; and presently he said, very slow:

"I was thinking of very old times, when the Romans first came here, nineteen hundred years ago—the other day .... Light came out of this river since—you say Knights? Yes; but it is like a running blaze on a plain, like a flash of lightning in the clouds. We live in the flicker—may it last as long as the old earth keeps rolling! But darkness was here yesterday. Imagine the feelings of a commander of a fine—what d'ye call 'em? —trireme[11] in the Mediterranean, ordered suddenly to the north run overland across the Gauls[12] in a hurry; put in charge of one of these craft the legionaries[13]—a wonderful lot of handy men they must have been, too—used to build, apparently by the hundred, in a month or two, if we may believe what we read. Imagine him here—the very end of the world, a sea the color of lead, a sky the color of smoke, a kind of ship about as rigid as a concertina—and going up this river with stores, or orders, or what you like. Sandbanks, marshes, forests, savages, —precious little to eat fit for a civilized man, nothing but Thames water to drink. No Falernian wine here, no going ashore. Here and there a military camp lost in a wilderness, like a needle in a bundle of hay—cold, fog, tempests, disease, exile, and death—death skulking in the air, in the water, in the bush. They must have been dying like flies here. Oh, yes—he did it. Did it very well, too, no doubt, and without thinking much about it either, except afterwards to brag of what he had gone through in his time, perhaps. They were men enough to face the darkness. And perhaps he was cheered by keeping his eye on a chance of promotion to the fleet at Ravenna[14] by and by, if he had good friends in Rome and survived the awful climate. Or think of a decent young citizen in a toga—perhaps too much dice, you know—coming out here in the train of some prefect, or tax-gatherer, or trader even, to mend his fortunes. Land in a swamp, march through the woods, and in some inland post feel the savagery, the utter savagery, had closed round him—all that mysterious life of the wilderness that stirs in the forest, in the jungles, in the hearts of wild men. There's no initiation either into such mysteries. He has to live in the midst of the incomprehensible, which is also detestable. And it has a fascination, too, that goes to work upon him. The fascination of the abomination[15]—you know. Imagine the growing regrets, the longing to escape, the powerless disgust, the surrender, the hate."

He paused.

"Mind," he began again, lifting one arm from the elbow, the palm of the hand outwards, so that, with his legs folded before him, he had the pose of a Buddha preaching in European clothes and without a lotus-flower—"Mind, none of us would feel exactly like this. What saves us is efficiency—the devotion to efficiency. But these chaps were not much account, really. They were no colonists; their administration was merely a squeeze, and nothing more, I suspect. They were conquerors, and for that you want only brute force—nothing to boast of, when you have it, since your strength is just an accident arising from the weakness of others. They grabbed what they could get for the sake of what was to be got. It was just robbery with violence, aggravated murder on a great scale, and men going at it blind—as is very proper for those who tackle a darkness. The conquest of the earth, which mostly means the taking it away from those who have a different complexion or slightly flatter noses than ourselves, is not a pretty thing when you look into it too much. What redeems it is the idea only. An idea at the back of it; not a sentimental pretence but an idea; and an unselfish belief in the idea—something you can set up, and bow down before, and offer a sacrifice to ..."

He broke off. Flames glided in the river, small green flames, red flames, white flames, pursuing, overtaking, joining, crossing each other—then separating slowly or hastily. The traffic of the great city went on in the deepening night upon the sleepless river. We looked on, waiting patiently—there was nothing else to do till the end of the flood; but it was only after a long silence, when he said, in a hesitating voice, "I suppose you fellows remember I did once turn fresh water sailor for a bit," that we knew we were fated, before the ebb began to run, to hear about one of Marlow's inconclusive experiences.

"I don't want to bother you much with what happened to me personally," he began, showing in this remark the weakness of many tellers of tales who seem so often unaware of what their audience would best like to hear; "yet to understand the effect of it on me you ought to know how I got out there, what I saw, how I went up that river to the place where I first met the poor chap. It was the farthest point of navigation and the culminating point of my experience. It seemed somehow to throw a kind of light on everything about me—and into my thoughts. It was somber enough, too—and pitiful—not extraordinary in any way—not very clear either. No, not very clear. And yet it seemed to throw a kind of light.

"I had then, as you remember, just returned to London after a lot of Indian Ocean, Pacific, China Seas a regular dose of the East—six years or so, and I was loafing about,[16] hindering you fellows in your work and invading your homes, just as though I had got a heavenly mission to civilize you. It was very fine for a time, but after a bit I did get tired of resting. Then I began to look for a ship—I should think the hardest work on earth. But the ships wouldn't even look at me. And I got tired of that game, too.

"Now when I was a little chap I had a passion for maps. I would look for hours at South America, or Africa, or Australia, and lose myself in all the glories of exploration. At that time there were many blank spaces on the earth, and when I saw one that looked particularly inviting on a map (but they all look that) I would put my finger on it and say, 'When I grow up I will go there.' The North Pole was one of these places, I remember. Well, I haven't been there yet, and shall not try now. The glamour's off. Other places were scattered about the Equator, and in every sort of latitude all over the two hemispheres. I have been in some of them, and ... well, we won't talk about that. But there was one yet—the biggest, the most blank, so to speak—that I had a hankering after.[17]

"True, by this time it was not a blank space any more. It had got filled since my boyhood with rivers and lakes and names. It had ceased to be a blank space of delightful mystery—a white patch for a boy to dream gloriously over. It had become a place of darkness. But there was in it one river especially, a mighty big river, that you could see on the map, resembling an immense snake uncoiled, with its head in the sea, its body at rest curving afar over a vast country, and its tail lost in the depths of the land. And as I looked at the map of it in a shop-window, it fascinated me as a snake would a bird—a silly little bird. Then I remembered there was a big concern, a Company for trade on that river. Dash it all! I thought to myself, they can't trade without using some kind of craft on that lot of fresh water—steamboats! Why shouldn't I try to get charge of one? I went on along Fleet Street, but could not shake off the idea. The snake had charmed me.

"You understand it was a Continental concern, that Trading Society; but I have a lot of relations living on the Continent, because it's cheap and not so nasty as it looks, they say.

"I am sorry to own I began to worry them. This was already a fresh departure for me. I was not used to get things that way, you know. I always went my own road and on my own legs where I had a mind to go. I wouldn't have believed it of myself; but, then—you see—I felt somehow I must get there by hook or by crook. So I worried them. The men said 'My dear fellow,' and did nothing. Then—would you believe it?—I tried the women. I, Charlie Marlow, set the women to work—to get a job. Heavens! Well, you see, the notion drove me. I had an aunt, a dear enthusiastic soul. She wrote: 'It will be delightful. I am ready to do anything, anything for you. It is a glorious idea. I know the wife of a very high personage in the Administration, and also a man who has lots of influence with,' etc., etc. She was determined to make no end of fuss to get me appointed skipper of a river steamboat, if such was my fancy.

"I got my appointment—of course; and I got it very quick. It appears the Company had received news that one of their captains had been killed in a scuffle with the natives. This was my chance, and it made me the more anxious to go. It was only months and months afterwards, when I made the attempt to recover what was left of the body, that I heard the original quarrel arose from a misunderstanding about some hens. Yes, two black hens. Fresleven[18]—that was the fellow's name, a Dane—thought himself wronged somehow in the bargain, so he went ashore and started to hammer the chief of the village with a stick. Oh, it didn't surprise me in the least to hear this, and at the same time to be told that Fresleven was the gentlest, quietest creature that ever walked on two legs. No doubt he was; but he had been a couple of years already out there engaged in the noble cause, you know, and he probably felt the need at last of asserting his self-respect in some way. Therefore he whacked the old nigger mercilessly, while a big crowd of his people watched him, thunderstruck, till some man—I was told the chief's son—in desperation at hearing the old chap yell, made a tentative jab with a spear at the white man—and of course it went quite easy between the shoulder-blades. Then the whole population cleared into the forest, expecting all kinds of calamities to happen, while, on the other hand, the steamer Fresleven commanded left also in a bad panic, in charge of the engineer, I believe. Afterwards nobody seemed to trouble much about

Fresleven's remains, till I got out and stepped into his shoes. I couldn't let it rest, though; but when an opportunity offered at last to meet my predecessor, the grass growing through his ribs was tall enough to hide his bones. They were all there. The supernatural being had not been touched after he fell. And the village was deserted, the huts gaped black, rotting, all askew within the fallen enclosures. A calamity had come to it, sure enough. The people had vanished. Mad terror had scattered them, men, women, and children, through the bush, and they had never returned. What became of the hens I don't know either. I should think the cause of progress got them, anyhow. However, through this glorious affair I got my appointment, before I had fairly begun to hope for it.

"I flew around like mad to get ready, and before forty-eight hours I was crossing the Channel to show myself to my employers, and sign the contract. In a very few hours I arrived in a city that always makes me think of a whited sepulchre. [19] Prejudice no doubt. I had no difficulty in finding the Company's offices. It was the biggest thing in the town, and everybody I met was full of it. They were going to run an over sea empire, and make no end of coin by trade.

"A narrow and deserted street in deep shadow, high houses, innumerable windows with venetian blinds, a dead silence, grass sprouting between the stones, imposing carriage archways right and left, immense double doors standing ponderously ajar. I slipped through one of these cracks, went up a swept and ungarnished staircase, as arid as a desert, and opened the first door I came to. Two women, one fat and the other slim, sat on straw-bottomed chairs, knitting black wool. The slim one got up and walked straight at me—still knitting with downcast eyes—and only just as I began to think of getting out of her way, as you would for a somnambulist, [20] stood still, and looked up. Her dress was as plain as an umbrella-cover, and she turned round without a word and preceded me into a waiting-room. I gave my name, and looked about. Deal table in the middle, plain chairs all round the walls, on one end a large shining map, marked with all the colors of a rainbow. There was a vast amount of red—good to see at any time, because one knows that some real work is done in there, a deuce of a lot of blue, a little green, smears of orange, and, on the East Coast, a purple patch, to show where the jolly pioneers of progress drink the jolly lager-beer. However, I wasn't going into any of these. I was going into the yellow. Dead in the center. And the river was there—fascinating—deadly—like a snake. Ough! A door opened, a white-haired secretarial head, but wearing a compassionate expression, appeared, and a skinny forefinger beckoned me into the sanctuary. Its light was dim, and a heavy writing-desk squatted in the middle. From behind that structure came out an impression of pale plumpness in a frock-coat. The great man himself. He was five feet six, I should judge, and had his grip on the handle-end of ever so many millions. He shook hands, I fancy, murmured vaguely, was satisfied with my French. *Bon voyage.*[21]

"In about forty-five seconds I found myself again in the waiting-room with the compassionate secretary, who, full of desolation and sympathy, made me sign some document. I believe I undertook amongst other things not to disclose any trade secrets. Well, I am not going to.

"I began to feel slightly uneasy. You know I am not used to such ceremonies, and there was something ominous in the atmosphere. It was just as though I had been let into some conspiracy—I don't know—something not quite right; and I was glad to get out. In the outer room the two women knitted black wool feverishly. People were arriving, and the younger one was walking back and forth introducing them. The old one sat on her chair. Her flat cloth slippers were propped up on a foot-warmer, and a cat reposed on her lap. She wore a starched white affair on her head, had a wart on one cheek, and silver-rimmed spectacles hung on the tip of her nose. She glanced at me above the glasses. The swift and indifferent placidity of that look troubled me. Two youths with foolish and cheery countenances were being piloted over, and she threw at them the same quick glance of unconcerned wisdom. She seemed to know all about them and about me, too. An eerie feeling came over me. She seemed uncanny and fateful. Often far away there I thought of these two, guarding the door of Darkness, knitting black wool as for a warm pall, one introducing, introducing continuously to the unknown, the other scrutinizing the cheery and foolish faces with unconcerned old eyes. *Ave!*[22] Old knittter of black wool. *Morituri te salutant.*[23] Not many of those she looked at ever saw her again—not half, by a long way.

☞ Notes

1. **Nellie:** name of a sailing ship, on which the story was told.
2. **Gravesend:** river port on the south bank of the Thames some 24 miles east (downriver) of London.
3. **a box of dominoes:** a set of small flat pieces of wood or plastic with different numbers of spots on, used for playing a game.
4. **mizzenmast:** the mast behind the main mast on a sailing ship.
5. **idol:** someone or something that you love or admire very much.
6. **from Sir Francis Drake to Sir John Franklin:** Sir Francis Drake (ca. 1540-1596), Elizabethan naval hero and explorer, sailed round the world in his ship *The Golden Hind*. Queen Elizabeth knighted Drake on board his ship, loaded with captured Spanish treasure, on his return. Sir John Franklin (1786-1847), Arctic explorer, in 1845 commanded an expedition consisting of the ships *Erebus* and *Terror* in search of the Northwest passage. The ships never returned.
7. **from Deptford, from Greenwich, from Erith:** Deptford, on the south bank of the

Thames, on the eastern edge of London, once (but no longer) an important dockyard. Greenwich is on the south bank of the Thames immediately east of Deptford. Erith is some 8 miles further east.

8. **"Change"** is the Stock Exchange. **"Interlopers"** were private ships muscling in on the monopoly of the East India Company, which was founded in 1600, lost its trading monopoly in 1813, and transferred its governmental functions to the Crown in 1858.
9. **fairway:** navigable part of a river, through which ships enter and depart.
10. **halos:** bright circles of light.
11. **trireme:** ancient Greek and Roman galley with three ranks of oars.
12. **Gauls:** ancient Celts, or ancient Frenchmen.
13. **legionaries:** members of a legion. Legion is the principal unit of the Roman army comprising 3,000 to 6,000 foot soldiers with cavalry.
14. **Ravenna:** city in Northern Italy once directly on the Adriatic Sea and an important naval station in Roman times. Now about 6 miles from the sea, connected with it by a canal.
15. **abomination:** someone or something that is extremely offensive or unacceptable.
16. **loafing about:** wasting time in a lazy way when you should be working.
17. **hankering after:** secretly feeling that you want something, over a long period.
18. **Fresleven:** the previous captain of the steamboat on the Congo River, and later Marlow would take charge of that boat.
19. **sepulcher:** a small room or building in which the bodies of dead people were put.
20. **somnambulist:** someone who walks while they are asleep.
21. ***Bon voyage*:** (French) used to wish someone a good journey.
22. ***Ave*:** the written abbreviation of avenue.
23. ***Morituri te salutant*:** "Hail! ... Those who are about to die salute you." The Roman gladiators' salute to the Emperor on entering the arena.

☞ Study questions

1. Why does Conrad have one of Marlow's listeners relate the story, rather than make Marlow the narrator of the novel who speaks directly to the reader?
2. Describe the situation and characters on board the *Nellfie*. How does Marlow differ from the other men, his audience, on board the *Nellie*?
3. Where are the characters at the beginning of the story, and why is this significant?
4. How is the Thames described? What does Marlow mean when he says that "this also has been one of the dark places of the earth"?
5. In describing the Roman conquest of England, Marlow suggests parallels to the main story of *Heart of Darkness*: what seems to be foreshadowed? How does Marlow define "conquerors"?

6. Marlow describes a map image of the Congo River in Africa as being like a snake. What snake-like qualities does this reference transfer to the river, and how does the transference set us up for the rest of the novel's events?
7. From his first few speeches, what can you tell of Marlow?
8. What is Marlow's attitude toward colonialism, or the "conquest of the earth," as he calls it?

☞ **Essay topics**

1. How can one's environment affect one's actions, feelings, and morals? Have you ever experienced a change in yourself that resulted from a change in your environment? What kind of change was it?
2. As briefly as possible explain the themes of the novel. Justify your choice of the theme?

8.4 William Butler Yeats

8.4.1 Life and career

Yeats(1865-1939) was born into an Anglo-Irish Protestant family in Dublin. His childhood was largely spent between school in London and his mother's native county of Sligo, where old Irish way of life and folklore were still very strong. After high school, Yeats entered the School of Art in Dublin where he met many artists and writers who encouraged him to be a poet. With a strong passion for Celtic legends, he read Irish poetry and the Gaelic sagas in translation. His youth was passed during the upsurge of Irish nationalist movement led by Parnell.

In his twenties, Yeats stayed in London for a time and got to know William Morris, Oscar Wilde and others. He also became associated with the Rhymers' Club—a group of poets who met regularly to discuss poetry. His early poetry was under the influence of the romantic poets, especially Blake, Shelley and Keats; but his Irish theme and his special use of language soon showed him to be a poet of distinction. In 1889 Yeats met and fell in love with Maud Gonne, a beautiful Irish actress and a fiery freedom fighter, who was to haunt him for the rest of his life. She inspired not only his poetic creation but also his patriotic feelings towards the nationalist movement. But she refused to marry him. Yeats visited Paris in 1894 and was introduced to modern French poetry, especially the Symbolists, by the poet-critic, Arthur Symons. Yeats met Lady Gregory and John Synge in 1896. With the common cultural ideals of reviving the Irish literature, they organized the Irish National Dramatic Society and opened the Abbey Theatre in 1904. Yeats served as its director and wrote 26 plays for the theatre.

Yeats finally married Miss Hyde-Lees in 1917, and lived a happy family life. When

Ireland won its independence in 1922, Yeats became a member of the new Irish Senate. In 1923, he was awarded Nobel Prize for literature. Yeats had a long poetic career and his creative power never diminished till his late years.

Yeats is considered to be one of the greatest poets in the English language; and his poetic achievement stands at the center of modern literature. He had a very long poetic career, stretching from the 1880s to the 1930s, and had experienced a slow and painful change in his poetic creation, starting in the romantic tradition and finishing as a matured modernist poet. Generally, his poetic career can be divided into three periods according to the contents and style of his poetry.

As a young man, Yeats began his poetic career in the romantic tradition. The major themes are usually Celtic legends, local folktales, or stories of the heroic age in Irish history. Many of his early poems have a dreamy quality, expressing melancholy, passive and self-indulgent feelings. But in a number of poems, Yeats has achieved suggestive patterns of meaning by a careful counterpointing of contrasting ideas or images like human and fairy, natural and artificial, domestic and wild, and ephemeral and permanent. The overall style of his early poetry is very delicate with natural imagery and musical beauty.

The first two decades of the 20th century were a period of transition to Yeats, during which his attitude towards politics, life and poetry had experienced a great change. His disgust at the bourgeois philistinism soured his political optimism, leaving him a disillusioned patriotic sentiment. His long-cherished but hopeless love for Gonne brought him only suffering and bitterness. Gradually, Yeats turned from the traditional poetry to a modernist one. Ideologically, he responded to Nietzsche's works with great excitement; artistically, he came under the influence of French Symbolism and John Donne's metaphysical poetry; and poetically, he accepted the modernist ideas in poetry writing advocated by Ezra Pound and T. S. Eliot. He began to write with realistic and concrete themes on a variety of subjects, exploring the profound and complicated human problems, such as, life, love, politics, and religion. The new vigor of his verse is reflected in the precise and concrete imagery, the strong passion, and the active verb forms. His style is simple and rich, colloquial and formal, with a quality of metaphysical wit and symbolic vision, which indicates that Yeats has already been on his way to modernist poetry. In his poem, "No Second Troy," Yeats expressed a strong feeling towards love and towards the Irish reality with scornful irony. Yet it is himself, not the lady, he blamed. In the poem, "September 1913," Yeats, with severe satire, assaulted the bourgeois philistines and their meanness of spirit and selfish materialism. His poem, "The Second Coming," raw and visionary, with political and religious overtones, gives an air of cyclic inevitability to the occurrence of the death and rebirth of the gods as part of the recurring cycles of history. It marks his maturity as a modernist poet and foreshadows his greater poems in the later years.

Yeats reached the last stage of his poetic creation when he was over fifty. The scorn so pervasive before was gone; but the loss of youth and the waste of life made him feel bitterer and more disillusioned. He yearned to move away from the sensual world of growth and change, and to enter the timeless, eternal world of art and intellect. Yeats came to realize that eternal beauty could only live in the realm of art. His concern has turned to the great subjects of dichotomy, such as, youth and age, love and war, vigor and wisdom, body and soul, and life and art. And this dichotomy has brought constant tensions in his works and revealed the human predicament. In this last period, Yeats has developed a tough, complex and symbolical style. In his famous poem, "Sailing to Byzantium," Yeats explored the problems of death, love, old age and art. Being at the junction of East and West, the city became a refuge from time, and, at once, purgatory and paradise, a haunt of spirit, symbolizing the unity of the opposites. "Once out of nature," or dead, the old man in "Sailing to Byzantium" will be gone into the "Monuments of unaging intellect," the "artifice of eternity," where art arrests change. The making of a work of art can be taken as another theme of the poem. It is man who has created the monuments, which are needed now to carry him beyond the sensual world, to transform him into a golden bird, which would sing of time, "Of what is past, or passing, or to come."

Yeats is also a dramatist, writing verse plays in most of the cases. The story threads of his early plays all came from the Irish myth or legends. In 1892, Yeats wrote his first play, *The Countess Cathleen* to impress Maud Gonne. The play is an Irish myth about a noblewoman who sells her soul to the devil in order to save starving peasants; and Yeats considered it as an appropriate symbol of the activities to which Gonne had dedicated her life. *Cathleen ni Houlihan* (1902), written largely in prose is a forceful play of patriotism, in which Cathleen, a poor and mysterious old woman, who symbolizes Ireland, calls on the young people to assist her in recovering her land from strangers and promises glory to those who make sacrifice in their fight. The play was a great inspiration to the Irish nationalists who were fighting against the English government for their own freedom and independence. In addition to the above mentioned, *The land of Heart's Desire* (1894), *The Shadowy Waters* (1900) and *Purgatory* (1935) are also regarded as fairly good plays by Yeats.

Toward the Irish Nationalist Movement, Yeats' attitude went through several different stages. When he was young, he took an active interest in nationalist politics. Later, when his love affair with Maud Gonne turned out to be fruitless and when his plays were denounced by the Dublin middle class as being anti-religious, he was apparently disillusioned with the state of the Irish Nationalist Movement and turned to praise the refinement of the aristocratic life. But when he heard the Easter Rising of

1916, Yeats was again inspired. Fairly speaking, Yeats was a moderate nationalist. Surely he had his national pride and his hatred for English oppression. But he never showed any enthusiasm towards the violent, heroic mass actions taken by the people for their national cause.

Not content with any dogma in any of the established religious institutions, Yeats built up for himself a mystical system of beliefs. In choosing the mystical belief of cyclical history over the modern conception of progress, Yeats owed a great deal to the Italian philosopher Vico and the German philosopher Nietzsche. He believed that history followed a circular, spiral pattern consisting of long cycles which repeated themselves over and over on different levels. And symbols like "winding stairs," "spinning tops," "gyres" and "spirals" were part of his elaborate theory of history, which had obviously become the central core of order in his great poems.

Yeats later disagreed with the idea of "art for art's sake." He came to see that literature should not be an end in itself but the expression of conviction and the garment of noble emotion. To write about Ireland for an Irish audience and to recreate a specifically Irish literature—these were the aims that Yeats was fighting for as a poet and a playwright. Starting from his twenties, he had been active in promoting the movement known as the Irish Literary Revival. He believed that the Irish art, poetry, drama, and legend would fill the people with national aspirations in striving for a new Ireland, and that only by "expressing primary truths in ways appropriate to this country" could artists hope to restore to the modern Ireland the "unity of culture" that was needed to bring an end to his country's internal division and suffering.

8.4.2 "The Lake Isle of Innisfree"[1]

I will arise and go now, and go to Innisfree,
And a small cabin build there, of clay and wattles[2] made:
Nine bean-rows will I have there, a hive for the honeybee,
And live alone in the bee-loud glade.[3]

And I shall have some peace there, for peace comes dropping slow,
Dropping from the veils of the morning to where the cricket sings;
There midnight's all a glimmer, and noon a purple glow,
And evening full of the linnet's wings.[4]

I will arise and go now, for always night and day
I hear lake water lapping with low sounds by the shore;
While I stand on the roadway, or on the pavements gray,
I hear it in the deep heart's core.[5]

☞ **Notes**

1. The poem is written in 1893. Tired of the life of his day, Yeats sought to escape into an ideal "fairy land" where he could live calmly as a hermit and enjoy the beauty of nature. The poem consists of three quatrains of iambic pentameter, with each stanza rhymed *abab*. Innisfree is an inlet in the lake in Irish legends. Here the author is referring to a place for hermitage.
2. **wattles:** stakes interwoven with twigs or branches.
3. **the bee-loud glade:** an open place in the wood where bees buzz loudly.
4. **full of the linnet's wings:** Here it refers to the fact that lots of linnets fly here and there. "**Linnet**" is a small brown singing bird.
5. **in the deep heart's core:** at the bottom of my heart.

☞ **Study questions**

1. Contrast the speaker's present location with the place that beckons him. What is the emotional effect of this contrast?
2. Instead of actually going to Innisfree, what is the speaker doing in the poem? How does hearing something "in the deep heart's core" differ from hearing it with one's ears?
3. How does Yeats use sound images to heighten the emotional effect of the poem?

8.4.3 "Down by the Salley Gardens"[1]

Down by the salley[2] gardens my love and I did meet;
She passed the salley gardens with little snow-white feet.
She bid me take love easy, as the leaves grow on the tree;
But I, being young and foolish, with her would not agree.

In a field by the river my love and I did stand,
And on my leaning shoulder she laid her snow-white hand.
She bid me take life easy, as the grass grows on the weirs;[3]
But I was young and foolish, and now am full of tears.

☞ **Notes**

1. Originally entitled "An Old Song Resung," with Yeats's footnote: "This is an attempt to reconstruct an old song from three lines imperfectly remembered by an old peasant woman in the village of Ballysodare, Sligo, who often sings them to herself."
2. **salley:** a variant of "sallow," a species of willow tree.
3. **weirs:** walls or barriers across a river to control the flow of water.

☞ Study questions

1. What is the speaker's attitude towards love? Do you think it right or wrong? Why?
2. What did the lady tell the speaker in the second stanza?
3. Why didn't the speaker listen to the lady's advice?
4. What can you learn from this poem?

8. 4. 4 "The Second Coming"[1]

Turning and turning in the widening gyre[2]
The falcon cannot hear the falconer;
Things fall apart; the center cannot hold;
Mere anarchy is loosed upon the world,
The blood-dimmed tide is loosed, and everywhere
The ceremony of innocence is drowned;
The best lack all conviction, while the worst
Are full of passionate intensity. [3]

Surely some revelation[4] is at hand;
Surely the Second Coming is at hand.
The Second Coming! Hardly are those words out
When a vast image out of *Spiritus Mundi*[5]
Troubles my sight: somewhere in sands of the desert
A shape with lion body and the head of a man, [6]
A gaze blank and pitiless as the sun,
Is moving its slow thighs, while all about it
Reel shadows of the indignant desert birds.
The darkness drops again; but now I know
That twenty centuries[7] of stony sleep
Were vexed to nightmare by a rocking cradle, [8]
And what rough beast, its hour come round at last,
Slouches towards Bethlehem to be born?

☞ Notes

1. This poem expresses Yeats's sense of the dissolution of the civilization of his time, the end of one cycle of history and the approach of another. The birth of Christ brought to an end the cycle that had lasted from what Yeats called the "Babylonian mathematical starlight" (2000 B. C.) to the dissolution of Creco-Roman culture.

"What if the irrational return?" Yeats asked in his prose work *A Vision*. "What if the circle begin again?" He speculates that "we may be about to accept the most implacable authority the world has known."

2. **gyre:** circular or spiral form or motion, which Yeats uses as the symbol for the winding up and winding down of circles of history (Yeats pronounced it with a hard g).
3. **The blood-dimmed tide ... full of passionate intensity:** These four lines refer to the Russian Revolution of 1917, seen as a portent, but later Yeats accepted the poem as an unconscious prophecy of the rise of Fascism also. Speaking in 1924, Yeats declared: "It is impossible not to ask oneself to what great task of the nations we have been summoned in this transformed world where there is so much that is obscure and terrible." **"The ceremony of innocence"** suggests Yeats's view of ritual as the basis of civilized living. Cf. the last stanza of "A Prayer for My Daughter."
4. **revelation:** disclosure; in Christian teaching, God's unfolding of His will to the human race.
5. ***Spiritus Mundi*:** the Spirit or Soul of the Universe, with which all individual souls are connected through the "Great Memory," which Yeats held to be a universal subconscious in which the human race preserves its past memories. It is thus a source of symbolic images for the poet.
6. **A shape with lion body and the head of a man:** referring to the sphinx.
7. **twenty centuries:** Yeats's cycles each lasted two thousand years.
8. **cradle:** the cradle of the infant Christ.

☞ Study questions

1. To what is Yeats referring when he mentions the "Second Coming?"
2. What religious event does the Second Coming refer to?
3. The poem begins with the image of a falcon flying out of control. Yeats is using this image to suggest the situation of the modern world. In what ways do you think the modern world is like the distant, circling falcon? Can you give specific examples of the "things [that] fall apart"?
4. What shape is the world in as described in the poem?
5. What is the significance of the poem's mention of the Sphinx myth?
6. What kind of creature suggested by Yeats seems to be coming? Does this creature seem to be positive or negative?
7. What country or area of the world seems to be the setting for the creature's arrival?
8. How long has the creature been sleeping? Is there any significance to this number?

8. 4. 5 "Sailing to Byzantium"[1]

1

That is no country[2] for old men. The young
In one another's arms, birds in the trees
—Those dying generations—at their song,
The salmon falls, the mackerel-crowded seas,
Fish, flesh, or fowl, commend all summer long
Whatever is begotten, born, and dies.
Caught in that sensual music all neglect
Monuments of unageing intellect.

2

An aged man is but a paltry thing,
A tattered coat upon a stick, unless
Soul clap its hands and sing, and louder sing
For every tatter in its mortal dress,
Nor is there singing school but studying
Monuments of its own magnificence;
And therefore I have sailed the seas and come
To the holy city of Byzantium.

3

O sages standing in God's holy fire
As in the gold mosaic of a wall,[3]
Come from the holy fire, perne in a gyre,[4]
And be the singing masters of my soul.
Consume my heart away; sick with desire
And fastened to a dying animal
It knows not that it is; and gather me
Into the artifice of eternity.

4

Once out of nature I shall never take
My bodily form from any natural thing,
But such a form as Grecian goldsmiths make
Of hammered gold and gold enameling
To keep a drowsy Emperor awake;

Or set upon a golden bough to sing[5]
To lords and ladies of Byzantium
Of what is past, or passing, or to come.

☞ Notes

1. Yeats wrote in *A Vision*: "I think that if I could be given a month of antiquity and leave to spend it where I chose, I would spend it in Byzantium (modern Istanbul) a little before Justinian opened St. Sophia and closed the Academy of Plato [i. e., ca. A. D. 535]. I think that in early Byzantium, maybe never before or since in recorded history, religious, aesthetic, and practical life were one, that architects and artificers spoke to the multitude in gold and silver. The painter, the mosaic worker, the worker in gold and silver, the illuminator of sacred books were almost impersonal, almost perhaps without the consciousness of individual design, absorbed in their subject matter and that the vision of a whole people."
2. **That is no country:** the sensual world where time passes and death is certain to occur.
3. **sages standing in God's holy fire/As in the gold mosaic of a wall:** wise old men (sages) depicted on the mosaic walls of Byzantine churches.
4. **perne in a gyre:** descend or spin with a whirling, spiral motion. "Perne" (or "pirn") is literally a bobbin, reel, or spool, on which something is wound. It became a favorite word of Yeats's, used as a verb meaning "to spin round;" he associated the spinning with the spinning of fate.
5. **To keep a drowsy Emperor awake;/Or set upon a golden bough to sing:** Byzantine Emperor Theophilus is said to have ordered his artisans to make him a gold and silver tree in which mechanical birds perched and sang.

☞ Study questions

1. In the first line of the poem, Yeats says about his homeland of Ireland, "That is no country for old men." Why is Ireland not appropriate for old men? How does the imagery in the first and second stanzas of the poem provide an answer to the question?
2. How do Ireland and Byzantium differ, according to the poem? Why might the speaker prefer Byzantium?
3. How does the golden bird described in stanza 4 differ from the birds mentioned in stanza 1? Why might the speaker choose the form of the golden bird over that of "any natural thing"?
4. According to the final stanza, what does the speaker hope to become? By extension, what kind of human accomplishment does he seem to value?

☞ Essay topics

1. What is the speaker's attitude toward aging and death? What does the poem say about the relationship between body and soul?
2. One of the important themes in Yeats's writing is his exploration of the relationship between the natural and the artificial, and particularly the relationship between nature and art. With particular reference to this poem, describe how Yeats characterizes this relationship. Does he prefer the natural to art, or art to nature?

8.5 Thomas Stearns Eliot

8.5.1 Life and career

Eliot(1888-1965) was born at St. Louis, Missouri, USA. He was first educated at Smith Academy in St. Louis. Between 1906 and 1914 he attended Harvard, studying widely in literature and philosophy. As a graduate student in philosophy, he furthered his studies in France, Germany and Britain. He took interest in Elizabethan literature, the Italian Renaissance and Indian mystical philosophy of Buddhism. He was also attracted by the French symbolist poetry. When the First World War broke out, he was doing his doctoral program at Oxford. So he decided to take up permanent residence in Britain.

Eliot got married to Vivien Haigh-Wood in 1915. His wife's mental instability caused lots of emotional difficulties in their marriage, which prompted some intense passages in Eliot's poetry. After a year or two of teaching, he became a bank clerk until 1925. During this period, he supplemented his income by lecturing, book reviewing and editorial work. His first important poem, "The Love Song of J. Alfred Prufrock," appeared in 1915. In 1922 he became the editor of *The Criterion*, which was one of the two most influential literary reviews of the 20th century. Eliot's most famous poem, *The Waste Land*, appeared in the first number of *The Criterion*. In 1927, Eliot took English citizenship and became a devout member of the Anglican Church. In his later career, Eliot busied himself with different kinds of literary work such as writing, editing, publishing and lecturing. He won various awards, including the Nobel Prize and the Order of Merit in 1948. Vivien Eliot, from whom he separated in 1933, died in 1947. Ten years later, in 1957, Eliot married Valerie Fletcher, his secretary. Eliot died on January 4, 1965, in London.

Eliot had a long poetic career, stretching from the beginning of the 20th century up to the 1940s. But his poetic output was not very large. His early poems were mainly collected in *Poems* 1909-1925 (1925). He also published *Prufrock and Other Observations* (1917), *The Waste Land* (1922) and two other small volumes of poetry. As a young man with bitter disillusionment and with boldness in the handling of language, Eliot had explored various aspects of social decay in the modern Western world, expressing a sense of the disintegration of life. Most of his early poems are about a state of mind. There is little "action" in a physical sense; the action is totally psychological. The poems are dominated by the dark horror of an earthly hell.

The Love Song of J. Alfred Prufrock is Eliot's first striking achievement. The poem is a sort of dramatic monologue, suggesting an ironic contrast between a pretended "love song" and a confession of his incapability of facing up to love and to life in a sterile upper-class world. Human predicament is the theme. Prufrock, the protagonist of the poem, is mentally ill, neurotic, self-important, illogical and incapable of action. He is a kind of tragic figure caught in a sense of defeated idealism and tortured by unsatisfied desires. The poem is intensely anti-romantic with visual images of hard, gritty objects and evasive hellish atmosphere. The surface tone is of over-civilized anxiety but the basic emotions are fear and malice. Individual lines or phrases are borrowed from past works, bringing a rich meaning to the poem. The meter varies within the conventional English line, and the rhyming is superb. *The Waste Land* (1922), Eliot's most important single poem, has been hailed as a landmark and a model of the 20th-century English poetry, comparable to the *Lyrical Ballads*. The poem is concerned with the spiritual breakup of a modern civilization in which human life has lost its meaning, significance and purpose. It has developed a whole set of historical, cultural and religious themes. With bold technical innovations in versification and style, the poem does not only present a panorama of physical disorder and spiritual desolation in the modern civilized world, but also reflects the prevalent mood of disillusionment and despair of a whole post-war generation.

In his later period, Eliot produced only two major volumes of poetic works: *Ash Wednesday* (1930) and *Four Quartets* (1944), both reflecting his allegiance to the Church of England. *The Four Quartets*, based on the Christian dogmas of incarnation and resurrection, is concerned with the quest for the immortal element, the stillness within time or history. Man, disillusioned and hopeless in his early poetry, now finds reconciliation in God. Thus, the *Four Quartets* is characterized by a philosophical and emotional calm quite in contrast to the despair and suffering of the early works.

Eliot was one of the prominent verse dramatists in the first half of the 20th century. Besides some fragmentary pieces, he had written five full-length plays: *Murder in the Cathedral* (1935), *The Family Reunion* (1939), *The Cocktail Party* (1950), *The Confidential Clerk* (1954), and *The Elder Statesman* (1959), in which he expressed the ideas of modern society with new accents of the contemporary speech. All the plays have something to do with Christian themes. Eliot was also an important prose writer. He wrote a large number of essays, articles and book reviews. His essays are mainly concerned with cultural, social, religious, as well as literary issues.

Like Wordsworth, Eliot has experienced a drastic change in his political attitude towards the world. When he was young, he was radical, pessimistic, satiric and explorative. When Eliot had himself well-established, his New England's religious background, his authoritative habit of mind, and his fears of the socialist revolution gradually turned him to the choice of conservatism and a hierarchic society. He came to believe that the illness of the modern world was of the sum of individual souls, and that the cure could only be obtained by the change of the individual souls through religious salvation. Thus, the quest for stability, for order, and for the maintaining of the bourgeois-status quo became his primary concern in his later works.

Eliot's primary goal in poetry is a search for detachment, or impersonality. In his essay *Tradition and the Individual Talent*, Eliot writes that "the emotion of art is impersonal." He argued that a poet's mind should remain "inert" and "neutral" towards his subject matter, keeping a gulf between the man who suffers and the mind which creates. "The progress of an artist is a continual self-sacrifice, a continual extinction of personality," and a continual surrender of himself to the past and the tradition. He holds that the past is not a dull and venerable ancestor but a living force which not only modifies the present but also provides the necessary conditions for the artist's creation of new forms.

By accepting Vico's cyclical theory of history, Eliot regards that the Western world has reached the last stage of the cycle in the 20th century. The post-war Europe has collapsed into a restless, pointless barren world in which the whole civilization has been degenerated and men are spiritually dead. So the subject matter of his poetry is to expose the sterility and futility of the Western culture, to reveal the breakdown of communication between human beings, to show man's disillusionment and frustration caught between his sense of meaning and his sense of meaninglessness, and to quest for a spiritual regeneration by finding salvation in religion.

Eliot's poetry is full of classical, biblical and mythical allusions, which call forth an immediate response in the reader's mind to the wonderful past so as to make the "truth" of his poetry transcend both time and space. Eliot also takes myth as an effective means of reaching beneath the level of present and conscious experience. In his poetry, ancient myth is not only used to convey man's struggle and failure in penetrating the mystical consciousness in a sterile world, but also to emulate a way of giving shape and significance to its structure. Another device used in his poetry is juxtaposition in which one of the elements ironically undercuts the other so as to produce striking effect. In order to illustrate man's sense of loss and the immense panorama of futility and anarchy, he throws into juxtaposition all kinds of conflicting images from ancient mythology, from past literature, from fragments of songs and scriptures, from history, religion and modern life.

An Anglo-American poet, critic, dramatist, and editor, Eliotis a major innovator in modern English poetry, famous above all for his revolutionary poem *The Waste Land*. His seminal critical essays helped to usher in literary modernism by stressing tradition, continuity, and objective discipline over indulgent romanticism and subjective egoism. In rejecting the poetic values of the English romantics and Victorians, Eliot, along with W. B. Yeats and Ezra Pound, set new poetic standards equal to those established by James Joyce and Marcel Proust in fiction.

8.5.2 "The Love Song of J. Alfred Prufrock"[1]

S'io credessi che mia risposta fosse
a persona che mai tornasse al mundo,
questa fiamma staria senza piu scosse.
Ma per cio che giammai di questo fondo
non torno vivo alcun, s'i'odo il vero,
senza tema d'infamia ti rispondo.[2]

Let us go then, you and I,
When the evening is spread out[3] against the sky
Like a patient etherized upon a table;[4]
Let us go, through certain half-deserted streets,
The muttering retreats
Of restless nights in one-night cheap hotels
And sawdust restaurants with oyster shells:
Streets that follow like a tedious argument
Of insidious intent
To lead you to an overwhelming question ...
Oh, do not ask, "What is it?"
Let us go and make our visit.

In the room the women come and go
Talking of Mickelangelo.[5]

The yellow fog[6] that rubs its back upon the windowpanes,
The yellow smoke that rubs its muzzle on the windowpanes
Licked its tongue into the corners of the evening,
Lingered upon the pools that stand in drains,
Let fall upon its back the soot that falls from chimneys,
Slipped by the terrace, made a sudden leap,

And seeing that it was a soft October night,
Curled once about the house, and fell asleep.

And indeed there will be time[7]
For the yellow smoke that slides along the street,
Rubbing its back upon the windowpanes;
There will be time, there will be time
To prepare a face to meet the faces that you meet;
There will be time to murder and create,
And time for all the works and days of hands[8]
That lift and drop a question on your plate;
Time for you and time for me,
And time yet for a hundred indecisions,
And for a hundred visions and revisions,
Before the taking of a toast and tea.

In the room the women come and go
Talking of Michelangelo.

And indeed there will be time
To wonder, "Do I dare?" and, "Do I dare?"
Time to turn back and descend the stair,
With a bald spot in the middle of my hair—
(They will say: "How his hair is growing thin!")
My morning coat, my collar mounting firmly to the chin,
My necktie rich and modest, but asserted by a simple pin—
(They will say: "But how his arms and legs are thin!")
Do I dare
Disturb the universe?
In a minute there is time
For decisions and revisions which a minute will reverse.

For I have known them all already, known them all—
Have known the evenings, mornings, afternoons,
I have measured out my life with coffee spoons;
I know the voices dying with a dying fall[9]
Beneath the music from a farther room.
    So how should I presume?

And I have known the eyes already, known them all—
The eyes that fix you in a formulated phrase,
And when I am formulated, sprawling on a pin, [10]
When I am pinned and wriggling on the wall,
Then how should I begin
To spit out all the butt-ends[11] of my days and ways?
    And how should I presume?

And I have known the arms already, known them all—
Arms that are braceleted and white and bare[12]
(But in the lamplight, downed with light brown hair!)
Is it perfume from a dress
That makes me so digress?
Arms that lie along a table, or wrap about a shawl.
    And should I then presume?
    And how should I begin?

* * * *

Shall I say, I have gone at dusk through narrow streets
And watched the smoke that rises from the pipes
Of lonely men in shirt-sleeves, leaning out of windows? ...

I should have been a pair of ragged claws[13]
Scuttling across the floors of silent seas.

* * * *

And the afternoon, the evening, sleeps so peacefully!
Smoothed by long fingers,
Asleep ... tired ... or it malingers,
Stretched on the floor, here beside you and me.
Should I, after tea and cakes and ices,
Have the strength to force the moment to its crisis?
But though I have wept and fasted, wept and prayed,
Though I have seen my head (grown slightly bald) brought in upon a platter, [14]
I am no prophet—and here's no great matter;
I have seen the moment of my greatness flicker,
And I have seen the eternal Footman[15] hold my coat, and snicker,
And in short, I was afraid.

And would it have been worth it, after all,
After the cups, the marmalade, the tea,
Among the porcelain, among some talk of you and me,
Would it have been worth while,
To have bitten off the matter with a smile,
To have squeezed the universe into a ball[16]
To roll it toward some overwhelming question,
To say: "I am Lazarus,[17] come from the dead,
Come back to tell you all, I shall tell you all"—
If one, settling a pillow by her head,
    Should say: "That is not what I meant at all.
    That is not it, at all."

And would it have been worth it, after all,
Would it have been worth while,
After the sunsets and the dooryards and the sprinkled streets,
After the novels, after the teacups, after the skirts that trail along the floor—
And this, and so much more?—
It is impossible to say just what I mean!
But as if a magic lantern threw the nerves in patterns on a screen:
Would it have been worth while
If one, settling a pillow or throwing off a shawl,
And turning toward the window, should say:
    "That is not it at all,
    That is not what I meant, at all."

* * * *

No! I am not Prince Hamlet,[18] nor was meant to be;
Am an attendant lord,[19] one that will do
To swell a progress,[20] start a scene or two,
Advise the prince; no doubt, an easy tool,
Deferential, glad to be of use,
Politic, cautious, and meticulous;
Full of high sentence,[21] but a bit obtuse;[22]
At times, indeed, almost ridiculous—
Almost, at times, the Fool.[23]

I grow old ... I grow old ...
I shall wear the bottoms of my trousers rolled.

Shall I part my hair behind?[24] Do I dare to eat a peach?
I shall wear white flannel trousers, and walk upon the beach.
I have heard the mermaids singing, each to each.

I do not think that they will sing to me.

I have seen them riding seaward on the waves
Combing the white hair of the waves blown back
When the wind blows the water white and black.

We have lingered in the chambers of the sea
By sea-girls wreathed with seaweed red and brown
Till human voices wake us, and we drown.

☞ Notes

1. A dramatic monologue in which the speaker builds up a mood of social futility and inadequacy through the thoughts and images which haunt his consciousness and by means of the symbolic landscape in which he moves. The title implies an ironic contrast between the romantic suggestions of "love song" and the dully prosaic name, "J. Alfred Prufrock."
2. *Epigraph*: These lines are taken from Dante's "Inferno", and are spoken by the character of Count Guido da Montefelltro. Dante meets the punished Guido in the Eighth chasm of Hell. Guido explains that he is speaking freely to Dante only because he believes Dante is one of the dead who could never return to earth to report what he says. Translated from the original Italian, the lines are as follows: "If I thought that my reply would be to someone who would ever return to earth, this flame would remain without further movement; but as no one has ever returned alive from this gulf, if what I hear is true, I can answer you with no fear of infamy."
3. **spread out:** This metaphor occurs many times in Bergson's *Time and Free Will* (1910), the work which Eliot, while in Harvard, quoted from most frequently in his writings about Bergson.
4. **Like a patient etherized upon a table:** Here the evening is compared to a patient who is etherized on an operation table. A contrast is perhaps implied between "ether" as the free sky and the word's medical connotations—helplessness, disease, the elimination of consciousness and personality.
5. **In the room the women come and go/Talking of Michelangelo**: Jules Laforgue, a French Symbolist, wrote: "In the room the women come and go/Talking of the

masters of the Sienne school." Eliot parodies Laforgue but creates a realistic scene of intellectual gossip, setting off as a kind of chorus. **Michelangelo:** great Italian sculptor, painter and poet.

6. **Fog:** According to Eliot, the smoke from the factories of his hometown St. Louis.
7. **And indeed there will be time:** Cf. "Had we but world enough and time," from Andrew Marvell's "To His Coy Mistress." The speaker of the poem argues to his "coy mistress" that they could take their time in courtship games only if they were immortal; ironically, Prufrock deludes himself into thinking there will be time to court his lady.
8. **works and days of hands:** "Works and Days" is a poem about the farming year by Greek poet Hesiod (8th century B. C.). Eliot's contrast is between useful farm labor and the futile "works and days of hands" engaged in meaningless social gesturing.
9. **dying fall:** In Shakespeare's *Twelfth Night* the lovesick Duke Orsino asks for an encore of moody piece of music: "That strain again! It had a dying fall" (1. 1. 4).
10. **sprawling on a pin:** Insect specimens are pinned into place for scientific study. Prufrock feels as though he is being brutally analyzed in a similar manner.
11. **butt-ends:** the ends of smoked cigarettes.
12. **Arms that are braceleted white and bare:** Cf. "A bracelet of bright hair about the bone" in John Donne's "The Relic." Eliot admires the line in his essay "The Metaphysical Poets" (1921).
13. **a pair of ragged claws:** Self-pitying remark that he would have been better as a crab at the bottom of the ocean. Cf. *Hamlet* (2. 2. 205-206), Hamlet mocks the unwitting and aging Polonius, saying that Polonius could become young like Hamlet only if he somehow went back in time: "for you yourself, sir, should be old as I am, if, like a crab, you could go backward."
14. **Though I have seen my head (grown slightly bald) brought in upon a platter:** *Matthew* 14:3-11, *Mark* 6:17-29 in the *Bible*; the death of John the Baptist. King Herod was enamored of a dancing girl named Salome. He offered her a gift of anything she wanted in his kingdom. Salome's mother told her to request the head of John the Baptist on a silver platter. Herod complied. Prufrock's observation of his "(grown slightly bald)" head parodies the event and gives it the flavor of mock-heroism found throughout the poem.
15. **eternal Footman:** Death.
16. **To have squeezed the universe into a ball:** Cf. Andrew Marvell "To His Coy Mistress" (41-44): "Let us roll all our strength and all/Our sweetness up into one ball, /And tear our pleasures with rough strife/Thorough the iron gates of life." The imagery is suggestive of phallic penetration of the hymen.
17. **Lazarus:** Another Biblical story. In *Luke* 16:19-31, a Lazarus is a beggar associated

with a rich man named Dives in a parable. When they died Lazarus went to Heaven while Dives went to Hell. Dives wanted to warn his brothers about Hell and asked Abraham if Lazarus could be sent back to tell them. Abraham refused saying, "If they hear not Moses and the prophets, neither will they be persuaded, though one rose from the dead."

18. **Prince Hamlet:** Shakespeare's most famous character, from *Hamlet*. Hamlet, like Prufrock, is indecisive and anxious about future consequences. Prufrock echoes Hamlet's famous "to be or not to be" (3. 1. 66) at the end of this line ("nor was meant to be"), a line that is about wondering whether it is worth existing ("to exist or not to exist") and couches itself in the passive tense ("to be").
19. **attendant lord:** Prufrock having an inferiority complex, stating that he will never be a main character with a purpose, like Hamlet, but rather an "attendant lord" (in this case Polonius), a mere auxiliary character who may slightly move the plot.
20. **To swell a progress:** An Elizabethan state journey made by a royal or noble person. Elizabethan plays sometimes showed full-blown "progresses" crossing the stage.
21. **full of high sentence:** sententiousness, in the habit of saying or writing things in a short and witty manner.
22. **obtuse:** dull witted.
23. **Fool:** Standard character in Elizabethan drama, such as a court jester who entertains the nobility and speaks wise nonsense (the Fool in *King Lear* is perhaps the best example).
24. **I shall wear the bottoms of my trousers rolled. /Shall I part my hair behind:** At the time, both styles were considered bohemian; the middle-aged Prufrock pathetically wonders if he can reverse his aging by embracing such youthful fashions.

☞ Study questions

1. To what social class does Prufrock belong? How does Prufrock respond to the attitudes and values of his class?
2. What does the description of the city streets tell you about the mind of the speaker?
3. When Prufrock starts talking about the "bald spot" in the middle of his head, what do you think he is worrying about?
4. When Prufrock starts talking about having known all the evenings already, what kind of a life do you think he has led?
5. Why do you think Prufrock keeps repeating that there will be enough time?
6. What is the real reason that Prufrock never asks his "overwhelming question"?

☞ Essay topics

1. What is the effect of the Biblical allusions in the poem?

2. What types of images show that people are dehumanized in modern life, and suggest that inanimate objects are alive?

8.6 James Joyce

8.6.1 Life and career

Joyce (1882-1941) was born into a Catholic family in Dublin. When he was young, his family was quite well-off; but gradually it became impoverished. Joyce got his education at Catholic schools where he received very strict religious training. During his school days, Joyce passed through a phase of religious enthusiasm; but he finally rejected the Catholic Church and started a rebellion against the narrowness and bigotry of the bourgeois philistines in Dublin. When he studied modern languages at Dublin's University College, he read a lot of books forbidden by the Catholic Church. Joyce finally decided to take the literary mission as his career. He refused to take any part in the nationalist activities of his fellow students. Influenced by Ibsen, Joyce regarded exile as the only way to preserve his integrity and to be able to recreate the Dublin life truthfully, completely and objectively.

After his graduation, Joyce went to study medicine in Paris. He was called back in 1904 by his mother's fatal illness. During his stay in Dublin, he met Nora Barnacle, an uneducated peasant girl, who charmed him with her liveliness and witty sense of humor. Together they went to France and lived as devoted companions without marriage, for Joyce was opposed to legal marriage. He eventually married her when he was around 50, thinking about writing his will. Joyce lived and worked in France, Italy and Switzerland for the rest of his life except a few brief trips back to Ireland. As an uncommercial writer, Joyce's life was largely one of poverty. He never had enough money for his family. His eye troubles and his daughter's mental illness added more sufferings to him. In difficult times, Joyce would take to drink. Sometimes the drunkenness inspired his imagination; more often he became very moody in his drunkenness. But he never wavered in his dedication to his career as an artist, and kept on writing all his life.

Joyce wrote altogether three novels, a collection of short stories, two volumes of poetry, and one play. The novels and short stories are regarded as his great works, all of which have the same setting: Ireland, especially Dublin, and the same subject: the Irish people and their life. In *Dubliners* (1914), a collection of 15 short stories, Joyce intended to write a chapter of the moral history of his country under four of its aspects: childhood, adolescence, maturity and public life. The first three stories proceed roughly through childhood and adolescence in a kind of autobiography; the next seven are about people in their maturity; and the last four deal with public life. The stories progress from simple to complex. Each story presents an aspect of "dear dirty Dublin," an aspect of the city's paralysis—moral, political, or spiritual. Each story is an action, defining a frustration or defeat of the soul. The whole sequence of the stories represents the entire course of moral deterioration in Dublin, ending in the death of the soul. The collection begins by presenting death as an inscrutable fact in a small boy's existence; it ends with a vision in which death is seen. To make the Irish see death and living dead in their life is perhaps the first step, in Joyce's opinion, to evoke the national spirit of the Irish people. The stories are also important as examples of Joyce's theory of epiphany in fiction; each is concerned with a sudden revelation of truth about life inspired by a seemingly trivial incident.

Joyce published his first novel *The Portrait of the Artist as a Young Man* in 1916. Its title suggests a character study with strong autobiographical elements. It is a kind of growing-up novel about a sensitive young man, who is at first shaped by excessively powerful and oppressive forces of his environment but gradually realizes the pressure and rebels against it and tries to find his own identity. Although the novel is partly in the tradition of autobiographical fiction, it is in many ways a revolutionary work with wide range of meanings: a study of the vanity of rebelliousness, an examination of the self-deception of adolescent ego, a revelation of personal betrayal, despair and alienation of an Irish young man, an objective account of its protagonist's inner-mind activities, and a symbolic portrayal of the gestation of an artistic soul. Adopting techniques drawn from such diverse sources as Flaubert, Wagner, Freud, the French Symbolists and impressionist painters, Joyce has managed to incorporate into his text different kinds of symbols borrowed from Greek mythology, Western literature, and the Roman Catholic liturgy in such a way that they impart both artistic unity and universality of meaning to Stephen's story. Thus, Joyce has not only raised *The Portrait of the Artist as a Young Man* above the level of the traditional Bildungsroman, but also succeeded in setting new standards of artistic excellence for the novel.

Ulysses (1922), Joyce's masterpiece, has become a prime example of modernism in literature. It gives an account of man's life based on a family during one day. By providing an instance of how a single event contains all the events of its kind, and how history is recapitulated in the happenings of one day, Joyce seeks to present a microcosm of the whole human life. With complete objectivity and minute details of man's everyday routines and his psychic processes, Joyce illustrates a symbolic picture of all human history, which is simultaneously tragic and comic, heroic and cowardly, magnificent and dreary. Like Eliot's masterpiece, *The Waste Land*, Joyce's *Ulysses* presents a realistic picture of the modern wasteland in which modern men are portrayed as vulgar and trivial creatures with splitting personalities, disillusioned ideals, sordid minds and broken families, who are searching in vain for harmonious human relationships and spiritual sustenance in a decaying world. In *Ulysses*, Joyce is mainly concerned with the psychic processes of his characters. But such a subject matter does not contain a clear and orderly pattern or form. To compensate for this, Joyce makes use of several means to superimpose patterns or forms on his formless subject matter, such as the unities of time and place, Homeric and Biblical patterns, symbolic structures, image or word-phrase motifs, cyclical schemes, and so on. He also takes great pains to create *Ulysses* from a complex of various techniques, shifting his style between naturalism and symbolism, between exhibitionism and mystification, and between parodies and verbal experiments.

Joyce spent 17 years working on his last important book, *Finnegans Wake* (1939). In this encyclopedic work, Joyce ambitiously attempted to pack the whole history of mankind into one night's dream. In the dream experience, there is no self-conscious logic, no orderly associations, no established values, no limits of time or space; all the past, present and future are mingled and float freely in the mind. Thus, *Finnegans Wake* is regarded as the most original experiment ever made in the novel form, and also the most difficult book to read.

Joyce is one of the most prominent literary figures of the first half of the 20th century. As a great artistic genius, he has created a body of work worthy of comparison with the other masterpieces of English literature. In his opinion, the artist, who wants to reach the highest stage and to gain the insights necessary for the creation of dramatic art, should rise to the position of a god-like objectivity; he should have the complete conscious control over the creative process and depersonalize his own emotion in the artistic creation. He should appear as an omniscient author and present unspoken materials directly from the psyche of the characters, or make the characters tell their own inner thoughts in monologues. This literary approach to the presentation of psychological aspects of characters is usually termed as "streams of consciousness." Joyce is regarded as the most prominent stream-of-consciousness novelist, concentrating on revealing in his novels the psychic being of the characters. Another remarkable feature of his writings is his style. His own style is a straightforward one, lucid, logical and leisurely; subtlety, economy and exactness are his standards. But when he tries to render the so-called stream of consciousness, the style changes: incomplete, rapid, broken wording and fragmentary sentences are the typical features, which reflect the shifting, flirting, disorderly flow of thoughts in the major characters' mind. To create his modern Odyssey—Ulysses, Joyce adopts a kind of mock-heroic style. The essence of the mock-heroic lies in the application of apparently inappropriate styles. He achieves this mainly by elaborating his style into parody, pastiche, symbolic fantasy, and narration by question and answer from an omniscient narrator. Many critics think that Joyce is a great master of innovation. His radical experimentation ranges from streams of consciousness to his fantastic engagements with rhetoric, sentimental romance, historical stylistics, counterpoint and expressionist drama. His mastery of the English language and style is always highly praised.

8.6.2 "Araby"[1] from *Dubliners*

North Richmond Street,[2] being blind,[3] was a quiet street except at the hour when the Christian Brothers' School set the boys free.[4] An uninhabited house of two storeys stood at the blind end, detached from its neighbors in a square ground. The other houses of the street, conscious of decent lives within them, gazed at one another with brown[5] imperturbable faces.

The former tenant of our house, a priest, had died in the back drawing-room. Air, musty from having been long enclosed, hung in all the rooms, and the waste room behind the kitchen was littered with old useless papers. Among these I found a few paper-covered books, the pages of which were curled and damp: *The Abbot*, by Walter Scott, *The Devout Communicant*, and *The Memoirs of Vidocq*.[6] I liked the last best because its leaves were yellow. The wild garden behind the house contained a central apple-tree and a few straggling bushes, under one of which I found the late tenant's rusty bicycle-pump. He had been a very charitable priest; in his will he had left all his money to institutions and the furniture of his house to his sister.

When the short days of winter came, dusk fell before we had well eaten our dinners. When we met in the street the houses had grown somber. The space of sky above us was the color of ever-changing violet and towards it the lamps of the street lifted their feeble lanterns. The cold air stung us and we played till our bodies glowed. Our shouts echoed in the silent street. The career of our play brought us through the dark muddy lanes behind the houses, where we ran the gantlet[7] of the rough tribes from the cottages, to the back doors of the dark dripping gardens where odors arose from the ashpits, to the dark odorous stables where a coachman smoothed and combed the horse or shook music from the buckled harness. When we returned to the street, light from the kitchen windows had filled the areas. If my uncle was seen turning the corner, we hid in the shadow[8] until we had seen him safely housed. Or if Mangan's sister[9] came out on the doorstep to call her brother in to his tea, we watched her from our shadow peer up and down the street. We waited to see whether she would remain or go in and, if she remained, we left our shadow and walked up to Mangan's steps resignedly. She was waiting for us, her figure defined by the light from the half-opened door. Her brother always teased her before he obeyed, and I stood by the railings looking at her. Her dress swung as she moved her body, and the soft rope of her hair tossed from side to side.

Every morning I lay on the floor in the front parlor watching her door. The blind was pulled down to within an inch of the sash so that I could not be seen. When she came out on the doorstep my heart leaped. I ran to the hall, seized my books and followed her. I kept her brown figure always in my eye and, when we came near the point at which our ways diverged, I quickened my pace and passed her. This happened morning after morning. I had never spoken to her, except for a few casual words, and yet her name was like a summons to all my foolish blood.

Her image accompanied me even in places the most hostile to romance. On Saturday evenings when my aunt went marketing I had to go to carry some of the parcels. We walked through the flaring streets, jostled by drunken men and bargaining women, amid the curses of laborers, the shrill litanies of shop-boys who stood on guard by the barrels of pigs' cheeks, the nasal chanting of street-singers, who sang a *come-all-you* about O'donovan Rossa, [10] or a ballad about the troubles in our native land. These noises converged in a single sensation of life for me: I imagined that I bore my chalice safely through a throng of foes. Her name sprang to my lips at moments in strange prayers and praises which I myself did not understand. My eyes were often full of tears (I could not tell why) and at times a flood from my heart seemed to pour itself out into my bosom. I thought little of the future. I did not know whether I would ever speak to her or not or, if I spoke to her, how I could tell her of my confused adoration. But my body was like a harp and her words and gestures were like fingers running upon the wires.

One evening I went into the back drawing-room in which the priest had died. It was a dark rainy evening and there was no sound in the house. Through one of the broken panes I heard the rain impinge upon the earth, the fine incessant needles of water playing in the sodden beds. Some distant lamp or lighted window gleamed below me. I was thankful that I could see so little. All my senses seemed to desire to veil themselves and, feeling that I was about to slip from them, I pressed the palms of my hands together until they trembled, murmuring: '*O love! O love!*' many times.

At last she spoke to me. [11] When she addressed the first words to me I was so confused that I did not know what to answer. She asked me was I going to *Araby*. I forgot whether I answered yes or no. It would be a splendid bazaar; she said she would love to go.

—And why can't you? I asked.

While she spoke she turned a silver bracelet round and round her wrist. She could not go, she said, because there would be a retreat[12] that week in her convent. Her brother and two other boys were fighting for their caps, and I was alone at the railings. She held one of the spikes, bowing her head towards me. The light from the lamp opposite our door caught the white curve of her neck, lit up her hair that rested there and, falling, lit up the hand upon the railing. It fell over one side of her dress and caught the white border of a petticoat, just visible as she stood at ease.

—It's well for you, she said.

—If I go, I said, I will bring you something.

What innumerable follies laid waste my waking and sleeping thoughts after that evening! I wished to annihilate the tedious intervening days. I chafed against the work of school. At night in my bedroom and by day in the classroom her image came between me and the page I strove to read. The syllables of the word *Araby* were called to me through the silence in which my soul luxuriated and cast an Eastern enchantment over me. I asked for leave to go to the bazaar on Saturday night. My aunt was surprised, and hoped it was not some Freemason affair. [13] I answered few questions in class. I watched my master's face pass from amiability to sternness; he hoped I was not beginning to idle. I could not call my wandering thoughts together. I had hardly any patience with the serious work of life which, now that it stood between me and my desire, seemed to me child's play, ugly monotonous child's play.

On Saturday morning I reminded my uncle that I wished to go to the bazaar in the evening. He was fussing at the hallstand, looking for the hat-brush, and answered me curtly:

—Yes, boy, I know.

As he was in the hall I could not go into the front parlor and lie at the window. I felt the house in bad humor and walked slowly towards the school. The air was pitilessly raw and already my heart misgave me.

When I came home to dinner my uncle had not yet been home. Still it was early. I sat staring at the clock for some time and, when its ticking began to irritate me, I left the room. I mounted the staircase and gained the upper part of the house. The high cold empty gloomy rooms liberated me and I went from room to room singing. From the front window I saw my companions playing below in the street. Their cries reached me weakened and indistinct and, leaning my forehead against the cool glass, I looked over at the dark house where she lived. I may have stood there for an hour, seeing nothing but the brown-clad figure cast by my imagination, touched discreetly by the lamplight at the curved neck, at the hand upon the railings and at the border below the dress.

When I came downstairs again I found Mrs. Mercer sitting at the fire. She was an old garrulous woman, a pawnbroker's widow, who collected used stamps for some pious purpose. I had to endure the gossip of the tea-table. The meal was prolonged beyond an hour and still my uncle did not come. Mrs. Mercer stood up to go: she was sorry she couldn't wait any longer, but it was after eight o'clock and she did not like to be out late, as the night air was bad for her. When she had gone I began to walk up and down the room, clenching my fists. My aunt said:

—I'm afraid you may put off your bazaar for this night of Our Lord.

At nine o'clock I heard my uncle's latchkey in the hall door. I heard him talking to himself and heard the hallstand rocking when it had received the weight of his overcoat. I could interpret these signs. When he was midway through his dinner I asked him to give me the money to go to the bazaar. He had forgotten.

—The people are in bed and after their first sleep now, he said.

I did not smile. My aunt said to him energetically:

—Can't you give him the money and let him go? You've kept him late enough as it is.

My uncle said he was very sorry he had forgotten. He said he believed in the old saying: "All work and no play makes Jack a dull boy." He asked me where I was going and, when I told him a second time, he asked me did I know *The Arab's Farewell to his Steed.*[14] When I left the kitchen he was about to recite the opening lines of the piece to my aunt.

I held a florin[15] tightly in my hand as I strode down Buckingham Street towards the station. The sight of the streets thronged with buyers and glaring with gas recalled to me the purpose of my journey. I took my seat in a third-class carriage of a deserted train. After an intolerable delay the train moved out of the station slowly. It crept onward among ruinous houses and over the twinkling river. At Westland Row Station a crowd of people pressed to the carriage doors; but the porters moved them back, saying that it was a special train for the bazaar. I remained alone in the bare carriage. In a few minutes the train drew up beside an improvised wooden platform. I passed out on to the road and saw by the lighted dial of a clock that it was ten minutes to ten. In front of me was a large building which displayed the magical name.

I could not find any sixpenny entrance and, fearing that the bazaar would be closed, I passed in quickly through a turnstile, handing a shilling to a weary-looking man. I found myself in a big hall girded at half its height by a gallery. Nearly all the stalls were closed and the greater part of the hall was in darkness. I recognized a silence like that which pervades a church after a service. I walked into the center of the bazaar timidly. A few people were gathered about the stalls which were still open. Before a curtain, over which the words *Café Chantant*[16] were written in colored lamps, two men were counting money on a salver.[17] I listened to the fall of the coins.

Remembering with difficulty why I had come I went over to one of the stalls and examined porcelain vases and flowered tea-sets. At the door of the stall a young lady was talking and laughing with two young gentlemen. I remarked their English accents and listened vaguely to their conversation.

—O, I never said such a thing!

—O, but you did!

—O, but I didn't!

—Didn't she say that?

—Yes. I heard her.

—O, there's a ... fib!

Observing me, the young lady came over and asked me did I wish to buy anything. The tone of her voice was not encouraging; she seemed to have spoken to me out of a sense of duty. I looked humbly at the great jars that stood like eastern guards at either side of the dark entrance to the stall and murmured:

—No, thank you.

The young lady changed the position of one of the vases and went back to the two young men. They began to talk of the same subject. Once or twice the young lady glanced at me over her shoulder.

I lingered before her stall, though I knew my stay was useless, to make my interest in her wares seem the more real. Then I turned away slowly and walked down the middle of the bazaar. I allowed the two pennies to fall against the sixpence in my pocket. I heard a voice call from one end of the gallery that the light was out. The upper part of the hall was now completely dark.

Gazing up into the darkness I saw myself as a creature driven and derided by vanity; and my eyes burned with anguish and anger.

☞ Notes

1. **Araby:** a term used to express the romantic view of the east that had been popular since Napoleon's triumph over Egypt. And, of course, the story is about Romantic Irony, for the unnamed boy has a romantic view of the world.
2. **North Richmond Street:** In 1894 little Jimmy Joyce was 12, and lived at 17 North Richmond Street.
3. **being blind:** referring to the street being dead end. But this also describes the condition of the boy's relation to reality.
4. **set the boys free:** Joyce uses this neat phrase to suggest that religion has imprisoned the boys.
5. **brown:** the most frequently used color in *Dubliners*. We note how quickly Joyce has been able to set a nearly hopeless and discouraged mood. In *Stephen Hero*, Joyce writes: "... one of those brown brick houses which seem the very incarnation of Irish paralysis."
6. ***The Abbot*, by Walter Scott, *The Devout Communicant*, and *The Memoirs of Vidocq*:** historical tale, a manual of religious instruction, and the recollections of a French adventure, respectively.
7. **gantlet:** an archaic spelling of "gauntlet."
8. **shadow:** Note the repetition of "shadow" (three times) in this paragraph. The people of Dublin are not living, but ghosts; the boys, who are very much alive, are

surrounded by shades of people.

9. **Mangan's sister:** Here Joyce makes the connection with the popular, but sentimental and romantic 19th century Irish poet, James Clarence Mangan (1803-1849). Mangan was himself fond of writing about "Araby," and even though he knew no Arabic he claimed that some of his poems were translations from Arabic. Joyce's use of "Mangan" is one of the strongest supports for the theme of romanticism in the story, while at the same time it serves to strengthen previous instances of hypocrisy and false sentiment.
10. ***come-all-you* about O'Donovan Rossa:** street ballad, so called from its opening words. This one was about the 19th-century Irish nationalist Jeremiah Donovan, popularly known as O'Donovan Rossa.
11. **she spoke to me:** Here is a good example of an important modernist technique: "Show, do not tell."
12. **retreat:** period of seclusion from ordinary activities devoted to religious exercises.
13. **Freemason affair:** international secret service society, also called the Free and Accepted Masons. His aunt shares her church's distrust of the Freemansons.
14. ***The Arab's Farewell to his Steed*:** popular 19th-century poem, which tells about an Arab boy who sells for gold coins the thing that he loves the most in the world, his horse, however, as the horse is being led away the boy changes his mind and rushes after the man to return to money and reclaim his love.
15. **a florin:** a former two-shilling coin. It was a considerable amount of money for this boy. The florin originated in Florence during the Renaissance and had a likeness of the Virgin Mary on one side and that of St. John the Baptist on the other.
16. ***Café Chantant:*** a French coffee house where musical entertainment is provided.
17. **salver:** tray, usually used for serving food.

☞ Study questions

1. What kind of conflict does the boy experience in the story between him and his environment, or between him and the adults?
2. How does the boy describe his feelings for Mangan's sister?
3. Why does the boy want to go to the bazaar?
4. What do you think about the boy's love for Mangan's sister? Have you experienced puppy love or momentary infatuation before?
5. What is the role of the boy's uncle in the story? What values and attitudes does he represent?
6. The story is an initiation story. What do you think the boy has learned?

☞ Essay topics

1. Why does the bazaar become a negative experience for the boy? What do you think the experience teaches him about dreams as opposed to reality?
2. In what ways did British rule of Ireland affect the everyday life of the Irish people?

8.6.3 An excerpt from Episode 8 of *Ulysses*

Pineapple rock, lemon platt, butter scotch. [1] A sugarsticky[2] girl shovelling scoopfuls of creams for a christian brother. Some school treat. [3] Bad for their tummies. Lozenge and comfit manufacturer to His Majesty the King. [4] God. Save. Our?[5] Sitting on his throne sucking red jujubes white. [6]

A sombre Y. M. C. A. [7] young man, watchful among the warm sweet fumes of Graham Lemon's, [8] placed a throwaway[9] in a hand of Mr Bloom.

Heart to heart talks.

Bloo ... Me? No. [10]

Blood of the Lamb. [11]

His slow feet walked him riverward, reading. Are you saved? All are washed in the blood of the lamb. God wants blood victim. Birth, hymen, martyr, war, foundation of a building, sacrifice, kidney burnt offering, druids'[12] altars. Elijah[13] is coming. Dr John Alexander Dowie, restorer of the church in Zion, [14] is coming.

Is coming! Is coming!! Is coming!!!

All heartily welcome.

Paying game. Torry and Alexander last year. Polygamy. His wife will put the stopper on that. Where was that ad some Birmingham firm the luminous crucifix?[15] Our Saviour. Wake up in the dead of night and see him on the wall, hanging. Pepper's[16] ghost idea. Iron nails ran in.

Phosphorus it must be done with. If you leave a bit of codfish for instance. I could see the bluey silver over it. Night I went down to the pantry in the kitchen. Don't like all the smells in it waiting to rush out. What was it she wanted? The Malaga raisins. Thinking of Spain. Before Rudy[17] was born. The phosphorescence, that bluey greeny. Very good for the brain.

From Butler's monument house corner he glanced along Bachelor's walk. Dedalus' daughter there still outside Dillon's auction rooms. Must be selling off some old furniture. Knew her eyes at once from the father. Lobbing about waiting for him. Home always breaks up when the mother goes. Fifteen children he had. Birth every year almost. That's in their theology or the priest won't give the poor woman the confession, the absolution. Increase and multiply. Did you ever hear such an idea? Eat you out of house and home. No families themselves[18] to feed. Living on the fat of the land. Their butteries and larders. [19] I'd like to see them do the black fast Yom Kippur. [20] Crossbuns. [21]

One meal and a collation[22] for fear he'd collapse on the altar. A housekeeper of one of those fellows If you could pick it out of her. Never pick it out of her. Like getting £. s. d.[23] out of him. Does himself well. No guests. All for number one. Watching his water. Bring your own bread and butter. His reverence. Mum's the word.

Good Lord, that poor child's dress is in flitters. Underfed she looks too. Potatoes and marge, marge and potatoes. It's after they feel it. Proof of the pudding.[24] Undermines the constitution.

As he set foot on O'Connell bridge a puffball of smoke plumed up from the parapet. Brewery barge with export stout. England. Sea air sours it, I heard. Be interesting some day get a pass through Hancock[25] to see the brewery. Regular world in itself. Vats of porter, wonderful. Rats get in too. Drink themselves bloated as big as a collie floating. Dead drunk on the porter. Drink till they puke again like christians. Imagine drinking that! Rats: vats. Well of course if we knew all the things.

Looking down he saw flapping strongly, wheeling between the gaunt[26] quay walls, gulls. Rough weather outside. If I threw myself down? Reuben J.'s son[27] must have swallowed a good bellyful of that sewage. One and eightpence too much. Hhhhm. It's the droll way he comes out with the things. Knows how to tell a story too.

They wheeled lower. Looking for grub. Wait.

He threw down among them a crumpled paper ball. Elijah thirty-two feet per sec is com.[28] Not a bit. The ball bobbed unheeded on the wake of swells, floated under by the bridge piers. Not such damn fools. Also the day I threw that stale cake out of the Erin's King[29] picked it up in the wake fifty yards astern. Live by their wits. They wheeled, flapping.

The hungry famished gull
Flaps o'er the waters dull.

That is how poets write, the similar sounds. But then Shakespeare has no rhymes: blank verse. The flow of the language it is. The thoughts. Solemn.

Hamlet, I am thy father's spirit
Doomed for a certain time to walk the earth.[30]

—Two apples a penny! Two for a penny!

His gaze passed over the glazed apples serried on her stand. Australians they must be this time of year. Shiny peels: polishes them up with a rag or a handkerchief.

Wait. Those poor birds.

He halted again and bought from the old apple woman two Banbury cakes for a penny and broke the brittle paste and threw its fragments down into the Liffey. See that? The gulls swooped silently two, then all from their heights, pouncing on prey. Gone. Every morsel.

Aware of their greed and cunning he shook the powdery crumb from his hands.

They never expected that. Manna.[31] Live on fishy flesh they have to, all sea birds, gulls, sea goose. Swans from Anna Liffey swim down here sometimes to preen themselves. No accounting for tastes. Wonder what kind is swan meat. Robinson Crusoe had to live on them.

They wheeled, flapping weakly. I'm not going to throw any more. Penny quite enough. Lot of thanks I get. Not even a caw.[32] They spread foot and mouth disease too. If you cram a turkey, say, on chestnut meal it tastes like that. Eat pig like pig. But then why is it that saltwater fish are not salty? How is that?

☞ Notes

1. **Pineapple rock, lemon platt, butter scotch:** As Bloom passes by a sweet shop, his eyes catch sight of the sweets.
2. **sugarsticky:** It means "sticky sweets;" here Joyce invents the word "sugarsticky," which vividly describes both her appearance and what she is doing.
3. **Some school treat:** The Christian brother is buying creams for the school children.
4. **Lozenge and comfit manufacturer to His Majesty the King:** These are the words on the shop window to show that the sweets are made by certain manufacturer for the king.
5. **God. Save. Our:** from the very words "His Majesty" Bloom's thought jumps to the national anthem of England, which is "God Save Our King."
6. **Sitting on his throne, sucking red jujubes white:** Bloom imagines the king as a child sucking gum on the throne.
7. **Y. M. C. A.:** the initials of "Young Men's Christian Association."
8. **Graham Lemon's:** the name of the sweets shop.
9. **throwaway:** a kind of advertisement leaflet.
10. **Bloo … Me? No:** Bloom's eyes catch the word "Bloo. …" he mistakes it for "Bloom."
11. **Lamb:** capitalized "Lamb" usually refers to Jesus Christ.
12. **druids:** priests of the ancient Celtic religion in Britain.
13. **Elijah:** the name of an ancient prophet of Israel. Here it refers to Dr. John Alexander Dowei, who was a Scottish-American evangelist and established the "Christian Catholic Church in Zion" in 1901.
14. **Zion:** a height in the northeastern part of Jerusalem.
15. **the luminous crucifix:** A crucifix is a cross bearing the sculptured figure of Christ. Here the crucifix is made of phosphorus, so that it shines in darkness.
16. **Pepper:** the name of the inventor of the crucifix.
17. **Rudy:** Bloom's son, who died in infancy eleven years before.
18. **themselves:** referring to the priests.
19. **butteries and larders:** Both words mean storeroom.

20. **Yom Kippur:** the Jewish day of Atonement, the most solemn day of the Jewish year, observed with fasting and prayers of repentance.
21. **Crossbuns:** sweet cakes indented with a cross.
22. **collation:** a light meal, especially at an unusual time.
23. **£. s. d. :** abbreviations, respectively, for pounds, shillings, and pence.
24. **Proof of the pudding:** an imcomplete English proverb: Proof of the pudding is in the eating.
25. **Hancock:** the name of some person Bloom knows.
26. **gaunt:** grim and forbidding.
27. **Reuben J. 's son:** Reuben J. Dodd was a solicitor in Dublin. His son fell into the Liffey River and was rescued by a man to whom Reuben gave two shillings as a reward. "One and eightpence too much" was the remark of Simon Dedalus, the father of Stephen Dedalus when he discussed the matter with Bloom earlier that morning.
28. **Elijah thirty-two feet per sec is com:** The pamphlet printed with "Elijah is coming" falls down at the rate of 32 feet per second.
29. **Erin's King:** the name of a ferry boat.
30. **Hamlet, I am thy father's spirit/ Doomed for a certain time to walk the earth:** a slightly misquoted quotation from *Hamlet* (I. v. 9-10).
31. **Manna:** the food miraculously supplied to the Israelites in the wilderness (see *Exodus*, 16:15).
32. **caw:** the cry of a gull or crow.

☞ Study questions

1. What pervades Bloom's thoughts when he passes by a sweet shop?
2. What does he think about when he is handed a religious pamphlet, with the opening phrase "Blood of the Lamb"?
3. What kind of feeling does Bloom have when he sees Stephen's sister, Dilly, in the street?
4. What does Bloom do when he watches the seagulls swoop around?
5. What facets of Dublin life are reflected in this episode?
6. What virtues and shortcomings of Bloom are highlighted in this episode?
7. What aspects of Bloom's personality are revealed in this episode?

☞ Essay topics

1. What does Bloom quest in this episode?
2. Comment on Joyce's use of symbolism in *Ulysses*.
3. Examine Joyce's use of stream-of-consciousness technique in *Ulysses*.

8.7 Virginia Woolf

8.7.1 Life and career

Virginia Woolf (1882-1941) was born into an intellectual family in London. She was educated at home by tutors while her brothers were sent to the universities. She got her learning mainly from her widely reading of books in her father's extensive library. As a young girl, Virginia was mentally sensitive and physically fragile, suffering from recurrent conditions of nervous stress which led to several suicide attempts.

Following the death of her father in 1904, Woolf moved with her sister Vanessa and two brothers to the house in Bloomsbury. Their home soon became the centre of the Bloomsbury Group, a loose organization of a number of free-minded intellectuals who would meet to discuss varieties of issues on politics, religion, philosophy, art, and moral values of the day. Within this intellectual circle, Virginia met Leonard Woolf, a writer of historical and political books; they fell in love and got married in 1912. Together she and her husband founded the Hogarth Press, which provided great help in publishing the early works of such writers like T. S. Eliot, E. M. Forster, Katherine Mansfield, and Maxim Gorky.

Virginia's health conditions became worse in her late fifties. With the imminence of the Second World War, she felt that civilization was done for, and that life was not of value at any price. After the completion of her novel, *Between the Acts* (1941), Virginia lost her last bit of strength to live on and drowned herself in a river near her country house in 1941.

Virginia Woolf began her literary career by writing reviews for *The Time Literary Supplement*. Her critical essays were collected in the two series of *The Common Reader* (1925 and 1932) and in a number of volumes published after her death. Besides the essays, another two books, *A Room of One's Own* (1929) and *Three Guineas* (1938), are worth mentioning, for Woolf discussed women's problems and expressed her feminist ideas in them.

Virginia Woolf wrote her first two novels, *The Voyage Out* (1915) and *Night and Day* (1919), more or less in the traditional way. But she was soon dissatisfied with the methods and outlook of traditional novelists. She started experimenting with new techniques in novel writing. *Jacob's Room* (1922) was her first attempt of such experimentation. Minimizing external action, Woolf made a subjective exploration of her characters' inner lives by presenting their interior monologues. Memories, thoughts and sub-thoughts blended with impressions of external objects. In her following novels Woolf made further experiments with the stream-of-consciousness technique and with the disruption of time. Her three innovatory novels are: *Mrs. Dalloway* (1925), *To the*

Lighthouse (1927), and *The Waves* (1931), which established her position as an important modern novelist. In 1928, she published *Orlando*, an imaginative analysis of gender, identity and creativity. Her final novel, *Between the Acts*, depicts the relationship between the writer and her audience and reflects upon the role of art in building civilization and defending it against lurking violence and male aggression.

Mrs. Dalloway, presenting the inner lives of the characters in the course of a single day, broke new ground with the stream-of-consciousness technique pioneered by James Joyce in *Ulysses* (1922). The central figure, Clarissa Dalloway, is an upper class hostess. She spends her day in London preparing for her evening party. Within this narrow frame of time and space, Mrs. Dalloway has very limited and trivial contacts with the outside world; but these contacts evoke in her and in other characters a rich flow of thoughts and memories that reveal Mrs. Dalloway's life story from girlhood to her present age of fifty. In one sense, the novel is a life story of Clarissa Dalloway, depicting a brave and resourceful woman, coping in her own way with a disappointing life of sexual repression, family trauma and the effects of illness. In another, it is about the human life itself. While probing the timeless values of human life on the poetic level, the novel presents, on the prose level, a wretched picture of the alienated modern world with its destructive forces of power-struggle, economic depression and war.

To the Lighthouse (1927) was Woolf's attempt to recapture in fictional form the characters of her parents and the atmosphere of the family holidays of her childhood at St. Ives in Cornwall. By using the stream-of-consciousness technique, she dramatizes the organic workings of the characters' psychological world with a most subtle and inward responsiveness. As her aim is to convey the spirit of life and to display the complex and inexpressible inner activities of man, Woolf adopts a symbolic structure in organizing her novel. It is arranged in three parts. Part Ⅰ is presented statically with a fixed scene; it is built around Mrs. Ramsay, who herself is a symbol associated with the flashing light of the Lighthouse, standing for the spirit of life and the subjective view towards reality. Thematically, the first part states the positive value of human life. Part Ⅱ conveys the passage of the clock time with a shadowy, menacing background that implies nature's hostility towards human life. This short part serves as a bridge to link the events happened in Part Ⅰ with those in Part Ⅲ; it carries the theme of the negative value of human life. Part Ⅲ poses a contrast with the static scene of the first part. It centers on Mr. Ramsay who represents the physical side of life and the objective view towards reality. Thus, the third part does not only reaffirm the positive view of the first part, but also presents a synthetic view towards the value of life by combining the subjective and objective views towards reality. In addition, the varied length of the three parts also resembles the pattern of the beams sent out from the Lighthouse, which is the central symbol of the novel. In fact, the novel is organized on a long-short-long, or light-darkness-light, pattern, which symbolizes a positive-negative-and-synthetic view of human value thematically.

Virginia Woolf is a conscious writer who takes novel as a form of art. In her opinion, the form of conventional, commercial novel is not true. As life, she thinks, is not a series of gig lamps symmetrically arranged, but a luminous halo, a semi-transparent envelope surrounding us from beginning of consciousness to the end, the writer should not base his work upon conventions but upon his own feeling, if he were a free man. "There would be no plot, no comedy, no tragedy, no love interest or catastrophe in the accepted style." What a writer should do is to record what life felt like to living beings, to communicate the impression made by one individual upon others, and to reveal human personality partly through its own self-consciousness and partly through the picture projected by it upon other minds. This desire to discover and record life as it feels to those who live it was the originating cause of Virginia Woolf's rejection of existing conventions and her invention of new forms and techniques which would express her own vision of life and convey the movement of things under the surface—the free play of thought, emotion and insight.

Virginia Woolf is a strong advocator of the feminist movement. In her whole life she has been concerned over the position of women. In her books *Three Guineas* and *A Room of One's Own*, she speaks at length of the injustices women have suffered from lack of legal rights, education, vocation opportunity, and independence. She holds that the totalitarian and patriarchal social structure is responsible for the deprivation of the women. To change the condition of women, the whole patriarchal structure, including marriage, should be changed first. But the extensive influence of the system has served men so well that it will take the feminist fighters great courage and enormous efforts to fight against it.

8.7.2 "The New Dress"[1]

Mabel had her first serious suspicion that something was wrong as she took her cloak off and Mrs. Barnet, while handing her the mirror and touching the brushes and thus drawing her attention, perhaps rather markedly, to all the appliances for tidying and improving hair, complexion, clothes, which existed on the dressing table, confirmed the suspicion—that it was not right, not quite right, which growing stronger as she went upstairs and springing at her, with conviction as she greeted Clarissa Dalloway, she went straight to the far end of the room, to a shaded corner where a looking—glass hung and looked. No! It was not RIGHT. And at once the misery which she always tried to hide, the profound dissatisfaction—the sense she had had, ever since she was a child, of being inferior to other people—set upon her, relentlessly, remorselessly, with an intensity which she could not beat off, as she would when she woke at night at home, by reading Borrow[1] or Scott;[1] for oh these men, oh these women, all were thinking—"What's Mabel wearing? What a fright she looks! What a hideous new dress!"—their eyelids flickering as they came up and then their lids shutting rather tight. It was her own appalling inadequacy; her cowardice; her mean, water—sprinkled blood that depressed her. And at once the whole of the room where, for ever so many hours, she had planned with the little dressmaker how it was to go, seemed sordid, repulsive; and her own drawing—room so shabby, and herself, going out, puffed up with vanity as she touched the letters on the hall table and said: "How dull!" to show off—all this now seemed unutterably silly, paltry, and provincial. All this had been absolutely destroyed, shown up, exploded, the moment she came into Mrs. Dalloway's drawing-room.

What she had thought that evening when, sitting over the teacups, Mrs. Dalloway's invitation came, was that, of course, she could not be fashionable. It was absurd to pretend it even—fashion meant cut, meant style, meant thirty guineas at least—but why not be original? Why not be herself, anyhow? And, getting up, she had taken that old fashion book of her mother's, a Paris fashion book of the time of the Empire, and had thought how much prettier, more dignified, and more womanly they were then, and so set herself—oh, it was foolish—trying to be like them, pluming herself in fact, upon being modest and old-fashioned, and very charming, giving herself up, no doubt about it, to an orgy of self-love, which deserved to be chastised, and so rigged herself out like this.

But she dared not look in the glass. She could not face the whole horror—the pale yellow, idiotically old-fashioned silk dress with its long skirt and its high sleeves and its waist and all the things that looked so charming in the fashion book, but not on her, not among all these ordinary people. She felt like a dressmaker's dummy standing there, for young people to stick pins into. "But, my dear, it's perfectly charming!" Rose Shaw said, looking her up and down with that little satirical pucker of the lips which she expected—Rose herself being dressed in the height of the fashion, precisely like everybody else, always.

We are all like flies trying to crawl over the edge of the saucer, Mabel thought, and repeated the phrase as if she were crossing herself, as if she were trying to find some spell to annul this pain, to make this agony endurable. Tags of Shakespeare, lines from books she had read ages ago, suddenly came to her when she was in agony, and she repeated them over and over again. "Flies trying to crawl," she repeated. If she could say that over often enough and make herself see the flies, she would become numb, chill, frozen, dumb. Now she could see flies crawling slowly out of a saucer of milk with their wings stuck together; and she strained and strained (standing in front of the looking-glass, listening to Rose Shaw) to make herself see Rose Shaw and all the other people there as flies, trying to hoist themselves out of something, or into something, meagre, insignificant, toiling flies. But she could not see them like that, not other people. She saw herself like that—she was a fly, but the others were dragonflies, butterflies, beautiful insects, dancing, fluttering, skimming, while she alone dragged herself up out of the saucer. (Envy and spite, the most detestable of the vices, were her chief faults.)

"I feel like some dowdy, decrepit, horribly dingy old fly," she said, making Robert Haydon stop just to hear her say that, just to reassure herself by furbishing up a poor weak-kneed phrase and so showing how detached she was, how witty, that she did not feel in the least out of anything. And, of course, Robert Haydon answered something, quite polite, quite insincere, which she saw through instantly, and said to herself, directly he went (again from some book), "Lies, lies, lies!" For a party makes things either much more real, or much less real, she thought; she saw in a flash to the bottom of Robert Haydon's heart; she saw through everything. She saw the truth. THIS was true, this drawing-room, this self, and the other false. Miss Milan's little workroom was really terribly hot, stuffy, sordid. It smelt of clothes and cabbage cooking; and yet, when Miss Milan put the glass in her hand, and she looked at herself with the dress on, finished, an extraordinary bliss shot through her heart. Suffused with light, she sprang into existence. Rid of cares and wrinkles, what she had dreamed of herself was there—a beautiful woman. just for a second (she had not dared look longer, Miss Milan wanted to know about the length of the skirt), there looked at her, framed in the scrolloping mahogany, a grey-white, mysteriously smiling, charming girl, the core of herself, the soul of herself; and it was not vanity only, not only self-love that made her think it good, tender, and true. Miss Milan said that the skirt could not well be longer; if anything the skirt, said Miss Milan, puckering her forehead, considering with all her wits about her, must be shorter; and she felt, suddenly, honestly, full of love for Miss Milan, much, much fonder of Miss Milan than of any one in the whole world, and could have cried for pity that she should be crawling on the floor with her mouth full of pins, and her face red and her eyes bulging—that one human being should be doing this for another, and she saw them all as human beings merely, and herself going off to her party, and Miss Milan pulling the cover over the canary's cage, or letting him pick a hemp-seed from between her lips, and the thought of it, of this side of human nature and its patience and its endurance and its being content with such miserable, scanty, sordid, little pleasures filled her eyes with tears.

And now the whole thing had vanished. The dress, the room, the love, the pity, the scrolloping looking-glass, and the canary's cage—all had vanished, and here she was in a corner of Mrs. Dalloway's drawing-room, suffering tortures, woken wide awake to reality. But it was all so paltry, weak-blooded, and petty-minded to care so much at her age with two children, to be still so utterly dependent on people's opinions and not have principles or convictions, not to be able to say as other people did, "There's Shakespeare! There's death! We're all weevils in a captain's biscuit"—or whatever it was that people did say.

She faced herself straight in the glass; she pecked at her left shoulder; she issued out into the room, as if spears were thrown at her yellow dress from all sides. But instead of looking fierce or tragic, as Rose Shaw would have done—Rose would have looked like Boadicea[4]—she looked foolish and self-conscious, and simpered like a schoolgirl and slouched across the room, positively slinking, as if she were a beaten mongrel, and looked at a picture, an engraving. As if one went to a party to look at a picture! Everybody knew why she did it—it was from shame, from humiliation.

"Now the fly's in the saucer," she said to herself, "right in the middle, and can't get out, and the milk," she thought, rigidly staring at the picture, "is sticking its wings together."

"It's so old-fashioned," she said to Charles Burt, making him stop (which by itself he hated) on his way to talk to some one else.

She meant, or she tried to make herself think that she meant, that it was the picture and not her dress, that was old-fashioned. And one word of praise, one word of affection from Charles would have made all the difference to her at the moment. If he had only said, "Mabel, you're looking charming to-night!" it would have changed her life. But then she ought to have been truthful and direct. Charles said nothing of the kind, of course. He was malice itself. He always saw through one, especially if one were feeling particularly mean, paltry, or feeble-minded.

"Mabel's got a new dress!" he said, and the poor fly was absolutely shoved into the middle of the saucer. Really, he would like her to drown, she believed. He had no heart, no fundamental kindness, only a veneer of friendliness. Miss Milan was much more real, much kinder. If only one could feel that and stick to it, always. "Why," she asked herself—replying to Charles much too pertly, letting him see that she was out of temper, or "ruffled" as he called it ("Rather ruffled?" he said and went on to laugh at her with some woman over there)—"Why," she asked herself, "can't I feel one thing always, feel quite sure that Miss Milan is right, and Charles wrong and stick to it, feel sure about the canary and pity and love and not be whipped all round in a second by coming into a room full of people?" It was her odious, weak, vacillating character again, always giving at the critical moment and not being seriously interested in conchology, etymology, botany, archeology, cutting up potatoes and watching them fructify[5] like Mary Dennis, like Violet Searle. Then Mrs. Holman, seeing her standing there, bore down upon her. Of course a thing like a dress was beneath Mrs. Holman's notice, with her family always tumbling downstairs or having the scarlet fever. Could Mabel tell her if Elmthorpe was ever let for August and September? Oh, it was a conversation that bored her unutterably!—it made her furious to be treated like a house agent or a messenger boy, to be made use of. Not to have value, that was it, she thought, trying to grasp something hard, something real, while she tried to answer sensibly about the bathroom and the south aspect and the hot water to the top of the house; and all the time she could see little bits of her yellow dress in the round looking-glass which made them all the size of boot-buttons or tadpoles; and it was amazing to think how much humiliation and agony and self-loathing and effort and passionate ups and downs of feeling were contained in a thing the size of a threepenny bit. And what was still odder, this thing, this Mabel Waring, was separate, quite disconnected; and though Mrs. Holman (the black button) was leaning forward and telling her how her eldest boy had strained his heart running, she could see her, too, quite detached in the looking-glass, and it was impossible that the black dot, leaning forward, gesticulating, should make the yellow dot, sitting solitary, self-centred, feel what the black dot was feeling, yet they pretended.

"So impossible to keep boys quiet"—that was the kind of thing one said.

And Mrs. Holman, who could never get enough sympathy and snatched what little there was greedily, as if it were her right (but she deserved much more for there was her little girl who had come down this morning with a swollen knee-joint), took this miserable offering and looked at it suspiciously, grudgingly, as if it were a halfpenny when it ought to have been a pound and put it away in her purse, must put up with it, mean and miserly though it was, times being hard, so very hard; and on she went, creaking, injured Mrs. Holman, about the girl with the swollen joints. Ah, it was tragic, this greed, this clamour of human beings, like a row of cormorants,[6] barking and flapping their wings for sympathy—it was tragic, could one have felt it and not merely pretended to feel it!

But in her yellow dress to-night she could not wring out one drop more; she wanted it all, all for herself. She knew (she kept on looking into the glass, dipping into that dreadfully showing-up blue pool) that she was condemned, despised, left like this in a backwater, because of her being like this a feeble, vacillating creature; and it seemed to her that the yellow dress was a penance which she had deserved, and if she had been dressed like Rose Shaw, in lovely, clinging green with a ruffle of swansdown, she would have deserved that; and she thought that there was no escape for her—none whatever. But it was not her fault altogether, after all. It was being one of a family of ten; never having money enough, always skimping and paring; and her mother carrying great cans, and the linoleum worn on the stair edges, and one sordid little domestic tragedy after another—nothing catastrophic, the sheep farm failing, but not utterly; her eldest brother marrying beneath him but not very much—there was no romance, nothing extreme about them all. They petered out respectably in seaside resorts; every watering-place had one of her aunts even now asleep in some lodging with the front windows not quite facing the sea. That was so like them—they had to squint at things always. And she had done the same—she was just like her aunts. For all her dreams of living in India, married to some hero like Sir Henry Lawrence, [7] some empire builder (still the sight of a native in a turban filled her with romance), she had failed utterly. She had married Hubert, with his safe, permanent underling's job in the Law Courts, and they managed tolerably in a smallish house, without proper maids, and hash when she was alone or just bread and butter, but now and then—Mrs. Holman was off, thinking her the most dried-up, unsympathetic twig she had ever met, absurdly dressed, too, and would tell every one about Mabel's fantastic appearance—now and then, thought Mabel Waring, left alone on the blue sofa, punching the cushion in order to look occupied, for she would not join Charles Burt and Rose Shaw, chattering like magpies and perhaps laughing at her by the fireplace—now and then, there did come to her delicious moments, reading the other night in bed, for instance, or down by the sea on the sand in the sun, at Easter—let her recall it—a great tuft of pale sand-grass standing all twisted like a shock of spears against the sky, which was blue like a smooth china egg, so firm, so hard, and then the melody of the waves—"Hush, hush," they said, and the children's shouts paddling—yes, it was a divine moment, and there she lay, she felt, in the hand of the Goddess who was the world; rather a hard—hearted, but very beautiful Goddess, a little lamb laid on the altar (one did think these silly things, and it didn't matter so long as one never said them). And also with Hubert sometimes she had quite unexpectedly—carving the mutton for Sunday lunch, for no reason, opening a letter, coming into a room—divine moments, when she said to herself (for she would never say this to anybody else), "This is it. This has happened. This is it!" And the other way about it was equally surprising—that is, when everything was arranged—music, weather, holidays, every reason for happiness was there—then nothing happened at all. One wasn't happy. It was flat, just flat, that was all.

Her wretched self again, no doubt! She had always been a fretful, weak, unsatisfactory mother, a wobbly wife, lolling about in a kind of twilight existence with nothing very clear or very bold, or more one thing than another, like all her brothers and sisters, except perhaps Herbert—they were all the same poor water-veined creatures who did nothing. Then in the midst of this creeping, crawling life, suddenly she was on the crest of a wave. That wretched fly—where had she read the story that kept coming into her mind about the fly and the saucer?—struggled out. Yes, she had those moments. But now that she was forty, they might come more and more seldom. By degrees she would cease to struggle any more. But that was deplorable! That was not to be endured! That made her feel ashamed of herself!

She would go to the London Library to-morrow. She would find some wonderful, helpful, astonishing book, quite by chance, a book by a clergyman, by an American no one had ever heard of; or she would walk down the Strand and drop, accidentally, into a hall where a miner was telling about the life in the pit, and suddenly she would become a new person. She would be absolutely transformed. She would wear a uniform; she would be called Sister Somebody; she would never give a thought to clothes again. And for ever after she would be perfectly clear about Charles Burt and Miss Milan and this room and that room; and it would be always, day after day, as if she were lying in the sun or carving the mutton. It would be it!

So she got up from the blue sofa, and the yellow button in the looking-glass got up too, and she waved her hand to Charles and Rose to show them she did not depend on them one scrap, and the yellow button moved out of the looking-glass, and all the spears were gathered into her breast as she walked towards Mrs. Dalloway and said "Good night."

"But it's top early to go," said Mrs. Dalloway, who was always so charming.

"I'm afraid I must," said Mabel Waring. "But," she added in her weak, wobbly voice which only sounded ridiculous when she tried to strengthen it, "I have enjoyed myself enormously."

"I have enjoyed myself," she said to Mr. Dalloway, whom she met on the stairs.

"Lies, lies, lies!" she said to herself, going downstairs, and "Right in the saucer!" she said to herself as she thanked Mrs. Barnet for helping her and wrapped herself, round and round and round, in the Chinese cloak she had worn these twenty years.

☞ Notes

1. The story was written in 1924 whilst Virginia Woolf was writing *Mrs. Dalloway*. It is possible that it was originally to have been a chapter in the novel with which it shares some characters and events. The stream-of-consciousness narrative concerns Mabel Waring, deeply self-conscious and insecure as she attends a party hosted by Clarissa Dalloway. Mabel's new, though old-fashioned dress symbolizing her insecurity; she has gone to great care to have it made but on arrival at the party she sees it in a mirror and immediately announces to herself "No. It was not *right*."
2. **Borrow:** George Borrow (1803-1881), English traveler and novelist.
3. **Scott:** Sir Walter Scott (1771-1832), Scottish poet, novelist, journalist.
4. **Boadicea:** queen in ancient Britain who led a revolt against the Romans, was defeated, and poisoned herself in A. D. 62.
5. **fructify:** bear fruit.
6. **cormorants:** large swimming and diving birds with webbed feet and voracious appetites. Greedy people are sometimes referred to as cormorants.
7. **Sir Henry Lawrence:** (1806-1857), English general and administrator in India.

☞ Study questions

1. What do we learn about Mabel from her reasons for choosing the new dress?
2. What kinds of activity and people does Mabel most and least enjoy? Explain how her preferences relate to her upbringing.
3. In what ways does her sense of inferiority become a barrier between Mabel and other people?
4. In what sense is "The New Dress" a stream-of-consciousness story?
5. What is the main theme of the story?

8.8 D. H. Lawrence

8.8.1 Life and career

Lawrence (1885-1930) was born in Eastwood, a coal-mining town near Nottingham. His father was a coal miner with little education; but his mother, once a school teacher, was from a somewhat higher class. As a boy, Lawrence was quiet, clever and rather fragile. He started his education by attending the local boarding school. At the age of 13, he won a scholarship to Nottingham High School. Then he went to work as a pupil-teacher for a few years. Meanwhile, the relationship between his parents was in a state of ongoing and violent disintegration, a trauma reflected in much of his early writing. In 1906 he took up a scholarship to Nottingham University College, studying for a teaching certificate. After completing it, he began to work as a regular teacher. In 1910 Lawrence's mother died of cancer. With deep grief, he produced several poems: "Sorrow," "The End," "Piano," and "The Virgin Mother." During this period, Lawrence also began writing novels. His first novel, *The White Peacock* appeared in 1911. His second novel is *The Trespasser*, came out in 1912. Lawrence was recognized as a prominent novelist only after he published his third novel, *Sons and Lovers* (1913).

In 1912 he met Frieda, Professor Weekly's wife, who was the daughter of a German baron, mother of three children. They fell in love with each other and eloped to the continent. They got married in 1914 after Frieda got a divorce from her husband. During the First World War, Lawrence was suspected as a spy and watched by the police because of his anti-war attitude and his wife's German origins. His important novel, *Rainbow*, was published in 1915, but was banned as a danger to public morality. When the war was over, Lawrence left England for Italy. Throughout the 1920s, Lawrence was constantly on the move, from Italy to Ceylon, Australia, New Zealand, the South Seas, America, and Mexico, then back to England, Italy, and finally died of tuberculosis in the south of France. During all these years of wandering about, Lawrence kept on writing. With strong endurance of pain and enormous power of creation, he produced a large number of letters, poems, stories, novels, plays, critical essays and travel books.

Lawrence is one of the most prominent English novelists of the 20th century, and, perhaps, the greatest from a working-class family. But critics disagree sharply on which are his masterpieces. However, the following are generally regarded to be his major novels: *Sons and Lovers*, *The Rainbow*, *Women in Love* (1920) and *Lady Chatterley's Lover* (1928).

Much of *Sons and Lovers* is taken from his early life. The story starts with the marriage of Paul's parents. Mrs. Morel is a strong-willed, intelligent and ambitious woman who married beneath her own class, while Mr. Morel is uncouth and often drunk, with no formal education, but a certain openness of nature and zest for life. After an initial stage of happiness in their marriage, the class difference between them starts to estrange them from each other. The disillusion in her husband makes Mrs. Morel lavish all her affection upon her sons. Thus, the sons gradually come under the strong dominance of the mother in affection, aspirations and mental habits, and see their father with their mother's eyes, despising their father whose personality degenerates step by step as he feels his exclusion. In the second part of the novel, Paul's psychological development is traced with great subtlety. Paul depends heavily on his mother's love and help to make sense of the world around him; but in order to become an independent man and a true artist he has to make his own decisions about his life and work. With many-layered richness, *Sons and Lovers* contains some of Lawrence's most characteristic themes: the dehumanizing effect of the bourgeois industrialization; the complexity of human relationships, especially those between husband and wife, mother and son, and man and woman; the emotional possession of one person by another; and the usual account of the spiritual liberation of the protagonist in search for identity and fulfillment as an artist.

The Rainbow is the story of three generations of the Brangwen family on the Marsh farm. It is primarily concerned with the living relationships of human beings. With the terrible corruption that accompanies the spread of civilization, human personalities are distorted; love is perverted to a kind of pure animal lust; and the relationship between man and woman in marriage is deteriorated into a conflicting one. Will's monstrous lust for Anna, Skrebensky's sinister animal desire of Ursula, and Ursula's fiercely corrosive and violently destructive activity in the moonlight are good examples to show the distortion of the individual personalities and the deterioration of the human relationships. In Lawrence's opinion, the mechanical civilization is responsible for the unhealthy development of the individual psyche, the perversion of sexual life, and the failure of human fulfillment in marital relationships.

As its title implies, *Women in Love* is a novel about two love affairs which are dramatically presented with a series of short, precise episodes. The two heroines are Ursula Brangwen and her younger sister Gudrun; and the two chief male characters are

Gerald Crich, the young coalmine owner, and Rupert Birkin, a school inspector. After a series of ups and downs, Birkin and Ursula have reached a fruitful relationship which sustains bodies and souls in balance. But the passionate love of Gudrun and Gerald experiences a process of tension and deterioration which leads to Gerald's final death and Gudrun's total perversion. Through the progress of the two love affairs, Lawrence explores two kinds of love: the destructive love between Gerald and Gudrun and the creative love between Birkin and Ursula. In this novel the individual consciousness is subtly revealed and strands of themes are intricately wound up. The structural pattern of the book derives from the contrast between the destinies of the two pairs of lovers and the subordinate masculine relationship between Birkin and Gerald. The two sisters, the two male friends, and the two couples are closely paralleled in ideas, actions and relations so that each is corresponding to and contrasting with the other. Thus, *Women in Love* is regarded to be a more profoundly ordered novel than any other written by Lawrence.

However, in *Lady Chatterley's Lover* (1928), Lawrence has returned to his early subjects and background of Nottioghamshire. It tells of the love affair between a wealthy, married woman, and a man who works on her husband's estate. By presenting an old romantic story about a dissatisfied aristocratic lady who deserts her half-man, half-machine husband to find love with a man of nature, Lawrence not only condemns the civilized world of mechanism that distorts all natural relationships between men and women, but also advocates a return to nature. With rich symbolic images, the nature is portrayed by Lawrence in its minute vibrations with a tragic quality in its loveliness, which seems to embody the emotional states of the characters. Through a combination of traditional realism and the innovating elements of symbolism and poetic imagination, Lawrence has managed to bring out the subtle ebb and flow of his characters' subconscious life.

Lawrence turned his eyes outward to human society in his short stories. He was not only telling a story, but also using them to expose the bankruptcy of the mechanical civilization and to find an answer to it. Irony, humor and wit are the characteristic features of many of his stories. *St. Mawr*, *The Daughter of the Vicar*, *The Horse Dealer's Daughter*, *The Captain's Doll*, *The Prussian Officer*, *Odor of Chrysanthemums*, and *The Virgin and the Gypsy* are generally considered to be Lawrence's best known stories.

Lawrence began his poetry writing very early and wrote quite a large number of poems in his whole career. His collections of poetry include *Look! We Have Come Through* (1917), *Birds, Beasts, and Flowers* (1923), and *Pansies* (1929). His poems fall roughly into three categories—satirical and comic poems, poems about human relationships and emotions, and poems about nature. Lawrence does not care much about the conventional metrical rules; what he tries to do in poetry is to catch the instant life of the immediate present. In several of his best animal poems, Lawrence reveals the sheer unknowable otherness of the non-human life.

Lawrence was a rebellious and profoundly polemical writer with radical views. In his writings, he expressed a strong criticism of the mechanical civilization. In his opinion, the bourgeois industrialization, which made its realization at the cost of ravishing the land, had started the catastrophic uprooting of man from nature. Those profit-seeking capitalists frenziedly worshipped the filthy materialism and made use of the mechanisms of matter to inflict their exploitative will on the workman, the society and the earth. Under this mechanical control, human beings were turned into in-animated matter, while the in-animated matter should be animated to destroy both man and earth. It is this agonized concern about the dehumanizing effect of mechanical civilization on the sensual tenderness of human nature that haunts Lawrence's writings.

Lawrence was one of the first novelists to introduce themes of psychology into his works. He believed that the healthy way of the individual's psychological development lay in the primacy of the life impulse, or in another term, the sexual impulse. By presenting the psychological experience of individual human life and of human relationships, Lawrence has opened up a wide new territory to the novel. But the writer's dilemma is that although those intimate feelings of love can be passionately experienced by individuals they can hardly articulate precisely in words without offending the authorities and middle-class readers who are narrow and bigoted in conventional moral ideas. To break the taboo, Lawrence defiantly makes a deliberate use of those "four-letter" words in his novels, especially in *Lady Chatterley's Lover*. He declared that any repression of the sexual impulse based on social, religious, or moral values of the civilized world would cause severe damages to the harmony of human relationships and the psychic health of the individual's personality. This frank discussion of sex in his novel is the chief reason why Lawrence had been accused of pornographic writing.

Lawrence's artistic tendency is mainly realism, which combines dramatic scenes with an authoritative commentary. The realistic feature is most obviously seen in its detailed portraiture. With the working-class simplicity and directness, Lawrence can summon up all the physical attributes associated with the common daily objects. In presenting the psychological aspects of his characters, he makes use of poetic imagination and symbolism in his writing. By using sets of natural images as poetic symbols to embody the emotional states of the characters and to illustrate human situations, Lawrence endows the traditional realism with a fresh psychological meaning.

8. 8. 2 "The Rocking-Horse Winner"[1]

There was a woman who was beautiful, who started with all the advantages, yet she had no luck. She married for love, and the love turned to dust. She had bonny children, yet she felt they had been thrust upon her, and she could not love them. They looked at her coldly, as if they were finding fault with her. And hurriedly she felt she must cover up some fault in herself. Yet what it was that she must cover up she never knew. Nevertheless, when her children were present, she always felt the centre of her heart go hard. This troubled her, and in her manner she was all the more gentle and anxious for her children, as if she loved them very much. Only she herself knew that at the centre of her heart was a hard little place that could not feel love, no, not for anybody. Everybody else said of her: "She is such a good mother. She adores her children." Only she herself, and her children themselves, knew it was not so. They read it in each other's eyes.

There were a boy and two little girls. They lived in a pleasant house, with a garden, and they had discreet servants, and felt themselves superior to anyone in the neighborhood.

Although they lived in style,[2] they felt always an anxiety in the house. There was never enough money. The mother had a small income, and the father had a small income, but not nearly[3] enough for the social position which they had to keep up. The father went into town to some office. But though he had good prospects, these prospects never materialized. There was always the grinding sense[4] of the shortage of money, though the style was always kept up.

At last the mother said: "I will see if I can't make something." But she did not know where to begin. She racked her brains, and tried this thing and the other, but could not find anything successful. The failure made deep lines come into her face. Her children were growing up; they would have to go to school. There must be more money, there must be more money. The father, who was always very handsome and expensive in his tastes, seemed as if he never would be able to do anything worth doing. And the mother, who had a great belief in herself, did not succeed any better, and her tastes were just as expensive.

And so the house came to be haunted by the unspoken phrase: There must be more money! There must be more money! The children could hear it all the time though nobody said it aloud. They heard it at Christmas, when the expensive and splendid toys filled the nursery. Behind the shining modern rocking-horse, behind the smart doll's house, a voice would start whispering: "There must be more money! There must be more money!" And the children would stop playing, to listen for a moment. They would look into each other's eyes, to see if they had all heard. And each one saw in the eyes of the other two that they too had heard. "There must be more money! There must be more money!"

It came whispering from the springs of the still-swaying rocking-horse, and even the horse, bending his wooden, champing head, heard it. The big doll, sitting so pink and smirking in her new pram, could hear it quite plainly, and seemed to be smirking all the more self-consciously because of it. The foolish puppy, too, that took the place of the teddy-bear, he[6] was looking so extraordinarily foolish for no other reason but that he heard the secret whisper all over the house: "There must be more money!"

Yet nobody ever said it aloud. The whisper was everywhere, and therefore no one spoke it. Just as no one ever says: "We are breathing!" in spite of the fact that breath is coming and going all the time.

"Mother," said the boy Paul one day, "why don't we keep a car of our own? Why do we always use uncle's, or else a taxi?"

"Because we're the poor members of the family," said the mother.

"But why are we, mother?"

"Well — I suppose," she said slowly and bitterly, "it's because your father has no luck."

The boy was silent for so" he asked, rather timidly.

"No, Paul. Not quite. It's what causes you to have money."

"Oh!" said Paul vaguely. "I thought when Uncle Oscar said filthy lucker, it meant money."

"Filthy lucre[7] does mean money," said the mother. "But it's lucre, not luck."

"Oh!" said the boy. "Then what is luck, mother?"

"It's what causes you to have money. If you're lucky you have money. That's why it's better to be born lucky than rich. If you're rich, you may lose your money. But if you're lucky, you will always get more money."

"Oh! Will you? And is father not lucky?"

"Very unlucky, I should say," she said bitterly.

The boy watched her with unsure eyes.

"Why?" he asked.

"I don't know. Nobody ever knows why one person is lucky and another unlucky."

"Don't they? Nobody at all? Does nobody know?"

"Perhaps God. But He never tells."

"He ought to, then. And aren't you lucky either, mother?"

"I can't be, if I married an unlucky husband."

"But by yourself, aren't you?"

"I used to think I was, before I married. Now I think I am very unlucky indeed."

"Why?"

"Well — never mind! Perhaps I'm not really," she said.

The child looked at her to see if she meant it. But he saw, by the lines of her mouth, that she was only trying to hide something from him.

"Well, anyhow," he said stoutly, "I'm a lucky person."

"Why?" said his mother, with a sudden laugh.

He stared at her. He didn't even know why he had said it.

"God told me," he asserted, brazening it out.[8]

"I hope He did, dear!" she said, again with a laugh, but rather bitter.

"He did, mother!"

"Excellent!" said the mother, using one of her husband's exclamations.

The boy saw she did not believe him; or, rather that she paid no attention to his assertion. This angered him somewhat, and made him want to compel her attention.

He went off by himself, vaguely, in a childish way, seeking for the clue to "luck". Absorbed, taking no heed of other people, he went about with a sort of stealth, seeking inwardly for luck. He wanted luck, he wanted it, he wanted it. When the two girls were playing dolls in the nursery, he would sit on his big rocking-horse, charging madly into space, with a frenzy that made the little girls peer at him uneasily. Wildly the horse careered, the waving dark hair of the boy tossed, his eyes had a strange glare in them. The little girls dared not speak to him.

When he had ridden to the end of his mad little journey, he climbed down and stood in front of his rocking-horse, staring fixedly into its lowered face. Its red mouth was slightly open, its big eye was wide and glassy-bright.

"Now!" he would silently command the snorting steed. "Now take me to where there is luck! Now take me!"

And he would slash the horse on the neck with the little whip he had asked Uncle Oscar for. He knew the horse could take him to where there was luck, if only he forced it. So he would mount again and start on his furious ride, hoping at last to get there. He knew he could get there.

"You'll break your horse, Paul!" said the nurse.

"He's always riding like that! I wish he'd leave off!" said his elder sister Joan.

But he only glared down on them in silence. Nurse gave him up. She could make nothing of him.[9] Anyhow, he was growing beyond her.[10]

One day his mother and his Uncle Oscar came in when he was on one of his furious rides. He did not speak to them.

"Hallo, you young jockey! Riding a winner?" said his uncle.

"Aren't you growing too big for a rocking-horse? You're not a very little boy any longer, you know," said his mother.

But Paul only gave a blue glare from his big, rather close-set eyes. He would speak to nobody when he was in full tilt. His mother watched him with an anxious expression on her face.

At last he suddenly stopped forcing his horse into the mechanical gallop and slid down.

"Well, I got there!" he announced fiercely, his blue eyes still flaring, and his sturdy long legs straddling apart.

"Where did you get to?" asked his mother.

"Where I wanted to go," he flared back at her.

"That's right, son!" said Uncle Oscar. "Don't you stop till you get there. What's the horse's name?"

"He doesn't have a name," said the boy.

"Gets on without all right?"[11] asked the uncle.

"Well, he has different names. He was called Sansovino[12] last week."

"Sansovino, eh? Won the Ascot.[13] How did you know this name?"

"He always talks about horse-races with Bassett," said Joan.

The uncle was delighted to find that his small nephew was posted with all the racing news. Bassett, the young gardener, who had been wounded in the left foot in the war and had got his present job through Oscar Cresswell, whose batman he had been, was a perfect blade of the "turf".[14] He lived in the racing events, and the small boy lived with him.

Oscar Cresswell got it all from Bassett.

"Master Paul comes and asks me, so I can't do more than tell him, sir," said Bassett, his face terribly serious, as if he were speaking of religious matters.

"And does he ever put anything on a horse[15] he fancies?"

"Well — I don't want to give him away — he's a young sport, a fine sport, sir. Would you mind asking him himself? He sort of takes a pleasure in it, and perhaps he'd feel I was giving him away, sir, if you don't mind.

Bassett was serious as a church.[16]

The uncle went back to his nephew and took him off for a ride in the car.

"Say, Paul, old man, do you ever put anything on a horse?" the uncle asked.

The boy watched the handsome man closely.

"Why, do you think I oughtn't to?" he parried.

"Not a bit of it! I thought perhaps you might give me a tip for the Lincoln."

The car sped on into the country, going down to Uncle Oscar's place in Hampshire.

"Honor bright?"[17] said the nephew.

"Honor bright, son!" said the uncle.

"Well, then, Daffodil."

"Daffodil! I doubt it, sonny. What about Mirza?"

"I only know the winner," said the boy. "That's Daffodil."

"Daffodil, eh?"

There was a pause. Daffodil was an obscure horse comparatively.

"Uncle!"

"Yes, son?"

"You won't let it go any further, will you? I promised Bassett."

"Bassett be damned, old man! What's he got to do with it?"

"We're partners. We've been partners from the first. Uncle, he lent me my first five shillings, which I lost. I promised him, honor bright, it was only between me and him; only you gave me that ten-shilling note I started winning with, so I thought you were lucky. You won't let it go any further, will you?"

The boy gazed at his uncle from those big, hot, blue eyes, set rather close together. The uncle stirred and laughed uneasily.

"Right you are, son! I'll keep your tip private. How much are you putting on him?"

"All except twenty pounds," said the boy. "I keep that in reserve."

The uncle thought it a good joke.

"You keep twenty pounds in reserve, do you, you young romancer? What are you betting, then?"

"I'm betting three hundred," said the boy gravely. "But it's between you and me, Uncle Oscar! Honor bright?"

"It's between you and me all right, you young Nat Gould,"[18] he said, laughing. "But where's your three hundred?"

"Bassett keeps it for me. We're partners."

"You are, are you! And what is Bassett putting on Daffodil?"

"He won't go quite as high as I do, I expect. Perhaps he'll go a hundred and fifty."

"What, pennies?" laughed the uncle.

"Pounds," said the child, with a surprised look at his uncle. "Bassett keeps a bigger reserve than I do."

Between wonder and amusement Uncle Oscar was silent. He pursued the matter no further, but he determined to take his nephew with him to the Lincoln races.

"Now, son," he said, "I'm putting twenty on Mirza, and I'll put five on for you on any horse you fancy. What's your pick?"

"Daffodil, uncle."

"No, not the fiver[19] on Daffodil!"

"I should if it was my own fiver," said the child.

"Good! Good! Right you are! A fiver for me and a fiver for you on Daffodil."

The child had never been to a race-meeting before, and his eyes were blue fire. He pursed his mouth tight and watched. A Frenchman just in front had put his money on

Lancelot. Wild with excitement, he flayed his arms up and down, yelling "Lancelot! Lancelot!" in his French accent. Daffodil came in first, Lancelot second, Mirza third. The child, flushed and with eyes blazing, was curiously serene. His uncle brought him four five-pound notes, four to one.

"What am I to do with these?" he cried, waving them before the boy's eyes.

"I suppose we'll talk to Bassett," said the boy. "I expect I have fifteen hundred now; and twenty in reserve; and this twenty."

His uncle studied him for some moments.

"Look here, son!" he said. "You're not serious about Bassett and that fifteen hundred, are you?"

"Yes, I am. But it's between you and me, uncle. Honor bright?"

"Honor bright all right, son! But I must talk to Bassett."

"If you'd like to be a partner, uncle, with Bassett and me, we could all be partners. Only, you'd have to promise, honor bright, uncle, not to let it go beyond us three. Bassett and I are lucky, and you must be lucky, because it was your ten shillings I started winning with ..."

Uncle Oscar took both Bassett and Paul into Richmond Park for an afternoon, and there they talked.

"It's like this, you see, sir," Bassett said. "Master Paul would get me talking about racing events, spinning yarns,[20] you know, sir. And he was always keen on knowing if I'd made or if I'd lost. It's about a year since, now, that I put five shillings on Blush of Dawn for him: and we lost. Then the luck turned, with that ten shillings he had from you: that we put on Singhalese. And since that time, it's been pretty steady, all things considering. What do you say, Master Paul?"

"We're all right when we're sure," said Paul. "It's when we're not quite sure that we go down."

"Oh, but we're careful then," said Bassett.

"But when are you sure?" smiled Uncle Oscar.

"It's Master Paul, sir," said Bassett in a secret, religious voice. "It's as if he had it from heaven. Like Daffodil, now, for the Lincoln. That was as sure as eggs."

"Did you put anything on Daffodil?" asked Oscar Cresswell.

"Yes, sir, I made my bit."

"And my nephew?"

Bassett was obstinately silent, looking at Paul.

"I made twelve hundred, didn't I, Bassett? I told uncle I was putting three hundred on Daffodil."

"That's right," said Bassett, nodding.

"But where's the money?" asked the uncle.

"I keep it safe locked up, sir. Master Paul he can have it any minute he likes to ask for it."

"What, fifteen hundred pounds?"

"And twenty! And forty, that is, with the twenty he made on the course."

"It's amazing!" said the uncle.

"If Master Paul offers you to be partners, sir, I would, if I were you: if you'll excuse me," said Bassett.

Oscar Cresswell thought about it.

"I'll see the money," he said.

They drove home again, and, sure enough, Bassett came round to the garden-house with fifteen hundred pounds in notes. The twenty pounds reserve was left with Joe Glee, in the Turf Commission deposit.

"You see, it's all right, uncle, when I'm sure! Then we go strong, for all we're worth, don't we, Bassett?"

"We do that, Master Paul."

"And when are you sure?" said the uncle, laughing.

"Oh, well, sometimes I'm absolutely sure, like about Daffodil," said the boy; "and sometimes I have an idea; and sometimes I haven't even an idea, have I, Bassett? Then we're careful, because we mostly go down."

"You do, do you! And when you're sure, like about Daffodil, what makes you sure, sonny?"

"Oh, well, I don't know," said the boy uneasily. "I'm sure, you know, uncle; that's all."

"It's as if he had it from heaven, sir," Bassett reiterated.

"I should say so!" said the uncle.

But he became a partner. And when the Leger was coming on Paul was "sure" about Lively Spark, which was a quite inconsiderable horse. The boy insisted on putting a thousand on the horse, Bassett went for five hundred, and Oscar Cresswell two hundred. Lively Spark came in first, and the betting had been ten to one against him. Paul had made ten thousand.

"You see," he said. "I was absolutely sure of him."

Even Oscar Cresswell had cleared two thousand.

"Look here, son," he said, "this sort of thing makes me nervous."

"It needn't, uncle! Perhaps I shan't be sure again for a long time."

"But what are you going to do with your money?" asked the uncle.

"Of course," said the boy, "I started it for mother. She said she had no luck, because father is unlucky, so I thought if I was lucky, it might stop whispering."

"What might stop whispering?"

"Our house. I hate our house for whispering."

"What does it whisper?"

"Why — why"— the boy fidgeted — "why, I don't know. But it's always short of money, you know, uncle."

"I know it, son, I know it."

"You know people send mother writs,[21] don't you, uncle?"

"I'm afraid I do," said the uncle.

"And then the house whispers, like people laughing at you behind your back. It's awful, that is! I thought if I was lucky —"

"You might stop it," added the uncle.

The boy watched him with big blue eyes, that had an uncanny cold fire in them, and he said never a word.

"Well, then!" said the uncle. "What are we doing?"

"I shouldn't like mother to know I was lucky," said the boy.

"Why not, son?"

"She'd stop me."

"I don't think she would."

"Oh!"— and the boy writhed in an odd way — "I don't want her to know, uncle."

"All right, son! We'll manage it without her knowing."

They managed it very easily. Paul, at the other's suggestion, handed over five thousand pounds to his uncle, who deposited it with the family lawyer, who was then to inform Paul's mother that a relative had put five thousand pounds into his hands, which sum was to be paid out a thousand pounds at a time, on the mother's birthday, for the next five years.

"So she'll have a birthday present of a thousand pounds for five successive years," said Uncle Oscar. "I hope it won't make it all the harder for her later."

Paul's mother had her birthday in November. The house had been 'whispering' worse than ever lately, and, even in spite of his luck, Paul could not bear up against it. He was very anxious to see the effect of the birthday letter, telling his mother about the thousand pounds.

When there were no visitors, Paul now took his meals with his parents, as he was beyond the nursery control.[22] His mother went into town nearly every day. She had discovered that she had an odd knack of sketching furs and dress materials, so she worked secretly in the studio of a friend who was the chief 'artist' for the leading drapers. She drew the figures of ladies in furs and ladies in silk and sequins for the newspaper advertisements. This young woman artist earned several thousand pounds a year, but Paul's mother only made several hundreds, and she was again dissatisfied. She so wanted to be first in something, and she did not succeed, even in making sketches for drapery advertisements.

She was down to breakfast on the morning of her birthday. Paul watched her face as she read her letters. He knew the lawyer's letter. As his mother read it, her face hardened and became more expressionless. Then a cold, determined look came on her mouth. She hid the letter under the pile of others, and said not a word about it.

"Didn't you have anything nice in the post for your birthday, mother?" said Paul.

"Quite moderately nice," she said, her voice cold and hard and absent.

She went away to town without saying more.

But in the afternoon Uncle Oscar appeared. He said Paul's mother had had a long interview with the lawyer, asking if the whole five thousand could not be advanced at once, as she was in debt.

"What do you think, uncle?" said the boy.

"I leave it to you, son."

"Oh, let her have it, then! We can get some more with the other," said the boy.

"A bird in the hand is worth two in the bush, laddie!" said Uncle Oscar.

"But I'm sure to know for the Grand National; or the Lincolnshire; or else the Derby. I'm sure to know for one of them," said Paul.

So Uncle Oscar signed the agreement, and Paul's mother touched the whole five thousand. Then something very curious happened. The voices in the house suddenly went mad, like a chorus of frogs on a spring evening. There were certain new furnishings, and Paul had a tutor. He was really going to Eton, his father's school, in the following autumn. There were flowers in the winter, and a blossoming of the luxury Paul's mother had been used to. And yet the voices in the house, behind the sprays of mimosa and almond-blossom, and from under the piles of iridescent cushions, simply trilled and screamed in a sort of ecstasy: "There must be more money! Oh-h-h; there must be more money. Oh, now, now-w! Now-w-w - there must be more money! — more than ever! More than ever!"

It frightened Paul terribly. He studied away at his Latin and Greek with his tutor. But his intense hours were spent with Bassett. The Grand National had gone by: he had not 'known', and had lost a hundred pounds. Summer was at hand. He was in agony for the Lincoln. But even for the Lincoln he didn't 'know', and he lost fifty pounds. He became wild-eyed and strange, as if something were going to explode in him.

"Let it alone, son! Don't you bother about it!" urged Uncle Oscar. But it was as if the boy couldn't really hear what his uncle was saying.

"I've got to know for the Derby! I've got to know for the Derby!" the child reiterated, his big blue eyes blazing with a sort of madness.

His mother noticed how overwrought he was.

"You'd better go to the seaside. Wouldn't you like to go now to the seaside, instead of waiting? I think you'd better," she said, looking down at him anxiously, her heart curiously heavy because of him.

But the child lifted his uncanny blue eyes.

"I couldn't possibly go before the Derby, mother!" he said. "I couldn't possibly!"

"Why not?" she said, her voice becoming heavy when she was opposed. "Why not? You can still go from the seaside to see the Derby with your Uncle Oscar, if that that's what you wish. No need for you to wait here. Besides, I think you care too much about these races. It's a bad sign. My family has been a gambling family, and you won't know till you grow up how much damage it has done. But it has done damage. I shall have to send Bassett away, and ask Uncle Oscar not to talk racing to you, unless you promise to be reasonable about it: go away to the seaside and forget it. You're all nerves!"

"I'll do what you like, mother, so long as you don't send me away till after the Derby," the boy said.

"Send you away from where? Just from this house?"

"Yes," he said, gazing at her.

"Why, you curious child, what makes you care about this house so much, suddenly? I never knew you loved it."

He gazed at her without speaking. He had a secret within a secret, something he had not divulged, even to Bassett or to his Uncle Oscar.

But his mother, after standing undecided and a little bit sullen for some moments, said: "Very well, then! Don't go to the seaside till after the Derby, if you don't wish it. But promise me you won't think so much about horse-racing and events as you call them!"

"Oh no," said the boy casually. "I won't think much about them, mother. You needn't worry. I wouldn't worry, mother, if I were you."

"If you were me and I were you," said his mother, "I wonder what we should do!"

"But you know you needn't worry, mother, don't you?" the boy repeated.

"I should be awfully glad to know it," she said wearily.

"Oh, well, you can, you know. I mean, you ought to know you needn't worry," he insisted.

"Ought I? Then I'll see about it," she said.

Paul's secret of secrets was his wooden horse, that which had no name. Since he was emancipated from a nurse and a nursery-governess, he had had his rocking-horse removed to his own bedroom at the top of the house.

"Surely you're too big for a rocking-horse!" his mother had remonstrated.

"Well, you see, mother, till I can have a real horse, I like to have some sort of animal about," had been his quaint answer.

"Do you feel he keeps you company?" she laughed.

"Oh yes! He's very good, he always keeps me company, when I'm there," said Paul.

So the horse, rather shabby, stood in an arrested prance in the boy's bedroom.

The Derby was drawing near, and the boy grew more and more tense. He hardly heard what was spoken to him, he was very frail, and his eyes were really uncanny. His mother had sudden strange seizures of uneasiness about him. Sometimes, for half an hour, she would feel a sudden anxiety about him that was almost anguish. She wanted to rush to him at once, and know he was safe.

Two nights before the Derby, she was at a big party in town, when one of her rushes of anxiety about her boy, her first-born, gripped her heart till she could hardly speak. She fought with the feeling, might and main, for she believed in common sense. But it was too strong. She had to leave the dance and go downstairs to telephone to the country. The children's nursery-governess was terribly surprised and startled at being rung up in the night.

"Are the children all right, Miss Wilmot?"

"Oh yes, they are quite all right."

"Master Paul? Is he all right?"

"He went to bed as right as a trivet.[23] Shall I run up and look at him?"

"No," said Paul's mother reluctantly. "No! Don't trouble. It's all right. Don't sit up. We shall be home fairly soon." She did not want her son's privacy intruded upon.

"Very good," said the governess.

It was about one o'clock when Paul's mother and father drove up to their house. All was still. Paul's mother went to her room and slipped off her white fur cloak. She had told her maid not to wait up for her. She heard her husband downstairs, mixing a whisky and soda.

And then, because of the strange anxiety at her heart, she stole upstairs to her son's room. Noiselessly she went along the upper corridor. Was there a faint noise? What was it?

She stood, with arrested muscles, outside his door, listening. There was a strange, heavy, and yet not loud noise. Her heart stood still. It was a soundless noise, yet rushing and powerful. Something huge, in violent, hushed motion. What was it? What in God's name was it? She ought to know. She felt that she knew the noise. She knew what it was.

Yet she could not place it. She couldn't say what it was. And on and on it went, like a madness.

Softly, frozen with anxiety and fear, she turned the door-handle.

The room was dark. Yet in the space near the window, she heard and saw something plunging to and fro. She gazed in fear and amazement.

Then suddenly she switched on the light, and saw her son, in his green pajamas, madly surging on the rocking-horse. The blaze of light suddenly lit him up, as he urged the wooden horse, and lit her up, as she stood, blonde, in her dress of pale green and crystal, in the doorway.

"Paul!" she cried. "Whatever are you doing?"

"It's Malabar!" he screamed in a powerful, strange voice. "It's Malabar!"

His eyes blazed at her for one strange and senseless second, as he ceased urging his wooden horse. Then he fell with a crash to the ground, and she, all her tormented motherhood flooding upon her, rushed to gather him up.

But he was unconscious, and unconscious he remained, with some brain-fever. He talked and tossed, and his mother sat stonily by his side.

"Malabar! It's Malabar! Bassett, Bassett, I know! It's Malabar!"

So the child cried, trying to get up and urge the rocking-horse that gave him his inspiration.

"What does he mean by Malabar?" asked the heart-frozen mother.

"I don't know," said the father stonily.

"What does he mean by Malabar?" she asked her brother Oscar.

"It's one of the horses running for the Derby," was the answer.

And, in spite of himself, Oscar Cresswell spoke to Bassett, and himself put a thousand on Malabar: at fourteen to one.

The third day of the illness was critical: they were waiting for a change. The boy, with his rather long, curly hair, was tossing ceaselessly on the pillow. He neither slept nor regained consciousness, and his eyes were like blue stones. His mother sat, feeling her heart had gone, turned actually into a stone.

In the evening Oscar Cresswell did not come, but Bassett sent a message, saying could he come up for one moment, just one moment? Paul's mother was very angry at the intrusion, but on second thoughts she agreed. The boy was the same. Perhaps Bassett might bring him to consciousness.

The gardener, a shortish fellow with a little brown moustache and sharp little brown eyes, tiptoed into the room, touched his imaginary cap to Paul's mother, and stole to the bedside, staring with glittering, smallish eyes at the tossing, dying child.

"Master Paul!" he whispered. "Master Paul! Malabar came in first all right, a clean win. I did as you told me. You've made over seventy thousand pounds, you have; you've got over eighty thousand. Malabar came in all right, Master Paul."

"Malabar! Malabar! Did I say Malabar, mother? Did I say Malabar? Do you think I'm lucky, mother? I knew Malabar, didn't I? Over eighty thousand pounds! I call that lucky, don't you, mother? Over eighty thousand pounds! I knew, didn't I know I knew? Malabar came in all right. If I ride my horse till I'm sure, then I tell you, Bassett, you can go as high as you like. Did you go for all you were worth, Bassett?"

"I went a thousand on it, Master Paul."

"I never told you, mother, that if I can ride my horse, and get there, then I'm absolutely sure — oh, absolutely! Mother, did I ever tell you? I am lucky!"

"No, you never did," said his mother.

But the boy died in the night.

And even as he lay dead, his mother heard her brother's voice saying to her, "My God, Hester, you're eighty-odd thousand to the good,[24] and a poor devil of a son to the bad.[25] But, poor devil, poor devil, he's best gone out of a life where he rides his rocking-horse to find a winner."

☞ Notes

1. This story was written in February of 1926 as a favor to Cynthia Asquith for a collection of ghost stories she was preparing. It's believed that the model for Paul was her autistic son, John, combined with Lawrence's own troubled past.
2. **in style:** to be fashionable.
3. **not nearly:** far from; much less than.
4. **the grinding sense:** the heavy sense.
5. **racked her brain:** thought very deeply and for a long time.
6. **he:** Here "he" is the grammatical subject, referring back to "puppy." Sometimes if the predicate verb is removed too far from the subject, a grammatical subject is inserted.
7. **lucre:** money or profit in its derogatory sense. Paul mistook "lucre" as "lucker."
8. **brazening it out:** saying it out unashamedly.
9. **She could make nothing of him:** She could not understand him.
10. **he was growing beyond her:** he was growing beyond her comprehension.
11. **Gets on without all right:** Gets on really without a name?
12. **Sansovino:** name of a racing horse, as are Daffodil, Mirza, Lancelot, Blush of Dawn, Singhalese, Lively Spark and Malabar, mentioned respectively later on.
13. **Ascot:** a horse-racing event, as are the Lincoln, the Leger, the Grand National and the Derby, mentioned respectively later on.
14. **a perfect blade of the "turf":** The "turf" means the racecourse, hence "a perfect blade of the turf," figuratively, comes to mean a person addicted to horse-racing.
15. **put anything on a horse:** put a bet on a horse.
16. **serious as a church:** very serious.
17. **Honor bright:** On your honor (to keep it between you and me). Here "bright" is simply used for emphasis.
18. **Nat Gould:** Nathaniel Gould (1857-1919). English journalist and novelist, who wrote

a large number of novels, all concerned with horse-racing.

19. **fiver:** five pound banknote.
20. **spinning yarns:** telling (often exaggerated or untrue) stories.
21. **writs:** a legal document that orders a particular person to do a particular thing, like paying a debt.
22. **as he was beyond the nursery control:** because he is no longer taken care of by the nurse.
23. **as right as a trivet:** perfectly. The trivet is a metallic plate-stand with three legs.
24. **to the good:** (used to describe a financial state) with a profit of.
25. **to the bad:** (used to describe a financial state) in debt by.

☞ Study questions

1. What clues does the title give to the author's intent and emphasis?
2. What is the conflict in the story?
3. What is the significance of the rocking horse?
4. How does Uncle Oscar take advantage of Paul?
5. What caused the death of Paul?
6. What are the major themes of the story?
7. What are the merits of the author's craftsmanship that help to realize the themes of the story?

8.9 W. H. Auden

8.9.1 Life and career

Auden (1907-1973) was born in York. He spent his early years in the landscape of the industrial Midlands which left a deep impression on him. He was educated first at Gresham's School and later at Oxford University. During the years at Oxford, he distinguished himself as a poet and a scholar. He worked as an editor for *Oxford Poetry*, and became the leader of a group of students. One of his early important works, *Poems*, was published in 1930. During the decade of economic and political crises, this book was enthusiastically received. The novelty of the alliterative meters, the causticity of the verse, and the unexpectedness of the allusions immediately established him.

After graduation, Auden became a school master. With a strong poetic vocation, he continued writing verse and published several volumes of poems: *The Orators* (1932), *The Dance of Death* (1933), and *Look Stranger* (1936). He also made extensive travels abroad. His brief spell as an ambulance driver in the Spanish Civil War and his trip to Japan and China with Christopher Isherwood greatly extended his range of experience. Auden also collaborated with Isherwood on several Brechtian topical plays such as *The*

Dog Beneath the Skin (1935), *The Ascent of F6* (1936) and *On the Frontier* (1938). In 1939, he settled down in the United States and became an American citizen in 1946. Starting from 1948, he spent half of each year in New York and the other half in Europe, writing poetry, literary criticism and doing translations.

Auden has a long poetic career and produced a large body of works in a variety of styles and on a wide range of subjects. His wide interests have always converged on the moral, the psychological and social problems of his time. His early poetry concerns with a diagnosis of the ills of the country, i. e. the physical waste land. His poems present a recognizable landscape of crisis: industries failed or failing, villages in miscommunication from one another, individuals afraid and ignorant. Every effort toward unity is frustrated. In these poems Auden has created an atmosphere of dread by uniting psychological disease with the economic decay of a class, and by imposing upon the whole scene a mysterious state of warfare, of love against death. With technical devices borrowed from Owen, Hopkins and Eliot, Auden has written some wonderful poems, which have an original vitality and powerful immediacy.

Auden's later poetry becomes more meditative, more abstract, more concerned with archetypal images and situations, and more religious in tones and feelings. Love has become his major theme: love as interpreter of the world, love as individual need, and love as redeeming power in the life of society and of the individual.

The essential qualities of Auden's style are: a quickness and lightness of touch, a clearness of phrase and sentence, a caustic wit, and an ironic hardness. But his style is not technically radical in the way Eliot's style is; neither is his style original in concepts of structure or organization. Many of the technical devices that make his poems impressive are borrowed from a variety of sources. Music hall, folk ballad and popular song also provide new elements in forming a strong rhythm for poetry.

For Auden, myth has served as a major and continuous mode of expression. Relying on a scientific structure provided by the new psychology, he approaches myth as a guide to unconscious drives in man and society. In his early poetry, myth reveals man's lonely struggle with the unconscious forces of his own nature; in the later poetry, myth reveals and celebrates the infinite in the finite, the spiritual essence of ordinary reality.

Another feature of Auden's work is the rendering of psychic states in terms of landscape. In his early poetry, landscape is usually an illuminating backcloth to some human social activity; while in his later poetry, landscape is often a symbol for an inner dilemma in human personality. His imagery easily translates time into space, or changes in personality into changes of location. And his great originality lies in his endlessly fertile invention of symbols. *Praise of Limestone*, one of his best poems, is a good example of the fusion of the scene observed in nature with the psychological symptom-symbol.

8.9.2 "Musée des Beaux Arts"[1]

About suffering they were never wrong,
The Old Masters: how well they understood
Its human position; how it takes place
While someone else is eating or opening a window or just walking dully along;
How, when the aged are reverently, passionately waiting
For the miraculous birth, there always must be
Children who did not specially want it to happen, skating
On a pond at the edge of the wood:
They never forgot
That even the dreadful martyrdom must run its course
Anyhow in a corner, some untidy spot
Where the dogs go on with their doggy life and the torturer's horse
Scratches its innocent behind on a tree.

In Brueghel's *Icarus*,[2] for instance: how everything turns away
Quite leisurely from the disaster; the plowman may
Have heard the splash, the forsaken cry,
But for him it was not an important failure; the sun shone
As it had to on the white legs disappearing into the green
Water; and the expensive delicate ship that must have seen
Something amazing, a boy falling out of the sky,
Had somewhere to get to and sailed calmly on.

☞ Notes

1. **Musée des Beaux Arts:** "Museum of Fine Arts." The reference is to the Museum of Fine Arts in Brussels, which contains Brueghel's *Icarus*. Auden visited the museum in 1938 and viewed the painting by Brueghel, which the poem is basically about.
2. ***Icarus*:** Icarus was the son of Daedalus, the cunning craftsman of ancient legend. Together they flew on artificial wings fastened to their shoulders with wax, but Icarus ventured too near the sun, which melted the wax, and so he fell and perished. The painting of the fall of Icarus is by the Flemish painter Pieter Brueghel (ca. 1520-1569): Icarus' legs are disappearing into the sea in one corner of the picture, the rest of which has nothing to do with him.

☞ Study questions

1. What, according to lines 3-4, did the Old Masters understand about suffering?

2. What disaster occurs in the second stanza? How does "everything" react to this disaster?
3. Does Auden sympathize with or condemn the behavior he describes? How do you know?
4. Why do people often react as they do in this poem? Do you think these reactions show human nature in a positive or negative light?
5. In what ways does the speaker of the poem seem isolated high above those he describes? What overall order does he see in these events?

8.10 Dylan Thomas

8.10.1 Life and career

Thomas (1914-1953) was born at Swansea, South Wales. He was educated at the local grammar school where his father was a teacher. From early childhood, Thomas was exposed to English literature. When he later recalled his past, he still remembered his early infatuation with the sound of nursery rhymes, the "colors" that words suggested to him, and the rhythms which excited him. After working for a time as a newspaper reporter, Thomas was "discovered" as a poet in 1933 through a poetry contest in a popular newspaper. When he published his first volume of poetry, *Eighteen Poems*, in 1934, Thomas was only 19. The book was widely noticed and enthusiastically reviewed by the critics. His early career was rounded off with two more books: *Twenty-Five Poems* (1936) and *The Map of Love* (1939), which includes poems and prose writings. In 1936 Thomas met Caitlin Macnamara and they got married the following year. By 1943 the couple had three children and mounting debt.

In 1939, Thomas moved to London to work for BBC, writing and performing radio broadcasts. The physical and psychic havoc of World War II deeply affected Thomas and shaped his third volume of poetry, *Deaths and Entrances* (1946), which contains many of his famous work. Thomas also wrote prose work. His best-known prose work was *Portrait of the Artist as a Young Dog* (1940), a collection of semi-autobiographical short stories, which stylistically and thematically bears comparison to Joyce's *Dubliners* and *Portrait of the Artist as a Young Man*. His radio play *Under Milk Wood*, first broadcast by BBC and later transferred to the stage, became extremely popular and was published in 1954.

In his later life, Thomas gained public attention as a touring bohemian poet, a captivating reader of his obscure poetry and highly sonorous prose. During this period his drinking became a serious problem, and the social aspect of the tours encouraged his drinking. He undertook three lecture tours to the United States, giving readings which attracted large audiences. During his third tour of America in 1953, Thomas slumped into a coma at New York's White Horse bar. He died shortly afterwards of alcoholic poisoning.

Thomas is essentially an individualist. His view of the world, which was shaped under the deep influence of Freud, Joyce, and the Bible, is very simple but pessimistic, i. e., the universe is a dynamic one, frighteningly active and alive; life is a continuous process of birth and death. But in his opinion, it is death, not life, that is the measure of time. To live is to burn; and death is present in the whole process of life, from beginning to end. Poetically, Thomas is a rebel against the classicist tendency of Eliot and Auden. He is also a rebel against the Oxford and Cambridge intellectualism in modern poetry. With a strong opposition to the King's English, he advocates for a language that is capable of harsh effects, coarse texture and violent colors.

Thomas was influenced by such modern movements as symbolism and surrealism, but he borrowed without adhering to any creed. He was particularly concerned with disassociating himself from the surrealist movement because he felt his conscious craftsmanship was contrary to the methods of that group. Thomas is a bold and original poet, probably the greatest lyric poet of his generation. His major poetic themes are limited but elemental—birth, childhood, sex, and death. And death casts its shadow on almost every poem. "The Force that through the Green Fuse Drives the Flower" is one of his most successful poems. Thomas draws the parallel between poet's and flower's, poet's and nature's vitality and confronts them with the universal fact of death. He sees the working of biology as a magical transformation producing unity out of identity, identity out of unity. The unity of life, the continuing process of life and death and new life link the generations to each other. He is often called a pagan, a mystic, and a humanistic agnostic; his God has been identified with Nature, Sex, Love, Process, the Life Force, and with Thomas himself.

One of his outstanding merits is his rich vocabulary, his sensual appreciation of words, and his intense persuasive idioms. The struggle with words is in a sense the primary struggle in all his poetry. One of his outstanding poems is "Especially When the October Wind" in which all that he experiences has a language, even the wind would punishing his hair "with frosty fingers." His busy heart "talks" and "sheds" the syllabic blood and "drains her words." He hears the "vowelled beeches," "oaken voices," "water's speeches," "the hour's word" and reads "the meadow's signs." The world itself is language. The poem turns back upon itself—the wind "punishes the land" too, "with fists of turnips" just as it punished him. Poet and landscape are momentarily fused.

His style is very much of his own: his imagery is said to be cosmic and sexual; syntax to be illogical and revolutionary. Like James Joyce before him, Thomas is obsessed with the sound, rhythm and multiple meanings of the words. He has made ample use of alliteration, assonance, internal rhyme, and approximate rhyme. His tone is usually grave and depressing, but the sound is rich in music. His acclaim is partly due to the idiosyncratic and surreal introspection which is his hallmark. However, his poetry is marred by his choking verbalism, his willful obscurity, and his overemphasized pathos, which mark his lack of maturity.

8. 10. 2 "Do Not Go Gentle into That Good Night"

Do not go gentle into that good night,
Old age should burn and rave at close of day;
Rage, rage against the dying of the light.

Though wise men at their end know dark is right,
Because their words had forked no lightning they
Do not go gentle into that good night.

Good men, the last wave by, crying how bright
Their frail deeds might have danced in a green bay,
Rage, rage against the dying of the light.

Wild men who caught and sang the sun in flight,
And learn, too late, they grieved it on its way,
Do not go gentle into that good night.

Grave men, near death, who see with blinding sight
Blind eyes could blaze like meteors and be gay,
Rage, rage against the dying of the light.

And you, my father, there on the sad height,
Curse, bless, me now with your fierce tears, I pray
Do not go gentle into that good night.
Rage, rage against the dying of the light.

☞ Study questions

1. Who is the speaker of this poem?
2. What do wise men know? What do they do in spite of this knowledge, and why?
3. How would you interpret the words *good night* and *the dying of the light*? What might dark and light symbolize in the poem?

☞ **Essay topics**

1. Describe the emotional impact of the poem and the view of life and death it expresses.
2. Which poet, Eliot or Thomas, touches you more? Explain.

8.11 Samuel Beckett

8.11.1 Life and career

Beckett(1906-1989) was born into a prosperous Protestant family in Dublin. He was sent off at the age of 14 to attend the legendary Portora Royal School, where he excelled in a variety of sports and showed little sign of the gloom that would later characterize his work and life. In 1923 he began his study of French and Italian at Trinity College, Dublin. Upon his graduation, he went to teach English at a French university in Paris, where he met James Joyce and became closely associated with him and his circle—an experience which was to prove significant in his own writing. In 1930, he returned to Trinity College as a lecturer in French, but gave it up after a year's teaching. He went again to the continent, wandering about for some years. In the course of his journeys, he came into contact with many tramps and wanderers, and these acquaintances would later translate into some of his finest characters. He finally settled down in Paris in 1937. During World War Ⅱ, Beckett joined the French Resistance Movement, fighting against the Nazi Germany, though Ireland kept a neutral position in the war. The arrest of some of his close fellow fighters in 1942 obliged him to move away to a remote part of the country. He returned to Paris after the war.

Beckett began his literary career in his early twenties, while teaching English in Paris. He wrote poetry, stories, novels, plays, and critical essays. He published two volumes of poetry: *Whoroscope* (1930) and *Echo's Bones* (1935), a collection of short stories entitled *More Pricks Than Kicks* (1934), and a critique of Proust in 1931. His first novel, *Murphy*, appeared in 1938. It deals with the philosophical problem of the relation of mind and body. His next novel *Watt* (1944) is a symbolic story set in Ireland, which concerns a meditative hero who goes to work for a mysterious householder. During an incredibly creative period between 1945 and 1951, Beckett produced in French a trilogy of novels under the titles of *Molloy*, *Malone Dies* and *The Unnamable* (1951-1953), which were translated by himself into English and published between 1955 and 1958. These novels, together with his later one *How It Is* (1961), have made him a fairly important and original novelist.

As a relaxation from the more arduous calling of novelist, Beckett wrote the play *Waiting for Godot*, which, with its successful production in Paris in 1953 and in London in 1955, made Beckett a famous writer. Over the next two decades, Beckett produced some twenty or so works for the theatre, radio, TV and the cinema. Among them the more important ones are: *End Game* (1958), *Krapp's Last Tape* (1959), *Happy Days* (1962), *The Last Ones* (1972), and some radio and TV plays such as *All that Fall* (1957), *Embers* (1959), *Cascando* (1964), *Breath* (1969), and *Not I* (1973). In his later years, his writing became very brief and highly abstracted in words with condensed ideas. For instance, *Breath* lasts perhaps one minute of stage time, reducing the whole world to a heap of rubble, and life to a single inspiration and expiration of breath bounded by two faint cries. Beckett was awarded the Nobel Prize for literature in 1969. He died in December, 1989.

Perhaps the most famous play written by Beckett is *Waiting for Godot*. The heroes of the play are two tramps, Vladimir and Estragon, who spend consecutive evenings waiting for somebody called Godot on a country road. While waiting, the two men occupy themselves with all kinds of trivial things or empty talks: they tell jokes, abuse each other, recall their past, wonder what they are doing, contemplate suicide, compare themselves to the two thieves who were crucified beside Christ, and so on. Two other characters, Pozzo and Lucky, come along as master and slave. Pozzo abuses and ill-treats Lucky, who is tethered at the end of a rope. Godot sends word that he will not come that day but will surely come the next. In Act Ⅱ the two tramps still wait at the same place. The two visitors appear again, Pozzo now blind and Lucky dumb. With difficulties, they pass on. Then the boy comes with the same message as yesterday. Then the two tramps declare their intention of leaving, but they still go on their waiting. Thematically, Beckett explores and examines man's life by taking away the illusory charms and by reducing him to the essential base. By so doing, he tries to make his audience see the negative side of man's life—a meaningless, hopeless and painful progress towards death. He concludes that man cannot find his true identity, cannot attain his real self, nor can he escape the hellish suffering and boredom; the only thing man can do is wait and pass time with meaningless trivial things or empty talks till death finally relieves him of the burden of life.

Under the influence of Jean Paul Sartre, Beckett accepts Existentialism, from which he has developed a very pessimistic view towards life and human society. Human thought, says Beckett, can reveal nothing to men in the final analysis. All ultimate truth is forever beyond the understanding of the human mind, and, therefore, truth does not, in effect, exist. He regards human existence as a very brief, unimportant event in an indifferent universe, a "flash of light between the darkness of the womb and of the tomb." Actually, Beckett is the prophet of negation and sterility. He holds out no hope to humanity in an alien and decaying world. His vision to man's entire life is a torment, a hell, an incomprehensible nullity enveloped by colorful patterns which, in essence, are composed of absurd and futile activities.

Beckett is an atheist, and his atheism springs from the scars left from a Christian belief once deeply felt. With rich religious images and symbols, Beckett presents in his works strong Christian nihilism, which shows his bitter rejection and blasphemy against his early beliefs. A typical example of this kind is the famous line about God from his play, *End Game*, "The dirty dog, he doesn't even exist!" which best reflects his grudge against God. Artistically, Beckett has come under the strong influence of James Joyce. His works, which parody the unsympathetic world and man's wretched lot, derive obviously from Joyce. If Joyce is concerned with portraying the richness and variety of life, Beckett is preoccupied with rendering the human impotence and nihilistic vacuum of life.

8.11.2 An excerpt from Act I of *Waiting for Godot*

Estragon, sitting on a low mound, is trying to take off his boot. He pulls at it with both hands, panting. He gives up, exhausted, rests, tries again. As before.

Enter Vladimir.

ESTRAGON: (*giving up again.*) Nothing to be done.

VLADIMIR: (*advancing with short, stiff strides, legs wide apart.*) I'm beginning to come round to that opinion. All my life I've tried to put it from me, saying, Vladimir, be reasonable you haven't yet tried every thing. And I resumed the struggle. (*He broods, musing on the struggle, Turning to Estragon.*) So there you are again.

ESTRAGON: Am I?

VLADIMIR: I'm glad to see you back. I thought you were gone for ever.

ESTRAGON: Me too.

VLADIMIR: Together again at last! We'll have to celebrate this. But how? (*He reflects.*) Get up till I embrace you.

ESTRAGON: (*irritably.*) Not now, not now.

VLADIMIR: (*hurt, coldly.*) May one enquire where His Highness spent the night?

ESTRAGON: In a ditch.

VLADIMIR: (*admiringly.*) A ditch! Where?

ESTRAGON: (*without gesture.*) Over there.

VLADIMIR: And they didn't beat you?

ESTRAGON: Beat me? Certainly they beat me.

VLADIMIR: The same lot as usual?

ESTRAGON: The same? I don't know.

VLADIMIR: When I think of it ... all these years ... but for me ... where would you be...? (*decisively.*) You'd be nothing more than a little heap of bones at the present minute, no doubt about it.

ESTRAGON: And what of it?

VLADIMIR: (*gloomily.*) It's too much for one man. (*Pause. Cheerfully.*) On the other hand what's the good of losing heart now, that's what I say. We should have thought of it a million years ago, in the nineties.[1]

ESTRAGON: Ah stop blathering and help me off with this bloody thing.

VLADIMIR: Hand in hand from the top of the Eiffel Tower, among the first. We were presentable in those days. Now it's too late. They wouldn't even let us up. (*Estragon tears at his boot.*) What are you doing?

ESTRAGON: Taking off my boot. Did that never happen to you?

VLADIMIR: Boots must be taken off every day, I'm tired telling you that. Why don't you listen to me?

ESTRAGON: (*feebly.*) Help me!

VLADIMIR: It hurts?

ESTRAGON: Hurts! He wants to know if it hurts!

VLADIMIR: (*angrily.*) No one ever suffers but you. I don't count. I'd like to hear what you'd say if you had what I have.

ESTRAGON: It hurts?

VLADIMIR: Hurts! He wants to know if it hurts!

ESTRAGON: (*pointing.*) You might button it all the same.

VLADIMIR: (*stooping.*) True. (*He buttons his fly.*) Never neglect the little things of life.

ESTRAGON: What do you expect, you always wait till the last moment.

VLADIMIR: (*amusingly.*) The last moment... (*He meditates.*) Hope deferred[2] maketh the something sick, who said that?

ESTRAGON: Why don't you help me?

VLADIMIR: Sometimes I feel it coming all the same. Then I go all queer. (*He takes off his hat, peers inside it, feels about inside it, shakes it, puts it on again.*) How shall I say? Relieved and at the same time... (*He searches for the word*) ...appalled. (*with emphasis.*) AP-PALLED. (*He takes off his hat again, peers inside it.*) Funny. (*He knocks on the crown as though to dislodge a foreign body, peers into it again, puts it on again.*) Nothing to be done. (*Estragon with a supreme effort succeeds in pulling off his boot. He looks inside it, feels about inside it, turns it upside down, shakes it, looks on the ground to see if anything has fallen out, finds nothing, feels inside it again, staring sightlessly before him.*) Well?

ESTRAGON: Nothing.

VLADIMIR: Show.

ESTRAGON: There's nothing to show.

VLADIMIR: Try and put it on again.

ESTRAGON: (*examining his foot.*) I'll air it for a bit.

VLADIMIR: There's man all over for you, blaming on his boots the faults of his feet. (*He takes off his hat again, peers inside it, feels about inside it, knocks on the crown, blows into it, puts it on again.*) This is getting alarming. (*Silence. Vladimir deep in thought, Estragon pulling at his toes.*) One of the thieves was saved. (*Pause.*) It's a reasonable percentage. (*Pause.*) Gogo.

ESTRAGON: What?

VLADIMIR: Suppose we repented.

ESTRAGON: Repented what?

VLADIMIR: Oh … (*He reflects.*) We wouldn't have to go into the details.

ESTRAGON: Our being born?

(*Vladimir breaks into a hearty laugh which he immediately stifles, his hand pressed to his pubis, his face contorted.*)

VLADIMIR: One daren't even laugh any more.

ESTRAGON: Dreadful privation.

VLADIMIR: Merely smile. (*He smiles suddenly from ear to ear, keeps smiling, ceases as suddenly.*) It's not the same thing. Nothing to be done. (*Pause.*) Gogo.

ESTRAGON: (*irritably.*) What is it?

VLADIMIR: Did you ever read the Bible?

ESTRAGON: The Bible … (*He reflects.*) I must have taken a look at it.

VLADIMIR: Do you remember the Gospels?

ESTRAGON: I remember the maps of the Holy Land. Colored they were. Very pretty. The Dead Sea was pale blue. The very look of it made me thirsty. That's where we'll go, I used to say, that's where we'll go for our honeymoon. We'll swim. We'll be happy.

VLADIMIR: You should have been a poet.

ESTRAGON: I was. (*Gesture towards his rags.*) Isn't that obvious. (*Silence.*)

VLADIMIR: Where was I … How's your foot?

ESTRAGON: Swelling visibly.

VLADIMIR: Ah yes, the two thieves. Do you remember the story?

ESTRAGON: No.

VLADIMIR: Shall I tell it to you?

ESTRAGON: No.

VLADIMIR: It'll pass the time. (*Pause.*) Two thieves, crucified at the same time as our Savior. One—

ESTRAGON: Our what?

VLADIMIR: Our Savior. Two thieves. One is supposed to have been saved and the other ... (*He searches for the contrary of saved.*) ... damned.

ESTRAGON: Saved from what?

VLADIMIR: Hell.

ESTRAGON: I'm going. (*He does not move.*)

VLADIMIR: And yet ... (*Pause*)... how is It—this is not boring you I hope—how is it that of the four Evangelists[3] only one speaks of a thief being saved. The four of them were there—or thereabouts—and only one speaks of a thief being saved. (*Pause.*) Come on, Gogo, return the ball,[4] can't you, once in a way?

ESTRAGON: (*with exaggerated enthusiasm.*) I find this really most extraordinarily interesting.

VLADIMIR: One out of four. Of the other three two don't mention any thieves at all and the third says that both of them abused him.

ESTRAGON: Who?

VLADIMIR: What?

ESTRAGON: What's all this about? Abused who?

VLADIMIR: The Savior.

ESTRAGON: Why?

VLADIMIR: Because he wouldn't save them.

ESTRAGON: From hell?

VLADIMIR: Imbecile! From death.

ESTRAGON: I thought you said hell.

VLADIMIR: From death, from death.

ESTRAGON: Well what of it?

VLADIMIR: Then the two of them must have been damned.

ESTRAGON: And why not?

VLADIMIR: But one of the four says that one of the two was saved.

ESTRAGON: Well? They don't agree, and that's all there is to it.

VLADIMIR: But all four were there. And only one speaks of a thief being saved. Why believe him rather than the others?

ESTRAGON: Who believes him?

VLADIMIR: Everybody. It's the only version they know.

ESTRAGON: People are bloody ignorant apes.

(*He rises painfully, goes limping to extreme left, halts, gazes into distance off with his hand screening his eyes, turns, goes to extreme right, gazes into distance, Vladimir watches him, then goes and picks up the boot, peers into it, drops it hastily.*)

VLADIMIR: Pah! (*He spits. Estragon moves to center, halts with his back to auditorium.*)

ESTRAGON: Charming spot. (*He turns, advances to front, halts facing auditorium.*) Inspiring prospects. (*He turns to Vladimir.*) Let's go.

VLADIMIR: We can't.

ESTRAGON: Why not?

VLADIMIR: We're waiting for Godot.

ESTRAGON: (*despairingly.*) Ah! (*Pause.*) You're sure it was here?

VLADIMIR: What?

ESTRAGON: That we were to wait.

VLADIMIR: He said by the tree. (*They look at the tree.*) Do you see any others?

ESTRAGON: What is it?

VLADIMIR: I don't know. A willow.

ESTRAGON: Where are the leaves?

VLADIMIR: It must be dead.

ESTRAGON: No more weeping.

VLADIMIR: Or perhaps it's not the season.

ESTRAGON: Looks to me more like a bush.

VLADIMIR: A shrub.

ESTRAGON: A bush.

VLADIMIR: A—What are you insinuating? That we've come to the wrong place?

ESTRAGON: He should be here.

VLADIMIR: He didn't say for sure he'd come.

ESTRAGON: And if he doesn't come?

VLADIMIR: We'll come back tomorrow.

ESTRAGON: And then the day after tomorrow.

VLADIMIR: Possibly.

ESTRAGON: And so on.

VLADIMIR: The point is—

ESTRAGON: Until he comes.

VLADIMIR: You're merciless.

ESTRAGON: We came here yesterday.

VLADIMIR: Ah no, there you're mistaken.

ESTRAGON: What did we do yesterday?

VLADIMIR: What did we do yesterday?

ESTRAGON: Yes.

VLADIMIR: Why ... (*angrily.*) Nothing is certain when you're about.

ESTRAGON: In my opinion we were here.

VLADIMIR: (*looking round.*) You recognize the place?

ESTRAGON: I didn't say that.

VLADIMIR: Well?

ESTRAGON: That makes no difference.

VLADIMIR: All the same ... that tree ... (*turning towards the auditorium*) that bog ...

ESTRAGON: You're sure it was this evening?

VLADIMIR: What?

ESTRAGON: That we were to wait.

VLADIMIR: He said Saturday. (*Pause.*) I think.

ESTRAGON: You think.

VLADIMIR: I must have made a note of it. (*He fumbles in his pockets, bursting with miscellaneous rubbish.*)

ESTRAGON: (*very insidious.*) But what Saturday? And is it Saturday? Is it not rather Sunday? (*Pause.*) Or Monday? (*Pause.*) Or Friday?

VLADIMIR: (*looking wildly about him, as though the date was inscribed in the landscape.*) It's not possible!

ESTRAGON: Or Thursday?

VLADIMIR: What'll we do?

ESTRAGON: If he came yesterday and we weren't here you may be sure he won't come again today.

VLADIMIR: But you say we were here yesterday.

ESTRAGON: I may be mistaken. (*Pause.*) Let's stop talking for a minute, do you mind?

VLADIMIR: (*feebly.*) All right. (*Estragon sits down on the mound. Vladimir paces agitatedly to and fro, halting from time to time to gaze into distance off. Estragon falls asleep. Vladimir halts before Estragon.*) Gogo! ... Gogo! ... GOGO! (Estragon wakes with a start.)

ESTRAGON: (*restored to the horror of his situation.*) I was asleep! (*despairingly.*) Why will you never let me sleep?

VLADIMIR: I felt lonely.

ESTRAGON: I had a dream.

VLADIMIR: Don't tell me!

ESTRAGON: I dreamt that—

VLADIMIR: DON't TELL ME!

ESTRAGON: (*gesture towards the universe.*) This one is enough for you? (*Silence.*) It's not nice of you, Didi. Who am I to tell my private nightmares to if I can't tell them to you?

VLADIMIR: Let them remain private. You know I can't bear that.

ESTRAGON: (*coldly.*) There are times when I wonder if it wouldn't be better for us to part.

VLADIMIR: You wouldn't go far.

ESTRAGON: That would be too bad, really too bad. (*Pause.*) Wouldn't it, Didi, be really too bad? (*Pause.*) When you think of the beauty of the way. (*Pause.*) And the goodness of the wayfarers. (*Pause. Wheedling.*) Wouldn't it, Didi?

VLADIMIR: Calm yourself.

ESTRAGON: (*voluptuously.*) Calm ... calm ... The English say calm. (*Pause.*) You know the story of the Englishman in the brothel?

VLADIMIR: Yes.

ESTRAGON: Tell it to me.

VLADIMIR: Ah stop it!

ESTRAGON: An Englishman having drunk a little more than usual goes to a brothel. The bawd asks him if he wants a fair one, a dark one, or a red-haired one. Go on.

VLADIMIR: STOP IT!

(*Exit Vladimir hurriedly. Estragon gets up and follows him as far as the limit of the stage. Gestures of Estragon like those of a spectator encouraging a pugilist. Enter Vladimir. He brushes past Estragon, crosses the stage with bowed head. Estragon takes a step towards him, halts.*)

ESTRAGON: (*gently.*) You wanted to speak to me? (*Silence. Estragon takes a step forward.*) You had something to say to me? (*Silence. Another step forward.*) Didi ...

VLADIMIR: (*without turning.*) I've nothing to say to you.

ESTRAGON: (*step forward.*) You're angry? (*Silence. Step forward.*) Forgive me. (*Silence, Step forward. Estragon lays his hand on Vladimir's shoulder.*) Come Didi. (*Silence.*) Give me your hand. (*Vladimir half turns.*) Embrace me! (*Vladimir stiffens.*) Don't be stubborn! (*Vladimir softens. They embrace. Estragon recoils.*) You stink of garlic!

VLADIMIR: It's for the kidneys. (*Silence. Estragon looks attentively at the tree.*) What do we do now?

ESTRAGON: Wait.

VLADIMIR: Yes, but while waiting.

ESTRAGON: What about hanging ourselves?

VLADIMIR: Hmm. It'd give us an erection!

ESTRAGON: (*highly excited.*) An erection!

VLADIMIR: With all that follows, Where it falls mandrakes grow. That's why they shriek when you pull them up. Did you not know that?

ESTRAGON: Let's hang ourselves immediately!

VLADIMIR: From a bough? (*They go towards the tree.*) I wouldn't trust it.

ESTRAGON: We can always try.

VLADIMIR: Go ahead.

ESTRAGON: After you.

VLADIMIR: No no, you first.

ESTRAGON: Why me?

VLADIMIR: You're lighter than I am.

ESTRAGON: Just so!

VLADIMIR: I don't understand.

ESTRAGON: Use your intelligence, can't you? (*Vladimir uses his intelligence.*)

VLADIMIR: (*finally.*) I remain in the dark.

ESTRAGON: This is how it is. (*He reflects.*) The bough ... the bough ... (*Angrily.*) Use your head, can't you?

VLADIMIR: You're my only hope.

ESTRAGON: (*with effort.*) Gogo light—bough not break—Gogo dead. Didi heavy—bough break—Didi alone. Whereas—

VLADIMIR: I hadn't thought of that.

ESTRAGON: If it hangs you it'll hang anything.

VLADIMIR: But am I heavier than you?

ESTRAGON: So you tell me. I don't know. There's an even chance. Or nearly.

VLADIMIR: Well? What do we do?

ESTRAGON: Don't let's do anything. It's safer.

VLADIMIR: Let's wait and see what he says.

ESTRAGON: Who?

VLADIMIR: Godot.

ESTRAGON: Good idea.

☞ **Notes**

1. **We should have thought of it a million years ago, in the nineties:** According to the context, Vladimir is saying that they should have committed suicide long ago.
2. **Hope deferred:** Hope delayed.
3. **the four Evangelists:** referring to the four of Jesus Christ's disciples who wrote the four Gospels. They were St. Matthew, St. Mark, St. Luke, and St. John.
4. **return the ball:** answer me.

☞ **Study questions**

1. How are Estragon and Vladimir alike? How are they different?
2. What is the barrier between the decision to act and action itself in *Waiting for Godot*?
3. Why do Estragon and Vladimir want to kill themselves?
4. What is the value of life in *Waiting for Godot*?
5. "Nothing to be done" is repeated two times in this section. In each case, who says it and why?
6. What is the worst kind of suffering we see in *Waiting for Godot*?
7. Soon after the play opens, Vladimir and Estragon discuss the theme of two thieves on the cross. What biblical story does this theme refer to?
8. Vladimir and Estragon are said to have complementary characters. What seem to be their complementary personal characteristics? In your opinion, does Beckett want them to represent themselves as individuals or do they stand for the entire humanity?
9. What are the main characteristics of the stage convention known as the Theatre of the Absurd? How are they shown in the play?

☞ **Essay topics**

1. Discuss the body/soul relationship in terms of Estragon and Vladimir's relationship.
2. Discuss Beckett's attitude toward hope in the play. Are there any real signs of hope?

8.12 William Golding

8.12.1 Life and career

Golding (1911-1993) was born in Cornwall, son of a schoolmaster. As a child, William was educated at the Marlborough Grammar School, where his father worked. He enrolled in Brasenose College, Oxford, in 1930. His parents intended to bring him up as a scientist, but the young Golding developed an interest in literature and then transferred to a program for English literature and philosophy. After graduation Golding worked as writer, actor and producer for a short time. He then became a schoolmaster at Bishop Wordsworth's School in Salisbury. During World War Ⅱ he served in the Royal Navy in command of a rocket ship. His wartime experiences played a large part in helping him to formulate his view of life. After the war, Golding devoted himself to teaching and writing.

In 1954, Golding published his first novel, *Lord of the Flies*. It was soon recognized as a major work of art and established him as a prominent contemporary novelist, dealing primarily with the innate evil and original sin in man. He continued to develop similar themes concerning the inherent violence in human nature. In 1955 he wrote a science fiction entitled *The Inheritors*. In his third novel, *Pincher Martin* (1956),

Golding dramatized a shipwrecked sailor who, while desperately struggling for his life by clinging to a barren rock, made a spiritual exploration of his evil doings in the past. The seemingly realistic account turned out to be a sheer illusion, for the sailor was drowned almost immediately after the shipwreck, never reaching the rock. *Free Fall* (1959) is an elaborate account of the life-drama of Sammy Mountjoy, who looks back on his evasive life which was full of wrong choices and failures. The title of the novel implies that one's fall or descent into evil is upon one's free will. In 1964, he published another novel entitled *The Spire*, which is a story about the building of the spire of a medieval Cathedral. But the holy-seeming project to the divine glory turns out to be not an innocent work with motives of pure worship but a filthy one with all sorts of ill intentions. *Darkness Visible* came out in 1979 after a long gap. The title is taken from Milton's description of Hell in *Paradise Lost*. In this novel, evil is even more terribly present; and the realistic setting embodies a moral fable with its suggestions of spiritual dimensions. In 1983, Golding received the Nobel Prize for literature.

Lord of the Flies remains his most famous work. Set sometime in the near future, the novel is about a group of schoolboys abandoned on a desert island during a global war. At first the boys are able to maintain themselves, but soon most of them relapse into a form of primitive savagery, throwing away nearly all the sanctions of civilization. The novel deals with the conflict between the forces of reason represented by Ralph and Piggy and those of irrationality represented by Jack and his party of hunters who paint their faces and bodies with colored earths and indulge in primitive ritual dances and human torture and murder. Through this adventure story the reader is presented with an analysis of some of the most important philosophical and psychological issues of modern thought.

Golding is a genuinely serious writer who holds a strong pessimistic view towards human nature, regarding man as inherently savage and violent, which reflects the mood of the postwar years. He thinks that modern civilization, the institutions and order imposed from without, is fragile and temporary, but that man's irrationality and innate evil are strong and enduring. Thus, his primary aim in his novel is to reveal this evil as a destructive force in man, which operates counter to the forces of reason and civilization. By stripping man of all sanctions of custom and civilization and by putting him in an extreme situation, Golding makes careful examinations of man's proneness to evil, his fear of unknown, and his use of technology for inhuman purposes. Golding is, in a sense, also a religious writer, emphasizing Original Sin in the Puritan tradition. His novels are permeated with the sense of man's sin and guilt.

Golding's fame has been in part due to his inventiveness in realistic fantasy, his richness in biblical symbolism, and his disposition to use the novel form as a fable. His novels are all in one way or another fables. By creating a mythology of his own, he has bridged a gap between the allegory of the past and the realistic fiction of the present. The structure of his novels is well organized and the narration is under heavy control. His prose is easy, smooth, but strenuous and compact, with a style rich in imagination, powerful in drama, and subtle in literary and mythic overtones.

8.12.2 An excerpt from Chapter 9 of *Lord of the Flies*

Long before Ralph and Piggy came up with Jack's lot, they could hear the party. There was a stretch of grass in a place where the palms left a wide band of turf[1] between the forest and the shore. Just one step down from the edge of the turf was the white, blown sand of above high water, warm, dry, trodden. Below that again was a rock that stretched away towards the lagoon. Beyond was a short stretch of sand and then the edge of the water. A fire burned on the rock and fat dripped from the roasting pig-meat into the invisible flames. All the boys of the island, except Piggy, Ralph, Simon, and the two tending the pig, were grouped on the turf. They were laughing, singing, lying, squatting, or standing on the grass, holding food in their hands. But to judge by the greasy faces, the meat-eating was almost done; and some held coco-nut shells in their hands and were drinking from them. Before the party had started a great log had been dragged into the center of the lawn and Jack, painted and garlanded,[2] sat there like an idol. There were piles of meat on green leaves near him, and fruit, and coco-nut shells full of drink.

Piggy and Ralph came to the edge of the grassy platform and the boys, as they noticed them, fell silent one by one till only the boy next to Jack was talking. Then the silence intruded even there and Jack turned where he sat. For a time he looked at them and the crackle of the fire was the loudest noise over the bourdon of the reef. Ralph looked away; and Sam, thinking that Ralph had turned to him accusingly, put down his gnawed bone with a nervous giggle. Ralph took an uncertain step, pointed to a palm tree, and whispered something inaudible to Piggy; and they both giggled like Sam. Lifting his feet high out of the sand, Ralph started to stroll past. Piggy tried to whistle.

At this moment the boys who were cooking at the fire suddenly hauled off a great chunk of meat and ran with it towards the grass. They bumped Piggy who was burnt, and yelled and danced. Immediately, Ralph and the crowd of boys were united and relieved by a storm of laughter. Piggy once more was the center of social derision so that everyone felt cheerful and normal.

Jack stood up and waved his spear.

"Take them some meat."

The boys with the spit gave Ralph and Piggy each a succulent[3] chunk. They took the gift, dribbling, So they stood and ate beneath a sky of thunderous brass that rang with the storm coming.

Jack waved his spear again.

"Has everybody eaten as much as they want?"

There was still food left, sizzling on the wooden spits, heaped on the green platter. Betrayed by his stomach, Piggy threw a picked bone down on the beach and stooped for more.

Jack spoke again, impatiently.

"Has everybody eaten as much as they want?"

His tone conveyed a warning, given out of the pride of ownership, and the boys ate faster while there was still time. Seeing there was no immediate likelihood of a pause, Jack rose from the log that was his throne and sauntered to the edge of the grass. He looked down from behind his paint at Ralph and Piggy. They moved a little further off over the sand and Ralph watched the fire as he ate. He noticed without understanding, how the flames were visible now against the dull light. Evening was come, not with calm beauty but with the threat of violence.

Jack spoke.

"Give me a drink."

Henry brought him a shell and he drank, watching Piggy and Ralph over the jagged rim. Power lay in the brown swell of his forearms: authority sat on his shoulder and chattered in his ear like an ape.

"All sit down."

The boys ranged themselves in rows on the grass before him but Ralph and Piggy stayed a foot lower, standing on the soft sand. Jack ignored them for the moment, turned his mask down to the seated boys and pointed at them with the spear.

"Who is going to join my tribe?"

Ralph made a sudden movement that became a stumble. Some of the boys turned towards him.

"I gave you food," said Jack, "and my hunters will protect you from the beast. Who will join my tribe?"

"I'm chief," said Ralph, "because you chose me. And we were going to keep the fire going. Now you run after food—"

"You ran yourself!" shouted Jack. "Look at that bone in your hands!"

Ralph went crimson.

"I said you were hunters. That was your job."

Jack ignored him again.

"Who'll join my tribe and have fun?"

"I'm chief," said Ralph tremulously. "And what about the fire? And I've got the conch—"

"You haven't got it with you," said Jack, sneering. "You left it behind, See, clever?

And the conch doesn't count at this end of the island—"

All at once the thunder struck. Instead of the dull boom there was a point of impact in the explosion.

"The conch counts here too," said Ralph, "and all over the island."

"What are you going to do about it then?"

Ralph examined the ranks of boys. There was no help in them and he looked away, confused and sweating. Piggy whispered.

"The fire—rescue."

"Who'll join my tribe?"

"I will."

"Me."

"I will."

"I'll blow the conch," said Ralph breathlessly, "and call an assembly."

"We shan't hear it."

Piggy touched Ralph's wrist.

"Come away. There's going to be trouble. And we've had our meat."

There was a blink of bright light beyond the forest and the thunder exploded again so that a littlun started to whine.[4] Big drops of rain fell among them making individual sounds when they struck.

"Going to be a storm," said Ralph, "and you'll have rain like when we dropped here. Who's clever now? Where are your shelters? What are you going to do about that?"

The hunters were looking uneasily at the sky, flinching from the stroke of the drops. A wave of restlessness set the boys swaying and moving aimlessly. The flickering light became brighter and the blows of the thunder were only just bearable. The littluns began to run about, screaming.

Jack leapt on to the sand.

"Do our dance! Come on! Dance!"

He ran stumbling through the thick sand to the open space of rock beyond the fire. Between the flashes of lightning the air was dark and terrible; and the boys followed him, clamorously. Roger became the pig, grunting and charging at Jack, who side-stepped. The hunters took their spears, the cooks took spits, and the rest clubs of fire-wood. A circling movement developed and a chant. While Roger mimed the terror of the pig, the littluns ran and jumped on the outside of the circle. Piggy and Ralph, under the threat of the sky, found themselves eager to take a place in this demented[5] but partly secure society. They were glad to touch the brown backs of the fence that hemmed in the terror and made it governable.

"*Kill the beast! Cut his throat! Spill his blood!*"

The movement became regular while the chant lost its first superficial excitement and began to beat like a steady pulse. Roger ceased to be a pig and became a hunter, so that the center of the ring yawned emptily. Some of the littluns started a ring on their own; and the complementary circles went round and round as though repetition would achieve safety of itself. There was the throb and stamp of a single organism.

The dark sky was shattered by a blue-white scar. An instant later the noise was on them like the blow of a gigantic whip. The chant rose a tone in agony.

"Kill the beast! Cut his throat! Spill his blood!"

Now out of the terror rose another desire, thick, urgent, blind.

"Kill the beast! Cut his throat! Spill his blood!"

Again the blue-white scar jagged above them and the sulfurous explosion beat down. The littluns screamed and blundered about, fleeing from the edge of the forest, and one of them broke the ring of biguns in his terror.

"Him! Him!"

The circle became a horseshoe. A thing was crawling out of the forest. It came darkly, uncertainly. The shrill screaming that rose before the beast was like a pain. The beast stumbled into the horseshoe.

"Kill the beast! Cut his throat! Spill his blood!"

The blue-white scar was constant, the noise unendurable. Simon was crying out something about a dead man on a hill.

"Kill the beast! Cut his throat! Spill his blood! Do him in!"

The sticks fell and the mouth of the new circle crunched and screamed. The beast was on its knees in the center, its arms folded over its face. It was crying out against the abominable noise something about a body on the hill. The beast struggled forward, broke the ring and fell over the steep edge of the rock to the sand by the water. At once the crowd surged after it, poured down the rock, leapt on to the beast, screamed, struck, bit, tore. There were no words and no movements but the tearing of teeth and claws.

Then the clouds opened and let down the rain like a waterfall. The water bounded from the mountain-top, tore leaves and branches from the trees, poured like a cold shower over the struggling heap on the sand. Presently the heap broke up and figures staggered away. Only the beast lay still, a few yards from the sea. Even in the rain they could see how small a beast it was; and already its blood was staining the sand.

Now a great wind blew the rain sideways, cascading the water from the forest trees. On the mountain-top the parachute filled and moved; the figure slid, rose to its feet, spun, swayed down through a vastness of wet air and trod with ungainly[6] feet the tops of the high trees; falling, still falling, it sank towards the beach and the boys rushed screaming into the darkness. The parachute took the figure forward, furrowing the lagoon, and bumped it over the reef and out to sea.

☞ **Notes**

1. **turf:** the surface of the soil with the grass and roots growing in it.
2. **garlanded:** to put one or more circle of flowers, leaves on someone.
3. **succulent:** thick and fleshy.
4. **whine:** to complain (too much) in an unnecessarily sad voice.
5. **demented:** mad; of unbalanced mind.
6. **ungainly:** not graceful; awkward in movement; clumsy.

☞ **Study questions**

1. How do Jack's leadership style and personality differ from Ralph's?
2. What does the face-painting have to do with the boys becoming more violent?
3. Who emerges from the jungle with the secret of the beast?
4. Under what circumstances did Simon die?
5. What is the most primitive, savage act committed in this novel?
6. At what point in the novel does Ralph start thinking that mankind is inherently evil?

☞ **Essay topics**

1. Where does Golding think evil come from?
2. In what way is *Lord of the Flies* a novel about power?

8.13 Ted Hughes

8.13.1 Life and career

Hughes(1930-1998) was born in Mytholmroyd, Yorkshire. When he was seven, his family moved to Mexborough, where his father ran a tobacco shop. As a kid, he roamed his countryside, the harsh landscape of the northern England moors, which had a strong influence over his future poetic creation. He attended the Mexborough Grammar School, where he received encouragement from his teachers to write. After leaving the grammar school, Hughes served two years in the Royal Air Force, spending much of his time reading Shakespeare and other English writers. Then he went to study English at Pembroke College, Cambridge, but he soon switched to archaeology and anthropology.

After graduating from the university, Hughes settled down in London, working as a zoo attendant, gardener, and script reader for J. Arthur Rank. He returned to Cambridge regularly where a number of his friends remained. It was at a launch party there that he met the American poet Sylvia Plath. They fell in love and soon got married. After spending couple of years in America, they returned to England. Hughes got a job of writing programs for the BBC as well as producing essays, articles, and reviews. The first few years of their married life went happily. They supported each other along with avidly pursuing their writing careers. Gradually their marriage began to fracture. Hughes' affair with Assia Wevill led to his separation from Plath in 1962. Plath moved to a new flat in London with her children. Following a state of depression, Plath finally committed suicide in 1963. The memory of Plath started to haunt Wevill, who killed herself and Shura, their four-year-old daughter in 1969. The following year, Hughes married Carol Orchard, with whom he remained until his death.

Hughes began writing poems when he was only fifteen. He published his first collection of poems, *Hawk in the Rain* in 1957. His second book of poems, *Lupercal*, appeared in 1960. These two volumes of poetry established him as a prominent poet of nature and animal in the 1960s. He also wrote two collections of poems for children: *Meet my Folks!* (1961) and *Earth Owl and Other Moon People* (1963). In the later period of his poetic career, Hughes published six more volumes of poems: *Wodwo* (1967), *Crow* (1970), *Season Songs* (1974), *Gaudete* (1977), *Cave Birds* (1978), and *Remains of Elmet* (1979). He also wrote short stories, plays for radio and stage, and some very fine critical essays in which he went straight to the heart of the matter, conveying somewhat single-minded critical insights with enthusiasm and power. In 1984, Ted Hughes was honored with the title of the Poet Laureate of the United Kingdom.

In his early poetry, Hughes mainly writes about animals. By creating hawks, jaguars, pikes and thrushes in the most vivid and vibrantly dynamic way, he manages to express the intense energy and physical presence of the animal and natural world. Poems like "The Hawk in the Rain," "The Thought Fox," "The Jaguar," "The Horses," "Hawk Roosting," "An Otter," and "Pike" may rank as the best of their kind since *Birds, Beasts and Flowers* by D. H. Lawrence. The title poem of *The Hawk in the Rain* is particularly powerful in presenting the conflict between vitality and death. The image of drowning in the rain and the image of the earth as a beast that swallows its human victims combine to present nature as a violent and brutal enemy. While man makes a desperate and uncertain struggle for life against forces of nature, the hawk, with his cool, superior calm, is above man's struggle, riding the air with a seemingly weightless effort. The weight and bodily limitations of man contrast dramatically with the "weightless quiet" of the hawk. But the real difference between hawk and man is that hawk is a creature of instinct whose will is in accord with nature, whereas man has lost that instinct and cannot be a part of the elements. "Hawk Roosting" from *Lupercal* is often regarded as a companion piece to "The Hawk in the Rain." The poem also emphasizes the strength of the hawk but does so with a greater insistence on the isolation of the bird and on the brutish quality of its strength. This time the poem is written in the first person; and the stress is put on the awful power of non-human life, contrasting it with the limitations of the power of human nature.

In his later poetry, Hughes is increasingly preoccupied with describing the divided nature of man and his relationship to the non-human powers of the universe. Poems in *Wodwo* express the tension between the experience of life in an unknown, hostile and meaningless universe and the refusal of man to give up fighting. The title poem of *Wodwo* is a dramatic monologue written in a stream-of-consciousness style, which expresses the thoughts of a creature half-man, half-beast, seeking knowledge of his identity and the meaning of the universe. In *Crow* Hughes has come to concern himself with a subjective exploration of the inner realities of man who lives in a dark, violent, death-ridden universe. To present this nihilistic universe and to show that beneath the feelings of complete despair there is still an active voice of unyielding energy and survival, Hughes creates a mythical figure Crow who, as a creature born into a very particular nightmare, embodies the inner experience of modern man. In *Gaudete* Hughes continues to explore in symbolic terms the divided nature of modern man's soul and the need to reconcile the inner and outer lives of man. However, with a suggestion that the division may be healed and the Crow-experience of life be overcome, *Gaudete* can be read as a counterpart to *Crow*.

Hughes thinks that a good poem is an organism, "an assembly of living parts moved by a single spirit." To write a good poem is to capture a spirit, or in his words, "to capture a wild animal." To achieve this, Hughes makes use of freer poetic forms, relies less on strict metrical schemes, and is more inclined towards an arrogant tone and an exaggerated diction. His images are usually simple, vivid but grim with a stark, hard-edged quality; his rhythms are bold, strong and rapid, with heavy stresses and obtrusive alliterations, producing an effect of urgent violence and primitive strength. His language, colloquial and varied, tends to move from comic levity and violence to grotesque surrealism. By mixing the Biblical and classical mythology with sharply topical allusions to motor-car accidents, pollutions, mechanized wars and nuclear devastations, Hughes creates a body of poetic myth that stands for the black and violent experiences of modern man.

Today, Ted Hughes has become reputedly one of the best English poets. He is often regarded along with Philip Larkin as representative of the English poetry since the Second World War. His point of view towards life is largely determined by two things: one is the aftermath of the two world wars which have brought about cultural, historical and psychological dislocations in Europe; the other is an "awareness of nature" and a fascination with the animal world. In his poetry, Hughes is preoccupied with the writing of nature, of animal life, and of the elemental forces of non-human life and the inner turbulence of modern man who is seen as being cut off from the instinctual sources of his power. With an acute sense of the inadequacy of humanism and the breakdown of all the traditional values, Hughes lays bare the sterility and nihilism in modern man's response to life.

8. 13. 2 "Hawk Roosting"[1]

I sit in the top of the wood, my eyes closed.
Inaction, no falsifying dream
Between my hooked head and hooked feet:
Or in sleep rehearse perfect kills and eat.

The convenience of the high trees!
The air's buoyancy[2] and the sun's ray
Are of advantage to me;
And the earth's face upward for my inspection.

My feet are locked upon the rough bark.
It took the whole of Creation
To produce my foot, my each feather:
Now I hold Creation in my foot

Or fly up, and revolve it all slowly—
I kill where I please because it is all mine.
There is no sophistry[3] in my body:
My manners are tearing off heads—

The allotment of death.
For the one path of my flight is direct
Through the bones of the living.
No arguments assert my right:

The sun is behind me.
Nothing has changed since I began.
My eye has permitted no change.
I am going to keep things like this.

☞ Notes

1. This poem is the monologue of a hawk sitting in the top of a wood. Hughes said he had in mid the personality of someone like Hitler so the poem can be read as an insight into fascist psychology. "roosting": a bird sitting comfortably through the night, perhaps sleeping.
2. **buoyancy**: the ability to float, either on water or (metaphorically) in the air.
3. **sophistry**: false but clever and believable reasoning or argument.

☞ **Study questions**

1. Who is the speaker? What traits make him seem human? Inhuman?
2. Describe the speaker's image of himself and of the world. How valid do you find his view of life?
3. Describe the emotional effect of the poem—is it amusing, frightening, moving, or something else altogether? Explain how Hughes creates that effect?
4. What does the poet's view of nature seem to be? Do you think the poem also portrays an aspect of human nature? Explain.

8.14 Seamus Heaney

8.14.1 Life and career

Heaney (1939-) was born into a Catholic family in County Derry, Northern Ireland. He grew up on his father's cattle farm. He attended local schools until 1957. Then he went to study at Queen's University, Belfast, where he graduated in 1961 with a first class degree in English. The following year he obtained a teaching certificate at St. Joseph's College, in Belfast. After one year as a secondary school teacher, he returned to St. Josephs to serve as a lecturer for three years. It was around this time that he began to write, joining a poetry workshop and publishing his work in university magazines. In 1965 he met and married Marie Devlin. They had three children.

Heaney became a lecturer at Queen's University in 1966. Partly to escape the violence of Belfast, he gave up his job and moved to the Irish Republic in 1972, working at a teacher training college in Dublin. Since 1981 he has spent part of each year teaching at Harvard University, where he is a Professor of Rhetoric and Oratory. Between the years 1989 and 1994 he held Professorship of Poetry at Oxford. Throughout this time he was publishing prolifically and dividing his time between Ireland and America.

His poetry is grounded in actual, local detail, often in memories of Derry or observation of his adopted home in the Republic of Ireland. His first two collections, *Death of a Naturalist* (1966) and *Door into the Dark* (1969), largely written before the renewed outbreak of the so-called "Troubles" in 1968, show Heaney alerting his audience to the violent history of colonization on his native ground, but preoccupied also by the rhythms of life in a rural setting remembered from his childhood. With *Wintering Out* (1972), Heaney sought to find historical and mythic analogies for the plight in which the minority found itself. In *Field Work* (1979) the political debate is out in the open in a more resonant and Yeatsian way than hitherto; with *Station Island* (1984), written after the deaths of the hunger-strikers and the so-called "dirty protests" in prisons, Heaney more openly ponders the relevance of his poetry in time of violence and polarization.

When his mother and father died respectively in 1984 and 1987, Heaney's poetry is filled with images of death and dying, but yet it is still firmly rooted in the life of this world. His tender elegies about friends and family members who have died serve many purposes: they mourn great losses, celebrate those who have gone before us, and recall the solace that remains to us in our memories. In the late-1980s, after the signing of the Anglo-Irish agreement, which brought about new administrative exchange between Dublin, Belfast, and London, a new tone of lightness and the exploration of new possibilities were brought into his poetry. This change was confirmed after the I. R. A. cessation of violence in 1994, and later the signing of the Good Friday agreement. Heaney's two most recent volumes of poetry, *The Spirit Level* (1996) and *Electric Light* (2001), have seen him turning away from immediate political issues to consider further ideas with visionary and allegorical views. Besides poetry, he also writes critical essays and does translations. His verse translation of *Beowulf* (1999) from Old English is highly praised. He received the Nobel Prize in Literature in 1995.

Heaney explores a wide range of subjects in his poems, including nature, love, the relationship between contemporary issues and historical patterns, and legend and myth. Viewing the art of poetry as a craft, he stresses the importance of technique as a means to channel creative energies toward sophisticated metaphysical probing. Like Yeats, Heaney combines all the conflicting poles of the Irish experience into a rich, embattled language: paganism and Christianity, repression and expansion, desire and chastity, country and city, ignorance and enlightenment, hope and despair. Extremely evocative yet clear and direct, balanced between the personal and the topical, his crafted poetry has been praised for its powerful imagery, meaningful content, musical phrasing, and compelling rhythms. The development of his poetry has often manifested a canny and clear-eyed responsiveness to changing patterns of violence and peace-seeking across the last thirty years of the twentieth century. His success in dealing with the murderous racial enmities of past and present, avoiding all the sins of oratory, and keeping his personal sense of balance, seems to be one of the most exhilarating poetic accomplishments in contemporary times.

8. 14. 2 "Follower"

My father worked with a horse plough,
His shoulders globed[1] like a full sail strung
Between the shafts and the furrow.
The horses strained at his clicking tongue.[2]

An expert. He would set the wing
And fit the bright steel-pointed sock.

The sod rolled over without breaking.
At the headrig, with a single pluck

Of reins, the sweating team[3] turned round
And back into the land. His eye
Narrowed and angled at the ground,
Mapping the furrow exactly.

I stumbled in his hobnailed[4] wake,
Fell sometimes on the polished sod;
Sometimes he rode me on his back
Dipping and rising to his plod.

I wanted to grow up and plough,
To close one eye, stiffen my arm.
All I ever did was follow
In his broad shadow round the farm.

I was a nuisance, tripping, falling,
Yapping always. But today
It is my father who keeps stumbling
Behind me, and will not go away.

☞ Notes

1. **globed:** formed into a ball-liked shape.
2. **clicking tongue:** making a short hard sound with the tongue, especially in order to get someone's attention.
3. **the sweating team:** here referring to the ploughing man and horses together.
4. **hobnailed:** marked by the short, hard-headed nails used as studs in shoes.

☞ Study questions

1. What images does the speaker use to describe his father working in the field?
2. What did the speaker do while his father worked? What did he want to do when he grew up?
3. What does the speaker say about his father today?
4. What do you think the last sentence of the poem means? What might the "stumbling" father who "will not go away" symbolize?
5. In what way can the past be both a gift and a burden?

Appendix

Acknowledgment

Acknowledgment must be made to the following works, from which we have benefited a lot in the course of compiling *A New Edition of Selected Readings in English Literature*.

Abrams, M. H., et al., eds. *The Norton Anthology of English Literature.* New York: Norton, 1986.

Barnard, Robert. A Short History of English Literature (2nd edn.). Oxford: Oxford University Press, 1994.

Bradbury, Malcolm. *The Modern British Novel.* Beijing: Foreign Language Teaching and Research Press, 2005.

Brooks, Cleanth. *Understanding Fiction.* Beijing: Foreign Language Teaching and Research Press, 2005.

Brooks, Cleanth. *Understanding Poetry.* Beijing: Foreign Language Teaching and Research Press, 2005.

Chen, Jia. *A History of English Literature*(4 vols.). Beijing: Commercial Press, 1986.

Chen, Jia. *Selected Readings in English Literature* (3 vols.). Beijing: Commercial Press, 1986.

Coote, Stephen. *The Penguin Short History of English Literature.* New York: Penguin Books Ltd., 1993.

Cronin, Richard. *Shelley's Poetic Thoughts.* London: The Macmillan Press Ltd., 1981.

Curran, Stuart, ed. *The Cambridge Companion to British Romanticism.* Cambridge: Cambridge University Press, 1993.

Drabble, Margaret. *The Oxford Companion to English literature* (5th ed. rev. and updated). Oxford: Oxford University Press, 1995.

He, Qixin. *A History of English Drama.* Nanjing: Yilin Press, 1999.

Head, Dominic. *The Modernist Short Story—A Study in Theory and Practice.* Cambridge: Cambridge University Press, 1992.

Hou, Weirui. *A Comprehensive History of English Literature.* Shanghai: Shanghai

Foreign Language Education Press, 1999.

Luo, Jingguo. *A New Anthology of English Literature* (2 vols.). Beijing: Beijing University Press, 1996.

Richetti, John, ed. *The Columbia History of the British Novel*. Beijing: Foreign Language Teaching and Research Press, 2005.

Rogers, Pat. *An Outline of English Literature*. Oxford: Oxford University Press, 1998.

Rosenthal, M. L. *The Modern Poets—A Critical Introduction*. Beijing: Foreign Language Teaching and Research Press, 2004.

Wang, Zuoliang. *A History of English Literature*. Beijing: Commercial Press, 1996.

Zhang, Boxiang. *A Course Book of English Literature*. Wuhan: Wuhan University Press, 2005.

Zhang, Boxiang. *An Introductory Course Book of English and American Literatures*. Wuhan: Huazhong University of Science and Technology Press, 2009.

Zhang, Dingquan and Wu Gang. *A New Concise History of English Literature*. Shanghai: Shanghai Foreign Language Education Press, 2002.